TOWARD

the Sea of

FREEDOM

ALSO BY SARAH LARK

TOWARD
the Sea of
FREEDOM

Sarah Lark

Translated by D. W. Lovett

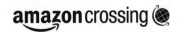
amazon crossing

Previously published as *Das Lied der Maori* by Bastei Lübbe in Germany in 2008. Translated from German by D. W. Lovett. First published in English by AmazonCrossing in 2015.

Published by AmazonCrossing, Seattle

www.apub.com

Amazon, the Amazon logo, and AmazonCrossing are trademarks of Amazon.com, Inc., or its affiliates.

ISBN-13: 9781503951532 (hardcover)
ISBN-10: 1503951537 (hardcover)
ISBN-13: 9781503948815 (paperback)
ISBN-10: 1503948811 (paperback)

Printed in the United States of America

First edition

Cover design by Shasti O'Leary-Soudant

Dedicated to Mary O'Donnell—
We will never forget you

Dignity

Wicklow County, Ireland

1846–1847

Chapter 1

Mary Kathleen's heart was beating quickly, but she forced herself to walk slowly until she was out of sight of the manor. Not that anyone would really have an eye on her. And even if Gráinne, the cook, did suspect something, two scones hardly amounted to anything—not compared to what Gráinne herself regularly filched from the wealthy Wetherby household.

Still, Mary Kathleen was trembling by the time she ducked behind one of the stone walls that defined the fields here, as they did everywhere in Ireland. The walls offered cover from the wind and even from prying eyes, but they could not shield Kathleen from her feelings of guilt.

She, Mary Kathleen, the model pupil of Father O'Brien's Bible study, she who had proudly placed the name of the Mother of God before her own at confirmation—*she* had stolen!

Kathleen still could not comprehend what had come over her, but when she had carried the tray with the scones up to Lady Wetherby, her desire had become all but overwhelming. The scones were freshly baked, with white flour and white sugar, and served with marmalade that came from England in sweet little jars. According to the label, which Kathleen deciphered with effort since she had only been taught the rudiments of reading and writing, the marmalade was made from oranges. Surely the contents of those little jars would taste delicious.

It had taken all of Kathleen's restraint to place the pastry tray carefully on the tea table between Lady Wetherby and her guest, curtsy, and whisper "Madam," without slobbering like the shepherd's dog. That thought made her want to giggle hysterically. She had almost been proud of herself when she went back into the kitchen, where old Gráinne was just then biting into one of the delectable little cakes—without giving Kathleen or the scullion maid so much as a crumb, of course.

"Girls," Gráinne liked to preach, "you already have enough to thank the Lord for, having gotten your hands on a post in this manor. The occasional heel of bread falls to you as is. Nowadays, with the potatoes rotting in the fields and people going hungry, a bit of bread can save your life."

Kathleen acknowledged this wholeheartedly—her family had been blessed with quite a bit of luck. As a tailor, her father always earned a little money, so the O'Donnells were not solely dependent on the potatoes that Kathleen's mother and siblings grew on their tiny plot. Whenever the need became too great, James O'Donnell drew from his meager savings and bought a handful of grain from Lord Wetherby or the lord's steward, Mr. Trevallion. Kathleen had no reason to steal—and yet she had.

Then again, why had Lady Wetherby and her friend left two of the scones untouched? Why had they not kept an eye on her while she cleared the table? The ladies had gone into the music room where Lady Wetherby played piano. They had no interest in the remaining scones, and Gráinne, as Kathleen had known, would not be suspicious either. Lady Wetherby was young and a gourmand. She rarely sent treats back.

So Kathleen had stuck the scones in the pockets of her neat servant's uniform and, later, in the pockets of her worn blue dress. Then she committed another theft by stashing the almost empty marmalade jar instead of following Gráinne's request to wash it. That was a venial sin, since she would bring it back clean once she had scraped the last of the marmalade from it. The theft of the scones, however, would burn in her soul until she could confess to Father O'Brien on Saturday. If she even dared to confess it. She was certain that she would die of shame.

Already, Mary Kathleen deeply regretted her actions, though she had not even eaten the scones. Yet notions of their taste and aroma consumed her. *God, help me!* The thought overcame her as she considered whether she might assuage the sin by giving the scones to her younger siblings. At least that would be active penance—and a much harsher punishment than rattling off twenty Hail Marys. But the children would doubtlessly flaunt their treats, and when Kathleen's parents learned of the matter . . .

No, that was not an option.

But that was not the worst of it. While Kathleen piously contemplated how she could expiate her sin, a desire flared up within her, making her heart beat more quickly again. Was it anxiety? Or guilt? Or joy?

She could share the scones with Michael. Michael Drury, the farmer's son next door, lived with his family in a cottage even tinier, sootier, and poorer than that of Kathleen's family. Michael surely had not eaten a morsel that day—aside, perhaps, from a few pilfered kernels of grain as he helped to harvest the crop for Lord Wetherby. Even that was considered a crime, one that Mr. Trevallion would punish with blows if he caught the boys.

The grain was for the lords, the potatoes for the servants. And when the potatoes rotted in the fields, the peasants understood just how low their standing was. Most of them accepted their lot in life. Michael's mother, for example, saw the mysterious potato blight as God's punishment and tried in her daily prayers to discern what had so enraged the Lord that He visited such misery upon them. Michael and a few other young men grew incensed at Mr. Trevallion and Lord Wetherby, who blithely reaped a rich grain harvest while the tenants' children starved.

Mary Kathleen pictured Michael's rakish expression when he had cursed the landlord and his steward: his furrowed brow under his dark, wiry hair, and the glint in his shining blue eyes. Would God consider it penance if she shared the scones with her beau? Yes, she would sate his hunger—but also her own longing to be with the tall, lean young man with the deep, beguiling voice. She yearned for his touch and to lose herself in his arms.

When times had been better, Michael had played music with his father and old Paddy Murphy on Saturday evenings and at the harvest festival every year. The villagers danced, drank, and laughed; and, later in the evening, Michael Drury sang ballads, his gaze fixed on Mary Kathleen.

These days, however, no one had the strength to dance. And Kevin Drury and Paddy Murphy had long since disappeared into the mountains. According to the rumors, they were running a flourishing whiskey distillery there. It was said that Michael sold the bottles on the sly in Wicklow. In any case, Kathleen's father wanted nothing to do with the Drurys, and he had admonished his eldest daughter strongly when he saw her with Michael one Sunday after church.

"But I think Michael means to ask for my hand," Kathleen had said, flushing brightly as she protested. "All, all officially and honorably."

James O'Donnell had snorted, his tall, slim frame shaking with displeasure. "Since when has a Drury ever done anything officially and honorably? The whole family is a bunch of ne'er-do-wells: fiddlers and distillers. Rascals, the lot of them. They wanted to ship that boy's grandfather off to the colonies. Little as I like the English, they'd have done a good deed there. But the fellow got away to Galway and then to God knows where. Just like his good-for-nothing son. As soon as things get too hot for them, they take off—and not one of them has left behind fewer than five kids. Keep your eyes off that Drury boy, Kathie, not to mention your hands. You could have any boy here, lovely lass that you are."

Kathleen had blushed again, this time out of embarrassment at her father calling her "lovely." Such praise was already suspect enough in Father O'Brien's eyes. A virgin should be virtuous and industrious, he always said, but under no circumstances should she put her charms on display.

Though in Mary Kathleen's case, this could scarcely be avoided. After all, she could not hide herself away altogether just to deny men a look at her delicate face, her soft honey-blonde hair, and her charming green eyes. Michael had compared the color of her eyes to the dark green of the glens before sunset. And sometimes, when they reflected joy or surprise, he said he saw in them sparks that shone like the first green of spring in the meadows.

Oh, Michael had a way with flattery. But Kathleen did not want to believe that he was really as much of a rogue as her father thought. After all, he worked hard every day in Lord Wetherby's fields. On top of that, he still fiddled on the weekends at Barney's Tavern in Wicklow—a long walk if no one lent him a donkey or mule. Sometimes Roony O'Rearke, the Wetherbys' gardener, was willing to do so. Roony was believed to be a drunk, but Kathleen did not want to consider a possible connection between moonshine whiskey and O'Rearke's loan of his donkey.

Kathleen stood up from behind the stone wall and began walking again. A copse divided the Wetherby estate from the cottages of its tenants. The landlords did not like to look directly at the houses of their servants and workers. Kathleen began to feel better—which was surely because rather than heading toward the village and her family's cottage, she was making her way to the wheat fields above the huts. The men would still be working there, but the sun was slowly setting. Trevallion would soon have to send them home.

Twilight always put the eager steward in a bind: there was still enough light to work—and Lord Wetherby was not running a charity, after all—but the twilight aided theft. The workers slipped stalks of grain into their pockets or hid them behind the stone walls to retrieve them when it was dark.

Kathleen hoped Trevallion would send his men home early that evening, even if it meant more dire hunger would prevail in the cottages. The families were waiting hopefully for their fathers' and brothers' takings. Not even Father O'Brien could seriously condemn the tenants' actions, though he assigned them sinners' prayers when they confessed their little thefts. Accordingly, the pious patriarchs spent half of Sunday on their knees in church. Meanwhile, young men like Michael roved across the fields trying to pinch a few more stalks, unobserved by the lord and lady, who spent Sunday riding and hunting with friends.

The full moon that rose over the mountains only strengthened Trevallion's fear of theft. As the moonlight brightened the landscape, the men, their wives, and their children would easily find the stalks of grain they'd hidden. Kathleen supposed that the overzealous overseer planned an early dinner and nap before riding half the night on patrol.

She had to force herself not to spit at Trevallion as he approached her. He sat high on the box of the last grain wagon while the exhausted workers dragged themselves home from the fields on foot.

"Hullo, little Mary Kathleen!" he said affably. "What are you doing here, blondie? Have they already sent you home from the manor? You all must be spending a lovely springtide in that kitchen. I'll wager old Gráinne isn't merely taking care of herself but the families of all her children and children's children with His Lordship's bread."

"His Lordship likes cake better," came a voice from the group of laborers shuffling tiredly behind Trevallion's wagon.

Kathleen recognized the voice of Billy Rafferty, one of Gráinne's sons. Billy was not the most clever, but he was crafty, and he liked to play the fool.

"Which you ought to know, Trevallion," Billy continued. "Don't you eat at his table?

The remark was answered with loud laughter. In truth, the English lord treated his Irish steward no better than he treated his tenants. Trevallion had a special position and would not starve. But he did not enjoy his lord's respect, nor was there any talk at all of raising him to nobility himself, an honor sometimes granted to stewards of very large properties. Though Lord Wetherby was a member of the nobility, his family was considered unimportant in England. His holdings in Ireland resulted from his wife's dowry and were rather small.

"At least my table is richly decked," Trevallion said. "With cakes, too, little Kathleen. In case you start to look for a husband who has something to offer."

Kathleen blushed deeply. No, the fellow could not know about the scones that seemed to be burning holes in the pockets of her dress. She must not act contrite, though. She lowered her eyes chastely. As a rule, Kathleen did not answer when Trevallion addressed her, especially not when he made such outrageously suggestive remarks. Too often, one heard of girls who surrendered to vice in the arms of their lords' stewards—though Kathleen could not imagine that this was due to the sin of lust.

Truly, Trevallion had nothing about him that could attract a girl. He was short, wiry, and redheaded like a leprechaun, but he lacked the wit of the mythical creatures for which the better-off Irish built houses in their gardens to secure help with farm work—and with moonshine whiskey distilling.

There was nothing kind to say about Trevallion. He was completely subservient to his English masters and cruel to their tenants. Even when the lord and lady were not residing on their holdings in Ireland, which was most of the year, he would not turn a blind eye. In times like those, most stewards would look away while the men went hunting or when some of the fruit and vegetables from the master's garden ended up in the pots of the farmers' wives. Trevallion fought for every carrot, every apple, and every bean on his master's land, though, in truth, Lord Wetherby only appeared at harvest time and during hunting season. The people hated the steward, and if a girl gave in to him, it would certainly be out of need, not love.

"Or is it that you have a young suitor here in the fields?" Trevallion now asked with a spiteful gleam in his eye. "Is there something I should know as the eyes and ears of His Lordship?"

Weddings had to be approved by the landlord, and he listened eagerly to Trevallion's whispers.

Kathleen did not dignify this question with a response either.

"I think I'll have a little word with the tailor O'Donnell soon," Trevallion said. Kathleen saw how he licked his lips before finally letting her go.

She was trembling. The fellow did not really mean to court her, did he? Her father was always speaking of a "good match," and he claimed that she could find her fortune thanks to her beauty as long as she waited demurely and chastely for the right man. That did not mean Trevallion, though, did it? She'd take the veil before marrying that pig.

Kathleen stopped at the side of the road with her head bowed, letting the grain wagons and men pass. She knew that Michael would soon arrive, and so she continued along behind the stone walls that enclosed the freshly harvested fields.

She felt burning rage at Trevallion as she watched the first hungry children from the village coming up to the fields. Everyone would try to find the last remains of the grain, and everyone would be disappointed.

Just at that moment, however, Kathleen caught sight of Michael, and she was filled with happiness. Michael approached calmly, as if strolling through the stubble field. He saw the women and children, of course, which was why he only waved surreptitiously for her to follow him. Anyway, Kathleen knew where he was leading her.

Their hiding place was a tiny bight below the town, near the fields on the river. There the reeds stood high on the shore and a mighty willow let its branches hang in the water. Both hid the lovers from view. Kathleen knew that it was a sin to meet there with a young man—not to mention one of whom James O'Donnell did not approve—no matter what lovely words he spoke. Yet something in her insisted on doing it anyway. She wanted to wring a little happiness from the joyless days of work in the manor and now the useless toil on her father's land in the evening.

Michael was sitting astride a lower branch of the friendly willow when Kathleen arrived. His eyes lit up at the sight of her, and he swiftly and gracefully stood to greet her.

"The sweetest girl in Ireland—and she belongs to me alone," he said with admiration in his soft voice. "People praise the Irish rose, but only he who knows the lilies can measure what beauty is."

Kathleen blushed and lowered her gaze, but Michael reached for her hands and kissed them. Then he brought them to his heart, pulling the girl closer. Softly, he kissed her forehead and waited until she finally offered him her lips. He gently wrapped his arms around her.

"Careful," she whispered nervously. "I . . . I brought something with me, and I don't want you to crush it."

Before Michael could press her to him, she pulled the scones and jar of marmalade out of her dress pockets. The young man, ravenous after working hard from sunup to sundown, eyed them covetously. But Michael Drury was not greedy. He took his time with enjoyments of every sort and, for the time being, deposited the delicacies on a large leaf in a fork in the willow. Then he continued kissing Kathleen, slowly and tenderly.

Kathleen did not understand the whispering of the other girls, some of whom were already engaged and fearing their wedding nights. Michael, she firmly believed, would never hurt her. Even now, she lost herself for a short time in his embrace, his earthy scent of work in the field, and his cool skin, on which his sweat was already dry.

But then Michael freed himself. He stared at the stolen scones. "They smell good," he sighed.

She smiled and was suddenly no longer so hungry.

"You smell good," she whispered.

Michael shook his head, laughing. "Far from it, dearest. I stink. And I think I ought to wash before you invite me to have tea like a gentleman."

Before Kathleen could protest, Michael had already thrown off his simple, dirty shirt. Kathleen tried to look away as he slipped out of his faded pants as well, but she did not manage it. The sight of his powerful legs, his flat stomach, and his muscular arms pleased her. Michael was slim, but he did not look half-starved like many other tenants. Playing fiddle in Wicklow seemed to have its benefits. Kathleen would all too gladly have accompanied him into the tavern sometime.

She laughed and crouched on the beach as Michael slid into the water with a splash. He dived under to wash his hair and face and then swam like a fish to the middle of the river.

"Why don't you join me? It's wonderfully cool," Michael called to her.

But Kathleen shook her head. It was too terrible to think about what would happen if someone saw Mary Kathleen O'Donnell swimming naked or even half naked—and not in the girls' sanctioned bathing spot but here, with a man, during the full moon and outside the village.

"Get out of there before I eat these scones myself," she teased him.

Michael obeyed her immediately and swam to shore. He shook the water out of his thick hair and slicked it off his body, pulled his pants back on, and sat down next to her on the rocky beach. Kathleen handed him his pastry and the jar of marmalade, into which she had just placed her finger to scrape out a bit of what was left. She spread it on her scone and took a tiny bite. It was the best thing she had ever eaten. The orange jam was sweet but also slightly bitter. The scone melted on her tongue.

Kathleen looked tenderly at Michael, who was eating with similar devotion.

"Gifted or stolen?" he asked.

Kathleen turned red again. "They were, that is, hmm, left over," she murmured.

Michael kissed her lips, and he tasted of orange.

"So, you filched them," he teased. "That makes them all the sweeter. But what will Father O'Brien say about it?"

"Maybe I won't even confess it," Kathleen said. She knew that Michael did not take confession too seriously.

Michael laughed and stuffed the last piece of scone into his mouth. Then he lay back and pulled Kathleen with him. He began to caress the tops of her breasts. He still had sticky jam on his fingers, and he held them up for her to lick clean when she complained.

"No, Michael!" Kathleen fended him off as he moved to unbutton her dress. "We can't."

"But Kathleen dearest, you'll have to confess anyway. I know you: you will. Father O'Brien will be shocked no matter what. So why don't we offer him a really good secret to keep?"

Kathleen sat up reluctantly. "God forgives, not the priest. And God only forgives those who repent with sincerity. But this . . ."

No matter what she did with Michael, she would never regret it.

Michael stroked her hair and face, quickly getting her to stretch out on the beach again.

"Kathleen, I want to make you my wife, you know. I want to give you my name—even if it's not worth anything. Give me a little more time. Look, I'm saving—"

"You're saving?" Kathleen interrupted him, raising her voice. "How in heaven's name can you save anything, Michael Drury? And don't tell me it's money from fiddling at the tavern."

Michael shrugged. "You don't want to know, Mary Kathleen—at least, Mary won't want to know. Kathleen may be curious, I suppose." He had teased her about her name since she had taken it at confirmation. "But it's nothing, nothing to be ashamed of."

"It's whiskey, isn't it?" Kathleen asked angrily. "And you really aren't ashamed to be fermenting barley and wheat and Lord knows what all to make whiskey? While children go hungry?"

Michael pulled her close. "I don't make it, dearest," he said. "If I tried my hand at it, it wouldn't do anyone any good. But if I don't sell it, someone else will. Old O'Rearke would be all too happy to do it himself. He's got a donkey to bring the barrels to Wicklow. But they don't trust him, the old drunk."

"Who are 'they'?"

Michael shrugged. "The mountain men. Dearest, it's really better if you don't know everything. But a few pence always fall to me. My mother gets most of it—our potatoes are all blighted, and without the whiskey money, my siblings would starve."

"Your mother takes sin money?" Kathleen marveled.

Michael arched his eyebrows. "Rather than burying her children."

It slowly dawned on Kathleen why Mrs. Drury spent so much time in church.

"But I get to keep a little for myself, Kathleen," Michael continued eagerly. "And for you. For us. When I've got enough, we'll run away. To America! Do you know what that means? The promised land. The sun shines all year there, and there's work for everyone. We'll get rich."

"And the ships that take people there are called 'coffin ships' because they turn into floating caskets long before they make it to New York. That's what I've heard. I don't want that, Michael."

Kathleen cuddled close to Michael. It was hard to think when she was in his arms. America scared her, and she did not want to leave Ireland. But she wanted nothing more than to be with Michael. She wanted to feel his hands and lips on her body. Kathleen wanted much more caressing than Father O'Brien could ever forgive, so much forbidden love that God Himself might punish her. There were worse things than fifty Hail Marys on a hard church pew.

Kathleen sat up. She had given into temptation much too often already.

"I need to get home," she said quietly, hoping it did not sound regretful.

Michael nodded and helped her smooth her dress and pluck the leaves from her hair. Then, in the shadows of the stone walls, he accompanied Kathleen to the village. The men in the fields must not see them. Neither could the thieves carrying their day's prizes home, nor the women and children gleaning every little kernel—and certainly not Trevallion, who rode tirelessly across His Lordship's fields meaning to catch some little sinner.

The landlord's bright, moon-bathed wheat fields gave way to the tenants' plots—small, impoverished, without a golden glow. The blight had not only blackened the roots but also the leaves of the potato plants. The dying plants cast ghastly shadows in the moonlight, and Kathleen was certain she could feel death. She took Michael's hand.

Finally, they parted at a fork between their farmsteads—the O'Donnells' small house and the tiny, dilapidated hut of the Drurys. It was late. Their family members would already be asleep on mats on the ground. Kathleen had four siblings, Michael seven. Even if their families could have afforded beds, there would not have been enough space for them. In the O'Donnells' cottage, a fire was burning. Kathleen might still get something to eat. It was dark at the Drurys'.

The next day was Saturday. In the morning, Michael would take his fiddle and O'Rearke's donkey into the town. And somewhere on the way to Wicklow, the saddlebags would fill with whiskey bottles as if by magic.

Chapter 2

"No, Father, I don't want to! I don't like him. You can't do this to me!" Kathleen spoke desperately, shaking her head forcefully.

"Now, don't act like that, Kathie. You don't have to marry him right away!" James O'Donnell yelled at her.

It was apparent that he did not think it right that his oldest daughter was arguing with him here, in front of the house and in the presence of most of her siblings. When Trevallion visited on Sunday, the children had excitedly assembled at the fire where their mother was roasting a few of the scant edible potatoes from the harvest.

The tenant farmers often cooked in front of their cottages to avoid filling the rooms with too much smoke. The chimney did not draw off the smoke sufficiently, especially in the wind and the rain. Now, the pan smelled of the bacon the man had brought.

"Mr. Trevallion very politely asked if he might bring you home after church next Sunday," her mother said. "Why should we deny him that?"

"Because, by rights, they should not let the brute into church in the first place!" Kathleen raged. "The O'Learys' baby died yesterday because Mrs. O'Leary's milk ran dry. With that"—she pointed furiously at the remaining bacon and the small sack of flour, which her mother gazed at almost in worship—"he might have saved it. But alas, Mr. Trevallion wants to accompany me at Mass, not Sarah O'Leary."

"Lucky for us, child," said her father. "And I'm not much upset that you don't like the man. At least then you won't allow him anything that isn't proper."

"At least not until he brings a whole ham by?" Kathleen asked importunately.

Her father's slap struck her so hard and so unexpectedly that she stumbled backward.

"You've gone too far, Mary Kathleen," said her mother. Although she did not sound very convincing; apparently sin was relative in sight of bacon. "And it wouldn't be so wrong to think a bit about the pantry when you think about love. Passion fades, Kathie. You'll love your children forever, regardless of who gives them to you. And you'll be grateful to a husband if he can feed them. With Mr. Trevallion you're on the safe side, whether we like him or not."

"I won't sell myself." Kathleen tossed her blonde hair and stepped aside in case her father might slap her again. "If I have children, it will only be by a man I love. Otherwise, I'll go to a convent."

Although her mouth watered at the scent of the potatoes roasting with the bacon, Kathleen turned on her heels and ran out. No, she wanted none of the meal that was Trevallion's payment for her companionship on the way back from church. What she wanted was Michael. She had to tell him about this.

She gave herself over to a moment of fantasy that Michael would run straight to Trevallion's house and challenge him to single combat. Like it had been in ancient Ireland, and in the sagas and fairy tales of knights and heroes that Father O'Brien sometimes told when he enjoyed a little too much of the whiskey that he claimed the leprechauns set at the rectory door.

Mary Kathleen smiled at the thought of the old priest who surely would not approve of Trevallion making claims on her. On the other hand, Father O'Brien did not approve of her keeping company with Michael either. Perhaps she should tell Father O'Brien she felt called and that she might go to a convent. Maybe then he would shield her from any more suitors. Or he might believe her and take her to the abbey in Wicklow.

Kathleen wandered across the fields to the river. The grain had not been harvested yet, and she risked running into Trevallion while he was on patrol. Yet Michael and his friends were, without a doubt, secretly harvesting and using the cover of the stone walls and the reeds by the water. Kathleen heard an owl call just as she stepped onto the path that led to the farthest fields. Then the owl's voice cracked.

Kathleen looked up toward where the call had come from and spotted Jonny, one of Michael's younger brothers, in the crown of an oak. He grinned at her conspiratorially.

"I'm the lookout, Kathleen," he said.

"You really can hardly be seen in the leaves, especially not in that bright red shirt," Kathleen said, rolling her eyes. "That owl call couldn't fool anyone. Just come down quick, Jonny Drury. Trevallion will have you whipped if he catches you."

Jonny dutifully lowered his gaze and feigned a serious expression. As he bowed in Kathleen's direction, he almost fell from the tree.

"It isn't forbidden for a boy to sit in a tree on a Sunday evening to make owl calls," he said. Then, in a high-pitched voice, he sang out, "Lookee, Mr. Trevallion, I've a slingshot. I call for the female, and when she comes, here's a rock, and we've meat in our pot."

Kathleen had to laugh. "Don't you dare tell him that. He'll take it as a violation of the hunting laws, guaranteed, and he'll have you hanged. Where's Michael? Down by the river? With the other boys?"

"Don't think so," said Jonny. "The others are already back in the village. With a bit of grain they found." The boy winked importantly. "Brian cut a whole sheaf. That'll make good flour, Kathleen."

Brian was another of Michael's brothers, but Kathleen did not believe all this about a whole sheaf of wheat. The boys wouldn't have dared to set aside so much grain in broad daylight—not even with as capable a lookout as Jonny. The Sunday raids of the fields did not save any family from hunger. It was more of a game—a chance to make a fool of Trevallion.

"But Michael didn't cut anything," Jonny confided. "He was angry, just hit at the grain as if he wanted to knock the whole field down. Could it be that he's angry at you, Kathie?"

Kathleen shook her head. "I'm not fighting with your brother."

Jonny grinned. "You're good friends, aren't you?" He giggled meaningfully and shook the branch back and forth. "If you bring me a scone like you did Michael, then I'll tell you where he is. And I'll stay here and keep watch for you two. How about that?"

"How did you know?" Kathleen blushed. Had Jonny eavesdropped on or even watched her rendezvous with Michael?

"The lookout knows everything," Jonny explained. "I even knew you'd come. And I know where Michael's waiting for you. So, promise me a scone from the manor kitchen. Then I'll tell you."

Kathleen shook her head. "You don't need to tell me. I can figure it out myself."

She suddenly felt an overwhelming longing to throw herself into Michael's arms. She probably would not even have to tell him what had happened between her parents and Ralph Trevallion. Michael must have listened in on the meeting or heard about it. Word got around lightning fast in the village, and faster still when it involved the steward visiting a tenant family on a Sunday—and bringing bacon, to boot. But Michael could not possibly believe she would have agreed to the meeting!

Kathleen made a decision. "No treats from the kitchen, Jonny," she said, "but an apple from the landlord's garden if you stay here and take your lookout job seriously. I'm going to meet Michael at the river—and if you hear anyone coming, make your owl noise. Although maybe you could imitate a bird that sings during the day?"

After Jonny had assured her he could do a convincing cuckoo, Kathleen ran down to the river. It was a sunny afternoon, and the Vartry River ran like a stream of liquid silver through the lushly green countryside. She made her way through the reeds on the bank.

"Kathie?" asked Michael before she even reached the little bight.

"Michael!"

Kathleen wanted to throw herself into the arms of her love, but he did not embrace her with the usual warmth. She breathed deeply. She had to tell him right away, so he would not get angry.

"Michael, I have nothing to do with it. I won't walk with Trevallion," she assured him. "Never! I, I only want you, Michael."

Michael looked hurt, furious. His face did not glow as it usually did at sight of her, and he did not have any beautiful words on his tongue. Nevertheless, he kissed her then—much, much harder and much, much more demandingly than usual. She was startled at first, but then she returned the kiss with equal passion. Something had changed in Michael's gaze. She saw ardor in his eyes, joy in the challenge and the fight.

Without a word, Michael picked her up and laid her down in a nest of reeds and grass, shielded by willow branches that hung so low that only dim greenly golden light penetrated. Kathleen thought about the church's varicolored windows and the colorful light that streamed from them during Mass. She thought about a wedding.

"I want to be your wife, Michael," she assured him.

Surely now, he would flatter her again, caress her, and kiss her.

"Prove it," Michael said in a tone that was strange to her.

Kathleen looked at him helplessly. And this time when he began to open her dress, she did not try to stop him.

***

Kathleen could not prevent Ralph Trevallion from accompanying her after Sunday Mass, though she exerted herself well enough to keep him from making any detours between the church and village or from parting from her parents and siblings. None of this seemed to bother the steward. He walked dutifully beside her, saying a few pleasantries and chatting with her mother and father.

For James O'Donnell, the walk through the village became a running of the gauntlet. The farmers did not approve of the tailor conversing with the steward, let alone his plan to seal family ties.

"Can't you walk around the village alone with the man, like the other girls with their beaux?" O'Donnell asked his daughter sharply after they had walked through the village with Trevallion for the third time.

"He's not my beau!" Kathleen retorted angrily. "And if you don't want to be seen with him, imagine how I feel!"

Kathleen did not make mention of Trevallion's presents, though her mother treasured the steward precisely because of them. The O'Donnells now always had enough flour to bake bread, and every Sunday, there was meat in the pot.

Michael Drury had to stand witness as Trevallion offered Kathleen his arm, as he walked beside her, and as he proudly led her through the crowd, which discontentedly made way, when the priest said good-bye to the parish after Mass. Michael was enraged as he watched, but he couldn't do anything about it. Yet during the long late-summer evenings after work, Michael pressed his claims in the fields along the river. He was usually already waiting for Kathleen, longing for the cuckoo call with which Jonny gleefully announced her. She came to him whenever she could. Sometimes Kathleen brought bread or fruit. Michael liked when she filched treats from the manor, but he wouldn't take anything that might have come from Trevallion's hand. Michael let her know that he would choke on that man's gifts.

These days she was always hungry—for food as well as affection. She knew she was sinning with Michael, and was ashamed of it—only afterward though, once the rush had died away. When Michael was making love to her, as when she thought about him at work or at night on her sleeping mat, she felt blessed, not guilty. Something so wonderful, so uplifting, could not be a sin. Besides, God did allow it, so long as a couple went into church and pledged themselves to each other first. Which Kathleen and Michael would have been prepared to do at any moment.

Once, she even pilfered a candle from the manor house, and the two of them solemnly recited wedding vows. Naturally, they knew this did not count. They were just children, playing at marriage. To make it real, they would need permission from their parents and the landlord, and Father O'Brien's blessing. They couldn't imagine how they would get all that.

"We'll marry in America!" Michael comforted Kathleen when, once again, these thoughts aggrieved her. "Or in Kingstown or Galway before we sail."

Kathleen no longer protested when he raved about their wonderful life together on the other side of the ocean. She had chosen him; she wanted to live with him, wherever that would be. And America was better than the convent—the only way to flee a marriage in Ireland.

***

The cold and rainy days of late autumn had arrived. Even under the thickest of the blankets Michael had scavenged, it was wet and uncomfortable in their love nest on the river. But the walks after church also grew shorter. Everyone took refuge in houses and cottages. Many people simply lacked the strength to do anything else.

There had been less and less to eat for weeks. Hunger held Lord Wetherby's tenants in its iron grip, although the lord himself did not notice. He and his wife had long since returned to their country house in England, where they sat drinking tea in front of the fireplace, cheered by the rich harvest of his Irish holdings. It was possible he was not even aware that no such blessings were bestowed upon his tenants and day laborers. His grain was sound. Why should Wetherby give a second thought to potatoes?

The few potatoes not blighted had long since been eaten. There had been so few, no one had been able to store any—not even seed potatoes for the following year. They would have to buy them, and God alone knew with what money. To survive the winter, the children gathered acorns in the forest, which their parents ground. The lucky ones, like Kathleen's family, added rye or wheat flour; others baked their bread from the coarse, unsubstantial acorn meal. The poorest—those who could hardly summon the strength to go into the woods to gather acorns or dig up roots—cooked soup from the meager grass that grew along the road. People fought over the last dry nettles.

Now and again, Father O'Brien would dispense donations in church. Collections were taken up in England for the Irish, and some of the charity even came from America. Nevertheless, it was never enough to last very long. Stomachs were filled once, but it only made the hunger hurt all the more.

Michael Drury's family found ways to make ends meet. Michael fiddled in Wicklow's tavern, but even the towns lacked money for diversions. Prices for groceries climbed in equal measure to people's hunger, and even the moonshine whiskey distillers in the mountains wanted for raw materials.

Through it all, Mary Kathleen was the only one on whom the strains of the famine could hardly be seen. While everyone around her became thin, she seemed to blossom and even to put on weight. The reason for that did not, however, lie in Trevallion's generous gifts. Old Gráinne cooked for the steward when the Wetherbys weren't there, and he would have enjoyed feeding Kathleen the extra pastries and cakes. She wouldn't take anything directly from him, though her mother joyfully accepted his boon and fairly distributed the treats to Kathleen's siblings. Kathleen could not be getting fat from that.

"It's my love making you more beautiful," asserted Michael when they met at the river to take a little walk on one of the few dry Sundays.

The countryside was covered in an early frost, the meadow seeming to wear a wedding dress, and the cold pressed through Kathleen's thin shoes. It would have been much too cold to lie down in the reeds. Outside, it was only tolerable when one was moving, so Michael and Kathleen strode quickly—they wished to put the village behind them as quickly as possible. On days like this, the gossip hounds curled up behind stoves, but one never knew if Father O'Brien might pass by on his way to a sick or dying parishioner.

Only when the young couple was a fair distance from the village did Kathleen dare to snuggle into Michael's arms. His caresses kept her warm. His hands moved beneath her threadbare shawl and her thin dress, and he stroked her shoulders and breasts.

"You're like a flower that blooms even in winter," he whispered, "because your gardener flatters you, tends to you, and pines for your blossom."

Kathleen bit her lip. "Do you really think I, I'm," she stammered, "taking on a more womanly form? I mean . . ."

"Your breasts seem to be growing at my touch," Michael laughed. "God knows they were always lovely and firm, but now—do you feel how my hands are no longer big enough to hold them?"

Michael caressed her breasts, and his hands wandered deeper inside her dress. "Everything about you is warm and wonderful. I long to curl up beside you and—"

Kathleen pushed him away. "Michael," she said in a concerned tone. "I, I don't know much about it, but I have seen the girls who marry and then . . . and then are in a family way. And I've seen my mother when she's carrying another baby. That's why, Michael, I, as wonderful as your love is, still, still—if a girl gains weight with nothing to eat, it often means she's got something growing in her belly."

Kathleen did not dare look at him. Michael let go of her, taken aback.

"You mean you might be pregnant?" he asked, disbelieving. "But, but how? It's too soon, Kathleen! I haven't put together the money for America yet."

Kathleen exhaled audibly. "The baby won't care a fig for that, Michael Drury! And I'm sure it wouldn't want to enter this world aboard a coffin ship. We'll have to marry, Michael. Very soon. Here."

"But Kathleen! Here, now? Where would we live? What will your father say? He's certainly not going to give his blessing."

"He's going to have to," Kathleen insisted bitterly. "Or live with the shame. Of course, I could just give myself to Trevallion quickly and say it's his. But we don't have that much time."

Michael roared. "That idiot touching you? Raising my child? Over my dead body! Listen, Kathleen, aren't there any other options?"

Kathleen glared at him. "You're not thinking of killing this child in me, Michael Drury."

Michael shook his head ruefully. "No. But it, it could be that you're wrong."

Kathleen shrugged. "That could be. I just don't believe it. I've made excuses to myself until today, Michael, but now that you've noticed it too . . . and it's going quickly. Quicker than for most girls. Soon everyone will see."

Michael took a few steps away from her, confused, unsure. He was quiet, which scared Kathleen, since it was so unusual for him.

"Aren't you happy at all, Michael?" she asked quietly. "Don't you want a baby? I mean, true, it's too soon and a sin and a scandal, and everyone will flap their mouths about it. But it is . . . we can finally marry, Michael. Even if it doesn't suit my father. If there's no other way, then Father O'Brien will have a word with him. Or don't you want to marry me, Michael?" Kathleen choked out her last sentence.

Remorsefully, he came back to her and took her in his arms with his accustomed tenderness. "For heaven's sake, Kathleen, of course I want to marry you! I want nothing more. And I want the baby. It's just, it's just, so soon." Michael sighed, then squared himself. "Listen, Kathleen, give me two or three weeks, aye? You take good care of yourself, and by then, I'll arrange something. I'll get the money for America, Kathleen. I don't want to approach the cross here on hands and knees and be dragged in front of the priest, like a poor sinner. I don't want them talking about you—not yet anyway. Later, of course, when we send them money from America or visit them with you wearing silk dresses and a velvet hat." He laughed. "Yes, I'd like that. We'll ride in a coach with two horses through this impoverished backwater and laugh down at Trevallion, or we'll buy the whole wheat harvest off his damned lord and give it to the people."

Kathleen could not help but laugh along with him. "Oh, that would suit you fine, Michael Drury. You're a show-off. But it'll be enough for me if old O'Rearke drives us to church in his donkey cart and I come out as Mrs. Drury."

Michael kissed her. "I can't promise you this particular church or donkey, dearest. But we'll find a church where we can join in union with pride and dignity." He straightened his posture, seeming to grow several inches.

"I, Michael Drury, am going to be a father. An exalted feeling. And I already know it will be a son. A handsome boy with my hair and your eyes." His own eyes now shone as joyfully as Kathleen had hoped they would when she sensed she was pregnant.

"And if it is a girl? You won't like your child at all then?"

Michael spun her around, laughing. "If it's a girl, we'll have to become rich even faster. So we can build a tower to lock her in. For a daughter of yours will be so lovely that a glance at her will lame a man and make him her slave."

Hand in hand, they walked across the fields along the river, dreaming of their new life. Kathleen did not want to think about how Michael would raise the money for the journey and wedding. She only knew she trusted him. She wanted to—had to—trust him.

Chapter 3

In the middle of December, when the water of the Vartry River had frozen at the banks and the famine in Ireland was at its peak, three sacks of barley and rye disappeared from Trevallion's barn. The grain for Lord Wetherby's horses was kept there. He owned three powerful hunting horses that needed to eat more than the mules and donkeys did.

Ralph Trevallion did not notice the theft at first—only when the animals' feed sack was empty did he go into the barn to retrieve fresh supplies and take stock. Then, however, his rage knew no bounds. The steward galloped into the village, upbraiding the tenants. Enthroned on the back of the largest hunting horse, he glared down upon the men and women.

"I will not rest until I've found the thief!" he spat. "That man will be driven from house and home, and his no-good family with him. And you all'll help me! Aye, don't look at me like that; you'll do as I say. I'll be accepting information starting today, and you have a week to deliver the thief to me. If you don't find him, you'll all go. Don't even think I couldn't answer for it to His Lordship. A pack the likes of you roams the streets by the dozen. With a flick of the wrist, I could fill the houses again—and just with men, you hear. No families whose brats we also have to feed."

Everyone looked at the ground, afraid. Trevallion was right. Lord Wetherby did not care who worked his fields. The streets of Wicklow were full of men fleeing the famine. Their children had long since been claimed, often their wives too. They simply lay on the side of the street starving when they could not find anything more to eat.

"Now hold on, Ralph Trevallion." Father O'Brien announced himself with a stern voice. "It was just a few sacks of grain—animal feed, like you said. It's a shame you didn't offer it long ago. Don't you see what's happening here? Can't your horses eat hay?"

"And by my faith, we don't know anything about it!" added Ron Flannigan, an older foreman. "We all bake our bread in the same oven, Mr. Trevallion, and believe you me, everyone here would smell it if someone was cooking mush or roasting grain in one of the houses. We dream of such stuff, sir."

Trevallion glared at him. "I don't care a fig what you dream about. I can only assure you I'll become your worst nightmare if you don't toe the line. A week, people, or you'll feel it."

With that, he turned his horse, leaving behind a village full of confused and despairing tenant farmers.

"But we haven't done anything," Flannigan shouted after him. He repeated the sentence again a second time, quietly and hopelessly.

Father O'Brien shook his head. Then he saw Kathleen standing somewhat off to the side with her parents. "Mary Kathleen, you must speak with him," the priest told her quietly. "You, he brings you home on Sundays with your parents' blessing and . . ." The old priest looked Kathleen's body over meaningfully. "You also seem to be close to him besides," he remarked. "He'll listen to you. Ask him for mercy for the tenants. For, for the sake of his child."

Kathleen blushed deeply. "Father, Father, what, what child? I, I've never had more to do with Ralph Trevallion than anyone else here."

The priest looked the girl in the eye. His gaze was questioning, severe— but Kathleen also recognized sympathy. Whether it was for her, the tenants, the child, or even Trevallion—whose hope to win Kathleen's love would be destroyed—Kathleen did not know. Nor could she stand his gaze any longer. It was not Trevallion with whom she needed to speak. It was Michael.

Where was he anyway? Kathleen wondered impatiently. She had not seen him during Trevallion's tirade. But she was firmly convinced that her beloved had something to do with the theft of the grain. Surely it was related to gathering money for the wedding and passage to America. But innocent people could not pay for it. Michael had to give the grain back. There had to be a way to put it back in the barn just as slyly as it had been spirited away.

If Michael had already fled, if he had left nothing to chance, he would doubtlessly retrieve her sometime. She hoped it wasn't too late, but it was possible that he could long since have sold the sacks in Wicklow or elsewhere.

While the villagers were still discussing what had happened, Kathleen ran down to the river. She did not really have much hope that Michael was hiding in their love nest in the cold, but she had to try to find him. When she passed Jonny's oak, no bird call sounded, but she heard voices as soon as she got closer to their hiding place.

"So little?" asked Billy Rafferty, complaining. "Four pounds? You can't be serious. I thought we were splitting it fifty-fifty."

"I did want to," Michael said, sighing. "But they wouldn't pay more than twelve. And I need eight pounds. With my savings, that will do for passage. And Kathleen and I—"

"Oh, Kathleen and you? But what about me? No golden shores of America for Billy boy? That wasn't the plan, Michael." Rafferty's voice sounded threatening.

"Billy, I did tell you! You get my job as the distributor. Starting next week, the whiskey will be flowing again—and of a quality like it hasn't been in years. Rye and barley, Billy. Otherwise, they only work with fermented potatoes, my friend. Anyway, you'll be able to supply the best taverns; you'll make a fortune." Michael spoke with an angel's tongue.

"Then why don't you do it yourself?" Rafferty asked.

"Well, because I have to leave, Billy. Kathleen . . ."

Kathleen's heart pounded. Was he going to spill their secret now? Though these two young men likely shared darker secrets than that of her child.

She could not help herself; she stepped out of the thicket of reeds.

"Is it true, Michael? For whiskey? You stole the grain so whiskey could be made from it? While children starve all around you?"

Michael and Billy jumped. They looked at Kathleen—at once guilty and defiant.

"Where else should I have sold it?" asked Michael. "They would have caught me right away if I'd tried anywhere else. The men in the mountains, they keep their mouths shut; never fear. They won't tell their lordships. They have their honor, Kathleen. No one talks; no one is betrayed."

"Except for Billy Rafferty," Billy grumbled. "You can do as you like with me."

"Oh, shut your mouth, Billy!" Michael yelled at him. "You've gotten plenty of money for loading three sacks of grain on a mule. I did the rest, as you know. Now pack your things and think about your tidy profit this weekend in Wicklow. You can take over this very Saturday. But think up a good excuse. Can't you play the tin whistle? Just say I got you a job playing music in the tavern."

Reluctantly, Rafferty withdrew. He would have liked to haggle for more money, but he did not like the thunderclouds in Kathleen's eyes. A woman's scolding was the last thing he needed. And besides, he felt more like celebrating than fighting. Four good English pounds in his hand! He was rich. Billy Rafferty forgot his anger and strolled back to the village, whistling.

"You want to send this idiot to Wicklow with whiskey?" Kathleen asked, horrified. "Michael, he'll give the scheme away as soon as he unpacks the stuff. If he doesn't choke drinking it all down on the way. Fine, it doesn't bother me if Billy Rafferty makes himself miserable. But you and I, Michael, we can't let Trevallion throw the families in the village out on the street."

Kathleen told him about Trevallion's appearance in front of the church.

Michael bit his lip. "He won't really do it," he mused. "But you're right—we ought to make ourselves scarce before someone suspects something and talks. The best thing would be to disappear tonight." Michael tried to put his arm around her.

Kathleen shook him off indignantly. "And if Trevallion does do it?" she yelled at him, disgusted at his cold-bloodedness. "Especially if I run out on him too. He has hopes—likely more than I supposed if I've understood Father O'Brien right. It'll put him in a rage if I up and vanish. Then he'll do even worse to the village."

Michael shook his head. "No. When I've vanished, he'll know who stole the grain. So he won't need to punish the others." His eyes flashed. "I'll just drop off a bottle of whiskey in the barn for him. As a thank you." He laughed.

Kathleen did not find any of it funny. "Michael, it's no good. We can't make our happiness off the unhappiness of others. Where would the villagers go? There's no work anywhere. It's bad enough you stole, and worse Trevallion's grain ended up in an illegal distiller's vat instead of the children's stomachs."

Michael shrugged. "I'll confess it," he assured her. "Sometime. But Kathleen, I'm thinking of our baby before anything. It ought to grow up in a better country where it needn't starve. I can't get the grain back from the vat and into the sacks. So, do you want to go with me now or not?" He wrapped her in his arms.

Kathleen briefly gave in to Michael's tender, comforting embrace. But then she found her way back to reality.

"Of course I'm coming with you!" she said. "But not right away. Not this week, when the village and Trevallion's head are cooking hotter than those distiller's vats. Father O'Brien's right: I should play nice with Trevallion. Try to distract him, make him think of other things. Yes, we'll do it that way; that's how we can save the village. You'll disappear before the week's out. Go with your idiot friend to Wicklow on Saturday and just stay there. Then people will suspect you, and the tenants will be out of the woods."

"And you?" he asked. "I'm supposed to leave you alone with Trevallion?"

Kathleen rolled her eyes. "God almighty, Michael, I'm not going to just give myself to him. I'll walk with him through the village, butter him up a bit, give him some hope . . . and then I'll come to Wicklow as soon as things have settled down. Just tell me where to find you."

Kathleen felt better having made this plan. This would work. But only if Michael played along.

Michael chewed thoughtfully on his upper lip. He liked his plan much better. But the village was also his home. The people there were close to his heart. His mother and his siblings . . . but they'd be driven out of house and home anyway when the villagers pointed their fingers at Michael. That hurt Michael—but his mother knew where his father was waiting for them. True, she would no longer be able to pray at church every day, but in exchange, the children would surely get more to eat in the mountains.

"All right, fine," he said reluctantly. "A week, Kathleen, but not a day more. You'll find me at Barney's Tavern. It's a bar on High Street; can't miss it."

***

Trevallion used the "Week of Truth," as he called it, to thoroughly mistreat the tenants. In the winter, there was little farm work to do, and the famine had so weakened the people that one could hardly ask anything of them. But that week, Trevallion made them all line up. They had to clean out the stables, haul rocks to expand the fences around the fields, and chop wood for the manor's fireplace.

"The fires need to be stoked, whether the lord's here or not," Trevallion explained. "Otherwise, mold will form in the walls. And the house can't be allowed to cool down, lest His Lordship decide to spend Christmas here after all."

That had never happened, but now the villagers almost wished for it. Lord Wetherby might be more amenable to reason than his overzealous steward. Gráinne claimed the lady, at least, was reasonable. Indeed, Kathleen, too, had come to know the young noblewoman as a superficial but ultimately good-natured creature. Surely she would not sit idly by while her farmers' children starved.

Saturday evening, Michael was half-frozen and exhausted from breaking rocks in the cold when he finally fetched the gardener's donkey. A few of the farmers watched him in silence, noting that this time Billy Rafferty was climbing onto the beast behind him.

"Where do you think you're going, Rafferty?" Ron Flannigan asked suspiciously. "A tour through the pubs in Wicklow? Do you have money to drink away, boy?"

Michael shook his head and, pointing to the tin whistle in Billy's pocket, answered for his friend. "I need him for the band, Ron. There's more money to be made together. They hardly pay a fiddler on his own."

Flannigan furrowed his brow. "And so you take the worst whistle player? Who's going to pay Billy for his playing? More like they'll give him something to stop."

The farmers laughed.

Michael laughed along. "People like the sound to be a bit rough around the edges," he said. "I know what I'm doing."

Ron Flannigan watched as they rode off. "Do you, now?" he finally murmured.

Kathleen had a hard time flirting, but she forced herself to do just that with Trevallion. She smiled at him when he walked into church on Sunday. Father O'Brien preached about forgiveness and clemency. In the end, he concluded, only God was the true judge, and no sinner could escape him, even if he avoided worldly judgment. The old priest even winked at Kathleen when she joined Trevallion immediately after Mass and spoke to him amicably. Did he thereby make himself guilty of the sin of procurement?

It amused Kathleen. She tried to maintain the light in her eyes, the smile on her lips, and the slight blush of her cheeks for Trevallion. For the first time, she allowed him to take her strolling all around the village without her parents by her side. She agreed with him in flattering terms as he described again and again how useful he was to his lord, how sure his station as steward was, and how respected the woman he took for his wife would be.

Kathleen was exhausted from all the smiling and lying when Trevallion finally delivered her to her parents' house. During the stroll she had experienced a strange sensation. It was almost as if she had not been alone with the steward, as if she were being watched. Had Michael sent Jonny to follow her?

That might have been the case. It had been hard getting her beloved to accept her mission with Trevallion. And for her part, Kathleen worried about Michael. Billy Rafferty had been at Mass that morning. He kneeled, visibly tired, next to his mother, who seemed rather perturbed. Kathleen could understand. Particularly in times like these, it was considered disgraceful to get drunk. Michael had never come to church on Sunday mornings any the worse for wear. Of course, the tavern owner would give the musicians a beer or two, but whoever got drunk on whiskey did not keep his job long.

Billy Rafferty did not seem to think that far ahead. Any form of strategy was foreign to him; Kathleen still thought him the worst choice for Michael's successor in the whiskey business.

But for Michael's sake, Billy's headache might not prove such a bad thing. The priest and the other villagers would assume that Michael, too, had been drinking the night before and thus had not come to Mass. Not until work on Monday morning would they finally note his absence.

In front of the O'Donnells' house, Trevallion handed Kathleen another sack of flour. "I know you won't take it, Mary Kathleen," he said formally. "You want to be sure no one will think you're for sale. But I do wish you would someday feel enough for me that my gifts would appear meaningless compared to my kiss."

The steward approached her, but Kathleen stepped back, startled. She felt panic at the idea of Trevallion's kiss—and not just because the thought of his lips on hers disgusted her. It was also because she was afraid of whoever might be following her. Little Jonny would not do anything dangerous. Nothing more could be expected from him than some stupid boyish prank, like a shot from his sling. He never hit anyway. But what if it was Brian who was following her?

What if it was Michael himself?

Kathleen lowered her eyes. "Mr. Trevallion," she said quietly. "Please, please, sir, I'm only sixteen. That's, that's too young for love." She blushed.

Trevallion smiled. "Oh, of course. I forgot myself."

Kathleen did not know if he meant it with affection or scorn.

"Then it's surely only a rumor that you have feelings for that village boy?" It sounded threatening.

Kathleen tried to lower her head even more demurely—and only then raised her eyes. She even managed a mischievous smile.

"My feelings might tend elsewhere, sir," she said. "But my mother instructed me to keep my eye on the pantry, too, when thinking of love."

Trevallion laughed resoundingly. "My, but you're a charming maid, Mary Kathleen."

He reached into his bag and added a packet of sugar to the sack of flour. "Here. Though it can't be sweeter than your lips."

Kathleen thanked heaven when she was finally able to flee into her family's small house. She knew they would be waiting impatiently, and that they would be ecstatic over Trevallion's wooing.

Sugar and flour. Now Kathleen could bake scones herself, though she feared they would taste bitter because of how she'd come by the ingredients.

***

On the Monday after Michael's disappearance, Kathleen continued her work in the manor as usual. Together with Gráinne, she lit the fireplaces, whose flames cast ghostly shadows on the walls.

At least it was warm for the women—and Trevallion did not bother them. Moreover, Kathleen stole a few moments to look more carefully at the Wetherbys' heavy velvet curtains and valuable furniture—she even dared to sit in one of the chairs, imagining an afternoon tea to which she had invited friends. If Michael was right, she, too, would one day have such lovely things, and a housemaid would light her fireplaces. In the New World, she would be free; she could earn money, become rich.

Kathleen gave in to her dreams for a few heartbeats—or rather, to Michael's dreams. She did not need a manor herself, or heavy chairs or velvet curtains. Kathleen would have been content with a cottage—a cozy little house, covered in ivy, with a cute garden where she could grow vegetables and trees. It should have a nice living room and a bedroom, a kitchen, and perhaps another room for the children. Not just one tiny room filled with smoke from the single fireplace as in her parents' house.

It suddenly dawned on Kathleen that she was dreaming of Ralph Trevallion's house. The steward lived in just such a cottage a little removed from the village and manor.

No! She chided herself for her thoughts. No house could ever make her marry someone as hard-hearted as Trevallion. Not to mention that she was carrying Michael's child.

As Kathleen stood up somewhat cumbersomely from the armchair to return to her work, she heard loud voices in the house.

"Oh, my Lord, no! Oh, merciful Mary!" said Gráinne. The old cook and housekeeper was screaming and moaning as if her heart had been broken.

Kathleen ran down the stairs and found Gráinne in the manor's vestibule, sunk down on the lowest step, lamenting and cursing.

"I can't do anything about it, Gráinne," Ron Flannigan was saying, his hand awkwardly on the old woman's shoulder. "I just thought I'd tell you myself. Before Trevallion hits you with it. And before, before . . ."

"Before the soldiers come? Before they—oh no, they wouldn't! They're not going to throw me out, are they? Tear down my house? Merciful God, Ron, I've eight other children."

Ron Flannigan shook his head barely noticeably. In his voice and entire comportment lay true regret. "I know it well, Gráinne. You're a good woman, and they're all good children. But you know the law."

"English law," Gráinne spat. "Ron, I've served the Wetherbys. These many years, I've always been true, never stolen—well, no more than a few bites of bread. If only the lord and lady were here. If I could throw myself at the lady's feet. She'd have mercy, to be sure."

"What's going on here?" Kathleen asked. "What can be so awful, Gráinne, that—"

A look at Ron Flannigan's face silenced her. Any encouraging word was inappropriate just then.

"They've arrested Billy Rafferty," Ron explained. "They're accusing him of stealing Trevallion's grain."

"But it wasn't him!" howled Gráinne. "Good Lord, you all know my Billy. A little braggart, but just like a rooster—all talk. He'd never come up with the idea of stealing the lord's grain. Who'd he sell it to anyway?"

"We don't know," Ron said seriously. "But they found money on him. More than three pounds; he can't have made it anywhere else. Certainly not playing the tin whistle."

"Playing the tin whistle!" yelled Gráinne. "The fiddler, that no-good Drury boy. I'd bet he . . ."

"Michael Drury has disappeared," said Ron. "And yes, we can assume he had something to do with it. But your Billy was in Wicklow on Saturday, Gráinne, and came home drunk. And last night he got into his cups again, with friends; he paid for half the village. This morning at work they all smelled of rotgut, and your Billy could not stand up straight. Are you surprised Trevallion was asking about it? No one told him, if that's what you're thinking, Gráinne. Even though he spilled a few things last night to his drinking buddies around the fire. About the whiskey, the distillers, his wonderful new job in Wicklow."

"Merciful Mother of God, if he tells that to the redcoats!" Gráinne crossed herself at the thought of English soldiers.

Ron sighed. "They'll beat it out of him sooner or later," he said. "But maybe it'd be better for him to talk. So far they're blaming him alone. When it turns out that the Drury boy was involved too . . ."

An icy chill shot up Kathleen's spine. Billy would betray Michael. It was as inevitable as the priest's amen during Mass. He might even betray her as well. After all, he knew why Michael had risked stealing. And more than anything—merciful God—she hoped he knew nothing about Barney's Tavern.

Kathleen's mind raced. She had to warn Michael. She needed to get to Wicklow before the soldiers interrogated Billy. And then it would be best just to stay with him. She could not do any more anyway. Now it all lay in Billy Rafferty's hands as to whether her family would be driven from house and home. When Trevallion learned that she had fled with Michael, he would accuse the O'Donnells of complicity.

Kathleen ran outside. Gráinne would not look for her; she now had bigger worries than the fireplaces in the manor. And Ron had hardly noticed her; he seemed not to know anything about her and Michael.

Heedless, Kathleen ran out onto the road. At least she had put on her shawl against the winter cold. There were a few things from her parents' house she would have liked to bring along, but there was no chance of that now. Her mother and siblings were surely at home, and they would be able to tell that something was troubling her.

Kathleen said adieu to them all in her heart. Then, determined, she turned toward Wicklow.

Chapter 4

The road to Wicklow stretched out long and wide before Kathleen. She sometimes walked and sometimes ran, moving as fast as she could. Still, anyone on horseback would easily overtake her, as two riders already had. Kathleen tried to remain calm as she continued along the road. It would grow dark before she reached town.

Suddenly, she heard a carriage rolling up behind her. Perhaps Billy was already being taken to prison in Wicklow. Half fearful and half hopeful, she turned to look and saw two powerful dappled horses in front of the cart and a familiar man on the box. It was Ian Coltrane, son of the livestock trader.

"Well, well, who do we have here?" Ian grinned down at her. "If it isn't little Kathleen O'Donnell. Whither goest thou, sweetheart?"

Kathleen forced herself to smile back. Ian Coltrane was handsome, a swarthy young man with flashing eyes. He was around twenty years old, somewhat older than Michael. He looked a bit like Michael, except his eyes were black like coal. People even whispered that the Coltranes had Gypsy blood.

Where his father, Patrick Coltrane, dealt in sheep and cattle, Ian specialized in horse trading. And he must have been making good money: his plaid jacket was new and padded and warm, his pants were made of leather, and his boots were solid. Kathleen looked at them almost enviously. Her own shoes were worn and not warm enough. Her feet already felt like ice blocks.

"To, to Wicklow," she answered. "I'm, I'm visiting an aunt. She's sick."

Ian grinned. "So your mother sent you off with nothing but a woolen shawl?" he said, looking at Kathleen's empty hands and her clothes, too thin for such a journey.

Kathleen blushed. Of course, she should have thought about that. True, the O'Donnells were poor, but her mother would have managed a little something for a sick relative, and surely she would have found a coat to better equip Kathleen for the cold. Likewise, Kathleen would have worn her Sunday dress for a visit to town.

"We, we don't have anything to give," she explained briefly. "I'm going to offer my aunt comfort and company."

Ian laughed. "I could use some of that as well," he teased her. "So if you'd like to offer me a bit, there's still a spot open next to me." He knocked on the box.

There was also a bench in the back of the two-wheeled cart where Kathleen would have much preferred to sit. But saddlery and tools lay strewn about, and beggars could not be choosers. So she climbed onto the box and took a seat next to Ian. He had the horses trot onward again. Behind the cart followed two more horses and a mule.

"And, and you?" Kathleen asked, though she was not at all interested. "Where are you going?"

Ian raised his eyebrows. "Where does it look like? Do you think I'm taking the nags for a walk? The horse market in Wicklow. Early morning in the square off the wharf. I hope I can make some money from these three."

Kathleen glanced at the horses. She knew one of them.

"The black one isn't young anymore, is he?" she asked.

That horse had pulled the cobbler's cart since Kathleen was a little girl. Or was she mistaken? Wasn't the cobbler's horse already gray around the eyes? And didn't it have a saddle sore on its back that was white? The horse that was now behind the cart was a gleaming black.

"That one? He's six years old and not a day more." Ian acted insulted. "Look at his teeth if you don't believe me."

Kathleen shrugged. The teeth would not have told her anything, but she could have sworn she had picked dandelions when it was waiting for its master in front of the cobbler's workshop. Those were better days, when people did not cook the weeds on the roadside into soup. The horse had a sort of twirled mustache over its nostrils. Kathleen had never seen that on an animal before, and the cobbler must have thought it peculiar, too, or he would not have called the horse Blackbeard. But Kathleen did not want to argue with Ian. She was much too happy about getting a ride for that. The dappled horses trotted merrily onward. Surely, it was not more than an hour or so to Wicklow.

So Kathleen tried to move the conversation from the horses to more innocuous subjects. She asked about Ian's father, whose business, according to Ian, was going rather badly.

"Doesn't have any money at the moment," Ian said casually.

This surprised Kathleen. Ian's father was a tenant of Lord Wetherby too, but he was in a much better position than the others. Patrick Coltrane was not working off his rent, since he paid it with his income from livestock trading.

"At least not from cows and sheep," Ian added, almost contemptuously. "What would they eat anyway? People are digging up the last roots themselves, after all."

"But you can sell horses?" Kathleen wondered.

Ian laughed. "There are always a few rich gentlemen. In Wicklow and Dublin, some still need a horse—or want one. You just need to make it clear to them that a horse'll make a lord out of a chandler. And in the country, the nags are cheap now."

Kathleen wondered just how much these chandlers knew about horses. They might well buy old Blackbeard once Ian made them believe it came from Lord Wetherby's stables.

"But I won't be staying here long," Ian ultimately revealed to her. "Not much money in this country. Enough to live, but if you want a bit more, no, I'm off overseas. I want to make a fortune."

"Really?" Kathleen asked, suddenly interested.

Ian was the first she'd heard speak of emigrating out of true excitement rather than pure need.

"A, a friend of mine also talks about that," she said. "And I, I . . ."

Ian looked at her curiously. "You want to as well? Well, that makes you the exception. Most of the girls you talk to about the colonies only tremble in fright."

"Well, there is the crossing."

Ian snorted. "The crossing. Fine, it's not going to be cozy, and there won't be much to eat. But compared to what you get to eat here, it would likely be better. Although you seem to me to be eating rather well, sweetheart. You are a lovely maid. And one with such vitality."

They rode on for a while in silence. Then Ian looked at Kathleen, who was shaking with cold, with new interest.

"You cold, sweetheart?" he asked, seeming concerned. He produced a blanket and put it around Kathleen's shoulders, pulling her a little closer as he did. "Come now, I'll keep you warm."

Kathleen was relieved they had just passed the sign for Wicklow.

Ian's hand wandered underneath the blanket, across Kathleen's shoulders and toward her neckline.

Kathleen pushed away from him.

"Could you, could you let me down here, please?" she asked.

Ian laughed. "Here? But we're still practically in the wilderness, sweetheart."

Indeed, this was a suburb in which cute cottages and gardens lay between small fields. They might still be a mile or two from the town center, the wharf, and Barney's Tavern.

"My aunt, she lives around here somewhere," Kathleen claimed.

"Oh right, the aunt," Ian mocked her. "Shouldn't I take you to her door?"

Kathleen shook her head. "No, no thanks. You've done enough; that is, I've had enough; I mean, I've imposed enough on your kindness. I can walk the rest of the way. Thank you very much, Ian."

Ian arched his brows and tugged on the reins. The team stopped at once. "If you insist, your wish is my command. And perhaps we'll see each other around." He tipped his cap.

Kathleen clambered down from the box, forcing herself to smile at him. "Sure, on Sunday in church, if you're ever there."

Even if she were going to be back at the village for church, Patrick and Ian Coltrane often spent their weekends at livestock markets. This was the reason Ian likely did not know about her situation with Ralph Trevallion. Otherwise, he surely would have teased her about it.

Ian saluted once more before bringing the horses back to a trot. Kathleen desperately hoped never to see him again.

On the horse cart's box, she had been nearly as cold as on foot. Now she had to force herself, quite stiff and exhausted, to put one foot in front of the other. But surely, it could not be much farther.

Indeed, it was not even completely dark when Kathleen reached High Street. She asked the very first passerby about Barney's Tavern.

He pointed out the way to her. "You can't miss it, child, just after the first turn. But what do you want with that place? You could earn more in others."

Kathleen could have died when she realized what the man had thought she was. She hastened her steps even more. When she finally reached the tavern, she was out of breath. She was hardly cold anymore.

Sighing with relief, she pushed the door open and was assailed by a gust of warm, stale air reeking of whiskey, beer, and tobacco. Kathleen struggled against the nausea that slowly gripped her. It did not seem that the baby inside her wanted to grow into a man who spent half his life in a tavern.

"What splendor in our poor hovel." A small, rotund man greeted her from behind the bar. "Golden tresses, alabaster skin, and eyes as green as Irish fields. If you're an illusion, lovely, you can stay, but otherwise this place is just for the boys."

Most taverns did not let women inside.

Kathleen forced another smile. "I'm Kathleen O'Donnell," she introduced herself. "I need to talk to Michael Drury."

The short, fat man eyed her in recognition. "Barney," he introduced himself. "You're the girl he wants to run away with? All due respect, but you could've caught a better man. How about me, cutie? At least I can offer you something. A tavern always has business."

Kathleen felt her anger rising. That was the last straw. She did not want to smile or play nice anymore. She wanted to see Michael.

"Listen," she said in a commanding tone. "I need to warn Michael. The redcoats are after him. So no games now, please."

The fat man grew serious at once. "Soldiers, girl? Damn it. I knew something was wrong. But no, 'Just a room for a few days, Barney! Just till my girl can break free. It's not easy, you know, for a girl like that, saying good-bye to her family.' He talked with a silver tongue, that one. And I got taken in. And in return he brings the English lobsters to my tavern?" Barney turned and roared into the room behind the barroom. "Michael!"

When he got no answer, he ran back there. Kathleen did not hesitate long. She followed him through the greasy kitchen and into a hallway that led to several doors.

"Michael!" Barney's call could not be ignored, and indeed, one of the doors finally opened. Michael stepped outside.

"Could you yell any louder, Barney?" he asked grumpily, but then he saw Kathleen behind the fat barman.

"Kathleen! I take it all back, Barney. She justifies any loudness. Aye, trumpeters and drummers should precede her wherever she goes, that the unworthy may turn away their gaze before they're blinded by too much beauty. Kathleen, that went faster than I'd dare dream." Michael moved to take her in his arms, but she forced herself to push him away.

"Michael, there's no time for that. They've arrested Billy. And he'll talk. We have to go!"

"They have Billy? Damn it, that little idiot. Couldn't put down the bottle, could he? And I warned him, I—"

"Michael!" Kathleen almost screamed. "Does he know about this hiding place?"

"I'd also like to know if he does," Barney said with the look of an angry bull terrier.

Michael shrugged. "I might have mentioned it. At least, well, we were here Saturday, right? If he names all the pubs . . ."

"I'm ruined!" cried Barney. "I have to get rid of the bottles. If they find them here, let alone if they find you . . . Just get out of here, Michael Drury!"

Michael began to gather his things. But while he was still tying his bundle and Barney was hurrying down the hall with his second armful of moonshine whiskey bottles, a young boy shot through the kitchen.

"Barney, Da sent me. You know, from The Finest Horse. The lobsters are there about the whiskey. And Michael Drury. You should . . ."

Barney cried out for heaven's help and ran all the faster while Michael looked around like a cornered beast.

"Kathleen, we need to get out of here. Fast. The Finest Horse is two doors down. When they're done there, they'll come here. Listen, you'll go first. From here, through the barroom."

"And you?" Kathleen stood there as if frozen.

"I'll go out the back door. We'll meet at the wharf. I'll find you." Michael tossed his bundle over his shoulder, but then something occurred to him. He rummaged a purse out of his pocket and pressed it into Kathleen's hand.

"Here, take that. Quick, what are you waiting for?" Michael pushed her into the hall.

"But, but . . ."

"No buts. Go, Kathleen. We'll meet later." Michael put a coin in the boy's hand. "Here, Harry. Take the lady to safety."

Voices could now be heard from the barroom. Loud voices, used to giving orders. Michael ran down the corridor. Little Harry, a smart, red-haired boy with the gentle, round face of a cherub, pulled Kathleen in the other direction. She had just enough time to cover her hair with her shawl before she found herself standing in front of two soldiers. The redcoats shoved her aside rudely and began tearing open the doors to the back rooms. As if numb, Kathleen followed Harry into the barroom, where immediately a wave of nausea swept over her again. This time it was because of not only the stench but also her fear.

Two more soldiers held the drunkards in check. "No one leaves the room until we know who you are and where you come from," one of them growled.

A few men fished for identification papers; others stumbled through explanations. Kathleen went pale with horror. She had no way of proving who she was. They would arrest her; they would find out where she came from and lock her up as Michael's accomplice.

Cries could be heard from the yard behind the tavern. But Michael had run away. Still Kathleen trembled.

But then she felt Harry's small, warm hand in hers. "Let's go, Ma. He's not here," said the little boy with a sweet voice. "Only the soldiers are here. Ma, just look at the pretty uniforms they have."

The little boy looked at the men with innocent admiration—pinching Kathleen's hand at the same time, however.

"Cry," he said out of the side of his mouth.

Kathleen sobbed. It was much easier to do that than it had been to produce the forced smiles of the previous hours.

Harry pulled her toward the door. "Good sirs, let us pass!" He turned to the square-shouldered soldier guarding the door. "We didn't find my da here. But we have to keep looking; otherwise he'll drink away all the money Grandda gave us."

The boy tugged emphatically on Kathleen's dress. She had to play along. She could not leave it to the child alone to lie their way out of there.

Kathleen whimpered. "He wanted to bet it on horses," she complained. "Can you imagine that, good sirs? And yet it was for our debts. And the farm, dear sirs. If we don't find Paddy soon, our landlord will throw us out on the street."

Now Harry cried too. His howls could have softened stones. The soldier cleared the door. The wailing likely played on his nerves, and he showed no interest in the woman. So Billy did not seem to have mentioned Kathleen when he had betrayed Michael. That was something, at least.

"Well, get going, woman," the soldier grumbled. "And I hope for your sake you find the man, but that's how they are, your Paddys and Kevins. Drinking and gambling good-for-nothings, the lot of them."

Kathleen was no longer listening. She hardly managed to stammer a thank-you as Harry pulled her out of the tavern with many a "God will reward you for it, sirs." Outside, his wailing stopped at once.

"Where to now?" Harry asked Kathleen.

***

Michael fled through the hallway. The back door was easy to find—after all, Barney had been running back and forth through it with the whiskey bottles. However, the door did not open to freedom but to a high-walled yard.

Michael squinted in the twilight as he hastened outside. There had to be a door or a gate. But the yard was filled with junk—empty bottles and barrels, old tables and chairs. Barney seemed to toss everything there that he could no longer use but did not want to throw away. Michael kept looking in the half-light and finally saw the gate.

Michael ran at the solid wooden gate, throwing himself against it—and found it locked. In desperation, he looked for the handle. Perhaps the key was already in the lock.

"Barney!"

It was useless. Barney was either back in the tavern, claiming innocence, or he had already escaped through this gate himself, knowing full well that he was throwing Michael to the wolves when he closed the gate behind him.

Back in the building, the redcoats were going through the rooms. It was only a question of time before they would come into the yard. Michael had to make a quick decision. Hide, or try to escape over the wall? The first was nonsensical; the men would search the whole tavern. Not to mention the space in the yard; where else would one hide moonshine? But there might be a way out over the wall if he climbed onto one of the barrels—or better yet, a barrel on top of one of the old tables.

Michael worked frantically. The first table broke under the barrel, but the second held. Michael quickly climbed on top of the table, but to get onto the barrel from the table required a balancing act. And the soldiers were already there. Michael prayed they would not spot him immediately in the near darkness, but the two men carried lanterns.

"There he is!"

Michael clambered onto the barrel with the courage of the desperate and heaved himself up so he could climb over the wall. A shot rang out. Michael smelled gunpowder smoke, but he did not let up in his efforts.

Yet—it was too late. One of the soldiers was already beside him and kicked the table and the barrel out from under him. Michael tried to hold onto the ledge of the wall, but the stone was slick from icy rain that had recently fallen. Michael's fingers slipped, and he fell hard on the ground.

"Michael Drury?" the soldier asked, pulling him to his feet.

Michael did not say a word.

***

"I don't know. Aren't you supposed to be looking after me?" whispered Kathleen. "To, to the wharf. If Michael . . ."

"If they don't nab him," Harry mused pessimistically. "Better find that out first. Before he tells them you're waiting at the wharf."

"He would never betray me!"

Harry shrugged. As he did, he seemed to come up with an idea. "Listen, lady, follow me. I'll take you to Daisy's. You won't stand out there—well, a bit, the way you look. But it'll do. Just don't show her your purse, or you won't have it anymore."

The boy pushed her energetically into a side street, but Kathleen resisted when she heard a loud noise from Barney's Tavern.

A pop. A shot.

"Michael! Michael! I need to go to him," howled Kathleen.

Harry held on to her dress with unexpected strength. "No way! I just got you out, and you want to go right back in? Are you mad? They'll probably hunt me down, too, once you give yourself away."

"But I . . ."

Harry was just as curious as Kathleen was desperate, but he held her out of sight. The two of them peered around the corner at the pub, from where they heard more noise and shouting. And then the door flew open. Two redcoats dragged out a man. He was resisting. Michael was in chains but seemingly unhurt.

"I told you they'd catch him," Harry said. Then he took Kathleen's hand. "Come on, you can't do any more for him. They won't hang him right away. Tomorrow you can ask where they took him. But for now, we need to get away."

Kathleen could not think anymore. She was frozen with fear and horror over Michael's fate. What would they do to him? They would not hang him right away? Surely they would not hang anyone for stealing three sacks of grain.

Harry pulled her through a doorway over which hung a red-painted sign that said "Daisy's," nothing more. But it did not take much imagination to picture what went on behind the door.

Kathleen's horror grew. "But this is, I can't . . ."

"Miss Daisy won't bite." The boy soothed her. "Nor the girls, for that matter. Anyway, they don't steal from the poor, and they always give me candy. So come on."

Kathleen entered the dark hallway behind the door, her heart pounding. Harry steered her up a staircase that led to another, narrower corridor along which were several doors. From behind one of the doors came the sound of laughing and chatter. Harry knocked, pushing the door open when no one responded.

"Miss Daisy? There's a girl here, from the country. Michael Drury, the whiskey distiller . . . she's his sweetheart. They just nabbed him, and now she doesn't know where to go."

Kathleen kept her head lowered, but she peered out anxiously from under her shawl. Her gaze fell on a room full of mirrors, gewgaws, and bric-a-brac. It seemed to be a sort of dressing room. Four or five girls, just barely dressed, were—to Kathleen's horror—in the middle of transforming into colorful birds of paradise with the help of bright red garter belts and ruffled dresses in flashy colors. One girl was lacing her corset; another was looking in a mirror and putting on her makeup.

Kathleen imagined the road to hell was like this, or similar. But the girls did not seem at all diabolical; rather, they looked quite normal. A few were also not as young as they looked at first glance. Miss Daisy had certainly already passed forty.

"And we're supposed to hide her? What is this, an inn?" Miss Daisy asked.

"Not hide," whispered Kathleen. "No one, no one is looking for me. And . . . I didn't want . . . I . . . I can just go." She turned around.

The woman laughed. "Oh, and where'll you go? A young girl, all alone on the street, in this quarter? Out there, the boys will all too gladly take for free what they have to pay for here. I know Michael; he's an honest one. His whiskey was always the best, especially the last batch."

Kathleen sighed. So Michael had delivered his moonshine to this establishment as well. How did the women pay for it? She felt something almost like rage arise within her.

The word "whiskey" seemed to make Miss Daisy think of something. She quickly drew a bottle out from under one of the dressing tables, poured a glass, and handed it to Kathleen.

"Here, drink. You look like you've seen a ghost."

"I should probably get going," said Harry.

Miss Daisy smiled at him and pulled some candy from the same hiding place. "Not without some provisions, my boy," she laughed. "The only man all of us here love," she explained, turning to Kathleen. "The girls are already fighting over who gets to take his virginity."

Kathleen blushed again, but Harry grinned at the good-natured madam.

"Not a chance, Miss Daisy. I'm looking for a proper girl like Michael did. That's what he told me: 'Harry, look for a good girl.' Then he mooned over his sweetheart and her beautiful eyes, green like Irish glens, and her golden hair."

Miss Daisy laughed even louder and pulled the shawl playfully from Kathleen's head. The shawl fell down to her shoulders, giving a clear view of Kathleen's hair and face.

Miss Daisy whistled; a few of the girls let out sounds of amazement as well.

"My lands, you," the madam managed. "A girl comes up from the country and you expect a shy little mouse. But you look like a real princess. He's kept you well fed, that Michael."

Miss Daisy looked longer at Kathleen's body. Kathleen pulled the shawl lower. Her stomach was still rather flat, but her gesture alone led Miss Daisy to draw the right conclusion.

"Oh, my little one. And here I hoped I might convince you to do some work, but you wouldn't be much use for long. Is Michael the lucky man?"

Kathleen yelled, "Of course it's Michael! What do you think? I, we, we were going to marry in America. We . . ."

Suddenly Kathleen felt like crying. She sobbed into the whiskey Daisy handed her, and despite her condition, she took the smallest of sips. It was her first-ever taste of whiskey, and it burned her throat like fire. She coughed.

"Well, nothing more is likely to come of that," said Miss Daisy. "You won't see him again anytime soon—at least not as a free man. You can visit him in prison if you give the guard a few pence. But by the time they let him out—if they even do—the baby will be grown."

"If they even do?" Kathleen asked, horrified. "Do you think they'll hang him? My God, they can't hang him for taking three sacks of grain."

"He stole too?" sighed Daisy. "Dearie, dearie. But no, they won't hang him. Just ship him out. Botany Bay, Van Diemen's Land. Ever heard of 'em, child?"

Kathleen tried at once to nod and shake her head. Naturally she had heard of the colonies. Of Australia, where prisoners were sent as forced labor. But they couldn't do that to Michael.

"If you get more than seven years, you've got it tough," said Daisy. "And they'll easily slap him with that. Even if he hadn't stolen. It's a shame, and I'm sorry for you. You can stay here if you want. How many months has it been anyway? Still early, isn't it? You can still get rid of it."

Kathleen stared at her. Get rid of her child? Was the woman in her right mind?

"I know a woman who does it well, so that girls hardly ever bite the dust. But fine, fine, I get it: there's no question. You'll be sorry, child."

Kathleen started crying again. Now the other girls started gathering around her. One laid a comforting arm around her. Kathleen shuddered at her luridly made-up face, but under all the powder and blush, she saw the features of an older woman who seemed much more motherly than Daisy.

"Now, let the little thing catch her breath first," the woman soothed. "She doesn't even know what she wants."

"Michael," sobbed Kathleen. "I want Michael, and the baby needs him. They can't . . ."

"Hush, hush." The woman rocked her back and forth. "Why don't we go look for that Michael of yours tomorrow?"

Kathleen looked up at her hopefully. "Look for him? You mean visit him? Where? In . . ."

"In prison, dearie. You can say it. But first we need to find him. It might be that they're holding him here, or they might take him back to your village. Or to Dublin. But I doubt it, at least not right away. In any case, we'll ask around. Maybe you'll get a chance to see him. But no more crying now; it's not good for the little one in there for Mommy to be sad."

The woman took one of the greasy cosmetic rags from the table and wiped Kathleen's tears away. "Anyway, I'm Bridget. No need to stand on ceremony with me. What's your name?"

"Kathleen," she whispered. "Mary Kathleen."

She had never before needed the Mother of God's help so desperately.

Chapter 5

Kathleen slept in the whores' dressing room, atop a mountain of worn ruffled dresses that stank of sweat and cheap perfume. Of course, she would have preferred not to touch anything that had surely seen sinful use. She wrapped herself in her shawl and in a blanket Bridget had brought her, which, though it was ragged, smelled clean.

Despite how tired she was, Kathleen woke once or twice when a man laughed or a woman squealed. Their voices sounded increasingly rollicking and drunk as the night wore on.

Yet Bridget seemed wide awake and cheerful and not particularly haggard when she woke Kathleen the next morning. She also looked much more trustworthy than she had the evening before. She had swapped her flashy red dress for a rather banal blue one, and she wore a tidy hat on top of her thick, curly brown hair. If she hadn't worn a layer of powder to try to conceal the traces of too many nights that had gone too late, she could have been taken for a typical housewife.

"Come on, Mary Kathleen," she said with a smile. "Shall we see what we can do for that Michael of yours?"

Kathleen ran a hand through her hair. She knew it must look terrible. Just like her worn and now dirty and wrinkled dress. How had she ever been able to fall asleep on that pile of laundry? Surely, she smelled of that horrible perfume now.

With a grin, Bridget handed Kathleen a comb. "Take it, dearie. None of us has lice. You may find everything here shocking, but it's really rather a nice little cathouse. Lord knows there are worse. Not even Daisy is as hardened as she acts."

"But, but, where are they now?" stammered Kathleen. "All the girls? And the men?"

Bridget laughed. "The customers, thank the Lord, are at home. We don't let them sleep here. And the girls are in their rooms. Most of them had a long night. Not me; they don't want me anymore. But Daisy lets me stay on anyway. There're almost always one or two lads a night too drunk to see how old I am, and I even do it a bit cheaper. Otherwise I do a little cleaning around here and put things in order. Ready, dearie? We should check the jail before they send your love off to Dublin or wherever."

Kathleen arranged her hair the best she could and pulled her shawl over her head again. This proved wise, for it was bitterly cold when she stepped onto the street alongside her new friend.

"Your love will be freezing in his cell." Bridget sighed in sympathy. "Do you have any money?"

Kathleen did not know how she should answer. On the one hand, Harry had warned her about mentioning her purse, but on the other hand, Bridget did not seem like a thief.

"I only ask because the officers can be bought," Bridget explained when she noticed Kathleen's reticence. "A cell here in Wicklow can either be hell or a decent enough place. But if you want a fire and something proper to eat, you have to pay. It's like a hotel. You have to pay for a visit too. But that's cheap. I can give you the penny for it."

Kathleen felt a wave of fondness and shame. This woman she did not know at all really meant to give away her hard-earned money. And Kathleen had looked down on her and distrusted her.

"That's not necessary! I have money," Kathleen quickly explained. "But, but thank you. And you, you, I don't think you're going to hell," she blurted.

Bridget roared with laughter. "Child, I've been there already. In and out again. More often than you can imagine. If the Lord God or the devil wants to top that, he's going to have to work pretty damn hard."

Kathleen tried to smile, but she was horrified. Bridget seemed such a good woman—but she blasphemed against God and challenged the devil.

Bridget led Kathleen through the little harbor town's less impoverished areas. The notorious Wicklow Jail was on the south side of town, next to the courthouse.

Kathleen was tired and frozen when they arrived.

"Look there: our new jail, barely ten years old. The old building was about to collapse, so they finally tore it down. Now, it's fully modern. They don't beat the prisoners so much anymore, just put them on the treadmill. It's more humane, they say. Only the new dungeon is supposed to be as ghastly as the old."

Kathleen did not quite understand what Bridget was saying, but the unadorned facade of the building, surrounded by high stone walls, filled her with dread.

Bridget headed determinedly toward the small guardhouse and pluckily requested entrance. The gatekeeper seemed to know her.

"Well, well, Bridie. 'Nother admirer of your gals locked up? Or your own true love?" he teased her.

Bridget smirked. "Now, now, sir. I've never more than smiled at a redcoat. If I were to have a rogue, then it would be one with something in his own purse."

The man laughed good-naturedly, then let them inside. Kathleen followed Bridget down a sad hallway into the main building, where Bridget joked with the guard they encountered. He became serious, however, when she mentioned Michael's name.

"That rascal from the county? The distiller?"

"Michael's not a distiller," Kathleen objected.

Bridget quickly motioned to Kathleen to be quiet. She arched her eyebrows at the guard. "The girl's not herself," she added briefly.

After that, the man paid no more attention to Kathleen, forging ahead with Bridget instead.

"That fellow's a hard nut to crack, Bridie. They beat the tar out of him last night already. The soldiers were angry because he resisted arrest. Gave 'em trouble. They had to drag him the whole way here; he didn't take one step himself. And the boy can hold his tongue! Not a word so far, despite all the beatings. Naturally, they wanted to know where that nest of distillers is. They found whiskey in several taverns, but it's more important to find the still."

"He doesn't know." Kathleen tried again.

Now she had the man's attention. "So you're part of it too, girl, that it?" he asked suspiciously. "Helped 'em make the booze, did you?"

"Oh, nonsense. The lass doesn't know a thing," Bridget declared. "Just came up from her village on the Vartry where the boy had been courting her by the book. And now she's out of sorts. She's a proper lass, sir. You ought to let her see her love, free of charge. I'm sure she'd have a good influence on the lad."

The guard laughed. "You'll use any trick, Bridie. But honestly, I don't give a damn if the boy talks or not. He's got his ticket to Van Diemen's Land in his pocket, either way—or to wherever they're sending the prisoners now. Botany Bay is supposed to be closed, I hear. So, whether the girl wants to pray with him or exchange a few quick kisses, it'll cost a penny."

Kathleen fished a coin out of her pocket. Earlier she'd hidden the bursting purse under her dress. She took a breath.

"Bridget here says you might be able to do something else for Michael, sir?" she asked quietly. "A better cell, better food?"

The guard shrugged. "He's got to come out of the dungeon first, miss. As long as they're having fun with him down there, there's not much I can do. And if he stays this stubborn, that could be till the trial. But after that he'll be here a few months—the ships won't leave till March. The sea's too rough in winter. I can probably make his stay better till then."

"Just bring him here for now," Bridget said. "Or does the lass need to go into the dungeon?"

The guard nodded, shrugging his shoulders. "The fellow's chained up down there. But now's a good time. The other guards are eating breakfast, and they like to wash it down with a little whiskey. Well, follow me, girl."

Trembling, Kathleen followed the man through drafty halls and down stairs into the vaulted cellar. Every step produced a ghastly echo. She did not say a word, nor did the guard. Only once did another guard pass them, herding a troop of ragged-looking prisoners. The men did not dare look up, though they stole side glances to get a look at Kathleen.

"Here we are."

The hall leading past the dungeon cells was lit only meagerly by miserable oil lamps. In the cells themselves, near total darkness reigned. Each prisoner only had a single candle to light his chamber. Kathleen squinted in the dark when she was allowed to enter.

"Wait a second," the man grumbled. He brought one of the lanterns from the hall into the cell. "Here, since it's you. Your beloved ought to be able to see you, at least. Just costs a halfpenny more."

"Only if you leave the lantern here until it burns out."

Kathleen did not know how it happened. She would never have believed she could summon the courage to say something like that. But just the first quick glimpse of Michael's body stretched out on a heap of straw made her shudder. She had to fight for him. She was all he had.

"Since it's you?" Michael's low voice asked suspiciously once the guard had gone. "What did you do to get them to let you in here, Kathie?"

Kathleen had already sat down beside him on the straw. She could hardly wait to put her arms around him and kiss him. But now she glared at him.

"What do you think, Michael Drury? That I behave like a girl of easy virtue just because everyone now thinks me the sweetheart of a criminal?"

"Kathleen." Michael sat up. "Forgive me, Kathleen. It was . . . It's been a long night."

He tried to sit up and lean against the wall, but she saw that his shirt stuck to his back and that the blood had soaked though the fabric. And now she noticed the chains on Michael's arms and legs.

"They whipped you?" she asked.

Michael shook his head. "Forget it, Kathleen. Let's not talk about it. I can only say I'm sorry. Good Lord, the last thing I wanted was to hurt you or your reputation. I wanted to marry you, Kathleen. Start a new life, raise our child together. And don't call me a criminal, Kathie. I didn't hurt anybody, never got in a fight, never betrayed anyone. I'm an honorable man."

Kathleen laughed weakly. "When you're not stealing grain or selling moonshine."

"Isn't it our right as the Irish to make our own whiskey on our land? Shouldn't we eat the grain—or drink something made from it—that we've sown and harvested ourselves? If Ireland belonged to the Irish, there'd be no famine. No, Kathleen, I'm not ashamed. Nor should you be ashamed of me."

Michael looked straight into her eyes. Kathleen almost felt afraid. He had never spoken so seriously to her before.

"They're going to send me away, Kathleen," Michael said. "I can't marry you and make you an honest woman. Although to me you're more than honest, Mary Kathleen—you're holy. And you'll raise our child with dignity. I trust you." He kissed her forehead as if to seal their bond.

She nodded mutely.

"What about the money, Kathleen? Do you have it?" Michael asked.

"Yes," she answered quietly. "What am I to do now?"

"Come closer."

She moved toward him and though he was chained, he caressed her as best he could. His touch was as gentle and comforting as ever, but it gave her no answer.

A penny bought an hour from the guard, and in that short time, Michael and Kathleen said their good-byes. Michael put his hand on his beloved's stomach as if he could feel the child already.

"Would you want to name it Kevin?" he asked. "After my father?"

Kathleen asked herself if she really wanted her son to be named after a whiskey distiller, but it was a beautiful name, a sainted name. She thought of all the stories Father O'Brien had told about St. Kevin. He had been strong and handsome, and so gentle and clever that sea monsters lay like lambs at his feet and birds roosted in his hands.

So she nodded and gave herself over one last time to Michael's kisses. It would have to last a lifetime.

Kathleen tried not to cry when she finally left.

"I'd like a smile to remember you by," Michael whispered.

Kathleen smiled through her tears. But then she thought of something. With a quick motion, she wrapped several strands of her hair around her hand and pulled them out, as she had often seen men do when shortening horses' manes.

"Here," she said. "I don't know if they'll let you keep it. But if so . . ."

Michael put the lock of her hair to his lips. "I'll fight for it," he said plainly, then tried tearing out a few strands of his own. His hair was not long enough, so he gritted his teeth and pulled out an entire tuft.

"Michael!" cried Kathleen, horrified. She did not want him to suffer any more pain.

"For you, my love. Forget me not."

The guard cleared his throat as Kathleen kissed Michael once more, this time on his forehead.

Michael held her hand until she finally withdrew it.

"I'll always love you," she promised with a firm voice.

"I'll come back!" he called to her as she stepped into the hall. "Wherever they send me, I'll come back."

Kathleen did not turn around. She knew she would have cried, and she did not want that.

You'll raise our child with dignity. I trust you. Michael had said that. She had made a promise, and she had to keep it.

***

"What now?" asked Bridget.

They had left Wicklow Jail, and Bridget had dragged the girl to the nearest cookshop that was already open. Kathleen was frighteningly pale. Bridget had thought she needed some hot tea—preferably with a shot of whiskey.

Now Kathleen was sipping indecisively at the steaming-hot drink.

"What can I do?" she asked listlessly. "I only know that I won't get rid of the baby. How could Daisy even think that? Bridget, I, I don't think I want to go back to Daisy."

Bridget shrugged. "Daisy isn't bad. And she did not mean you any harm, believe me. It's just she knows all too well what you're in for if you bring a bastard into the world. And that's what they'll call your child, dearie, no matter how much love conceived it. It's not pleasant for the child, Kathleen. I'm a bastard myself, and I've often thought what a blessing it would have been if my mother had killed me in the womb. But so be it. No one is forcing you, Daisy least of all. If, however, you want to go back . . ."

Her eyes wide, Kathleen looked at Bridget, who continued to talk, undisturbed.

"Look, dearie. Basically, you have three options. One, you stay here, with Daisy. She made you the offer. You're a vision of loveliness, lass. She'd make a fortune from you, and you'd do well for a few years. You could give the baby to someone to raise and pay for it."

"But then I won't even see it," protested Kathleen. "Other people would raise it."

Bridget shrugged. "You can't raise it into a good Christian in a whore-house either."

"And the other options?" asked Kathleen, dispirited.

"Well, you could go back to your village. And the smartest thing would be to look for someone who would take an experienced woman."

"What do you mean by that?"

"A man who'll marry you. Despite your child. You're so pretty, there must be dozens of lads who want you. They'll just have to take the child too. Besides, you do come with a certain dowry, don't you?" Bridget looked at Kathleen sharply. She must have guessed about Michael's money.

Kathleen nodded. "Aye," she admitted. "But I love Michael. I can't, with another—"

"Dearie, you won't even believe all that a person can do," Bridget interrupted her bitterly. "But fine, you could also remain unmarried. Your parents will probably make your life miserable, but if you're lucky, they won't throw you out right away. And there is one more alternative."

"What's that?" Kathleen was grasping at straws.

"Take the money and buy yourself passage on a ship," said Bridget. "Go to America like you two planned. But I'll tell you right now, no one knows what happens to people there. Neither I nor anyone else, no matter what the people say. Maybe it really is the promised land, where milk and honey flow from springs. Maybe it's even shabbier and dirtier than here. Particularly for girls. I've never yet heard of a country where the girls are free. It's a risk. If you want to take it, we'll take care of you somehow until the next ship."

Kathleen thought it over, her heart beating heavily. She was scared. Of the coffin ships, of the unknown country. Even in America, she supposed, it would be a scandal to raise a child out of wedlock.

"You could say you're a widow." Bridget seemed to read her thoughts.

An idea occurred to Kathleen—for her and her new friend.

"Would you come with me, Bridget?" she asked quietly. "I have, we had, money for two passengers. I could pay for you. And I, I wouldn't be so alone."

Bridget thought about it for a heartbeat but then shook her head. "No, dearie," she said quietly. "I don't have the courage. I no longer believe in the New World, child, and not in heaven, and not in forgiveness, but not in scandal anymore either. What can the poor kid do about the fact that his father stole? Not to mention that he did so for the noblest reasons? But that won't save you, and I don't have strength for a new hell. Who knows what waits for us on the other side of the world?"

Bridget sighed. "What I have here, I know. Not paradise, but better than many others have. I don't dare risk it. But don't listen to me, Kathleen. I'm probably just too old. If I were still sixteen, then I might do it. But no longer, lass. I'm sorry."

The older woman laid her hand comfortingly on Kathleen's arm. Kathleen sighed. She knew she would not risk it alone. America had never been her dream; it was Michael's. With him, she would have gone. Without him, it was hopeless.

So Kathleen chose the second path. After she parted from Bridget, thanking her a thousand times, she set out on the long road home to her village.

This time no cart stopped next to her, and that suited her fine. She was in no hurry to arrive. Either way, people would gossip about where she had been and what she had done.

When she was halfway there, a redcoat wagon came from the opposite direction. As it passed her, she recognized Billy Rafferty, who lay in straw in the back of the wagon. He was chained to the prison bars. Apparently they were taking the other thief to Wicklow. Kathleen pulled her shawl over her face, and Billy Rafferty took no notice of her.

In the village, her return caused less commotion than she would have thought. Indeed, the villagers were focused on Gráinne Rafferty and her family. The law had come down with all its might on the old cook, and Trevallion, the only one who could still have objected, knew no mercy.

The soldiers had stormed the Raffertys' house that afternoon, driving out Gráinne and her children. Though the cook cried and begged, the soldiers stood deaf and dumb. As the family stood in the open air with the few possessions they had been able to save in haste, the redcoats tore down the cottage's walls and set it on fire.

Gráinne and her children had remained behind, sobbing. They did not even have the option of staying with another villager temporarily. They had to leave Wetherbys' land by sundown.

"The only guilty one is that Drury boy," Gráinne said, pointing at the smoking ruin that had once been the Drurys' hut. But Fiona Drury and her children had not given Trevallion the satisfaction of forcing them onto the street. They knew what was coming, so the night after Billy's imprisonment, they made for the mountains.

"They always acted so Christian, but in the end, they were the same rats as their forefathers," Gráinne said.

Yet Kathleen was sure Fiona had left in tears herself. Michael's mother had never wanted to live in the mountains. But at least she had a refuge. There was no hope for Gráinne.

"Perhaps you'll find work in the city," Kathleen's mother said to try to comfort Gráinne. "The girls will soon be old enough to find jobs for themselves too."

One after another, the village women approached the ostracized family, handing them little presents. With a heavy heart, Mrs. O'Donnell gave them the last little sack of grain from what Trevallion had gifted them.

Gráinne nodded bravely. Then she led her children off into the unknown.

Kathleen bore her mother's accusations and father's slaps without complaint. She did not tell them where she had been; her parents knew anyway.

"And now Trevallion knows what was going on too," her mother said. "He would have been such a good choice, Kathleen. But no, you had to get involved with a rascal, a thief, and a distiller. It will take a long time before that wound has healed. Let's just hope you're still a virgin."

Kathleen did not comment on this either. Her mother would notice the truth soon enough.

Chapter 6

Days in the dungeon were hell, and it did not get better when, two days after Michael's arrest, Billy Rafferty was locked away in the cell. On the contrary, now Michael also heard Billy's screaming and crying during his interrogations. Again and again, the British accusers tried to beat any information they could out of the young criminals, but Michael remained firm, and Billy had long since told them everything he knew.

Michael could hardly stand to hear the whip rain down on his friend's back; it almost hurt him more than the blows he received himself. He forgave Billy's betrayal. Michael believed it had been his own fault. Billy could not handle money, nor could he have continued the whiskey sale. Bringing him into the theft had been careless.

Michael would have done better to fetch an assistant from the mountains or work with his younger brothers. Jonny and Brian could hold their tongues. But he hadn't wanted to encourage his brothers toward crime, and Billy had not required much convincing.

The jailers considered Michael hopelessly stubborn. They cut his meager portion of the porridge on which the prisoners in Wicklow Jail lived to try to get him to talk, but Michael wouldn't bend. He spent Christmas of 1846 drinking water and eating moldy bread in the pitch-black dungeon, thinking of Kathleen and listening to Billy's sobbing in the next cell. Desperately, he clung to the lovely scenes of the past. He conjured Kathleen's white body in the grass beside the river. He recalled every kiss and every caress, and he thought of their baby in her womb. Michael was determined that it would not end this way. He would return to Kathleen, even if they shipped him to the ends of the earth.

By year's end, the redcoats' ardor to wring new confessions from Michael and Billy had cooled. Instead, a man appeared. Though his suit had seen better days, he introduced himself as an attorney. Michael listened as Billy told the story again, crying through the whole tale. Michael kept his silence with this man as well. He did not believe this sad-looking lawyer could do anything for him. With theft came banishment. They would be condemned. And the length of the sentence was more or less irrelevant. Once you landed in Australia, you never came back.

Still, Michael stubbornly believed he would find a way back. There was no prison one could not escape. Walls couldn't be put up around an entire country, and if Australia were an island, he would just swim for it.

Michael yearned to write to Kathleen, at least. Like most of the village youths, he had mastered the fundamentals thanks to Father O'Brien. As long as he sat in the dungeon, though, there was nothing he could do. Even if Michael had a penny with which to bribe the guards, he would have needed not just pen and paper but also a lamp. The lantern Kathleen had gotten from the guard had long since burned out, and in his cell, Michael could hardly see his hand in front of his face.

The attorney told the prisoners the date of their trial. The sentencing was scheduled for the beginning of January, just next door in the courthouse. This news caused new rivers of tears for Billy, but Michael looked forward to it. Once they had been sentenced, there would be no more reason to torture them. Michael also thought they would be moved out of the dungeon to the cells, where it was surely warmer and the food might be better. He drew new courage from these hopes, and he made it through his trial without saying a word.

"You two could shorten your sentences by showing remorse," said the judge—a short, thin man, wearing a giant white wig, who reminded Michael vaguely of Trevallion.

At that, Billy almost fell to his knees before the man, and crying and lamentation arose in the courtroom too. Gráinne Rafferty and two of her younger sons were present, but Michael had hardly recognized the old cook at first glance. The once rotund Gráinne looked haggard and emaciated, her children dirty and ragged. Apparently they had been cast out of the village and were struggling through life on the street. Michael wondered how a woman could make money out there without selling herself. With a guilty conscience, he thought of Gráinne's daughters, who had not come with her. Were they standing on some corner of the wharf, offering their bodies to the sailors?

Michael's parents had not come either, but as he let his eyes roam for the third time over the people in the courtroom—among them, other prisoners to be sentenced and their families—he caught sight of Brian and Jonny in the last row. Jonny grinned at him, and Michael smiled in return. It was good to know the two of them were over there and not in chains next to him.

When the judge saw Michael's smile, he became annoyed. He angrily accused him of contempt for the law, but Michael let the accusations bounce off him, just as he had the judge's earlier admonition. The English occupiers could mistreat him, condemn him, and exile him, but they could not force him to take them seriously.

Finally, the sentences were announced. Billy's seven years of exile were no surprise. That was the usual sentence for theft. Michael received ten years. The Irish in the courtroom found that too hard a sentence, and they reacted loudly.

Michael received his sentence in silence. He did not move or say a word until the other prisoners were led out and Jonny could finally make his way to him.

"Jonny! How's Ma? Is everyone well?"

Jonny nodded. "Aye. Ma sends her love, but it was too far for her to travel in this cold. And she's not mad at you." He grinned. "On the contrary, I'd almost say she and Da were one heart and one soul. Wouldn't surprise me if we have another brother or sister before long."

"Jonny!" Michael laughed, if a little forcedly. "And . . . Kathleen?" he asked quietly.

Although his family no longer lived in the village, he was sure Jonny still talked to his old friends.

Jonny shrugged. "Don't know. I haven't seen her. Or hardly anyone from the village. Seems the O'Donnells didn't throw her on the street. But people are talking, you know. So, is it true what Pat Minoghue says? Is there a baby coming?"

Michael bit his lip. Of course, Kathleen must now be in her third month. A pregnancy could not be kept secret forever. And naturally, her parents were in a rage and punishing her, but at least they had not sent her away.

He did not know whether he was relieved or disappointed. Of course everything would be easier if Kathleen waited for him in the village. But being thrown out might have given her the courage to try her luck in the New World. Australia might even be closer to America. Perhaps he could flee straight there.

"Tell her I'm thinking of her," Michael called to his brother as the guards pulled him away. Until then, they had allowed him the conversation—perhaps out of surprise that their stony prisoner could actually talk—but regards to his beloved proved too much for them.

***

Indeed, they did not take the men back to the dungeon. Finally, the relief Kathleen and Bridget had worked out for Michael was taking effect. The corrupt but affable guard was convinced to extend favors to Billy too. Bridget was in the courtroom when Billy and Michael were sentenced, and the old whore was happy to pay an extra penny for Michael's desperate accomplice.

Kathleen had left plenty of money with the good woman, and Bridget felt sorry for Billy and his family. Since the trial, he had shared a halfway spacious four-person cell with Michael and two other men. There were even a few logs for the fire and plenty to eat every day.

"What happens now?" Billy asked.

"Now, we wait," one of their fellow prisoners explained, "until the next ship leaves for Australia. And that might take a while. If the winter is long, they won't send us over until May."

"Probably also depends on how quick this place fills up," the other speculated. "If the jail's bursting at the seams, they'll sail—they don't care if the tub sinks, after all."

Michael thought the latter point was likely untrue. The English Crown might not care about the prisoners, but a ship was valuable and its crew consisted of Englishmen, probably experienced seamen. Michael had never heard of a prison ship going down.

Half of the prisoners in Wicklow Jail were serving shorter sentences and were employed for labor, mostly doing simple and rather boring tasks. The other half were waiting to be shipped out, and those were the more serious criminals being shoved off to Australia. They were mostly thieves who were driven to their crimes by pure need. But there were also brawlers and murderers among them, always looking for trouble.

Boredom took its toll: there was bullying, abuse, and fighting. And there were draconian punishments if someone was caught in the act. Michael, who was considered a troublemaker because he neither treated the guards with reverence nor let the other prisoners push him around, quickly became acquainted with punishment.

The guards in Wicklow Jail would have preferred to be rid of him sooner rather than later.

***

At the beginning of March, Michael and the other prisoners whose deportation was planned for that spring were ordered to the prison doctor. Only healthy and halfway hardy men were sent away. The traveling conditions were not easy, after all, and England did not want to be accused of causing the deaths of prisoners. However, one always had to reckon with losses. The oppressive compactness on the ships and the insufficient food and fresh water encouraged epidemics, infections, and fevers.

Dr. Skinnings—a tall Englishman who, with his red hair and freckles, could also have passed for an Irishman—examined and cared for the bloody welts on Michael's back.

"Those will have to heal before we can send you to sea," he said. "Open wounds quickly become infected there."

Michael laughed bitterly. "Then tell your friends the guards to spare me their attentiveness for a couple of days. It's not my fault the wounds don't close, believe you me."

While the doctor examined him, listening to his lungs and heart, Michael looked around the infirmary. He had been thinking about escape for weeks—since he had left the dungeon, in fact—but Wicklow Jail had proved a modern and secure prison. The walls were high and thick, the guards alert. So far, no opportunity for getting away had presented itself.

The prisoners, some of whom had been in Wicklow for years, confirmed Michael's observation. Since the prison's renovation ten years before, no one had escaped. But Michael was not prepared to give up easily. He had hoped that perhaps the doctor's office would present an opportunity, but things did not look good here either. If he had correctly figured out the prison floor plan, the infirmary did not include a wall facing outside. Even if he had been able to flee out a window, he would only have found himself back in the prison yard. Moreover, the window in the doctor's office was barred just like those in the cells.

A few things had stood out to Michael and awakened his interest. There were pencil and paper in the doctor's desk, as well as a notebook and a pen atop the medicine cabinet beside the scale.

As Dr. Skinnings turned to write Michael's information in the notebook, Michael seized his opportunity. Quickly, he made the pencil and two pieces of paper disappear into the pockets of his wide prisoner's trousers. When the doctor turned back toward him, Michael smiled obediently.

Dr. Skinnings looked severe. "What did you just take?" he asked with a firm voice. "Don't lie. You took something. You can give it back to me, or I'll call the guards. The latter would not be good for the healing of your back."

Michael felt his face becoming red. Now even this doctor would think him a common thief. Wordlessly, he pulled the paper and pencil from his pocket and laid them on the doctor's desk.

Dr. Skinnings furrowed his brow. "Paper and pencil? Nothing from the cabinet?"

Michael looked in surprise at the bottles and pill boxes on the shelves. "What would I want with them?"

Dr. Skinnings shrugged his shoulders. "Who knows? Get drunk? Kill yourself? The men are always trying it—and yet most of them can't even read what the bottles say. But that's not the case with you, now, is it?"

"I could read them," Michael informed the doctor. "But that's about it. That's Latin, right?"

"Latin and sometimes Greek. Well, well, you can recognize that. You've a clever head, Michael Drury. What a shame you seem only to want to make it through the wall. Why do you want the paper and pencil? Do you hope someone outside will free you? Do you belong to some organization perhaps planning an assault on the prison ship? You can tell me, or the guards will beat it out of you." Dr. Skinnings eyed Michael with arched eyebrows.

Michael laughed. "No one beats anything out of me, Doc," he said. "I can keep quiet—and die, if it comes to that. But there's no dark secret here. I don't have any friends with magic weapons. Just a girl in a village on the

Vartry who is pregnant with my child. I'd like to write her a farewell letter, to give her a little hope."

Dr. Skinnings shook his head. "Hope for what, Drury? Do you think you're coming back? My God, man, be reasonable. No one comes back. You'll spend the rest of your life in Australia, in Van Diemen's Land, likely. But that needn't be so bad. You're still young. You have a ten-year sentence to serve, of course, but after that, you can apply for land as a free settler. Over there is more land than anyone knows what to do with, Drury. As for those ten years, I'll mention in my report that you can read and write. That'll make you valuable. You'll be employed in more skilled jobs than just clearing the land. Only if you behave, of course. Use these ten years, Drury. Get to know your new country. Don't see this punishment as an exile but a chance for a new beginning."

Michael shook his head. "And what should I tell Kathleen?" he asked. "I promised to marry her."

The doctor shrugged. "Forget the girl. It sounds harsh, but it's the best advice I can give you. You won't see her again. And now, feel free to take paper, a pen, and some ink, and write her a beautiful letter. Tell her to take care of herself, but don't give her any hope."

Dr. Skinnings permitted Michael to write his letter in the office while he examined the next patient. The doctor promised to send the letter himself— free of charge. A few of the corrupt guards did post letters but demanded a horrendous charge, and Michael did not trust them.

He couldn't be sure that the doctor would send the letter without reading it first, but Michael did not want that to dictate what he wrote to Kathleen: "Trust in my love, Mary Kathleen, and pass it on to my child. Though I don't yet know how I'll manage it, I'll come back!"

A few days later, the prisoners condemned to deportation were loaded into prison wagons and driven to the wharf. Michael once again hoped for an opportunity for flight, but the guards were on alert. Plus, troublemakers like Michael had their hands and feet restrained and had to be dragged, with their chains clanking, into the wagons. Then the chains were pulled through special rings attached to the beds of the vehicles. In order to flee, the prisoners would have had to dismantle the wagons.

Billy Rafferty was sobbing again as he sank next to Michael onto the filthy straw that covered the bed of the wagon.

"Now it's final," he wept. "They're sending us away. We'll never see our home again."

"I will," said Michael assuredly, grasping Kathleen's lock of hair, which he had hidden securely in the sleeve of his shirt. "I'll see Ireland again and marry Kathleen. They can't keep me in chains for ten years!"

Chapter 7

Kathleen's pregnancy could no longer be hidden. Her mother had stopped screaming at her, and her father didn't hit her anymore. It would not do anything, after all. The first months, in which a merciful hand could still have led to a natural loss of the child, had passed. Kathleen's parents and siblings punished her with silence and disdain instead of fighting and lamenting. In the village, people whispered behind her back.

After the worst of the winter was over, the tenants' lives shifted back outside. They had had enough of the oppressive crowdedness of the small, smoky huts. Kathleen left the house as rarely as possible, and she was often alone in the stuffy cottage.

Kathleen, who always felt tired, spent whole days lying on her mat—dreaming about Michael, mourning for him—until, one day, her mother said something that forced her to her feet.

"Make yourself useful," she ordered angrily, pointing to the spinning wheel. "Or shove off with your bastard. It'll cost us enough."

Kathleen dragged herself to the spinning wheel, but when her mother went outside, she pulled Michael's purse out from under her straw mat and counted the money once again. Spring was coming; ships would be sailing for America. If only she could summon more courage and strength. But it seemed the baby in her womb was robbing her of the last of her energy—or perhaps it was the contempt and cruelty of the people around her that exhausted her. The only one in the village who showed Kathleen any kindness was Father

O'Brien. The old priest had, no doubt, seen his share of women fall from grace, and he seemed to recognize that recriminations would do no good.

When Kathleen confessed the whole story to him in tears, he even tried to intervene with the prison chaplain in Wicklow.

"If Michael's willing to marry you, perhaps the chaplain will do it," Father O'Brien said. Kathleen had some hope, but just a few days later the response arrived: the chaplain strongly advised against marrying a prisoner before deportation. His opinion was clear in his letter to Father O'Brien:

> No blessing lies in sealing a union that can no longer be con-
> summated. On the contrary, we would be encouraging sin
> thereby. The young man will remain in the colonies forever,
> and the young woman in Ireland. Is she to remain chaste her
> whole life? Naturally, we might wish for that, but the flesh is
> weak. A marriage before his deportation would, moreover,
> nourish the hope that he might return. Thus, he would not
> integrate himself in the colonies. We would be fomenting
> recalcitrance and resistance, not to mention that Michael
> Drury is not counted among the obedient and God-fearing.
> It would be better if this Kathleen O'Donnell was to accept
> her fate and view it as expiation for her sins. May she serve
> as an example to the other girls of her village.

Father O'Brien expected tears from Kathleen as he read his colleague's opinion. But her eyes remained dry—and the priest recognized more anger than sorrow, let alone remorse.

"And what about the baby, Father?" she asked harshly after a pause. "Whom the church is denying a father and an honorable name? Should I have it baptized with the name 'Example'?"

O'Brien shrugged his shoulders. He could have admonished her for disparaging the church, but there was no point. In his heart of hearts, he agreed with her.

***

The first days of March were sunny, and Kathleen remembered her happy days by the river with Michael. She would have gladly left the dark hut to enjoy the outdoors, but her mother brought her plenty of wool to spin, enough to keep her busy all day.

Kathleen was just considering whether she should move the spinning wheel out in front of the cottage and whether that would invite the scorn and mockery of the passing villagers, when there was a knock at the door. When she opened the door, she was amazed to see Ian Coltrane standing there.

The young horse trader smiled at her. "A good day to you, Mary Kathleen O'Donnell," he said formally.

Kathleen bowed slightly and returned his greeting. "What brings you here, Ian?" she asked, not unfriendly but reserved. "We don't have any horses to sell, and my father doesn't mean to buy any."

Ian grinned. "No, nothing about a horse," he said. "I didn't come for that. I wanted to see you, Kathleen. But should we go inside or to the village square? It could put you in a bad light if a passerby sees you talking with me here."

Kathleen wondered if he was serious. "You can't sully my name any more; that's been done already," she said casually. "I don't care what the people say. So, what brings you here, Ian?"

Ian smiled. "Well, I need to get back to Wicklow in the coming days. And I wanted to offer you another ride. In case you'd like to visit your aunt again."

Kathleen sank her head. Was he mocking her? Well, she would not show any reaction. She would not be shamed by him. "My aunt got better a long time ago."

Ian shrugged. "Good for her," he said with a note of sarcasm. "But perhaps something else takes you to Wicklow. They say a ship is sailing soon, for London."

Kathleen frowned. "Ships are always sailing from Wicklow," she said.

Ian nodded, and something flashed in his black eyes. Was it mischievousness? Cruelty?

"But not every ship has condemned lads on board on their way to Australia. And I've heard one of them sailing on this tub has some connection to you."

"To London?" Kathleen blurted. "They're sending Michael to London? And thence on to, to . . . Do you think I could see him one more time?" In her excitement she grasped Ian's arm.

"I don't know," Ian replied curtly. "I only know I'm driving to Wicklow early Monday, to the horse market. And if I meet you somewhere outside the village, then I'll gladly take you with me."

Kathleen thought it over. There would be plenty of trouble if she ran away without telling her parents anything. They might refuse to take her back in afterward. But that would certainly be the case if she told them about the ride. And what exactly did Ian Coltrane have in mind with this offer? He would not drive her to town out of pure neighborliness.

"What do you get in exchange, Ian?" Kathleen asked distrustfully.

Ian shrugged. "I'll get to see golden hair blow in the wind and green eyes shine. Perhaps I'll even hear a thank-you from tender red lips."

"Oh, enough," Kathleen said. "You don't need to flatter me. And I'll tell you right now: I don't have more than a few looks and a few words to offer. Whatever people say."

Ian bowed gallantly. "I would never have thought of asking anything indecent of you, Mary Kathleen," he said. "On the contrary, I admire you. Such a dutiful girl who is always on her way to act as a nurse for her old aunt."

Kathleen pressed her lips together. Her instincts told her it was not a good idea to take Ian's offer. But her heart yearned to see Michael once more, even if she couldn't speak with him.

"I'll think about it," she told Ian.

He laughed. "I'll wait for you on Monday."

***

At barely first light on Monday, Kathleen heard Ian's cart rolling through the village, and she slipped out of the house while her family slept. Ian and his two-wheeled cart, with two donkeys attached this time, were waiting at the edge of the village.

"You didn't have to think long," Ian teased when Kathleen climbed onto the box. "I can understand someone finding it lovely to watch the ships sail. But how much lovelier it would be to sail with them."

"If you're eager to go, you only need to take three sacks of Trevallion's grain," she said impudently, "and they'll book you passage free of charge."

Ian laughed. Then he began to talk about the horse market in Wicklow. It was early spring, the time of year when people bought work animals. He hoped the donkeys would fetch a good price. At least, that was what he told Kathleen. She cast a fleeting glance at the animals and thought she recognized the gardener's donkey as one of them. Lately, old O'Rearke had cursed about the animal all the time. It was old and lame. Now, however, it seemed quite nimble and did not drag its leg. Ian Coltrane seemed to have a talent for rejuvenating his wares.

He laughed uproariously when Kathleen remarked on this.

"Aye, you could call it that," he said and then began to brag shamelessly of his success.

Kathleen did not listen. She had no desire to converse. Her thoughts were only with Michael, and she guarded as a treasure the letter Father O'Brien had given her the day before.

"I should not support it," the old priest had said, almost with remorse, when he stopped Kathleen after Mass. "My brother of the cloth, who sent me this, advised me to throw it away. But alas, I have a too-soft heart." With that, he had pressed a letter into her hand, furtively and quickly, so her parents would not notice.

Kathleen had waited hours to open the letter. She knew it was from Michael, and she wanted to be alone when she read his farewell. His words warmed her heart: He had not forgotten her. He would come back. And surely it would be a comfort to him to see her in the crowd when his ship sailed. Michael's letter was the final push toward accepting Ian's offer.

Ian let Kathleen off at the wharf before proceeding with his donkeys. He would pick her up on his way back.

"Excuse me, sir, which is the ship bound for London?" Kathleen shyly asked a sailor who was just unloading a cutter. The man grinned at her.

"The prison ship?" he asked meaningfully. "Can't miss it, lass. See there where all the people are standing? They're also hoping to get a last look at the rascals bound for Van Diemen's Land. Is it your brother or sweetheart, my dear?"

The sailor let his gaze wander over Kathleen's body. "Oh, the husband, is it?" He grinned. "Well, you won't see much more of him in this life. But if you're looking for a new one, I'd be happy to have you, sweet. Such a pretty thing, a fellow'd gladly take the stowaway as part of the trade." He nodded toward her belly and reached for her arm.

Kathleen pulled herself free and ran in the given direction. Some fifty people were already waiting there, Gráinne Rafferty among them.

When Kathleen moved to join her, Gráinne spat.

"Well look here: the whore who dragged my Billy into misfortune," she shrieked. "Fine little Mary Kathleen who could have had the steward but took the worst rogue. Trevallion don't want you no more, that it? They should send you away, not my Billy who never did a bad thing in his life."

Gráinne cursed and howled as those standing around looked rather compassionately at Kathleen. Finally, she managed to get away from the old cook—without learning where Gráinne and her family lived now or how they were doing.

It had turned not into a radiant spring day but rather a gray, rainy morning. Kathleen was freezing in her thin maternity dress. It had belonged to her mother, who had worn it through all five pregnancies. Now it was ragged, and Kathleen's shawl did not keep her warm either. And she was getting hungry. She hadn't had breakfast before sneaking out of the house. The baby in her womb kicked in protest.

Nothing was happening on the wharf. Though the crowd of those waiting grew larger, the prisoners were nowhere to be seen. Around noon, sailors appeared on deck to adjust the sails. And then, as Kathleen shivered with cold and hunger, a train of six prison wagons approached. Prison guards were on the boxes of the wagons, and soldiers guarded the train. The soldiers were well armed, and as the train got nearer, they took up posts between the waiting crowd and the wagons. Kathleen's hope of exchanging a few words with her beloved sank.

Worse still, the wagons were driven right up alongside the ships. The prisoners only had a few steps to take on land before they were pushed on deck. A few threw themselves, sobbing, to the ground to kiss Irish soil one last time. Others walked stoically without looking back. Still others tried desperately to glimpse their loved ones in the crowd on the wharf.

The men in the last wagon hardly had this opportunity. Their hands and feet were heavily chained, and they dragged themselves onto the ship, driven roughly by the guards who struck at them, yelling. Kathleen cried out when she recognized Michael among these unlucky souls. She called his name, but all the others in the crowd cried out to their husbands, brothers, and sons. There was no way the prisoners could pick out the voices of their loved ones.

Michael did not look around. He could not guess, after all, that she was at the wharf. When he disappeared into the belly of the ship, Kathleen collapsed, sobbing.

"Now, now, don't cry, lass. It's not good for the baby," said a sympathetic voice beside her. "And you must take care of it. At least you have that from him."

A careworn but motherly woman helped her to her feet and led her to the wharf wall where she could sit down.

Kathleen looked at her, uncomprehending. It felt good to have someone say something friendly about the child growing within her. And the woman was right. She had lost Michael, but the little one inside her was a piece of him. She should be happy about it instead of quarreling with her fate.

"How about you?" she managed, pointing to the ship now setting sail.

The woman understood at once. "My son," she said quietly. "And he didn't leave a grandson behind for me. He had two children, but the famine . . . In the end, he stole a sheep—he thought a little meat could keep the last one alive. But he just wasn't a good enough thief. They caught him and locked him up. I buried his wife and the child. What are these days we live in, lass?"

The woman put her arm around Kathleen, and the two of them watched the ship move away from land. The rain did what it could to make it disappear quickly into the mist. Kathleen wept noiselessly. The woman beside her had no more tears left. Neither of them heard the cart making its way through the slowly dispersing crowd.

"Ready?" asked Ian Coltrane, who seemed to suddenly appear before her.

Kathleen was startled. "I, I . . ." She felt she had to explain to the woman next to her. But the woman merely shrugged her shoulders.

"It's all right, lass. You're right to look forward. And he must be a good lad to drive you here to say farewell." They stood and the woman hugged Kathleen again, lovingly and maternally. "I must be going myself. God be with you, lass."

Agitated, shivering with cold and weak with hunger, Kathleen climbed onto the cart's box. Without a word, Ian handed her a blanket in which she could wrap herself.

"Help yourself," he said curtly as he gestured to a bag of hot meat pies under the seat.

Kathleen bit voraciously into what was surely an expensive treat and wondered again: Why was Ian doing all of this for her?

The whole way home, Kathleen feared that Ian would demand his payment for being her driver. She could hardly have stopped him. There was no one on the road on that wet, cheerless day. But nothing happened. Ian even accepted her persistent silence. When they had almost reached the village, she risked asking him once more.

"I'm not much company, Ian. I'm sorry. And what's worse, people will talk when they see you with me. What do you get out of this?"

"Perhaps I just want you to think I'm a good fellow."

"What do you care what I think?" Kathleen asked wearily. "And what do I care whether you're a good fellow or a . . ." The word "swindler" almost slipped out of her mouth, but she managed to hold it back.

Ian shrugged. "In any case, I wanted you to see him sail away." His eyes gave him away: he wasn't at ease. "Now you know he's gone and can forget him."

Kathleen was relieved when she caught sight of the first village houses. They were close enough that she had an excuse to get off the wagon. Now she need not have anything more to do with Ian Coltrane.

As she walked the rest of the way home through the rain, Kathleen thought about the old woman's words. Michael was gone, but he had left her his child. A bond would always exist between them. And she had his promise to return. Kathleen hummed a nursery rhyme as she arrived at the village.

Her father's reception sobered Kathleen up at once. She had expected difficulties when she reached home, but the brutal slap in the face with which her father welcomed her took her by surprise. She almost fell backward.

"Where did you get the money, you little whore?" James O'Donnell waved Michael's purse around in front of her face. "You hoard a fortune in my house and say nothing about it. Where did you get it, Kathleen? What did you do for it? Is it whore's wages?"

Kathleen sobbed. The words hurt more than the blow. "It's from Michael," she finally managed. "And it belongs to his child. You have no right."

"I have all the right in the world," he roared at her. "I'm to be the bastard's guardian, after all. So, this is Michael's. And where did he get it? Distilling? Stealing?"

"Would it be worth less if so?" asked Kathleen.

She knew it sounded impudent and rebellious, but in truth, she was only tired. She wanted to put all of this behind her. Let him take her money, let him beat her. As long as she could sink down onto her straw mat and pull the blanket over her head at some point.

But then her mother made her presence known. "It doesn't matter where it's from," Erin O'Donnell said, her lips thin. "What's important is where it goes. Don't you understand, James? This money is a gift from God. It will save our honor!"

Kathleen's mother looked at her with a thoughtfully furrowed brow, and Kathleen stared back, uncomprehending.

Erin O'Donnell clasped her forehead. "My God, James. With that we can buy a husband!" She took the purse from him and waved it triumphantly in front of Kathleen. "This money, my sweet Mary Kathleen, is your dowry."

Chapter 8

Ian Coltrane appeared in church the next Sunday, less conspicuously dressed than usual. He had exchanged his checkered jacket for a dark, dignified coat. After Mass, he politely asked to speak with James O'Donnell.

And a short time later, before the fire in the O'Donnell's humble house, he asked for Mary Kathleen's hand.

"I can keep your daughter fed, Mr. O'Donnell, better than most of the lads here. Though I still live in my father's house, I can have a few stable rooms furnished for us. It won't be for long anyway."

"Not for long?" asked O'Donnell sternly. "Now, what's that supposed to mean? You're not planning on a long marriage?"

Ian laughed. "No, I want Kathleen for all time. No one will take her from me; that I swear. But I've had enough of this famine, Mr. O'Donnell. And enough of English lords I have to flatter to keep my trade license, and of rent and taxes that eat up what little I earn. I don't mean to say anything against Ireland, Mr. O'Donnell. It's a beautiful country. A man could love it if he were allowed. But I've no talent for rabble-rousing, nor for bootlicking. That means I need to leave. And I'm prepared—"

"To America?" asked Erin O'Donnell. "Mr. Coltrane, that may sound like an adventure to you, but half of the emigrants die on the ship! And Kathleen . . . Do you know she's pregnant?" Kathleen's mother blushed.

Kathleen was following the conversation, and she wanted to say something, but it was as if her throat were tied shut.

Ian Coltrane raised his eyebrows. "I know that, Mrs. O'Donnell. I'm not blind, after all. Nor a fool. Nothing draws me to the coffin ships. Or to factories in New York either. A cousin of mine is over there and writes sometimes. It's a different sort of hell than here, but a hell nevertheless. No, Mrs. O'Donnell, I mean to make my fortune. I mean to go to a new country, a brand new one where no one spits at an Irishman and calls him 'Paddy,' and where the ships have better oversight. The journey is longer, but the Crown sends inspectors who look closely at the room and board. It also does not lead to a foreign land indifferent to the British—the British remain citizens, and we become them. The journey is more expensive than to good old America, so I still have some saving up to do. But in a year, two at the most . . ."

James O'Donnell furrowed his brow. "And what is this promised land called?" he asked skeptically.

Ian smiled. His eyes shone as he did—and Kathleen suddenly knew what frightened her. When he had spoken of marriage, he had looked predatory, like a trader making a deal. A swindler hiding his true motives.

"New Zealand," Ian said. "Discovered a hundred years ago, I believe. It's supposed to look a little like our country, but sparsely settled. A few Indians or the like, but peaceful, mostly. Anyway, where I want to go, out on the Canterbury Plains, there are just sheep. Ideal for livestock trading and breeding. All the animals had to be brought over. In the country itself there were only birds."

"Where is it?" Kathleen finally managed to get out a word. "And to whom does it belong?"

"No one!" Ian crowed. "Well, I suppose it's an English colony, but anyone can go. And where is it? Far, very far away, somewhere in the South Seas. But it doesn't matter. The captain'll know where he's going. And for us there'll be land and freedom and a new life! Passage costs thirteen pounds each. I've got the money for one ticket already, but I'd love to take Kathleen with me, Mr. O'Donnell."

"And her child?" Erin asked severely.

Ian shrugged his shoulders. "It'll come one way or another. No matter where. Better it be born in a land that has never heard the name Drury. Alas, I won't gather the money that quickly. But I promise you, Kathie, that we'll be gone from here before the child is old enough to understand the word 'bastard.'"

Kathleen felt strangely touched. Was Ian really worried about her child? Would he raise it as his own? With all the consequences that implied? She wished she could trust him.

Erin O'Donnell breathed deeply, giving her husband and Kathleen a triumphant look.

"Don't worry about that, Mr. Coltrane. This girl has a dowry, and not just one that cries and wets itself. You can book your passage. But first make your proposal, and be sure you both say 'I do' before Kathleen rips the seams in all her clothes."

"What about me?" Kathleen cried. "Is anyone going to ask me what I think of this?"

Three pairs of eyes looked at her. Were they uncomprehending? Or unfeeling?

"No," said James O'Donnell curtly. "At least not until you stand before the priest. And God help you if you don't . . ."

Erin O'Donnell snorted. "Don't worry about that," she scoffed. "She can say yes. She had trouble with no."

While her parents raised a glass with Ian to the trade they called a marriage proposal, Kathleen ran outside. She did not want any of the whiskey Ian had brought along, which she thought she recognized by the bottle as the kind Michael used to distribute. Instead, she felt she needed to talk to someone desperately. Anyone who meant good by her. Kathleen yearned for Michael. Or for Bridget, the prostitute. Or the old woman from the wharf; it would be wonderful if Kathleen could speak to her now.

She ended up in front of Father O'Brien's rectory. The priest smiled as she stood disheveled, with wild hair and a tear-streaked face, before his door.

"Do come in, Mary Kathleen," he said amicably. "You know you're welcome here. Do you want to confess, my child?"

"What do I have left to confess, Father?" Kathleen blurted. "Everyone can plainly see the evidence of my old sins. And sitting at the spinning wheel, it's hard to add new ones."

"Even in our thoughts we can sin, Mary Kathleen," Father O'Brien said with feigned severity. "But step in, step in. You'll catch a cold in that thin dress."

Mary Kathleen entered the tiny rectory.

"What's wrong, Mary Kathleen? Come sit down."

Kathleen sat. Then she inhaled deeply. "Ian Coltrane wants to marry me," she said.

O'Brien listened silently to her somewhat confused explanation of Michael's money and Ian's plans. "Ah, and you think young Coltrane knew about the purse?" he asked at the end. "The way you put it . . ."

Kathleen shrugged. "I don't know, Father. It's not really possible. But Ian, he's eerie, Father. Sometimes I feel he knows everything."

The priest laughed. "I doubt that, child. Unless you mean to imply he's in league with the devil. And I can't imagine that, even if he's undoubtedly a swindler. That mule he foisted on William O'Neil . . . But let's forget that. You don't have much of a choice, Mary Kathleen, if you want a father for your baby."

"But the baby has a father!" cried Kathleen. "Michael will come back. He promised! And then, then he might not find me. Then I might be in, in . . ."

"New Zealand," the priest helped her. "But then you'd be a good bit closer to that Michael of yours. Of course, even the thought of another will be forbidden you once you're Ian's wife."

"Closer?" Kathleen sat up.

The old priest was amused by how quickly life returned to the girl's green eyes. "Come, take a look." O'Brien pulled a globe out of a cabinet in which he kept the instruments for his school lessons. "Look, here's Ireland. And there's London, where they're taking Michael now. From there he's going to Australia. Here, through the channel and into the Atlantic, around Africa, past Madagascar. And then here, clear across the Indian Ocean. This is Botany Bay, Kathleen, and Van Diemen's Land. It's an island offshore. Here, you see?"

Kathleen followed the priest's finger as it traced the endlessly long path across the globe. She lost all hope as he did. Never, never would Michael find his way back to Ireland. It was completely impossible. Perhaps you could escape a prison, but you couldn't sail halfway around the world without money or papers.

"And down there"—Father O'Brien pointed to two small islands to Australia's southeast—"this is New Zealand."

"That's, that's really very close," she said excitedly.

The priest shrugged. "Something more than a thousand miles, if that seems near to you. But like I said, it's closer than Ireland, however you look at it."

"And the country: I've never heard about it before. The islands in the South Seas, aren't they full of cannibals?"

O'Brien laughed. "Well, this one has rather more Protestants, who, in general, show themselves harder for the missionaries to convert. Most of the immigrants are Scotch or English—a few Germans too. I haven't heard anything about the natives so far. And there aren't many settlements yet, either, just a few whaling stations, some seal catchers, fortune hunters. I wouldn't like to see you in their camps, Kathleen. But Ian'll hardly go to those anyway. After all, they don't buy many horses."

"Ian said something to my parents about the Canterbury Plains."

The priest nodded. "Yes, I've heard of it. The Church of England is supposed to be founding a city, and the area is supposed to be good for livestock husbandry. Ian will make money there, in any case. So think about it, Mary Kathleen. Don't fear; I'll not marry you to any man you don't like, regardless of what your parents want. But think about it. As I said, you don't have many options."

Kathleen sighed. Then she looked again at the endlessly long way from Ireland to Australia—and the comparative stone's throw to New Zealand.

"I've thought about it, Father," she said. "I want to go to New Zealand."

The old priest shook his head. "That's not right, Kathleen," he said softly. "It should be 'I want to take Ian Coltrane for my lawfully wedded husband, in sickness and in health.'"

***

Father O'Brien married Ian and Kathleen two weeks later in his little church. Beforehand, Kathleen had thought up every possible excuse to delay the wedding. She did not want to marry until she got to her new homeland.

Her mother dismissed this with a disdainful glance at Kathleen's belly.

"There'll be no question of that, Mary Kathleen," she said sternly. "You can't travel with Ian without being married. And who'll do the ceremony down there? An Anglican reverend? A blind one if possible, so he won't notice you're ready to give birth at the altar? And what if the baby is born on the way? If you give birth on the ocean before you're married, the poor bastard won't just lack a father but a homeland too."

"He's getting a father. That's why we're doing all this, isn't it?" Kathleen grumbled. She saw that her objections were childish. Father O'Brien was right: Going to New Zealand meant she had to marry. And no matter how close she would be to Michael on the map, once married she would be as far as was possible.

Kathleen was ashamed when she stood at the altar with Ian. She wore a new wide-cut green dress, and she stuck Michael's letter and lock of hair in her cleavage, so that they were next to her heart. In principle, she was already betraying her husband, but no one would learn of it, of course. Mary Kathleen had long stopped confessing every sinful thought.

Ian had set aside a portion of her dowry for a proper celebration, so at least the good food stopped the mouths of her worst mockers. But it did not matter what people in the village said about Kathleen's union with Ian. Just three days after the wedding, the young couple would set out for Dublin. From there, a ship would leave for London the next day. And just a few days later, on April 5, the *Primrose* would depart from London for Port Cooper, a harbor near the future pastures of the Canterbury Plains.

Kathleen was not afraid of her wedding night with Ian. Though she had qualms regarding her new husband, his body did not disgust her, and her memories of making love with Michael were all good ones. She had hoped Ian might spare her for a bit; it seemed the baby in her belly would be an obstacle. Ian, however, would not be deterred. He took possession of his young wife that very first night.

Of course he would not have phrased it so, but for Kathleen that was what it felt like. The deal was made, hands were shaken, and now the horse could be ridden. Ian performed this last act with little sense of tenderness. He dispensed with any caressing and pushed very quickly into her. When Kathleen groaned in pain and surprise, he yelled at her. "What's this? Surely you're not going to pretend you're a virgin."

At that, Kathleen held her tongue and lay still until it was over. She hoped he had not harmed the baby, but she did not worry too much. In the tenants' tiny cottages, children knew when their parents had sex, however much they tried to suppress every noise. Kathleen's father had always insisted on his rights until nearly the very end of her mother's pregnancies. Erin O'Donnell had accepted it; now, Kathleen accepted it—and she had the feeling of finally avoiding a sin.

She would never be able to think of Michael while Ian lay with her.

Goodness

London, England

Van Diemen's Land, Australia

Port Cooper, New Zealand

1847–1850

Chapter 1

Lizzie Owens would have liked to have been a good girl. She even half knew how to go about it; the pastor in the orphanage had talked about it endlessly, after all. Good girls did not steal and did not tell lies, and they did not give themselves to men for money. That was why everyone treasured them, God was pleased by them, and they went to heaven when they died.

Lizzie's dilemma was that she was only just seventeen years old and did not want admission into heaven so soon. Refraining from all the forbidden things would have brought a quick death from hunger, and it would have taken her dear friend Hannah and Hannah's children, Toby and Laura, with her. Try as she might, she simply could not avoid stealing, lying, and whoring, and so she would end up in hell.

On this day, she woke hungry as ever. Even worse, it was cold. She removed the thin blanket and pushed the children carefully aside. Toby and Laura had liked to sleep snuggled against Lizzie ever since Hannah had brought her sweetheart, Lucius, into their wooden shed in Whitechapel. As if that drafty spot in the recess between two stone buildings, which barely protected them from the rain, was not already too small for four people.

Lizzie hated having to duck behind a threadbare curtain with her customers when the children were nearby. Still, she managed to grit her teeth and keep quiet while the men used her. Hannah could not be quiet, however, which was why Lizzie always tried to go out with the children. Or sometimes she would sing to them, but then the men cursed and complained.

Now it did not matter, because Hannah had Lucius and the children knew what the two of them were doing in the second bed near the door.

"But it's gaining them a father," Hannah had said, quite matter-of-factly. "Lucius will make money and protect us."

Yet Lucius was usually too drunk by midday to stand upright. He could not have protected himself, let alone anyone else. He wasn't in any danger, though, since there was nothing to take from him. Just yesterday, Hannah and Lucius had fought about how he did not work.

Lizzie looked over at the dirty mattress that Hannah and Lucius shared. She had expected to find them in a close embrace, but, to her disbelief, only Hannah was there. Lizzie had not imagined all that noise early that morning. Lucius must have actually gotten up to go to work.

It was not that hard to earn something, in truth. The ships from or bound for overseas had to be loaded and unloaded, and day laborers were hired for that. But you had to be at the harbor by daybreak—and good-for-nothings like Lucius didn't manage that often.

Lizzie threw on her shawl and went to the stove. She sighed with relief when she found embers still burning. Two logs were there as well; they would provide a little warmth until the children woke and the sun was higher in the sky.

Lizzie stretched. Not a bad day at all. It was not raining; the buckets they placed under holes in the ceiling were empty. She knew a piece of bread had even been left over the night before. She'd save most of it for the children, but a bite or two would fortify her, and then she would walk down to the harbor.

It was likely that ships had landed overnight—and those ships would be full of sailors hungry for a woman's body. Hannah—who liked to sleep late—did not believe her, but Lizzie often found the best customers in the morning, and she rarely had to bring them home. Before the sun rose, the hourly hotels rented their rooms cheaply.

Lizzie looked for the bread, but without luck. That damned Lucius. He'd taken the last crumb of bread away from the half-starved children.

Her first impulse was to wake Hannah and make harsh accusations, but she could imagine how her friend would defend Lucius: "Is he supposed to go off to find work on an empty stomach?"

There was no talking to Hannah these days. Her love for Lucius had robbed her of reason. Lizzie doubted the rat would even bring a penny home.

If Hannah and Lizzie were lucky, he would share his last bottle of gin with them. He never thought of the children.

Lizzie had to change her plans. She was plenty familiar with how to pick up men, and making her smile charming, so she would look beautiful to them, required little energy. But the men did not like it when her stomach growled while they exerted themselves on top of her. She had to eat something, even just a bit of bread.

Lizzie went over to the washbasin and thanked the heavens when she found that Lucius hadn't used the water she had hauled in the day before. She splashed the cold water on her face, shivered, rubbed herself dry, and brushed her hair.

She always tried to look neat when she left the house, and during the day she refrained from the garish cosmetics of her trade. That did her no harm either. Some of the boys liked going off with a girl who looked as young and honest as she did. As she put on her dress and hat, she occasionally looked in the sliver of mirror little Toby had found in the trash somewhere and given her as a present.

Toby had just turned five, but he already knew what was valuable. When they let him crawl around in the trash cans of the rich, he found glass and scrap metal they could sell and so contributed more to supporting the family than Lucius did. Hannah knew this and often would simply send him out alone to go looking—another thing for which Lizzie reprimanded her. The boy was still too small to fight off the other street urchins. And what was worse, he could be kidnapped by the gangs of men in London who forced small children to pickpocket and beg.

She set in place the handsome little hat she had bought last year at the charity clothing market. Really, she had not been able to afford it, but the vendor woman had fallen for her smile and given it to her for a pittance. Lizzie practiced her smile in front of the mirror. But without breakfast or someone across from her, it did not work.

She wished she could be as beautiful as Hannah had been before she had two children and then gave herself to gin and men like Lucius. Hannah was curvy, pale, and blessed with an abundance of red hair. Her eyes shone blue, and she had thick eyelashes—she was the kind of woman men could hardly resist.

Lizzie, in contrast, was petite, her body scrawny like a boy's. She had small breasts and doubted, since she was already seventeen, that these would grow any fuller. Her face was round, though her cheeks were sunken and pale. The proportions of Lizzie's nose suited her face, at least when people saw her from the front. From the side, it seemed a little too long, mischievous but not coy. Her hair was somewhat wiry and a boring dark blonde, her eyelashes and brows were so light-colored and sparse that they were hardly noticeable if Lizzie did not emphasize them with charcoal, and her eyes were a common blue.

Lizzie was not a girl you noticed at first glance, but she possessed a peculiar talent that helped her survive nonetheless. She had the ability to make the sun go up with a smile. Sometimes the air around her seemed to vibrate when she smiled. A radiance emanated from her eyes that people simply had to return—whether man, woman, or child. Their hearts seemed to warm; they talked to Lizzie and joked with her. Merchants sold things to her for less or gave them to her outright.

Lizzie's smile could open doors otherwise closed to girls like her. Some mean, brutish customers stopped and approached her with respect and care when she offered them a smile. And misers thought twice about running out without paying Lizzie as they often did with other whores. Sometimes the men would take her to a cookshop after her work was done to buy her a pie and gin—just to see a grateful smile.

Unfortunately, she had not possessed this talent for bewitching people when she was a child. Lizzie often dreamed of how differently her life could have gone if she had been an adorable, irresistible little thing. If she could have beguiled the people in the orphanage with a smile, perhaps parents could have been found for her.

Little Lizzie—found on a street in the East End where she clung, howling, sniffling, and crying, to the legs of passersby—was a scrawny, recalcitrant child no one wanted. She did not discover her smile until later, at thirteen or fourteen, once she was already back on the street.

She used to dig discarded clothing out of the trash in order to sell it, and she remembered how once she had gone into a sweetshop with her hard-earned pence. She should have bought bread, but she couldn't resist sugary treats. In sheer happiness at the sight of all the wonders in the glass cases and dishes, she had smiled at the seller—and had promptly gone out with a whole bag of sweets. They were broken candy canes and stuck-together bonbons—nothing the man could sell. But he did not have to give them to Lizzie.

"Here," he had said, with a smile to match hers. "Sweets for a sweetheart."

***

Lizzie lowered the mirror and went on her way. Now, where could she scrounge something to eat? She considered first going to the pier and trying to pick someone up, but just the thought turned her stomach. What was more, the scents from the bakery a few streets over had her spellbound.

She could do nothing else; she had to follow the scent of fresh bread. It would have been much smarter to go begging at the back door. The baker's wife might have had some leftover bread, and perhaps she had woken up on the right side of the bed. It happened; now and again, she had given Hannah some leftovers when Toby and Laura had looked too hungry. But something had gotten into Lizzie. She entered the shop through the front door.

The baker was standing there, which was good. Men often fell for Lizzie's charms, whether her smile worked or not. In front of her, another customer was buying two rolls. Lizzie waited until the baker had helped him. Then she smiled, greeting him politely. However, she noticed that her magic was not working that morning. She could manage a pleasant smile, but nothing more.

Nevertheless, the baker responded amicably. "Well, my lovely girl, what can I do for you?"

What could he do for her? Lizzie let her starving gaze pass over all the baked goods on the shelf. "A loaf of bread," she said longingly, "and two sweet rolls for the children, and some croissants."

Lizzie was not serious; she simply whispered the objects of her longing. It was so warm in there, so wonderful. She was surprised when the baker handed a bag across the counter.

"There, that'll be three pence."

Lizzie took the bag. "I," she whispered, "I don't have any money right now. Is it possible for me to come by later with it?"

"You don't have any money?" The baker's previously friendly demeanor darkened. "Dear, you don't have any money, and I don't have anything to give away. So what are you doing here? Give me back that bag and get out of here. Pay later? I can just mark that down as a loss."

The bag in her hand was real. And the counter was high. The man could not leap over it. What madness was this?

Lizzie pressed the bread and pastries to her chest. "I'm, I'm sorry," she stammered. "But I'll come back with the money." Then she ran out of the store.

The baker yelled "Thief!" after her.

She ran down the street as fast as her feet would carry her. Not toward her shed, since they could find her there, but to the market. Surely it was already bustling; she could disappear in the crowd and then return home the long way to give the children something to eat.

Lizzie was afraid, but she also felt a prickling of power. She would never have thought herself capable of such a brazen theft. Yet it seemed to be going well. The baker would not catch up to her quickly, and the few passersby at that early hour seemed too tired to chase her.

Then suddenly, a hugely fat police officer stood in front of her like a wall. She had never before seen the police in this quarter of London. An unlucky coincidence.

"Well, aren't we in a hurry, lovely." The officer held her with one hand. "I'll bet your husband's waiting for his breakfast?"

Lizzie tried to smile. "My children, sir, I, I, they should have something in their stomachs before they go to school."

"I see, I see. You've already got children who go to school. Good, very good. And your husband makes plenty of money—and the call from over there is for a whole different thief." The officer pointed toward the bakery, where the baker was still yelling.

The baker's wife ran down the street to Lizzie and the officer. "That's her! I'm sure of it; that's her!" she yelled. "Bring the little thief back so my husband can look at her. Everything should be done proper. But I know her. Walks around here haughty as can be. How could my husband have ever been fooled? You'd think her a proper girl, but really she whores herself. Everybody knows that. A pretty face, and the fellows get weak. Don't let the beastie go, officer. She'll just run away."

Lizzie made no move to run. It would have been senseless anyway. The officer was much stronger. If anything could help her in this unfortunate moment, it was begging and pleading.

***

"Sir, hear me out, please!" The baker seemed inclined to listen to her. "I was in a daze; I did not mean to order anything I can't pay for. I meant to ask from the start if you would put it on a bill. But the children, sir, if you let them lock me up, then they'll get nothing to eat. And I would have brought you the money, without fail. I'm not, not some . . . I'm honest, I . . ."

The baker's wife answered Lizzie's words with a mocking laugh.

The baker breathed out sharply. "So, hungry children, is it? And a loaf of bread wouldn't have been enough? You had to take some pastries?"

Lizzie bit her lip. "I didn't want . . ."

"Do you want to report the theft or not?" the officer asked.

The baker's wife ripped the bag from Lizzie's hand. "Of course we do. It just gets better and better! Look at these rolls and croissants. All smashed; we can't even sell them now. And more than that, she's a whore; I'm telling you, officer. Just ask around."

Lizzie turned one last time to the baker. "Please."

But he knew no mercy either. He shook his head. "Take her away," he said to the officer.

"Get that dumb thing out of his sight before he gets weak again," his wife said.

Lizzie closed her eyes. Now all she could hope for was a merciful judge. And for Hannah. She would at least confirm Lizzie's story about the children.

***

Newgate Prison was filthy and crowded. Lizzie felt she could hardly breathe when they pushed her into a long room lit only by a small barred window high up on the wall. At least fifteen other women were in the room, and for all of them together there was only one toilet in the corner, which stank abominably. For furniture there was only a bench, and two powerful women occupied it. Some women leaned against the walls; others sat on the dirty straw-covered ground. Lizzie stood at the door and lowered her gaze. In the straw were fleas; she was sure of it. She hated fleas.

A nagging voice suddenly called out: "I must be mad. Lizzie Owens, who always thought 'erself better."

Lizzie looked up.

Candy Williams, a prostitute from her neighborhood, smirked at her. "What did you do?"

"Got caught stealing bread," Lizzie said. Why deny it? Besides, Candy was not mean. She was simply teasing Lizzie.

A few women laughed.

"What a dumb little girl," one of the women on the bench said. "If you're going to steal, it 'as to be worth it. Look, that girl there." She nodded her head toward a beautiful dark-haired girl staring, unresponsive, at nothing. "She pinched a gold watch. Would 'ave gone fine, but the fence snitched."

"My man will come get me," whispered the girl.

More of the women snickered.

"That fine knight of yours probably got you into this mess," said the fat woman on the bench. "Didn't 'e make a deal with the fence? Couldn't 'e have taken the blame? Nah, girl, 'e's washed his 'ands of you."

"What happens to someone who steals bread?" Lizzie asked quietly.

The fat woman grinned. "The same thing that 'appens when you steal a watch. Theft is theft. Depends on your lawyer too. If 'e lets your kids in the court, and they 'owl a bit—"

"She doesn't 'ave any children," Candy said.

The fat woman furrowed her brow. "No? Didn't I see you on the street with two brats? I'd wanted to talk to you about my cathouse. You've got something about you. But I don't take anyone with brats; that's only trouble."

Lizzie now remembered having seen the woman once before. Franny Gray. She owned a brothel on Hanbury Street.

"How did you land here?" Lizzie asked. "I thought . . . if you had a house . . ."

The whores on the street had always envied Franny Gray's girls a bit—not to mention the brothel owner herself, who seemed to be raking in money.

"I'm asking the questions here," Franny clarified. "And don't you worry about me. I'll be out of here before you can even say 'bail,' though that's not as fast as Velvet can pull a watch out of a man's pocket." She indicated the dark-haired girl again, and the others laughed. Then she returned to interrogating Lizzie. "So, where'd you get the brats? Stole 'em? Showing 'em the ropes? Did you already sell 'em? Love, I wouldn't 'ave thought you the kind."

Franny frowned disapprovingly.

Lizzie exploded. "How dare you talk to me like that! As if, as if . . . My God, yes, I whore and sometimes steal, but that doesn't mean I'd teach children to do so. The little ones are Hannah's—the redhead who works Dorset Street. I live with her, and the children, damn it, the children always . . ."

With that, Lizzie turned away. She could well imagine what would become of Toby and Laura if Hannah had to care for them alone.

Candy laughed. "I told you, I did, Franny. A sweetheart. An angel. She's just hiding 'er 'alo. It just won't 'elp you, Lizzie. And as for Hannah, I wouldn't rely on 'er either."

Lizzie had hoped Hannah would soon come visit her—word of arrests spread quickly in the neighborhood, and everyone knew about the comforts a few pence could buy a prisoner. If it had been Hannah who'd been caught by the police, Lizzie would have taken another customer so she could help her friend.

Suddenly two guards appeared to let Franny out. "It proved to be a mistake, the matter with the gentleman's wallet," one of them explained reluctantly. "He had misplaced it after all. Anyway, he has his wallet now and regrets the misunderstanding."

Franny signaled her triumph and rushed out of the cell. Lizzie wondered how the woman had arranged the matter—from a cell, no less. But she was probably always prepared for such eventualities. The customer who had been robbed had gotten his wallet back. How Franny's people had made him apologize on top of that defied Lizzie's understanding.

***

Lizzie did not receive a visitor until the next day, after a hellish night in the holding cell. Franny's share of the bench had been immediately occupied—this time by a woman far less affable than Franny. The new cell boss was a fighter and, by appearance, a beast. She made direct overtures to terrorize the others.

"We should try to get out of here," Candy sighed. "Tomorrow she'll want better food, and then she'll take all of ours away to make money from it."

"But we don't have anything." Lizzie said.

Candy laughed derisively. This was not her first stay in jail. She had served two years for prostitution and expected a similar sentence this time. Though they might send her to the colonies as a repeat offender.

"We still 'ave our clothes," she said. "If you look around . . ."

Lizzie looked at the other women. A few were only wearing ragged underskirts over which they pulled their holey shawls in embarrassment. At least it wasn't cold in the cell; all those bodies kept it warm.

"And that little 'at of yours, you should try your luck selling it to one of the guards," Candy said. "He might take it 'ome to his wife. In any case, you might get lucky and 'ave 'im move you to another cell."

Lizzie was willing to part with her hat, but her name was called before she had the chance to haggle with a guard.

"Elizabeth Owens," a bored guard read aloud from a piece of paper. "Your lawyer is waiting outside. Speak with him; your trial is this afternoon."

Lizzie gathered new hope. Perhaps she really would be free soon. For a loaf of bread, they couldn't possibly punish her as severely as a jewelry thief like Velvet.

Her lawyer was completely uninterested in Lizzie's story. As she learned immediately, he represented her and Candy and Velvet and all the women who did not have the money to afford a better attorney.

"It might be that the judge takes extenuating circumstances into account," he said placidly, "but I would not count on that. The prisons are full."

"But if he lets me go, there'll be an open spot," Lizzie said, bewildered.

The lawyer laughed. "Love, they can't just let you all go. Where would we be if you could all steal and prostitute yourselves and the next day we let you all go free? No, just forget that. If the judge is kind, you'll get five years."

"Five years? Five years in prison for a loaf of bread?" Lizzie looked at the man, horrified.

"It was more than a loaf though. From what I hear, you took a few pastries with it; that doesn't fit with robbing because of hunger. Which is why I don't think the judge will make a mild ruling. Sentence could run seven years, love, and seven years means deportation."

"You, you mean they'd send me to the colonies?" Lizzie could not believe it.

"That's what it would amount to, so be prepared."

"But isn't there anything that can be done? If the judge sees the children . . . no one will care for the children when I'm gone."

Lizzie did not want to cry; indeed, she had meant to smile. But now tears ran down her cheeks. She was not really afraid of Australia. It could not be worse than London. But Toby and Laura . . . and seven years, seven years in prison.

Her lawyer shrugged. But Lizzie was determined to fight. She pulled her little hat out of the pocket in her dress.

"Here, sir. I don't have any money, but you can sell this."

The attorney's threadbare suit looked as if it had come from a market like the one Lizzie's clothes had, and it was in worse shape.

Lizzie confirmed. "That will earn a few pence. But please go down Whitechapel Road and speak with my friend. She should bring the children to court and testify for me. Please! You are my lawyer, after all. You have to help me!"

The lawyer took the hat without a word, knocked the dust off, and returned it to its proper form. "I'll see what I can do," he said, "but I can't promise anything."

***

At least the man kept his word. When Lizzie was led into the courtroom in chains, Hannah was sitting, stony-faced, with the children beside her. Lizzie saw that Toby and Laura wanted to call something to her, but Hannah reprimanded them sharply. Lucius was with them, and his tense expression did not bode well.

The official removed Lizzie's chains and pushed her onto the defendant's bench. Shaken, she stood up before the judge, who looked like a being from another world in his dark robes and white wig.

"Name?" asked the clerk.

"Elizabeth Owens," Lizzie answered quietly.

"Year of birth?"

"1830, I think."

The judge furrowed his brow. "Where?"

"In London, I assume."

"Is there anything you know for sure?" the judge asked sarcastically.

Lizzie lowered her gaze. "No."

"Impudence will not get you far, girl."

"I'm not being impudent. I'm just an orphan. Although I don't know that for sure either. I don't even know my real name. They gave me the name Owens after the man who turned me in to the police. He found me on Cavell Street, he said. I think that's true. I think I remember it. But I'm not sure. They said I was three years old."

"Well, you've remained true to the street," remarked the judge. "Did they not try to raise you to be a better person in the orphanage?"

"Of course, sir."

"And? Why are you here, then?"

"They only tried, sir," Lizzie answered abjectly.

The court filled with laughter.

The judge banged his gavel indignantly. "What's that supposed to mean, girl?"

"I ran away, sir," Lizzie admitted. "Because I wanted to be a good girl, but I did not want to get beaten. I was always the smallest, sir. I did not get much to eat, and now, please, sir, you must believe me. I never steal otherwise. I wanted to put it on a bill, and I only wanted a loaf of bread. Please, look at the children. It's plain to see that they don't get anything to eat."

Hannah seemed to want to leap up, outraged, at this charge, but Lizzie's attorney got the first word.

"Your Honor, the woman faced extenuating circumstances. She did not steal the bread for herself, or at least not only for herself, but for two starving children for whom she cares."

"Who are not her own, however?" asked the judge incredulously.

"No, Your Honor, they belong to a friend, and the family is present. If it pleases the court?" The lawyer gestured to Hannah, who would no longer be restrained.

She leaped to her feet. "It's a groundless effront'ry, Your, Mr., uh, Judge. The police says I let my children starve. I've got to straight away defend myself against this orphan brat who wants to tell me 'ow to raise my kids. I take good care of the little ones, and now I'm getting married, too, to get 'em a proper father." Hannah pointed to Lucius. "And 'e'll buy us a nice house and nice clothes. My little ones ain't going to starve."

Glaring at Lizzie, Hannah sat back down. Lizzie wished she could disappear. Of course Hannah could not tell the truth. Otherwise, they might take the children away.

The judge turned to Lizzie. "Do you have anything to say, Miss Elizabeth Owens?"

Lizzie said nothing. Indeed, she thought Toby's and Laura's emaciated faces spoke for themselves, but at least Hannah had outdone herself that day and cleaned the children's faces. Their clothing looked new—secondhand, of course, but clean. Lucius really must have earned something, and Hannah had summoned the energy to take it from him before he could drink it away. Perhaps she would do that more often in the future. Lizzie could only wish her the best.

The rest of the trial passed in a fog: her lawyer's meaningless words, the judge's admonishments and recriminations, and finally the verdict. Deportation, seven years, as her attorney had predicted. As she later learned, it would not have been hard to foresee. Nearly all her fellow prisoners received the same sentence. Only the cruel fighter, who had likely almost killed someone, was sentenced to ten years.

Candy cried. She had a lover she liked and whom she did not want to leave. Velvet seemed to have grown another shade paler. Her man testified against her, which did not help him in the end. He, too, was sent to the colonies.

The prison chaplain explained to the condemned precisely what fate awaited them. "Van Diemen's Land is a large island near Australia, an independent colony. It's been settled a long time already, so don't be worried about the natives—everything there is British. The women's prison is very modern. And you'll be going soon. The *Asia*, under command of Captain John Roskell, weighs anchor at the end of March. Only women will be on the ship—at least that's the plan."

"'Ow long does the voyage take?" asked one of the women.

"The voyage will take roughly three months. You will first be sent to a female factory. There's sewing and laundry to do there. But some of you will also work as housemaids, or in the gardens, and some of you might marry. There are few women down there. Whoever behaves well and finds a respectable husband may be pardoned. So don't lose courage. God knows what He's doing. He will be with you in this strange land, and if you work at it a little,

Jesus will save you. Now, let's pray together . . . or do you still have a question, miss?"

Lizzie had shyly raised her hand. "If we do work over there, will they give us something to eat, Reverend?"

The reverend laughed. "But of course, child. The Crown doesn't let its prisoners starve. True, the food here might not always be the best, but in the colonies . . ."

Lizzie nodded. Even in the prison in London, she was not made to starve. Yes, the food was abysmal, but there was plenty of it. She had often had less and worse in her stomach than the constant porridge here. There was supposed to be fruitful land in the colonies, and Lizzie was thoroughly willing to work it herself. Someone just needed to show her what to do. And if "being good" no longer meant starving, she was happy to try it again.

That night she fell asleep full of hope, despite the fleas and lice in the cell, and despite the tears and sobs all around her. She wanted to live a life pleasing to God, even if she did not completely understand God. Perhaps he was sending her to Australia to save her.

But then, who would save Toby and Laura?

Chapter 2

The morning of March 23, the condemned women were taken aboard the *Asia*. The ship was imposing, but it almost looked small beside the many-story prison hulks at the dock. It was not just the women's prison in London that was bursting at the seams. The prisons for men were so overstuffed that they had resorted to ships docked in Woolwich. Conditions inside were supposed to be horrible. Merely the sight of them filled Lizzie with dread.

The *Asia*, which had already made five trips to Australia and back without a problem, seemed inviting in comparison despite how crowded it was. Alongside some hundred paying passengers, there were at least one hundred and fifty prisoners, thirty guards, and Captain John Roskell's crew.

Lizzie was horrified when they led her down a ramp into a gigantic dark room. Separated only by wooden partitions that were necessary to secure their pallets, one hundred female prisoners were housed in the tween deck. The guards took other prisoners farther down to the ship's hold. Finally, they also brought twelve men inside, each chained to the others.

The women listened as the some of the prison attendants argued with the captain of the ship. "Oh come on, you're not even fully occupied. And we can't possibly stuff more of these criminals into the prison hulks. So just take them, Captain Roskell—no need for them to show up on the manifest."

"And their food doesn't appear either, does it?" grumbled the captain.

"We'll deliver their food. We just won't note it, if you catch my meaning." The warden laughed and made a gesture as if he were pocketing money. "Now, just say aye, Captain Roskell. What difference does another dozen scoundrels aboard make?"

The captain must have relented, because not long after that, the men were shoved down the ramp. The ship's carpenter followed behind to set up a barricade for them.

Lizzie felt a vague sympathy. Below the waterline, where the men would stay, it was surely even gloomier than on the tween deck, where at least the women could orient themselves a little. Not that there was much to see. It was one three-tiered berth after another—no other furniture, no luggage either.

"Don't complain. At least we don't chain you up," declared the guard who was supervising the loading of the women into their berths.

Lizzie, Candy, and Velvet agreed about their bunks without fighting. Candy wanted to sleep on the bottom, and Velvet volunteered for the top, just under the ceiling. That left the middle for Lizzie.

In other areas, women were arguing over their bunks. The guards had to get involved—and they did so forcefully. They immediately broke their word about putting the women in chains. Lizzie couldn't help but notice that every pallet was equipped with them.

"Just until we set sail," grumbled one of the guards, a soldier of the Crown like the others, "so you don't do anything stupid."

Lizzie smiled at him. She had accepted her fate, and she could do it again. She had smiled at the reverend and immediately received a Bible as a present. The man was delighted that she could read and, in the days before her deportation, Lizzie was moved to a roomier and cleaner four-person cell.

Her magic had worked on the doctor too. He attested to Lizzie's malnutrition—which was the case but also applied to most of the other imprisoned women—and prescribed better food for the voyage. Now for the guard . . .

"But you don't need to chain us up, sir. What trouble would we cause? You don't really believe that women as little as we are could take the ship by force and free all the prisoners, do you?"

Lizzie managed to look afraid of the men belowdecks. Really, she thought the men were harmless—just desperate ne'er-do-wells like the women. Though that was far from certain. Even among the women there were a handful of serious criminals—murderers, most of them sentenced to death before having their sentences commuted to a lifetime of hard labor in the colonies.

The colonies did not like to take these people in, and even the captain feared them. During the voyage, they were lodged deep in the ship's hold, where no light and hardly any fresh air entered, and they were kept in chains. Lizzie had seen that the cruel fighter, the terror of the holding cell, had been taken belowdecks.

The guard looked almost sympathetically at the three young women. His gaze first paused on the beautiful Velvet before landing on the smiling Lizzie.

"A ship taken under such lovely force wouldn't be the worst thing," he said, grinning. "But it'll cost you, my sweet. Might I pay you a visit once we're at sea?"

Lizzie sighed in her mind but maintained her smile. *So much for a life pleasing to God*, she thought. She should not have even tried flirting with him. But if she rejected him now, he would become angry, and she could not afford that. She needed an ally on the ship.

"If you think it'd be fun among all the girls here," she said softly. "I'd be a little embarrassed, myself."

The man laughed. "Be embarrassed, will you? Are you that fine a girl? Well, I'm sure there's a little spot where we can be alone, never fear. Now just hold still, my sweets, and don't scream or howl when we weigh anchor. It might also get a little stormy tonight." He stole a quick kiss from Lizzie. "Take it as a taste of sweeter storms to come," he whispered.

She wiped her mouth as soon as he left. She was already disgusted. No doubt there would be no opportunity during the voyage to wash herself after sleeping with her new admirer.

"Getting an early start," a disapproving voice remarked from the bed across the way.

Lizzie lay just a couple of feet away from her neighbor at the same height. In the dreary light that came through the spaces in the deck planks, she saw an older woman. Even in these circumstances the woman wore her hair tightly tucked under a bonnet, and she had been permitted her dress and the modest head covering. So she could not be entirely without means.

Lizzie realized that her new admirer hadn't chained the women who had been fighting in the berths across from hers.

"Sooner or later," Lizzie answered calmly, "the boys do what they want. Besides, aren't you happy you weren't chained up?"

"I don't care either way," said the woman. "They could have hanged me for all I care." With that, she turned her face to the wall.

Lizzie closed her eyes and tried to imagine herself out of the stuffy tween deck. She did not succeed, of course. She could not help thinking of the men and women who were chained up even deeper down. She listened to the dozens of them who wept and prayed.

She was only leaving Hannah and the children behind, but most of the other women were mourning husbands, lovers, and children of their own. She did not wonder what or whom the woman next to her was leaving behind or how she had ended up here. She did not look like a criminal, but Lizzie did not feel guilty herself either.

Finally, she tried reading the Bible, hearing the calls and commands from the deck above, the rustling of unfurling sails, and then the droning of the wind caught in them. Most of the women screamed when the ship began to move—as did the few men in the hold.

***

Michael Drury had screamed along with the other prisoners when his ship had left Ireland. Now, however, he was silent. For him, England was just as foreign and perhaps more hostile than far-off Australia. He had been lucky that in London, he had not seen more than a length of harbor wall. Originally, the prisoners from Ireland were supposed to be put on one of the prison hulks that lay at anchor in Woolwich. But then some space had been found on this ship, which was transporting women to Van Diemen's Land.

They had moved the Irish prisoners directly from one ship to another, and now Michael, in chains for half a day, lay on his pallet in the darkest corner of the darkest deck in the *Asia*. The captain had given the men transport only on the condition that they remain strictly separated from the female prisoners at all times. So they could not hope for much freedom of movement. And yet no one had thought to provide the men with chamber pots or bottles into which they could relieve themselves.

In every row, there was at least one man frozen in silent agony who did not respond to the calls of his fellows. Billy Rafferty was among them. The young man had fallen into a sort of numbness after screaming and crying for hours during the departure from Ireland. He had already suffered occasional fits of claustrophobia in his cell in Wicklow, and the tightly sealed dark rooms belowdecks on the rocking ship to London caused him to lose his mind. Now he lay next to Michael in chains, whimpering.

The stench on the lowest deck quickly became worse and worse, the air stuffier. Michael was happy when the ship finally began to move. Maybe they would finally remove the prisoners' chains now.

Indeed, that was the case on the tween deck, but Michael and his companions in misery remained fettered. Adding to the existing stench came that of vomit, for the first days at sea proved stormy.

"The English Channel," the man in the berth next to Michael's explained. He was a sailor who had killed another man during a brawl. "As far as the Bay of Biscay, it's mostly rough weather. The molls will be puking their guts out. But damn it, I'm hungry anyway. Is there nothing to eat around here? Even any of those dry crackers?"

Before the guards had distributed a meager ration of hardtack that morning, they had sent a few women down from the tween deck with buckets and mops to wash up at least the worst filth. A watchman stood next to each of the women as if, despite their chains, Michael and the other men might jump them.

"At least your beds aren't stacked on top of each other," one of the women said, trying to comfort Michael, "or you'd have to wipe it off your face. Happened to a few of us. And the seasick ones still don't always make it to the privy. How long does a trip like this take?"

"About a hundred days," the imprisoned sailor informed her.

The men groaned.

"I thought four weeks maybe," mumbled Michael. "Like to America."

The sailor laughed bitterly. "New York is a stone's throw compared to this. But they'll take us up on deck. They can't let us rot here for three months. The queen, she's a good woman. She wouldn't allow it."

Michael did not comment on this. After Queen Victoria had let half of Ireland starve without a word, he couldn't attribute much goodness to her. But perhaps she at least showed mercy to her landsmen. The majority of prisoners in Van Diemen's Land were Englishmen, after all.

Michael yearned for light and air, but even more to be able to stretch his legs. He was already feeling the pressure of the hard wooden pallet to which he was chained. Like most of his fellow prisoners, he was undernourished, and his shoulder blades poked out and quickly became sore from lying on the pallet. Worse still were the barely healed welts on his back, which burned after the women emptied a few buckets of seawater over the fettered prisoners. Now, the men were clean but wet, and though it was humid in the belly of the *Asia*, it was not very warm. Likely, it would be days until Michael's linen pants and shirt were dry, and then they'd be filthy again.

***

Lizzie and the other women in the tween deck also struggled with seasickness, but at least they had a bucket on hand for every six women. In Lizzie's partition, it had hit Candy and two other women the worst. Velvet didn't seem to notice anything happening around her, and the older woman—after two days of silence, she had finally introduced herself as Mrs. Portland—was apparently too busy to be sick.

It appeared it was Mrs. Portland's self-appointed duty to care for the other women. She ran from one to the next with pitchers and buckets full of drinking and wash water, forcing them to eat at least a little bit of the hardtack but not complaining when they immediately vomited it up.

"A few are so weak," she explained to Lizzie, "I'm afraid they'll die of exhaustion."

Following Mrs. Portland's directions, Lizzie was tending to Candy. "So when will this get better?"

"When the sea calms down," replied a man's voice.

Lizzie spun around. For four days she had been expecting the guard with whom she had flirted during embarkation to claim her services, but apparently he'd had too much to do on deck.

"Sometimes it also gets better when you get out in the air. How about it, sweet? Want to take a walk with me?"

Lizzie would have done anything to get out in the air, but on the other hand . . . "These two are doing a lot worse than me," she said, pointing to Candy and another of the women.

This woman was tiny and could hardly be more than fourteen years old. She would not survive long if she continued spewing all her food.

The guard thought a moment. "First, be good to me," he finally said, "and then we'll see. It's about time you all went on deck anyway. I'll speak with the lieutenant."

Giving him a gentle smile, Lizzie followed him up the stairs. Cold, damp Atlantic air struck her immediately. She held her face happily into the wind and looked around curiously. Lizzie was not the only girl on deck. Apparently, a few of the guards were giving one another alibis so they could go topside with the girls of their choice. Lizzie's guard—he introduced himself as Jeremiah—had even thought of protection from the rain. He pulled her into a lifeboat over which he had spread a tarpaulin. There was a blanket for bedding, and what was more, he produced a bottle of gin from under the planks with a triumphant grin.

Lizzie took a long swig; the alcohol warmed her body and calmed her stomach. Then she let herself sink, content, onto the blanket. She had plied her trade under less conducive circumstances before. Though she found it difficult to feign passion when Jeremiah finally entered her, he fortunately proved easy to please. The man also proved to be normally sized—it did not hurt too much, though she was anything but ready for him. Lizzie let the business pass over her and then asked him for the promised walk. To her surprise, Jeremiah agreed. He seemed to be truly thankful to her; perhaps he had even fallen for her a bit.

He led her across the deck, showing her the structures for the passengers' cabins and the crew's quarters. By the end, Lizzie's hair was wet from the rain, and she felt refreshed. It was almost too much when, on top of that, Jeremiah handed her the bottle of gin, still more than half full, and a small bag of flour.

"Here, it's good for the stomach. Perhaps you can get the little one in your partition back on her feet. Mix the flour with water; it'll help her."

Lizzie thanked him profusely. When she got back to their stuffy, stinking lodgings, she put the bottle to Candy's lips first. Candy drank greedily and seemed to feel better immediately.

"Mrs. Portland?" Shyly, Lizzie held the bottle out to the older woman.

Mrs. Portland looked disapprovingly at the gin. "I've avoided that my entire life," she said, "but what's to be done? When in Rome . . ." She looked at Lizzie, then took the bottle and sipped. She coughed and struggled for air.

"I don't drink it for fun either." Lizzie felt she had to defend herself. Her instinct told her this was a good woman who had lived a life pleasing to God.

Lizzie would so have liked to know how she had ended up on the ship. "Do we still have water?" she asked.

The guards distributed the drinking water to the partitions in pitchers, though it hardly sufficed. Again and again, ugly scenes arose; in some of the partitions, the women were fully at odds. They begrudged each other every sip of water and every bite of bread.

Mrs. Portland nodded, and Lizzie dissolved some flour in the water as Jeremiah had advised. She gave some to Mrs. Portland's charge, who drank it and managed to keep the mixture down.

The next day the guards did, indeed, open all the portholes for the women held in the tween deck.

"Step up in groups of twenty-four," said the lieutenant who commanded Jeremiah and the other guards. "Limit yourselves to the separated deck space and move around. Loitering will not be tolerated. Contact with the passengers will not be tolerated. Do not speak to the sailors or guards."

Lizzie supported Candy, and Mrs. Portland carried the sick girl onto deck. Then they walked around. The women seemed a bit like wild animals on display at the fair; after all, there were plenty of spectators. The sailors treated themselves to prurient looks, and the passengers gathered in front of their cabins and stared at the prisoners. Most of the passengers were middle-aged, retired people who had finished their military or police service and were now taking advantage of the generous land apportionment in Australia. In England, their pensions hardly sufficed to live on, but in Australia they would be rich. Servants were, after all, abundant—the wives of these future settlers would have their pick from among Lizzie and her fellow sufferers.

***

Going outside awoke the prisoners' desire to live, but there was a problem. It rained constantly, and the storerooms were not sealed tight. All their clothes were damp, and the spring chill of the Atlantic did nothing to dry them. At least the water that washed over the deck in rough seas did not stand on the tween deck. It seeped through to the lower level and collected there. In some places belowdecks it stood knee-high and stank.

The women were taken outside daily, but the men remained heavily fettered. Not much movement was possible for them, so they were soaking wet and shivering with cold. And they were suffering their first cases of fever and diarrhea. Michael often drifted off in fever dreams and half sleep; his wounds had become inflamed and hurt. But it was not yet so bad that he lost all his strength. He forced himself to eat, and now he could keep the food down. Mostly, Michael suffered from the cold and wet.

"It will get warmer one of these days, once we reach the Bay of Biscay," his neighbor, the sailor, consoled him as he shivered and coughed.

The sailor was right, but the warmth, followed by the heat of the Indian Ocean, did not improve the prisoners' situation. The women on the tween deck were happy about their dry clothing, but Michael and the other heavily guarded men were not so lucky. Belowdecks it remained damp, and the warmth encouraged rot. On top of that, bugs gained the upper hand. Michael had the feeling he was being eaten alive by fleas and lice.

When they were taken up on deck, the men tried to master the infestation and their itching a bit by splashing each other with seawater. But the guards did not allow them to undress. The passengers, suffering from yawn-provoking boredom, still liked to watch when the prisoners were led out on deck. The daily "show" was almost their only distraction. Since Michael and the others went back to their berths with wet clothing, no one was surprised by the outbreak of cholera.

***

Lizzie was horrified when the first people died. The disease quickly took the young girl in her partition, despite Mrs. Portland's care and the additional food all six women in the partition owed to Lizzie's relationship with Jeremiah. She shared his presents generously and was angry that Candy did not always do the same after she disappeared with one of the sailors.

The prohibition against looking at the men could not be maintained. A lively trade quickly developed between the women on the tween deck and the lustful sailors and soldiers. Candy was in high demand and soon forgot her love back home. For that, the gin helped her more than anything. While she was good about sharing food in their common pantry, she kept the booze for herself.

The captain held a short ceremony for the dead, and then the bodies were given over to the sea—an entrancingly beautiful blue sea in which dolphins played but in which a shark fin also cut the waves, its owner hoping for prey. "It's behind them now," Mrs. Portland sighed. "Who knows what still lies ahead of the rest of us."

Mrs. Portland no longer held Lizzie's relationship with Jeremiah against her. She often asked Lizzie to accompany her when she went to visit other partitions to care for the sick. Lizzie was eager to help, and Mrs. Portland patiently instructed her in the most important tasks.

"Where did you learn all this?" Lizzie asked.

Until recently, Mrs. Portland had never said anything about her past, but she had begun to open up to Lizzie. "I helped in a Poor Law hospital," she explained. "Out of gratitude. They patched me up often enough for free, and I don't like to take without giving back. They need all the help they can get, especially with the women. It doesn't feel good to be touched and bandaged by a fellow when your own has just beaten you black and blue."

She did not say more, but Lizzie could imagine the rest. Mrs. Portland had been married—and her husband had beaten her. Had she left him and thus fallen into disrepute?

"Oh no, child, she killed him." It was one of the patients who finally cleared it up for Lizzie. Emma Brewster was an aged prostitute who suffered from terrible pains and fluid retention in her legs. Mrs. Portland treated her with cool compresses and gin poultices. Lizzie was applying one such treatment when the subject of Mrs. Portland and her misdeed came up.

Lizzie almost dropped the gin bottle. "She did? Mrs. Portland?"

Emma Brewster nodded. "To be certain, child, I was at the trial. You know how they try us in groups. Anna Portland was up right after me. She did not do a very skillful job, as far as her defense goes. Doesn't show a scrap of remorse. The bastard beat her over and over, she says. But she took it because she wanted to be a good and righteous woman, and who knows what all else. Till he went after her daughter. She was thirteen. He knocks her down and is standing over her, pants already open, when Anna comes into the house. So she beats him to death with the fire poker. She's strong enough, all right. And she doesn't regret it, she says. She'd do it again. And if God don't like it, she says, well, she can't do nothing about that; she must just have more in common with the devil."

Lizzie did not know whether she should laugh or cry. "Wasn't she sentenced to death, then?" she asked.

Her patient nodded. "Of course, but it was commuted. They commute almost all the women's sentences."

"But, but the murderers are all on the lower deck." Lizzie still could not believe it.

Emma Brewster rolled her eyes. "Child, they locked Anna up half a year in Newgate. They saw pretty quick that she wasn't scum. The doctor, the reverend, everyone spoke on her behalf, to keep her in England too. That poor woman left seven children behind. The daughter she protected was the oldest. But nothing could be done. They had to send Anna overseas. The children went to the orphanage."

Lizzie sighed. She thought of her own, unknown mother. Until then she had never thought very highly of her. To Lizzie, it was a crime to put a child on the street. But then again, perhaps her own mother had acted in the same desperation as Anna Portland had.

Chapter 3

While the *Asia* sailed slowly through the Doldrums—where the light winds often brought ships to a complete stop—the fever epidemic reached its high point. Though the rates of illness remained reasonable among the women on the tween deck, down below, the situation was quite different. No one in the lower deck was still able to stand.

The guards were completely overburdened by this crisis situation. At first, they still tried to force the men onto the upper deck; then they took off their chains and left them to their fate. An appeal asking the few still-capable men to care for their comrades wasn't followed; an attempt to force them to do so was resisted. Soon, even the strongest were too weak to wash and feed the sick and dying every day.

A solution did not present itself until the guards dropped an especially high number of dead into the sea. The passengers, naturally, observed the ceremonies. When they ended, Caroline Bailiff, the brave spouse of a retired police officer, offered a suggestion to the captain.

"Why don't you have the women take care of them?" she inquired. "True, half of them are good for nothing, and the last thing the poor devils down there need is a whore to finish them off, but there must be a few that have kept some remainder of responsibility and perhaps only faltered once out of necessity. The earlier you select them, the better—for the poor souls down there now, and for the families who will later be looking for servants."

Understandably, the future free settlers received this idea well, though the guards still had their doubts.

The next time the women were allowed to walk around freely, Caroline Bailiff started looking for helpers. The first to volunteer was Anna Portland.

"D'you really want to do that?" Emma Brewster asked Anna. The old whore had taken the berth left open in Anna and Lizzie's partition after the frail girl had died. She slept better there than in her previous corner, which she had shared with five very enterprising young girls.

"Ain't you had enough of the fellows?" Emma asked. "Me, I don't look at a prick if I don't have to, let alone if a man's going to give me a fever instead of cash." Emma kept her distance from Caroline Bailiff and the sailors who accompanied her noting the names of the volunteers. "You might just come across one who beat his wife to death."

"They're not all that bad, you know," Anna said. "Perhaps I'll save one who stole a bit of food for his children. There are a lot of Irish among them, and the whole world's talking about their famine."

Though Lizzie had never heard anything about the famine herself, she knew that Anna had moved in better circles. Her husband had been an artisan, and she had lived in a proper house. She had been able to feed her children and even buy a newspaper from time to time.

"Anyway, I can care for the sick; others will have to dress them." Anna said. She turned to Lizzie. "How about you, Lizzie? Are you coming?"

Lizzie followed Anna, her heart pounding, into the office Caroline Bailiff had improvised beneath a sunshade. Mrs. Bailiff immediately noted Anna's neat little hat, which, when it was new, must have resembled her own. Anna's hat clearly pleased Mrs. Bailiff, but she looked at Lizzie rather skeptically.

"And what motivates you to care for the men, girl?" she asked Lizzie after Anna had explained her work in the hospital.

Lizzie shrugged. "I've been helping Anna since we got here," she said. "There's nothing else to do, after all."

Mrs. Bailiff arched her eyebrows. "And have you always taken care of men?" she asked sarcastically. "You do count among the girls who offered, hmm, special cures in the streets of London, don't you?"

Lizzie looked at her candidly. "Not by choice!" she said. "Just for money. And really, they were never sick. On the contrary, they were, if anything, too . . . They had rather too much vim, madam."

Mrs. Bailiff maintained her straight face, but amusement shone in her eyes.

"I'll keep an eye on the girl, madam," Anna said. "She's a good girl and quite capable."

Lizzie smiled. Her heart swelled. No one had ever said that about her before.

Mrs. Bailiff asked for some time to think it over, but she was soon prepared to accept any offer. The women weren't clamoring to undertake nursing duties in exchange for minor improvements in their food and living conditions, or for vague promises of good employment in a house in the new country. After all, most of them had long since seen to improving their living conditions themselves. Some of them had made good friends among the guards or sailors who visited them and brought them supplies; some offered their attentions to anyone interested, in exchange for a bit of salted meat or a few swigs of gin. In any case, hardly any of the women wanted to trade her work as a whore for filth, drudgery, and the risk of contagion. And so, in the end, only four female prisoners and two ladies from the group of future free settlers ventured into the ship's hold with wash water and gin, the only medicine the ship's doctor provided.

Anna Portland and Mrs. Bailiff went straight to work. When they entered the lower deck, they withdrew in horror.

"It is impossible to work here," Anna said, not bothering with the formalities of a proper lady. "You cannot see your hand in front of your face, everything is covered in filth, and there's nothing to do about the heat and damp. Go to the captain, Mrs. Bailiff, and ask that the men be brought on deck. We can care for them there, and the weather is fine."

The *Asia* was on the Indian Ocean. No one had seen land for weeks, but the weather remained good and the seas calm. They didn't have to reckon with waves that washed over the deck as they did in the Atlantic. A mutiny by the prisoners, which the captain had mentioned to quash the women's desire to erect a hospital, also seemed unlikely.

"They might be felons, but at the moment they're more dead than alive," Mrs. Bailiff pointed out to him. "And even if they captured the ship, where precisely would they go? All I see is water, water, and more water. I wouldn't know whether to sail right or left, not to mention I don't know how to sail. The same is true for those poor devils below, seeing as they come from the darkest corners of Ireland and London."

Finally, Captain Roskell relented. He ordered the guards to remove the sick men's chains and, with the help of the few men who were still able, they carried the sick on deck. The women laid them down on beds of blankets and removed their damp clothing. As Lizzie washed them, she could see how they must have been strong before all this and much handsomer than most of her customers. Of course, now they were emaciated and reeked of sweat and sick, but a few of them . . .

Lizzie ran her sponge over the chest of a tall, dark-haired man whose square jaw and full lips hinted at his formerly attractive appearance. She flinched when he whispered, "Thank you."

"Are you awake?" she asked, astounded. Most of the men she had cared for so far could no longer speak. Two had already died in Anna's care, likely grateful for some fresh air before their final breaths.

"No," whispered the man. "I'm dreaming, dreaming I'm free, that I've no more chains to wear, that the sun's shining on me, and I see an angel. Angels also only exist in dreams. Or am I already dead?"

Lizzie laughed. "Just open your eyes, and you'll see I'm no angel," she said and found herself immediately looking into two eyes, tired and feverish, to be sure, but incredibly blue. When the man looked at her, life stirred within his eyes.

"Aye," he sighed. "An angel and a cloud. I was promised a cloud from which I could look down."

Then he closed his eyes and sank back into fever dreams again. It did not seem to be going as badly for him as for most of the others, but he needed more fluids.

She filled a cup with tea and held it to his lips. "Drink. It's good for you." The man swallowed obediently but seemed to remain in his own world.

"Kathleen," he whispered as Lizzie cooled his forehead.

She did not know why she was disappointed. Of course a man like this had a sweetheart. Or maybe this Kathleen was his wife.

***

Michael had held onto consciousness as long as possible, even as his head and limbs began to hurt and the first men around him died. He had only given up when he heard Billy scream. In his fever, the boy seemed plagued by all the devils hell had to offer. At some point, Michael could no longer bear it and willingly slipped off into his own world. He hoped the fever might offer him sweet dreams, but that did not prove true.

Michael's pain followed him into unconsciousness. The welts on his back burned and wept, his shoulders and hips were sore to the bone, and the chains caused bloody chafing on his wrists and ankles. Every movement hurt, and it was impossible to find a position in which some part of him was not in pain. Michael was aware enough to know that he vomited and wet himself, which only worsened his stench, but even if the chains had not held him to his pallet, the strength to get up had long since left him. On top of all of that, he suffered a burning thirst. Though the guards brought them drinking water, no one made the effort to distribute it, let alone hold it to the lips of the feverish men. Michael had tried to gulp something down when the unwilling guards on cleaning duty had emptied pails of seawater over him, but the saltwater made matters worse.

The noise around him, too, grew ever more infernal, making any thoughts or dreams of better times impossible. The feverish men called for their mothers and their wives; Michael murmured Kathleen's name. At least, he thought he did. He could not be sure. The only thing he could be sure of was that he would die. There, on an English ship, in his own filth.

Michael was ashamed of his weakness, but at some point he wept, whimpering just as desperately and helplessly as Billy, whom they had long ago carried away wrapped in sailcloth, ready for his burial at sea. Michael struggled against the image of the hungry sharks tearing apart and devouring his friend—just as they would eventually do to him.

He resisted desperately when the guards finally removed his chains and directed a few of the other prisoners to carry him away. "I'm not dead yet. I'm not, not yet, not dead."

Could it be that they were going to feed him alive to the sharks? Or was he already dead, but instead of ascending to heaven, his soul was trapped in his body?

In the end, a merciful slap woke him and there was fresh air for him to breathe and a girl washing him. Michael whispered something nice to her, as if to Mary Kathleen. Their shared words allowed him to slip into lovelier dreams, dreams in which it was warm and the wind blew in the fields by the river . . . only here it smelled like salt. And the water tasted bitter.

Michael coughed when the unsweetened tea washed over his gums. "Drink. It's good for you."

Her warm, friendly voice spoke to him. Michael felt her lift his head. The bitter brew slowly ran down his throat. He swallowed obediently. It was liquid, anyway; it would slake his thirst.

***

Slowly pouring the tea into the Irish prisoner's mouth, Lizzie suddenly saw the inflamed red welts on his back and was horrified. The women prisoners at Newgate had occasionally been struck with clubs, but these were the marks of a whipping.

"Anna!" Lizzie shouted. Someone who understood more about nursing needed to see to this matter.

Moments later, Anna Portland and Mrs. Bailiff bent over the Irishman's flayed back.

"Horrible," Mrs. Bailiff pronounced. "How medieval. Where does the man come from? Ireland? What a state they must be in. It's good that you noticed this, child. Go examine the others. These men will surely die of fever and infection if this goes untreated. You'll help me, won't you, Mrs. Portland?"

Lizzie noticed that Mrs. Bailiff no longer talked down to Anna. The two women had recognized their similarity of spirit and treated each other with respect.

Lizzie reluctantly parted from her patient to check on the others, and she immediately discovered similar injuries on two more men. She returned to the prisoner to comfort him while Anna and Mrs. Bailiff washed his back and treated his wounds with gin.

He cried out in pain. It was all Lizzie could do not to speak soothingly to the sick man and ask his nurses to be more careful with him. But she held back. Anna and Mrs. Bailiff knew what they were doing. And if she showed even the slightest personal interest in the handsome, dark-haired man with the beguiling eyes, they would doubtless remove him from her care.

The women tried to wrangle salve from the ship's doctor. He wasn't sober but the doctor managed to recall that in earlier times, doctors had spread wood tar over such wounds. Mrs. Bailiff reacted even more violently to this than to the sight of the welts and withdrew into her cabin, only to emerge almost at once with her store of marigold salve.

"Really, I'd meant to have it for my own medicine chest," she said regretfully. "Who knows if there's anything like it in Australia. And until the marigold seeds I brought have sprouted . . . But we need the salve here and now; we can't just let those poor fellows die like animals."

When Lizzie finally dared to return her attention to the young man who had captivated her so, his wounds had been cleaned and bandaged. But he was still suffering from a high fever and shaking all over. Lizzie poured more tea and water into his mouth and brought him another blanket. She would have liked to stay with him, but night was falling, and the guards insisted on taking the imprisoned women back to the tween deck. Mrs. Bailiff and one of the other nurses, a bony, humorless woman named Amanda Smithers, were to continue caring for the men on deck.

Lizzie did not notice how tired she was until she stretched out on her pallet. But she was to get no rest.

"Are you back, sweetheart?" whispered Jeremiah.

He was accompanying Candy, whose turn it had been to retrieve dinner for their group of six. She had a pot filled with a casserole that consisted mostly of potatoes.

"You must be hungry. But this is nothing. Come with me. Topside I've got bread and meat for you," Jeremiah said with a smile.

Lizzie's mouth watered. She knew, however, that Jeremiah's unwashed body would be on deck for her along with the delicious meal. And Mrs. Bailiff and Mrs. Smithers might see her. It was out of the question.

Lizzie attempted a seductive but simultaneously bashful smile. "A little later, Jeremiah. Please. When . . ." She tried to blush and even succeeded. "The ladies . . ."

Jeremiah grinned. "You really are a shy one. You could be mistaken for a virtuous little thing from a good house. But that suits me fine. A little later, then, when the passengers are served dinner."

Though the settlers on the *Asia* were not traveling first-class—as they did on other emigrant ships, where there were luxurious accommodations for high-paying passengers, and animals were brought on board to provide fresh meat for meals—they still gathered in a communal dining room. Naturally, the food set in front of them was far better than that fed to the prisoners. Mrs.

Bailiff and Mrs. Smithers would not miss dinner. After their hard work, they were just as hungry as Lizzie and Anna.

Nevertheless, Lizzie struggled with a pounding heart when Jeremiah led her up the stairs an hour later. Would she really avoid meeting the other women? This was the first time they'd been together on deck at night. The stars sparkled in the sky as Jeremiah satisfied himself with her.

"The stars look different than in London," Lizzie said, reluctantly cuddling with him.

She knew he liked it, and though she could not bring herself to caress him while he was entering her, still she could at least summon a few displays of affection for him before or after. Mostly after—he showed little interest beforehand. And if she applied herself too much, she risked arousing him again. But Lizzie felt she owed it to him. At heart, Jeremiah was a nice fellow.

"Of course," he responded proudly, as he always did when he could explain something. "We're almost on the other side of the globe, you know. The Southern Cross, there, you see it?" He pointed to four shining stars that formed an easily recognizable cross. "The lengthwise line points south. That's why they call it that. People once needed these constellations to orient themselves at sea. Oh yeah, and the Australians want to put the Southern Cross on their flag—once they decide exactly how that should look."

Lizzie nodded and looked into the night sky, fascinated. The stars seemed much brighter here than in London—but of course, that was because the *Asia*'s deck was dark and there was nothing else around.

"Beautiful," she whispered. "So, have you already been to Australia? Is it nice there?"

Jeremiah shrugged his shoulders. "Well, not yet. But I could stay there. I think about it sometimes. A fellow can get land; I could marry. What do you think, Lizzie? Could you see yourself living like that?"

Lizzie looked at the young man, taken aback. Was he proposing? Did he really . . . ?

"But I, I'm imprisoned. I . . ."

"Oh, I asked around. They'll pardon you quick if you find a husband. That's what they want, after all. That you lot all become upright and live virtuously. You do your time, two years in the colony, and then it'd still take a little time. I'd have to work a few short years." He laughed. "Well, you won't be running away from me, eh?"

But on your next trip the next girl would run into you, Lizzie thought soberly. She wondered why none of it excited her anymore. Marry! Become an honest woman. Be free to have children. True, she did not love Jeremiah, but he was good-natured. So far she had not seen him strike the prisoners or even treat them rudely. Marrying him was more than a girl like her could ever dream. And her own land on top of it, a house, even? She was relieved that she did not need to decide right away. Anyway, a few years from now, Jeremiah might well have changed his mind.

Her thoughts wandered to the dark-haired man with the blue eyes and the flayed back; she simply could not forget him. She hoped she wouldn't arouse any suspicion when she asked Jeremiah if she might check on the sick men once more before he took her back down to the tween deck.

As she had hoped, Jeremiah remained in front, away from the section of the deck where the feverish men were located. The guards were just as afraid of contagion as the prisoners. It seemed it hadn't even occurred to him that he might catch the fever by way of Lizzie.

She approached the young Irishman's bed and took fright. He was no longer shivering, or moving at all. Then she realized his eyes were open and he was staring at the starry sky, just as she had been a few minutes before. She suddenly felt connected to him.

"It's all so strange, Kathleen," he said, barely audibly. "Heaven, I thought I'd look down, but I'm looking up into the sky above . . . how strange, Kathleen."

"You're not in heaven," she whispered, "just almost to Australia. They're our stars, and look—the moon!"

The thin crescent moon was just about to set beneath the dark blue horizon.

"I'm not Kathleen either." Lizzie realized she sounded rather sad. "I'm Lizzie, Lizzie Owens. Elizabeth."

The man smiled weakly, feeling for her hand. "You're beautiful, Kathleen," he whispered. "More beautiful than all the stars."

Lizzie didn't try to clarify any more. She would have loved to know his name. And she would have especially loved to be beautiful.

Chapter 4

Kathleen and Ian Coltrane's journey to New Zealand passed calmly. Except for a storm off the Cape of Good Hope, there were no incidents. Kathleen almost enjoyed the voyage.

Naturally, she suffered like all the others in the cramped steerage deck—for a thirteen-pound fare, one could not expect too much luxury. Ian and Kathleen shared a cabin with a couple and their two children, a whiny girl and an insolent little boy who was always snickering or adding commentary when his father or Ian insisted on their marital rights. It was unpleasant for Kathleen and the young, already worn-looking Mrs. Browning to sleep with their husbands in front of the children and the other people, but neither Ian nor Mr. Browning had any compunctions.

The deck of the *Primrose* was not sealed, and water sloshed into the lodgings of the poorer passengers just as it did on the prison ship. The sanitary conditions were a little better than what Kathleen had heard was common on the prison ships—there were lavatories on the tween deck on this ship. Unfortunately, there were too few for all the passengers, so they often overflowed and needed cleaning. The food was simple and had usually cooled off by the time it reached steerage, but it was satisfying.

Half-starved when they boarded, the Irish did not understand why the English complained about the kitchen's inadequacy. Many of the Irish were eating their fill every day for the first time in years. In general, once they overcame their farewell pains, the Irish provided atmosphere on board. Many of the men had brought tin whistles, fiddles, and harmonicas, and their music encouraged dancing at night; the girls and women sang the songs of their old homeland. Kathleen could not help thinking of Michael almost constantly. No one played the fiddle as beautifully as he, and she kept imagining she heard the deep voice with which he used to sing for her.

When they had finally left the Atlantic behind—along with clammy clothing and water in the cabins—the sailors and the men from steerage tried fishing, as a means of expanding the food offerings. At first it seemed to be a diversion, trying to haul in, with hook or harpoon, the dolphins, sharks, and barracudas that followed the ship. But over time, their technique matured, and the aroma of grilled fish wafted over the deck. Birds, too, especially albatross, fell victim to the men's hunting. They caught them using a long line that trailed behind the ship, with hooks and fish for bait.

Kathleen was cheered by the occasional meals with fish and the sight of the still foreign-seeming starry sky, which she saw when she strolled the deck with other steerage passengers at night. Only first-class passengers were meant to promenade there, but the longer the voyage lasted, the more the captain and sailors turned a blind eye. Besides, no one could deny anything to a girl as pretty, or as pregnant, as Mary Kathleen. She only hoped the baby would not be born at sea. When Ian revealed to her—only once they were aboard— that the voyage would last at least three months, she had been horrified and accused him of being inconsiderate. Kathleen's baby was due at the beginning of July, and there was no guarantee that they would reach their new homeland by then, let alone have established themselves.

Ian let her anger roll off him—like everything else she said or felt. Kathleen quickly got the feeling she was nothing more to him than a pet or doll. He talked to her and seemed to expect certain reactions, but she could have just as easily been mute or a Chinese speaker. Ian did not bother with any objection or any concerns about their short- or long-term plans, and even when Kathleen simply told him what she liked or did not like, as a rule, he did not comment on it.

But Ian's silence was not the only thing spoiling Kathleen's voyage and their young marriage. It was also his constant mistrust. Whenever she wasn't by Ian's side, whatever she did without him, he pried about it. He never simply asked her where she had been or what she had done. Instead he acted like a detective, spying on her and asking other people where she had been.

The Brownings clearly found this unpleasant, and it was more so since Elinor Browning assumed Ian's concern was that he suspected her husband of pursuing Kathleen. During the evening entertainment, Ian jealously watched his wife's every movement—even though almost no one made an attempt to get close to visibly pregnant Kathleen. When she was asked to dance—there were considerably more young, unmarried men than women on board, and most of the married men allowed their wives to dance with the boys without a grumble—Ian always responded no. At first, he was friendly and made the excuse of Kathleen's advanced pregnancy, but after a glass or two of whiskey he became belligerent. All it took was one near fistfight, and their fellow travelers began to avoid Kathleen—the men because Ian expressly suspected them, the women because gossip spread quickly. If a man had to watch his wife the way Ian Coltrane did, then the bored emigrant wives were sure he had a reason. And she was pretty, of course, Mrs. Coltrane. Dangerously pretty. They had better keep an eye on their own husbands.

After two months on board, Kathleen felt almost as isolated as she had in her home village after word of her pregnancy had spread. There was nothing anyone could accuse her of, but everyone from Ian to the young children looked at her suspiciously.

Kathleen accepted it and sought time alone. If she managed to flee the constriction of her cabin for a few moments, she admired the starry sky and spoke with the baby in her womb, who now moved ever more often.

Ian was annoyed if she took too long with an evening visit to the lavatory, but Kathleen enjoyed her moments of freedom. Beneath the foreign stars, she felt closer to Michael. Perhaps he was even looking at the Southern Cross, too, and thinking of her. If only she could have informed him somehow that she was there, following him to the other side of the globe.

Finally, the last part of the voyage began. After Sunday service on deck, the captain explained to the passengers that they were crossing the Tasman Sea between Australia and New Zealand.

"How close are we to Australia?" Kathleen asked after the ship's doctor had inquired how she was feeling.

She hoped he would not have to deliver her baby; she did not think much of his qualifications as a doctor. Nevertheless, he was a good teacher. On board, he taught the children as a second job, and almost all of them learned to read or write during their passage.

"Far," laughed the doctor, "very far. We were a little closer but we've sailed past it. If we were bound for Botany Bay, Mrs. Coltrane, we'd be there already."

Kathleen forced herself to smile. "They don't send anyone to Botany Bay anymore," she said.

The doctor nodded. "True, just to Van Diemen's Land and, more recently, to Western Australia, on the other side of the continent."

Kathleen felt a deep disappointment. "So you can't get there from New Zealand?" she almost whispered.

"What could you want in Australia?" the doctor asked. He meant it amicably, but Kathleen flinched in terror. He was speaking dangerously loudly. Ian might hear him. "If you want my advice: stay in New Zealand once you get there. It's a peaceful country—no wild animals except for a few birds, no snakes, nothing that could be dangerous. In Australia, on the other hand, half of the animals are poisonous, the natives are aggressive, the weather is extreme, and every five minutes there's a wildfire. There's a reason they send the ne'er-do-wells there. Although now they're trying to get respectable settlers in the new colonies—the first in the west are already half-starved."

The doctor continued his good-natured explanation until he saw Kathleen's tortured face and stopped. "Now, now, if someone wants to go there, he'll get by. There must be ships that go from New Zealand's West Coast to Fremantle—maybe even from the North Island. Ask when you get there. But wait till your child is born. It won't be long now."

Kathleen was too agitated to concentrate. It was as if she could feel Ian's gaze on her even when she could not see him. And if he was watching, he would immediately ask everyone he could if they'd heard her conversation with the doctor. She looked around nervously. Mrs. Browning stood near her and looked over the railing. Kathleen hoped that, of all people, Mrs. Browning had not heard anything. But then again, this woman who shared her cabin was likely more on her side than anyone; after all, Ian's constant distrust got on Mrs. Browning's nerves as well.

Kathleen put on a smile as she returned to her husband. Anyone else would simply have asked what she was talking about with the doctor. But Ian looked past Kathleen and turned to Mrs. Browning.

"What sort of important conversation was my lovely wife having with our doctor?" To an outsider, the question would have sounded moody. To Kathleen it sounded threatening.

Elinor Browning forced a smile. "Well, what else? It was about her baby," she said. "Whether it's going to be a boy. Of course, the doctors say you can't see it in the stomach, but if you ask me, you carry a girl lower down, so you get a rounder stomach. But her little boy there, he sits higher and almost makes the stomach pointy."

Kathleen smiled gratefully at the woman. She had made it around those rocks. If only it were as easy to sail around all the rocks surrounding New Zealand and Australia.

***

The *Primrose* reached Port Cooper after precisely one hundred and two days, not a day too soon for Kathleen's baby. While the immigrants were assembling on the main deck—called by the ship's horn, announcing the first bit of land they had seen for weeks—her water broke. Despite the beginning of her labor, she hauled herself on deck to catch sight of the new country. It did not make a very promising impression. On the contrary, New Zealand's South Island lay hidden behind a veil of rain, behind which a rocky coast took shape. They saw the outlines of distant mountains that looked snow covered. *This is supposed to be a country that resembles Ireland?* thought Kathleen. *With sheep in green pastures?* She was disappointed but had other concerns at the moment. It might be hours before they made landfall. What if the baby would not wait so long? Regardless of how the land looked, she did not want to deliver on the ship.

The baby took its time. Elinor Browning and a few other women took care of Kathleen until they reached the port—and then promptly left her alone so they could celebrate their arrival. While the first of the new settlers, drunk with excitement and joy at having survived the voyage, stumbled onto the land and kissed the ground of their new home, Kathleen was dying a thousand deaths of pain and fear. What if the women did not return? What if she were forgotten there? Of course, Kathleen told herself, Ian would think of her, but she had not seen her husband since they had sighted land. In her worst nightmares, she imagined him already negotiating his first horse sale in Port Cooper while she was stranded, in labor on the ship. After all, she was not delivering his child. Surely, he could not care less what happened to the baby.

But Ian did appear, and he looked appalled at the sight of his wife shaking and covered in sweat in their cabin. He seemed indignant. Apparently, he expected her to give birth to her child as quickly and easily as a mare birthing a foal.

"Get up, Kathleen, we have to go. And you need someone to care for you. I've spoken with people in town. We'll take you to the smith's house."

"To the what?" asked Kathleen, horrified. "The, the blacksmith? You don't mean he will deliver the baby?"

"Of course not, but his wife is supposed to be a midwife. Now come on! And put some clothes on. I can't drag you onto land in your nightshirt. How would that look? We want to open a business here, Kathleen. So get to your feet and act like a lady."

She bent over with a contraction every few minutes—how was she supposed to force herself into a dress and fix her hair? But Ian's demeanor left no room for discussion. Arduously, interrupted by cramps and despairing sobs, she put on her loosest dress, stuck her hair under a bonnet, and struggled out of the cabin. On Ian's arm, she finally left the ship.

Kathleen hardly noticed anything about her new homeland. A gangplank and a primitive, pear-shaped harbor—likely a natural harbor; not much had been built there yet. Above it, hills, a settlement. Kathleen broke out in a sweat again as she struggled down the gangplank. She had to stop again and again. If Ian had not held her, she would have fallen and perhaps delivered the baby on the street.

You'll raise our child with dignity. Kathleen thought she could hear Michael's voice. She clenched her teeth. Fortunately, the smith's house was not far—nothing in Port Cooper was far from the bay in which the ships anchored. The settlement was tiny. Yet each of the wooden houses was far larger and statelier than the tenants' cottages in Ireland.

Kathleen's hopes rose when Ian knocked on the door of a neat little blue-painted house. A mule stood in the pen beside it. From the shed next door came the sound of a smith's hammer. Kathleen slumped against the door. At least she would get out of the rain. She had to smile at the possibility that the primary similarity between New Zealand and Ireland was constant bad weather. But when the door opened, she froze. The woman who opened the door was short and stout, her hair dark and frizzy. But more than that, she had dark skin.

Kathleen was confused. She thought black people only lived in Africa. No one had ever said they were in New Zealand. Well, Father O'Brien had mentioned natives. They were supposed to be rare. And peaceful.

When Kathleen looked at the woman more closely, she had to admit that she did not make a frightening impression, although . . . her face was covered in blue designs. Tattoos. Was Kathleen trapped in a nightmare?

At that moment her next contraction seized her, accompanied by nausea. She tried to get ahold of herself. She did not want to vomit in this stranger's doorway.

"Oh! Baby comes quickly now." The woman smiled—and her wide smile immediately made her face less frightening again. "Come in, woman. I help, don't worry."

All too happily, Ian let Kathleen go as soon as the short woman offered herself as a support. At least the midwife wore normal clothing. And she had pinned up her hair just like a good English or Irish housewife.

Kathleen allowed herself to be led into the small, cozily furnished house. In fact, everything here was normal except for the skin of the dark-skinned woman and her broken English. Was Kathleen dreaming? Finally, she found herself in a clean bed—apparently the house's master bed, which even stood in its own little bedroom. Kathleen only knew of such luxury from the manor house or Trevallion's cottage.

The short woman felt Kathleen's stomach with skillful hands. "Comes soon," she said soothingly. "First baby?"

Kathleen nodded. And then dared to ask a question. Politely—after all, she was supposed to comport herself like a lady. "You, you're not an Englishwoman?"

The midwife all but shook with laughter. "Of course." She giggled. "I from London, related to queen, little cousin."

Kathleen doubled over with the next contraction. Was that a joke? She no longer knew what was dream and what was reality, how she had arrived there, or what awaited her. Perhaps she would wake up in a moment lying next to Michael in the fields by the river.

"You, sit up. Baby comes easier when kneeling. I know is not your custom. And no, I not cousin of queen. Although niece of chief! My name is Pere. I Maori. Ngai Tahu is my tribe." The short dark-skinned woman pointed, self-assured, at her chest and smiled at the uncomprehending Kathleen. "Before *pakeha,* white settlers, Maori came across sea with Tainui, this tribal way of birth. Many summers and winters ago. But now everyone lives here, not enemies with *pakeha.* My husband *pakeha* and smith."

So she was a native who had married the local smith. Ngai Tahu seemed to be her tribe or her village. And she did seem peaceful. Kathleen did not want to think anymore. Exhausted, she gave herself over to Pere's skillful hands.

A few hours later, Kathleen's son was born. She was enraptured by the little one, and Pere seemed to share her enthusiasm, but Ian hardly glanced at the newborn. Only when Pere quite unassumingly introduced the baby as Kevin James Coltrane did he react vehemently.

"James is fine," he said. "But she shouldn't dare name him Kevin! Tell her that. I'm warning her, woman, if she tries to play games with me . . ."

Although she'd already heard his threatening words, Kathleen sighed when Pere brought her the message as directed. "Your husband is not very friendly," the Maori remarked.

Kathleen began to apologize for Ian—an act that was soon to become a habit. "Then I'll call him Sean," she affirmed finally.

She had always liked the name—and as far as she knew, it appeared in neither Michael's nor Ian's family.

Ian, fortunately, had no objections to the new name, and he immediately turned his attention from his wife and baby. Seeming satisfied that Kathleen would stay with John and Pere Seeker for the time being, he left to sleep in the tent-like provisional lodgings that the residents of Port Cooper offered its new arrivals. A few of the settlers wanted to stay here; others were in a hurry to get over the mountains and to the interior, where there were supposed to be better conditions for the establishment of a farm. Though there was fertile land around Port Cooper, the residents had already divided it among themselves. Whoever wanted to live in the Canterbury Plains—the name the first white settlers had given to the flat land below the mountains—had to negotiate with the Maori.

Ian had no intention of doing that. Nor did he see the necessity of learning even a few words in the Maori language—after all, it was rather unlikely that the natives would be buying horses from him anytime soon. They kept few livestock; instead, they relied on hunting, fishing, and primitive agriculture.

Kathleen, on the other hand, liked talking with Pere. She learned the Maori word for Port Cooper first: Te Whaka-raupo—Harbor of Reeds.

"And they call New Zealand Aotearoa," she explained to Ian when he visited her for the second time.

During his first visit, she was still completely exhausted from the birth, but now she sat in bed, holding her baby in her arms. She felt almost like the old Kathleen again.

Ian noticed she seemed happier and, if it was even possible, she was even more beautiful. Ian eyed little Sean with an expression that almost bordered on jealousy.

Pere watched Ian with pursed lips. Her English was not perfect, but she read people's faces like books.

"The great white cloud," Kathleen continued. "John says it's supposed to be beautiful. This is just the harbor, just a bay with rocks all around. But the land itself is vast and fertile."

"What's so important you have to talk to the smith about it?" Ian asked.

Curt as he was, at least he addressed Kathleen directly this time. He did not seem to consider the Maori woman worthy of asking.

Kathleen shrugged. She wanted to answer amicably that she could learn important information about her new country from just about anyone, but anger seized her. She could not let Ian keep spying on her.

"Well, I am lying in his bed," she replied, "so I ought to be able to exchange a few words with him."

Ian glared at her. "You lie in John's bed with Michael's baby in your arms. How remarkable you can be proud of that, Kathleen. But it won't continue like this. If you would listen instead of chattering so, I would already have told you that part of your Te-whaka-whatever now belongs to me. I bought a plot of land and a house."

With Michael's money? The question was on the tip of Kathleen's tongue, but she managed to stop herself. The expression on Ian's face was already frightening enough; she did not want to antagonize him any more. The news—exciting as it was—heightened her anger.

Her own land! Her own house. She had always wished for that in her dreams. But couldn't Ian have waited until she could look at it with him? And how could he decide to settle in Port Cooper while beyond it much more extensive, better land might be available?

Kathleen bit her lip. "Ian that's, that's lovely, I'm sure. But, but didn't you think about perhaps buying land elsewhere? Over the mountains? Perhaps it would even have been cheaper. Have you already signed for it?" Surely there was a way they could talk reasonably.

Ian frowned; Kathleen knew that her objections angered him.

"Of course I signed; I don't need your permission, after all. And of course I thought of everything. I'm not stupid, you know. This here is the only large settlement for a long way. And new settlers come through here. They have to. So it's the best place for a livestock trader. The only place. I think I can come get you tomorrow, Mary Kathleen. In the meantime, I'll take our things to the house; then you can make a home of it."

It was hard for Kathleen to imagine making a home when she could barely stand. The birth after the long sea voyage had drained her more than she had expected. But Pere and John had showed her a great deal of understanding. Tall, strong-as-an-ox John Seeker had simply taken his bedding into the smith shop, and Pere had lain down next to Kathleen. At night, they had whispered to each other and exchanged stories. Pere told little Sean the first fairy tales from his homeland, Aotearoa.

"He needs to know his history," she had explained to Kathleen. "For us is important; we call *pepeha*. Everyone can tell in what canoe forefathers come to this country, where settled, what they did. Also, history of ancestors."

After Ian left in a huff, Kathleen and Pere lay on the bed with Sean between them. Pere said, "Your husband not happy with baby. Why? Is son! Everyone want son."

Kathleen had learned that *pakeha* was the Maori word for the white European settlers. *Pakeha wahine* meant "white woman," *pakeha tane*, "white man." The Maori called themselves "moa hunters." "Moa" was a bird that had lived on Aotearoa when they had arrived. By now, however, the beast had died out.

Kathleen sighed. She did not know how to answer. But Pere was already speaking again.

"Is maybe from other man? We don't act so, children welcome. But *pakeha* . . ."

Kathleen was horrified. Was it so easy to recognize? Would everyone know? Alarmed, she reached for Pere's arm.

"For God's sake, Pere, just don't tell anyone!" Kathleen pleaded. "Please, this child is a Coltrane. I did all I could to give him a name and a father. No one can know that, no one, please! Please don't even tell John."

Pere shrugged. "I don't care. I no tell anyone. But you only gave baby name. Not father. Father is more than name. And your husband is nothing."

Chapter 5

For three whole days the prisoner believed Lizzie Owens was a proper girl. And Lizzie had never felt happier.

The men from belowdecks recovered slowly from their fevers. Lizzie and the other women still spent many hours washing the sick men, rubbing them with vinegar and gin, and pouring water, tea, and finally some soup into their mouths. To Caroline Bailiff and Anna Portland's satisfaction, none of the men died under their care. And on the third day, the dark-haired man even managed to smile at Lizzie and call her by her own name rather than Kathleen's.

"Elizabeth," he said softly. "You see, I remember. You told me your name when I was sick, and you claimed not to be an angel. But I don't believe that. You're an angel all the same. My name is Michael Drury."

Lizzie smiled, and Michael thought she looked lovely. Until then she had looked nondescript—surely warm-hearted, but unimpressive to him. Now, however, her warm, all-indulgent smile charmed him.

"An angel doesn't land on a prison ship," she replied. "Unless it got really lost."

Michael smiled back and drank a sip of the tea Lizzie handed him. "You said it yourself: an error, doubtless. Why are they sending you to Van Diemen's Land, Elizabeth?"

"Lizzie," she corrected him, although she felt flattered. Elizabeth sounded lovely, important, and—good. "I stole some bread," she admitted. "I was hungry. And you?"

Lizzie's heart pounded. She had been afraid of the answer—which was why she had thus far avoided asking Mrs. Bailiff, let alone Jeremiah. Michael had been in chains; obviously he counted among the serious criminals. But she could not imagine him as a robber or murderer.

"Three sacks of grain," said Michael. "Our whole village was hungry."

Lizzie felt weak with relief. So, he, too, had erred out of need. And to help others.

She smiled happily. "That doesn't count," she said. "The judges, they've just never been hungry."

For a few days, Lizzie walked on clouds. Michael was no criminal; he could prove himself and be set free—just like her. As she lay on her pallet at night, she dreamed of such freedom. Fields, a garden, a house—and Michael, who would ask her shyly if she would want to share that with him.

But those were just idle dreams. This Kathleen, whom Michael obviously loved, was still out there somewhere. *Kathleen*—Lizzie did not want to be jealous, but she felt something like hate for his sweetheart in his homeland. She had cautiously asked, making a joke of being only too eager to know about the girl for whom he had mistaken her. Did they really look so similar?

Lizzie had felt hurt when he responded to this question by laughing. No, of course she had nothing in common with this Kathleen and her locks of gold hair, shining green eyes, and tall form. Michael seemed never to tire of crowing about his girl.

Lizzie could only practice patience. Fine, she could never compete with this charming girl in the flesh. But when one looked at it practically: Kathleen was far away. Michael would never see her again, and someday her image would fade. Lizzie, on the other hand, was in front of him every day—and even if she was not beautiful, Michael was a man. In due time, he would need a woman, and why should Lizzie not be happy for once? Among the deportees were but a few truly beautiful women, and they would quickly be married off.

The master of the ship had decided on the beautiful Velvet for himself. She surrendered to him reluctantly, and her prudish manner seemed to excite him. Velvet would not bother with a prisoner in her new homeland. A free settler or soldier could offer her more—early release and then a large house and servants.

And Michael—Lizzie could already tell that he did not count among the simplest people. He was friendly and smart, and she loved his jokes and his flattery. Yet she also knew from all the time they'd spent talking that he was proud and easily excited. Lizzie now knew why they had chained him up with the serious criminals. Michael Drury would not conform, and if he nevertheless wanted to survive in a system that demanded good conduct and humility from prisoners, he would need a woman who stood by him.

Lizzie did not follow any particular strategy to catch Michael's eye. She had too often been forced to fool men. She just wanted to be there for Michael, and she wanted only to be good to him. In doing so, she created a predicament. Now when she met Jeremiah on deck and did his bidding, she asked for salt meat and sausage. She claimed it was to fortify the sick men's food, but in truth, she only brought it to Michael. And to Michael she said, "We get it in payment for taking care of the sick. But you need it more than I."

The atmosphere between the sick men and the women grew ever more informal. Some of the men were already strong enough to seek their pleasure in the arms of the wilder girls—which caused the number of women prepared to care for the men to increase daily. Lizzie was not the only one to fall in love with one of the young men; the others had also had enough of the relationships of convenience with sailors and guards. Besides, the voyage was approaching its end, and many girls yearned for a man who could perhaps be a support in the new country.

***

"She is a charming girl," Michael said to Hank Lauren, one of the other Irishmen from the jail in Wicklow. The guards had moved Hank to Billy Rafferty's berth when he died, and Hank and Michael had become friendly. "The English are crazy to deport such a nice girl just for stealing a loaf of bread."

Hank's laugh boomed. "She might well have stolen some bread," he said, "but only because she was too lazy just then for the next customer."

"What's that supposed to mean, Hank? You seem to think every girl's a whore."

Renewed laughter ensued, strengthened this time by the sailor whose bunk was on Michael's other side. "And you like them ones with the halos," he mocked Michael. "'Mary Kathleen'—just the way you say it sounds like a prayer."

"There's still hope that at least Mary Kathleen is as holy as she made you believe. Little Lizzie here whores herself, though," teased Hank, who was known throughout Wicklow as a rogue and a pimp.

"And she didn't exactly start here on the ship," the sailor added.

Michael looked over at Lizzie, who was just then showing one of the men her warming smile. She cared for the man lovingly, but nothing indicated any interest beyond caring for the sick.

"And how did the two of you come upon this knowledge?" Michael asked reluctantly.

"We're just not country bumpkins like you," Hank teased him. "My Lord, you can see it in the way a moll like that moves, the way she touches you—and dare I ask where you think that comes from?" Hank Lauren pointed at the salt meat and hardtack, some of which Michael was just then licking from his fingers. "Extra rations for nursing? Don't make me laugh."

"And what do you think she's doing up here alone on deck almost every night before she takes another quick peek at you?" the sailor asked. "Did she let herself out of the prisoners' deck? Uh, no, Michael. So Miss Lizzie lets one or two of the guards mount her and then rewards herself with a look in them lovely eyes of yours."

Michael said nothing, but from then on, he watched Lizzie more alertly. And he did hear her whispering with Jeremiah before coming over to him.

Lizzie was disappointed when Michael only greeted her frostily, employing none of his usual flattery. The day before, he had called her his "evening star" and, smiling, made her pick out a star he would name after her.

Now he limited himself to a "Good evening, Lizzie. Done with work?"

Michael did not say aloud what he knew, nor did he accuse her of anything. Nevertheless, Lizzie cried her eyes out in her berth. Her beautiful dream had dreamed itself out; she had seen it in his eyes. Elizabeth was Lizzie once again; the angel once again the whore.

***

On a cool morning in July, after a voyage of exactly one hundred and ten days, the *Asia* dropped anchor in Hobart Harbor. Jeremiah had told Lizzie that it was the middle of winter in Australia, and the island off its coast proved suitably cold and rainy. The master of the ship handed over the prisoners and their papers to the governor of Van Diemen's Land. Michael did not register any of this; he and the other serious criminals had been taken belowdecks as soon as land was sighted.

"The devils are all better," the captain had explained to the indignant Mrs. Bailiff. "And if they see land now, that will give them renewed vigor. I'm not about to risk a mutiny a few hours before I'm free of my cargo."

The women were allowed to watch from the deck as the ship landed. The little town that surrounded the harbor did not seem all that threatening. The buildings looked new and inviting, nothing like a prison.

"The prison is in Port Arthur," the talkative Jeremiah revealed to the curious Lizzie. "But they only send the serious criminals there. Only those who backslide here in the colonies—the lowest scum. They throw the rest into the work camp, so they're not nearly as closely watched."

"And the women?" Lizzie asked, scared.

"There are special accommodations," Jeremiah said. "But it's all only supposed to be half as bad."

Lizzie did not believe his reassurances, but for now she looked out at Hobart. The town lay on the mouth of the Derwent River at the foot of a mountain. It looked cleaner than London, more manageable; the air seemed clearer, despite the rain that obscured her vision. Most importantly, however, this was finally land again. Lizzie felt her anxiety dissipate. She would not have admitted it, but the knowledge that she was sailing across a mighty ocean, miles away from the nearest shore, had frightened her.

The passengers and future settlers were the first ones permitted off the ship. Mrs. Bailiff and Mrs. Smithers said fond farewells to Anna Portland and offered some friendly words for Lizzie and the others who'd helped with the sick men.

It was nearly time to say good-bye to Jeremiah, and Lizzie was relieved on one hand and almost reluctant on the other. She had not loved the guard, and worse, she assumed Michael's rejection had to do with her relationship with Jeremiah. But he had helped her survive the voyage. Lizzie had needed a protector, and she had paid Jeremiah to be that—with the only currency she had. If Michael could not understand, there was nothing that could help.

Lizzie wiped the tears determinedly from her eyes. Touched, Jeremiah kissed her. He must have thought she was crying for him, and Lizzie let him think that.

***

"Cascades Female Factory." A stout, austerely dressed female attendant pointed out the transport's destination after she had assigned the women into covered wagons with the help of soldiers. Lizzie, Candy, and Anna Portland clung to each other. They had spent such a long time at sea, the ground beneath them seemed to sway. Anna almost fell as she was ushered down the gangplank, and in the wagon, Lizzie felt less steady than she should now that they were on ground. The women could hardly see out from where they sat, but through a tear in the tarpaulin, they caught glimpses of small, clean streets, wooden houses, and red stone buildings.

"All built by prisoners," said Velvet.

She sounded apathetic. Lizzie wondered if she was missing the captain who had taken her to bed almost every night the past week. Even with his influence it would be a while until Velvet was released, but as usual, the beautiful black-haired girl did not reveal anything.

The female factory—the workplace of the female prisoners—was built of stone, a complex of extensive, unadorned buildings and cell blocks.

The moment they arrived, the supervisor ordered the women into a waiting room, where they bathed and then received their prison uniforms. Anna Portland sadly tossed her bonnet in with the rest of the clothing the women had worn all those days at sea. As a rule, these articles, which were ragged and filthy after the voyage, were burned.

"Now the hair cutting," the supervisor ordered—a direction that brought cries of indignation.

Anna watched as her gray-streaked brown hair fell to the ground. Candy sobbed desperately as they cropped her glorious red locks. Even Lizzie cried as a bored guard sheared her long, soft hair. Though her hair wasn't all that pretty to begin with, it grew slowly, so it would be years before she looked even halfway good again.

Velvet was silent as her thick black tresses fell away, but Lizzie thought she saw a flash of anger behind the stoic gaze of her dark eyes—more feeling than Velvet had shown during the whole voyage.

Anna, Lizzie, Candy, and Velvet occupied a bunkroom along with eight other prisoners. It proved roomy and, like everything else in the female factory, spotlessly clean.

The leader of their block immediately gave a speech about what shape the women's righteous life would take. Every day, they would pray before starting work and again at night. The prison director led the prayers, while the guards, who were all women, inspected the cells for cleanliness and order. Work began at six and continued until sundown, interrupted only by meals. There were no other breaks.

At last, Anna's and Lizzie's work—and Velvet's relationship to the captain—while they were aboard paid off. The three of them received the status of first-class prisoner, which brought with it a few privileges—not the least of which was that they were employed doing less difficult work. Anna had a post in the infirmary, while Lizzie and Velvet were assigned to the kitchen, where they were hardly supervised.

"You could run away," Candy said, almost a bit jealous. She was still with the second class, but after three months of good behavior, she could be promoted as well.

Anna shook her head. "Where are we supposed to go, child?" she asked gently. "This prison is in the middle of nowhere."

The female factory lay in a sort of light scrubland, uncultivated and miles from the next settlement. "They would catch you before you ever got to town. And even if you made it town, what would you do there? Return to your old profession? They'd catch you before you even made it to your third customer."

Indeed, escape from the Cascades Female Factory proved unnecessary. Reasonable behavior seemed to lead to commutation—as did marriage.

Candy saw how it worked after only two months in the sewing factory, where she had been assigned. "You can't imagine," she informed the others excitedly. "We all 'ad to form a line—the first-class girls in the front, of course, and the rest behind—then three men walked past us. Two were new settlers; one was a soldier. One of the settlers already knew what 'e wanted. 'E'd gotten to know Annie Carmichael on the ship. Anyway, he dropped a handkerchief in front of her first. She turned red as a beet when she picked it up—and just like that, she was engaged."

Lizzie and the others looked at Candy, mouths agape. She raved on without a pause.

"The fellows eyed us like mares at the horse market," Candy continued. "I was just waiting for them to check our teeth. Then the other two let their handkerchiefs fall—one of the girls picked it up; the other began to 'owl. She probably was still pining for some sweetheart in England. I thought, now the man will tell 'er 'e'll come back. It's what you'd expect, right? But no, 'e just picked out another one. The three of them will get clemency now and be married. Can you believe it? I was still too shy this time, you see, and with this short hair, I look like a plucked chicken. But next time, I'll show 'em. I'll get me a fellow like that, and then I'll be out."

Two men visited the prison's kitchen and cleaning personnel. They had to line up as Candy had described, and the men had their pick. Lizzie felt she could die of shame. Naturally, the men on the streets of London had had their choice. Lizzie had often strolled down the alleys alongside other whores. But then, when and how she presented herself had always been up to her. She could hide behind her makeup or her neat little hat. It was self-deception, but she had really felt her fate was in her own hands. Here, however—call it a horse market or a slave market—Lizzie did not smile.

Of course, Velvet did not force a smile either, but a man chose her nonetheless. The man was neither young nor handsome. Lizzie wondered why Velvet picked up the handkerchief.

The men never wasted a second glance on Lizzie, but one afternoon the prison director summoned her. Normally that only happened when a woman broke some rule—or was picked for marriage. Lizzie could not remember breaking any rules, so might one of the men have decided on her after all? And how could she refuse without losing her status as a first-class prisoner?

Fearful, she slipped through the long, cheerless halls of the factory, in which there was always a draft.

It was not a man sitting across from the severe prison director but a well-dressed woman. Lizzie recognized short, bony Amanda Smithers and curtsied properly.

"Elizabeth Owens"—the prison director had an oddly sharp, high-pitched voice that always made the women tremble—"you know Mrs. Smithers, I take it."

Lizzie nodded. "I hope you're well," she said politely.

Mrs. Smithers smiled. "Very well, my girl. We—"

The director interrupted her. He seemed to have no intention of letting Mrs. Smithers state her own business, preferring to hear himself talk.

"Elizabeth, Mrs. Smithers needs a maid. And since you made an excellent impression on her on the ship, she has expressly asked to employ you."

Lizzie blushed and curtsied again. Sometimes female prisoners were put to work outside the factory. The women sought these posts in high-society houses—after all, one spent all day outside the prison, saw some of the town, and missed evening prayers. Moreover, the food was much better than at Cascades, where their meals were sufficient but boring: bread and porridge for breakfast, bread and vegetable soup for lunch and dinner. Workdays, Sundays, holidays. Every day. No one went hungry, but Lizzie had long since ceased looking forward to meals.

"We have a special case on our hands," the prison director continued. "Mr. Smithers oversees work on the road from Hobart to Launceston. His house is near Campbell Town, so, closer to Launceston than Hobart. Indeed, it would—"

"Even for a girl from the Launceston factory, it would be too far away to return every day," Mrs. Smithers interrupted. "What the director means to say, Lizzie—Elizabeth—is that you would have to live in our house if you took the job. Would that suit you?"

Lizzie was startled. She knew most of the girls would have cheered, but she was of two minds. She had never thought she might be able to leave the female factory so soon, and if she was being honest, the offer did not mean all that much to her. Lizzie rarely had felt as secure as she did in this prison. The work was not hard—the cook, a fat, friendly woman, laughed and joked with her girls and had not yet struck any of them. Even in Lizzie's bunkroom, all the women were pleasant, and everything was clean and orderly.

All the praying sometimes bored her, but she relished the feeling of being truly good without compunction for once in her life. The overseers and the pastor were friendly to her. On Sundays, she sometimes read the Bible or some other books with other prisoners' children. A few women had been deported with their offspring, and if a female settler in Van Diemen's Land broke the law, she and her children went to the female factory. Lizzie enjoyed interacting with the little ones, and she didn't have to worry about them as she would if they were her own.

She hoped taking care of the children might become her job at the prison, and then, eventually, she could get a job as a nanny outside it. In any case, she had prepared herself to spend the next three and a half years at Cascades. After serving half their time, women were usually pardoned. Then they could look for work in town and perhaps even find a husband.

Recently, Lizzie had permitted herself to dream again. The face of her fairy-tale prince was concealed by clouds, so she did not need to admit that his body still resembled that of Michael Drury.

And now, this unexpected offer to move in with Mrs. and Mr. Smithers near Campbell Town.

"We have moved into a very grand house," Mrs. Smithers explained, smiling. "The owners will be in England for some time and have left it in our care for as long as this section of road is under construction. In any case, I desperately need a maid, and I think you would feel at home with us. You'll have a lovely room, the cook is friendly, and the gardener"—she winked—"well, I hope you won't be married out from under us. Lizzie, what do you think?"

"Above all, of course, it matters what the Cascades Female Factory thinks," said the prison director strictly. "But since the girl has behaved herself so far . . ."

Lizzie hardly knew what was happening to her, but within an hour, she was sitting next to Mrs. Smithers in a neat little chaise traveling toward Campbell Town.

Chapter 6

Kathleen Coltrane hauled herself up the hill. It was a beautiful spring day, and far beyond the hills that surrounded Port Cooper, she could see the majestic peaks of the southern mountains. Grassy plains were supposed to lie between them—Kathleen often dreamed she might see them someday. Especially as she once again had to climb the stony streets of Port Cooper to her house, on foot and with two children.

Almost all the houses in the growing harbor town lay in the hills. This included the little blue-painted cottage that Ian had acquired two days after their arrival. Kathleen thought of the day she first had to overcome the climb. She had almost crumbled.

Three days after her son's birth and so soon after the long sea voyage, a dark chasm had seemed to open before her when she stood up and attempted to walk. But Ian knew no mercy. He had bought a house, and he wanted to move in with his young wife right away.

When she had entered the cold, barren residence, Kathleen had burst into tears. The previous owner—he had moved to the Canterbury Plains—had only left behind furnishings he did not need for his new house, so this one was nearly bare.

"Where should I put the baby? Where are we supposed to sleep?"

Ian just shrugged. "We'll buy a bed. As far as I care, a cradle too. We'll need it often enough. You can see to the house. I'll give you money. Don't act like this is so awful, Kathleen. Remember, your family slept on the floor."

That was true, but they had had mats, and a fire was always burning. And Kathleen had not been exhausted from childbirth and a long voyage.

"Like I said, Kathleen, see to it," Ian commanded. "I have to go to the stables. I'll probably be taking the first horse there later. The miller's nag. He says she's difficult, nearly ran away from him with the bread wagon. Well, I'll fix that. But the household is really your affair."

She realized Ian had not bought any groceries either, not even milk. There was only a sack of flour on the table. Kathleen would have baked bread from it if she hadn't felt so bad. Then she cast a hopeless look at the stove in the kitchen—which was not burning and for which there was no wood at hand. Surely there was some outside. But she could not summon the strength to go outside. Not as long as the ground seem to sway underneath her.

Fortunately, the baby had fallen right to sleep on a blanket, and she was making plenty of her own milk with which to feed him. Pere had made sure of that by providing her with soup and strange vegetables called sweet potatoes.

She looked around a bit more and discovered that the house itself was quite lovely. Simple, but purposefully built: a living room, a bedroom, another room in which Sean could sleep, and a rather large kitchen. By Irish standards, it was a grand home. No one in Kathleen's village had this much space. Even Trevallion's cottage was smaller. Surely there were also stables and pastures. After all, Ian always thought first about his four-legged wares.

Kathleen had to admit that her husband had not made a poor purchase. The kitchen windows opened out to the harbor, so Kathleen would always have something to see when she was busy about the house. And even her first glance outside revealed a happy surprise. Pere was already coming up with a basket on her arm, and she was joined by another, younger woman.

"Bringing presents for moving in," the Maori woman called to her. She proudly handed her new friend a basket full of sweet potatoes and seeds.

Pere's companion smiled broadly at Kathleen. "I'm Linda Holt. My husband's the miller here," she said, "and he told me that you've just moved in. Without furniture, without supplies, and with a newborn baby to boot. These men! Carl did not even think to give your husband a pitcher of milk or some ham. We do a little farming, you see."

The women did not wait for Kathleen's invitation to enter; instead, they walked right into the house.

"My God." Linda got excited. "The Shoemakers didn't leave you a thing. And how are you? You're shivering all over."

Kathleen was unable to answer, but Pere told Linda the story of how the Coltranes came ashore in Port Cooper. After that, the two women went straight to work. Pere carried in a pile of wood and set to lighting all the stoves in the house.

"Must get cold out. Not good for the baby," she explained when Kathleen protested. Surely wood was expensive.

Linda had run home to retrieve the cradle her own daughter had just grown out of. "And by the time the next one comes," she said, tapping her stomach, "you'll already have your own."

She brought her daughter—a blonde-haired, cute little thing—with her when she returned. Kathleen looked after the child while Pere baked bread— strange flatbread, which had almost nothing in common with the loaves she was used to—and Linda drove to the carpenter with her husband's fractious horse. She must have done so very skillfully: the nag did not get away from her, and she came back with a bed, a table, and two chairs in the wagon.

"This is what the carpenter had around. Anything else you're missing, you'll have to order. Help me set up this bed, Pere. What a pain. You Maori sleep on mats, right? That's so much more practical."

"Practical" was Linda's favorite word, and Kathleen soon became fond of the tall, slender blonde woman. She had no idea how she would have survived her first days in Port Cooper without her neighbors' energetic help. Linda and Pere; Veronica, the carpenter's wife; and Jenny, the petite but exceedingly plucky wife of the lumber seller, cooked for her, lent her furniture and uten- sils, stoked the stoves, and, most of all, always had a comforting and friendly word for her.

Ian eyed the feminine invasion of his house with more than distrust. The women soon noted that he found them bothersome, and they stayed away when they saw his cart in front of the house. This suited Ian fine, but Veronica and Jenny often asked their husbands for help for the new settlers. The car- penter took measurements and delivered furniture; Jenny's husband sent their son by with firewood. When Ian became aware of these visits, he reacted with anger that increased as more time passed. Two weeks after Sean was born, Ian began getting on top of his wife again.

"No," Kathleen said. She wanted to push him away. "Not yet; it's too soon. I'm, I'm still very sore."

Ian held her arms tightly. "So, you're sore are you? That can hardly still be from the birth. Who's been seeing you, Kathleen? Who have you been having fun with while I toil? The boy I saw coming out of the house when I came home yesterday looked handsome."

"That was Jenny's oldest son," Kathleen explained, struggling against Ian's grip, "barely thirteen years old. He brought firewood. My lands, Ian, what do you take me for? A bitch in heat who would—"

"Spread her legs for any man? Well, so far you haven't proved the contrary. And I'm not going to take the risk of raising another stranger's bastard. This time *I'll* get you pregnant."

Ian forced her beneath him and quickly thrust into her. She could not suppress a cry of pain. Sean whimpered, and Kathleen bit her lip. She hoped desperately that the neighbors had not heard her.

***

Only three weeks later, Ian had realized his intent, and Kathleen conceived again. She gave birth to her second son, Colin, just a little more than ten months after her arrival in her new country. But while she had carried Sean without complications, her second pregnancy had its share of challenges. Kathleen struggled against weakness and nausea and, on top of that, she had to quickly wean Sean because her milk was running dry. The baby was outraged at this. He cried constantly, and Kathleen could not keep him quiet when Ian came home.

Fortunately, Ian was often away. His business was doing well, and it often took him to the Canterbury Plains for several days at a time. There were not yet any livestock markets in New Zealand like the ones in England and Ireland. Ian had to ply his trade as a sort of traveling salesman. He would buy a few horses, sheep, or cattle; herd them across the countryside; and offer to sell them to the next farmer. Of course, this worked better with horses, mules, and donkeys than with grazing animals, the moving of which demanded herders and dogs. This was especially true for trade between the settlers of Port Cooper and the farmers in the plains. It was almost impossible to lead non-haltered animals over the steep, rough pass that separated the harbor from the interior.

So in Port Cooper itself, Ian focused on the horse trade—and he quickly managed to make his new neighbors distrust him.

***

Kathleen thought about all this as she climbed up the hill, the ungainly toddler Sean on one hand and baby Colin bound to her back in a sling. In her other hand she hauled her purchases: vegetables from the harbor market, milk, and milled grain to bake bread and make porridge for the children. As if all that weren't enough, she pulled a cumbersome sack of wool behind her. It needed to be washed, teased, and spun. Kathleen was skillful with such things, and Linda, the exuberant miller's wife, liked to take advantage of this. She had grown up on a farm and kept a few animals in stalls near the mill. While she readily sheared her five sheep herself, handiwork like spinning or weaving didn't come easily for her.

Once, Kathleen had the bitter thought that Linda or her husband could have brought the material to her door in their wagon. But their horse was dragging its leg again, and even if Linda did not come out and say it, Kathleen thought they were punishing her for Ian's deception about the horse.

"Just what was your husband thinking, selling my Carl that old nag?" Linda said. "Sure, our other mare was a little peculiar—she would come home without Carl." A stifled giggle slipped into Linda's voice. She came from the country; her husband, from a suburb of London. He was an excellent baker and miller, but he had no talent for animals. "But still, it would move. This new one, though . . . I'd bet it's hauling at least twenty years on its back."

"Can't you tell?" Kathleen objected shyly. "By the teeth?"

"Oh, there are ways," said John, the smith. He was just entering the mill to look at the horse's leg again. "You rub this and that off the teeth; horse traders are creative."

"But, but Ian would never . . ." Kathleen defended her husband.

John rolled his eyes.

"I've yet to meet a horse trader who's not a rascal," he said. "But, of course, I agree with you, Mrs. Coltrane. You shouldn't sell your neighbor a lame nag. That comes back around to you. So let's just assume your husband simply knew nothing about the previous owner's schemes."

Kathleen would have liked to believe that, but there was already too much talk in the little town for it to be the case. Almost no one was satisfied with the animals Ian had sold them—only George Hancock, one of the farmers, was happy at first with a gorgeous dark-black broodmare. But she still had not birthed a foal, and Hancock had just learned that its previous owner had sold it for that very reason. The argument that Ian had not known didn't work this time. The previous owner swore he had revealed the reason he was selling it.

"Had no reason to lie, either," said an excited George Hancock at a picnic after the prayer meeting one Sunday. "Penny's a fine horse, just not for breeding. And Ian Coltrane—forgive me, Mrs. Coltrane, but that fellow lies as naturally as you or I breathe."

Kathleen had pretended she did not hear—after all, Colin was working himself up to cry as loud as he could, and she had to prevent Sean from joining him. Still, what they were saying hurt, and it poisoned her newly formed friendships. Ian preferred it that way, naturally. He never stopped torturing Kathleen with his jealousy and had grown angry because she did not get pregnant immediately after Colin was born. By now, he, too, had realized that Port Cooper was not the ideal place for him to settle.

Shortly after the Coltranes' arrival in New Zealand, the Canterbury Association in England had formed an organization of faithful Anglicans determined to establish a large settlement in the new colony. They had acquired land a day's march from Port Cooper for a new city—Christchurch, finally a diocese on the English model. A road would be built across the mountains in the near future.

People would need animals for transportation and work. The new citizens of Christchurch would assuredly not be buying those in Port Cooper if there were closer alternatives. So Ian was contemplating a move, while just the thought of leaving her new friends made Kathleen fearful and uncertain. When Ian once again unleashed his anger on her and accused her of infidelity, she contradicted him for the first time.

"You of all people accuse me of cheating! Who here cheats his customers? I can hardly still look people in the eye, the way people curse the old, lame, or barren nags you've sold them. And you don't really think it will be any different if we move to Christchurch, do you? Or are you suddenly going to turn into an honest trader?"

"As honest a trader as you are a wife," Ian roared at Kathleen, hitting her and throwing her on the bed.

Lately, he had started to insist on his marital rights at unexpected times. Apparently, he feared she would do something to prevent a pregnancy if he did not take her by surprise. And the struggle for sex seemed to excite him, so he increasingly forced himself on Kathleen while Colin cried and Sean was in danger of falling into the fireplace or some other horror.

Kathleen could never relax. What Ian insisted on had nothing in common with the joys of love she had shared with Michael in the fields by the river. Kathleen asked God to forgive her, but she began to hate Ian.

***

That day in spring, Ian's problems with the neighbors escalated. Kathleen had just carried her sons and her supplies past John Seeker's smith shop and considered whether she ought to take a rest. Sean was already whining; the climb was long for him, too, and the weather was unusually warm for the spring month of November. Surely Pere would have a glass of water for Kathleen and milk for the little ones. The Maori woman was the only one who still treated Kathleen as kindly as when she had first arrived. Knowing the secret of Sean's paternity, Pere, of all people, had reason to scorn her. But apparently the Maori thought about things differently.

"Every child reason for joy, every child property of tribe, every woman mother, every old woman grandmother," Pere had soothed Kathleen. She told her repeatedly about the customs of her people, among whom even a child out of wedlock was no reason to feel ashamed. "If a man knows woman is fertile, she valued much more."

Even little Sean pulled her toward the house. He liked to visit Pere because she told him fairy tales and spoiled him with sugary treats. The Maori loved sugar—and Pere enjoyed that, as the wife of a *pakeha*, she could get all the sugar she wanted. She baked bonbons, candy canes, and sweet cakes she generously gave to all the neighborhood children.

But as Kathleen was still considering whether she wanted to knock or go straight home and start working on the wool, she heard a loud argument coming from the smithy. One of the voices was Ian's, and indeed his horse, a strong chestnut, was hitched in front of the house.

Kathleen's first impulse was not only to go home but to run there. If Ian saw her here, he would accuse her of wanting to see John or fetching some means of preventing a pregnancy from Pere. It would be far better if she were at home washing and teasing the wool. But then what she heard from inside the shop made her too curious to leave. Kathleen ordered Sean to quit his whining and listened by the door of the smithy.

"What do you mean you won't do it?" Ian asked. "Come, I'm just asking you to hammer in the nails a little higher. The seller gave me the horse because its shoes wouldn't hold."

John snorted like an angry horse. "Don't tell me your tales, Coltrane. If the shoes don't hold, you change smiths, not horses. The man sold his horse because it's unsteady. Something's wrong with the left back leg; bad hipbone, I take it. And now you want me to hammer the nails so tight the shoes pinch? Then both legs will hurt, and he won't drag that one, eh? But I won't do it, Ian Coltrane. It goes against my professional honor."

"Bah. What's honor, John? Now do it. I'll pay three pence more." Ian's voice sounded relaxed. "If you don't do it, I'll do it myself, but I can't get the nails in a neat row. People notice that."

Kathleen was startled when John tore open the gate to the smithy and commanded Ian to leave. "I believe you, boy, that you don't know what honor is. But I do know, so get lost with your lame nag, and shame on you."

The powerful smith rushed Ian outside with a shove. Ian tripped and fell. The horse, which he held by the reins, shied. Kathleen hoped she could still flee unnoticed, but Ian had already seen her.

"You, you little whore," Ian seized her arm and shook her. "Caught you in the act, huh? You were listening at the door to see if everything was quiet and you could get to your lover."

Kathleen shook her head desperately. The children began to scream.

John Seeker opened the door to his smithy again. "Be gone, Coltrane," he growled. "On my land you'll neither cheat your customers nor beat your wife. The poor thing, she's really done nothing to deserve an ass like you. Leave her alone, ride home, and calm yourself. And woe to you if tomorrow I see you've hit your wife. Are you all right, Kathleen?"

Kathleen nodded, her face red with shame. So now the neighbors knew Ian beat her too. And worse still, in his rush to defend her, John had called her by her first name. Ian would hold that against her. Normally her friends' husbands respectfully called her Mrs. Coltrane, especially in Ian's presence.

Ian shoved Kathleen rudely toward home. "Get out of here," he whispered to her. "You've caused me enough trouble. Now get home; I'll see you there. And this time, I'm giving you a new baby."

***

Indeed, Kathleen was pregnant when Ian sold their house in Port Cooper two months later. John Seeker had talked about the scene at the smithy all over town, and since then, everyone had avoided Ian Coltrane. Kathleen received no more invitations to Bible study or the prayer meetings on Sundays at which the settlers of all faiths met. So far, there were neither Catholic nor Anglican pastors in Port Cooper, so they had to fend for themselves. Kathleen, who could sing or read from the Bible with a full, sweet voice, had been a welcome addition. But Ian had spoiled that for her too. On the other side of the mountains, he explained, there would be no neighbors with whom she could flirt. Ian had bought a farm on the Avon River, not far from the new settlement, Christchurch, but still too far to offer Kathleen any opportunities for socializing.

"You can care for the children; we'll have a few sheep too. For diversion you can shear your own wool for once." It was clear that Ian was cheered by the thought of soon being able to lock up his young wife on a solitary farm.

Yet despite all the bad omens, Kathleen was excited about the world beyond the mountains. Finally, she would see more of her new country than a bay and a few hills. So she tried to look at the future with optimism as she carried Colin and Sean and a few of her things over the trail to Christchurch. Since the people of Port Cooper were expecting an onrush of new residents bound for Christchurch, the trail had been smoothed, and traveling it no longer presented a great challenge. Nevertheless, mounts were usually led, mostly by assistants who knew the region and held the halters of the horses or mules for a small fee. This practice gave the route its new name: the Bridle Path.

At the time of their move, Ian and Kathleen owned three mules, but Ian needed them to carry the household accessories and furniture. Though one could send cumbersome items up the Avon by ship, Ian was stingy about the price. After the voyage and the purchase of their first house, there was nothing left of Michael's money. Ian bought the farm with the income from his own business.

Kathleen told herself that a part of that money still belonged to her and Sean. She was no longer ashamed that it was made selling whiskey. Distilling alcohol had always been met with a wink. What Ian did was much worse.

In any case, Kathleen and the children had to walk—like most settlers who came to New Zealand in steerage. They had an advantage because they weren't weakened by the long voyage and they were practiced in climbing the hills of Port Cooper. Kathleen no longer ran out of breath so quickly, but the first part of the climb up the Bridle Path was, nevertheless, a challenge. She had to pull behind her a whining Sean, who did not see why he had to climb up the pass or why they had cleaned out their house. The thought of having to live somewhere else, far from his beloved Aunt Pere, scared him as much as it did Kathleen.

Worse still, the steep path was stark. The grassland quickly gave way to barren rock. For a long time, they walked along crater rims through a desert of bare gray volcanic rock. Sean clamped onto Kathleen's hand and Colin onto her neck. Kathleen was worried before they had even made it a third of the way, and even more so since Ian did not bother to encourage her or help. It wasn't until they stumbled at a dangerous spot that he finally took Colin's carrier and packed it on one of the mules.

"He can't stay up there, Ian. If he moves, the whole thing will fall down, and he'll fall off the mountain." Kathleen was exhausted—probably even more so since she was pregnant—and relieved not to have to carry Colin around anymore, but that rickety seat on the mule . . .

"As clumsily as you move, he really would fall," Ian spat back. "I won't allow you to endanger my child."

Kathleen had a sharp response on the tip of her tongue, but she swallowed it when Ian reluctantly buckled the carrier onto the mule's back. A lot could be said against him, but he loved Colin. He sometimes returned from his business travels with something for the boy—wooden horses or woven balls crafted by the natives. Colin still did not know what to do with them, but Sean was delighted. Kathleen would not let herself think about how he would react when he was old enough to realize that Ian brought the gifts exclusively for his brother and not for him.

The climb over the rocks and along the extremely narrow path seemed not to want to end, but then, suddenly, a plateau leveled off before them. Ian suggested they rest and tied the mules to a tree. Kathleen ought to have unpacked the bread she had brought along, and she longed for a drink of water. But curiosity overtook her. She felt carefully, while holding Sean's hand, for the edge of the shelf.

What she saw overwhelmed her: a world that she had left behind nearly two years ago. Before her lay her homeland. Ireland. The fields. The river.

Kathleen blinked to make sure she was not dreaming. She stared down, uncomprehending, at a green landscape of gentle hills through which the Avon wound. It was broken up by copses and rock formations, just like the ones she remembered from Ireland. What was lacking were human settlements. There were no villages and no manors—only small individual farmhouses. And something else was missing: the endless stone fences that divided the land into smaller entities. This was free, open land.

Kathleen felt her heart pound with a strange sensation of happiness. She looked at the land of which she had dreamed with Michael. Bathed in sun, but green, just as green as Ireland—a land reflected in Kathleen's eyes.

"Good Lord, Ian, it's so beautiful," she said admiringly. "It's just, just like my country."

"Your country is nothing," Ian informed her moodily. "This is the land of our children. By the time they're grown, I'll own a great deal of it, enough for a grand farm. Sheep perhaps, and horses. We'll be rich."

Kathleen wondered if he was also thinking of Sean when he spoke of these children. He could not disown the boy. Ian had received Michael's money—Kathleen was now sure that he had known about the purse in her possession when he courted her. Sean carried his name in exchange. A fair trade, on paper. Sean was also her son, and Kathleen would fight for him. Their land in Port Cooper had not been important to her. But this? This should belong to Michael's child.

Chapter 7

The journey from the female factory to Campbell Town had lasted three days, and the two overnight stops were more comfortable than Lizzie could ever have imagined. First they stayed with Mrs. Smithers's acquaintances in Green Ponds. There Lizzie was welcomed by their maid, Lisa, who was a former prisoner and who had only good things to report about her current life. Lizzie and Lisa chatted half the night, and afterward, Lizzie could hardly believe they had exchanged harmless gossip and romantic stories like normal girls instead of tales of whoring and hunger.

Mrs. Smithers and Lizzie spent the next night in a small hotel in Jericho, which lay along an already finished stretch of the road to Launceston. She rented a room for Lizzie as if it were completely natural, and then joked that she should not run away in the night. Lizzie had no intention of that. For the first time in her life, she was sleeping alone in a room between immaculate sheets and on soft pillows scented with roses and lavender. Why would she leave this lovely dream?

The journey itself was exciting. The road between Hobart and Campbell Town was already well paved, but parts of it went through the wilderness. Lizzie peered, spellbound, into the darkness of the rainforests where, she was quite sure, mischievous animals like the Tasmanian devil were about. She was shocked when a kangaroo leaped across the road and just as startled when she saw the first chain gang.

When things had gone so well for Lizzie in the female factory, she had stopped worrying about Michael. Now, however, she realized that the English Crown treated male prisoners very differently.

The overseers of the chain gang were armed and carried whips, which they used without hesitation. The men's mostly bare backs showed the marks of this treatment. The overseers mercilessly forced them to break rocks to make way for the road and to clear the forest for new settlements.

Lizzie covered her eyes with her hands.

"Well, no, it's not pretty, Lizzie," Mrs. Smithers said. She told their driver to pull the covering over their prim chaise; it had just begun to rain. "But the poor devils haven't deserved any better. Whoever has to labor here, especially in the chain gangs, did wrong elsewhere. Most of them were already serious criminals in England. I know it hurts you to see, but remember they're robbers and murderers!"

"But some, some are just escapees," Lizzie risked objecting.

There was talk in the female factory of how a few men were always trying to escape imprisonment. For the girls, they were romantic heroes, unyielding rebels who could not be broken by even the harshest treatment. Their attempts always ended, however, in a chain gang or the dreaded prison in Port Arthur.

"A few, certainly," said Mrs. Smithers dismissively. "But if you ask me, idiocy is also punishable. Where do the fellows think they're going? Into the rainforests? Where the snakes or wild beasts will get them? The towns are too small to hide in: Jericho, Hobart, Launceston—they're not exactly London. Moreover, they don't know anyone here. Escape is simply hopeless."

"What if they stole a ship?" asked Lizzie. "To sail home?"

"Home?" Mrs. Smithers laughed. "Child, you know what that journey is like! Across the Tasman Sea, the Indian Ocean? Around the Cape of Good Hope? The Atlantic? If one of them had the makings of a ship's captain, he would not be here. Although I have heard that some occasionally escape to New Zealand, that's just hearsay. Whether they are stuck on this island or that one, in the end, it doesn't matter."

It does to someone who wants to be free, thought Lizzie, trying to forget the longing in Michael's eyes. His gaze had made her melt and dream of freedom. Yet he had only been thinking of that girl he called Mary Kathleen.

***

Though Mrs. Smithers had said the house in Campbell Town was grand, in truth it was nearly a castle. Lizzie marveled at the many rooms, and her eyes wandered, disbelieving, from the heavy furniture to the silver to the porcelain from England.

In Lizzie's eyes, the greatest of these wonders was the chamber she had been assigned in the servants' quarters. It was small—besides a bed, a table, a chair, and herself, not much would fit inside. But it didn't matter because all of it was hers. No one else would bother her with their snoring, crying, or talking in their sleep. The bed was simple but clean—and if Lizzie dried some flowers, she could make her pillow smell just like the one in the hotel in Jericho. That could not be too hard. There were roses in the garden.

Even Lizzie's fear that the other servants might look down on her because she was a prisoner immediately proved unfounded. The cook, Martha, immediately revealed that she was a pardoned deportee.

"Stood lookout on a burglary for my man," she confessed. "Lord, was I a fool back then, but I really thought he'd make a load of money. Instead, he shot someone. Still, I was lucky I didn't end up on the gallows."

Every night, the gardener went back to the prison where he was serving his sentence. He was thankful he had escaped having to build the road, but he was such a puny little man that Lizzie couldn't imagine he'd have managed the work. He fell madly in love with Lizzie right away, and it was not long before she was drowning in rose petals. Pete, the male servant, was big and strong enough for road work, but he was also older. He hoped to be pardoned soon, and planned to marry Martha then. The two of them would remain at the house, in apartments prepared for them. It seemed clear to Lizzie that for many convicts, deportation was more of a blessing than a curse.

She happily received her maid's dress and bonnet, and Mrs. Smithers took the time to explain each of Lizzie's household tasks. Polishing, dusting, waxing, serving tea and meals—none of these tasks was particularly fun, but all of it was far better than wandering the streets and serving one man after another between filthy sheets. For the first time, Lizzie was living up to the standards of the reverend in the orphanage: she was being good, living righteously, and keeping it so.

If it were not for Mr. Smithers.

Amanda Smithers's husband was often away for days at a time, managing the road construction. Some of the prisoners were skillful, but few of them had experience in this work. As a rule, the prisoners from Ireland and Scotland were farmers. They knew about agriculture and husbandry and did excellent work on simple tasks like clearing forest for the new roads. But they had no expertise breaking rocks and securing roads.

The crew overseers almost all came from military careers rather than a background in engineering. So it was up to Martin Smithers to instruct his colleagues and decide every detail himself. He slept in a tent or barracks hardly more comfortable than the prisoners', and it was only on the weekends that he returned to the grand house that his wife and the household servants made comfortable for him.

Lizzie first met Mr. Smithers just a week after she arrived. Though he showed no outward interest in the formal introduction his wife made, Lizzie immediately saw the glimmer in his eye, and it didn't bode well.

He confirmed her first impression when he came into the breakfast room the next day. "Ah, so here we have the charming new house kitten," he said.

Lizzie, who did not know how to take that expression, vacillated between her desire to ignore him and continue her work of setting the table and the curtsy propriety demanded. To avoid any issue, she did the latter with her eyes chastely lowered. But Mr. Smithers did not leave her alone.

"Why don't you look me in the eyes, kitten?" he asked. With a salacious smile, he put his finger under her chin and lifted her head with gentle force. "Are you afraid I might see some desire? Are you really as good a little thing as my wife tells me?"

Lizzie looked up at him, examining his wide, sunburned face. Mr. Smithers was a tall, heavy man who hardly seemed to fit his short, lean wife. His brown hair was already thin, his eyes watery blue. Desire was about the last thing Lizzie felt at the sight of him. Rather, the former whore in her sighed as she imagined how his weight would crush her when he collapsed on her, satisfied.

"I don't understand what you mean, sir," Lizzie claimed, hoping she might blush. But she had heard such speech too often to feel shame. It was tiresome to her. Yet she felt fear rise up within her.

"Then think it over, kitten." The man grinned, and his fingers wandered from her chin over her cheek to her temple. "You're a pretty little thing. Don't make me wait too long until you're in heat."

Mrs. Smithers was coming down the hall and Lizzie heard her with enough time to flee Mr. Smithers's grip before his wife entered the room.

Lizzie tried to avoid him the rest of the weekend, but it was almost impossible. He leered at her every time he passed her, and when she served meals, he would sneak a grab under her skirt or pinch her. Naturally, Lizzie couldn't allow herself any outward reaction.

She was frazzled when she slipped into her room after Saturday's dinner—only to discover Mr. Smithers waiting for her.

"Such a sweet kitten wouldn't let me go to bed without a good-night kiss."

Lizzie dodged him just as he reached out for her. "I believe," she said through clenched teeth, "it's supposed to be bad for the health to hug and kiss your pets."

It was meant as a joke—on the streets of London, one learned to use quick wit not only to attract men but also to keep them at bay. Lizzie thought her quip was clever, but Martin Smithers took a step back, as if she had attacked him.

"What is that supposed to mean, girl? Are you threatening me? What's got into you that your claws come out first? I thought you'd just stolen something. If you're violent . . ."

Fear spread through Lizzie. She had not done anything. But the prison director would believe whatever Mr. Smithers might say about her. Frightened, she inched out of her room to the hallway, where she raised her hands defensively.

"I've never hurt anyone, sir, I swear it. Nor would I you."

"So, that was no allusion to cats clawing?" Smithers asked mistrustfully.

Lizzie shook her head, frightened. "Of course not, sir. Of course not. Only, the doctors say pets eat rats and the like, and have fleas," she stuttered in her desperate attempt to explain her joke.

And Smithers did show belated amusement, but his laughter was threatening, not sincere.

"They'll have deloused you in the female factory. Think about where you've come from when you talk back to me! The rats are still waiting for you."

With that, he seized Lizzie and pressed a kiss to her mouth. Not more brutally than most of her customers, but Lizzie was shocked and disgusted. Just then, Mrs. Smithers called for her husband. Lizzie sighed with relief and silently thanked her employer and her God. As soon as Mr. Smithers turned away, she ran back into her room and locked the door behind her.

***

The next morning, Lizzie went to church with her employers. A picnic followed the sermon, and after Martha was finished serving, she and Pete invited Lizzie along with them on a walk to visit the other pardoned or first-class prisoners.

Lizzie stayed behind, though, wanting nothing more than to sit on her blanket and enjoy the sun and the new sights around the neat little church and Campbell Town.

Mr. Smithers pounced the moment she stood up to stretch her legs. Under the pretense of showing her the birds and trees, he led her around the back of the church and into a copse where he kissed her again.

"Now that's better, pet. A soft, cuddly kitten."

Lizzie tried desperately to free herself. "Sir, please, please not here. If someone comes . . ."

The copse behind the church was the only place where young lovers could go. The cook and her beau had already disappeared here themselves.

Smithers grunted, understanding. "Yes, yes, you're right. I just can't keep still when I see that spark in your eyes and the way you move, quick and graceful like a house kitten ought."

"But, but . . ." Lizzie fought back tears. If someone caught them . . .

"And a little shy, that's not bad either. All right, fine, not here. But soon we'll find a secret little corner, and then you'll keep your promise."

Lizzie had no idea what she had promised him, but when he finally let her go, she was so relieved that she nodded. She was off work the rest of the day, and when they returned to the house, she went straight to her room to pray that Mr. Smithers would not come after her again.

On Monday, Mr. Smithers returned to the construction site, but Lizzie was so upset that she could not concentrate on her work. First she broke a teacup; then she forgot to clear the tea table, which she was swiftly admonished for. Later in the afternoon, when she was helping Martha, she cut her finger and her blood dripped into the salad bowl.

"What's gotten into you?" said the cook. She grabbed the bowl away from Lizzie. "You're usually so helpful."

Lizzie burst into tears and buried her face in her hands. After she got her story out between sobs, she fell into wild self-doubt.

"He can see it in me," she said. "Yet I want to be good. Really, I want, I want to live a righteous life."

Martha had listened with a stony face. "So it's begun again." She sighed. "No, enough, enough! It has nothing to do with you!"

Lizzie would not listen. "Can, can it be that I'm destined to be a whore?" she asked despairingly.

The cook shook her head. "For men like Mr. Smithers, every girl who wears a bonnet is fair game," she said calmly. "Somehow it drives him mad. He even pinches my backside sometimes, and I'm no younger than the missus. Why do you think Tilly got away so fast?" Tilly had been the maid before Lizzie. "She was quite happy here before Mr. Smithers took over the house. The Cartlands were always hosting parties. Tilly made tips like you would not believe. She meant to save for three years before marrying that Tom of hers. But the new master would not give her a moment's rest."

"But, but, couldn't she . . . She was pardoned, right?" Lizzie stammered.

"Sweetie, that doesn't mean much. The man would have needed only to make a silver spoon disappear and blame her. That would have been it for her freedom. And it's no different for you. You . . . ."

"I could ask to go back to the factory," Lizzie said. Just then, Cascades seemed liked a heavenly refuge.

Martha shook her head. "What reason would you give? Do you mean to tell the truth? Then they'll both be at your throat, both mister and missus. Be careful, for heaven's sake. These things can end at the gallows. Best thing would be to keep a stiff upper lip and try to find a fellow to marry as soon as possible. Take the gardener. He's not handsome, but he's a good man. Although then they'll ask you to stay on and work, which means cheating on the fellow first thing."

"But where am I supposed to find someone else? How long will that take? Is there nothing else I can do?" Lizzie looked at the older woman desperately.

"You really could steal something," she said harshly. "Something small. I'll blame you. Say you took some salted meat—you could tell them you had a friend in a nearby chain gang and wanted to get it to him."

Lizzie rejected the idea. "I don't want to be convicted again. I won't survive it a second time. And backsliding would mean third rank—I'd rot in a jail."

The cook shrugged. "Then keep old Mr. Smithers happy."

Lizzie surrendered the next Sunday night. Sadly, in so doing she also profaned her refuge, her own room, in which she had been so happy. Mr. Smithers saw this as proof that she lay with him willingly and joyfully, but for Lizzie it was simply the best way to avoid discovery. If Mrs. Smithers found out, it would all be over. Her freedom of movement, her status as a first-class prisoner—all done. They would send her back to prison in shame and scandal. As soon as he left, Lizzie changed the sheets, washed herself with the water she had set out—which was even still warm—and cried herself to sleep.

She gave up hope that she would ever be allowed to be good. Once again, Lizzie Owens was merely fighting to survive.

Chapter 8

Ian Coltrane's new farm lay among lovely surroundings on the Avon River, which would flow through Christchurch once the city was developed. It offered a rather large but already somewhat dilapidated farmhouse and stables for keeping livestock. It comprised more acreage than all of Kathleen's village. The Coltranes suddenly had more property than their former landlord, Wetherby, though they lacked the fences and tenants.

Ian and Kathleen would never have been able to work all of their land themselves. Plus Ian quickly filled the stables with animals of every sort, and Kathleen was overwhelmed by the task of caring for the livestock. She came from the country, and she had a good understanding of planting a garden and working a field. In good years, her father had sometimes kept a goat, a few chickens, and a sheep or two. But here, whole herds of animals scattered across vast pastures, which Ian only provisionally fenced.

Ian never kept the animals long since he sold them through his livestock business. He often just let them wander and trusted that limits might be set by the presence of barley to eat and the shepherding efforts of the farm dog—though the dog's lack of skill and instinct indicated Ian had been the one cheated for a change. Unfortunately, the sheep proved limitlessly fond of wandering, and, oddly, they were especially attracted to the construction sites for what would become Christchurch.

Most of the social contact Kathleen had in her first months in the Canterbury Plains was through visits by outraged foremen or aggrieved boatmen who had to forge a path among the bodies of peacefully ruminating sheep. Then, despite her pregnancy, Kathleen would swing up on one of the mules or horses and try to herd the sheep back. Often a few men helped her with that—Kathleen's beauty and her desperate situation touched their hearts, and they were happy to try their hands at herding.

Naturally, they expected a cup of tea or, even better, a whiskey, by way of appreciation, but Kathleen only said her thank-yous to the men with a pounding heart, and then thanked heaven when they moved along. It did not bear thinking about what might happen if Ian caught her sitting around the table with one or more, often good-looking, strangers.

In general, the new settlers in the plains were not half-starved emigrants from Ireland or Scotland but Anglicans from good families looking for adventure. Many of the men were construction workers, specially hired in England, and they were mostly friendly and had good manners. None of them attempted to get too close to the isolated farmer's wife, although some of them likely dreamed of her at night.

Kathleen had no interest in them anyway—if she still found the strength to dream at night, Michael was the only one who appeared. But even his face was fading in her memory. Kathleen's life was a singular drudgery of tending to the garden, the fields, the stables, and, of course, the children, whom she had to watch constantly. Colin, especially, who could hardly be kept out of the stables as soon as he could walk, was always up to something. Sean was less interested in the animals. He only liked the farm dog, and Kathleen often found them together, sitting side by side on the wooden porch and staring at the river. Sometimes he whispered something in the dog's ear, and Kathleen wondered if Sean was telling the dog fairy tales. Could Sean remember Pere's stories about canoes and Maori demigods? Or was it his mother's stories from Ireland, of fairies and leprechauns, that he told the dog?

Besides the children and occasional complaint bringers from Christchurch, Kathleen's social contact was limited to Ian's customers, but Ian told her she was only to present herself to them silently and with a lowered head. She did that willingly after twice she let slip some information Ian didn't want revealed about animals for sale. Both times he beat her so brutally that she was afraid she would lose the baby. But even when she said nothing, Kathleen looked forward to these rare visits. After all, Ian would offer a glass or two of whiskey to seal the deal, and then he'd chat with his customers. This was the only way Kathleen heard any scraps of news from the outside world.

The onrush of settlers to Christchurch hardly abated. After the first four ships arrived, more and more people in the Old World became interested in the new country on the other side of the globe. Ian's customers always emphasized that, in contrast to Australia and Van Diemen's Land, New Zealand was not being settled by prisoners but by good Christians. They were proud of it, and Ian drank with them to that—although the Coltranes were Catholic and thus had considerably less respect for an English Protestant than for an Irish convict.

Ian did not allow Kathleen to drive to Christchurch for Sunday service in the Anglican church. She would have liked to do that—surely God would have seen past the false faith of her surroundings and heard her prayers anyway. But Ian would not budge.

Ian's customers reported about Port Cooper, and this interested Kathleen. She still missed Pere and her other friends in the little town, which, though it had also been called Port Victoria, had received yet another name. Now the town was to be called Lyttelton, after an important man in the Canterbury Association, and the tiny settlement was slowly growing into a city. The traffic through it to Christchurch brought money to Lyttelton.

John, the smith, had established a transport service for the new settlers, which the well-off immigrants liked to use. For a certain fee, one could be led over the Bridle Path on a mule. John did not buy his mules from Ian, however, which embittered Ian enough that he thought the better of cheating John's competition in Christchurch. Ian provided the man with beasts of burden that were healthy and strong. Yet he could not prevail. John simply had a better location in Lyttelton; he was immediately at hand when ships arrived.

Now Lyttelton had a tavern and a hotel, and recently, a pastor had settled there as a doctor. News of this filled Kathleen with envy: she was due in a few weeks, and this time there was no hope of Pere or another midwife—let alone a doctor—to help with the delivery. Theoretically, Ian could call somebody from Christchurch, but the Coltranes hardly knew anyone there, and Ian took no steps to make new acquaintances. And there was nothing to guarantee Ian would even be home when Kathleen gave birth. He promised not to ride away during the time in question, but if the baby was early, Kathleen would be alone. She simply tried not to think about it.

***

Kathleen checked the fences near the house, work she hated, and not just because her belly hampered her. After an hour, she was already bathed in sweat, although it was winter—a cool, dry, day in June, unusually sunny for the season. Anyone who had an eye for natural beauty could enjoy a distant view as far as the majestic southern mountains and even make out individual peaks. Kathleen only knew the name of the tallest: Mount Cook. In Port Cooper, Pere had told her everything about the local bay and the Port Hills that separated Lyttelton from Canterbury. Here in the plains, there was no one to teach her. For Kathleen, the mountains and plateaus had no names, and she did not bother to name the landmarks.

Little Sean excelled at this, however. He had begun to talk early. So he would dub a copse in the middle of which a natural clearing appeared the "Fairy Place," and a large rock standing in the middle of a meadow "Leprechaun."

The children were good company as she worked. Colin would attentively hand her a tool while Sean tried to teach the dog to shake hands.

"Good boy, give me good paw," he explained to the agreeable but completely useless mutt.

Recently, Ian had come to believe he needed to teach his sons manners. "It impresses the customers," he once said. "Especially the higher class. For the farmers, it mostly doesn't matter how you lot act. But the gentlemen like a 'yes, sir' and 'no, sir.' 'How good you look on the horse, sir.' 'Of course, this is no horse for a farmer, sir, it's got too much vim. But if anyone can tame it, it'd be a master rider like you, sir.' And at that, you'd bow and smile."

At thirteen months, Colin hadn't understood anything his father was saying, but he liked to laugh and imitate Ian bowing. Sean, however, had furrowed his brow. He was two years old and asked questions all the time.

"Some can tame a horse, some can't," Ian had said, more to himself than anyone. "The main thing is the customer believes he can. When it turns out he can't, well, at least he'll come back and admit it. And, boys, if the man comes right back with the horse, give him your good hand and bow."

"What's that, good hand?" Sean had inquired, though he risked a slap for being insolent. "Other hand good too."

Now the dog he was trying to teach seemed to be having similar trouble understanding the difference. When he raised a paw at all, it was the left one. But Sean was distracted anyway. Over the path that led from the farm to Christchurch, a donkey was trotting toward them, a conspicuous little animal with friendly, upright ears. It was properly bridled and bearing a rider who looked no less strange than her mount.

As they approached, Kathleen could see the woman was young, somewhere around her own age, so about twenty. She was thin and delicate. However, Kathleen immediately thought she recognized the first signs of a pregnancy. The waist of the elegant brown velvet riding dress seemed to be a little high, and the fabric strained a bit around the breasts. However, the woman sat very elegantly in her English sidesaddle—a relaxed, upright posture like the one Lady Wetherby in Ireland also had. On a donkey, one so small at that, both the large saddle and the prim appearance of the rider seemed more than out of place.

Kathleen couldn't help but laugh when she caught sight of her. The young woman returned the laugh at once. She had a lovely smile and a little nose set in an oval face framed by a few dark-brown corkscrew curls, which had come loose from under her hat. Her friendly brown eyes looked out from strong brows and thick eyelashes.

"Hello," the rider greeted her, bowing and graciously lowering her hand, which held a riding crop. Kathleen also recalled this gesture from the lady in her homeland. "How lovely to meet another person. And a woman at that. Even if you laugh at me first thing. I do admit I must look a little like Sancho Panza on his donkey."

"Like who?" Kathleen asked shyly.

The young woman ignored the question. Instead, she looked over Kathleen and the children inquisitively.

"Well, I see your two knights are still too little to help me from the saddle," she said regretfully before gliding nimbly down from the donkey without help. Smiling, she approached Kathleen.

"Allow me to introduce myself. I am Claire Edmunds, of Stratford Manor, farther upriver."

"Stratford Manor?" asked Kathleen, awed. That sounded grand. The houses of many wealthy Englishmen in Ireland also had fine-sounding names.

"Well, yes, after Stratford—Stratford-upon-Avon, you know. Shakespeare's hometown. Such foolishness, calling the river the Avon and then the city Christchurch. Bigoted folk, all of them would-be missionaries. Anyway, I named the farm. Sounds better than Edmunds' Farm, don't you think? My husband laughs at me for it, though. What do you call your farm?"

Kathleen shrugged. "Coltrane's Livestock Trade," she said. "I'm Kathleen Coltrane."

Claire Edmunds furrowed her brow. "Ah yes, your husband sold Spotty here to mine." She pointed to the donkey.

Kathleen now recalled having the animal in the stables for a short time.

"A nice animal," Claire continued. "But your husband ought not to have told mine that this little fellow could do all the farm work. He claimed he was worth two mules in front of a wagon or a plow."

Kathleen blushed. "My husband . . ."

"Is a horse trader. I understand; they all lie. One simply can't believe anything they say, and Spotty makes that plain. But Matthew has no notion of horses. And, of course, he doesn't listen to me."

"Spotty?" asked Sean, stroking the donkey's nose.

Claire nodded. "Indeed. And what is your name, young man?"

Sean held his hand out to her—the left, unfortunately, but he bowed. "Sean, Madam."

Claire Edmunds laughed and shook Sean's hand blithely. "What a sweet child. And so well raised. So, as I was saying, I'm not angry about all that with Spotty. *Au contraire.* Since he can't do farm work, I have him to myself."

"Your saddle's funny," said Sean.

"It's from England," Claire explained. "I brought it with me. I would have loved to bring my horse too, but we could not afford it." Her face became sad. "But what can you do? It's not important for happiness." The woman looked cheerful again. "In any case, I have my saddle and my riding dress—and Spotty. And I've finally found a woman who does not live so far away and with whom I can talk." She looked questioningly at a daunted Kathleen. "You will talk to me, won't you?"

Kathleen smiled and decided she could not afford to be shy. "Of course," she said. "You're the first woman I've seen in seven months, and I'm not supposed to talk to you? I'm just a little surprised."

Claire nodded, understanding. It did not seem to be any different for her. A mischievous smile flitted across her face. "Nothing wrong with that. But you ought to think of inviting me to tea now, as I'll need to go soon. When my husband comes home in the evening, he has to eat right away. I take that very seriously, the fastest way to the heart being through the stomach." Claire made this assertion sounding thoroughly convinced. "It's just I can't cook very well," she admitted.

Kathleen laughed and invited Claire into the house. The other woman took her little hat off, revealing a thick knot of dark hair, which she loosened, freeing her corkscrew curls. Kathleen wondered how she would look with such a hairstyle, and suddenly she was aware of her worn dress and her stringy hair.

Claire seemed to read her thoughts. "I don't have that many good dresses either," she confessed. "In truth, really just this one, since I haven't had it on since I left home. And it won't fit me much longer. Nor the others. Matthew says I should simply sew myself a new one, but I don't know how." Claire sighed. "Anyway, I dressed up today to go riding. And I even found someone." Her face brightened. "Matthew will be very happy for me. He's so considerate! Truly, you know . . ."

"So, where was your home, originally?" Kathleen inquired.

"Liverpool," Claire answered at once. "How about you? You're Irish, are you not? Matthew said something like that." She blushed.

Kathleen had to laugh again. "'Those damned Irish.'" She imitated in a deep voice what Matthew Edmunds was almost sure to have said: "'Thieves and cheats, the lot of them.'"

Claire giggled, at ease. "Quite close," she confirmed. "I just didn't want to say it and insult you. And I'm sure not all Irish are like that. Surely many are very . . . nice." She bit her lip and changed the subject. "Tell me, you wouldn't happen to be a midwife, would you? I, I'm having a baby, you see."

Kathleen swallowed. In her homeland, people were not nearly as prudish as in England, but even the Irish would not have broached the subject of childbirth after a mere half hour of acquaintance. Only Pere spoke so casually about having children.

Claire blushed again. "I'm sorry. Certainly that wasn't proper. But I really must go soon, and it weighs on my heart. Mrs. Coltrane, I . . . I have no idea how the baby will get out." She bit her lip.

Kathleen should have been moved by her embarrassment, but Claire amused her. They were the same age, but this girl seemed so innocent and naive. It was hardly imaginable that she was married and soon to have a baby.

"Well, out the same door it came in, generally speaking," Kathleen answered drily.

Claire looked at her, disbelieving. "You mean there, where my husband . . . but, but it's not big enough. It's hardly big enough for my husband." Her face was now completely red. She looked like a ten-year-old in Father O'Brien's classroom.

Kathleen smiled. "Claire! May I call you Claire?" She could hardly call this girl Mrs. Edmunds. "I hope it's all right if we call each other by our first names at this point. The entrance widens."

"You're sure?" Claire asked suspiciously. "I know I'm ignorant in these matters. My father's a doctor, but one simply does not talk about such things with her father. My mother would have an attack of asthma if I asked her something like that."

"I'm sure," Kathleen soothed her. "You don't need to worry about that. But someone gave you away in marriage. Did no one tell you anything about having children?"

Claire chewed on her lower lip. "Strictly speaking, no one gave me away," she said. "I gave myself away. Really, I was supposed to marry my cousin; he's going to be a doctor and take over Father's practice. But he's a boring oaf. Well, and then I got to know Matthew." An otherworldly radiance spread over Claire's face. "In the city, at market. Kathleen, he's so funny. He was always making me laugh. And he tells such lovely stories. About all his travels—imagine, he's been to America! And to Hawaii. And Australia. But New Zealand was best, he said back then. A little like England, but everything new, no bigwigs, no limitations—Matthew wanted to buy land and settle. With me! Oh, Kathleen, it was so romantic when he asked me. And the way he described everything. The river here, the Avon—don't you think it's a sign? I'm Juliet; Matthew is Romeo. But my parents would never have accepted it. So I simply did it."

Claire got up and assumed a histrionic posture. "O Romeo, Romeo! Wherefore art thou Romeo? Deny thy father and refuse thy name, or, if thou wilt not, be but sworn my love, and I'll no longer be a Capulet."

She beamed.

Kathleen frowned. Was her new friend crazy?

Claire looked just as taken aback. "Don't you know it?" she asked, disbelieving. "Shakespeare. *Romeo and Juliet*. It's a very famous story. Don't you have any romance over there in Ireland?"

Kathleen did not reveal her romance with Michael or their time in the fields by the river. Nevertheless, she learned every detail of Claire's flight from her parents' house, her precipitous wedding in London, and her voyage to New Zealand.

"I wrote my parents again, but they did not want to see me. I don't miss them, particularly, either. Only I do miss my horse, although now I have Spotty. And I have my Matt, too, of course. He is wonderful, truly. Only, well, at first it was exciting here in the new country on the farm, but now . . . I'm all alone, Kathleen." Claire vacillated between euphoria and disappointment.

"Matthew bought himself a boat. He fishes in the river and ferries people who want to get from Lyttelton to Christchurch. He says we could get rich if only I would manage the house better. He is, well, he surely loves me very much, but he, I think he's not very happy with me." Claire sounded like a child who has received a bad mark at school. "And yet, I try hard. I just don't how to do all of it. Have you ever milked a cow? Before you came here, I mean."

Claire's outburst did not really call for an answer, which probably was for the best. A report of Kathleen's experiences husbanding sheep and cows would probably have awed the young woman into silence. As it was, Claire kept talking, and an astonished Kathleen learned that no one had ever particularly bothered her new friend with practical matters. Her parents possessed a large house. There were servants who did everything for them. Her mother had not taught Claire and her sisters even a modicum of housekeeping. Instead, they could do what they liked—as long as they behaved within the bounds of proper breeding. Claire liked to ride. Besides that, she liked to read and study. She knew French, Latin, and Italian. She played the piano and the violin. She had read books about astronomy and had always wanted to discover a new star.

"It was always so wonderful with Matthew," Claire said enthusiastically. "We would look into the sky together, and he would name the stars. And tell me about the Southern Hemisphere, about the Southern Cross." She smiled, lost in thought at the memory, but then she suddenly looked sad. "Now I discover stars every day," she said soberly, "though not with Matthew. He, he hasn't the time. Yet I'm sure he knows their names. I could look them up, of course, but I can't find a book with them in it. I can't find any books anymore, Kathleen! Otherwise I could read about childbirth. Where, where did you learn everything about babies? Did someone tell you before you were married?"

Kathleen sighed. "I learned it too early, alas. When is yours expected, anyway?"

"There's still time," Claire said, leaving unsaid whether she knew how long a pregnancy normally lasted. "But yours is coming soon, right? Do you have someone who'll help you?"

Kathleen shook her head, and Claire seemed to sense that her more experienced friend was not much less afraid of giving birth than she was.

"You know what? When the time arrives, I'll come here and stay with you," Claire said—and it sounded comforting, although Claire clearly did not know whether she was trying to calm Kathleen or herself. "True, I can't do anything much, but I'll see it. Then at least I'll know what's waiting for me. And in any case, it's better than being all alone."

Chapter 9

"You must think that I don't know what's going on between you and my husband."

Mrs. Smithers made this devastating revelation quite casually as she laid freshly cut long-stem roses in Lizzie's basket. Table decorations. Mr. Smithers was expected that evening, along with a business friend. Lizzie felt all the blood drain from her head, and she almost dropped the basket, but then there was only resignation and exhaustion. Fine, it was out. She had lost. But at least she would no longer need to worry.

Lizzie tried to breathe deeply and compose her thoughts. She gazed at the overgrown garden, modeled, only somewhat successfully, on an English park. The roses grew well; the grass grew too lushly, though—it was not velvety smooth but hard like reed. Acacia had overtaken a large part of the garden instead of forming a neat hedge, and eucalyptus trees overshadowed the mani-cured English fruit trees.

It was a cool but rainless summer day in Van Diemen's Land. Lizzie had been trying for almost six months now to keep the secret of her relationship with Mr. Smithers. It was not easy because Mr. Smithers often lacked caution and tact. When he saw Lizzie in her blue dress, white lace apron, and bonnet doing any kind of work, he lost control of himself. He would want to take her on the nearest divan or even on the carpet, and he reacted poorly when she refused. She had nothing for which to blame herself. She did not provoke him and only lay motionless in her chamber until he had satisfied himself. In England, her customers would have complained, but Mr. Smithers did not seem to care as long as she wore her bonnet and apron. Just as Martha had suggested, the uniform aroused him more than the girl who wore it.

And now, after all her efforts not to let the matter come to light . . .

"Madam, I . . ." Lizzie began to stammer, but words failed her.

"Don't lie to me," said Mrs. Smithers sternly. She glared at Lizzie from beneath the brim of her straw sun hat. Apparently, she had counted on denial. "If anything is going to save you, it's only absolute honesty."

Save her? Lizzie felt as if the ground beneath her was swaying—much more so than back on the ship.

"I . . ."

Mrs. Smithers didn't give her a chance to explain herself. "Do you expect something from it?" she asked curtly. "Do you have hopes of some kind?"

Hopes? This had destroyed them. Lizzie almost could have laughed. Perhaps this was just a bad dream.

She shook her head helplessly.

"Are you expecting some benefit? Early pardon? Hush money?"

Lizzie shook her head more strongly.

Mrs. Smithers furrowed her brow. "Do you love him, perhaps?"

"No!" Lizzie yelled, her voice finally firm.

"Then why do it?" Unlike all the others, this question sounded like it was asked out of honest interest. Mrs. Smithers seemed startled at this—and then gave an answer before Lizzie could. "Well, you girls can't control yourself. That's why you're here, after all—I was warned, you know."

Lizzie lowered her head. She should have been angry, but she just did not want to hear any more. She wanted Mrs. Smithers to hand down her sentence so she could finally be done with this.

"You're aware that I could send you back to Cascades?"

Lizzie nodded abjectly.

"But on the other hand"—Mrs. Smithers looked at Lizzie with an odd expression of pity—"the next one wouldn't likely be any better. And at least you're not pretty."

Lizzie wanted to yell at Mrs. Smithers and tell her that she could probably get her husband back to her bed if she would only wear a bonnet and apron. She held her tongue, of course—and she felt a certain strange curiosity. What did Mrs. Smithers have up her sleeve?

"You're useful otherwise, so you can stay. I've thought of something else: You'll be married. You can have Cecil, the gardener. He'll be delighted, I'm sure, and you can move into the old coach house. But whether that will satisfy your lust . . ." Mrs. Smithers reddened.

Lizzie felt panic well up within her. If she lived in the coach house, she would be fair game for both men. And she would be deceiving Mrs. Smithers and her own husband. At some point she would be caught again. Lizzie saw no way out.

"But, madam, your husband—"

"Not a word against my husband," Mrs. Smithers thundered. "It's decided. I'll talk with Cecil, and he'll make his proposal." She tore the basket of roses out of Lizzie's arms and strode with dignity into the house.

Lizzie remained helplessly behind. Now explaining was the only solution. She had to talk the matter over with Cecil. The gardener was a prisoner himself. He had to understand.

That night Lizzie remained unmolested—Mr. Smithers was getting drunk with his guest. The man was a soldier who coordinated the employment of prisoners in the region, and he wanted to do his host a favor by sending a chain gang to clear the acacias from the garden.

Lizzie eavesdropped on the conversation while she was serving, and Mrs. Smithers inquired about dangers the men might present.

Sergeant Meyers, a short, stocky man with the face of a bulldog, comforted her with a laugh. "The bears are all chained up, madam—for months, at that. They've given up on foolishness. Over time they all become peaceful here. We raise them into good Christians, each and every one of them." He raised his glass to Mr. Smithers.

Lizzie turned away in disgust. She spent the night brooding desperately. How should she begin her conversation with Cecil, and what solution should she propose? In the end, it would depend on him anyway. Perhaps he wouldn't even care about sharing her with Mr. Smithers. Then she would be lost. But with a little luck, he would refuse to take her for his wife under those circumstances. In that case, she would need to find a new betrothed as soon as possible—best would be someone influential enough that she would no longer have to work in the Smitherses' house. Lizzie would never have imagined it possible, but she began to long for Jeremiah.

The next morning, Cecil the gardener was busy directing the men of the chain gang. Sergeant Meyers had not exaggerated. At sunrise, an overseer drove the twelve chained men to work. Lizzie watched from the house, waiting for Cecil to be done so she could talk to him. Before she even had a chance to try, Mrs. Smithers had him called up to the house.

"What does she want now? New plants to show off?" grumbled the cook.

Mrs. Smithers was a passionate gardener, but she did not understand that most plants from her homeland did not thrive on their own. And she took no interest in native plants, which she thought of as weeds.

"Well, it has to do with husbandry," said Lizzie, sighing. She busied herself with the dusting just across the hall from Mrs. Smithers's receiving rooms so she'd know when Cecil left.

He seemed beside himself with joy when Mrs. Smithers finally dismissed him. Lizzie heard him thank her what seemed like a thousand times. Her own courage sank. This conversation would not be easy. Perhaps it would be better to wait until Cecil had calmed down a bit. No, it had to be now. Lizzie put her feather duster aside and walked determinedly to the garden.

She was not prepared for his greeting.

"Lizzie!" The short gardener beamed across his entire gnomish face when he saw her. He ran up to her, twirled her through the air, and kissed her unrestrainedly on the mouth.

"I knew you would want it too. You were just shy, says the missus, and that's fine by me. But now we ought to show our love."

Lizzie's heart all but broke at having to destroy his joy. Though she was anything but in love with the gnome, she valued him as a kind person and a friend.

"It's not that simple," she began, drawing him out of view of the house and into the shadow of a eucalyptus tree. "Cecil, I, the mistress . . ."

As she spoke, first the joy and then the color drained from the gardener's weathered face.

"So you don't really want to marry me?"

Lizzie sighed. "Cecil, what I want has nothing to do with it. I'd be happy to marry you, but I'd remain Mr. Smithers's property."

The smile returned to Cecil's face. "But not forever," he said. "We'll save a bit, and then move elsewhere. And the Cartlands will come back sometime too, you know. Then we'll work for them."

"But not for half a year," said Lizzie. "At the earliest. Until then . . ."

"Oh, I can stand it until then," Cecil declared generously.

But I can't! Lizzie wanted to scream. Most of all, she did not want to marry an idiot who did not even recognize the risk of sacrificing her to every horny goat without a fight. Or did Cecil expect some advantage from the arrangement? Would he allow Mr. Smithers's continued adultery with his own wife for more money and a better position?

"The offer stands until tomorrow," Cecil said, beaming with joy. "The missus'll handle things with the reverend. And you'll have your pardon!" Cecil had received a pardon himself four weeks before, and with her marriage, Lizzie would be free too. But she had rarely felt so confined.

Cecil returned to his flowers. Pensively, Lizzie looked over at the chain gang. Martha had charged her with bringing water to the men. She might as well do it now.

Lizzie filled a pitcher at the well. The men were supposed to have their own cups. She made her way to the acacia jungle in the rear section of the garden, keeping her head lowered as propriety demanded.

***

"That's enough water. Don't you recognize me at all, Lizzie?"

Lizzie was just pouring water for the first man in the row, after politely greeting the overseer, when a tall, dark-haired convict spoke to her excitedly.

"Lizzie Owens, my little angel on the ship?"

Lizzie looked up, disbelieving, but she recognized the soft, deep voice with the Irish accent from his first words. Michael Drury's shining blue eyes flared almost rakishly at her.

"And once again, you don't leave anything out," he teased. "What a greeting that just was. Since when do you favor leprechauns?"

"Excuse me?" Lizzie asked, confused.

She was already upset, but Michael's sudden appearance completely rattled her.

"Leprechauns, gnomes, dwarves—that's what we call fellows like your short friend there, in Ireland."

Michael gestured deprecatingly at Cecil, who was just then toiling to prepare the hard soil for new seeds from England.

Lizzie pulled herself together. If she were to show weakness now, if she were to reveal the feelings that welled up anew at the sight of Michael, she would never again be able to approach him unselfconsciously.

"A short man, but a free one," she mocked. "You, on the other hand, Michael Drury: a year in Van Diemen's Land and still in chains? Yet all you did was steal a few sacks of grain. Or was that a lie?"

Michael shrugged. "Perhaps something of an understatement, like yours about the bread." He winked at her. "Maybe I sold a little whiskey too. How about you?" He smiled.

Lizzie smiled back, pained. "To be in chains here, you must have done more than that."

She struggled to remain calm and, above all, to keep her expression under control. The overseer did not need to know that the two of them were old acquaintances. Slowly she went from one man to the next, pouring them water while she continued to banter with Michael.

"Three escape attempts," Michael admitted. "The first on the very first day. I thought it was a good idea to sneak back on the *Asia*, since I already knew its darkest corner. Direct passage back to Ireland." He laughed.

Actually, not such a bad idea. "What went wrong?"

"I should have waited for them to clean and unload that tub," Michael said resignedly. "So, they caught me straight away. And then . . ."

Lizzie had finished pouring water. Everyone had drunk, and the overseer was watching her, likely wondering why she was still hanging around the prisoners. She had to return to the house.

"Michael, I have to go," she whispered. "But tomorrow is Sunday. I'm free in the afternoon. Where can I find you?"

Michael arched his eyebrows. "You mean, where can you find *us*? We stick together, as you can see. Outside a cell, you'll only find a chain of us. But Sunday afternoons we are allowed a little fresh air. Somewhere between the twenty-fourth and twenty-fifth devotional."

The other men laughed.

"Simply walk down the new road. Our barracks are on the river. The old ones from the bridge construction workers. They're accordingly bug ridden."

The overseer raised his whip meaningfully and looked at Lizzie. "Break's over, men."

Lizzie waved and raised her pitcher toward the overseer. "I'll come," she whispered to Michael.

***

The next morning, she was to see yet another old acquaintance.

As on every Sunday, she followed the Smitherses to church, although this time she was on the arm of the beaming Cecil. Mr. Smithers looked sheepish. His wife had probably not left him in the dark about why she cared so much about Cecil and Lizzie's marriage. Lizzie walked with an unhappy face. She could not even muster a smile at the reverend's congratulations. The cook patted her shoulder comfortingly.

Suddenly, Sergeant Meyers and his wife demanded all her attention. The soldier greeted the Smitherses from the church entrance. His wife stood, tall and elegant, next to him. She wore a simple brown dress adorned with a lace collar and lace gloves over her delicate hands. A lovely little hat with a cream-colored band sat atop her hair, which she had tied at the nape of her neck into a supple bun. She had black hair, eyes like dark diamonds, and a delicate complexion.

Lizzie stared in astonishment at Velvet, the watch thief from London. Velvet politely offered Mr. Smithers her hand, saying a few obliging words. Only with a wink did she reveal to Lizzie that she, too, recognized her old cellmate. Then she followed her husband, whom she towered over by half a head, into the church.

Lizzie could not concentrate on the service. So that was why Velvet had consented to be married. Sergeant Meyers held an elevated post; no doubt he was well paid and could count on a good pension and several acres of land when his military career was over. Lizzie had not known that even such well-off men sought their wives among the convicts, but Velvet was a beauty. Sergeant Meyers was ugly; in England, he might have found a more virtuous wife, but certainly not one nearly as attractive.

After the service, Velvet and her husband took a ride with the Smitherses. The women had not seen the progress of the road construction in a long time, and Mrs. Smithers wanted to know what her husband did during the week. Velvet climbed gracefully into the chaise, waving surreptitiously to Lizzie.

Lizzie merely intimated a wave. Neither of them would gain anything from publicizing their acquaintance.

Lizzie needed to escape Cecil's company if she was going to see Michael that day. Unfortunately, the little gardener stuck to her like a barnacle, laying out his tragic life story to her while leading her on a long walk.

Born the youngest of fifteen children on a farm in Wales, he had fled poverty and hunger and gone to Cardiff. He made a few trips as a sailor but was not very good at it, then made another attempt at farming. Finally, he stole a sheep and was promptly apprehended. That brought him to the colonies.

"And next time, you'll tell me your story," he said. Then, to Lizzie's great surprise, he said, "Now I'm going to meet with a couple fellows." Cecil furtively withdrew a pint of whiskey from his pocket. "The master gave this to me to celebrate the engagement."

Lizzie shook with rage. Could he not share the booze with her? Good Lord, she could use a couple swigs after the last few days. And worse yet, it had already begun: Mr. Smithers was giving Cecil whiskey, which he accepted gratefully. The two were getting to be well acquainted. What was a wife between friends?

Lizzie walked down the new road, which was not all that new. Convicts had built the red bridge over the river almost twenty years earlier. Now they mostly did expansion and repair work. On the Elizabeth River, near the bridge, lay the barracks.

The men in Michael's gang were enjoying themselves by the river. Two of them had built a makeshift rod with which they tried to fish, but it looked like they were new at it. A few of the others tried to explain what they were doing wrong, but they went ignored.

Michael gave Lizzie a warm smile as she walked down to them and sat next to him on the riverbank. The river was lovely and peaceful. Plants that Lizzie would have called water lilies floated on it. Probably, though, they were something completely different—nothing in Van Diemen's Land was quite what Lizzie expected.

"You're late. Did your leprechaun keep you so long?" he teased.

"My betrothed took me on a walk," Lizzie said with dignity.

The chain gang laughed, and the men yelled bawdy jokes at her. Each of them offered to marry her, promising greater pleasure than she could enjoy in Cecil's arms.

Lizzie frowned and cut them short. "Boys, as it is, you couldn't have me alone anyway. Now, out with it, Michael Drury. What did you do that they still have you in chains?" She glanced at his wrists, which were red and raw where the chains rubbed. "Heavens, you're hurt again. You're lucky it doesn't get hot here; otherwise you'd have flies bringing you another fever."

Michael shrugged. "I'm smarter now, you see. But it takes time to learn. It was stupid to run away unprepared. But I had hoped there would be bigger cities here where a fellow could disappear."

"Even prepared, it's just as hopeless," said one of the convicts. He was not shackled, and he also seemed to know how to fish, having apparently caught three that now lay next to him on the beach. "The cities are glorified villages, and the whole thing's an island, in case you lot haven't noticed. You can't get out."

"I wouldn't say that," one of the other men declared. Lizzie recognized the sailor who had come over on the *Asia* in the berth next to Michael's. "We have a plan, anyway. As soon as they let us out of these chains, we're off."

Michael nodded and threw a rock into the water.

"You still want to escape?" Lizzie asked, stunned. "If you're caught again, you'll spend your whole sentence in chains. Accept it, Michael. Without a ship, captain, and crew, you won't reach Ireland."

"Ireland, no," said Michael, sticking a blade of grass in his mouth. "But . . ."

"Now, don't reveal the plan," warned the sailor. "The moll is after a pardon. You hear it, don't you? She'll betray us."

"You're doing a good enough job of that yourselves," Lizzie said angrily. "Who's behind this brilliant plan, anyway? The twelve of you?"

Unsurprisingly, two other Irish were there, and Lizzie thought there might be something to the talk of their incorrigibility. Dylan was a squarely built, red-haired young man who one could tell was Irish at first glance. His upper body was muscular. Will looked just as strong, and he was taller. He was a giant of a man with blond locks, a sloping forehead, and the small, vicious eyes of a pit bull.

"The three of us, and Connor here as navigator," Michael said proudly. "Connor's sailed at sea. He'd find it blind."

"What is *it*? What would he find blind?" Lizzie stared at him.

Dylan lamented about betraying the "secret." Lizzie shook her head about the supposed secret, shared with twelve others—and probably half the other residents of the barracks. Not that it was a problem. No one would betray the men. Fleeing Van Diemen's Land was so hopeless that those in charge did not bother to advertise rewards for betraying others' escape plans.

"New Zealand," announced the former sailor. "It's right nearby; the trip'd be easy as you please."

"That's why half the convicts've already gone there," the fisherman mocked them.

"When you know what you're doing . . ." the sailor retorted.

"What is New Zealand anyway?" Lizzie asked. "Another colony?"

An hour later, her head was swimming with contradictory information. Will and Dylan depicted New Zealand as a promised land; Michael had heard it was supposed to resemble Ireland; and Connor, whom they most believed, told fantastic stories of whale and seal hunting. The West Coast was mentioned again and again. Once more, Lizzie longed for Jeremiah. His reports had mostly been reliable.

***

Lizzie tried to learn some things on her own. There was a globe in the Smitherses' study, and she looked around Australia for islands, but besides Van Diemen's Land, she only found New Guinea and few smaller islands on the other side of the country. Sailing there seemed like madness to Lizzie. You would have to sail along the entire Australian coast.

But then she discovered two islands on the other side of the Tasman Sea: a long one and a smaller one shaped similarly to Van Diemen's Land. New Zealand. So it did exist, and its western coast lay toward Van Diemen's Land. But getting there meant crossing an ocean. Lizzie tried to estimate the distance, and she became dizzy.

"What are you doing there, kitten?" Lizzie winced when she heard Mr. Smithers's voice. "Dusting the globe? Yet you don't even have your bonnet on."

Lizzie sighed. "I'm off this evening, sir," she whispered. "But if you want, I, I can go put it on for you. Just don't tell . . ."

"Don't tell what? That you were a little curious how the earth looks? Of course not, sweet, why would I? With your wedding imminent, you are surely dreaming of returning to England with Cecil. But look how far you have to sail, kitten. England is fifteen thousand miles away."

He kissed the nape of her neck.

"And New Zealand?" Lizzie asked hoarsely.

Mr. Smithers laughed. "You can't quite swim there either. But it's only two thousand four hundred miles. There's even a ship from Hobart. But I'm warning you, kitten, the sea is stormy. And what would you and Cecil do there? Hunt whales? Seals? Cecil wouldn't hurt a fly. And there are no jobs for house kittens like you either. Unless they're as bawdy as you." He embraced her and let his hands wander over her breasts. "You'd find plenty of customers on the West Coast."

"Have you been there before, sir?" Lizzie asked, fighting back her disgust.

"No, but it might be that we'll move there when the work here is done," Mr. Smithers said, seeming rather disinterested. "They're building a new city on the East Coast. There'll be work for me there. David Parsley is looking into it soon." David Parsley was Mr. Smithers's assistant, a young engineer whom he regarded highly. "If you're a good little kitty, we'll take you and Cecil with us."

Martin Smithers covered Lizzie's neck with more wet kisses.

Traveling with him and Cecil to New Zealand was really the last thing Lizzie envisioned. Even if a new city sounded rather enticing, whenever something new came into being, everything went topsy-turvy. But there did not seem to be convicts in New Zealand, so surely there would be no soldiers there to look for escapees.

***

"So, what exactly is your plan for New Zealand?" Lizzie asked Michael when she saw him the following Sunday. The chain gang was still working nearby. Lizzie had feigned a headache to get away from Cecil and seek out the men once more. "There's no sea anywhere near here."

"We're not free yet either," said Dylan. "It'll still be a few months until they take off our chains, and then we'll be in Launceston."

"Then we'll be in Hobart," Michael corrected him optimistically. "We'll break out, steal a ship . . ."

"What kind of ship?" asked Lizzie.

"A sailboat. It's a little too far to row, right, Connor?"

Connor nodded. "What I have in mind," he mused weightily, "is a sleek, little sailboat."

"We'll make it," Will added, sounding less convinced.

So, a glorified raft. Lizzie thought with horror about the wide sea and the storms Mr. Smithers had mentioned.

"Have any of you ever sailed before? I mean, aside from Connor?" she asked the men.

Michael, Dylan, and Will shook their heads.

"But you pick it up quick," Connor insisted.

Lizzie could not help herself: she began to doubt even Connor's experience on oceangoing ships. Probably, he had only sailed to sea as a cabin boy. He could not be much older than eighteen or nineteen. In her opinion, their plan was bound to fail. The escapees could count themselves lucky if they were caught in Hobart Harbor. They might otherwise pay for their nonsense with death at sea.

In any case, Lizzie did not want Michael exposed to the hazard. Let alone herself. And then there was the fact that she could not wait for some blind agent of the Crown to commit the foolishness of removing Dylan's and Will's chains. Lizzie would have left those two in the chain gang until they were old and gray. It would have to be different.

That evening, she tried to picture herself in better places while she stoically lay under Martin Smithers's sweaty, thrusting body.

Lizzie developed a plan.

Chapter 10

After Claire Edmunds's visit, Kathleen's silent brooding, resignation, and surrender to loneliness gave way to a liveliness she had not felt of late. Was it possible she had found a friend? Was it possible they would visit each other regularly, be present for each other's births, and talk easily with each other as she had with her neighbors back in Ireland and during her first months in Port Cooper?

Kathleen was going to wash the teacups Claire and she had drunk from, but she wanted the proof that Claire had been there. She had not imagined Claire, and she was not on her way to going mad. Kathleen tucked Claire's teacup in a cabinet as a keepsake. The next day she would return the visit. If Claire's house was also along the Avon, there had to be a faster way to get there than taking the road to Christchurch.

The next day she tended to only her most necessary duties before setting her boys on the calmest and surest mule Ian had in the stables and climbing up behind the two of them. They got on their way quickly, but it soon became difficult to make her way through the reedy, tall grass and the low-hanging branches of the trees on the banks. Kathleen dismounted and led the mule, but she was not discouraged. If she went along the banks a few times, a path would form on its own. The banks were overgrown but passable.

And indeed, Kathleen's effort paid off. It took her an hour—so only about three miles lay between the Coltranes' farm and Stratford Manor. The Edmunds' estate didn't awe her as much as she had imagined it would. Despite its lovely-sounding name, it was no manor, just a meager cottage hammered together out of boards, quite similar to her own but in worse shape.

Kathleen remembered Ian cursing in frustration when they had taken ownership of the farm. He had spent the first few weeks on repairs alone, until he had fixed the house and stables well enough that the wind would no longer blow through the cracks in the wall and the roof kept out the rain.

Claire's husband took his boat toward Christchurch every day to ferry people and their households up the Avon from the sea to their new town. From his farm, this was laborious and time consuming. So far, at least, he had not had the time or the money to weatherproof or even repaint the house. The old paint, a matte yellow, had long since begun peeling off, which made the house look even more dilapidated. And the fences to the paddocks—in which the donkey, Spotty; a fat cow and its newborn calf; and a few sheep meandered—did not look very sturdy. Though plenty of grass was growing there now, once that was eaten, the animals would wander elsewhere for sustenance, and Claire would have to go off looking for them just as Kathleen did with their livestock.

Kathleen took her children off the mule, tying it as securely as possible to the most trustworthy-looking fencepost, and they crossed a ramshackle porch to the front door. When she knocked, Claire opened the door lightning fast—clearly she was just as eager for company as Kathleen herself. Today, however, she had not dressed finely. Her dark hair was carelessly put up, and she wore an old housedress that stretched over her stomach just like the riding dress. Why didn't she just let the clothes out a bit?

Claire's whole face beamed when she saw Kathleen and the children. She immediately wrapped her arms around her new friend.

"How lovely you've come," she said. "Come in; I'm brewing tea. You can also have some of the stew I'm making, but I'm afraid it's not very good."

Kathleen refrained from trying the sweet potatoes, which were indeed completely overcooked.

"It's best to peel them first," she said when she looked in the pot.

"But the skin falls off by itself if you cook them long enough, and then . . ."

"But then they're mushy, and you get dirt in your cooking water—or do you clean the skin thoroughly beforehand? If you want to make a stew, you need to peel them and cut them into little chunks. And I'd add something more than the sweet potatoes and that piece of meat. What is that anyway?

In any case, you can't cook it long enough for the fiber to come off the bone. I'd cut the meat off now. Do you have any onions or proper potatoes? It looks like there's a garden around the side of the house."

Claire was astonished. She had not planted the garden herself; that must have been the wife of the farm's previous owner. And she had no idea anything edible grew there. Her efforts were limited to planting a few young rata bushes.

"They're quite lovely, don't you think?" she said excitedly, pointing at the red blossoms.

Kathleen nodded. "Yes, but you can't eat them." For the tenants in Ireland, the yield of their small gardens was necessary for survival. No one would have planted trees for the sake of decoration. "Here, look: potatoes and carrots. And herbs. You can use all of these."

Claire reacted joyfully to every dug-up tuber as if it were an uncovered treasure.

Back in the kitchen, Kathleen set to work to save the stew. Together she and Claire chopped up the sweet potatoes and other vegetables from the completely overgrown garden. Claire handled the knife so clumsily that Kathleen feared she might cut herself. Kathleen put all of the vegetables in the pot along with the meat she had removed from the bones.

"Didn't you have a garden at home?" Kathleen asked once the pot was back on the fire.

"Sure," Claire said, "and a gardener too. The most my mother did was tend to the roses. And we girls made garlands."

Claire had worked hard to beautify her cottage. The rata bush blossoms, as well as shining green pohutukawa and yellow blooming kowhai branches, stood in handsome porcelain vases on the floor. Decorations aside, the furnishings were humble. The Edmundses possessed even less, and considerably more decrepit, furniture than Kathleen and Ian. Their three-legged table was, however, covered with a beautiful linen tablecloth, and Claire now set filigreed porcelain dishes upon it. Fascinated, Sean fingered one of the paper-thin teacups; Kathleen took it warily out of his hand before he broke it.

"Oh, that wouldn't be the worst thing. A few already broke on the way over," Claire said, at ease. "I have sets for twelve people. That many people don't even live in this whole county."

Kathleen had to laugh. The house and its contents were just as much at odds as her new friend who could not cook a simple stew but served tea with skilled hands and elegant motions. It all reminded Kathleen of Lady Wetherby, who had taught her maids herself how to prepare and serve this most English of drinks. Was that all English girls learned of housekeeping?

Claire freely admitted this when Kathleen dared to ask it aloud. "Yes," she said. "Rather. Though, of course, I do also know how to set the table for meals with several courses and the like. And how one suitably places the guests—for example, when one has a bishop and a general as guests at the same time. But that isn't much use here. Just as little as the tableware." She looked regretfully at her treasure of Chinese porcelain.

"Why did you bring it then?" Kathleen asked. No one could think so impractically, and Claire did show a settler's spirit.

Claire frowned. "My mother sent it to me. I told you that I wrote to my family in London after the wedding. My father wanted nothing more to do with me, but my mother sent me a trousseau. It would break her heart if I went abroad so completely without means, she wrote."

"But there would have been other things she could have sent," said Kathleen, thinking of pots, fabric—or simply money.

Claire smiled understandingly at her new friend. "I thought so too. My violin, for instance. Or a few books, notes, a dictionary. I have no idea how I'm supposed to raise my child. How am I supposed to teach him anything when we don't even have a dictionary?"

Kathleen sighed. Claire's situation was obviously worse than she had feared. Claire was highly educated and cultured, but she possessed none of the skills that were natural for Kathleen and necessary for survival in this country. She could not sew, nor had she practiced using a broom or scouring brush.

"When our maid back home cleaned the floors, they got clean," the young woman explained helplessly. "When I do it, everything is just wet."

Nevertheless, Claire had not let her failings discourage her. She was diligent and tried everything, having had the most success with stable work. Her charm and her friendly manner also worked on the animals. So she was able to add fresh milk to the tea. Claire reported, not without humor, that she had dubbed the cow Minerva and reached a sort of "lady's agreement" with her. If she fed the animal and sang to it, it would hold still for milking.

"And then last night she had a calf," Claire reported enthusiastically of her latest adventure. "It came out her rear." She blushed. "You were right that, hm, it stretches. Is it like that for us too?" She felt her belly.

Kathleen nodded.

"We had to pull, though, Matt and I. It was difficult. And are human children also so, so slippery?" Claire kept chattering on pleasantly. "Well, anyway, there the calf is, and its mother ought not to be called Minerva, since she was a virgin."

"The cow was still a heifer?" Kathleen interrupted her, confused. "I thought Ian sold her to you pregnant. She was giving milk, after all."

Claire's eyes grew wide. "You knew she was pregnant?"

Over the next hour, Claire learned that cows only gave milk when they were pregnant or had delivered a calf. And, transfixed, little Sean listened to the story of the goddess Minerva who sprang from her father's head and never took a spouse.

"Although she really missed out there," Claire said, sounding very convinced.

Kathleen would not have signed onto that statement without reservations. She had long since begun to question her marriage to Ian. Would she someday trust Claire Edmunds enough to talk about it?

On this day, too, Kathleen was reluctant to part from her strange but exceedingly engaging new friend. But she expected Ian back from a trip that night, and she did not want him to find the house empty. Claire generously gave her half of the vegetables they had dug up from the garden. Kathleen's garden had yet to yield any produce.

"Then you can cook your husband stew too," Claire said. "Matt will certainly be astonished when he returns later." The aroma of the finished stew wafted from her kitchen. "And next time, you can bring me yeast, or whatever one calls it."

Claire's efforts at bread baking had so far limited themselves to the mixing of roughly ground grain with water. The result was inedible, hard-as-bone unleavened bread. Kathleen had told her about the existence of leavening that afternoon.

***

Kathleen was happy for Claire's friendship, but Ian Coltrane did not prove as enthusiastic about his wife's new acquaintance. Kathleen would not have told him anything about Claire at first. Since Ian so readily misconstrued her remarks as attacks and harmless stories as confessions of infidelity, she had become exceedingly careful, only telling her husband what was necessary.

But Sean blurted out the news as soon as Ian came home. He mocked—as well as he could at his age—Mrs. Edmunds's strange saddle.

"'potty, 'potty," Colin squealed, laughing.

"Are they talking about that upper-crust bitch and her donkey?" Ian asked.

Kathleen explained the children's comments and told him where Claire's residence was.

"With the sailor husband trying his hand as a ferryman?" asked Ian. "He's not getting anywhere. And that woman—I have to warn you, Kathleen, the respectable women in Christchurch won't talk to her."

So that was why Claire had feared Kathleen might rebuff her.

"Why not?" Kathleen inquired. "Granted, she's a bit strange. But quite friendly and open."

"She's stuck-up, is what she is," Ian said. "And forward. The woman at the dry goods store in Christchurch says she asked such inappropriate questions that she blushed like a schoolgirl. And what's more, she's slovenly. Even her husband says so. All the women feel sorry for him, the way he runs around. She can't patch his clothes, can't cook. And their house—I've seen it myself, Kathie. A real shame. I don't think it's right for you to associate with her."

Kathleen shrugged her shoulders. "Well, the fine ladies of Christchurch won't know about it anyway. Although I find it interesting how much of their gossip you hear. But no matter what the whole world says about Claire Edmunds, I'm having a baby soon. And the only woman within ten miles is Mrs. Edmunds. She's promised to stay with me and—"

"Her?" Ian laughed. "She still believes storks bring babies. I'm warning you, Kathleen."

Kathleen lowered her head. But then she continued anyway. She and Claire had not shared any secrets, but contact with the lively girl had given her strength.

"That's because no one will answer her inappropriate questions," Kathleen said curtly. "And besides, Claire Edmunds is pregnant. Someone has to help her when the baby is born, and that will be me. It's my Christian duty, Ian. Whether you like it or not."

To Kathleen's amazement, Ian did not talk to her any more about Claire Edmunds, nor did he expressly forbid contact with her. Probably, he recognized that he had no way of enforcing this.

"I'll hear about it, Kathleen, if you make too nice with Matt Edmunds," was all he said, standing up from the table and ordering Kathleen into the bedroom with a dark look. Kathleen followed him—but while she lay beneath him, bearing his thrusts and rough kisses, she did not think of some other man but instead of the armored, warlike goddess Minerva.

***

"Oh, Matthew doesn't like that we're friends either," Claire said when Kathleen cautiously alluded to Ian's opinion.

As it happened, Claire knew very well what people said about her. She had also heard a bit about Kathleen, which she now reported. "They say you don't want to have anything to do with the parish since you're Catholic. Irish, you're all supposed to be Catholic. And who knows what strange observances you might have."

"Observances?" asked Kathleen, who did not know the word.

"Customs. Something about actual blood and flesh in your services—if you asked the chandler's wife, you'd think you all ate babies." Claire laughed, but Kathleen was horrified.

"Seriously, Matt says I'll have to keep an eye on the little one. But he's just angry at that Ian of yours because of the matter with the donkey. He's nursing a grudge. And he'll need a mule soon—hopefully your husband won't trick him again. Couldn't you have a word with him?"

Kathleen shook her head regretfully. Ian did not inform her of his sales plans, but naturally, he was still cheating people. For Kathleen, the worst of it was that now he had the boys watch as he transformed an old, lame nag into a shiny young horse with a charming temper in time for a sales conversation. The children did not understand much of it yet, but they both felt very important when their father took them into the barn to explain his "craft." If this continued, they would become swindlers before they could even speak properly.

Kathleen tried to impart a healthy moral foundation for the children with as many Bible stories as she could tell, but these stories were of no interest to

Sean. Claire quickly became his idol. Other than Pere no one could tell more and better stories than she, and she was happy to exchange them for practical guidance in everyday matters from Kathleen.

Soon the women were visiting each other as often as three times a week. The path along the river became so worn down that Claire's donkey and Kathleen's mule could trot along without getting stuck. Claire's cooking skills improved, and her house now gleamed, just like Kathleen's.

In turn, Claire was helping Kathleen with her reading. Father O'Brien had taught her the basics, but she was never truly at ease with it, so her return to it was halting and slow. The Bible was all she needed at first. But then Claire lent her one of her few exciting books. Kathleen exerted herself, and very soon, she read almost as naturally as her friend. At night, she found the greatest pleasure in taking out Michael's farewell letter, which she had strenuously hidden from Ian since their marriage. Now that she read easily, it was as if she heard his soft, low voice as she read.

Mary Kathleen . . . I'll come back . . . Oh, how long it had been since she'd heard him call out her name.

Roughly one month after the women's first meeting, Kathleen gave birth to a girl. It was an easy birth. Heather was quite small compared to the boys; Claire could hardly comprehend how delicate and well formed her little toes and fingers were, how cute her little mouth, and how soft her blonde hairs. Despite his assurances that he would be home for the birth, Ian was off on yet another business trip. Claire stayed with her friend as promised—although her help consisted largely of making tea and offering encouragement. Kathleen had never thought someone would manage to make her laugh during her contractions. But Claire compared Kathleen's delivery so seriously and insistently with that of a cow that Kathleen could not hold her laughter inside.

"I'm glad I didn't have to reach into you," declared Claire as she finally laid the baby in Kathleen's arms. In the meantime, lambs had been born on both farms, and Kathleen had expertly helped when there were complications. Claire had watched the events with interest but only roughly understood what Kathleen did to deliver twin lambs, wound up in each other, one after the other into the world. "But, of course, if it had come to it, I would have done it!"

***

Claire's own delivery did not pass without complications. After her friend spent two days in labor, Kathleen seriously feared Claire would not survive the birth. Matt was not prepared to send for a doctor in Christchurch. When Kathleen asked him why, he pointed out the high cost.

"You two can do it alone," he complained. "The animals don't have any problems."

"Then you'll be sure to help out like you did with the cow, right, Mr. Edmunds?" Kathleen responded angrily.

That did not happen. After the first few hours of Claire screaming and moaning desperately, Matthew Edmunds climbed into his boat and let the gentle current take him to the nearest tavern.

Kathleen was frothing with rage. To her astonishment, Matt's disappearance filled Claire with hope.

"I'm sure he's looking for a midwife," she wheezed, "or a doctor, even. It can't be that expensive. He, he loves me, after all."

In the end, the young woman also proved considerably tougher than Kathleen had judged her to be. When the baby was finally ready, Claire pushed with all her might, and with a bloodcurdling scream, her daughter slid into the world.

"I'll never be a lady," groaned Claire. "My mother said . . . my mother said, 'Ladies don't scream. A lady lets every pain pass without complaint.'"

"Really, now?" said Kathleen. "Well, we don't need any ladies here. They can all just stay in Liverpool. Look what a lovely baby you have. Do you know what you want to name her?"

Claire agreed that her baby was delightful. "I think I'll name her Chloe," she said. "That goes well with Claire." She stroked the baby's delicate little face, which still looked a little wrinkled after the birth.

"But I don't know if I want to do that again." Claire considered. "I admire you, Kathleen. Three times through this torture? I find once to be enough."

Kathleen took a confused Chloe out of her arms and began to bathe and swaddle the baby. "Matt probably won't ask you to," she said bashfully. "Ian, on the other hand . . ."

"So, you only have three children because Ian insisted?" Clair asked curiously. "And I thought . . . well, I thought I was the only one." She bit her lip.

"The only what?" inquired Kathleen. Ian was not wrong. These conversations were a bit more than inappropriate. Yet she was curious.

"The only one for whom it isn't fun. That is, hm, the, well, act of love."

Shocked, Kathleen did not know whether she should laugh or hold her peace, but Claire was already continuing.

"In books it says it's supposed to be nice. Well, it doesn't really say anything, of course, but the wedding is always the high point, and they live happily ever after. Only, I, I thought it nicer before the wedding. Matt had always spoken so kindly to me, and when he kissed me, it was tender and soft. But now . . . Have you ever thought it nice, Kathie? What, what, that is, what people do in bed?"

Kathleen smiled and thought she could feel Michael's kisses on her skin again. All at once she felt the urgent desire to share her secret with someone. Or at least to hint at it.

"It doesn't necessarily have to do with a wedding," she said. "With before or after one, I mean."

She left it at that. After giving birth, Claire was too tired to solicit more.

***

Summer and winter passed. Over time, Kathleen saw that Matthew Edmunds disappointed her friend far more than she'd initially thought or than Claire would portray. By the stories Claire had told, Kathleen could not have imagined the uncommunicative fellow who did not even show particular interest in his new daughter. Yet Claire persisted in depicting her handsome sailor as a daredevil and lively storyteller who had taken her heart by storm. She seemed to judge him based on this, and indeed, Matt Edmunds was quite good-looking. He was tall and blond, but Kathleen thought he always wore a sullen expression, which made him seem unapproachable and unlikeable. Claire's husband seemed to nurse a grudge against the whole world, especially his lovely, vivacious, and charming wife.

Apparently, Matt had imagined emigration and life in this new country differently, although Claire and Kathleen could not quite figure out what displeased him. Considering they arrived with little more than some china and a few books, the Edmundses were not doing poorly. Matt had invested his meager savings wisely, and he now earned enough from his ferry business to support his family. Over time that would increase, for the growing city of Christchurch promised all citizens a secure existence. Perhaps Matt simply missed the adventure his life at sea had offered. And it was clear that Claire, for all her charms, could not make it up to him.

Claire, however, did not want to admit this. "I'm sure he loves me," she said defiantly when now and again a less-than-flattering comment about Matt's behavior escaped from Kathleen's lips. "Even if he thinks I'm stupid and boring."

She left open whether she only assumed this or whether Matt had said these things to her face. "It's because I can't do anything right," she said by way of excusing Matt's behavior.

Kathleen did not respond, although a sharp retort lay on her tongue. Claire had learned to manage her household quite well. She lacked practical experience, and her talent for handicrafts was mediocre at best. But with regard to intelligence and originality, she surpassed Matt Edmunds effortlessly.

Kathleen could not get enough of Claire's lively stories and her constant new ideas. She had imagined the Edmundses' evenings to be considerably happier and more entertaining than her joyless coexistence with Ian. But Kathleen had begun to think even Claire held her tongue in her husband's presence. She occasionally seemed to wince when Matt came home unexpectedly while she sat at the kitchen table chatting with Kathleen.

Granted, that may have been because Matt reacted with rage to anyone who bore the Coltrane name. Whenever he saw Kathleen in his house, he couldn't refrain from making comments about "lazy molls," "good-for-nothing Irish," and "rogues and cheats." Kathleen tried not to take it personally, since she could completely understand his aggravation with Ian's business practices. Matthew had paid heftily for Spotty, but when there was heavy work, he had to lease a mule from a faraway farm, and it required great effort to bring the mule there and back. And the nearest horse trader other than Ian lived even farther away.

Kathleen was not at all surprised when one day she heard Matt and Ian in the stables.

"There, look at that brown mule mare. Strong, young, and friendly. I send my own children out with her," Ian said. "Go, Sean, get the brown one from the pen."

Sean, who was now almost three years old, gripped the halter ardently. The two boys vied to assist their father whenever he was there. Fortunately, Sean did not yet recognize that Ian's indulgent looks fell on Colin while he was chastised more often than praised. Because he was older and more skilled, Sean still dominated his brother. Serious problems would only arise when Colin closed this gap.

Kathleen proudly watched as Sean entered the pen, carefully shut the gate behind him, and ran to the old brown mule that had been in the stables a week. Ian had used this time to grind down her teeth, work on her hooves enough that her irregular gait could no longer be seen, and make her fur shine with coloring agents and oils. The hairs above her eyes and beneath her scant forelock were no longer gray, and her eyes shone thanks to plenty of oats and compresses of a special mixture Ian called "eye comfort." Kathleen was concerned that whatever methods Ian might have used to improve the mare's energy might endanger Sean, but the mare was as compliant as ever. Good-natured as she was, she was still at least fifteen years old.

"There, just look at the teeth—no more than six years old, this one. She'll pull her weight; look at those sturdy legs. And she's a lovely sight, too, don't you think? Your wife values such things, I hear." Ian smiled winningly.

Matt Edmunds glanced politely into the mule's mouth—looking just as helpless as Claire had during her first visit to the vegetable garden. Ian had not needed to go to any trouble with the teeth. Matt Edmunds had no idea.

"And she's not expensive. I'll make you a good offer. I could sell her for more, but for you, Matt, well, I have a bit of a bad conscience because I vastly underestimated your farm. I thought that little donkey—otherwise an excellent animal, as your wife is always telling mine—would be enough to do the work. But you've got quite a bit of land to plow—my admiration. And that alongside your true calling as a ferryman! Your wife lends quite a hand, I'd wager."

Kathleen reluctantly had to admire her husband's sales skills. Matt Edmunds willingly swallowed the bait and reported extensively on Claire's failings. They were finished viewing the mule.

Kathleen went to do her work in the garden, and when she finally entered the house, the men were just drinking a second glass of whiskey to wrap up their business deal. Kathleen would have liked to scream, but her decision was affirmed. She would not allow Ian to cheat Matt a second time. She could not bear it if Claire turned away from her as the women had back in Port Cooper because of Ian's dishonesty.

Once Matt Edmunds had gone, she stood up to Ian. "Ian, this won't do. In a few days Matt will notice that the mule is old as stone, and no later than her next shoeing she will start dragging her foot again. Claire might even see it straight away; she knows a lot about horses. And then they'll never talk to us again."

Ian laughed and poured himself another drink—good whiskey, not cheap moonshine. Ian Coltrane was doing well for himself. One could tell by looking at him too: he was no longer a muscular but slender giant. Increasingly, he resembled his stocky father: his face was fleshy, the contours of his muscles ill defined; and though he was not fat, he looked heavy. Over time he had adopted the horse trader habit of carrying a gnarled stick, which he could use to lean on during sales negotiations or to motivate the horses quickly and effectively. He'd used it on Kathleen, too, and even on little Sean.

Kathleen had long stopped caring one bit for her husband. Ian Coltrane disgusted her. She could endure the nights with him only because she had Michael's letter among her clothing. After Ian had climbed off her and fallen asleep, she would slink over to her dresser and run her hands over the letter and hair as if to purify herself.

"Why should we care if the Edmundses talk to us?" Ian burst out laughing. "The fellow's an idiot and his wife is a stuck-up shrew. What do we need with them?"

Kathleen shook her head, despairing. "Ian, the Edmundses are our neighbors! If anything happens, we're reliant on them and they on us. Claire and I were present for each other's births. We're friends."

"And I told you from the beginning that I don't approve of your friendship," Ian said with composure. "If this deal keeps you from constantly running over to that stupid goose and allowing her to fill our kids' heads with her nonsense stories, then all the better."

Kathleen sighed, but she continued doggedly. "Ian, she's not filling their heads with any nonsense. She's teaching Sean to read, even though he's still so young. And she'll teach Colin next year. Where else are the children going to learn it? I can't exactly send them to school in Christchurch every day. Please, Ian! If you won't give up cheating your customers, at least think more carefully about whom you can cheat without punishment and whom it's better to leave alone."

Ian stood up threateningly. "Kathleen, I don't like to be called a cheat! Least of all by a whore like you. God knows you have no idea of what's right and what's not!"

Kathleen knew she would not make it through the night without bruises and worse humiliations, but she could not stop. Above all, finally, she wanted answers.

"So why were you in such a hurry to marry this whore?" she asked in a surge of courage. "You knew I was pregnant, Ian. You knew about Michael. If you find me so disgusting—"

Ian laughed and took a swig from his whiskey bottle.

Kathleen trembled. She hoped she had not gone too far.

Ian gripped her hair almost tenderly. "Who could find you disgusting, sweet? The prettiest girl in Wicklow County, even if a little spoiled, but only a little. In the end, you chose me and not a job at Miss Daisy's."

Ian had known about the offer from the brothel owner?

Ian grinned at her. "Aye, girl, did you think I lived like a monk in Wicklow?" he asked snidely. "Kathleen, my heart, I trade horses. And a good horse trader knows everyone and everything. That Michael of yours, I bought moonshine from him often enough. He didn't steal Trevallion's grain to feed the poor, and that had to be clear to anyone not head over heels for him. And Billy Rafferty! I took him home in my wagon after his drinking bout. Couldn't get over how Michael had only given him a piece of what was due him, because he needed to pay for his little Kathleen's passage, after all."

Kathleen listened, stunned, her eyes wide. So her suspicion had not been wrong. Ian had known about Michael's money the first time he had taken her to Wicklow. Might he have sent the police after Billy Rafferty?

In any case, Ian had made sure that Kathleen had seen her beloved in Wicklow—once and once again for good measure. Although the second time, she had, of course, only watched him sail away. He had not let her take a last look at Michael out of kindness, but simply to be sure. One way or another, Michael would get the money from his robbery to his sweetheart—after all, he could not do anything more with it.

"You, you knew about my dowry?" Kathleen inquired flatly, wanting to be sure.

Ian shook with laughter. "Of course! I put two and two together. The privileges Michael got in prison, for example. Old Bridget has a soft heart, surely, but to pay for two bumpkins like Michael and Billy out of her whore's pay—I wasn't about to believe that."

"And how did you know about their privileges?" asked Kathleen.

Ian made a dismissive gesture. "Billy Rafferty's sister. Back then she was walking the street near the horse market. I talked to her, gave her a drink of whiskey—you know how it is, Kathleen. Now, don't look so appalled! Haven't I managed your money wisely? Aren't you and your bastard doing well?"

Kathleen turned away, but Ian wasn't done yet.

"And I heard about Miss Daisy's offer, too, Mary Kathleen," he crowed. "Tell me, was it hard to decide? You could've had an easy life back in Wicklow. Why did you choose me anyway, Kathleen? Just for the little bastard's sake?"

Kathleen did not say another word. Not when Ian pushed her to the bed in a rush of drunkenness and desire for mastery. Not even when she thought she might suffocate under his weight and that of her new certainty.

***

In the morning, she got up before her husband even stirred. She hastily gave the children some porridge, then fastened Heather onto the chestnut-colored mule's back and set the boys up there, too, before she climbed up behind all three of them. She rode them as quickly as she safely could over the riverbank path and reached Matt Edmunds while he was still putting his boat in to set out for Christchurch.

"Mr. Edmunds." Kathleen presented the mule to him. "My husband sent me to bring you your purchase from yesterday. It's quite a lovely animal. I think you'll be happy with this one. I'll ride it up to the stable for you."

Matt Edmunds did not notice that the mule had been exchanged, but Claire was amazed when she took the animal into the stables along with Kathleen.

"Your own mule? Ian sold Matt his best mule? What did Matt pay for that? Ought I to reckon with being driven from house and home if we can't come up with the money?" She laughed and patted the new mule. Spotty reacted with a jealous bray.

Kathleen was not in the mood for jokes. "Best thing would be for you to take your animals a little farther inland today," she advised Claire. "Take Spotty and this one out to graze at the Leprechaun rock, or even better, hide them at the Fairy Place. Most of all, don't let my husband see you or the mules. Oh yes—and come by tomorrow to look for me. If you find he's killed me, look after my children."

Chapter 11

Rather than living in the makeshift barracks, Sergeant Meyers and Velvet had rented two rooms at a small inn. When Lizzie knocked, the proprietress immediately let her inside. Instead of her apron and bonnet, Lizzie wore a dark dress and a carefully coiffed hairstyle so she would not be recognized as a maid gone astray. It was a weekday, and she had used an errand to grant herself a free hour.

Lizzie followed the proprietress with a pounding heart. Sergeant Meyers should not be home at that hour. One never knew, of course, but Velvet greeted her alone. She dismissed the proprietress at once, amicably but firmly, to fetch tea and pastries.

"I really can't stay that long," Lizzie said nervously, looking around the room. "You've got it nice here. You've become a real lady, Velvet."

Velvet smiled. "It's not as nice as your bosses have it," she said. Misreading Lizzie's unhappy facial expression, she qualified her statement: "Well, if I had to dust all that shiny stuff every day, I'd probably see it with other eyes too."

Lizzie shook her head. "That's not the problem. I don't mind cleaning. But . . . we don't have much time, Velvet. You have to listen to me. I need your help."

Velvet held up her hand to stop her and gestured with her chin toward the door. The proprietress was just coming in carrying a platter with teacups and rolls.

Once the tea and treats were on the table, Velvet thanked her with a smile and motioned for Lizzie take a seat. "Now we can talk," she said once the woman had gone. "So, what can I do for you? You want to marry, I heard?"

"I want to flee," Lizzie corrected her. She had no time for polite conversation. "Together with Michael Drury. But first he needs out of his chain gang."

"Wait a minute, wait." Velvet poured the tea. She did not seem perturbed by Lizzie's revelation, but she had always been like that. "You're going a little fast. Are you aware that no one has ever escaped from Van Diemen's Land before?"

"So they say, but if I was the governor and someone ran away, I wouldn't admit it either. But it doesn't matter. We'll just be the first."

"But Lizzie, why?"

Velvet saw in Lizzie's impatient expression that she did not want to discuss it. Lizzie looked at the clock in the corner of the room.

"I should get to the butcher's, Velvet. The cook's waiting for the meat."

Velvet nodded. "All right, fine. You absolutely want to make yourself miserable with Michael Drury. How can I help?"

"You can ask your husband to mark Michael as a lower security risk so they take off his chains," Lizzie said. "That's the first thing. Then we need to get to Hobart somehow."

If she were being honest, her plan did not extend much further. And everything needed to go quickly since her wedding already had been announced at church.

"Somehow," Velvet said mockingly. "Now, don't sit here like there's a fire under you, Lizzie. It won't help. You need to take a little time."

"I don't have any time," Lizzie burst forth. "This swine, Mr. Smithers, throws himself on me every night he spends at the house. And more or less with his wife's blessing. She thinks she can only stop him by marrying me off. In four weeks they're going to hitch me to the gardener who's agreed to continue sharing me with Mr. Smithers. And Michael Drury is chained up with a few violent idiots who rave to him about fleeing to New Zealand—and yet they can't even row a boat, let alone sail one across the Tasman Sea. So you see . . . I don't have time, Velvet. I need papers and passage on the next ship."

"The ships to England are searched thoroughly," Velvet said.

"But not the ones to Auckland or Greymouth or all the other funny-named places in New Zealand. The idea isn't that bad, just its execution. With those fools, Michael will never make it."

Velvet nibbled on a roll. "Well, first, you have more time than you think," she said. "No, not now, of course. You need to hurry to the butcher; I see that. But with the wedding. Before your pardon, they'll interrogate you one last time. Likely they'll send you to Hobart. That will take at least two months, so don't drive yourself mad. And second, I see that you want to get away. And the idea's ingenious. If only I'd thought of that! But why, for God's sake, do you need Michael Drury?"

Lizzie lowered her gaze.

Velvet moaned, brushing a strand of her gorgeous black hair from her fair forehead. "Yes, I know, you love him. Even on the ship you couldn't miss it. But Lizzie, the man will make you miserable. He's a dog who—"

"You don't even know him," Lizzie said, defending the man she loved.

Velvet rolled her eyes. "I've heard enough about his adventures. Although dog is perhaps the wrong word. It might very well be that Drury is a good fellow. But in the end, he's still given his whole heart to that girl he knocked up in Ireland."

"He knocked . . . he . . . Mary Kathleen?"

Lizzie had not yet touched her tea, but Velvet could see she needed some fortification. She pulled a bottle of rum out from behind the sofa and poured some into Lizzie's tea.

"Yes, Michael knocked up his girl. Didn't think about how he was supposed to feed the kid until afterward either. As if he'd fled into a forest full of poison snakes and only then considered how he was supposed to get out again. At first, he didn't even know that this was an island. The man will keep getting into trouble, Lizzie! He's too emotional, too impulsive. You saved him once when he had a fever. And now you want to save him again. He doesn't even love you." Velvet poured rum in her own cup as well.

"He will, though . . . if only I . . ."

A tiny furrow formed over Velvet's nose. Lizzie remembered from their days as cellmates that this always happened before Velvet indulged in a fit of excitement. "If only you do *what* for him? Lie, steal, whore? I thought that way once too. I'd have done anything for Murphy, and then he foisted all the guilt onto me. He claimed he hadn't quite known that pinching watches was illegal and suddenly I just slipped the thing to him. And yet I'd been stealing for him for two years. At first, I thought I'd die. But you don't die that easy . . ." Velvet lowered her gaze.

"But Michael . . ." Lizzie tried once more.

"Forget Michael," Velvet said sternly. "Get yourself to safety. You'll find someone else in New Zealand. These colonies are crawling with fellows. And over on the islands, they're all free."

Lizzie chewed her lip. "I won't make it alone," she whispered. "I need him."

Velvet shook her head. "You don't need him. He needs you."

"Same thing," Lizzie said. "So, will you help me? Please, Velvet, please! You said yourself: he's a good fellow."

Velvet gripped her forehead. "All right, fine, Lizzie," she finally said. "But promise me you won't rush. Think it over again calmly."

Lizzie nodded halfheartedly, but now Velvet was the one thinking—and an idea came to her. "Listen, Lizzie. Michael came from the country, right? Do you think he knows anything about horses?"

Though she had no idea, Lizzie nodded eagerly. "Of course," she said.

"Good. There's a constant lack of drivers here. They have heavy teams for clearing the forests and transporting building material, but most of the convicts come from the city. They don't know how to drive the wagons, and worse, they're afraid of the giant nags. If my husband frees Michael, and he behaves for a couple of weeks, he might get a wagon to drive. That's your ticket to Hobart. But that'll take a little time. Will you make it?"

Lizzie nodded bravely. "I'll try. If Michael doesn't take off the moment they remove his chains."

Velvet rolled her eyes. "Then you can take it as a sign," she said. "Really, it's the best thing that could happen to you. Now get to the butcher. Otherwise you'll catch trouble."

She accompanied Lizzie to the door, and suddenly hugged her.

"Good luck, Lizzie!" she whispered. "It'd be nice if one of us got to be happy."

***

A week later, Lizzie's pardon hearing was delayed. While Mrs. Smithers and Cecil were rather disappointed, Mr. Smithers was delighted that the wedding had to wait. Apparently, Mrs. Smithers was of the opinion that with or without a marriage certificate, Lizzie ought to start taking her pleasure with Cecil rather than her husband. But she no longer spoke to the girl about it directly.

Michael was freed from his chains three weeks after Lizzie and Velvet's conversation. He easily adapted to the post of stable boy, where Sergeant Meyers placed him after a short questioning about his previous experience. Michael was used to mules. The heavy workhorses with which he now had to contend were larger but hardly any more difficult to handle. Michael fed and cleaned them, and to the satisfaction of the stable master, he even knew how to hitch them.

"Might you be able to drive too, boy?"

Michael nodded and soon accustomed himself to the giant wagon with which he transported the building materials and logs. The horses were less of a problem than the size and weight of the wagon, but Lord Wetherby's grain wagons had not been all that much smaller. Michael handled it all well, and he would have been called to be driver, but he wasn't yet trusted enough to be sent out alone on the roads.

***

"Just don't do anything stupid," Lizzie urged Michael.

She tried to see him as often as possible. Though it wasn't easy, the best time to sneak in a visit was during the week, when she was out running errands. Martha played along with these rendezvous good-naturedly enough, though Lizzie hadn't told her about the escape plan, since she knew the cook had her misgivings about Michael.

"How's that supposed to end, child? Love one and marry another, and the third takes what he wants. Just watch out, girlie. Cecil, he can't like what's going on with the master. But he can't do anything either. But if he hears about you and the handsome driver . . ."

Lizzie shrugged her shoulders. Before Cecil heard anything, she intended to be on a ship to New Zealand—or in prison again in Hobart. Once she ran away, there was no turning back, but now almost anything seemed better than becoming Cecil's wife while staying Mr. Smithers's whore.

Now, Lizzie tried not to look at Michael. He was atop the box of a wagon, and she was walking inconspicuously alongside him toward the store. "Behave for a couple of months. Let Sergeant Meyers start to trust you." She could hardly keep herself from casting at least a comforting look at his handsome face and into his shining eyes.

"An opportunity will surely arise," she said under her breath.

"Of course." Michael sounded cheery and carefree. He seemed to enjoy the job of driver. Might he not want to leave at all anymore? Lizzie's heart skipped a beat. If she arranged everything now, and then he said no . . .

"I can't do anything on my own anyway. I have to wait for Will and Dylan and Connor. Without Connor, it's hopeless."

Lizzie sighed. So he did still want to flee. She would dissuade him yet.

And then, a couple of weeks later, events came to a head. It began with Mrs. Smithers summoning Lizzie. Of course she obeyed, but her heart was pounding. Were things taking too long for her mistress? Would she level more charges that Lizzie was seducing her husband?

Mrs. Smithers, however, did nothing of the sort. Instead, her news was positive.

"Tomorrow you will ride to Hobart. They want to question you again, and then things will hopefully go faster with your wedding. Pete's driving to Hobart anyway; he's taking David Parsley to the ship." Pete was not just house servant but also driver for the Smitherses.

"Mr. Parsley means to travel?" Lizzie asked without inflection.

"For business. New Zealand; it concerns a contract. It seems they're thinking of a road between the east and west coasts, something like that. I'd rather return to England, of course, but that's no concern of yours. We can't leave here for two or three years anyway. In any case, ready yourself. You leave at sunrise."

Lizzie went back to her work and tried to sort out what was happening. It was Thursday. She would be traveling Friday and Saturday, so the ship would leave either Sunday or Monday. She could easily take care of Mr. Parsley; the man was a coward, and he had often winked at her when he was a guest of the Smitherses and Lizzie served dinner. Did he know that she belonged to his boss? The blood rose to Lizzie's face. But that did not matter either. More important than anything now was getting to Michael. She quickly set the dinner table, then ran to Martha.

"I have to go! Give me an errand, any errand."

The cook frowned. "What do you want to do now, child? The missus wants you to serve. Mr. Smithers is expected."

Lizzie looked at her, horrified. "Today? No! I've got to go, Martha! Tell them anything. Tell them I'm with Cecil, giving him the news that I'll be pardoned soon. Or tell them you sent me to get eggs, and I'll claim I sprained my ankle in the chicken coop."

Martha shook her head. "The chickens are already asleep. Off with you, girlie, but hurry. I'll think of something. The missus is in a good mood. And Master, well, if you get back in time . . ."

Lizzie nodded. She knew her duties. But for now, she took her apron off as she ran out, and wrapped herself quickly in Martha's shawl. It was late summer, and in Van Diemen's Land, it was already cold. It was also raining lightly as Lizzie ran across the village streets to the stables near the barracks. If she was lucky, Michael would still be there. He had to be there.

Michael was feeding the horses and whistling to himself. Lizzie went weak with relief.

"Michael, Michael, thank God you're here." She had to restrain herself from throwing her arms around him.

"My little angel," he laughed. "Hey, is the house on fire, or are you having trouble with your little lover? Should I beat him for you?"

Michael seemed to be in a good mood and not quite sober. That was no wonder. Whenever there was contraband whiskey circulating among the convicts, the drivers always got a few swigs. Michael put his arm around Lizzie, who was leaning against a stall, trying to catch her breath.

"Stop your nonsense and listen." Lizzie's fear made her rebuff him more strongly than she actually wanted to. She hoped he was not too drunk to understand the plan. "Michael, Sunday or Monday a ship is leaving for New Zealand. You'll get papers and a ticket—no, no questions now; there's no time. But you have to make it to Hobart. I'll meet you . . ."

"At Battery Point, in Mayfair Tavern," Michael said quickly. "It's a tavern, supposed to be easy to find."

Lizzie rolled her eyes. "Just say: the soldiers will search there first," she mocked. "But fine, it's somewhere at least. But don't go inside. Stay somewhere nearby. Or, better: look for the ship to New Zealand and hide on the pier.

I'll come there with a man. Follow us inconspicuously, and at some point, I'll meet you and give you the papers."

"But how do you mean to—" This was all happening a bit too fast for Michael.

"I don't know yet, but it's worth a try. Just come to Hobart. But don't tell anyone. Not even your friends from the chain gang."

"But they . . . I can't just . . . They'll wonder . . ."

"Let them. It's better they stay in the dark than betray you. Michael, between now and when the ship leaves, you'll have to hide for three days and cover more than a hundred fifty miles. It'll be better if no one knows where to look for you."

Michael was quiet for a moment, seeming to weigh his loyalties. But then he shrugged. "So be it. I'll leave tonight," he declared.

Lizzie squinted. "Don't you think it would be better to go tomorrow with the team?"

"A team would draw too much attention. I have a better idea. I'll take a horse. Wish me luck, Lizzie."

Lizzie was moving to go when he kissed her. First on the forehead, then quickly on the mouth. "And good luck to you too," he said.

Lizzie managed to smile when Martin Smithers came to her bed that night. She knew it was the last time, so she endured his caresses and thought of Michael.

***

Michael needed all the luck he could get—starting with his escape. Among the horses in his charge was an unruly young stallion. Gideon was a Shire horse—gorgeous, dark brown, white-footed, and almost fifteen hands tall. A farmer near Launceston had ordered the horse from England, and one of the drivers had brought it from Hobart. Now it stood in a stall with Michael, waiting to be transported to the farm—though the stable master was in no hurry. He planned to have the stallion cover all the mares in his stables before sending him onward. And nearly all the settlers in the area who had mares had spoken with him. They handed him a small fee, and the stallion performed his service. The farmer would never be the wiser.

The animal could hardly believe its luck. Every day he became unrulier, and he beat on the stall wall nervously whenever a mare was in heat. Michael had repaired his stall three times already. It would be completely believable for the stallion to manage to escape one day. And the horse was strong. It could easily make it to Hobart and take Michael with it. If it would carry a rider.

Michael was not sure it would. His heart raced as he started to take out the largest saddle. No. If the stable master noticed the missing saddle, it would be a giveaway. Michael swallowed but decided to take the risk of riding bareback. He merely put an old harness on the stallion, bridled it with a shabby bridle, and spoke kindly to it as he led it outside.

All that was missing was a note. Drivers logged their routes on a board in the stable, so Michael found the chalk and wrote across all the columns: STALLION RAN AWAY. FOLLOWING TRACKS TO WEST—MICHAEL.

That should keep the stable master calm for a few hours. And busy. He would send out search teams; the stallion was valuable. Michael, meanwhile, would be riding east—or breaking his neck.

Michael needed a rock or some other means of getting onto the giant animal's back. And he could not risk moving over soft ground. Otherwise, the stable master would find hoof prints, which were unmistakable for the giant stallion. Michael muttered a prayer and thought of Kathleen as he swung from the box of his wagon onto Gideon's back. The stallion pranced a bit but remained calm, and Michael thanked heaven. Then he spurred the horse onward. Gideon took the first few steps, giving Michael a taste of what was awaiting him. Without a saddle, the movements of the powerful horse would rattle him such that everything would hurt afterward. But that did not matter to him now. They were on their way.

***

Lizzie was in the coach to Hobart with David Parsley. She kept trying to have an agreeable conversation with him, but he was rather grouchy in the morning. Finally, Lizzie gave up and waited until Mr. Parsley was fully awake. She managed to charm him with her warm smile, and then she hit upon a topic of conversation that interested him: road construction.

Parsley talked and talked. Lizzie no longer needed to contribute a word but, nevertheless, she felt ground down when Pete stopped that evening at the same small inn where, on her way to the Smitherses', Lizzie had spent the most pleasant and promising night of her life so far. *And that without any man*, she thought bitterly. In fact, she had yet to enjoy a man's company. The lavender-scented bed was enticing, and David Parsley had just begun to court her a bit, but caution was better.

"We'll sleep in the hay," she told Pete, the driver. He, at least, would not touch her.

Lizzie sighed and acted as if it were difficult to part from Parsley. And luckily, the magic worked. Her smile brightened the heart of the aloof engineer, and she got a decent dinner. Lizzie drank really good wine for the first time, and the French Muscat Blanc charmed her palate. She could have sat at the candlelit table forever, regardless of what Parsley was saying, so long as she could drink this wine.

"You don't waste any time," murmured Pete when she finally came, tipsy indeed, to sleep in the hay.

His comments sobered her at once. So far Martha and Pete had held a high opinion of her, but in a few days, they, too, would think Lizzie Owens a whore.

The next day passed similarly to the first in the coach, but Parsley was quite conversational and Lizzie began to flirt in earnest.

"Don't you have a wife, Mr. Parsley? Don't you sometimes miss soft arms as you travel the world providing all the colonies with roads?"

Parsley blushed, hemming and hawing. "I, hm, I've simply never encountered, well, one as sweet as you, Miss Owens."

Lizzie smiled and let herself dream. What if he meant that? What if she truly won over this somewhat boring but rather good-looking and seemingly honest man? He would be able to care for a family—she would even get to see the world if she traveled around with him for a few years. But that was a fantasy. Never ever would she be able to convince Mr. Parsley to take her straight to New Zealand—especially before she was pardoned. And when he returned, she would long since have been married to Cecil. No, there was no alternative. It was impossible, once again, to be good. On the contrary: Lizzie would be adding one more entry to her registry of sin.

The second evening, she ate with Mr. Parsley again, and this time it was not easy to fend off his advances. David Parsley had drunk the majority of the two bottles of wine they had emptied, and he was swaying a bit when they stood up and he accompanied Lizzie outside.

"Come now, Miss Owens, it'll be warmer beside me than in the hay. And, well, if I've understood Mr. Smithers correctly, you're not usually nearly so prudish."

Her heart froze. So this young man, who had seemed so simple to her a moment before, also knew of her shame. Mr. Smithers had boasted about her.

Lizzie breathed deeply. She could not be offended. She had a role to play.

"Perhaps, perhaps tomorrow. When we're no longer on the road. When does your ship depart, Mr. Parsley?"

Chapter 12

Pete was supposed to drop Lizzie at Cascades Female Factory on Sunday evening. She was to spend the night there and be questioned Monday. When they reached Hobart on Sunday afternoon, however, Mr. Parsley slipped a pound into the coachman's hand—a small fortune for a convict.

"Forget about the girl for tonight," Mr. Parsley ordered. "My ship departs early tomorrow, and I'd like a little enjoyment. I'll take her to the hotel."

"But the master will inquire," Pete said, uncertain. "And the factory, the girl's expected there."

"I'll get there, Pete, don't worry," Lizzie said soothingly. "Just a little later. I'll knock ever so primly on the door, so no one gets the wrong idea, and then I'll tell them our axle broke."

"I'll deliver her myself," said Mr. Parsley, grinning at Lizzie.

"You know best, sir." Pete shrugged. "As do you." He gave Lizzie a severe look and steered the wagon toward the rental stables where he would find a place to sleep.

Lizzie sighed. Time for the final act. And Michael; she hoped he had made it to Hobart too.

"Now, let's find ourselves a cozy little inn," whispered Parsley, linking arms with Lizzie.

She smiled at him. "Perhaps in the harbor?" she asked. "Then it won't be so far for you to go tomorrow morning. And I'd love to see the ship. If I were a man, oh, I believe I'd sail to sea."

"What a pretty sight you'd be in a sailor's uniform," he teased her.

Lizzie shuddered. Did all men like uniforms?

The ship was a modern three-master, and as far as Lizzie could tell, it gave a seaworthy impression. It was smaller than the *Asia*, but she was not about to spend three months at sea on this journey. Parsley told her that the voyage to New Zealand would take between twenty and thirty days. Lizzie's heart beat heavily. If only she were already at sea.

And then she saw Michael. He was squatting on the pier with a fishing line. Just another poor devil trying to fish for his supper with a load of goods as shelter from the wind. Lizzie tried not to give him a second look. But he must have seen her because he started reeling in his line.

Lizzie placed her arm determinedly through Parsley's. "Come on; I'm getting cold. Perhaps we should buy a bottle of whiskey."

She had noticed the previous evening that he could not hold his liquor. If a little wine made him wobble, half a bottle of whiskey should make him sleep like the dead. That would absolve her of the unpleasant task of knocking him unconscious, which Lizzie did not really trust her ability to do.

Parsley pulled her closer. "So, you like whiskey too, Miss Owens. Well, look at you. And in the Smithers house, you always acted so virtuous. Oh, you girls."

He giggled as if he had discovered something embarrassing. Lizzie laughed with him mirthlessly. She had to persevere, not letting any of his words affect her. Fortunately, he decided on an inn and not some hourly hotel. Its proprietress did not ask for a marriage certificate when Parsley entered them as a married couple, and she offered them a spacious room with clean sheets.

***

Lizzie watered down her own whiskey but left Mr. Parsley's undiluted. She was almost too nervous to wait until he was drunk and considered hitting him over the head with the fire poker after he dozed off, exhausted, after their first time together. But no, Anna Portland had killed her husband that way. Lizzie could not risk it. Even if she wasn't meant to be a good person, it didn't mean she had to be a murderer. She shook Parsley awake and smiled at him.

"So, you haven't had enough of me yet. You can't get enough of me. Here, take another drink. And then make me happy again."

Lizzie had rarely worked as hard as she did that night, but by three in the morning—boarding was at five and departure at seven—David Parsley had emptied more than three quarters of the whiskey bottle. He slept like a dead man. Lizzie could empty his pockets at her leisure. Why wouldn't she just take everything? Michael and she would need bags. It would be conspicuous to travel without them. Cold-bloodedly, Lizzie pocketed David's wallet and carried his travel bag downstairs.

"My husband will be down in a moment," she told the proprietress, moving past her before she could even ask.

Lizzie hoped the woman would not run upstairs and try to wake Parsley. But that was unlikely. As long as the man remained in her hotel, she could wait for the bill to be paid. And what did she care what "Mrs. Parsley" was doing in the middle of the night with her bag?

Michael stepped out from a niche as soon as Lizzie emerged.

"Finally! I thought you'd never be done. Who was the fellow? And what, what did you do?"

Lizzie tiredly handed him her victim's passport. "That was David Parsley. And now you're David Parsley. You don't need to know more than that."

As casually as possible, the two strolled along beside each other. Michael had thrown Parsley's bag over his shoulder. He smelled of horse.

He told her of his adventures with Gideon. Amiably and tirelessly the stallion had carried him to Hobart. On the second day Michael had detoured onto side roads, and he told Lizzie colorful tales of the exotic animals he had encountered. "I swear to you, one of the beasts was a Tasmanian devil."

Though he described a ferocious-looking black animal armed with powerful teeth, it had not dared get too close to giant Gideon. During the day, Michael had slept peacefully in the shadow of the massive stallion—and he attributed being intact to its protection. Though Lizzie thought she had heard that the snakes and insects in Van Diemen's Land actually presented more danger than that strange, rather cute Tasmanian devil, she said nothing. Michael had clearly grown fond of the stallion.

"There would, naturally, have been a tidy sum in it if I had sold the horse," he finally said regretfully. "But he drew too much attention. There would have been suspicion."

"That was very clever of you," Lizzie said. "What did you do instead?"

"I let him run free," Michael said. "He'll show up somewhere later today, probably in the pen of a nice mare. That farmer can decide between looking for its owner and figuring possession is nine-tenths of the law."

Lizzie thought that a fitting solution.

"This is the ship," she said when they finally reached the pier. "The *Elizabeth Campbell*. And here are the tickets." She handed Michael a couple more papers. "There's also plenty of money in the wallet. You can . . ."

"Lizzie, I don't know how to thank you for all you've done for me." Michael looked desirously at the illuminated gangplank. The ship was being loaded, and passengers were already boarding. "But tell me, isn't it a risk for you? If this fellow wakes . . ."

Lizzie looked at him, stunned. "Is it a risk for me?" she asked, disbelieving. "Michael, that fellow is Mr. Smithers's assistant. And of course he'll wake up. He'll not be dead from a bottle of whiskey."

"But then, then he'll report you." Michael looked concerned.

Lizzie rolled her eyes. "Michael, by the time he wakes, we'll have long been at sea."

"We?" asked Michael. "You want to come too?"

"What did you think?" Lizzie was too taken aback to feel hurt. "That I'd help you flee and then return like a good little girl to marry my—what do you call him? Leprechaun?"

"But how is this going to work?" Michael moved David Parsley's travel bag from one hand to the other.

Lizzie was getting angry.

"Simply," she told him. "You go to the skipper, or whoever's responsible, and book passage for sweet Elizabeth Parsley, your loving wife. There won't be any problems. Worst comes to worst, you'll have to share a berth with me."

"But they'll get suspicious. Where did this David Parsley's wife come from?"

Lizzie forced herself to be patient. "Michael, the captain doesn't know Parsley. He could have been married ten years or just found the love of his life for all the captain knows, and for all he cares. He only wants the money. So go tell him you decided to bring your wife after all."

"I don't know."

Lizzie saw Michael struggling with himself. On the one hand, he owed his chance to escape to Lizzie—who, seen in the light of day, was not very honest. Making off with a ship of the Crown as he had planned with Connor and the others, though it doubtlessly carried more risks, probably suited him better than what Lizzie had done. Now, however, there was no going back. It would be suicide to look for Parsley and give him back his stolen papers. On the other hand, though, she imagined Michael did not want to burden his new free man's life in New Zealand right away with a theft and a whore.

"Well, I know!" Lizzie yelled as she grabbed Parsley's wallet from a stunned Michael. "You're coming with me or not at all. Think it over."

Lizzie dangled the wallet provocatively over the pier wall. If Michael said the wrong thing now—or if she was startled by a clumsy movement . . .

"Fine. Then I'll tell the skipper, tell him that . . ."

Lizzie sighed. "Don't tell him anything. I'll come with you," she said resignedly. "And I'll do the talking."

***

"I do so hope there's still room for me on the ship. There is, isn't there?" Lizzie asked. She was fluttering her eyelashes in a manner meant to be demure, but to Michael's overwrought imagination, every one of her expressions had a salacious echo. "Imagine, my husband's letting me travel with him now. Though at first he was so concerned for, for us." Lizzie stroked her entirely flat stomach with a fleeting motion and even managed to blush. Her smile was heart-warming.

The skipper grinned. "Of course, madam. And not to worry; you'll travel as safely as in Abraham's bosom on the *Elizabeth Campbell*. For a small additional charge, we'd even have an exceptionally comfortable cabin."

"That would be wonderful," Lizzie beamed. "Oh, did you hear, dear? The ship is called Elizabeth, like me."

Michael acquiesced, grinding his teeth.

The "small additional charge" would consume almost all of their starting money, but the cabin was truly luxurious. Lizzie marveled at the white sheets, the porcelain washbowls, and the massive mirror. She looked herself over carefully and sighed.

No one could tell what she had done by looking at her. She looked proper and even somewhat homely in the gray dress Mrs. Smithers had given her for her questioning at the factory. She also wore a bonnet—not as jaunty as her flower-adorned little hat in London, but suitable for a lady.

"I'd like to wash," she said, somewhat sheepishly, to Michael. "Could you . . ."

Michael immediately withdrew outside. Lizzie wondered if he held a grudge against her for something. He could not really hold it against her that she had stolen from David Parsley. And the circumstances . . . Lizzie blushed a bit. Why was it really so much worse to feign love than to steal boats and make moonshine?

While Lizzie felt halfway safe in their cabin, Michael strolled nervously across the ship's deck. He should have asked what exactly had happened to Mr. Parsley. Had Lizzie really only gotten him drunk? What if he awoke early? They could not be caught now—he would die of shame, having profited from Lizzie's betrayals and then been found out anyway. This would be the most embarrassing escape attempt since one of the convicts in Hobart had the idea of dressing as a kangaroo and trying to hop away.

Yet Michael's fears did not come to pass. The *Elizabeth Campbell* weighed anchor punctually at seven, and the skipper steered it safely out of Hobart's natural harbor and out to the high seas. Michael's heart beat heavily with joy when, after a short time, the land disappeared from view. How would he have felt if he were sailing a stolen boat with Dylan, Will, and Connor now? Twenty days. After Lizzie had revealed the general voyage length, it became clear to him what kind of adventure he had planned to undertake. He had to admit that Lizzie had been right. This was the only way to escape to New Zealand without danger to life and limb, and the realization of this improved his attitude somewhat.

He returned to their luxury cabin. Lizzie sat at the porthole looking toward the strange land she had lived in for a year but had never really gotten to know.

"Now I'll never see a Tasmanian devil." Lizzie turned to Michael and smiled. Apparently, she held nothing against him. And her smile was captivating. Gentle and warm, it enchanted her unassuming face and dark-blonde hair. Moreover, she had scrubbed herself clean. Her skin shone; a wet sheen lay on her lips.

Michael suddenly became aware that he had not held a woman in his arms in a long time. He smiled back. "I could show you an Irish devil," he said suggestively as he sat down next to her.

Lizzie moved away from him nervously.

"Lizzie, I, I don't have anything I could give you." Michael's voice sounded pleading. "But I, look, we'll be living here for three weeks. Lying beside each other like man and wife."

"Or brother and sister," Lizzie said, amused. It had been good to have patience. At first he might not have understood, but now—now, he was making an effort to declare himself.

"Lizzie, have mercy. I can't! I'm a man, and I haven't had a woman in so long. Would you, could you see . . . Please, Lizzie, share the bed with me!"

Now it was out. Michael looked at her imploringly. His eyes no longer shone; now they burned.

Lizzie smiled, then allowed him to embrace her.

Michael had learned the art of love in Miss Daisy's brothel in Wicklow—and if the women there did it for free, they wanted to get something out of it. Daisy had personally instructed him, and he had enjoyed every moment with the older woman. Later, he had given Kathleen pleasure with his slow, tender lovemaking, and he would not disappoint Lizzie now either.

Lizzie, who had always associated physical love with pain or, at best, indifference, had until then been convinced she could never enjoy it. Men needed it, while women basked in amiable words, gentle kisses—and above all, the hope that men would protect them and make them a home. Lust had always been strange to Lizzie before, whatever Mrs. Smithers and others believed.

But that first day on the ship to New Zealand, Michael aroused sensations that she had not even known existed. He stroked and kissed parts of her body she had not bared to her customers, and when he pressed into her, he did so slowly and gently, as if he were approaching a virgin. At some point, Lizzie forgot everything around her. She no longer knew where her body ended and his began. Finally, she arched up beneath him, digging her nails into his back with lust, pressing her face against his throat and his strong chest.

"Michael," she whispered. "Michael."

Michael nestled his face into her breasts, breathing in her scent. "Kathleen," he said quietly.

With that, something died inside Lizzie. She lay quietly, not bothering him—trying, though she knew better, to hold on to some magic. Michael caught his breath at some point. He propped himself up beside her and playfully stroked her breasts and stomach.

"That was wonderful," he said softly. "I can't thank you enough. Lizzie, you're, you're such a good person."

Lizzie did not say a word. That night she slept for the first time next to the man she loved. But she cried herself to sleep.

Strength

Nelson, Kaikoura, Canterbury Plains
1850–1858

Chapter 1

Lizzie and Michael spent twenty-two untroubled days on the *Elizabeth Campbell*. They shared the bed in their luxury cabin at night, and during the day, people treated them like a married couple. Only a few passengers were traveling on the small ship, a fact that unsettled Michael.

"They'll all remember us precisely when the soldiers come looking for us," he said. "We'll have to leave the city we land in—what was it called again? Nelson?—right away."

"Their investigation won't go that quickly," Lizzie said. "As for descriptions of us, we didn't hide our faces in Van Diemen's Land either. But who's going to look for us? Naturally, the Australian officials will inform the police in New Zealand, such as they are. That won't happen right away. And you don't really believe that the New Zealand authorities are going to spend all their energy on finding two escapees among thousands of free settlers, do you? I think we'll be able to look around at ease."

Lizzie feigned calm, but in truth, the thought of arriving in Nelson filled her with increasing dread. It had less to do with the fear of discovery and arrest and more to do with the end of forced cohabitation with Michael. Lizzie did not know what Michael had planned for this new country, but she sensed that his plans did not include her.

Regardless, her first look at Nelson, a new but already almost city-like settlement on the northern tip of the South Island, announced the breathtaking beauty of her new homeland. As the ship entered Nelson's natural harbor, the area glistened in the sunlight. There were beaches, green hills, and prim little wooden houses. Mountains rose up behind the harbor.

"And palm trees!" Lizzie cried as the ship came closer to land. "Michael, have you ever seen a palm tree before? It must be warm here. Oh, I love it, Michael. Shouldn't we just stay here?" In her euphoria, Lizzie spontaneously nestled against the man beside her.

But Michael rebuffed her. "Stay here? Are you mad, Lizzie? We're not coming as settlers, you know, we're—"

"We're what?" She did not at all want to ask questions, but the time had come. Even if it hurt, she had to know what to expect. "Naturally, we could leave this town as quickly as possible. But you don't really believe you'll make it off this island, do you?"

Michael laughed, a little forcedly. He turned his gaze from Nelson and looked almost longingly at the sea.

"Of course I do," he said with total confidence. "I'll stay here just long enough to earn the money for passage. Then it's farewell, New Zealand. Home calls."

Lizzie held tight to the railing to keep herself from shaking Michael. "You want to go back to Ireland? You can't be serious. They'll arrest you on the spot and send you on the next ship back to Van Diemen's Land."

Michael shook his head. "Nonsense. I have friends in Ireland. I'll go into hiding. And it won't be for long anyway. I'll fetch Kathleen and the baby, and then we'll leave."

Lizzie swallowed. "Michael, what you call a baby is more than two years old by now. You haven't heard anything from Kathleen. You don't know where she is. Or if she might have married."

"Mary Kathleen? My Mary Kathleen?" Michael shouted angrily. "I told her I'd come back. I swore to her I'd come, and she knows I will. Kathleen's waiting for me. I'm sure of it." He ran a hand through his thick, dark hair, which was tousled by the wind.

"And where is she waiting?" Dear God, they might part in anger, but it had to be possible to make him see straight. "In your village? Do you think her parents were so eager to keep feeding her? Her and her bastard?"

"Well, perhaps she isn't in the village," Michael said. "Perhaps she lives in a big city like Dublin, and"—a light shone in his face—"perhaps she's even gone on to America. I gave her the money to go. Maybe she's there."

"Walking down to the shore every day to watch for your arrival?" Lizzie mocked him. "I don't know anything about America, Michael, but they send a lot of ships there from London. One departs every week or so, most of them filled with hundreds of people. So I take it it's a big country. How do you mean to find her? And how is she supposed to make a living for her child? Heavens, Michael. It's not that simple for women."

Michael spun around. "What do you mean by that? That Mary Kathleen might have lowered herself? That she could be like you?"

Michael's words revealed all of his disdain for fallen women. Lizzie turned away, but then rage welled up within her, and once more, she faced him.

"Of course not! Absolutely unthinkable! Mary Kathleen is far too holy to spread her legs for a bite of bread. I don't doubt she'd rather die. Maybe she's already thrown herself in the sea with her bastard and her shame. Often enough that's the only choice a woman has, Michael: whore yourself or starve. Sorry I've been too cowardly for the second. Though it's all the same when it comes to damnation: whoring and suicide. God sends both types of sinners to hell. Only Michael Drury makes a distinction. How can you live with yourself knowing my whore money bought your freedom?"

Lizzie ran to their cabin and quickly retrieved her few possessions. Michael could keep David Parsley's clothes and travel bag. From under the mattress, she pulled out Mr. Parsley's wallet. There was not much left, but half of the remaining ten shillings belonged to her. *Half?* Defiantly, Lizzie took every penny. She had worked for it. And Michael still held that against her. Damn it all, if only he had paid her for every bit of pleasure she had granted him on the voyage.

She put on her hat and ran down the gangplank to the pier of the placid little harbor. Michael, she would have to forget. It was time for a new beginning. Somewhere in this lovely country, in which the air seemed clearer than Lizzie had ever thought possible, there had to be a place for her. She would look for employment, and perhaps she would finally make her life pleasing to God.

Lizzie strolled down the new, clean streets of Nelson and felt her anger abate. She hoped it would be replaced with courage and optimism, but in truth, there was only an endless sadness. However Michael had treated her, she had loved him. And now she would probably never see him again.

***

Michael was upset when he disembarked a short time later. Angry, on the one hand—he had noticed the missing money—confused on the other. His fight with Lizzie weighed on his heart. After all, he couldn't dismiss everything she had said about Kathleen. Naturally, Kathleen would never lower herself to whoring or thievery. Of course she would wait for him. But indeed, it might be difficult to track her down.

He could not let the matter go as he roamed Nelson's streets, though he had other, more urgent, problems. Where, for instance, could he earn enough money for his next meal? Still, that paled in comparison to how he might find Kathleen, wherever she was hiding.

Father O'Brien. The priest would surely know where Kathleen was. Michael only needed to write to him and inquire. First, though, he needed an address to which Father O'Brien could send his reply.

Michael sighed and finally began to look around. Damn, this Nelson place had the most spick-and-span harbor he had ever seen. Everything looked tidy and navigable. But still, it was a port. Michael Drury, or rather David Parsley, could not be the only man stranded in town without any money or future. He entered the nearest tavern, put on a winning smile, and looked over the barkeeper behind the counter and the drunkards in front of it.

"Well met, lads! Anything I can do here to earn a beer? Just got in from Australia and my girl stole my money."

The barkeeper boomed with laughter, and one of the drunks made room for Michael. He waved for a glass. A few hours later, in the tavern yard, Michael slept off his first night of drinking in this new land. The next morning he made his way to what would be his new workplace.

"Go south to Kaikoura," one of the men had advised. "There's a whaling station, Waiopuka. There's always work there for a good lad, and no one asks for papers."

"But I'm not a sailor," Michael said.

The man shrugged. "Doesn't matter. They haul the critters onto land."

***

Lizzie wandered Nelson's right-angled streets, in a rush from her recovered freedom. She had hated her life in London, but now and again, there had been wonderful little moments. She remembered sunny days when a kind customer had handed her a few shillings and she was able to stroll through the market streets admiring a display or trying on a hat. In those times, she had been the happy, innocent young girl whose life she always imagined.

She had missed that these last couple of years. In Van Diemen's Land, everyone had known who she was, and she had not even had a penny to her name. Thus, she felt all the richer now as she entered a tearoom in one of the whitewashed wooden houses adorned with bays and balconies. Lizzie sat, smiled at the server, and ordered tea and rolls. She felt confident enough that she almost succumbed to the temptation of asking about employment. But Michael was right: it would be madness to settle straight away in Nelson. And madder still to work in a tearoom into which someone like David Parsley could walk as soon as he finally got to New Zealand . . .

Lizzie almost had to laugh. If she spent a few more hours in this carefree spirit, she would soon come to view her life as an adventure. But it was not, and Lizzie forced herself to think seriously. Her money would not last long; she needed to do something.

"Pardon me, might I ask you something?" She turned with a shy but heartwarming smile to the server. "I had hoped to reunite with an old family friend, from my village back in England. He arrived two years ago and wrote to us, but I forget the name of the town he settled in. Something near Nelson, I know that much. Not in the city itself. Are there other settlements nearby?"

The young woman shrugged. "Settlers have been arriving in Nelson for ten years now, miss. Few stay, though. There's not much to be done here. They spread out all over the area—to the villages and farms. The next-biggest town would be Sarau. But there it's almost all Germans."

Germans? Lizzie wondered, but the heritage of her future fellow citizens did not really matter. She had to improvise now. "Now that you mention it, my friend wrote us something about German settlers. And Sarau, yes, that could be it. How do I get there from here?"

"The gentleman over there comes from the area." The woman gestured at a tall, heavy man with thick brown hair and a wide, weathered face. He was sitting in the corner of the tearoom, thoughtfully shoveling meat pies and sweet potatoes into his mouth. He was drinking coffee with his meal. "Just ask him if he knows your friend. Perhaps he can take you as well. He's quite nice. Comes by whenever he has business in town."

Lizzie chewed on her lip. "But I can't simply sit across from him. What would he think of me?"

The server smiled. "I'll talk to him for you."

A short time later, Lizzie was curtsying politely before Otto Laderer, a farmer from Sarau.

"There are English in area. But stay with themselves, like we too," he said in hard, somewhat broken English. "So, can be, your friend there is. Can ride with and look if you want."

Lizzie thanked him courteously and waited until Laderer had finished his meal, then climbed onto his wagon, which was pulled by two powerful horses. Laderer had bought wood and tools in Nelson, and a few supplies like coffee and tea. Not much though.

"We farm with dairy cows, pigs, chickens. And fields. Feeds itself," Laderer explained when Lizzie asked him about his farm.

Lizzie was fascinated. She had never been in the country before, and the thought of being able to sate one's hunger with produce from one's own fields seemed paradisiacal.

"Is Sarau a pretty place?" she inquired. "You see, really, really I'm supposed to have come to marry my friend." Lizzie was becoming intoxicated by her story, which was taking on a life of its own. "But if I don't find him? And well, anyway, I don't find the idea of marrying somebody I haven't seen in ten years very appealing."

The big German gave her a quick sidelong glance. "Will be fine," he muttered.

Lizzie offered him a sweet smile. "Maybe. Well. But if not, do you think I could find employment in Sarau? I'm a maid. I worked for a very fine family."

"No fine families in Sarau," the farmer informed her. "But work. Much work. If you want, I take you as maid. Food and clothing, a pound a week. But hard work."

Lizzie nodded. "I'm used to it," she declared, self-assured. Even in Campbell Town she had worked from sunup to sundown, after all.

The farmer gave her an appraising sidelong look. His eyes wandered over her petite figure, her narrow shoulders and hips. Lizzie was used to such looks, but she realized to her surprise that there was no lust there.

"Will see," he said and shook the horses' reins.

The team trotted through copses behind which the majestic view of the mountains became visible. Lizzie felt confident about the future.

***

Kaikoura lay more than a hundred miles from Nelson, but Michael's drinking buddy was a sailor, and he told him he'd ask his captain to give Michael a ride on his ship, which took train oil and whalebone to Europe. It had taken on some freight on the West Coast but would mainly be supplied in Kaikoura.

"Can't I just come along to England?" asked Michael, who could hardly believe his luck. "I'll make myself useful, I swear."

The vessel's very small crew did not need any more members, and the captain showed little interest in teaching a landlubber. He did agree to take Michael to Kaikoura, but he immediately made it clear that passage was not free.

"Old Fyfe'll pay your way when we get there," the captain said. "A big, strong lad like you, he'll be licking his chops. You'll have to work it off, of course. But not to worry."

Robert Fyfe was the founder and proprietor of the whaling station, and it did sound as if he were hungry for workers. In any case, the captain was willing, so Michael boarded a ship once again, leaving Nelson—and Lizzie Owens—behind without a second thought.

Kaikoura proved an idyllic peninsula separating two bays with beaches that were part rock and part sand. In one of these bays lay the whaling station, Waiopuka, which was dominated by a stately manor, its founder's house.

"Built on a foundation of whalebone," Michael's drinking buddy explained. "There's hardly any wood here, you see."

Indeed, even the tombstone crosses of the men who met their end in Kaikoura were made of whalebone. The bodies of the powerful sea creatures could be used in a number of ways, and their capture must have been profitable. Robert Fyfe, a wiry man with sparse red hair and skin weathered by wind and sea, readily advanced Michael the money for his voyage.

"You can build a shack up there," he instructed his new worker, pointing at a meager settlement past his house.

The whalers built their shacks from tree bark and fern branches. They hung doors and windows with tarpaulin or sackcloth to keep out the worst of the wind and rain. Michael's future neighbor, Chuck Eagle, invited him right away into his shack, which he had furnished only with a cobbled-together table and chair made of whalebone. It smelled beastly—apparently the bones had not been boiled long enough. Or did the stench emanate from Chuck and his clothing?

"You get used to it," Chuck said amicably when he noticed Michael crinkling his nose. He held out a bottle of whiskey, and Michael took a deep drink. "The fishies stink—especially if we don't get 'em on land right away. We try to keep 'em on the hook and pull 'em onto the beach, but sometimes the harpoons get loose, and then the body sinks down. Not so bad, really. It fills with gas, and after a few days, floats back up. But stinks something awful."

"On the hook?" asked Michael. "You hook these monster fish?"

He had never seen a whale, but the skeletons on the beach had given him an impression of what he had to expect.

Chuck laughed uproariously. "Nah, then we'd have to hunt the bait too. A sperm whale'd swallow a whole shark. No lie, the beasties gobble fishes more than twenty feet long. In one bite. Though they're not fish themselves, they say. 'Cause they feed their young like cows. Anyway, we hunt them with harpoons."

What that looked like, Michael saw the very next day. Which, according to Chuck, was a stroke of luck.

"We used to net one every week, but now they're getting careful. Or maybe the area's fished out; who knows? Sometimes it's bad for weeks, and then you don't make much either."

Earnings at the station were graduated. The harpooners, who had to fire their massive weapons as accurately as possible in order to weaken the whale with the first shot, received the most. The barbs had to bite deep into the whale's flesh. If they fell out, the contest was lost, as a rule. Wounded, the whale would submerge, surviving or perhaps dying who knows where. The beasts could cross monstrous distances when they swam, so there was no hope of finding the body if a whale survived a harpooning.

Yet if the shot landed right, the whale truly did hang "on the hook," so to speak. The harpoons trapped it on a long rope tied to the boat. The whale would pull the boat behind it as it fought for its life, a hellish ride that also justified the high pay for the six rowers and the helmsman. Boats were always flipping over, their occupants losing their lives in the water. The most skilled and bravest rowers and harpooners at Fyfe's station were uncommonly strong men with brown skin and dark, sleek hair, which they often wore tied in a sort of knot.

"Maori," said Chuck. "They came to New Zealand as settlers a few centuries before us whites."

Michael was surprised. Since there had been no "savages" in Van Diemen's Land for a long time, he had not expected any natives in New Zealand, either. The Maori at the whaling station did not seem particularly savage, however. They were actually quite approachable, once one had gotten used to the tribal symbols tattooed on their faces. They wore the same work clothes as the white whalers: loose shirts, linen pants, and wide hats. They also spoke English—not perfectly but comprehensibly. They laughed at the same jokes as the whites, or at least pretended they understood the innuendos, and they did not say no when a bottle of whiskey made the rounds. However, they did not live in the provisional shacks at the station but at night went home to their village—a walled settlement consisting of wooden houses decorated with complicated carvings.

"They all sleep in one room," Eagle told a stunned Michael. "The girls too."

The Maori girls were not particularly lovely by English standards of beauty. Like the men, they were of stocky build and, even as young women, often plump. Their faces were also tattooed, which revolted Michael at first. Yet they were friendly and exceedingly sexually free. They often went topless in the warm weather, walking around the village or staging dances with their breasts swinging, and slept with any man they liked. Apparently, no one checked on whether a girl was sneaking out of the sleeping lodge at night.

"And they don't even want anything for it," Chuck said excitedly. "Although, naturally, they're happy if you give them some trinket. Strange customs, but very pleasant."

Michael did not think of girls at first. After he slaughtered a whale for the first time, he had no desire for company, really for anything but a great deal of soap and water—and a bottle of whiskey in order to forget it all. Michael was not yet allowed on a boat.

"Have to see if you can row first," said Fyfe.

Michael, who was after increased pay, did not reveal to him that he had never done it before. He was sure that after years of forced labor in chains, he could muster the strength for it without a problem.

Fyfe seemed able to read the lie on his face, however. "Well, watch for now and help cut up the whale. Then we'll see."

Michael watched from the shore as the whale dragged the harpooners' boat behind it. Once it tired, the helmsman shoved a lance into its body—leaving scarcely enough life in the whale that it remained just under or just above the water. Then the boat dragged the whale ashore, and the men began to eviscerate it.

"It's not dead yet," Michael shouted. He was horrified as the first knives were stuck into the massive body to remove the layer of fat beneath the skin.

"Less chatter, more work," Eagle instructed him.

The body had to be dismembered, and Michael tried not to look toward the animal's eyes as he stuck his own wide knife into its flesh. The fat was white-gray, slippery, and disgusting. Michael did not want to touch it. He preferred to operate the winches that transported the pieces of fat to the kettles, where they were boiled down.

The yellowish fluid was then poured out of the kettles and into barrels. One whale yielded up to twenty barrels, and they fetched a good price. In the meantime, the butchers had made it down to the bones and were separating them from the meat. The men divided the bones and told Michael and a few others to bury them in the sand.

"Then they won't smell as bad while the meat rots," Chuck explained.

Though Michael wondered how much difference it would make, he dug energetically. In a few weeks, they would dig the bones out again and sell them. Ladies' corsets were made with them in England, and the light, flexible, yet sturdy material was also used for hooks and in the suspensions for coaches.

Michael found the slaughtering disgusting. He also did not want to eat any of the whale meat, which the men cooked in the same kettles they had used for the blubber. He was happy when they finally opened a water pipe through which the rest of the dismembered whale was washed back out to sea. It cleaned the beach, but even after a thorough bathing Michael thought himself foul-smelling and soiled. Fyfe kept half Michael's pay as a first payment for his passage; Michael drank away the other half.

"Eh, you don't make much on land," Chuck comforted him, thinking his mood was a result of the paltry and quickly liquidated pay. "Next time, you'll row with us; then you'll make more."

A few days later the next whale emerged, and by then, Michael had figured out the rudiments of rowing. Tane, one of the strong Maori men, sat beside him and offered instruction.

"We've always done," he said amicably when Michael had some difficulty at first. "We came in canoes—many, many lives ago. My family come with Aotea, great, proud canoe."

"You came here in a rowboat?" Michael asked, taken aback. "From where?"

On his trip to Kaikoura he had thought more kindly of Lizzie Owens, as he did again now during his first attempt at rowing. What would have happened if she had not taken the initiative and instead had let him set out with his comrades did not bear thinking about. Even the little assistance he had been allowed to offer on the boat had shown him how hard it was to maneuver a sailing ship. And that was just the Tasman Sea.

"From Hawaiki, land we come from. Far, far away. Kupe, first man in Aotearoa—what we call this island—killed husband of Kura-maro-tini. Was very beautiful woman. Then fled with her here."

"That was a while ago though, right?" Michael asked Chuck Eagle later.

He laughed. "Six hundred years. But anyway. They're settlers too. The land belongs to them same as to us. And besides, they take a good bit of money when they sell us some of it."

Chuck was saving for his own bit of land. He dreamed of a farm, but it wasn't clear whether he'd done any farming in England. Probably he had gone to sea instead, but Michael did not ask. Except for the Maori, everyone there was running from something.

The Maori were also the ones who coped best with the gruesome work. Tane muttered a sort of invocation in his language as he crouched down next to Michael in the boat the next time they went whaling. The harpooner had just pulled the trigger, and the hooks dug into the flank of an imposing sperm whale.

"Telling sorry to Tangaroa, god of sea," Tane explained. "Sorry that we kill and thanks for sending us whale. And ask for help with hunt."

While the Maori was still talking, the struck whale tossed about. For Michael and the others, the hellish ride began. As the whale shot back and forth in a panic to free itself of the harpoon, it wrenched the rowboat behind it. Water soaked the men. Michael swallowed a swell of the salty drink in fright. When the boat threatened to capsize, he was sure he would soon die. Tane and the others tried through skillful use of oars and their weight on the benches to maintain balance, but Michael could no longer even think.

In the end, the whale exhausted itself in the water—and Michael vomited over the side of the boat when the helmsman stabbed his lance into the helpless animal. When they began to row again, Michael felt as if the dying whale's eyes were following him. Surely it was an illusion. He did not look at them to convince himself, but the whale's silent accusation did not let go.

Michael had caught fish and hunted rabbits before. He'd trapped little animals and broken their necks. In times of starvation, one ate what one could get, so Michael had never felt guilty. But this was something else. This was merciless slaughter for goods that, strictly speaking, no one needed. England would survive without whalebone and train oil, no matter what price it all fetched. Michael was firmly convinced that Tane's prayer had not been heard. The god of the sea could not forgive this.

That evening Michael drank the memory away—for which he needed far more whiskey than usual. The other men ate the whale meat, unbothered by the killing and seeming not even to perceive the stench around them. Michael never wanted to ride along in the rowboats again, and by no means was he eager to take the post of helmsman or harpooner. He silently bore the laughter of the men, who teased him for having gotten scared and sick, and he considered how he could get away from the whaling station as quickly as possible. He had to work off his debt. But to stay until he had earned enough for passage to Ireland? Unimaginable.

Chapter 2

Never before had Lizzie been as close to a righteous life than as a maid at the Laderers' farm in Sarau. Their farm lay just outside the little village in the Marlborough region at the edge of the Waimea Plain. The earth was fruitful, and the settlers showed their gratitude for that—especially since their first few years in the new country had not been blessed with good fortune. Closer to Nelson, there was little farmland and, worse yet, they had been plagued there with flooding.

But Otto Laderer was not frightened by these setbacks. After first settling in Nelson, he had risked a second new beginning here in Sarau. He was always clearing more land, and his cattle breeding flourished as well. His wife, Margarete, a strong, sturdy woman, worked just as hard as he, as did his two sons. Neither their father nor the two sons, for whom wives had already been found, regarded Lizzie lustfully.

The Laderers began their work before dawn and went to bed when it was dark. They expected the same of Lizzie. The work was hard, but the meals were regular and ample, and she was paid on time at the end of each month.

The Laderers called their new maid Liese or Lieschen and did not even ask for her last name. "How could come from England with only one dress?" was the only question Mrs. Laderer ever asked Lizzie. She seemed not to care at all about Lizzie's previous life.

Lizzie might have been quite content to stay a while and save money, but she found little joy in her work, which was all the worse since it seemed that work was all she did. Lizzie was not lazy. Her skill as a house and kitchen maid had always earned praise. The Laderers, however, needed a milkmaid.

Lizzie was supposed to collect eggs and help slaughter animals, which she struggled to do. Cleaning out the barn bothered her less, except that pushing wheelbarrows full of heavy cow manure to the compost pile made her bone-tired. Then there was the milking, feeding, and herding of the cows and horses. Lizzie didn't trust the big animals and nearly died of fright when a cow so much as lifted a leg during milking or turned to look at her.

Lizzie had more skill with plants than animals, so she had better luck with the field work and the kitchen garden. On Sundays she often pulled flowers in the forest and planted them in the garden to beautify it.

"What it does, this flower bush?" Mrs. Laderer asked when she saw the garden. "You could plant an apple tree."

The Laderers, in general, declined anything that was not useful or yielded no produce. Lizzie caught herself missing the Smithers house—the beautiful furniture, the tea parties, the flowers in vases, the rose garden. She had been able to dream herself into a lovelier life, no matter how dirty and fretful reality was. With the Laderers, she had nothing to fear, but there were also no dreams and nothing she could look forward to. She also missed her own language. Neither the Laderers nor their neighbors spoke English more than they absolutely needed to—and in truth, they used their own language rather sparingly. The Lower Saxons were rather curt, and Lizzie never really warmed to them.

So Lizzie was particularly cheered when, after four months, Margarete Laderer asked her to help in the house one afternoon.

"You said you were in a fine house," she said. "Today comes a fine Englishman, the British Resident and a councillor of the Bay of Islands."

Lizzie knew nothing about the Bay of Islands, but a councillor sounded important to her.

"On visit wants he to speak with someone who can English, so Otto."

Otto Laderer did indeed speak better English than most of the settlers.

"Surely drinks he tea. You make tea, or?"

"Can I make tea? Oh yes," Lizzie said with a smile. "I can serve it too. Oh, please, Mrs. Laderer, let me set the table and serve it properly. Like fine people do. Please."

"We are good people, not fine," said Mrs. Laderer, but she didn't resist.

Lizzie took a look at the pantry and fished out the tablecloth the Laderers only used on the most important holidays. With great enthusiasm, she set the table with the Laderers' fine tablecloth, folded napkins, and cut rata blossoms, which she arranged beautifully. The farmers only drank coffee, so she had no luck finding a proper teapot, but they owned a handsome earthen coffee set, blue with white dots, from which tea would surely also taste good. Lizzie prepared everything and then put on her dress with a white apron over it. She was only missing a bonnet to make her maid's uniform complete. Lizzie shook off an uneasy feeling as she looked at herself in the Laderers' tiny mirror. She hoped the councillor did not have the same perverse tendencies as Mr. Smithers and would appreciate her work, not her appearance.

When she heard voices welcoming the councillor, she went to the door, curtsied, and took the cape that had protected the tall, slender man from the light rain. He smiled amicably and gave her his tall hat as well. Then he followed Mr. Laderer into the living room, where Mrs. Laderer waited.

"James Busby." With a perfectly executed bow, the guest introduced himself to the woman of the house, who seemed unsure of how to reply. She somewhat awkwardly invited Mr. Busby to sit, and Lizzie brought out the tea after letting it steep exactly three minutes. She positioned herself to the right of the guest, asked politely about milk and sugar, and curtsied when the man thanked her.

Otto Laderer and his wife both looked at her, awestruck, and Lizzie struggled to maintain a solicitous face instead of beaming. Finally, she was making an impression on her masters.

"I heard that a few of the German settlers here in the Marlborough region know a thing or two about viniculture," Mr. Busby said after exchanging a few words with Otto. "They needn't be experts, you know; I'd be managing them. But a bit of experience would not be bad. Our native workers have no knack for it, you see. They've never drunk wine before, and when you let them taste it, they don't like it!"

Mr. Busby said this with a horrified expression, as if the Maori had blasphemed against his god, but the Laderers did not react. Lizzie thought it completely possible that they had never tried a sip of wine either. They drank little, and when they did, it was usually homemade schnapps. Lizzie thought it very tasty but rather strong.

"We make no wine," Laderer said. "Maybe the Bavarians. But I believe not. They prefer beer."

"You don't have any vineyards here either," said Busby, as if anyone who had tasted wine and understood something about its manufacture would certainly plant grapes. "Well, there's nothing to be done. Forgive me for taking up so much of your time." Then Busby looked at Mrs. Laderer and Lizzie and smiled. "And thank you for the tea. It was excellent."

"Would you like another cup?" Lizzie asked.

Really, Mrs. Laderer should have asked this question, but Lizzie couldn't resist the opportunity.

Busby declined the tea but arched his eyebrows in surprise. "You're English, dear child?" he asked amicably.

Lizzie nodded and curtsied again.

"And excellently trained. My compliments, Mr. Laderer. It's a rare thing here. In the larger towns, there's talk of recruiting English servants from the orphanages in London. Especially here on the South Island, where there aren't as many natives available—even if they are more compliant than the natives in the north. You've really had a stroke of luck with your girl. Where do you come from, child?"

Lizzie considered whether she should lie. But he was a Scottish man, and if he knew even a little about England, her accent would tell him where she was from.

"From London, sir," she answered. "Whitechapel."

Busby smiled. "But not one of the ingenuous orphanage imports, I take it. A strange idea, skimming the scum off to here."

Lizzie blushed. "No, my, my father was a carpenter."

Anna Portland's husband had been a carpenter.

"Very good. As I said, you're lucky, Mr. Laderer. I couldn't acquire her from you, could I?" Busby turned to Mr. Laderer with a smile that made it seem as if his question wasn't a serious one.

Otto Laderer pursed his lips. "Acqu—?"

"Acquire. It means . . . Mr. Busby would like me to work for him," Lizzie said.

She was being impertinent again, but Lizzie could not keep it inside. Busby seemed to assume that she belonged to the Laderers, body and soul, and that they were happy with their housemaid. But if she could set him straight . . .

"Liese is milkmaid by us," Mrs. Laderer said.

Mr. Busby looked at Lizzie. He had sharp, piercing eyes. "Milkmaid. Is that true Lie . . . ?" The name obviously presented difficulties for him.

Lizzie curtsied. "Elizabeth, sir. Lizzie."

"And your family name, child?" Busby asked.

Lizzie breathed deeply. Now, no mistakes. "Portland, sir. Elizabeth Portland. And yes, it's true. I primarily work in the barn. Here, they don't much need a housemaid." Lizzie tried to express herself such that Mr. and Mrs. Laderer would understand her too.

"But then why don't you seek employment elsewhere? In Nelson or Christchurch or on the large farms. People would lick their chops for you. Doubtless you have letters of recommendation."

Lizzie needed a good story. One that explained why she had no papers and no recommendations. She bit her lip. Best would be a story as true as possible. It need not be her own story, but it shouldn't be the kind you would think up on the spot either. She cursed her lack of foresight. After all, her boring months in Sarau had given her plenty of time to think something up.

"Mr. and Mrs. Laderer were good to me when I came from Australia," she said, then lowered her gaze. "They did not ask me, and I, I would have been ashamed to tell them everything."

Busby smiled. "Australia? But you can't be a convict?" He wagged his finger playfully at Lizzie.

Lizzie looked at him, pained. "Not I, sir, but my mother. Anna Portland. In London . . . well, in London everyone heard about the case, and my employers there no longer wanted to keep me. Then I thought I could join my mother if I went to Australia. My inheritance from my father just sufficed. But . . . I couldn't find her."

Though the Laderers listened with interest, they surely only understood half of what Lizzie said as she stuttered out the tragedy of Anna Portland to the councillor. He could easily convince himself of the story's truth with a letter to London—or disprove her story with an even quicker letter to Australia about escaped female convicts.

At the end of her story, Busby was visibly touched. "Naturally, I'll have that looked into, Elizabeth. But as it stands, if your masters here will let you go, I'd gladly take you with me to Waitangi. It's on the North Island, so I hope you don't get seasick."

***

The Laderers let their ill-suited milkmaid go easily, and James Busby informed all of the many acquaintances they met on their journey back to the North Island that his wife would finally be happy with him.

"Usually, I only bring grapes back. When, instead, she gets an English housemaid, she won't be able to contain her joy."

It was quite clear to Lizzie that Mr. Busby was devoted to his wife and six children. Even during their long journey together, the wine connoisseur and politician did not get too close to his new employee. Lizzie found it difficult to form an opinion of him. Busby had fixed convictions and opinions for which he was willing to fight. On the way to Waitangi, an area on the far edge of the North Island, they often entered the houses of his political friends and foes, and occasionally Busby and his hosts had heated discussions. Lizzie heard again and again that her new master was wrong-headed—but on the other hand, he was highly respected and must have been something of a good diplomat.

As Busby told Lizzie, he had worked out the famous Treaty of Waitangi, in which the chieftains of thirty-four Maori tribes pledged themselves to the Crown without a fight. True, William Hobson had received more fame for it, but Busby had represented the British interests in New Zealand long before him. Now, as a councillor of the Bay of Islands, he functioned as a sort of advisor for the Waitangi region.

The bays and islands of this region were sparsely settled, and the Maori long since Christianized and assimilated. At the beginning of the century, missionaries had settled the area, rather than whalers and seal hunters as in the rest of New Zealand.

No one actually wanted advice from Busby. He had burned too many bridges among the settlers and missionaries for that. He seemed to get along best with the Maori, but they didn't need a councillor either. Thus, Busby found plenty of time for his own interests. One of these was viniculture, but Busby also published a newspaper and tried his hand at trading and farming. Above all, he liked to see himself as a teacher, at least as long as his students never talked back. He had taught agriculture and viniculture in Australia and seemed to miss it sometimes.

Busby knew New Zealand well and entertained the knowledge-hungry Lizzie with information about its flora and fauna. She marveled at forests of ferns and strange birds that dug holes. She learned everything about sheep husbandry—wherein Busby primarily saw the future of the South Island—and more all the time about viniculture. Busby was trying his luck with a vineyard near Waitangi, so far without much success.

Nelson and Sarau could not compare to the terrain around Waitangi. The natural beauty on the North Island stunned Lizzie. The deep-blue bays with their little rocky islands, the fern forest with its impenetrable green, and the mountains whose color changed with the angle of the sun—she had always pictured paradise like this.

***

With the Busbys, on the North Island, Lizzie felt she finally achieved her righteous and satisfying life. Agnes Busby managed a grand, open house and was truly happy about her new housemaid. She only had Maori servants and maids otherwise but spoke not a word of their language. Either someone had to translate, or she mimed to make herself clear. Neither proved satisfactory.

Mrs. Busby loved beautiful things and would gladly have managed her house like a British country manor. She had grown up in New South Wales but came from a noble family. Alas, neither her husband nor the Maori servants were interested in the waxing and polishing of the heavy furniture or the proper hanging of the velvet drapes. No one brushed Mrs. Busby's riding dresses properly or ironed the lace on her clothing. Lizzie had learned most of this from Mrs. Smithers, and she shared her new mistress's joy in well-kept rooms and stylish house management. Lizzie also enjoyed caring for the Busbys' children, and she gladly took them off the hands of the Maori girls, who were loving but overtaxed by the British style of raising children.

Overall, the Maori were friendly and skillful—they just required certain accommodations. Though Mrs. Busby had a limited view of them, Lizzie quickly realized, much to her surprise, that there were more similarities than differences between the Maori and the English. She had never seen a dark-skinned person in England, and the representations of savages in the Australian reverend's sermons had led her to picture beings that weren't quite human. The strong, tattooed people with their strange hairstyles and habit of running around half naked would almost have confirmed this for Lizzie, but then she noticed that girls conversed with each other, giggled, and joked, just as Lizzie had once done with friends. Although Mrs. Busby didn't speak with Maori in their language, the Busby children picked up the language of their caregivers, and they understood the Maori just as they did their own people.

When Lizzie interacted with the Maori, she did not mime, nor did she adopt Mrs. Busby's unpleasant tendency simply to speak English louder and louder. Instead, she asked anyone who knew enough of both languages for the Maori words, and in that way began to learn it herself. After a few months, she could laugh along with the scullery maid, Ruiha, about how there was simply no Maori word for "buffet" or "calling card."

She learned that all the foreign customs of the Maori had their own significance: the dances and cries that had scared her at first were often merely greeting rituals, and the tattoos designated people's tribal loyalties. Ruiha and the other servants soon invited Lizzie to their *marae*, and Lizzie admired the artistic woodcarvings on the Maori's meeting place and sleeping lodge.

There was something that completely surprised Lizzie: among the Maori it did not seem to be particularly important who was married to whom, and there was no such thing as a "woman of easy virtue." In the evenings, Ruiha would disappear with the gardener. The housemaid had a little boy whose father's identity was unknown. Paora, the stable boy, made open advances toward Lizzie, but he only laughed when she rebuffed him in a panic. At first, Lizzie feared that this would anger him enough that he might approach her with force, but then she realized that the members of the tribe were making fun of his rejection rather than her bristling behavior. As two of the Maori girls began to act out a parody of how one properly courted a *pakeha wahine*, Paora slunk away.

Lizzie's tension quickly disappeared, and she laughed as one of the actresses offered the other flowers and bowed repeatedly. The actress portraying the *pakeha* girl played coy for a while until she finally "surrendered" to her admirer, which the actress expressed in dance motions that seemed rather obscene to Lizzie's eyes. The other onlookers weren't embarrassed at all—they couldn't stop laughing when the lover tripped over his pants and did not seem to know whether he should take them off or keep them on for the act.

Later, Lizzie heard that Paora had disappeared with another girl while Lizzie returned, alone, to the house.

Mrs. Busby was of mixed minds about Lizzie's friendship with the Maori. Lizzie's ability to communicate with them made her life easier, but she didn't like her fraternizing with the natives. It seemed strange to her for a good English girl to do so.

Mr. Busby viewed the whole situation with satisfaction. He thoroughly respected the Maori, despite their lack of interest in wine. They simply did not understand that it mattered precisely when the grapes were gathered and whether the mash was fermented before or after it was pressed. They thought thinning out the grapes was a waste, so there was a lot of wine but none of it very rich.

Mr. Busby could discuss these problems for hours, but aside from one of his sons, Lizzie was the only other person interested in the particulars of wine manufacture. Busby imported wine for his table from the most diverse growing regions, and he let Lizzie taste the wines, just as he did his less enthusiastic family members. On Sundays he took Lizzie to the vineyard, ostensibly to lay out a picnic for the family, but really as an audience for his endless stories about the grapes. Sometimes, Lizzie asked him a question or two or even expressed her opinions about the winemaking, which delighted Busby.

"Goodness, you two could make me as jealous as a schoolgirl," said Mrs. Busby with a wink. Then she ducked contentedly under a parasol to read while her husband led Lizzie and the children among the grapevines to explain the importance of early harvesting and of pruning the vines.

For the first time in her life, Lizzie was almost unreservedly happy. She liked her work with the Busbys, and it fulfilled her. Naturally, she occasionally thought of Michael, the strange attraction he had exerted on her, and her unexpected bliss in his arms. In the end, he had hurt her, and she had suffered enough hurt. Lizzie did not want to mourn Michael, and she did not want to be disappointed and frightened anymore.

Summer and winter flew by, but she was still barely twenty-two years old. Lizzie needed a few years to learn to dream again, but she was confident that she would fall in love again. With a good man. Lizzie still believed in living a life pleasing to God, with children and a small house.

"We're looking for a vintner for our Lizzie," James Busby liked to joke when someone in the Busbys' large circle of acquaintances teased Lizzie for not having a fiancé. "What do you think, Lizzie? Should he be a smoldering-eyed Frenchman from Languedoc or a blond German with blue eyes?"

"A dark-haired man with blue eyes," Lizzie said. "But I fear they're all making moonshine in Ireland."

Chapter 3

Michael could not get used to killing and dismembering the whales, but the other jobs that presented themselves in Waiopuka were no more appealing. When he saw how seals were killed and skinned, he drank a whole bottle of whiskey to stop thinking about the little creatures' howls as they were beaten to death and the cries of their mothers. He would take whales over that, but since he never worked his way up to harpooner or helmsman, his pay remained meager—and he needed enough of that to drink himself a nicer life in the evening. It would take years for him to pay off his ship's passage from Nelson and be free—a gloomy outlook indeed.

It was two years of loveless work before an opportunity appeared. One day, the old sea dog, Robert Fyfe, ordered his men to build a pen next to his house. The wood for it came from the West Coast. Apparently, Fyfe was sparing nothing for his new project.

"What's he got brewing? Farming, livestock?" Michael asked his neighbor, Chuck Eagle.

Chuck shrugged his shoulders. "Maybe horses? I could see him doing that. No matter what, he has to start something new. The whales are staying away. Just one in the past month."

"It's winter," said Michael.

Chuck shook his head. "That hardly makes a difference. Besides, they're all males. It's always too cold here for the females. We used to hunt through-out the year, but now—well, the critters ain't fools. It took them a while, but they've figured out this area's trouble. Old Fyfe needs to either buy another ship or think of something else. And the seven seas don't call much to him anymore."

The residents of the new pens arrived a few days later, and Michael could hardly get enough of looking at them. Since he had left Ireland, he had hardly seen a sheep. And even in his old homeland, he had never seen such beautiful, well-fed examples as these three hundred animals now rushing into the enclosure in Fyfe's yard.

"Romney sheep—two rams, three hundred ewes," Fyfe declared proudly. "Look at the strength of those two fellows, Parsley."

The two rams attacked each other. Such small confines seemed to make them aggressive.

"I'd separate them before they kill each other," said Michael. "But truly beautiful animals. First-class quality. My respect."

"You know something about sheep, do you?"

Michael nodded. "A little," he said. "We had some. In the village I come from. Or, rather, the landlord had some. We tenants could feed at most two or three, then later, none. In the famine years, we ate the grass itself."

Fyfe laughed. Michael bit his lip.

"Then I guess I know who to turn to when there're problems," Fyfe said affably, but Michael hardly listened.

Fyfe was known for insisting on being right. As long as the whaling station had existed, he had never asked for advice. Even buying the first-class sheep was surely a stroke of luck. A livestock trader could just as easily have tricked him.

Michael did not think much more about the sheep for the next two weeks. Two mighty whales fell into the whalers' clutches, and Michael sank deep once again, first into blood and fat, then into whiskey.

One morning, four weeks after the arrival of the gorgeous Romney sheep, Captain Fyfe appeared at Michael's hut.

"Parsley? I, well, you know about sheep, you said."

Michael stumbled outside. The night before, he had once again drank his fill of whiskey.

"Better than whales, at least," he mumbled.

"Was that bragging, or is there something to it?"

Michael yawned and tried to collect himself. "I herded the landlord's sheep when I was a boy," he said. "After that, I was mostly in the field. I'm no shepherd, but I've picked things up along the way. All Ireland's full of sheep."

"Well," Fyfe said, "you sure can't know less than me. So come by and take a look at them. To me, they seem as if they're not all doing well. Mostly, they limp. I'd like to know why."

Michael cleaned himself up and walked over to the house. He was shocked by what he saw. The sheep's wool was matted and filthy, and the grassy ground of the pen had turned into a wasteland of mud. The hay for them to eat was wet and muddy, and several animals dragged their legs.

"And? Any idea?" asked Fyfe. Clearly, it did not please him to have lost hold of the reins.

Michael nodded. "Of course. The pen's too small. The ground's too wet and muddy."

"And that's why they're limping?"

Michael nodded again. "It's called foot rot," he said. "Hoof inflammation. Take a look." He went over to a sheep, flipped the protesting animal onto its back in one motion, and grabbed one of its hooves. "Here, it starts in the cleavage. Give it a smell. Stinks, don't it?"

Michael pointed to the ulcerous mass that had already formed in the cleavage, and the captain crinkled his nose. Michael, himself, did not think the stench of the foot rot nearly as sickening as the stink of rotting whales, but he marveled that Fyfe even had a sense of smell anymore.

"So what do you do?" Fyfe asked, revolted. "I'll be damned if the breeder didn't trick me."

Michael shook his head. "I don't think so. They were in top form when they first got here. It's from the mud—foot rot, like I said. It's a problem with the environment."

"So we need a bigger pasture, more wood. Will we be able to herd them back into it? And are they always going to limp?"

Michael smiled. "You can't fence off the pastureland for six to nine hundred sheep," he said. "And soon that's how many you'll have when these ladies lamb." He gestured at the ewes. "Let them graze freely. The hooves need to be properly trimmed. And get some copper sulfate from a pharmacist. We'll smear that on, or herd the sheep through a bath of it. Then it'll heal."

"Trim?" asked Fyfe, frustrated. "Trim something off their hooves? Can you do that? That is, without killing them?"

Michael laughed. "If you can get me a hoof cutter."

Robert Fyfe left right away for Kaikoura while Michael began caring for the hooves. Some of the other workers built a basin through which he could herd the animals to treat their inflammation. Two days later, additional wood arrived for more fences. Clearly Fyfe was determined to take the care and breeding of his sheep seriously.

The wet winter gave way to a no-less wet spring, and the new pens soon resembled the old when it came to the condition of the ground.

"You need to herd the sheep out," Michael advised once again.

"And if they don't come back?" Fyfe asked, concerned.

"Send a shepherd along," Michael advised. "One who likes to rove."

Fyfe snorted. "You'd like that," he scoffed. "Admit it: you're after the job. Looking at the scenery all day and pocketing money for it."

Michael shrugged. "If you leave the sheep here, you'll soon have to pay me to trim their hooves again."

And with that, Michael seized his opportunity. Fyfe had paid just as much for trimming the sheep's hooves as he did for harpooning a whale. Now, he was looking for the cheapest possible alternative.

"Can girls do it too? Shepherd, that is."

Michel laughed. "Anyone who's not blind or lame can," he said.

***

A few days later Michael took an evening stroll to look at the sheep but found the pens empty. Fyfe must have finally followed his advice. Michael wondered whom he had hired as shepherds and decided to ask the old sea dog right away. Fyfe was just then walking out of his manor and looking with suspicion at the hills behind the whaling station. Apparently, he was expecting his sheep.

The first of them could already be seen as Michael approached the captain. They were trotting down the hill, flanked by a few Maori girls.

"Took little longer to find all today," said the first to reach Fyfe. "Kere and Harata had to run far. And I climbed." The girl was clearly proud of herself and her friends.

"You didn't lose any animals, did you, Ani?"

The girl shook her head.

Michael had to laugh.

"What's so funny?" Fyfe asked.

"I'm just enjoying the lovely sight, sir," Michael said. He stole a glance at the slender, agile Ani, whose long black hair fluttered in the wind. "And I'm wondering why they use dogs to herd sheep in Ireland when girls look so much better. Although I'd wager the dogs are faster. Maybe that's why they've replaced the girls. After all, 'collie' comes from 'colleen.'"

Fyfe looked at him and furrowed his brow. "Dogs?" he asked. "That probably costs more money?"

The Maori girls understood more quickly. The next day, they brought two fat, yellowish-brown mutts along. The dogs waggled happily and greeted every person enthusiastically but did not take any interest in the sheep.

Fyfe sent for Michael. "Can you train them? To replace the girls?"

Michael tried, but the Maori dogs had no shepherding in them. Yet they found the whaling beach irresistible and rolled around in the remains of the slaughtered whales.

"If a sheep runs away from them, it'll only be because they smell so bad," Michael said.

Tane pursed his lips. "But they're dogs," he said.

Michael nodded. "Just not the right kind. Is there another sheep farm anywhere? Perhaps somewhere farther inland?"

Tane asked the members of his tribe and finally found something. The next weekend, Michael went with Tane and two other Maori boys, three of the eager shepherdesses, and two bitches in heat up the Clarence River. Michael sometimes had difficulty keeping up with the quick strides of the Maori, and roads rarely crossed the copses and scrubland through which the river flowed. Finally, though, they reached cleared land and pastures.

"Coverland Station," one of the Maori boys exclaimed. "House there." He pointed to the west and counted the miles off on his fingers.

Ultimately, Michael and the Maori camped about a mile away from the sheep farm's main house. Tane and the other boys caught fish in the river while Michael made a fire and the girls cooked sweet potatoes in the embers.

The dogs did their part. They disappeared during the night, and when they returned in the morning, a gorgeous long-nosed black-and-white collie followed them.

"That's the kind we want," Michael said contentedly, and enjoyed the next two days he spent fishing, hunting, and in the arms of the lovely Ani.

***

A few months later, the Maori village was crawling with puppies, all of which had more herding instinct than their mothers. Most of them were black and white, and some of them looked exactly like their father.

"We'll use them to keep breeding," Robert Fyfe cheered, happily paying Michael and the Maori a bonus.

Michael concentrated fully on training the dogs, and Fyfe reluctantly accepted him as a shepherd. After all, there were now much more demanding tasks than the herding of the animals: lambing and shearing. The former proved no great problem. The young Maori shepherdesses understood what they had to do after Michael showed them just once how to help the ewes when there were complications. The shearing was more difficult. Michael had done it a few times in Ireland and managed again, after a little practice, to produce acceptable fleece. But he was slow—shearing all three hundred, which would soon be around a thousand, was out of the question. Teaching the girls was no use. They lacked the strength to flip the sheep onto their backs and to use the shears efficiently.

Ani and her friends sheared two or three sheep and then stopped—as the Maori often did, without grand announcement or even excusing themselves. Yet Tane and the other Maori men soon proved willing. The number of whales continued to decline, but the Maori had gotten used to extra income from the *pakeha* and were no longer solely dependent on hunting, fishing, and the meager yields of their fields. They pushed for work on the farms, and almost all of them showed skill in handling animals. Shearing, though, was once again a challenge: it presented moral problems for Tane and his friends.

"Sheep don't want this," Tane said as Michael seized one of the animals and held it between his legs while he sheared it. The ram bleated in protest.

"Well, and?" Michael said, taken aback. "Whales don't want to be harpooned either. That hasn't stopped you so far."

"Whale something different," responded Tane. "With whales we call on Tangaroa before harpoon and ask forgiveness. Then whale forgive us."

Michael doubted that but shrugged his shoulders. "Fine, just ask him for forgiveness with the sheep too."

Tare shook his head. "Tangaroa, god of sea," he said. "Sheep not of sea. Sheep not from here at all. Came with *pakeha*."

Michael understood. In Aotearoa's pantheon, there simply was no one responsible for sheep. But there was a solution. Michael silently thanked Father O'Brien for his comprehensive teachings on the many saints in the Catholic Church.

"For us, St. Wendelin handles sheep," Michael told Tane. "We could all address a small prayer to him."

***

"Now we just need to get them to put a little effort into it," Michael said to Robert Fyfe and his cousin George, newly come to Waiopuka.

The time had come for shearing again. George Fyffe—he never neglected to point out that he spelled his name with a third *f*—had just taken possession of a piece of land north of Kaikoura and named it Mount Fyffe Run. He planned to raise sheep there in grand style.

"So far, they're hardly managing more than one or two sheep per day. What if we made a sort of contest out of it? The fastest shearer gets a bottle of whiskey?"

This arrangement soon proved its worth: Michael took home only the first bottle. After that, the skillful natives surpassed him. However, the problem had to be solved of when to say the prayer to St. Wendelin. So far Tane and his friends had been calling on the saint before the shearing of each sheep, but now they agreed to collectively ask for absolution before they started work each day. Because of this, George Fyffe and his foreman, Michael Parsley, soon gained a reputation as especially reputable and God-fearing men. After all, no other sheep farmer called his men to prayer before work.

***

While Michael made a name for himself, ultimately giving up his shack in Waiopuka to move into better accommodations in Mount Fyffe Run's barracks, a priest in Ireland was working through a difficult task.

Letters lay before Father O'Brien: a few from Kathleen Coltrane, who wrote about her children in, to his joy, an ever more fluent and lively style. And there was an awkward—but no less astounding—letter from Michael Drury that told of his flight from Van Diemen's Land, a feat for which he was thoroughly proud. After all, not many men had accomplished that before. Michael wrote that he was in New Zealand and well on his way to making a fortune by whaling. He intended, within a short time, to earn enough money to fetch Kathleen and his child. Michael asked for news of his "fiancée" and sent her his love.

Father O'Brien needed to know more before he replied to either of them. He went to Dublin, where he visited libraries in search of information about far-off New Zealand. Christchurch and Kaikoura might well be hundreds of miles apart or even be located on different islands, and then he could discourage Michael without needing to lie to him. But really, it wouldn't matter. In his heart, the old priest knew that Michael Drury would sail across half the world to see Kathleen O'Donnell again.

Father O'Brien soon learned that Kaikoura was less than a hundred miles from Christchurch. Michael could reach Kathleen and their son in a few days. But then what? Would Michael blame her? Would Kathleen commit a deadly sin and leave her husband when she saw Michael again? Father O'Brien had known when he married them that Kathleen had not loved Ian, and her letters did not make it sound as if that had changed. Indeed, she hardly wrote about Ian at all.

The more Father O'Brien thought about it, the less wise it seemed to inform Michael of Kathleen's whereabouts. It must have been one of God's strange occasional jokes to bring them close enough that they could be together again. Or was this an act of the devil to test all those involved? Father O'Brien did not want to be guilty on any account, so he decided on the following reply:

> As for Mary Kathleen, my son, shortly after your deportation, she married the livestock trader Ian Coltrane. The two of them emigrated, and the last I heard from her she had three children and was leading a God-fearing life overseas. This news may disappoint you, but God has surely directed Mary Kathleen and He will hold her and her children in His hand. The oldest goes by the name Sean. The boy was

born but a few months after the wedding and has, according to Kathleen, a sharp mind and dark hair like his father. I include Mary Kathleen and her family in my daily prayers, as I will you now, as well, my dear Michael. I remain ever concerned for your health and for that of your everlasting soul.

Father O'Brien

Chapter 4

"Look what I have!" Claire pulled Kathleen into her house and pointed excitedly to the tea cakes she'd baked. "Oh wait; let's take care of the children first. I don't want sticky fingers on everything."

Kathleen set Heather next to Chloe, who was playing with little building logs in a corner of the living room, and Claire gave each of the girls a fresh-baked tea cake. She made these cakes astoundingly well, while her bread only met the lowest of expectations.

"I once stole two pastries something like these," Kathleen said, lost in thought. How long ago that was. "I didn't want to, but I was so hungry."

Claire laughed. "Well, now you have plenty of them. Here, take another. Matt only needs three or four." She generously placed two little cakes on the fine porcelain plate she had set out for Kathleen.

The two women were sitting, as they did almost every afternoon, in Claire's living room, which still was not very comfortably furnished. Almost two years had passed since the births of their daughters and the incident with the mule, and Matt Edmunds and Ian Coltrane seemed to have halfway reconciled themselves to their wives' friendship. Matt, at least, no longer held a grudge against Ian. Since the chestnut mule did good work for him, he viewed the first bad deal as a misapprehension on the trader's part and was open to being good neighbors.

Ian traveled farther through the country to buy and sell animals. He still primarily traded in horses, but now he also had a herd of gorgeous sheep, which, in Kathleen's opinion, absolutely needed to be shorn. The women considered bringing professional shearers onto their land. Such bands had been forming recently, ever since sheep breeding and wool producing had developed into important industries in the Canterbury Plains. Among the large farms, people already talked of "sheep barons," and Ian frequently went off to try to do business with them while Kathleen remained behind to work with the animals and take care of the children.

Not much had changed in the couple's relationship; Ian had taken the exchange of the mules with comparative calm. But he had not bought Kathleen a new mule. Instead he left the old mule that had actually been meant for Matt Edmunds on the farm.

"Now let's see how much you need your friend," Ian said, hoping to punish Kathleen more by keeping her from riding to visit Claire than he could with any beating.

Kathleen solved this easily enough. She fed the old mare plentifully and gave it to Claire, who took it to a smith in Canterbury. He gave the animal new shoes, handed Claire a salve for its leg, and advised her not to overburden it.

"She can still do a bit of work," Claire repeated to her friend, trying to mimic the smith's deep voice. "Carrying around such a pretty little thing must be a pleasure for it." She laughed conspiratorially, then added in her normal voice, "I think he's a little in love with me."

Kathleen wasn't sure about the state of the love between Claire and Matt. She was surprised her friend had not gotten pregnant again in the last two years. For a woman so young, this was rather unusual. Ian had impregnated Kathleen twice in that time, but both times she had miscarried.

"You probably work too hard," Claire said sadly after Kathleen had lost a baby in the fifth month.

Kathleen saw the cause in Ian's increasingly brutal assaults. Though they had regularly slept together during her first pregnancies, he had treated her with greater care. Now he entered her with no regard and struck her when she resisted or showed even a measure of unwillingness. He had also put on more weight, while Kathleen had only gotten thinner. At least, though, she no longer went hungry as she had back in Ireland. Her garden put out vegetables, her fields delivered grain, and Ian slaughtered animals several times a year, so meat was always on hand.

But Kathleen worked from morning to evening, and she was under constant stress. Ian was naturally the reason for that. Though she had come to terms with what he did to her, she could not accept Ian's treatment of Sean. Kathleen's sons were now five and six years old, and a difference hardly existed between Colin and Sean when it came to comprehension and physical adroitness. Sean could no longer outshine his younger brother—at least not in the skills important to Ian.

In all things related to horses and the stables, Colin proved more dexterous and clever than his brother. And he already knew how to employ his impish smile to enchant customers. Colin was blond and had Kathleen's attractive features. With his dimples, lively eyes, and friendly manner, he charmed women above all, while he impressed men with his absolute obedience to his father.

Colin worshipped Ian. And Ian did everything to encourage that. He praised him, gave him presents, and let him ride the horses, sometimes even out to the buyers. Ian brought Colin on his shorter trips, and Colin sat next to his father in the tavern while Ian chatted with customers to whom he had successfully made a sale. Sean, on the other hand, got nothing, which increasingly weighed on him. The boys fought often, and Sean received beatings from Ian when he defied instructions and talked back. He clenched his teeth and did not make a noise when Ian struck him unrestrainedly.

Kathleen wondered where Sean drew the courage for his defiance, but of course, Michael had never been one to duck a fight. It wasn't lost on Kathleen that Claire might have enhanced her favorite student's fortitude by reading to him about heroes like Robin Hood and King Arthur.

Kathleen and Sean listened with indefatigable excitement. Claire often had to laugh when she watched two pairs of enthusiastic green eyes hang on her every word.

The green of Sean's eyes was not bright like Kathleen's but instead pale and veiled. In Sean, Kathleen saw Michael's dark hair and square features as well. He was an extraordinarily smart young man, with a pronounced sense of justice. Sometimes it took him hours to feed the horses because he counted out the hay straws so as not to give one more than the other.

"Maybe he'll become a judge." Claire looked hopefully at her friend.

Kathleen shrugged. She could also see Sean as a farmer or—if he could attend seminary—a priest.

Chloe and Heather were still too young to show particular traits. Claire hoped Heather would one day be as beautiful as Kathleen, and Kathleen wished for her goddaughter, Chloe, Claire's effervescent nature and openness to new things—like to the colorfully sprinkled tea cakes, which Kathleen now looked at distrustfully.

"What is this anyway?" she asked, trying to pick a bright red piece of candied cherry out of her pastry to examine it more closely.

"Candied fruit," Claire said eagerly. "Cooked and pickled in sugar and juice. I don't quite know how it's done, but aren't they delicious? I haven't had any in years."

"Where did you get it?" Kathleen asked.

Before Claire could explain where the delicacies came from, the boys stormed into the living room and attacked the tray with the cakes. Colin pushed Sean to the side, but he hit right back. Kathleen separated the brothers, holding them apart by their collars as if they were two growling puppies to be grabbed by the scruffs of their necks.

"We eat; we don't wrestle," she said sternly. "And we say hello first." She indicated Claire, whom neither boy had taken notice of yet.

Sean responded, immediately sobered, by offering his hand and a perfect bow. Colin grinned winningly at Claire, bowed, and asked how she was. Kathleen noticed this difference more and more. Sean was polite but discreet whereas Colin used every opportunity to engage someone in conversation and thereby wrap her around his little finger.

"The fruits are from my mother," Claire finally answered. "I wrote her about Chloe's birth, and now she's sent a crate of things."

"More porcelain?" Kathleen asked skeptically.

"No, books! A dictionary! And candied fruit because I like it so much. Material for a new dress—I wrote her that I've been sewing for myself."

Kathleen smiled. This was a slight exaggeration. Claire showed just as little talent for sewing as for all other housework, but at least now she could mend her and Matt's things, and she even managed to make simple children's clothing.

Claire searched the generous crate from England for the material and held the fabric up just under her face. "Won't it look good on me?"

It really was lovely, a light gold-brown that made Claire's eyes shine. The crate also contained cream-colored hand-fashioned lace. She could adorn the dress with it or even make a bonnet.

"You'll help me sew it, won't you?" Claire asked. "Look, I'll show you what I want. Can we make it?"

She pulled a stack of magazines out of the crate and spread them out in front of Kathleen, who studied them, wide-eyed. At twenty-two, Kathleen Coltrane was looking at women's magazines for the first time, and she was stunned by the drawings of women wearing the latest Paris fashions and by the design variations: puffed sleeves, round and square collars, whalebone corsets.

Claire pointed to the dress she had already picked out. The tight bodice would emphasize her slender waist and, naturally, would be worn with a corset. The skirt fell in flounces, which would look good decorated with lace. The neckline was round and could also be set with lace. Claire could never sew a dress like that. But Kathleen?

"It needs to be a little shorter," Kathleen finally replied. "If you let it touch the ground here, you'll ruin it. Otherwise, it's beautiful. And of course, we'll manage it. Matt will love it."

Claire nodded but did not seem overly hopeful, which filled Kathleen with concern. What had happened to Claire's frothy optimism and her conviction Matt loved her more than anything? In the past Claire would have replied immediately to such a remark with an excited smile, but now she needed a few moments to compose herself after Kathleen mentioned her husband. Only then did she laugh.

"We'll start right away," Claire said, pleased. "You can take my measurements and cut. And then I'll help sew. Will there be enough material?"

The material not only sufficed for a dress for the petite Claire but also for a skirt for Kathleen. She suggested a little dress for Chloe instead, but Claire refused.

"If you're going to do all this work for me, you should have something for yourself. Ian's just like Matt—he'll never buy anything for you."

That was true, though Kathleen was surprised by how Claire had said it. "Just like Matt"—was Claire's unlimited enthusiasm for her husband cracking? Yet it could hardly be missed that neither Matt nor Ian was very generous with his wife. Claire was always mending her old clothes, and Kathleen had not worn anything for years but cotton dresses, the material for which Ian acquired cheaply. Whether it suited Kathleen's complexion, hair color, or eyes did not matter at all to him.

The fabric from Claire was lovely—so lovely that even as a skirt it emphasized the gold tone of her hair and made her eyes shine. It was just a shame that her blouses were made from the same cheap material as her dresses. Claire, generous as ever, insisted Kathleen take the rest of the lace and use it to decorate her delicate green blouse.

Kathleen could hardly get enough of her appearance when she finally looked at herself in Claire's old mirror. And Claire looked even more enticing in her new outfit.

"I don't believe it," Claire said. She turned around in front of the mirror, which was, of course, too small for her to see herself fully. "It fits perfectly. Really, Kathleen, in Liverpool we had the city's best tailor make our clothes, but he never did anything this lovely. Where did you learn to do this?"

Kathleen shrugged. The use of needle and thread had always been easy for her. Her father had been a tailor, and she had been able to pick up a thing or two, but James O'Donnell had rarely sewn such elaborate women's dresses. In good years, there had been an order for a wedding dress, and even Lady Wetherby had ordered something altered now and again. Making dresses had always interested Kathleen, and when she served in the manor, she took care of alterations for Lady Wetherby.

"You could make money with this," said Claire enthusiastically. "You know what we'll do? When Ian's gone for a few days again, we'll go to Christchurch together."

Claire occasionally went on such excursions now that the Edmundses possessed the new mule, Artemis, which Claire named after the virginal hunter. If Artemis—or Missy as Kathleen and Matt called her—was not needed for work, Matt had nothing against it. Though he seemed to find it tiring when Claire came home bubbling with excitement and spread out all her novelties in front of him. Kathleen had twice seen the way he sharply criticized her for it. Her friend had fallen silent, disappointed.

"We'll put on our new clothes and go in old Mrs. Broom's shop. Her eyes will fall out of her head. And then we'll stop by the hotel and perhaps go see the reverend. Yes, what a good idea. His wife's horribly vain, and they have a stupid, ugly daughter as well. When they see us, they'll believe even that girl could be pretty if she only had nice clothes."

Kathleen had to laugh. "But there's nothing as nice as this cloth in Christchurch," she said.

Claire shook her head in disbelief. "You haven't been there in a long time, have you?"

Strictly speaking, Kathleen had never been to the bustling little city. She had visited Mr. and Mrs. Broom's shop once or twice with Ian, but everything was still being built then.

"There's an abundance of fabric in Christchurch, and even a men's tailor," Claire said. "In a few years, you'll be able to get anything there you could in London. The city's growing so rapidly. But you'll see all that. We'll stroll as we shop."

Kathleen smiled wearily. This enterprise would falter on the fact that neither she nor Claire had her own money. But her friend was in such a radiant mood that she did not raise the subject, nor did she object by bringing up what Ian would say if he discovered that Kathleen had strolled the streets of Christchurch in her Sunday best.

No, going to town without her husband's blessing was unthinkable.

But Claire could be very convincing, and once she had decided on something, she was loath to let it go. This time, without even asking, she showed up with her wagon in front of Kathleen's house. She climbed down from the box in the manner of a princess in white gloves, which she had to remove to hitch the mule. These gloves had also come from her mother's gift crate; while not at all useful in New Zealand, they clearly made Claire happy. Claire had done her hair, and her corkscrew curls showed from beneath an old hat to which Kathleen had added some lace so it would suit the dress, and her eyes shone adventurously.

"Let's go. Get dressed: Christchurch awaits!" she called to Kathleen. "All the children may come. Into the back, boys, but don't let Chloe or your sister fall out."

The Edmundses, of course, did not possess a chaise. Claire had yoked Artemis to a covered wagon. There was only room for two on the box, so the children would need to ride in back. Sean and Colin found that especially exciting, though, and Kathleen had to work to convince them to wash up and change for the adventure. Claire waited outside until everyone was ready and was taken aback at first when she saw Colin. He strutted proudly in a checkered jacket, which made him look like a cute caricature of his father.

"Well, didn't you get dressed up?" said Claire when she had composed herself. "Now, who sewed that for you? Kathleen, did you?"

Kathleen looked at her, pained. "The tailor in town. Ian brought it home last weekend. He had one made for himself, and there was material left over."

"Not for me, but I wouldn't wear something like that anyway," said Sean, but his voice betrayed his aggrievement. "You look like a leprechaun!"

Claire burst into laughter. While Claire loved to tell stories, Kathleen possessed a remarkable gift for drawing. She particularly liked to draw the fairies and gnomes of Irish stories, and the similarity between Colin in his suit and Ireland's rustic dwarves was obvious.

"You're just missing a top hat," Sean added mockingly. He was wearing his own Sunday suit, which, though it was made of cheap fabric, had been properly tailored by Kathleen. "I'd rather wear a sailor's outfit."

Claire let the boys climb into the wagon and handed them the little girls.

"When your mommy makes some money, she'll sew you a sailor's suit," Claire promised Sean. Once everyone had finally sat down, she snapped her mule's reins and they were off.

Kathleen shook her head. It was a crazy idea. No one would pay her for her sewing. And surely she would regret this "shopping stroll"—no matter how happy it made her.

The first thought quickly proved wrong, the latter correct.

Starting in Mrs. Broom's shop, their clothing met with praise. Two customers immediately showed excitement about the designs and, a short time later, they bent over the fashion journals Claire had brought in anticipation. Both found the dresses of their dreams within, but neither trusted herself to sew it.

"Kathleen will do that for you," Claire suggested, "though not for free, of course."

Kathleen blushed deeply, hardly daring to name a price when the women asked. "I don't know, a pound?"

Claire was just as perplexed, but now fat, gossipy Mrs. Broom interceded. She was best known for dispensing advice, but she was also a businesswoman.

"A pound? Do you mean to insult the woman? The men's tailor, Mr. Peppers, wouldn't thread his needle for that!" she yelled at her customers. "No, no, Mrs. Coltrane, don't do that. You can't make that dress for less than two, more like three, pounds. If someone can't pay that, she'll have to try to sew it herself."

Mrs. Broom gave her two customers a look that immediately put their reputations as well-off citizens in question, so they quickly ordered the dresses.

"I can't make the corsets for them, however," Kathleen explained carefully. Both customers had decided on dresses for hourglass figures.

"I'll order those from England," Mrs. Broom said. She winked conspiratorially at Kathleen as the two customers left happy. "And you can make this one for me," she declared, pointing at a sophisticated black lace dress that had caused a furor in Paris. "But for one pound—after all, I just got you two customers."

"While selling cloth and two corsets for you," retorted Clair. "We really ought to get some of those profits. No, if Mrs. Coltrane gives you a discount, then no more than two shillings."

The women finally agreed that Kathleen would sketch the dress designs from the fashion magazines and leave the pictures with Mrs. Broom. For every customer she acquired this way, Kathleen would give her a discount of one shilling on her own orders.

"You'll end up sewing her that dress for free," Claire said. "And she'll look horrible in it. Like a cream pie in mourning. But she'll provide you with more customers than you'll know how to handle."

The next stop was the parsonage. "Reverend Baldwin is getting his hopes up about Christchurch as a diocese. Could you tell him you've already done work for, what do I know, the wife of the pope?"

Kathleen crossed herself. "One, I don't lie, and two, Catholic priests can't marry," she said distractedly.

Claire furrowed her brow, obviously thinking of an alternative. "But they wear rather spectacular robes, right? A ball gown for the Bishop of Ireland?"

Kathleen categorically refused to tell any lies, especially one that involved blaspheming against her church. As a Catholic, she was even a little ashamed to pay her respects to the Anglican priest, but the reverend's scrawny wife and fat daughter each ordered a dress. Claire rejected Mrs. Baldwin's attempts to negotiate as shrewdly as Mrs. Broom.

"Although it would not be bad to place a few fashion magazines in the church," she considered on the way back, "or at least in the parsonage. Old lady Baldwin would do it if she could get her dresses made more cheaply, but I think the reverend would say no."

Claire insisted they celebrate their success with tea at the Crown Inn. She entered the tearoom with the assurance and grace of a well-bred lady. But Kathleen was uncomfortable among the heavy, expensive furniture, the baroque curtains, and the silver chandeliers. Though she kept her head lowered, she received admiring looks. Claire was cute, but Kathleen's beauty outshone that of all other women and girls in the room, despite her shyness. Claire watched with a smile as the waiters tried to outdo each other in serving Kathleen. Male guests pulled her chair out for her, and all the other women looked at her jealously.

Only Claire did not begrudge her the luck, which her friend could not properly savor.

"Well, smile at least," she instructed Kathleen. "You're something special here. Everyone's admiring you."

The attention made Kathleen so uncomfortable that she felt as if she could barely keep down her tea and cake, so she focused instead on feeding Heather and Chloe small bites of the pastries. Sean ate a piece of cake very properly. He tried to use the dessert fork as naturally and skillfully as Claire did. He said please and thank you and tried to show perfect manners. Colin stuffed pastries into his mouth. Even though he showed poor manners, he smiled through it all, winning over the people in the tearoom.

Colin had certainly garnered a lot of attention, but Claire couldn't help but feel as though everyone was suppressing a "but why do they dress him like that?" as Colin proudly reached for his checkered jacket when they were on their way out of the tearoom.

Claire had knowingly deposited it at the tearoom's wardrobe, hiding it under the other coats. "Here, it's better we don't say you're a tailor," she whispered to Kathleen.

***

As Kathleen expected, news of her trip to Christchurch quickly reached Ian. He came home in a rage, and by the end of the evening, he had beat Kathleen black and blue and taken her customers' advance payments for himself.

"Whore's wages!" he screamed.

The next day, Kathleen sobbed to Claire about the lost money. She would need to sew for a month without receiving a shilling for it.

"I thought I could save something, to send Sean to university."

"And you will. Something like this won't happen to us again." Claire hugged Kathleen and spread cooling balm on her bruised face. "I'll bring in the next orders myself, and you hide the work when Ian's home. And it's best you show Colin as little as possible, the little traitor."

Kathleen looked at her indignantly. "Colin is only five."

Claire arched her brows. "But he brags about his adventures. You hear the fantastical things he reports from his excursions with Ian. He told his beloved daddy every compliment the waiter at the Crown Inn paid you, guaranteed. You know very well what Ian makes of these things. And Colin knows what Daddy wants to hear. Yes, even at five. Don't fool yourself."

The new arrangement worked well. Claire drove to Christchurch once a month, delivering finished dresses and bringing in new orders. She also asked her mother to send a new batch of fashion magazines. They weren't needed too urgently, for Kathleen had been inspired to create her own designs ever since she had sketched the dresses during that first visit to Mrs. Broom's shop. Claire was enthusiastic about her designs, and their customers even more so.

Soon Kathleen had to refuse work because she could not keep up with all the sewing. That was in no small part because she could only pick up the needle at night when she finished the farm work and Colin was asleep. Kathleen didn't want to admit it to Claire, but she, too, noticed that the boy was acting as Ian's spy at home.

In the meantime, the sheep were shorn, fortunately without precipitating a new crisis in Kathleen's marriage. Claire had sent the shearers over on one of the few days when Ian was at home, and Kathleen did not set foot outside. Ian used the opportunity to sell their leader a horse.

"That means we'll have to find different people next time," Kathleen said, sighing. She glanced at the lovely fleece and the animals properly freed of their wool. "The man will soon notice that the gelding is lazy as sin and lame on top of that. But maybe we won't have any sheep by this time next year."

"Oh, we will!" said Claire.

The Edmundses did not change their livestock continuously, and in contrast to Kathleen, who only saw the sheep as runaways and manure factories, Claire rather liked the animals. She was also on the best of terms with the sheep shearers and had even shorn two sheep herself. Now she was eager to learn how to work the wool. Kathleen showed her, and it was not long before Claire achieved some skill in spinning. She offered her wool for sale in Mrs. Broom's shop—and the town's women loved it.

"I told you we'd do well with the wool," Claire said, packing another load into her wagon. "Teasing wool and dyeing and spinning it—you can't do it in a town house, and it's really only worth it if you have your own sheep."

Kathleen and Claire sold the whole wool yield of both their farms—and were happy their husbands didn't think to demand the money from them. Neither Ian nor Matt had ambitions to become a sheep baron. For Ian, the animals were merely burdensome things that ate money; he was trying to sell them as soon as he could. And Matt rode back and forth between Christchurch and Lyttelton day after day. He did good business transporting the settlers' belongings to the plains or merchandise from the plains to the ships. It must have occurred to him that he was loading more and more wool for England. Either he did not think his own dozen sheep worth mentioning, or he simply did not take interest in the goods he moved.

There were indeed strong indications of this lack of interest, as Matt appeared increasingly bored and in a bad mood. The absence of high praise for the wonderful, humorous, and tender Matt Edmunds was an indication of Claire's disenchantment with her husband.

Claire was unrestrainedly happy about the money she and Kathleen made, though. "We'll be rich yet, Kathleen." She smiled, but then grew serious. "We'll run away together."

Kathleen looked up, surprised, from her money. She was just counting it all again, hardly able to comprehend her fortune. But this ripped her out of her trance. Claire Edmunds was thinking of escaping her marriage?

"They say," whispered Claire, who seemed finally to need to express herself, "well, the women in Christchurch, they say Matt has a lover in Lyttelton."

Kathleen laid her arm around her friend's shoulder. "That can't be true, Claire. It's surely just gossip."

"But it might be true," Claire said bitterly. "After all, in the first few years, the sea was rarely so rough that he had to stay overnight in Lyttelton. But now it happens all the time. I see it, too, Kathleen. I'm not blind, you know."

"But do you not let him into your bed anymore?" Kathleen asked, blushing. "I mean, you haven't gotten pregnant again."

Claire wiped the tears from her eyes. "It's not that I don't let him," she said quietly. "He just doesn't want to. Matt is so . . . I don't know what makes him so dour and unhappy. I do love him, even though he's so different than he used to be. But well, I think, I think, for all he cares, the sooner I'm gone the better."

Claire Edmunds, the eternal optimist, broke down in tears.

Chapter 5

Kathleen Coltrane's and Claire Edmunds's marriages didn't grow any happier over the next few years, but their business together developed into an unexpected success. Kathleen couldn't keep up with all the orders she received for dresses and even evening gowns. They hired two women in town to do the sewing, and Kathleen concentrated primarily on the clothing designs and cutting the patterns. Claire focused on weaving filigreed wool cloth, and she was very skillful at creating new effects with different shades of coloring. She worked nearly all the wool from her sheep herself, and she took Kathleen's yield when the Coltranes had sheep during shearing time.

Certainly Claire contributed to the family's income, which was bitterly necessary.

Claire complained about how Matt's business never flourished. While the other boatmen and fishermen had already acquired bigger and more modern boats, Matt had made no progress. The money he earned he drank away either in the taverns or in boats with friends.

Even Ian grumbled occasionally about Matt: "He entertains the whole tavern with his sailor's stories. But those won't catch him any fish or carry any loads—and there's less and less of that to do the more they pave the Bridle Path."

Coaches could now travel along the pass, and when Ian was away for several days and took Colin with him, Kathleen and Claire gathered up Sean and the girls and ventured to make an excursion to Lyttelton. Kathleen wanted to see her Maori friend Pere again, and Claire, who had been seized with ambition when it came to wool, hoped to learn about fabric dyes from the native woman.

Naturally, Pere was overjoyed. She raved about how big Sean had grown and spoiled him and Heather and Chloe with sweets. Kathleen marveled at how the primitive settlement of Port Cooper had developed into the large town of Lyttelton. She enjoyed being able to talk with Pere's husband, John, and learn more about their new country's course of development.

"They found coal in Westport; they're starting to mine there," John explained. "But more important than that, they found gold in Otago. All the madmen and adventurers are rushing to the gold sites hoping to make a fortune. Not many are going to manage that, but it'll bring people to the country. Unfortunately they're not exactly the best sorts, but they're founding towns too. Dunedin on the coast in the south—settled by Scots mostly. Blenheim in the north—bunch of Germans around there. So the land's slowly filling up."

"And does that not disturb your people?" Claire asked Pere, who was just explaining the night sky to the children.

It was a warm summer evening, and they had enjoyed the view of the sea while Pere grilled fish and sweet potatoes. Now, the clear night sky emerged before them, and Claire was thrilled that Pere knew the names of the stars—though only in her own language, not English.

Pere shook her head. "Not here on South Island, Te Waka a Maui. Never were many. Only one tribe, Ngai Tahu, and a few others far to north. Have nothing against *pakeha*—when they pay honest for our land and work. You must watch out; many swindlers. But our chieftains smart, not much fighting with each other. On North Island different. Many tribes there, much treaties. In Waitangi, chieftains made treaty with *pakeha* but still, there is often trouble."

"Here the people are just happy when they get work," John added.

Pere grinned at him. "And money and pots and blankets and warm clothing," she said. "Who doesn't want to live little better life?"

Kathleen and Claire nodded in agreement. Their lives lacked luxury despite the good income they earned. Claire hid her money in the barn beneath the manure pile, and Kathleen hid hers behind a loose brick in her fireplace. They couldn't spend anything without making their husbands aware of their income. Now they looked longingly at Pere and John's comfortable home, the cushions on the chairs, the wall hangings woven by Maori women, and the small sculptures out of pounamu jade.

"These *hei-tiki*," said Pere, generously giving Claire and Kathleen two tiny jade fetishes on leather bands.

Claire looked reverently at her pendant while Kathleen quickly hid hers beneath her clothes. It made her happy to have a good luck charm, but she dared not think of what Ian would do if he found it. The best thing would be to hide it in the secret compartment in which she kept her money—and Michael's letter and lock of hair.

Claire now joined the little stargazers, pulling Chloe into her arms. "That's the Milky Way," she explained, pointing at the sky.

Pere smiled. "We call it Te Ika o te Rangi," she explained. "And that's Matariki, very important for attitude of new year—so we have grand festival."

"The Pleiades," Claire interpreted. "But what do you call that star there, Pere? I don't know any name for it." As soon as Pere told her the name of one, Claire would point to yet another star.

Pere answered patiently, and finally Claire's wish to learn more about her new stars was being fulfilled.

Kathleen did not care at all about the night sky. While Claire and the children laughed, repeating Maori words, she memorized the names of the *pakeha* settlements John mentioned: Greymouth and Westport, Nelson and Blenheim, Dunedin and Queenstown. She would certainly never travel to the stars. But maybe she would find a place for herself and her children right there on New Zealand's South Island where she could be safe from Ian's presumptions and abuse.

***

More years passed, and it was 1858 before Kathleen seriously thought about realizing her escape plans. Ultimately, it was not Kathleen's growing desperation or Sean's increasingly worse relationship with Ian that provided the impetus. It was Matt Edmunds, of all people, who started the ball rolling.

Sean was eleven, Colin ten, and both boys were attending school in Christchurch. It was a long trip, but Sean was happy to ride the ten miles—he hungered for knowledge, and he'd found a place for himself at school. Thanks to Claire's instruction, he had been able to read and write for a long time, was good in math, and even understood a little Latin. He had read halfway through the dictionary, and in doing so developed remarkable knowledge. Sean impressed his teachers so much that they skipped him one, then three grades. Even among the older students, he was one of the smartest, and people already talked of his being admitted into Christ's College, which was being built.

Colin enjoyed school less. Thanks to Claire's lessons, he could skip first grade and would surely not have had to attend second grade either, but he showed little initiative. For his later career as an animal trader—he was already declaring that now—he claimed that all he needed to know was math and that the rest of the subjects were a waste. Colin wanted to spend his time preparing the horses for sale and breaking them in, and of course there was nothing better than traveling with Ian on his business trips.

Ian rode from farm to farm, though Kathleen had the feeling he avoided the biggest and most important estates. People like the Wardens on Kiward Station, the Barringtons, or the Beasleys could not be tricked, and they undoubtedly had too much dignity to even receive Ian. They either ordered their animals from England or bred them themselves. Ian mostly did business with small farms, and he swindled people over and over again. Naturally, whiskey played a big role in this, and Ian even drank during the day now.

Aside from Colin, the whole family was relieved when Ian went on sales trips. Ian increasingly showed Sean his disdain, and he didn't even take notice of Heather. Having just turned nine, Heather had begun to fear her father more, and when Ian was gone she did not miss his bullying of her beloved brother Sean and his beatings of her mother.

In fact, on that spring day in November, Colin was the only family member in a bad mood. Ian had set out that morning on a trip that would last several days, but he had left Colin at home so he would not miss school. Colin was mistreating the horse with which he was working in the paddock in front of the house. Sean was cleaning out the stables, and every time he came out with the wheelbarrow, he argued with his brother about how harshly he was treating the young horse. Kathleen was in the house, and Heather was picking red rata and yellow kowhai blossoms. Like Claire, Heather insisted on being a lady and decorating her house.

Suddenly, Claire's chestnut-colored mule came galloping down the unpaved path between Kathleen's house and the paddock as if pursued by the

Furies. Claire sat on its bare back, steering it as best she could with a rope for a bridle. Spotty, her donkey, followed just behind, also at breakneck pace, with Claire's daughter, Chloe, on top. Chloe was now almost as good a rider as her mother and rode either sidesaddle or stock saddle, but that day Chloe held onto Spotty's bony back with great effort. If mother and daughter had ridden all three miles at that pace, the girl must have been sore.

Claire and Chloe got down from their mounts as soon as they stopped. The little girl went to hitch the animals, but Claire seemed incapable of any reasonable thought or action.

"Kathleen! Kathleen!" Claire shouted.

When Kathleen stepped out of the house, Claire threw herself, sobbing, into her arms. "Kathie, Kathie, I, we, our house, Matt . . ."

Kathleen embraced her friend, pulling her close to comfort her. Her thoughts raced through all the possible catastrophes. Had the house burned down? Might Matt have died in the flames?

"A, a fire, Claire?" she asked.

Claire shook her head but did not manage a single word.

"Some people came," Chloe said when her mother couldn't explain. "A man and his wife and two boys. With a big wagon and furniture. And they, they threw us out."

Chloe sounded more taken aback and disbelieving than unsettled, as if she didn't quite yet understand the seriousness of the situation.

"They threw you out?" Kathleen did not understand either, although memories of Ireland suddenly assailed her. Gráinne Rafferty on the dock in Wicklow. The Drurys' hut, torn down and burned. "But that can't be, Claire; this is a free country. There aren't any noble lords—"

"The people say they bought it," Chloe said. "With all its in . . . in . . ."

"Inventory," Claire finished the word, seeming to regain her speech. "They had proof too. The bill of sale was without a doubt correct. Matt, the dog . . ."

"Matt sold the house out from under you?" Kathleen asked, horrified.

Claire nodded. "Maybe he sold us as items in the inventory too," she said bitterly. "The buyers were very angry to find us still there. They claimed Matt had already left. He had used the money from the farm to buy shares in a schooner, a cargo ship. He's sailing to China on it as we speak."

Kathleen looked at her dear friend who was so wholly beside herself and suddenly became completely calm. She had put the decision off for a long time, but now fate was handing her an opportunity. She could not let Claire go—everything in her rebelled against returning to her joyless life before Claire's arrival. And Claire was too well bred to survive on her own in Christchurch or Lyttelton. Kathleen breathed deeply.

"What about your clothes, Claire?" she asked.

Matt had never taken an interest in Claire's wardrobe, but her mother had continued to send her material that Kathleen crafted into beautiful pieces. Claire and Chloe owned an extensive wardrobe that was their pride and joy, and of course, the dresses were like new since they never had the opportunity to wear them.

Claire's eyes flashed with anger. Apparently, now she was really coming back to herself, and her despair was giving way to a healthy rage.

"Part of the inventory. I wanted to pack some, but the woman saw right away that I had more than this old thing I'm wearing." Claire was wearing a tattered housedress, so she must have been working in the garden when the people stormed in. "In any case, she plopped down, plump and greedy, in front of my wardrobe and said she bought all the valuable items with the farm."

"You could fight it," said Kathleen. "A lawyer from Christchurch . . ."

Claire waved the idea away. "Oh, forget it. They'll have it all sold before the lawyer even shows up. Besides . . ." She smiled grimly. "We got the animals in exchange."

"They must have belonged to the inventory, didn't they?" asked Kathleen. "How did you manage to get them away?"

"They were in the forest, at the Fairy Place," she said. "And the new people had enough to do making sure I didn't take anything from the house. So Chloe and I ran to the river and then rode around the farm into the copse. And here we are."

"You two shouldn't stay too long," Kathleen said. "They'll report the theft, guaranteed."

"You, you're not serious," Claire whispered. "You're, you're not throwing us out, are you? I thought . . ."

Kathleen shook her head impatiently. "Stop that nonsense. Of course I'm not throwing you out. But you have to know they'll look here first. At least, they will once they learn we're friends. Besides, Ian won't tolerate you here. But that doesn't matter. We'll run away. The two of us and the children."

"We'll run away?" Claire's eyes were huge. "You mean to leave Ian?"

Kathleen nodded decisively. "I have for a long time. I just didn't dare do it alone. But forget it; we need to plan. First, the animals need to go into the stables. Sean . . ." Kathleen turned around, looking for him, and saw Sean and the other children too. Sean sat on the paddock fence listening patiently; Colin was on his horse, eyes and ears open; and Heather was whispering with Chloe.

Missy and Spotty could no longer be seen. Sean winked at his mother. Kathleen gave him a warm smile. How clever the boy was. He'd already gotten the animals out of sight.

"Good. Then let's go into the house now and pack our things," Kathleen said to her children. "Ian has the wagon. We need to take the carriage and the mule. So don't take too much. It'll be tight with six of us already." Kathleen breathed deeply and readied herself for the most important question. "Claire, do you have your money?"

Kathleen exhaled when Claire nodded. "Yes," she whispered. "Chloe grabbed it from the barn while I argued with the woman about the clothes. Otherwise these people might have laid claim to it too. But here it is."

She fished the bills and coins from the pockets of her housedress. She had stored her money in a handsome mahogany box—another piece from her largely useless trousseau—but she couldn't have ridden with it.

"Good!" Kathleen's relief was so great that she embraced Claire suddenly. "Then it all won't be so bad. See, you have your animals, your money; you're rich, Claire, and me too. We'll run away. We'll start over somewhere else!"

"But where?" Claire asked as she followed Kathleen into the house. Kathleen boiled water and placed bread and butter on the table—no matter how eager they were to go, Claire needed tea and something to eat. Chloe seemed starved, and she started eating right away.

Kathleen's children did not make any move to gather their things. They listened, fascinated, to the conversation their mothers were having.

"It has to be a city," Kathleen said, "and preferably not one that's grown out of a whaling station or the like. There won't be any women there, so whom would we sell our dresses to? Only places like Christchurch make sense."

"But that's too close," Claire said.

Kathleen rolled her eyes. "Of course we're not going to Christchurch. Ian would find us within a day, and you'd lose your animals, not to mention face charges for theft. No, we should either head north to Nelson or south to Dunedin."

"I would argue for Nelson, Mother." Sean spoke up in his sometimes-stilted formal mode of expression. "Or even for the North Island. That's where all the big cities are—Wellington, Auckland—and Father would never find us there."

Sean was the only one of the children who did not seemed surprised by Kathleen's plan to flee. On the contrary, it was as if he had already considered it.

"But I don't want to leave Da!" Colin shouted. It seemed he had only just then realized what was happening. "We're not really going, are we, Ma? We, we belong . . ."

"We don't belong to your father at all, Colin." Kathleen informed him, more harshly than she intended. "He's kept me locked up for years, and I've had enough. We're going to—"

"I'm not going anywhere!" Colin got agitated. "I'm staying with Da."

Kathleen shook her head. "It's not your decision to make, Colin. You've already picked up too many bad habits for my taste. From now on there'll be no more cheating. You'll go to school and learn a proper trade. My God, ever since I married your father, people have complained to me of his swindling. I couldn't look at myself in a mirror if I heard such things about my own son."

Colin leaped up. "You've lived quite well from that swindling, you and your, your . . ."

He did not pick up words as well as his brother, but Kathleen could feel her face flush as Colin tried to repeat the recrimination Ian had thrown at her so often. It was long past time she got the children away from Ian. It did not bear thinking about what would happen once they understood what "bastard" meant. Claire immediately sensed what the boy wanted to say. She, too, reddened and looked down.

Kathleen slapped Colin. "That's enough from you, Colin! Sean, take your brother in your room and help him pack. A change of shirt and pants for both of you, a few little things if there's anything you want to take. Yes, Sean, for God's sake, the dictionary too."

"You still have it here?" Claire's face brightened.

Kathleen turned her eyes to heaven, but Colin was not defeated yet. "Didn't you hear me, woman?" he asked in the same tone and in the same words as his father. Cold shivers ran up Kathleen's spine. "I'm staying right here. I'm not about to run away behind Da's back. And you can't take the carriage. It's new. Da bought it and—"

"Your da," said Kathleen calmly, "bought everything here with my money. So if I take a carriage and mule, he's still been well paid for his costly name." She spat these words. "Now get to it, children."

"So? And what are you going to do?" asked Colin provocatively. "Are you going to tie me up in the carriage? Tie up my hands and legs? Then you better do it well, Ma—'cause when I get out, I'm going to ride to Da. I know where to find him, Ma. Then he'll come to Nelson and get you, or to this North Island or wherever you hide."

Claire looked at her friend. Kathleen could tell from her expression, which was half sympathy and half fright, that she believed Colin. And Claire's face was reflected in Sean's. He did not trust his brother either.

"You'll have to let me go sometime," said Colin. "Then I'll go to the police and report you. And they'll find Da if we're too far for me to."

"Colin." Kathleen felt her heart breaking. "Colin, I'm sorry about the slap. But we can't go without you. We're all going together."

"I belong with Da!" yelled Colin. He was now almost to the door. "And I'm going to find him now."

Colin fled out of the kitchen. Sean did not wait a moment. He ran right after him.

"We can't leave him behind," Kathleen said helplessly.

Claire poured tea. Now she was the one thinking with a clear head. "We can't take him either," she said, determinedly. "We could never be sure of him. We never have been. Think of our visit to Christchurch."

"But he's just a little boy," whispered Kathleen. "He's not bad."

Claire shrugged. "There's not a big difference between good and bad with little boys," she said. "Colin's influenced by his father. He loves him and admires him, and he should, of course. For Colin, Ian can do no wrong. But you, Kathleen, you do all kinds of wrong in his eyes. For years he's been listening to Ian's accusations. You'll have to tell me sometime what exactly happened. Sean . . ."

Kathleen nodded, putting her finger to her lips. "Not in front of the girls," she said. "But if I leave him behind now, that means . . . it would mean giving him up."

Claire looked her in the eyes. "You can give up Colin or yourself," she said firmly. "Or should I say 'give up Sean'? Because once he understands whatever it was you did for him, if you leave today, he may love you for it. If you stay, he'll hate you."

Kathleen tapped her fingers against her teacup. At that moment, the door opened, and Sean entered.

"He's gone," he said, out of breath. "I'm sorry, Ma, but he was faster than me. He went toward the woods. I'm going to the stables to watch the animals. If he gets to the horse, it's all over."

"You mean you want to take the horse with us too?" Kathleen asked weakly.

Sean nodded. "There's no other choice. We're lucky it's the only one we have now. But if we leave a horse for him . . ."

"He'll come back," Kathleen whispered, "if we just wait a while."

Sean rolled his eyes. "Of course, when he gets hungry. But then? Do you want to tie him up?"

"Go to the stables, Sean," said Claire, "and hitch the mules. We'll leave in half an hour."

Sean shifted from one foot to the other. "Ma?" he asked.

Kathleen bit her lip. "Do as your Aunt Claire says, Sean."

Kathleen packed her patterns and designs, and clothing for herself and Claire. Fortunately, she was the taller of the women, so she would be able to alter the items for Claire. Finally, she retrieved the money from her secret compartment in the fireplace. Not a fortune, but enough, along with Claire's savings, for a small business. She considered whether she should take some of Colin's expensive clothes for Sean but recoiled from the thought. Doubtless, Sean would grow up with the idea that his mother was a thief and a whore, but she didn't want to steal from her son. Sean wouldn't want any of Colin's things anyway. So she only packed Sean's own suits and the dictionary.

Sean was driving the carriage around as she came out of the house with her few possessions. Claire and the girls were already waiting outside.

Claire had helped Heather pack, and she took a few things for Chloe as well. "Is that all right?" she asked, looking embarrassed.

Kathleen waved away her concern.

The black carriage was a four-wheeled vehicle, relatively new and almost a bit stately. Ian rode in it when he sold horses to townspeople. Sean had hitched

Kathleen's and Claire's mules to it. The donkey was tied to the rear, and the horse walked alongside. It was still wearing the saddle and bridle from Colin's ride. Kathleen realized that Colin had made it into the kitchen so quickly after Claire's arrival because he had not bothered to take off the animal's saddle. Or perhaps he'd left it on purposely, the idea of fleeing to his father already on his mind.

Sean cleared the box for Kathleen and went over to the small black horse. "I thought I'd ride, so you'll have more space," he said, securing his things in the saddlebags.

The women nodded; the girls took their bundles and climbed into the backseat of the carriage. Kathleen stowed her things beneath the box.

Then they were under way.

"Nelson, how far is that anyway?" asked Claire as Kathleen took the reins.

"Around two hundred miles, maybe more," Kathleen said.

"What about Colin? He's really not coming?" Heather asked.

Kathleen glanced at her daughter in the backseat. Heather looked back unhappily. The farm on the Avon disappeared behind a bend in the road.

"Sweetheart, Colin threatened to betray us if we force him to come." Claire sounded as if she were telling a story of something that happened long ago, perhaps at King Arthur's court. "So we had to leave him to do as he wanted."

"That rat will betray us anyway!" said Sean, trotting alongside the carriage. "We shouldn't take the highways, Ma. Maybe we should even make a detour."

Kathleen shook her head. "I know," she said with pressed lips. "But Nelson is too far, Sean. The road over the mountains is a challenge. We wouldn't make it with the carriage. We could only do it on foot or mounted. And then Kaikoura, the whalers, two women and two girls—it's simply too risky, Sean, though you're surely right about the North Island."

"Where are we going then?" asked Claire.

Kathleen made her final decision. She turned south.

"To the Scots. To Dunedin."

Chapter 6

Lizzie's righteous life among the Busbys lasted seven years.

For New Zealand's North Island, they were exciting years, and James Busby's household often stood at the center of events. Following the initial sluggish immigration of people from England, Ireland, and other corners of Europe, new settlers came in droves after the Treaty of Waitangi was signed. The settlers founded cities and established agriculture and coal-mining regions. As a councillor of the Bay of Islands, James Busby organized land measurements and road construction, received the more important immigrants, and served these visitors his own wine—although, to his dismay, the results of his efforts never approached those of France or Germany's winemakers.

While Busby's family remained uninterested in the wine, Lizzie did her best to put Busby's vision of proper viniculture into practice, and she never shrank from work among the vines. She worked wonders among the Maori vintners. Since she now spoke their language almost fluently, she could explain how Busby wanted to improve the quality, not the quantity, of the vineyard's produce.

Lizzie would have grown lonely if she had not spent so much time with the hospitable Maori. The maids and gardeners were happy to take her into their tribe, which welcomed her without prejudice and without asking penetrating questions about her past. This gave Lizzie a feeling of freedom— besides, there was reason to believe that they would not have judged her, even with a better understanding of her previous life. The concept of prostitution was as foreign a notion to the Maori as strict *pakeha* sexual morality. If there was anything about Lizzie that made the Maori wonder, it was her declining to choose a partner. Ruiha once asked her quite plainly about this.

"Do you not like men?" she inquired, playing with a strand of her long black hair, which was always breaking out of the polite braids Mrs. Busby prescribed. "Do you prefer women? I have never seen it, but they say it happens."

Lizzie blushed. "Perhaps," she stammered, shyly but honestly, "I've already had too many—men that is, not women. I've never been with a woman. I did not even know such a thing existed."

Ruiha nodded. She might not understand Lizzie's behavior, but she accepted her.

Mrs. Busby was not so accepting—of either the Maori themselves or Lizzie's relationship with them—especially as the climate between the Maori and *pakeha* worsened with time. The natives were no longer as welcoming to new settlers as they had been at first. Their island was getting more crowded, and disagreements became more frequent. At the missionary schools the Maori learned English and math—and the cleverer among them quickly began to question the treaties and land sales.

James Busby had to wrestle with the complaints of the Maori and the settlers. And Mrs. Busby was aggravated that her native servants still were not perfect despite their years of working in the house. She absolutely couldn't understand what would drive her otherwise impeccable English maid into the natives' village.

"You could stay here and read a good book," Mrs. Busby said to Lizzie. "I'd be happy to lend you one. Or you could sew yourself a dress. Why don't you just do what the other housemaids do?"

There weren't any other *pakeha* maids in the area, so Lizzie was never sure where these comparisons came from. She read slowly, and she could not sew particularly well, but she did take pleasure in the activities she performed along with the Maori women. She helped them harvest, braid, and weave flax; learned to play the flute; and roasted meat and vegetables in earthen ovens. Lizzie, the city girl, learned to light fires and catch fish among the tribes. She brought Mrs. Busby honey from the blossoms of the rongoa bush and a powder of koromiko leaves for her headaches. It was all completely harmless, but Mrs. Busby remained distrustful, nevertheless.

"You don't follow those lads into the bushes, do you, Lizzie?" she asked. "There's no black lover who'll leave you to take care of his bastard someday, is there?"

Lizzie could say no to the first question with good conscience, and the second as well—although there was a man who was trying to woo her. Kahu Heke was a tall, strong, but (by Maori measure) slender young man who came from the best of families but preferred to spend his time in the whaling camp of Kororareka instead of perfecting the Maori traditions: storytelling, hunting, and dance. Kahu Heke bore the name of a famous ancestor. Lizzie did not entirely understand whether the great Chief Hone Heke who had caused commotion in the English colony and set off the Flagstaff War was his father or uncle.

In any case, Kahu was a nephew of the current Chief Kuti Haoka, who often reprimanded Kahu when he wandered back to the tribal fire after another adventure. Like his great ancestor, Kahu liked to knock over an English flagstaff or steal a Union Jack. He improved the breeding among tribe's sheep by occasionally bringing back a few exemplary animals, which had "simply followed him," from the *pakeha* breeders, and he wrote letters of complaint for any Maori who had been upset by the whites. Kahu had perfectly mastered reading and writing, having enjoyed an excellent education in a missionary school. Although he was officially Christian, he was happy to invoke the rights of the old gods when contesting *pakeha* settlers' use of a piece of land that was holy to his people.

After years of missionary school, Kahu seemed to have some difficulties with the promiscuous customs in his tribe's *marae*. He obviously liked Lizzie, and he wooed her in a manner that seemed not to quite fit either culture. Sometimes he made bawdy jokes that made her blush. Then he would give her small presents, or he would even pick flowers in the *pakeha* manner. All this amused the tribe members, and Lizzie imagined they might well make bets about if and when Kahu would have success with her.

She did not encourage his attention. Though Kahu was a rather good-looking man, as a member of the Maori nobility his face was adorned with tattoos that simply repulsed Lizzie. Moreover, she did not want to fall in love with another young man who always had one foot in trouble. She feared the discovery of Kahu Heke's thieving raids and the rebellious thoughts he voiced aloud.

His attitude was somewhat unexpected because Kuti Haoka's *hapu*, or clan, belonged to the Ngati Pau tribe, which was originally welcoming to the whites. The Ngati Pau's great chieftain, Hongi Hika, had been one of the first to sign the Treaty of Waitangi. Now, however, even that tribe doubted the new settlers' honesty. Too often, the *pakeha* had cheated the *hapu* and *iwi*—the Maori terms for their tribes—in purchasing land, and limitations on trade seemed only to apply to the Maori, not the whites. Kahu Heke always had new cases to report when he came to the village.

"They take our land, offend our *tapu*, and cut down our forests for their ships. And what do we get in exchange? Their whiskey and their diseases."

"Well, you seem to like their whiskey," Ruiha teased him.

Lizzie's friend obviously had a weakness for Kahu. Kahu was right with regard to the diseases, however. Many natives died of childhood illnesses like measles. And not every tribal warrior knew how to handle his whiskey, which also led to conflict.

"Soon we won't tolerate it," Kahu announced loudly. "Listen to my words. Sooner or later it will come to war."

Lizzie did not like to hear that. After all, it brought her into a conflict of loyalties with her employers. James Busby would doubtless have expected her to report such seditious speech. But she kept quiet—in the presence of the Maori as well as that of the whites.

***

Ultimately, it was anything but rebellion that put an end to her happy life with the Busbys. Lizzie's confrontation with her past caught her completely off guard.

"This evening there'll be a grand dinner, Lizzie," Mrs. Busby said, at ease, when Lizzie and the other housemaids came into her receiving room for the morning review. "So everyone please appear for service in neat, clean uniforms and with polished shoes. Keep an eye on the others, Lizzie; you know they don't take that seriously enough."

The Maori girls regarded the peculiar European shoes included with the maids' uniforms as rather suspect.

"Ruiha will serve at the table, Lizzie will handle the reception, and I'll discuss the menu with Cook later. Polish the silver again. The gentlemen come from England, and they will be used to the finer things."

"How many people are we expecting, madam?" Lizzie asked politely.

Mrs. Busby shrugged. "Two British engineers or architects, something like that, and a few men from Russell. It's about some road construction project. I'll be bored all evening again. Oh yes, and bring up a few bottles of the French wine, Lizzie. Maybe we'll manage to open them before James can bring out that sour stuff of his."

Lizzie curtsied and began the preparations. In contrast to the Maori girls, she enjoyed setting out the porcelain and polishing the silver and crystal until they shone.

By the time the guests were due to arrive, even the maids shone, clean and neat, having let Lizzie order them around good-naturedly until even the last bonnet sat perfectly in place. Lizzie waited at the entrance to take the coats and umbrellas from the guests. It was winter, and even if it was not very cold, it rained in buckets all day. A curtain of rain hid the beauty of the bays and forested hills.

Lizzie did not recognize the man at first as he hastened, in the middle of a group, to come out of the weather. Only when the tall, red-faced road construction engineer took off his coat and hat did it strike Lizzie like lightning. Martin Smithers stood in front of her. And he looked just as flabbergasted as she.

Her first impulse was to flee—perhaps she could get away before he recognized her. Of course that was impossible, and he recovered from his surprise much faster than Lizzie. Smithers's water-blue eyes shone lustfully. He smirked at Lizzie as he handed her his coat.

"Look here, it's the house kitten. What a pleasure. And look, you're respectable once again." His eyes darted around with the speed of a ferret's, and once he saw that all the other visitors were deep in conversation, he leaned into Lizzie. "I was not at all happy about your leaving, sweet. Do you know who my wife got to replace you? A pale, scrawny fellow who trained as a butler before stealing from his employers. No fun, my kitten."

Lizzie took a step back from him, then brought his coat and hat to the closet to give herself a moment to think. Smithers would give her away. He would make sure she was arrested and returned to Australia. But perhaps the Busbys would want to keep her; perhaps it was not so bad. Perhaps . . .

Lizzie could feel Smithers's gaze follow her as she curtsied before the other visitors. She thanked heaven that Ruiha was assigned to serve the meal. All she had to do was look at the food in the kitchen one last time to make sure its arrangement suited the European sense of beauty. The cook sometimes indulged in somewhat exotic creations, which the family was willing to try but which they spared their guests.

James Busby would not, however, be denied the presentation of his own wine. Ruiha appeared immediately after the first course with a task for Lizzie. "You're to fetch one of our late vintages and de . . . dec . . ."

"Decant it," Lizzie said, with a sigh.

That meant Mr. Busby wanted the wine served with the main course, and she would have to pour it. James Busby liked to present his own English housemaid together with his own New Zealand wine. Usually she did not mind, but on this day . . .

"Kitten, wait for me in the hall." Smithers whispered these words to her as she filled his crystal goblet with wine. "We have a few words to speak to each other."

Lizzie thought once more of fleeing, but it was doubtless better to hear what Smithers had to say. Perhaps she could negotiate with him. She left the kitchen immediately after the next course and stood in the hallway. Martin Smithers did not make her wait long.

"Kitten, you won't believe how I've missed you."

He pressed Lizzie against the wall and kissed her as if to save his life. Lizzie tasted juice from the roast with a sour tinge of wine. She felt nauseous.

"But you haven't missed me, have you? Mr. Busby surely keeps an open house; lots of clients for a sweet little whore like you."

Lizzie tried to struggle free.

"I'm a respectable woman, Mr. Smithers," she said. "I've done nothing wrong since I escaped Australia. Only work. And, and after seven years with the Busbys, I've served my time."

Smithers laughed. "You can't be serious, kitten! Served your time? Perhaps for the little theft in London. But what about the money you took from poor Parsley? After you seduced him and tricked him. He became the laughing stock of the colony. Do you think he wouldn't report it? They're looking for you, kitten. And this time you won't get an escape or pardon. They keep girls like you in the factory ten, fifteen years."

Lizzie pictured the walls of the factory, remembered the never-changing daily routine. Back then, none of it had seemed so bad to her. But now she was used to freedom: the vast sky over the bays, the forests and their secrets, her Maori friends.

"Mr. Smithers, please." Lizzie did not know why she pleaded. Surely this man knew no mercy. But perhaps she really could bargain with him.

"Mr. Smithers, perhaps, perhaps I did miss you, after all." She tried to smile but knew it came out miserably.

Smithers laughed again. "Oh, don't lie, kitten. But you do look cute when you smile. This bonnet deserves a smiling face. Oh I, I could eat you up." He kissed her again.

"Mr. Smithers, you can have me, but only if you don't give me away."

Smithers let her go and furrowed his brow. "Oh?" he asked threateningly. "And just who is dictating that to me?"

"I am," said Lizzie calmly. "If you don't swear by, by, by your God you won't give me up, then I'll cry out right here."

Smithers smirked. "But no one will believe you, sweet. I'll say you attacked me."

Lizzie felt a burning desire to kill the man. She had heard the Maori legends that told of female warriors. In ancient battles, women had fought at the sides of their husbands. The girls had shown her old war clubs made for women's hands. Lizzie had only felt a creeping feeling at the time, but now she imagined smashing this man's skull in with one of the clubs. Again and again until his wide, sweaty face and evil smile were unrecognizable.

"Sir, I've served in this house for many years," she said with dignity. "And I have yet to attack a gentleman. So they won't simply believe you. You could tell them of my escape. But then they'll arrest me. I'll spend tonight in police custody. Do you mean to sneak off to the station to bribe an officer? Do you mean to rape me in the tiny jail where the walls have ears? You're too cowardly for that, sir. All of New Zealand would hear of it."

Smithers bit his lip. He did not like it, but she was right. And she had the leverage.

"Very well, kitten, what would you suggest?"

He no longer smiled, but desire burned in his eyes.

"I'll come to your hotel room. You need only sneak me inside, but that won't be hard. The inn has a back entrance." Lizzie had often been present when wine and other products of Busby's farm were delivered there. However, Smithers interpreted her knowledge of the inn differently, of course.

"You go there often, do you, sweet?" he asked, once again with his puerile smile. "Very well, but I'm expecting an unforgettable night."

Lizzie nodded. If it bought her freedom, she would let him have his way in everything. Though, in her experience, he was not hard to please so long as she wore her bonnet.

***

Smithers ended the evening early—he was the most important guest, but he seemed unfocused to the other guests, and so did not succeed in convincing the notables from Russell of his plan for a road to Auckland.

"As if he had plans for later," Busby said with astonishment to friends with whom he was having a last drink in his study. "Odd fellow. Maybe it's better we look for someone else."

If only Mr. Busby had thought of that earlier, Lizzie thought as she performed her last duties. Ruiha and the others went home, cheerful, with some of the remaining food for their families. The cook was generous about that, and Mrs. Busby hardly kept an eye on her.

Lizzie slunk into her room. Should she take a bag? Should she flee, just to be safe, after satisfying Smithers? But where? She loved her work at the Busbys. She quickly packed a change of dress and some underclothes. She had promised Smithers the whole night. If he insisted on that, she would have to go straight to work for the Busbys the next morning.

***

Martin Smithers was already waiting at the back door of the inn when Lizzie cautiously knocked. He succeeded in sneaking her into his room, unseen by the innkeeper, without difficulty. Lizzie sighed with relief. She would have died of embarrassment if the old lady who managed the inn caught her with a guest. Smithers wanted Lizzie to wear only her apron, and he found it exceedingly arousing when she obliged. Lizzie just prayed all of this would pass without further incident, and without pregnancy. Lizzie had stopped noting her monthly cycle but hoped not to be in her most dangerous days. Still, she would douche herself afterward—something she used to do as a matter of course—just to be on the safe side.

Smithers insisted on the whole night, but did not demand much of Lizzie. It nauseated her, but he mauled her with wet kisses and asked her repeatedly to curtsy in her apron and bonnet and say phrases like: "Dinner is served." His advances hardly caused her pain. He was rather an unimaginative lover. Nevertheless, Lizzie did her best to make the night special for him. She held up her end of the bargain and proved more active, tender, and willing than in Campbell Town.

Early in the morning, Smithers fell asleep. Lizzie lay next to him a while longer, as if on coals. She wanted to go home. The sooner she took a vinegar douche, the better. And a little sleep before work would be nice, of course. She was deathly tired. But she could hardly hope for rest. It was five in the morning, and her work began at half past six.

Lizzie cast a final glance at the man in bed as she gathered her bag and stole quietly from the room. She hoped never to see him again.

Unfortunately, the innkeeper was already awake and busy in the kitchen wing. The back door was blocked, and Lizzie did not dare slink out the front. She waited impatiently until the innkeeper went into the front of the house, then she ran back to the Busbys. It was cold on the road and in the kitchen, but Lizzie took a pitcher of icy water to her room and washed herself as thoroughly as she could. She had forgotten the vinegar. Once, she had always kept a small bottle on hand, but this was her first douche in years.

Lizzie ran to the kitchen, hoping to get the vinegar before the cook arrived. If she had to she could make up some story for the cook, but a pregnancy could not be hidden. On the way back to her room from the kitchen, she suddenly heard voices.

"At this hour, Mr. Smithers?" James Busby's aggravated voice came from the receiving room. "Could your urgent news not have waited a bit? You've dragged us from our beds, sir."

"By the time you woke on your own, the criminal might well be on her way to the next town," Martin Smithers said.

That bastard! She had given him his night, but here he was to betray her.

"I was not sure yesterday if it really was the girl, but when she came to my hotel last night . . ."

Lizzie felt sick. All Lizzie had was the desire to weep. She had not managed to protect her virtue. Worse, she had sold herself anew.

But for now she was still free. By the time the sleepy Busby had made sense of Smithers's frantic telling of the story and taken action to seize her, she could be gone. If only she had a destination. Lizzie could not hide in Russell, or Kororareka as the Maori called it. Though it was not far, it was too small, and in a whaling camp, a woman on her own was fair game. She might get by as a whore, but as soon as there was a small bounty for her, her next customer would hand her over.

The Maori village, she suddenly thought, and a great relief washed over her. Why hadn't she thought of this the day before? Her Maori friends would not betray her, and the *pakeha* would not dare press into a Ngati Pau village on suspicion alone.

Lizzie couldn't risk returning to her room, but on her way out of the house, she met the cook, Ruiha, and Kaewa, the other kitchen girl.

The three women listened to Lizzie's confused story. She did not know if they understood everything, but at least there was no doubt that she was welcome in the village.

"You can stay as long as you want," said Kaewa.

"Could you . . . my things?"

Lizzie wanted to ask the girls to bring her bag, but she was so exhausted and overwhelmed, her ability to express this in Maori faltered. The bag she had packed the night before was still in her room. She somehow made herself clear enough, and Ruiha nodded gently and thoughtfully, as was her manner.

***

Despite the early hour, the tribe's *marae* was already bustling with activity: the women were preparing flatbread on an open fire and feeding the *hangi* ovens, the children were playing, and the men were caring for the livestock—the tribe now kept sheep. Lizzie was received with excitement. No one asked what she was doing there on a workday, but the women noticed her confusion and fear.

"Are you sick?" Ruiha's mother asked. "Go to Tepora. She's speaking with the gods, but afterward, surely she'll have time for you."

Tepora was the village midwife. She also knew about healing and served the gods as a priestess. Lizzie did not completely grasp the range of duties of a *tohunga,* as they called Tepora, but Lizzie knew Tepora to be helpful and calm. She received Lizzie without many words, roasted bread for her, and heated water and herbs. Lizzie felt better as she ate and drank. Then she began to tell—of London, of Australia, and finally of the previous, horrible night.

Tepora gently stroked her hand. "I know you suffered through yesterday," she said kindly. "All of that defines your life today, but you must not let it rule you."

"Is that supposed to mean that it's my fault?" Lizzie said angrily. "I never desired that bastard."

Tepora shook her head. "You don't understand, child. You don't see the difference between *taku* and *toku. Taku* tells you how important you are for your story. And *toku* tells you how important your story is for you. You are not important to London or to Australia. And this man is not important for you."

"I'm running away from him anyway," said Lizzie bitterly. "And I have to leave a life that I like well."

"Perhaps you are running to a destination that waits for you in the past," said Tepora quietly. "All times are one, Lizzie. You can define them for yourself."

Lizzie sighed. She didn't understand Tepora—even if she knew the meanings of the words. Clearly the old woman could not help her. Or could she?

"Do you know of any herbs that will keep me from getting pregnant?" Lizzie asked hopefully.

Tepora shrugged. "Not completely sure but somewhat sure," she said. "Wait, I'll fetch something for you. It will cause a bleeding."

Lizzie waited patiently in front of the wise woman's house. She was not permitted to enter. That, too, counted among the tribe's many taboos. Tepora soon appeared with a cup, and Lizzie drank the bitter brew with a sigh of relief.

Just as she was leaving the wise woman, Lizzie saw a possible ally who was likely anchored in the here and now. Kahu Heke strolled, self-assured, through the camp. The young warrior smiled at Lizzie as she approached him.

"There you are, Elizabeth," he said happily. He always called Lizzie by her proper name, although she thought it sounded strange from his mouth. "I was sent to find you. The chief wants to speak with you. The women say you ran away from the *pakeha.*" Kahu's whole face shone, making the blue tattoos on his cheek seem to dance. "As it should be. Perhaps now you understand why I don't like them."

"It was something completely unrelated."

Kahu arched his brows. "If I understood the women correctly, the *pakeha* sold you to an old lecher."

Lizzie once again felt the blood rise to her cheeks. It was difficult to explain in the foreign language what had happened to her. But, of course, Kahu spoke fluent English, like most of the younger Maori. He accompanied her to the chieftain's house, and she was happy he did—regardless if it was as protector, as interpreter, or simply out of curiosity.

Kuti Haoka received Lizzie in front of the *wharenui*, the village's meeting house. It was not raining that day, so he spared them the extensive ceremonies necessary, according to Maori custom, to admit a visitor. The setting was awe-inspiring enough as it was. Kuti Haoka, an old warrior, stood in traditional clothing in front of the *wharenui*, which was richly decorated with thousands of carvings. Against the wintry cold, he had wrapped himself in a voluminous shawl, which made him look like a powerful, dangerous raptor. The mountains reared up behind him and the village, and, despite the rain the day before, the air was crystal clear.

Lizzie, Kahu, and an audience from the village kept a respectful distance. The tribal chieftain was *tapu* as well. He could not be touched.

"You are here, *pakeha wahine*, to ask our aid?"

Lizzie swallowed when she heard his deep, husky voice. She nervously began to tell her tale, but Kuti Haoka soon bade her to stop and, with a few curt words, asked Kahu to translate.

"Just speak English," Kahu encouraged her. "That will make it easier for everyone. The chief appreciates that you speak our language, but he also sees that yesterday's burdens are weighing on your speech today. I'll translate for him."

Lizzie smiled gratefully. Then she began to explain in English what had happened to her. Kahu translated, and the chief listened to everything quietly and carefully.

"As a punishment, they took you from your tribe to an island with strange stars?" he asked. "Because you wanted to feed children and so took a few flatbreads from a neighbor's fire?"

"Something like that," said Lizzie. Kahu's translation had sounded rather free to her as well. "Only, I don't really have a tribe."

"And then a man you did not want took you, and the other women did not intervene?"

Lizzie nodded.

"Any woman would have run away," Kahu said.

The chieftain nodded but then reflected a long time before offering Lizzie a response.

"I would very much like to help you, *pakeha wahine*, but I don't want any trouble," he finally said—or at least this was how Kahu translated his flowery expressions. "There is ever more bad blood between Maori and *pakeha* lately, and arguments among the tribes as well. So, it is difficult to send you to another tribe. Perhaps to the Waikato; they now host our king. What do you call that, Kahu? Asylum?"

Some time ago the Maori chieftains had voted on a king from among moderate leaders like Hongi Hika. They hoped to be able to negotiate better with the whites if they could oppose their queen with a *kingi*. However, it had been hard to find volunteers for the office of *kingi*, and Queen Victoria had so far mostly ignored Potatau I of Aotearoa.

Kahu Heke shook his head. His eyes flashed willfully, as if he were planning another strike against the *pakeha* just then. "Potatau won't even understand what this is about, Uncle!" He paused a moment so the chief could consider this. "Besides, he doesn't have the slightest influence. This will only lead to aggravation, believe me. If you lend me the big canoe, the chief's canoe, I'll take her to the Ngai Tahu."

"To whom?" asked Lizzie. She had never heard of the tribe.

"On the South Island," Kahu said quickly and quietly, so as not to disturb the chief in his consideration of the bold proposal. "They'll never find you there."

"But, but . . . the South Island. That's where I came here from. We'll have to cross the whole country." Lizzie grew dizzy when she thought of the days of traveling with James Busby. "We'll never manage that without them finding me."

Kahu shook his head but gestured for her to be quiet. "What do you say, Uncle? It would increase both our *mana* to bring the *wahine* to safety. All the tribes will speak of us." The Maori recognized a warrior's influence and renown with *mana*.

The chieftain looked severely at his nephew. "The men around the fire may amuse themselves with such a story, Kahu, but will the spirits grant that your *mana* will grow? Isn't the battle we wage for Aotearoa too serious and too holy to be decided by escaped women and broken flagstaffs?"

Kahu shrugged his shoulders. "Depends on the spirit," he said in English. "Chief Hone Heke in Hawaiki will slap his sides at it."

His forebear Hone Heke had died a few years before and now, according to Maori belief, held court on the legendary island Hawaiki.

Kahu winked at Lizzie but then pulled himself together and reformulated his response somewhat more eloquently in his own language.

The chief did not seem impressed. "Do you also carry the blame for something, Kahu? Do you want to go? Will we see the canoe again? Why would you take part in a journey like this that may cost you your life?"

Kahu laid his hand on his heart. "Uncle, what are you thinking? Of course the canoe will come back. Nor will this cost me my life. I'm a good sailor. And why do I do it? Well, why did Kupe steal Kura-maro-tini?"

Lizzie did not understand these last words, but she did see the chieftain grin. "So the voyage would lead us to new islands blessed by the gods," he said. "But Kupe also returned, as is well known." The chief seemed to eye Lizzie critically.

"What did you tell him?" Lizzie whispered to Kahu. "Why do you want to take me?"

The young Maori looked at her innocently. "Because we have a common enemy," he explained. "And there's no better friend than the enemy of an enemy."

Lizzie frowned. None of that involved words she did not know in Kahu's language. Really she ought to have understood better. Perhaps the Maori were speaking in allusions. They often did that, and Lizzie thought it would take more than a lifetime to hear all the legends and stories about Aotearoa and its ancient heroes, and to understand their meaning.

Kuti Haoka made his decision. "Very well," he said, turning to the people of his tribe and raising his voice. "Kahu Heke, chieftain's son of the Ngati Pau, will travel with the big canoe. May he journey with the blessing of the gods. Tangaroa may accompany his journey. We will prepare the canoe."

"And you," he said, turning back to Lizzie, "will be safe here until tomorrow. But if you want to accompany my nephew, so accompany him to the meeting house. I know the customs of *pakeha*. And no man of my blood is to besmirch your honor." With that, the chief walked back inside the *wharenui*.

Lizzie leaped at Kahu. "What does he mean? We're supposed to marry? Why?"

Sleeping together in the tribe's *wharenui* meant marriage. Men and women who simply wanted to have fun together slipped off outside. In the Maori view, they did not thereby dishonor the women.

"The chief misunderstood something," Kahu said offhandedly. "Don't worry. I won't do anything to you. Not here, not on the journey."

Lizzie readily let the subject drop. There were other things that unsettled her far more. "How do you picture the journey, anyway?" she asked, thinking of Michael and Connor's outrageous scheme to flee from Australia to New Zealand on a sailboat. "Do you mean to sail? Or row? The two of us all alone? Do you know how far it is? We have to go all the way around the island. That's a long way, and it's winter."

Lizzie remembered that England did not send prison transport ships until it was spring. The ocean was considered too unruly in winter, and surely that was true of the Tasman Sea too.

Kahu looked at her sternly. "So do you want to get away from the old dog looking for you now or not?" he asked, almost angry. Apparently, he had been counting on more gratitude than penetrating questions. "And don't you tell me how far it is. You seem to forget we were navigating around these islands ten generations before Tasman was even born. In summer and in winter, in spring and in fall. And now, excuse me. I must take possession of the chieftain's canoe."

Chapter 7

Putting the chieftain's canoe into the water seemed to be a highly complicated and spiritual matter. The men of the tribe spent the day on the beach, leading dances, songs, and blessings. The women busied themselves with preparations for an opulent dinner. Lizzie helped them cut, season, and cook vegetables, fish, and pork for the farewell celebration.

Everyone was in high spirits, and by the afternoon the younger girls were wearing their traditional dancing clothes—woven upper body coverings and skirts of hardened flax strands—over which they wrapped blankets against the winter cold. The men were still celebrating on the beach when it grew dark, and the women greeted Ruiha and Kaewa as well as the Busbys' cook. Lizzie was desperate for news from the councillor's house and she was cheered when Ruiha waved at her right away with her bag. She had found it and taken it before Lizzie was even missed.

"It took a while for the master and mistress to understand everything that Mr. Smithers said about you," explained Kaewa.

"And? Did they believe him?"

Lizzie had to ask even though she knew the answer. She couldn't help but hope the Busbys appreciated her and her many years of tireless work. Perhaps they had simply thrown Martin Smithers out. Or maybe they were sending a letter to Van Diemen's Land requesting pardon. Surely it would be granted—so many years with a family like the Busbys had to count for more than an escape.

But Ruiha nodded. "Yes, in the end, they did. Especially since you were gone. Perhaps if you had stayed . . ."

"Nonsense!" Kahu Heke shouted. He was returning from the beach. With him came all the other men, starving from all the singing and dancing for the god of the sea. "Don't even think of going back, Elizabeth. The whites only believe the worst about people, even their own."

Kaewa nodded. "The mistress said you had become suspicious lately anyway, being here in the village. She lost trust in you right away."

Lizzie swallowed her tears. It was no use crying over injured pride. After all, it did seem that a righteous life was not to be her fate.

"Here, eat something," Kahu said, handing her a bowl of meat and sweet potatoes. "And take a drink." He held out a bottle of whiskey. "Forget the Busbys. Tomorrow we'll be at sea."

***

In the morning, Kahu and Lizzie loaded the chieftain's canoe with provisions and water. She felt better as soon as she saw the craft. Until then she had always imagined the canoe as a sort of rowboat. But the *Hauwhenua* was a gorgeous outrigger canoe decorated with carvings, the pride of the tribe under Kuti Haoka. It only had its shape in common with the little boats in which the Busbys' children liked to paddle around the bays. It offered space for at least twenty rowers or passengers, but as a rule, a sail, not muscle, powered a canoe like this. The outrigger ensured it would not capsize in rough seas.

Kahu explained to Lizzie that the sail, which was not square but oval and tapered into two blades, provided safety.

"It makes the boat faster," he said. "And besides, it will help the boat sit more securely in the water when the wind blows. A very important innovation—only the *pakeha* still haven't happened upon it." Kahu smiled encouragingly as he tossed Lizzie's bag on board. "You really don't need to fear, *pakeha wahine*," he added gently. "I'm sorry if I was gruff with you yesterday. I was unaware that you were afraid of the voyage."

Lizzie nodded. She had since then thought about the words Kahu had said to his uncle the day before. Kupe had been the first settler to reach New Zealand from Polynesia, and Kura-maro-tini became his wife. Kahu must have compared himself and Lizzie to those two; the chieftain had supposed that

Kahu hoped to earn her love with a voyage to the South Island. Though the chief had not liked it, Lizzie understood that Kahu did not want to marry her right away. She was prepared to give herself to him as thanks for her rescue. After all, men insisted on such payment, and even if his face repulsed her, Kahu's body was taut and agile. Sleeping with him would, no doubt, be more pleasant than her nights with Martin Smithers.

"What does *Hauwhenua* mean?" she asked, hoping to bring the conversation to neutral ground.

Kahu smiled. "Wind that blows from land. The canoe is to carry us forth from the coast."

Finally it was time to depart. Almost the entire village led the travelers to the water. Ahead of everyone strode the chief, his untouchable daughter, and several priests. Their departure with the *waka ama*, the outrigger canoe, did not pass without songs and blessings.

Kahu gallantly helped Lizzie into the boat. She had to smile. Here they were, on the beach of Aotearoa, surrounded by a few half-naked singing and dancing natives, but Kahu behaved like a polite suitor inviting his sweetheart onto a rowboat in Hyde Park's Serpentine lake. Kahu's behavior was a mixture of tribal custom and an English education from his European teachers. Lizzie wondered if one would triumph over the other in the end.

Kahu first directed the *Hauwhenua* away from the South Island. Even though that was their destination, he thought it made more sense to sail along the west side of the North Island in the Tasman Sea. Lizzie gasped, almost panicking, when the land disappeared from view.

"You really don't trust me, do you, Elizabeth? Is it because I'm not white? Or because you think me a dodger?"

Lizzie pulled her scarf more tightly around her head. It was sharply cold at sea. She tried to smile. "I, it's just, it's just the boat is so small for the wide-open sea. And, and you're not a sailor."

Kahu laughed. "I'm a born sailor, Elizabeth, like all men of the tribes. Have you never seen the Maori children in the bays with their little canoes? But I can ease your mind otherwise. I sailed on an English three-master from Tamaki Makau Rau to London." Tamaki Makau Rau was the Maori name for Auckland.

"You've been to London?" Lizzie could hardly believe it.

Kahu nodded. "Aye, I wanted to see it once. So I hired on to an English ship. You have to know your enemy if you want to fight him successfully. And I wanted to know what the *pakeha* had planned. What they wanted to make of our country if we let them. I'll tell you now, I didn't like it."

Lizzie shrugged her shoulders. "Well, London. It's not evil, but the docks . . ."

"It's a sewer, Elizabeth." The words burst out of Kahu. "You know that yourself. There are beautiful houses, big houses, and rich people, of course. But the tribe does not stick together. Society is rotten. I've seen the children in the bad quarters who must choose either to steal or to starve. I can imagine what your past life was like."

Lizzie blushed. "Did you . . . ?"

"Did I buy a *pakeha* girl for the night?" Kahu shook his head. "No. But not because I'm such a good person—sorry if I have to disappoint you on that. I went into town with the sailors. Only, the girls didn't want me." He pointed at his tattoos.

Lizzie smiled bravely. "I don't mind," she claimed. "So if you'd like . . ."

Kahu exhaled sharply. "So, you think that's why I'm doing this?"

Lizzie shrugged.

"That's not why," said Kahu. He did not look at Lizzie though. "It's something else entirely. If I'm ever to sleep with you, Lizzie, then it will only be in the meeting lodge in front of the eyes of the elders. I want to be part of your future, not your past. And I will be *toku* for you, not *taku*."

Lizzie's shy smile was real this time. "Was that just a declaration of love?" she asked carefully. "And what about the conflict between the Maori and *pakeha*? Or about the war you think is coming?"

Kahu was still looking out at the sea. "All wars end one day—for good or ill. And if you really want to know, I don't believe we can throw the *pakeha* back out of the country. In the end, we'll have to share it. We must learn respect for each other. Unfortunately, many of you only understand the language of war. Not you, though, Elizabeth Portland. You and I, we could make something new."

Lizzie sighed. "You don't know me, you know," she said quietly. "Portland is not even my real name."

Kahu looked at her, confused. He seemed embarrassed. But then he smiled.

"But I know the name of the canoe you came to Aotearoa in."

Lizzie wished she wanted to kiss him, but she felt nothing except a vague form of peace as Kahu calmly shifted the sail.

"Will we go ashore at night?" she asked.

Kahu shook his head. "No. At first we'll travel close to the coast, but later we'll move away from it a bit, and then navigation becomes easier at night—as long as the gods let the stars shine. We'll only land now and again to take on more water and provisions. But you really need not fear. This isn't some voyage of discovery, Elizabeth. We're sailing around a country that has belonged to my people for centuries—even if your people are only now reaching their hand out for it. You can go to sleep unconcerned. And tomorrow we'll be looking in the direction of Hawaiki."

To her surprise, Lizzie slept rather well in the swaying canoe, wrapped up in numerous blankets against the biting, winter cold. The air was fresh and made her sleepy. She awoke relaxed and no longer afraid. Lizzie started to prepare a breakfast, but Kahu called her to him first, pointing toward the coast. Imposing cliffs fell steeply into the sea. They were craggy and without vegetation. Only rarely did a kauri tree cling to a projecting rock on which a little soil seemed to have collected.

"Look, that's Cape Reinga, the northernmost tip of Te Ika-a-Maui and, so, of all Aotearoa. From there wander the souls of dead Maori back to Hawaiki, the island from where the first canoes came."

Kahu pointed out onto the sea. They could spy a little island, but after that, all was ocean—and no one knew where Hawaiki had really been located. Kahu's ancestors must have sailed from unimaginably far away.

Lizzie shivered. "So Hawaiki lay to the north?" she asked. "Was it colder than here?"

Kahu took the dried meat and bread she handed him, and laughed. "Elizabeth, *wahine*, how long have you been on this side of the globe? Seven years or more? And in that time, have you still not realized that things are different here than in England? Hawaiki was warmer than Aotearoa. That's why many of the plants our ancestors brought could not take root. In fact, only the *kumara* thrived, the sweet potato. You *pakeha* have fared better; your climate is similar to ours. Your plants flourish, and your animals all the more. You will all shape this country more strongly than we. You can do more with it. But that is still no reason to appropriate it without paying properly."

Lizzie nodded but did not want to think too much about the fighting between Maori and *pakeha*. The land along which they sailed was too lovely— a pristine, wild, mountainous landscape dotted with white beaches and green hills. Toward evening, the land fell out of sight again and would remain invisible for several days. The thought unsettled Lizzie anew.

The weather was worse too. After two days, they were caught in a terrible storm. True, the *Hauwhenua* could hardly capsize, but it did not offer any protection from the weather. Waves washed into the canoe; Kahu was busy with the sail, so Lizzie bailed water out of the boat. She was soaked through within the shortest time, and her whole body shook with cold.

"But we're making good progress," Kahu declared, pleased, as lightning raged across the night sky. Indeed, the canoe only moved ahead, and the voyage seemed nothing but fun to the sailor.

Lizzie, on the other hand, only felt the need to pray. She asked herself seriously whether it was better to turn to Jesus Christ or Tangaroa, the Maori god of the sea.

Kahu shook with laughter when she inquired to whom he was praying.

"You may find it funny, but I don't want to blaspheme against God," she said, annoyed. "Least of all in this storm. If you made someone angry up there . . ."

The tall Maori looked tenderly at the delicate girl who now looked like a wet, frightened cat. Lizzie could not guess how similar to his people she was. Kahu, at least, had never met a European who approached questions of religion so practically. Most *pakeha* had always struck him as bigoted.

"So you'd risk it in good weather?" he teased her, having to yell over the wind. "Pray to whomever you want, Elizabeth. You're not in danger anyway. The wind will die down soon. We Maori learn that Tane is the god responsible for the wind, Tangaroa for the sea, and Papa for the earth. Yet in the missionary school, we sang songs about Jesus the shepherd, the sailor, the gardener in the Lord's vineyard."

"In the vineyard?" Lizzie asked. Her study of the Bible had not gotten as far as the vineyard, but that interested her.

Her question didn't deter Kahu from his theological considerations. "Sometimes," he continued, "I ask myself if that doesn't all get to be too much for him."

Lizzie had to laugh despite herself. "Look, there's a star," she called, point-ing to the sky where the first clouds were drifting apart.

Kahu nodded. "There, you see? It's clearing up. For which you can thank Rangi, the god of the sky."

As it started to grow light, Kahu steered toward land. They needed sup-plies and to dry themselves.

"This is the region of the Ngati Maniapoto," Kahu said as he pulled the canoe onto the beach. "In truth, they're very warlike, but now that they host our king, they act very diplomatically. We'll make a fire, you can warm your-self, and I'll look around for drinking water."

The area surely had plenty of water. It was defined by green hills and thick forests over which defiant rocks towered like giants. Lizzie was nervous when Kahu left her alone, but she took the opportunity to remove her completely soaked clothing, though all she had to cover herself with was an equally wet blanket.

Kahu smiled tenderly when he returned and saw Lizzie sitting by the fire. She had let down her hair and untangled it. It hung halfway down her back, unruly and stiff from saltwater but dry, at least. Her slender body was wrapped in a blanket held in place somewhat securely by a belt around her hips. She was grilling fish on sticks and sweet potatoes in the embers, and she had built a frame out of fern wood on which their clothes now hung to dry. To him, she was no longer a *pakeha wahine* but a Maori girl he would gladly have taken in his arms.

Kahu brought skin bags of fresh water and a bird he had killed. They would eat royally that day. He plucked the bird, rubbed its meat with sea salt, and then laid it on Lizzie's improvised grill.

"How did you shoot that thing?" Lizzie asked, amazed. Kahu had set out unarmed; he only carried the small knife he always did. "What kind of bird is that anyway? The feathers looked more like fur."

Kahu nodded. "Aye, at first glance. And I didn't shoot him; I dug him out. Don't look so surprised. Kiwis are nocturnal. During the day, they dig themselves holes in the woods. Once you have a bit of experience, you can find those holes and dig them out and kill them. The English would surely find that dastardly, but we're hungry."

Lizzie did not care how Kahu had caught the bird; it was delicious. She was dry and felt better when they finally took the canoe back out to sea.

"How much farther is it now?" asked Lizzie.

Kahu shrugged. "We could be there in a day or two. Depends on how the wind blows. And where exactly we want to go."

"Maybe to Nelson?" Lizzie said.

Kahu furrowed his brow. "That's the last place I'd go ashore," he said. "There are hardly any Maori left in the area since the whole thing with Wairau."

"There was war there, right?" Lizzie looked fearful. "The German settlers talked about it. Are the, the Ngai Tahu very aggressive?"

Kahu shook his head and laughed bitterly. "Quite the contrary. They're much too peaceable. Not a single uprising against the whites beforehand. The Ngati Toa lived in Wairau—they actually come from the North Island, but they once had a very warlike chief who expanded their domain as far as the South Island. There were a few fights with the Ngai Tahu then too. The Ngati Toa are not especially patient. When the *pakeha* measured their land before there were even negotiations for sale, the Ngati Toa attacked. Twenty-two dead on the whites' side, four on the Maori's. I wouldn't call that a war."

"You're not dead, though," said Lizzie. "No one takes it seriously unless they're in the middle of it."

Kahu smirked. "A pronouncement worthy of Tepora. But apart from all the wars, fights, conflicts, or whatever you want to call them, do you really think it smart to go back into hiding where once Busby hired you? They'll look for you there first."

Lizzie chewed on her lip. "But are there even other cities? I mean . . ."

Kahu rolled his eyes. "The South Island is considerably bigger than the North Island, although less densely populated. The Ngai Tahu number perhaps two thousand. Thus, they also tolerate more *pakeha*. From where we are, the closest area is the West Coast. However, I don't like the idea of leaving you there alone with whalers and seal hunters, a savage heap of the vilest sorts your England has to offer. Those towns are still growing too—the only things finished so far are the taverns."

Lizzie sighed. She could well imagine the options for women to earn money in these towns.

"On the East Coast, there's Dunedin and Christchurch. Both are rather far; we'd need to sail a few days. But God-fearing people live there." He winked.

Lizzie waved him away wearily. "I know. The Canterbury Association. And a Scottish organization . . . I can't remember the name . . . Mr. Busby knows them all. We always had representatives come visit. Kahu, I don't dare go to Christchurch. I'd probably run right into another man like Smithers."

Kahu nodded. "Or even the man himself," he said. "They build roads on the South Island too. Do you intend to work as a housemaid again?"

"What else?" Lizzie let her hand dangle over the edge into the water. "I can't do anything else. Perhaps in a less important family, though. A smaller house; a farm if I have to."

"You could stay with the Ngai Tahu," Kahu suggested.

Lizzie shook her head. "No, no, don't be mad, Kahu. I, I like you Maori. But I'm a *pakeha*. I liked it at the Busbys. And the Ngai Tahu won't want me anyway. What would they do with me? No, we . . . Are there other towns?"

Kahu thought. "Kaikoura," he said reluctantly. "Another whaling station, really. But there are supposed to be more farmers settling there now—though certainly no gentlemen like Mr. Busby. No one will look for you there." He smiled. "And you'd be closer to me. The legend says the demigod Maui caught the mighty fish that later became the North Island near Kaikoura."

Lizzie looked at Kahu. This time she succeeded at her soul-warming smile. "Like that, we could easily catch a fish and have an island for just the two of us."

Kahu shrugged. "Alas, only the gods have that option. People take their canoes and sail the seas until they find land. Like Kupe and Kura-maro-tini once did. So if you want, Elizabeth . . ."

Lizzie lowered her gaze when she saw the love in his eyes.

***

A few days later, they were just off the shore of Kaikoura. The peninsula on which the town lay fascinated Lizzie even from the sea. The beaches, the hills, the daunting mountain landscape of the southern mountains, which almost reached to the sea—everything seemed even bigger and less civilized than in the north. She was startled when suddenly a whale emerged in front of her.

"It, it, it could gulp us down in one bite," gasped Lizzie as the giant whale performed coltish leaps.

"But he won't," Kahu soothed her. "He'll be happy if we don't do anything to him. The people here are slowly killing them. There aren't as many as before."

It was clear to her where the legend of Maui and his fish came from. One could imagine that such a giant beast really could become an island.

Kahu suggested presenting Lizzie in the local Ngai Tahu settlement, but she preferred to go straight to town.

"I can go myself and say hello to the tribe if it's necessary," she said. "But I need to find employment and lodging in Kaikoura, and they can't help with that."

More than anything, she did not want to enter the Maori settlement with Kahu. Everyone—at least every woman—would clearly see during his introduction what Kahu felt for her. People would believe she was his wife, or at least his lover. The natives would not imagine a platonic relationship, and Lizzie did not want to begin her new life with misunderstandings.

"You'll need money," Kahu said.

Lizzie shrugged. "Will the Ngai Tahu give me some?" she asked.

With a sigh, Kahu drew a money pouch from the bag in which he kept his things. "I'll give you some. But it's not much. You won't be able to live more than a day or two from it."

Lizzie blushed as she took the small pouch. "This is . . . you don't need to do this, Kahu."

He waved her objections away. "You have nothing to give back, at least nothing you'd be willing to give and I could accept. Don't say it, Elizabeth. It's fine. If the gods desire it, we'll meet again. Then you can pay me this amount back, if you're rich by then. *Haere ra*, Elizabeth."

He meant to bow slightly, but Lizzie pressed against him and put her nose and forehead on his. *Hongi*—the Maori salutation. "Why, why do you still call me Elizabeth, anyway?" She didn't want to drag out their good-bye farewell, but she had wanted to ask him that for a long time.

Kahu looked at her seriously. "Because that's your name. Maybe not Portland. But not Lizzie, either. Lizzie is a name for a servant. Elizabeth is a queen's name."

Lizzie bit her lip. Did he really see her that way? As a queen? Michael had only seen the whore in her. She did not know why she thought of Michael just then.

Lizzie raised her hand and gently stroked the tattoos on Kahu's cheek. The symbol of a chieftain. "*Haere ra*, Kahu Heke," she said softly. "I hope the gods mean well by you."

Chapter 8

Lizzie waded onto land—Kahu had not wanted to sail the conspicuous chieftain's canoe into the small harbor of Kaikoura, so he let her out on a beach near the settlement. Now she put her shoes back on and made her way to town. Or was it better to call it a village? From the sea Kaikoura had looked very attractive in the sunlight. Up close, the sun also shone on dirt and squalor.

Kahu had told her it had originally been a whaling station, and that was exactly what it looked like. Of course Lizzie had never seen a whaling station, but she knew the docks in London, and she knew how a place looked when primarily men—and young, lost, and not very domestic girls—lived there. Kaikoura consisted of cheap, thrown-together wooden houses, many in various states of disrepair. People had not settled here in the same way they had in Nelson. Everything was tailored to providing temporary roofs over the heads of men who whaled and skinned seals. No one stayed long, no one took a woman for longer than a few hours, and no one had anything of his own. Housemaids weren't likely in demand at the fishermen's huts. A general store sold all sorts of goods, from food to fishing hooks, but the owner shook his head when Lizzie asked about work.

"I manage with just my wife," he said, "and—good heavens—a maid, with a bonnet and apron, I'll bet. Allison'd laugh herself to death if I brought you to her."

"I'd throw you out," responded the gruff, squarely built woman who was just coming out of the shop's backroom. She was a head taller than her rather dwarfish-looking husband and, no doubt, held the reins. "Everyone knows what goes on in grand houses between the masters and the chambermaids."

Lizzie wondered how everyone was supposed to know that. She blushed again. "I'm an honest girl," she said. "And I, I have references."

She did in fact—written by Kahu Heke, whose education in the missionary school ensured he had covered everything. Lizzie had been deeply touched when she discovered the letters in the pouch Kahu had handed her. And she had not even been able to thank him for them.

The merchant laughed. "They won't help you make a sale, either, girl. Honest or not, no one here needs a maid. Maybe the sheep farmers farther inland. Though there aren't any homes as grand and fine as those in the plains. The farmers were all whalers and seal hunters before. If they need a house-cleaner, they take on a Maori girl—she'll stick around for bed, too, and not make a production of it. Nah, sweet. Look for another town or another job."

That was discouraging, but Lizzie continued through the town. Kaikoura, however, had only one shop, one smith, one carpenter (who was also the undertaker), and three taverns. In front of one of the taverns, she met a girl, somewhat younger than her and heavily made-up.

"Do you work here?" Lizzie asked. "On, on the street or in a house?"

The girl looked at Lizzie, amazed. She was blonde, her hair put up in a complicated coiffure, her dress too shiny and red for an honest merchant's daughter. Lizzie, on the other hand, looked exceedingly demure in her neat, dark maid's uniform.

"In the tavern," the girl answered. "No one walks the street here. Too cold and wet. Besides, the barkeepers always need new blood. And pay halfway fairly too. Are you looking for work?"

Lizzie nodded. "Yes, but not that kind."

The girl laughed. "Sure, I hear you. You're picturing a convent's kitchen, or do you mean to become a nun yourself? Your dress would suit that. There ain't any proper convent nearby, alas. Otherwise, I'd already be there. I'm Irish and a good Catholic."

Lizzie furrowed her brow. She did not know anything about convents, but the girl, doubtless, was teasing her.

"I worked as a housemaid before," Lizzie said. "And as a milkmaid too."

"Well at least the stench from the customers won't scare you off," the blonde said. "Honestly, sweet, they stink like animals here. Blubber, blood, who knows what all. Whalers aren't for delicate sensibilities." She looked at Lizzie appraisingly. "But you ain't got no delicate sensibility, do you, little sister? Now what is it that tells me you're not new to the profession?"

Lizzie sighed. So people could see it on her. She had always thought that was the case. "I haven't done it in a long time," she said.

The girl waved that away. "You don't forget how."

Lizzie bit her lip. "I don't want to do that anymore."

The girl snorted. "Sweetheart, I don't do it because it's such great fun either. But look around: there's nothing but this backwater for far and wide. Right behind're the mountains; a little to the south, Waiopuka; and the whaling station on the coast. That's where the customers mostly used to come from. But now less and less; they need ships if they want to go after the critters. They anchor here, and we serve the lads. It was nicer with regulars. They would wash up occasionally. What can you do? The Fyfes, who ran the whaling station, now raise sheep too."

Lizzie grasped at straws. "I heard that on the big sheep farms, well, that there were fine people who might need servants."

"The Fyfes are old salty dogs. They need good whiskey and the occasional girl, but certainly not to clean. And they're not big farms, either, around here. The big ones are in the plains. And there are supposed to be rich people's houses in Christchurch too."

"I simply can't go there," said Lizzie wearily.

"I can't either. I robbed a customer," the blonde said. "Wasn't even my fault. The fellow didn't want to pay, so I smashed a chair over his head and took off with his wallet. Stupid me, it was the brother of a police officer. Anyway, they're looking for me. But Christchurch is too pious to make anything there anyway. And Dunedin is worse, full of Calvinists."

"There has to be something else. I'll work hard. I know how to fish. Do you think I could make something at one of the whaling stations?"

The blonde shook with laughter. "A girl on a whaling station? I'd like to see you wade around half naked in blubber and blood to butcher the beast. Lands, sweet, you don't want to do that. You're cute enough; you've got work experience. What do you mean to do, ask around if the fishermen need help with crawfish?"

"Crawfish?"

"Aye, they drag loads of them out of the sea. They taste great too. But I don't think the fishers'd hire a girl. Even if they take their wives out now and again, the poor, overworked little things. If you're set on it, maybe one of them will marry you. They're all crazy for women. Whenever they can scrape the money together, they come to the taverns, and the girl they call upon gets a marriage proposal straight away. But is that what you want?"

Lizzie confessed that it wasn't. The fishers' huts looked dilapidated and impoverished. Their wives probably wore themselves to the bone, first at sea with their husbands and then at home, and likely with children waiting for them too. That might please God, but Lizzie's piety had its limits.

"I'll think it over," she told the girl. "What's your name, anyway?"

"Claudia. And you?"

"Lizzie."

Another world in which first names sufficed.

She tried her luck with the coffin maker, who told her she was indeed very nice but his customers did not need encouraging anymore. She strolled once more around the fishermen's huts and then went on to the Maori village.

The Ngai Tahu were friendly, and considerably more open than the tribes on the North Island. Lizzie felt comfortable with them at once, in part because they wore more Western clothing and only a few young people were tattooed. Apparently the Maori on the South Island acclimated more willingly to the customs of the *pakeha* than those on the North Island. Economically, however, things were going badly for the tribe. Many men had worked at the whaling station, always as day laborers. Now that there was less whaling to do, they had no earnings. For the women there was little to do anyway. A few helped on sheep farms, but only occasionally in the barns. As for house servants, the reports of the *pakeha* in town were confirmed: no one had ever taught a Maori to be a butler, gardener, or coachman, let alone a chamber or kitchen maid.

Lizzie stayed the night in the village, which resembled a campsite more than the proper *marae* of the Ngati Pau. It seemed the Ngai Tahu had to abandon their settlement often.

"In the spring, when the stores are low," one of the tribe members said, "we wander to better hunting grounds in the mountains. If you want, you can come along, but there are hardly any *pakeha* and certainly no large houses."

Being so close to the sea, the tribes could always feed themselves with fish, but the *pakeha* were competing with them more and more for the fishing grounds. Lizzie was surprised that their response was not like that of the tribes on the North Island, but the Ngai Tahu had a different perspective.

"Before the *pakeha* came, things were actually worse for us," the women reported. "True, there were fish, but no seeds, no sheep. It is cold in winter. Now we have warmer clothing, we tend our fields, and for a long time, we received work from the whites."

The connection with the *pakeha* could be seen in the way the tribe lived. They had comforts that were more familiar to Lizzie: the women weaved wool, so there were blankets and mats. Their diet seemed more varied, and they cooked their food in pots and pans purchased from the *pakeha* rather than in earthen ovens or with sticks over the fire. Of course, their geographic situation was also different. Lizzie noticed at once that it was colder here than on the North Island. Surely it was more difficult to make it through the winter.

Lizzie did not want to live at the tribe's expense for too long. After two days, she gave the women some money, said good-bye, and returned to town.

The tavern in front of which she had met Claudia was called the Green Arrow, and from what Lizzie could tell, it was also the cleanest in Kaikoura. Lizzie entered and asked for work.

Pete Hunter, the stocky barkeeper, didn't ask for references or her name. He eyed Lizzie briefly, mumbled something, and then pointed her to a room on the second floor.

"You need to keep it clean yourself, do laundry once a week at the Chinese cleaners. If you want to change your sheets more often, you have to wash them yourself."

Lizzie spent the first hours of her new old life scrubbing the room halfway clean and fighting the fleas.

"Should I lend you a dress?" asked Claudia as they went down to the tavern that evening. "Hunter'll advance you the money for materials if you want to sew yourself one, but he'll want it back with interest."

Lizzie shook her head. She had spent the previous few hours lowering the neckline on her maid's dress and raising the skirt under the apron so that it was shorter in front and gave a view of her legs. Her face was made-up and her hair coiffed, and she wore her bonnet somewhat askew.

She placed herself sheepishly next to the door of the tavern and curtsied as the first man entered. "May I take the master's coat?" Lizzie smiled mischievously up at her customer, recognizing the coffin maker.

Lizzie had her first customer.

***

Kahu Heke sailed north, thinking of the girl he was leaving behind. The first girl who seemed capable of wandering with him between the worlds of the Maori and the *pakeha*. For now, the *pakeha* still held on to her. As for him? Kahu Heke had no answer. Probably, they would elect him chief after his uncle Kuti Haoka. The Ngati Pau respected him. But if he wanted even a chance to win over Lizzie, he would have to become a farmer instead, cutting through all the *tapu* that surrounded a warrior chief, acclimating like the Ngai Tahu, whom he looked down upon. He could bring his worlds closer together for Elizabeth's sake. In truth, he would only be speeding up a development that was inevitable anyway.

Kahu decided not to bother with Kororareka and negotiating with the whalers anymore. It would be better to learn something about agriculture— perhaps even about what fascinated Lizzie so much: viniculture.

The young Maori smiled grimly as the *Hauwhenua* flew over the waves. If he wanted, once he was chief, he could even get himself crowned king. So far, no one was fighting for the post. To the Maori, the idea of centralized rule was foreign. If someone like Kahu, with his knowledge of *pakeha* culture and his fluent English, applied, everyone would be excited.

In the rush of speed and wind, Kahu gave in to his daydreams. Elizabeth was his queen, and one day, he would take her with him to London. The young Maori saw himself as *kingi*, and he laughed as he pictured Elizabeth curtsying before Victoria and having Prince Albert gallantly kiss her hand. Elizabeth would prove herself worthy of her name, a queen who warmed the hearts of others with her irresistible smile.

Chapter 9

Over the previous few days, Michael and his Maori helpers had freed more than four thousand mostly unwilling ewes and rams from their wool—all the sheep of the farms in the Kaikoura district. It had long since become custom for Michael to hand the Fyffes' farm over to the Maori girls for a few weeks in the spring and travel from farm to farm with his shearing company. The men earned a considerable additional income doing it, while the girls helped lamb and herd the ewes into the mountains for the summer. Fyffe was the only owner who employed women for that job; the other farms exclusively hired men to work as shepherds.

Now that the sheep were shorn, Michael had money in his pocket and a powerful thirst. A march through the taverns in Kaikoura sounded just about right to him. There would still be something left over to set aside for the voyage back to Ireland.

Michael was saving for his return home, although he was not sure how serious he was about it anymore. Since the letter from Father O'Brien had arrived, his zeal had markedly decreased. After all, he would not be seeing Kathleen now. She was gone. Somewhere in America with that swindling ass, Ian Coltrane.

Michael wondered how, of all the men in Ireland, she could have fallen in with that one; when he thought of his son calling that livestock trader his father, it horrified him. Worse still, all of it had been done with Michael's money. Ian Coltrane would never ever have been able to pay for passage on his own. And Michael did not believe that Ian loved Kathleen. From what he knew, Ian had kept a girl in Wicklow—a red-haired whore, impudent and stuck-up, the exact opposite of the reserved, gentle Kathleen. And Kathleen could not have loved Ian. Perhaps her parents had forced her to marry him.

Whenever Michael rode alone across the country, he imagined traveling to America and looking for Kathleen. He would flush her out somewhere in New York and knock Ian Coltrane out of her bed. Of course he knew that it would be harder to search New York than all of Ireland. Besides, the normal route to New York led to Australia—where Michael absolutely did not want to go—and then to China. So for now, Michael put off the decision. His savings grew so slowly that he would have to work for years to afford the passage. The whiskey and the blondes in Kaikoura ate up much of what he earned. When Michael's longing became overwhelming, he would treat himself to a girl, like cute little Claudia from the Green Arrow—and he paid so well that none of the girls ever complained when he called out Kathleen's name as he climaxed.

That evening, too, after shearing, he felt the need for a night with Claudia or one of the other blondes. Michael left his Maori friends Tane and Maui at the first tavern, where the beer was weaker and the women cheaper. As he opened the door at the Green Arrow, he was taken aback to see a peculiar figure standing there.

"Good evening, sir. May I help you out of your coat?" A petite, dark-blonde girl in a simple maid's dress, with a shorter skirt and a lower neckline than most, looked at Michael amicably. "It would be my pleasure to serve you tonight, sir." The girl sank down in a low curtsy but smiled seductively.

Michael could not help himself. He laughed uproariously. "Lizzie Owens! And still not respectable."

Lizzie glanced at Michael's ragged appearance, his tattered breeches and dirty raincoat. "Michael Drury," she said, "and still not rich."

Michael had long since forgotten the discord between them when they had parted. Laughing, he took Lizzie in his arms and swung her around.

"Lassie, it's so good to see you again. I've wondered a long time what became of you."

Lizzie broke free. She was also happy to see Michael, but by no means did she want to let him hurt her again.

"Shouldn't you long since have returned to Ireland?" she asked. "To marry your Mary Kathleen?"

Michael sighed. "Oh, Lizzie, that's a long story."

He began to tell it, but then Claudia shoved her way between them.

"Hands off of this one, Lizzie. He's a regular of mine." She rubbed her body against Michael and looked him seductively in the eye.

Lizzie stepped back. "I don't want him. I just know him from long ago."

Claudia smirked, whereas Michael looked embarrassed. Lizzie turned to Michael. "Do what you came for. We can talk later."

He still looked terrific with his curly black hair, which he wore longer now than before. Lizzie had almost forgotten how blue his eyes were and how they could melt her in an instant.

"You really don't mind, Lizzie, if she and I go . . . ?"

Lizzie rolled her eyes. "No, Michael. I'm just happy when no one calls me Kathleen in bed. Though I'd love to know what happened to your lady. We'll have a drink once you've made Claudia here a happy girl."

With a smile, she returned to her post. As every evening, she did not have to wait long. Men went mad for her maid outfit, especially after she altered it and started calling every insignificant whaler or shepherd "master." Lizzie earned enough to get by and to afford a new dress or two. Claudia and the other girls made fun of the dresses Lizzie picked out, which were always made of good material and quite staid. Sunday church dresses, Claudia called them.

However, Lizzie did not go to church. The reverend was an easygoing man who looked after his sheep more than his God, so he allowed the girls to come to services. But Lizzie no longer wanted to pray to a God who, in Kahu's view, was, at best, overtaxed by His faithful and, at worst, did not care about them at all. Lizzie was long-suffering. She understood that God could not make it too easy for people to lead a life pleasing to Him. But she could not forgive Him for the obstacles He had put in her way: Martin Smithers had been one test too many, not to mention life in the Green Arrow.

Lizzie hated serving the whalers and seal hunters who stank of blubber and blood, and the intense smell of sheep emanating from the shepherds disgusted her almost as much. Selling herself had not been as bad with the sailors on the docks in London. They had often treated themselves to a bath after the long sea voyage, so they were cleaned up for the girls and were cheerful when they told their stories of foreign lands and strange customs. The men in Kaikoura, on the other hand, slogged through their sad, failed existences, gambling and whoring away what little money they earned. In bed they were clumsy and stiff—although Lizzie did attract the best of the lot for herself. After all, the men needed a modicum of humor and imagination to go for her little game. But even her "masters" wanted to get the most for their money as quickly as possible, and each of them left a few fleas or lice behind on the pillow.

Lizzie's life was a constant battle against stench, filth, and vermin. She washed her bedsheets daily herself, but really, she would have had to change them after every customer for them to stay halfway clean.

While the other girls spent their nights drinking, Lizzie mostly stayed sober. She had Pete pour her cold tea when the customers bought her whiskey. It was enough that her nights resembled nightmares; she did not want to have to deal with morning headaches too. Besides, she did not like the booze Pete Hunter served. It wasn't that the cheap booze insulted her palate after the Busbys' wine; even inveterate whiskey drinkers shuddered with every swallow. Lizzie didn't know where the stuff came from, but whoever made it ought to have been banned not to Australia but to the North Pole.

Lizzie did her best to remain hopeful that there really would be another alternative to her sad existence in the inn. It could not be that she was to spend her whole life there. She often went out to look for other work in the town, and occasionally Lizzie and Claudia or one of the other girls would rent a coach for a Sunday excursion. Lizzie's wish to find an out-of-the-way sheep farm—perhaps operated by an English gentleman and his wife who yearned to hire a well-trained housemaid—never came true. When even her Maori friends left Kaikoura to go on their wanderings, Lizzie ran the danger of sinking into hopelessness.

She yearned for Kahu Heke and dreamed of him and his canoe the way other girls did of princes and their white horses. In her daydreams, he landed on the beach near Kaikoura, she climbed inside, and they fled her sad existence.

Lizzie often thought that it would be better to turn herself in and face the risk of being shipped to Van Diemen's Land again. She had felt better in the female factory than she did in the Green Arrow, and at some point even serious criminals were released. Lizzie even had caught herself dreaming of a life with Cecil, the Smitherses' old gardener.

And now Michael had come.

Lizzie thought of him while she lay under a whaler who just that morning had harpooned a gray whale. The man had proudly told her of it right away, though his catch had hardly escaped her notice. After all, he stank as if he had bathed in train oil. His whole body was covered by a greasy layer.

Lizzie absolutely had to distract herself while he worked himself out on top of her. She ran the risk of vomiting. So she tried to envision Michael's face. He still looked good, maybe even better. The hard life and the work outside—perhaps even his concern for Kathleen—had etched wrinkles in his face that she found attractive. And while he looked older, he still seemed to be an adventurer, and his life was still young—as was hers. Did she still long for him? Did she feel a desire to share her life with him like she had when they had played husband and wife on the way to New Zealand? One thing was for certain: she did not picture him as a lover. At the moment she felt no desire for physical love. Yet Lizzie was happy Michael had come back into her life. She felt something. Almost like hope.

Naturally, that was foolish. Michael had never had the air of a fairy tale prince. Yet somehow she really wanted him around again. It was as if he were turning a page within her—damn it all, he was not going to help her onto the back of his white horse so they could gallop away together, but he was a man. Granted, he had hardly ever proved rich in ideas or success—not in his wooing of Mary Kathleen and certainly not in his interaction with Lizzie. But he was not so stupid or so proud that he wouldn't listen to a woman, and Lizzie believed she could take the horse's reins and lead the prince onto the right path. Now she just had to think of something.

Lizzie's heart beat heavily as the whaler finally grunted and pulled out of her. If what Michael had told her about Ireland was true, there was a possibility of becoming both rich and respectable.

She did not return immediately to her work post. With a shudder, she washed the traces of the last customer from her body and put on one of her good dresses. Then she excused herself to Pete Hunter.

"Pete, sorry, but I suddenly received a visitor." She blushed. The whores used this expression when they got their periods.

Hunter looked at her unhappily. "Again, Lizzie? Weren't you visited just last week?"

Lizzie looked at her feet. "I, it seems I caught something. Anyway, I cured that, but now, well, it seems I'm bleeding again."

She hoped that the innkeeper did not know enough about women's matters to question her.

"Fine, fine. The main thing is you're not running around here with a heavy belly. Do you mean to go out still?" He looked at her dress. "Wouldn't it be better to lie in bed?"

"Pete, I need to see the woman again. About this matter now. I don't want to be out from work longer than I have to, you know."

Fortunately, Michael was already standing back at the bar with Claudia, and he watched Lizzie walk outside. She hoped he would follow her, and indeed, he caught up with her at the next corner.

"So, I still have to meet you in unlit streets." He grinned and put an arm around her. "Tell me what you've been doing, Lizzie. Or no, we'll find a nice tavern where we can drink as we talk."

Lizzie shook her head. "There's nothing like that here, Michael. All three pubs are whorehouses, too, and I can't be seen at the Golden Horseshoe or in Paul's Tavern after sneaking out on Pete. If we want to drink, you're going to have scare up a bottle somewhere, and we'll go down to the docks."

Lizzie waited for Michael on the pier, and finally he showed up with the whiskey.

"What miserable booze," he complained after taking a gulp and passing the bottle to Lizzie. She smiled, having expected that reaction.

"I wanted to talk to you about that," she said. "But first, tell me: What happened to your plans for Ireland?"

Michael gave her the broad view of what had happened, and Lizzie laughed. "So, she did replace you, your Mary Kathleen," she mocked him. "She who was supposed to wait until the end of her days, ever with a prayer for her lost love on her lips."

"I'm sure she couldn't help it!" Michael defended his love. "I'm sure."

Lizzie rolled her eyes.

"Anyway, I haven't saved up enough money for Ireland, yet," he continued, "or for America. You don't make much as a shepherd. Old Fyffe pays just enough."

Lizzie nodded, although she was tempted to mock him again. In fact, good shepherds earned considerably more than most whalers or seal hunters. But she'd just seen where Michael's money went.

"And what happened to you?" Michael changed the subject. "Stayed true to the old calling?"

Lizzie shook her head and told him about the Busbys and then about what had happened with Smithers.

"Unbelievable," he laughed. "There are supposed to be about sixty-five thousand whites in New Zealand now, and of all people he runs into you. It seems to be fate, Lizzie. Accept it. And you have a new job now, right?"

Lizzie glared at him. "I'd be happy to give it to you, Michael. I'd even trade with you. The sheep don't smell worse than the boys, and at least I wouldn't have to smile at them, I wouldn't get pregnant from the work, and the rams wouldn't give me any disgusting diseases. Damn it, Michael, I want out of there!"

Michael shrugged. "I can ask old man Fyffe," he said. "We employ a couple of Maori girls for the sheep. But a girl like you from the docks of Kaikoura? My God, Lizzie, the lads at the whaling station would go mad."

Lizzie sighed. "I don't want to herd sheep either, Michael. I want to do something else. Listen . . ."

"Can we go somewhere else? What do you think?" Michael interrupted her. He shivered. "To the stables, maybe; it's warmer near the horses."

"That's another thing supporting my idea," said Lizzie.

Michael eyed her, confused. "You want to go to the horse stables?"

Lizzie grabbed her forehead. "I want to go under a roof with a whiskey bottle," she explained. "Or put another way, with loads of whiskey bottles. There'll have to be something better in them than what's in here. Michael, you used to sell the stuff. Do you know how to make it?"

Michael thought. "My father did the distilling, but it's not all that hard. You need a few things for the still, as well as a pot and grain. Besides that, wood plays a role. You need oak or ash. There's none of that here."

Lizzie waved off that concern. She was not interested in details. "Can you do it or not?" she asked coolly.

Michael nodded. "I can. But, but a whiskey distillery—is that allowed here?"

Lizzie rubbed her eyes. She had not thought it would be this difficult. "Did you lot care much about that back in Ireland? Michael, there's a jungle in those mountains right outside of town. Build yourself a hut. Nobody's going to look there for a whiskey still. If you can't get around it, just pay a few taxes. Kaikoura is full of thirsty people who don't like this swill"—she pointed at the bottle—"any more than you do. Our own stuff need only be a bit better, and we'll sell it with ease."

"And what does all this have to do with the horse stables?" asked Michael. He was just then opening the door to the Green Arrow's pen. His horse, a small chestnut, greeted him with a quiet snort.

Lizzie forced herself to be patient. "It has to do with there not being a tavern in this town where women aren't for sale, where a fisherman can take his girl without being ashamed or freezing half to death on the docks. We'll rent one of the old houses."

"We. You keep saying 'we,'" Michael said.

Finally, he seemed to understand that Lizzie meant all of this seriously and that her plans were not for him alone. Of course, he'd had trouble with that before, and Lizzie tried not to let her disappointment from the past flare up again. She needed to think clearly about how she wanted a business relation-ship with Michael—not to marry the prince, just to lead his horse.

"I thought I'd run the tavern," Lizzie said, excited. "And you'd supply me with the whiskey. The other tavern owners would soon want our stuff, but I'm sure there are differences. You could make extra good whiskey for us and not quite as good whiskey for the others. Then they'd go to our place to drink and to the Arrow for the girls. And everyone would be happy."

"But we would have to invest money first," Michael said. "Copper pots are expensive. And I would need to experiment a bit. We would need bottles."

Lizzie nodded. "I've saved a little," she said. "And you have too, right?"

"For Ireland," Michael said.

Lizzie would have liked to shake him. "Good God, Michael, if the distill-ery and tavern are a success, you'll earn enough in a year to go to Ireland and find three girls named Mary who can recite their book of prayers backward and forward. But like this, you'll never make it, and I'll never make it out of the Green Arrow. Let's try it, Michael. You owe me."

***

Over the next few weeks, Michael chopped wood in the mountains with the help of Tane and Maui. The three men built a hut and experimented with burning different sorts of wood.

"If it's wet or old or smokes too much, it's no good," explained Michael. "Then they'll see it from town, and I might as well set up trail signs for any investigators."

Lizzie praised him for his caution, but there wasn't even a police force in Kaikoura. Lizzie's concerns were different. Kaikoura lay in a remote area. There was hardly any agriculture. Where would they get the large quantities of grain?

For the time being, Lizzie ordered a variety of grains from the store in town. She gave the excuse of wanting to bake something for which she was feeling nostalgic.

"What can you make from malt and rye?" asked the grocer's wife mistrustfully.

"Oh, German bread," Lizzie said.

Mrs. Laderer in Sarau had produced dark, coarse bread from every possible ingredient. Lizzie could no longer recall most of them, but they could completely have resembled those from which one made whiskey.

"Are you German?" asked the woman, astounded. "To me you sounded like you came from somewhere in London."

Lizzie nodded. "We, we immigrated to England when I was still very little," she said, quickly making up a story for the woman. "But really, I'm from, from St. Pauli."

That was the name of the ship that had brought the first Germans to Nelson, and Lizzie seemed to recall it having to do with a location.

"Well, it's no business of mine," said the grocer's wife, handing Lizzie her supplies.

To acquire a copper pot and still, Michael had to make his way to Christchurch. Among all the pious Anglicans, however, he could find no one selling the materials for making whiskey. Finally, Michael haggled with a pharmacist for his equipment. The pot and distillation flasks were smaller than those his father had used, but he would just make smaller quantities.

A few days later, Michael distilled the first batch of alcohol with Lizzie and the somewhat astonished Maori, Tane and Maui, watching. The men poured the liquid into an empty barrel they had found in one of Fyffe's sheds.

"That'll turn into whiskey," said Michael after trying a few drops. "It should sit for a few years though."

"A few years? Are you crazy?" Lizzie, who had been waiting patiently until real alcohol appeared in the distillation flasks, tapped on her forehead for an idea. "Think of some recipe that works right away. I'm ready; I want to open my tavern."

Michael did not disappoint her. Just a week later, he had a drinkable product to offer—although he spent the next stretch of time making liquor from the most adventurous things, up to and including New Zealand sweet potatoes. For simplicity's sake, Lizzie called them all whiskey. How would her customers know what they were supposed to taste like? If it came to it, she was prepared to mix them with other liquids; Mrs. Busby had occasionally drunk cocktails, and Lizzie had noted a few recipes. Mrs. Busby's friends had particularly enjoyed a combination of coffee and whiskey—that way, no one smelled the alcohol, which was frowned upon for women far more so than for men.

Lizzie, who was hoping for female customers, christened her new tavern Irish Coffee. The very day she opened, she was already cheering up the overworked fishermen's wives, who always came home exhausted and frozen to the bone from the morning catch, with some of the tavern's namesake. Their husbands could not object to a chat and a coffee with the nice proprietress, the more so since Lizzie never charged them more than a penny per drink. The fishermen, too, drank at a discount. After all, they had helped Lizzie find a place for her tavern. It was right on the harbor, in a hut a seal hunter had built before moving to the West Coast. The rundown shack had stood empty since he'd left, but Michael and the two Maori were able to fix it quickly. Lizzie painted it green and coffee brown and hung a handsome sign above the door.

"Now the customers just need to learn the barkeeper's only to be looked at and never touched," Michael said, laughing.

Lizzie was already indicating with her clothing that she was no longer for sale. She wore one of her good dark dresses, a little more low cut than for church, but modest enough. She wore a snow-white apron over that, but she did not stick a bonnet in her properly coiffed hair.

"They'll learn quickly," laughed Lizzie.

Indeed, she knew how to put importunate customers in their place with a smile. And it seemed a Maori man was always leaning on the bar, sipping a beer and ready to order any troublesome drunks, amicably but firmly, outside. Lizzie's tavern drew fishermen and craftsmen who wanted to drink in peace and chat with others like them or the friendly proprietress. The drunks were often lonely, but they couldn't afford to pay for the company of whores. Lizzie's heartwarming smile was free, and she offered sandwiches and snacks to sate her customers' hunger. The mostly single men lived in primitive lodgings and hardly ever cooked. The Irish Coffee soon became like a warm, comforting home to them.

After a few weeks, a fishwife shyly offered to cook seafood for the tavern.

"Shrimp," said the woman, a Maori married to a white man. "They're what the area is named for. Kaikoura means 'meal with shrimp.' There's nothing that can compare to them."

Lizzie agreed after she had tasted them, and from then on she also served shrimp and fish soup at affordable prices. Michael was astounded when, after the first six months, she laid out a hearty meal along with the first reports of their accounts. She had completely taken over the distribution of his whiskey. What she did not sell at the Irish Coffee made its way into the other taverns.

"That's unbelievable," muttered Michael. "I didn't make that much in two years."

Lizzie nodded, satisfied. "And what's more, you can save more since you no longer have to buy the whiskey you drink," she said, teasing him.

Michael looked at her seriously, for the first time in a long time. And he liked what he saw. Lizzie had put on a little weight over the previous few months and no longer looked like a starving cat. Her hair was thicker and shiny. Perhaps best of all, her face reflected her satisfaction. She was not beautiful like Kathleen but cute, to be sure. He thought of how tender she had been on the ship and how warmly she could smile. No wonder half of Kaikoura was in love with Lizzie.

Michael reached out and tenderly stroked her hair and face, pulling her close to him. "I can think of another way to save money," he whispered in her ear. "What do I need with the girls from the Green Arrow when I can have the Irish Coffee's owner herself? Seriously, Lizzie, you're so lovely. What do you think? Shouldn't we partner in other ways too?"

Lizzie fought back the weakness that had momentarily seized her at Michael's touch. Damn it, she was still not immune to him. She quickly freed herself from his arms, got up, and took two steps back.

"You want to be rich; I want to be respectable," she said adamantly. "And I'm doing my best to help you, so please respect my wishes too."

Gold

Dunedin, Kaikoura, Tuapeka, Otago

1858–1862

Chapter 1

Dunedin was similar to Christchurch in some ways. This city, too, was young and still growing. The first Scottish settlers had only arrived ten years ago. Before that, the whaling outpost and the nearby seal rookery had drawn hunters.

The three hundred and fifty determined Scots who arrived in two ships in 1848 put an end to the primitive settlements of tents and wooden huts. They had the founding of a city in mind, and one built for eternity. A new Edinburgh should rise. The devout adherents to the Church of Scotland immediately set to constructing monumental stone buildings. They were all fanatic Calvinists and thought the traditional Scottish church was too liberal on questions of faith. The new citizens of New Zealand saw themselves as God's elect and tried to prove themselves worthy of this by working tirelessly to acquire economic wealth. They insisted on strict modesty and order.

Claire had heard all of that and explained it now to Kathleen and the children as the mules pulled their buggy southward. "I hope the women like fashion even if they are as ascetic as they're rumored to be. It's possible they see nice clothing as a superfluous luxury."

Kathleen shrugged. "They have to wear something. And they won't all be Scottish, right?"

"I don't know," Claire replied, "but they're supposed to be very, very hard-working, and we are too. We'll make it yet, Kathleen."

Since they had been traveling, Claire's mood had improved considerably. Kathleen thought she moved past her thief of a husband astoundingly quickly, but Claire was an optimist and a dreamer, after all. The beauty of the environment through which they drove cheered her too. There was already a somewhat well-paved road along the coast, and again and again there were views over blue lagoons and jagged rocks. The mountains also seemed to inch closer as they left the flat Canterbury Plains and entered mountainous Otago. For Claire, new wonders seemed to wait around every bend in the road. She never tired of joking with Chloe and Heather or telling the girls stories.

During the first few days, Kathleen often looked around anxiously—though she knew that Ian could not actually be following them. Even if he had come back early for some reason, Colin would have sent him to Nelson. But she would not rest easy until she was in as big a city and could hide among as many people as possible. If she ever rested easy. Kathleen had long dreamed of her escape, but her guilty conscience already bothered her. In the eyes of her church, she had just failed for the second time. First, she had not entered marriage as a virgin, and then she had left her husband. She did not dare to think what Father O'Brien would say about his former favorite student.

Sean acted more like Claire. The new scenery intoxicated him, and the farther away they were from their home, the lighter he seemed to feel. The Calvinists considered education important, and Claire had heard good schools were being built in Dunedin; there were even plans for a university. Here, no one would reprimand him for neglecting work in the stables, and he would not need to ride for miles to get to school. Sean was nothing but excited about his new life, and he enthusiastically eyed the new buildings and the bustling streets when they finally reached the city.

Heather and Chloe were less charmed by their new home.

"But Mama, nothing's even done yet," Heather objected as they passed the third scaffolding. "Where are we supposed to live?"

During their travels, the children had slept in the carriage and Kathleen and Claire beneath it. That would be impossible in Dunedin—particularly for future businesswomen. Kathleen was as unsure about the new city as her daughter, and she looked to Claire for an answer to Heather's question.

"Well, in an inn at first," Claire said. "Until we've found a house we can rent."

Kathleen looked around skeptically. "Where would we rent something? Heather's right. All the houses are still being built."

Claire shrugged. "The builders have to be staying somewhere. And once one of the new houses is ready, an old one will become available. Don't worry so much, Kathie. We'll find something."

Kathleen first looked for some stables they could rent, which she quickly found. Next to the stables, a hotel was being built, but only the foundation had been laid.

"An inn?" The stable owner was clearly surprised.

He was a bear of a man whose name, Duncan McEnroe, conjured images of warrior clans and stories of heroes in Claire. However, McEnroe did not seem very heroic, just suspicious and grumpy. Even his emphasis on the word "inn" made one think of a whorehouse.

"Well, yes, there must be a nice, clean hotel in which respectable women could spend a few nights safely," Claire said.

McEnroe arched his brows. "Now, whence do ye come?" he asked rudely. They did not seem to think much of politeness or even restraint in Scotland. "Two women alone with a buggy full o' children and nary a man?"

"My husband is a sailor," said Claire. "And Mrs. Coltrane is a widow."

Kathleen lowered her head.

"And why're you traveling alone through the area?"

Duncan McEnroe was not the only one who wanted to know. The two innkeeper widows he'd finally sent the women to also asked piercing questions. The first categorically refused to take in Kathleen, Claire, and the children. The second didn't quite believe Claire's wild story about lost husbands and a poor harvest that had forced the women to give up their farms in the Canterbury Plains.

"Whosoever is devout and properly tends his fields will receive a rich harvest from the Lord," the small old woman informed them before slamming the door in their faces.

"Well, she's never heard of the potato blight," remarked Kathleen.

"She never left Edinburgh before emigrating," said Claire. "She was probably married to some very strict Calvinist, but he died during the voyage and now she has to rent rooms just to have enough to eat."

With a gesture, Kathleen stopped her friend. "Claire, don't waste your imagination on the old witch. Instead, think of what we're going to do. We need to stay somewhere."

Followed by their tired, whining children, the women walked through the center of town, where the streets formed a massive octagon. The plans for the city were clear, and surely one day it would be very beautiful, but for now, there were few houses in Dunedin. On top of that, it began to rain.

"It would be best to get the carriage and look farther out," said Kathleen, discouraged.

Claire was not listening. She had just seen a strange construction site in the middle of the octagon, where someone had erected a tent.

"Take a look. Someone's camping," she said excitedly. "Perhaps that's what someone does when they intend to build later. Maybe that's how you get land. If you stay there long enough, it's promised to you. Come, let's ask."

Kathleen raised her brows. Claire had strange ideas about land acquisition, which likely resulted from reading too many legendary stories. In Claire's fairy tales, the gods would grant heroes the land they could walk around in a day, throw a spear onto, or fit under an ox's hide as Dido had with Carthage once upon a time. Kathleen could not imagine such archaic games in the middle of Dunedin. Most likely, the land here was either rented or sold, and if you pitched a tent where it was forbidden, you would be chased out of town.

Claire couldn't be stopped, though. She tapped on the tent fabric until there was movement inside. Finally, a tall man stepped out into the rainy evening.

Kathleen did not hear what her friend discussed with him, but she sighed with relief when he immediately waved them inside.

"Come in, come in, before you get soaked," he said.

The man had a pleasant voice and friendly brown eyes, straight light-brown hair, a high forehead, and dimples, as if he laughed often. He wore a priest's collar.

Kathleen and the children followed Claire out of the rain and into an unexpectedly comfortably furnished tent. There were armchairs and a sofa, a heavy wooden buffet, and a table with chairs. The space was cramped; surely the furniture had been purchased for a larger house. But it did not seem as if the pastor considered his living space provisional.

"Reverend Peter Burton of the Anglican Church, at your service," he introduced himself. "The Anglican diocese of Dunedin, to be more precise. But so far it's without a bishop."

"And would you become said bishop?" asked Claire respectfully.

Reverend Burton laughed. "No. Quite certainly no. At least, it would surprise me very, very much. I'm more of a placeholder. In the truest sense of the word."

"There, you see," crowed Claire, looking triumphantly at Kathleen. While the girls politely curtsied to the priest and Sean offered his hand, Claire explained her theory of land acquisition in Dunedin. The reverend laughed loudly at that.

"No, my dear, it's not that simple, although in my case you're not entirely wrong. In my case, Johnny Jones, a former whaler out of Waikouaiti who now maintains a few farms, has donated this site to us. One day it will be known as St. Paul's Cathedral—although St. John would surely have seemed more fitting to our noble patron and doubtlessly increased his willingness to give. I suggested that, too, but no one listens to me."

The reverend invited Kathleen and Claire to sit. Then he also sat, and continued speaking.

"Now, the location of our future house of worship is rather central, as you've no doubt noticed, which does not suit our Calvinist city fathers. The Church of England in the middle of New Edinburgh! In any case, they're contesting the site, and so that no one will think of placing a statue to Calvin or the like here, I'm camping on the spot." Reverend Burton smirked. "I'm something like Peter the Rock, on which we'll someday build our church. I hope the bishop doesn't take that literally and build me into the foundation in some heathen sacrifice for luck."

Kathleen looked confused.

"But they won't really do that, will they?" asked Sean anxiously.

Reverend Burton laughed once again. "There are people who'd think it rather a good idea. But I think you're right, my child. It wouldn't be Christian, and the bishop will surely turn away from it."

Claire gave the reverend her dimpled smile. "I take from your words that you don't exactly hold the most desirable position in the Anglican Church," she said. "But we should introduce ourselves. Claire Edmunds and Kathleen Coltrane. And this is Chloe, Heather, and Sean."

Reverend Burton held out his hand formally to the women. Kathleen stood back up and curtsied shyly.

"Chloe and I are Anglican," Claire added. "Kathleen, well, she's Irish."

Reverend Burton nodded. "My parish has just grown by two members. Which puts us at five all together, I believe. Mrs. Coltrane, you and your children are welcome, too, naturally. You'll see that the differences are not at all that great."

Kathleen nodded. She had already visited the Anglican Sunday service in Lyttelton.

"But what brings you here now—other than that you would like to acquire land quickly and easily?"

Again Claire told her story about their respectively missing and dead husbands. "We want to open a dress shop," she explained. "Perhaps we could put up a few sketches here? The pastor's wife in Christchurch was one of our best customers."

Kathleen blushed deeply, but Claire dug a few pictures out of her travel bag.

Reverend Burton whistled mischievously through his teeth. "Very nice," he said enthusiastically. "But I'll tell you now: these will attract about as many people as my preaching does. Have you seen the women here? They outdo each other in trying to look as much like a crow as possible."

Claire giggled, and Kathleen had to laugh. In contrast to her optimistic friend, it had already occurred to her as they drove the city how sad and unassuming the Scottish wives' dresses were. The second innkeeper had looked very much like an evil crow.

Reverend Burton regarded the women. So far, Claire had steered the conversation, but now he noticed Kathleen's honey-colored hair, her aristocratic features, and her enticing green eyes.

"This here," said the reverend, pointing to one of the drawings—an evening gown with a fitted bodice and low neckline—"must look like the straight road to hell to a Puritan. After all, it would give any man sinful thoughts."

His smile took the sharpness from the words. Claire winked at him conspiratorially, but Kathleen looked at him anxiously.

To Reverend Burton, Claire Edmunds appeared unselfconscious, but Kathleen Coltrane did not seem like an adventurous and so far successful entrepreneur. Rather, she seemed to be browbeaten. Or even on the run?

"Now, what're we to do with you?" he asked the circle. The women looked visibly tired, and the children, too, seemed exhausted. "I think, first thing,

I'll grant you all sanctuary for tonight. Although you have to imagine it's a sturdier refuge."

"You mean we're to sleep here with you in the tent?" Claire asked, frowning.

Reverend Burton shook his head. "For heaven's sake, the bishop would . . . Well, there's likely no lower post in New Zealand, but elsewhere in the world, there are supposed to be cannibals to whom he urgently needs to send missionaries."

"What exactly did you do?" asked Claire, seizing the moment. "That is, to be banished here—if not quite to be among cannibals."

But Kathleen had heard enough talk. Heather had been leaning, exhausted, against her for a while, and even Sean looked as if he were ready to fall over. She, too, needed a bed desperately.

Agitated, she turned to the pastor. "Please, do tell us where we're to sleep. Because otherwise we'll have to look for something else. It's already getting dark. And I don't think that Mr. McEnroe will let us sleep in the stables."

"Hardly," Reverend Burton said drily, "lest you seduce the horses! No, as I said, I'm granting you sanctuary." He quickly lifted the tent flap and pointed to a second, similar structure a few yards away. "Do you see that? That's St. Paul's Cathedral. We celebrated the placing of the cornerstone, and I pitched that tent over it. For now it belongs to you, although we do celebrate Sunday service in there. Of course, you won't need the whole cathedral anyway. It's to have space for five hundred of the faithful, the bishop tells me."

Kathleen smiled shyly at the reverend. "That is, it's very nice of you."

Reverend Burton dismissed this. "There's nothing to thank me for. Though I might thank you all if you'd do me the favor of sharing my meager meal with me. In fact, it need not be so meager if I might send this young man here off to the butcher." He indicated Sean. "I was not counting on company. But they don't let me starve, and I have a stove. So I would be happy to feed you and your children, if I may."

Kathleen wanted to express her tiredness and decline timidly, but Claire was already nodding with a grin. "Of course you may! We're starving. Should we do the cooking? That is, I can't cook very well, but Kathleen is an excellent cook."

In the end, Kathleen took over Reverend Burton's kitchen inside the tent while Claire and the children went over to the future church with the pastor. It was dry and warm enough, but aside from a few wooden benches and a cross, there were no furnishings and certainly no beds. Claire suggested retrieving the blankets and bedding from their buggy to make the space more comfortable. She happily accepted the reverend's offer to accompany her and the children to the stables.

"Although you'll be sure to compromise yourself in Mr. McEnroe's eyes," Claire teased him.

Reverend Burton shrugged his shoulders and opened a huge black umbrella over her head. "In Mr. McEnroe's eyes, we're all damned to hell. And better yet, we can't do anything to change that. From the very beginning of time, God determined that Duncan McEnroe would go to heaven and we wouldn't. No wonder he keeps his nose so high; he didn't even have to earn it. Damnation could just as easily have happened to him. In any case, we'll fetch your things now, and tomorrow you can look for new stables. There's an Irishman who lives on the other side of town: Donny Sullivan. Does a bit of horse trading and is Catholic, of course. But otherwise, a good fellow."

***

"Now, what did you do?" Claire inquired for the second time an hour later, after everyone had taken a seat around Reverend Burton's large dinner table.

The reverend had said a prayer and eagerly scooped himself food from the steaming bowls of meat, potatoes, and other vegetables. He did not scrimp on praise for the cook. Kathleen blushed with embarrassment and sipped nervously at her wine. Reverend Burton toasted the women, without compunction, after he opened the bottle with a grand gesture.

"To my first visitors in the new diocese! And to our fabulous cook, Mrs. Coltrane," he declared, smiling at Kathleen. Kathleen lowered her gaze shyly and peered through her lashes at Claire, looking for help.

This brought them back to Claire's question. She would not let go until the reverend told them his story.

He looked at her searchingly. "If I confess now, I want to hear your story once again afterward," he replied. "And something better than all that with the poor harvest. I passed through Christchurch a few months ago, ladies. There was no poor harvest in the plains. You should either tell the truth or show more skill in lying. Otherwise, everyone will be onto you."

Kathleen reddened again.

Even Claire chewed guiltily on her lip. "A storm flood?" she asked. "The river flood? Yes, we did live on the Avon."

Reverend Burton rolled his eyes. "You're lucky I don't need to hear your confession," he said. "Your friend doesn't lie as shamelessly. Wouldn't you like to tell me the truth, Mrs. Coltrane?"

Kathleen lowered her head so much that he could hardly see her face. "I, I, well, it was not originally a flood," she stammered, "but, but it does have to do with the fields on the river and, well, also with a bad harvest."

The reverend and Claire looked at her, equally uncomprehending. Then the reverend dismissed it.

"Well, maybe I don't even need to know. And I'll agree that it's my turn to confess." He grinned at the women and then went to his bookshelf, drew out a magazine, and opened it to some marked pages. "I take it you're not familiar with this."

Kathleen had still not recovered from the questioning, but Claire reached for the magazine, interested, and Sean likewise peered at it curiously. It was a reprint of papers by Charles Darwin and Alfred Russel Wallace: *On the Tendency of Species to form Varieties; and on the Perpetuation of Varieties and Species by Natural Means of Selection.*

Claire furrowed her brow. "What is it about?" she asked.

"A fascinating theory," the reverend replied with gleaming eyes. "It discusses the origins of plant and animal species. Darwin supposes that one species develops from another, so to speak, over the course of many thousands of years."

"Well, and?" Claire asked and took a sip of wine. "It's like with sheep breeding. You cross one sort with another so that the wool becomes more beautiful and the sheep themselves more resistant to weather. That's right, isn't it, Kathie?"

Kathleen nodded absentmindedly.

"But perhaps it could be applied to humans as well," Reverend Burton said.

"Nothing new there, either," Claire agreed. "I'm dark-haired with brown eyes; my husband has, had, hm, has"—by now Claire had told so many versions of her story that she no longer recalled whether she had declared herself or Kathleen the widow—"blue eyes and blond hair. And Chloe has black hair and blue eyes. What's the problem?"

Reverend Burton bit his lip. "You need to see it on a larger scale, Mrs. Edmunds. People are suggesting that this Mr. Darwin will conclude that mankind descended from apes."

Claire furrowed her brow. "I saw a monkey once," she said. "It was very cute. A little like a person. It seemed very clever. It collected the money for the organ grinder."

Reverend Burton had to laugh. "The greed highly developed species seem to have in common seems so far to have escaped Mr. Darwin."

Claire giggled, but Kathleen hardly seemed to be listening.

"But now what does that have to do with you defending a piece of land in Dunedin against the Church of Scotland instead of preaching somewhere in the Canterbury Plains?" Claire asked. "I don't quite see the connection."

Reverend Burton pointed to the volume. "I preached about this," he explained, "about how it will make a whole new interpretation of the Bible necessary."

Claire understood. "Because then all that with Adam and Eve can't be true. But I could not imagine that anyway; I wasn't made from anyone's rib." She threw her head back proudly, and Reverend Burton could hardly contain his amusement.

"Whereby we both seem to have made ourselves guilty of blasphemy," he teased her. "In contrast to you, Mrs. Edmunds, my bishop insists—and with him, it seems, the whole Anglican Church—that Mr. Darwin is wrong and the Bible right. So you'll have to make your peace with the rib, even if you like the monkey better."

"But what bothers the bishop about this new interpretation?" Claire sniffed with satisfaction at her wine glass. "Does it really matter in the end if God made the world in six days or if it took him a little longer?"

Kathleen raised her head. She had seemed uninvolved yet had been listening attentively. "If the bishop admits that the story of the rib isn't true," she said calmly, "then he has to accept that maybe the rest of it isn't true either. All that about, about the Virgin Mary maybe, and the Immaculate Conception. Or with the indivisibility of marriage."

Reverend Burton did not know why, but he had the impression that the beautiful blonde woman felt a bit comforted by this conversation.

Chapter 2

Finding a home for two women and three children in Dunedin proved as difficult as finding an inn. There were indeed some finished houses, and a few of them were lovely, several-storied stone buildings, but the owners resided in most of them, and if anything was for rent, they could pick out their renters. An Anglican and a Catholic with no husbands were at about the bottom of their wish lists.

"And things look bleak for our tailoring too," sighed Claire. The women had shopped and cooked for their second night as guests, along with their children, at the reverend's table. "Literally, the women here don't seem to wear anything but black."

"Do you have other skills to offer?" Reverend Burton asked. "Aside from cooking. You've done another marvelous job, Mrs. Coltrane. Though I fear hiring a cook would seem as much of a luxury to the Scots as the purchase of beautiful clothing."

"Farm work," said Kathleen quietly. "I always worked in the garden, in the fields, and with animals. Sean can do that too."

The boy nodded sadly. He had been hoping he would no longer be bothered with feeding animals and spreading manure, but he understood the seriousness of the situation. Of course he would do whatever work was needed.

Reverend Burton thought for a moment, but then his face brightened. "Well, if you don't have your hearts set on Dunedin, farm work gives me an idea. I've already mentioned Johnny Jones, haven't I, our generous patron?"

The women nodded.

"As I said, he originally had a whaling station, but for a while now, he's made his money in trading and shipping—and he runs a farm. That is, there are actually several farms in Waikouaiti, a small town not far from here. Several farmers have settled there since Dunedin was founded. They provide the city with its groceries. As far as I know, everyone there is doing well for themselves."

"Where exactly is it?" Claire asked, but then she was already somewhere else with her thoughts. "Oh right, I remember: I could also teach piano!"

Both Kathleen and the reverend saw better chances in Waikouaiti, if only in regard to piano lessons for the Scottish children.

"Soon you'll be thinking of playing the organ in their services," chided Kathleen when she noticed that Claire was loath to let go of her latest business idea.

"Assuming they don't consider music blasphemous too. On the farm, we'd surely be able to weave again. We might even be able to sell wool in sober colors here."

"We'll go there tomorrow," said Reverend Burton, in good spirits. He opened another bottle of wine.

Claire seemed somewhat unhappy about having to live outside a city again, but Kathleen appeared to like Reverend Burton's idea. She came to life as he told her about settlers in the small town. Johnny Jones had brought them over to New Zealand from the Australian city of Sydney.

"But were they really allowed to leave?" she asked. "Aren't they all convicts?"

"First of all, not all Australians arrive in the country as convicts," answered Reverend Burton. Her sudden and lively interest surprised him. "And second, only a few people there are condemned for life. Most serve seven to ten years. As soon as their sentences are served, they're free. They can go wherever they'd like, though they never make enough money for passage back to England. Why Jones would bring over Australians and whether they were convicts or not, I have no idea. But you can ask the people tomorrow yourself."

Sean yoked the mules; the women had not yet changed stables, which seemed odd to Reverend Burton. He thought Kathleen Coltrane would be happy to meet a landsman. Not to mention Donny Sullivan charged less money than McEnroe. But Kathleen and Sean acted downright skittish, if not repulsed, when talk turned to changing stables. Apparently they had something against horse traders.

Reverend Burton rode his horse beside Sean and just behind the women and their two daughters in the carriage. He noted how surely the boy sat in the saddle of his small black horse. True, most farm children knew how to ride a horse, but Sean seemed like an expert; he handled the young animal with facility and care. Still, he blushed when Reverend Burton paid him a compliment about it. A quiet boy, like his mother. Reverend Burton thought them both equally fascinating, even if Kathleen never seemed to warm up to him. Perhaps she had reservations about his religious affiliation. The Irish had certainly suffered considerably at Anglican hands. But Reverend Burton was in no hurry. He would be there a long time yet, and Kathleen, too, it seemed. She might thaw someday.

***

Waikouaiti lay several miles outside of Dunedin's borders, and it couldn't be compared to the Scottish settlement. Here, people settled on the coast, and the area was entirely flat. Otago's hilly terrain did not begin until a mile west of the farms. Two miles farther lay the mouth of the Waikouaiti River. It immediately reminded Claire of the Avon, and in truth, Waikouaiti was more comparable to the Canterbury Plains than Dunedin. The little town consisted mostly of cabins similar to the farmhouses Kathleen and Claire had left behind.

Reverend Burton headed straight for a neat red-painted school, which stood beside an equally well-kept church. There was also a parsonage.

"My brother of the cloth, Reverend Watgin, also serves as the teacher here," he informed Sean, who was listening attentively. "He's been here for almost twenty years now and is very strict—so, please, not a word about Mr. Darwin's ideas. Reverend Watgin thinks me dangerous; the bishop must have warned him about me. In any case, Johnny Jones brought him here to offer his settlers spiritual and moral support. He really thought of everything."

Reverend Watgin and his wife did not seem any less bigoted and ossified than the Scottish settlers of Dunedin, but the couple had been on the South Island longer and seemed to have lost their pioneering spirit. They showed only a modicum of politeness to Reverend Burton, and they viewed Kathleen, Claire, and the children with skepticism.

"So, from the plains," said Reverend Watgin, a tall, haggard man with piercing eyes. "Widows?"

"My husband is at sea," Claire rushed to assure them.

"And why aren't you waiting at the harbor like a good wife?" Watgin asked sternly. "Whenever you are involved in something, Reverend Burton, we see the effects of modern times. Priests deny the Bible; women leave their homes . . ."

Kathleen and Claire said nothing to his grumblings, as Reverend Burton had advised them.

"We briefly had to pay our respects there first, but Reverend Watgin does not have much say," he told them later. "The main thing is that Mrs. Jones is like you. Johnny is at sea most of the time; his wife holds rank here, and she's an uncrowned queen."

Mrs. Jones resided on Matanaka Farm, named for the strips of coast on the north end of Waikouaiti Bay. She ruled over a large, tidy farmhouse surrounded by gardens of lushly blossoming flowers, which Claire noticed first. The farm buildings were painted in fresh colors that also spoke of a person who embraced her life—and what was more, the mistress of the house seemed to have a weakness for good-looking young men. Her small blue eyes shone when she opened the door for Reverend Burton.

Mrs. Jones was plump, and a smile spread across her greasy face at the first glimpse of her male visitor. Excitedly, she adjusted her coiffure, which seemed to consist of a thousand blonde corkscrew curls. Doubtless it took her hours with her curling irons every day to give it shape, but it made her look younger. Her cheerful, high-pitched voice contributed to people liking her at once.

"Reverend Burton! Are you bringing those dangerous thoughts of yours back to our tiny little town?" she teased him, all her little curls bobbing with pleasure. "Now what have you brought us here? Not any fallen women, I hope?" She shook her finger at the reverend. "Recall: 'our descent hearkens back exclusively to decent, well-regarded citizens of South England.'" She spoke these last words with a high-pitched, almost nagging voice, apparently imitating someone. "So please don't entrust any little sheep that have faltered in any way to our Mrs. Ashley. They could blacken the whole herd!" Mrs. Jones winked at the reverend and the women.

"And so she denies heredity too," laughed Reverend Burton. Apparently, they were talking about a mutual acquaintance. "But Mrs. Jones, you should be ashamed. We've just got here, and you start mocking your brothers and sisters in Christ. Is that Christian?" He did not wait for an answer. "I think it's time for a good work—as atonement, so to speak—and you'll suffer in silence what Agnes Ashley has to say about it."

At that, the reverend described the women and children's situation to Carol Jones.

"You know the Scots, Mrs. Jones. They immediately assume eternal damnation when a woman is alone, no matter the reason. Mrs. Edmunds and Mrs. Coltrane will never have any luck in Dunedin, and I can't let them sleep in the church forever. People are already wagging their tongues. Even our own ladies are no angels, after all, as you well know."

Mrs. Jones giggled. "Aye. Do you have any experience with farm work?" She turned to Kathleen and Claire. "Or can you make yourselves useful some other way?"

Kathleen nodded, wanting to say something about herself, but Claire beat her to it. "We had a sort of business in Christchurch," she declared courageously. "Ladies' fashion in the styles of Paris and London."

With a grand gesture, she pulled out a few of Kathleen's drawings and held them out to Mrs. Jones. The town founder's wife looked at them with an increasingly covetous facial expression.

"You can tailor this here?" Mrs. Jones' tiny curls bobbed again. "Truly?"

***

A short time later, Kathleen, Claire, and the children moved into a shanty on the coast. It had no window, but Claire was delighted they could hear the sea.

"We'll have some windows put in," said Mrs. Jones, unconcerned. "That's important; otherwise you'll ruin your eyes sewing. You really think this crinoline will look good on me, Reverend?" Mrs. Jones could hardly tear herself from the fabrics and designs. She had already found a favorite dress too. "Won't it make me look fat?"

Kathleen was cleaning the shanty and making it comfortable while Claire said a heartfelt good-bye to Reverend Burton.

"You will come to visit occasionally, won't you?" she asked.

The reverend nodded. "Of course. I'll also look forward to seeing you Sunday at service. It's a little far, naturally, so now and again you'll want to attend the sermons of my esteemed colleague here for a change." He winked at her. "And you must bring this back to me as well." He pointed to the Darwin papers Claire had borrowed to study with Sean.

Kathleen was not overly excited about that. Sean would be going to Reverend Watgin's school from now on and should not offend him right away. Yet on the other hand, his hunger for knowledge could hardly be sated.

"I'm expecting a new book," Reverend Burton continued eagerly. "*On the Origin of Species*; it's to be published soon. In it, Mr. Darwin will provide evidence for this hypothesis. Keep your eyes open. It will cause an uproar in the next few years. The world will change."

Reverend Burton's last statement would be proven right when it came to Otago. However, it was not the writings of Charles Darwin that would turn everything topsy-turvy in Dunedin and its environs.

***

At first, life in Waikouaiti traveled a familiar course. To Claire, it hardly differed from her existence in Christchurch. At least, she did not find any friends, except for the cheerful Mrs. Jones.

Kathleen looked forward to meeting the settlers from Australia, hoping to learn information about the country to which Michael had been banished. Yet even the mention of penal colonies seemed to anger the farmers, and even more so their wives.

"That's how it always is," said Mrs. Ashley, who didn't require an introduction. Mrs. Jones had done a perfect impression. "Hardly does one mention that accursed land but it's about rogues and thieves and murderers. You can't even tell people you come from there, because they assume you were hauled there in chains. But, ladies, we are honorable people driven by a pioneering spirit. We left the south of England willingly. Keep that in mind. We come from highly esteemed families and . . ."

"I just was curious about what it's like there," said Kathleen, "the country, the weather, the people."

Mrs. Ashley was not assuaged. She gave Kathleen and Claire disapproving looks.

"It depends on where you wash up in that hellish country," answered Mr. Ashley in her stead. He was not quite as prejudiced and cantankerous as his spouse, but the women didn't like the brawny, dim-witted farmer any more than they did his wife. "There're deserts where you burn up, but also regions where it rains all the time, like here. There are plains, rainforests, swamps. Anyway, it's not like it should be. And the animals: everything that creeps and crawls carries death inside it—snakes, scorpions, massive spiders. The big animals don't birth their young normally but carry them in pouches of fur and skin. It's unnatural is what it is."

"Or different than in the south of England." Mrs. Jones grinned.

The group had met on the way to church, and their "queen" was wearing her new dress for the first time. The crinoline and puffy sleeves weren't perhaps the best choice for her figure, but Carol Jones was overjoyed with the powerful marine blue of the silk she had chosen. The other women looked at her with a mixture of fascination, disapproval, and jealousy.

"Don't listen to our friends, girls. They were disappointed by Australia; that's why they're here."

"But the worst are the convicts," Mrs. Ashley took up her husband's tirade. "You lose your good reputation as soon as you set foot in that country—and what's worse, you can't be sure of life and limb. They let the people run free, you know, once they've served their time, and often enough even before that. You can imagine, a whole country settled by ne'er-do-wells."

"Surely they weren't all ne'er-do-wells," Kathleen dared to object, but that only turned the upright English even more against her. Everyone had a story to tell about how he or one of his neighbors was robbed, lied to, or cheated by a former prisoner.

"I'm sure there's something to what they say," Kathleen said glumly to Claire after church. "No doubt some prisoners are dangerous. And then there are the forest fires and wild animals. They say many of the convicts die there."

Kathleen could no longer keep it to herself. On that second Sunday in their new home, she finally told Claire about Michael. She breathed a sigh of relief when Claire did not damn her for her love but instead found the whole thing rather romantic.

"He wrote he'd come back," she said, enthralled, as Kathleen showed her the letter from Michael she had carefully kept all those years. The sight of his lock of hair almost moved her to tears. "Oh, Kathleen, maybe you should have waited for him."

***

Mrs. Ashley and her friends found Kathleen's interest in Australia strange; they also found the women and children without male protection strange. To them, cute, lively Claire and the quieter but extraordinarily beautiful Kathleen seemed a constant temptation for their husbands. They gossiped about every little conversation between the women and a farmworker or settler. Nevertheless, these pious women delighted in London fashion. So they slunk repeatedly to Kathleen and Claire's house to place orders for clothing—only to complain about the high costs later.

"We'll never make as much as in Christchurch," said Claire with concern. "I had been looking forward to city flair. Instead, we're sitting in the country again washing wool. If only they'd let me help out more with the sheep and horses at least. But, no, I might seduce Mr. Ashley in so doing. As if he were any more attractive than one of the rams." Claire was more than unsatisfied.

Kathleen settled markedly more easily into her uneventful life. At least no one was beating and insulting her anymore. Sean was unthreatened, and Heather no longer witnessed ugly scenes. The children attended Reverend Watgin's school, and thanks to their education from Claire, they easily overtook the settlers' children. Sean, in particular, could learn nothing more in the village school. Were it not for Reverend Burton, he would have been disappointed with Otago. At least once a month, Claire insisted on attending Sunday service in Dunedin, usually driving there on Saturday afternoon, having dinner in Reverend Burton's tent, and sleeping in the "church" or at the house of another parishioner. The Anglican parish grew slowly but steadily, and naturally, Reverend Burton did not want to gain a reputation for housing female visitors overnight.

Still, Claire and Kathleen were always welcome, as were the children, especially Sean, whose sharp intellect fascinated the reverend. He loaned the boy books and talked with him as with a grown-up about history and philosophy. Claire also treasured conversation with the reverend. Kathleen mostly only listened silently, but she never objected to the visits to Dunedin and never seemed bored. When she did on occasion interject something, it was usually striking and sharp-witted. Still, she could have lived without the discussion of Mr. Darwin's ideas.

Kathleen often wondered what drew her to spend time with Reverend Burton. She did notice that she felt safe and comfortable in his presence—more comfortable than anywhere else since she had fled Ian. She still felt guilty—not about Ian, but Colin. She should not have left her son to himself and his swindler father. Moreover, Kathleen feared retribution. The escape had been so quick that she hadn't thought much about Ian coming to look for her. In fact, she had assumed he would let her go. Now when she thought about his fits of jealousy, she couldn't imagine how he would tolerate her leaving him. Ian may never have loved her, but he had seen her as his property. And he would not like her being stolen from him.

All these thoughts fell silent when Kathleen was around Reverend Burton. She recognized that he admired her beauty, but he never got too close. She appreciated the way he conversed with Claire—not as man and woman, but as two people who shared similar interests. Reverend Burton did not flatter like Michael, and he did not flirt with the women. Yet surely he kept his word and bore the consequences of all he said and did. His adherence to Darwin's theories and rebellion against his own church impressed her. The Bible was a big book, and Reverend Burton could preach about everything and anything, not just the creation story. And yet he would not let go of this subject, and as consequence, he bore his exile to a tent in Dunedin patiently.

Nevertheless, he recently had been worrying more and more about his future. "They're talking of ordaining a bishop and sending him here." He sighed. "Will I keep my position here then? I rather doubt it. They'll find something else for me. Perhaps I'll be sent to preach to the Maori."

"The Maori believe the world was made when two lovers were forcefully separated," said Kathleen.

She now often worked with Maori women. There was a settlement near Waikouaiti, and Reverend Watgin made every effort to convert the Ngai Tahu, and they came politely to church. However, during their mutual exchanges of patterns and secrets about wool dyeing, they told Kathleen and Claire their people's mythology: Papa was the earth, Rangi the sky, and only once their children pushed them apart could plants, animals, and humans come into being.

"So, even worse," laughed Claire. "Natural selection and divorce. They can't set you loose among the Maori, Reverend; you'd come back with even more shocking ideas than you had before."

***

Thus passed the summer and winter. Claire and Kathleen lived a quiet, not very exciting life in their little town on the South Island. But then, on a cool autumn day in 1861, something happened that would influence not only the Anglican church but also the life of every single citizen of Otago. The first in Waikouaiti to learn of it was Carol Jones, because she allowed herself the luxury of a daily newspaper. Occasionally, delivery of the *Otago Witness* was late and she received three or four issues at once. Still, she did learn the news before everyone else, and that day, she gladly shared her knowledge with Claire, who was helping her in the garden.

"They found gold near the Tuapeka," Mrs. Jones said. "An Australian; seems he's completely beside himself. 'Shining like the stars of Orion on a dark, frosty night,' he said. So he might make a decent geologist, but he'd starve as a poet."

Claire laughed. "And now? Is everyone running to the Tuapeka?"

The small river where Gabriel Read was supposed to have found gold flowed some thirty-five miles from Dunedin.

Mrs. Jones shook her head. "Stuff and nonsense. You know the Scots. Wheat's more precious than gold, and heaven forbid any wealth without work. The city sent out a hundred and fifty people first thing to see if there's anything to it. Maybe this Read fellow just dreamed it up."

For a while, no one heard any more about Gabriel Read's gold find. Even Reverend Burton didn't know any news. "The bishop in Canterbury has been warning about people chasing after gold; so far, there have been rumors of more finds but no reports about them in the papers."

A few weeks later, Kathleen, Claire, and the children were spending another Saturday evening with the reverend. He had invited a young married Anglican couple that had immigrated from Australia a short time before. Of course, Reverend Burton knew of Kathleen's interest in the neighboring country. He bathed in Kathleen's gratitude but also registered that her face looked increasingly clouded over with sorrow as she heard the couple's report.

"The country is very fertile," said Mr. Cooper, an agricultural engineer, "but a large portion is very dry. And not without its dangers. Some regions are breathtakingly beautiful, but in the grass wait poison snakes and other beasties. Nor are the natives always friendly; no comparison with the Maori here. The aborigines aren't looking to give anything away. They feel threatened by the white settlers. Well, and the many convicts there have not done us any favors either. Most of them, it's true, aren't half so bad, but there are also plenty of scoundrels the others don't even like."

"Is it, is it true that many die?" Kathleen asked quietly.

Mr. Cooper shrugged his shoulders. "That depends a bit on the region. For instance, Tasmania—what they used to call Van Diemen's Land—has a bad reputation, true, but nature is not nearly so dangerous there. In the interior, however . . ."

"What about the forest fires?" asked Claire.

Kathleen had admitted that she had been suffering nightmares since hearing the Ashleys' reports. She pictured Michael trapped in a fiery hell. And sometimes herself as well. Kathleen did not know whether these images related to hearing of the fires or more to her own sins and the purgatory they made inevitable.

Mr. Cooper nodded. "Indeed," he confirmed, "forest fires occur. Or rather, brush fires. When they first catch, the fire spreads with unbelievable speed. Anyone caught in it has no chance. New Zealand is the more pleasant land in every respect. But the convicts in Australia don't die in droves either. On the contrary, most receive a pardon, and many end up acquiring land of their own and becoming completely normal settlers. Do you have family there? Or you, Kathleen? You're Irish, right?"

Kathleen blushed deeply, but before she could say anything, Sean, now fourteen, and Rufus, the Coopers' son, slipped through the entrance to the tent. The two boys had become fast friends and had walked through Dunedin a bit after dinner.

"Ma," Sean now reported excitedly, "they say ships have arrived in the harbor. Loads of them!"

"More than sixty!" Rufus crowed. "There are hundreds of people there."

The reverend furrowed his brow. "The Spanish Armada?" he teased the boys. "Or some other fleet come to conquer the British Empire?"

"I don't know," said Sean, "but they're supposed to be from England. Or Australia?"

"People are saying lots of different things," said Rufus.

Claire nodded, laughing. "Exactly, and it's not all going to be true. Probably it's just a ship or two more of Scots."

But in the morning, when Kathleen and Claire awoke in the Coopers' house, the two boys announced the next sensation.

"Look, there on the hills."

The Coopers lived on a street that led steeply upward toward the mountains and offered a good view of the hills all around the city. Until the day before, there had only been trees and bushes to see there, but now the hills seemed sprinkled with white.

"Those are tents," called Mr. Cooper. He was still wearing his morning robe and looked just as taken aback as the boys at the many new arrivals around the city. "Merciful heavens, the boys were right. Dozens of ships must have arrived to bring all these people here. But what do they want?"

Mr. Cooper's wife raised her eyebrows. "Well, what else, Jason? Gold. Those there are just the first wave. Tomorrow they'll be gone toward Gabriel's Gully, but the day after, new men will arrive."

"We should go to the church," suggested Kathleen.

If the boys were right, and the gold seekers had come from England, a crowd would also have come to the reverend.

Indeed, this was the first Anglican service in Dunedin for which Reverend Burton's church tent was literally bursting at the seams. The reverend had to open the flaps and preach loud enough that even the men outside could hear. The established parish members eyed the new arrivals suspiciously, but in truth, the men made a thoroughly good impression. They looked a little haggard, of course, and weakened by the voyage, and it was clear from their clothes that they were not wealthy. Yet they were polite and reserved, seeming almost fearful in their new country.

The reverend took up the men's request to thank God for a safe voyage. Most of the men came from England and Wales. A few Irish held themselves off to the side; though they had an urgent desire to pray, they mistrusted the Anglican rites. Reverend Burton saw with pleasure that, after service, Kathleen welcomed her own. The new arrivals looked at her like an angel made flesh. During the voyage, they explained, they had only seen men. As soon as news of the new find had reached Great Britain, ship owners had specifically advertised to gold seekers. Within two days, a ship had been filled and its sails set.

"First come, first served," said a friendly young man named Chris Timlock who immediately started talking with Claire. "When it happened in Australia, I was too young. But now, I didn't even give it half a day's thought. My wife wasn't so excited, but she'll see: this is our chance to get out of poverty."

A large portion of the men had not even paid for their passage. The captain had transported them trusting that they would soon earn the money in the gold mines. The young church attendees doubtlessly wanted to pay their way afterward, but as for the other gold seekers . . .

"Some of them are real bastards," said Chris Timlock, shaking his head. "Some of the lads on the ship, horrible. And in the camp too—there's a rough air over there, I'll tell you that, Mrs. Edmunds."

The diggers did not all come from the Old World. Some of the men who arrived in Otago Harbor were veteran gold diggers from Australia.

"You've got to stick by them," Chris said with shining eyes. "They know what they're doing."

The fact that they had not yet achieved great wealth didn't unsettle them. Each of the men believed firmly in his own luck.

In those days, the merchants in and around Dunedin were assured wealth. Shovels and bowls with which to pan for gold were sold out first thing Monday morning. The diggers fought each other for the last tools. And the city certainly wasn't prepared for the need for food and other supplies. Within the shortest time, the farmers of Waikouaiti had sold all their grain. All around Dunedin, the number of animals plummeted. The gold miners shot at anything that moved and promised a meal—as well as at freely roaming sheep, cats, and dogs. The sanitary conditions of the improvised camps were horrendous. Otago's fresh air gave way to a pervasive stench of excrement as soon as one approached the city of tents. Nevertheless, as Mrs. Cooper had predicted, the gold miners moved on over the next few days toward Gabriel's Gully, the name given to the first gold mine on the Tuapeka. The Scots sighed with relief and hoped to be done with them. But Reverend Burton shook his head.

"It would be better to steel oneself for the next wave," he told Kathleen and Claire.

They had stayed a few days with the Coopers, helping the other women in the parish arrange tea and soup kitchens to serve the hungry men. In the camps, rule had already fallen to the strong. The poor and optimistic churchgoers from the country or working families could not prevail against the old adventurers from Australia or the West Coast. It was not all dreamers who filled the hills around Dunedin—the scum from the whaling and seal hunting camps; luckless gold seekers from Collingwood in the northwest; and released convicts from Australia, who surely had not made the money for their passage by honest means, all came too.

These men poured through the city; it was almost impossible to make it to the Tuapeka River without passing Dunedin. In Dunedin, the gold seekers got their bearings and acquired tents, digging implements, and provisions—and if someone really did find gold, he would turn it into money there. The small Scottish community was wholly overwhelmed by this onrush of men without much in the way of Calvinistic sensibility. The merchants disdained the men but still did their best to satisfy their customers. It was not long before they began ordering groceries from the Canterbury Plains and importing whole ships' worth of tools from England.

In Dunedin, construction boomed. After all, not only were gold seekers pouring into the city but also people who wanted to stay. Craftsmen's workshops, businesses, and banks opened swiftly, as did taverns and brothels. Just six months after the arrival of the first gold seekers, the population of the city had doubled—and more men were arriving, many with their wives and children.

"I have good news and bad news for you," the reverend said.

Kathleen and Claire had just made another trip into the city, their wagon fully laden with wool goods from the farms. Recently, people in Dunedin had been ripping the woven blankets, sheepskin, and knit goods from their hands. It was cold in the gold miners' camps—and even if the hardened diggers could bear it, the women and children needed warm clothes.

"Though you might not even take the bad news as such. You might not even miss me."

Reverend Burton smiled, but he looked at them searchingly, particularly at Kathleen. He knew he should not think of her as lovingly as he did. For a pastor's wife, he needed an upright Anglican, as courageous and unproblematic as possible. Kathleen was Irish, Catholic, and burdened with a dark secret to boot. Yet Reverend Peter Burton could not help himself—his heart always danced at the sight of the beautiful blonde woman with deep-green eyes.

Kathleen raised her brows. "You're leaving, Reverend?" she asked quietly.

Peter nodded, feeling hope. Was there disappointment in her eyes?

"Off to the cannibals?" Claire said, teasing him. "Is it far? Have you overdone it with your preaching?"

"Not quite," he answered. "They're going to begin construction on St. Paul's in earnest next year, so they want to install a pastor a little firmer in his faith than I, or one who at least knows something about carpentry—or both. However it works out. In any case, I'm to serve the gold miners in the camps."

"Do they require spiritual comfort?" asked Claire. "From what I hear, they reach for girls more than Bibles." The first provisional brothels had opened in the mountains already.

Peter Burton smiled. "All the more reason to offer them spiritual guidance, says the bishop. And who better to turn to than me?"

The reverend was answering Claire, but his eyes never left Kathleen. She had lowered her gaze once again. Peter hoped his feelings did not deceive him, but she seemed concerned.

"Now, I won't be falling off the edge of the world," he said. "We needn't fall out of touch. I, I may visit you, may I not? Kathleen?" Peter now looked plainly at her.

"In Waikouaiti?" she asked with lowered eyelids.

The reverend shook his head, beaming. "No, in Dunedin. This is the good news. Kathleen, Claire, I've rented a storefront for you. A new parishioner, Jimmy Dunloe, has purchased a building in the center of town."

"A gold miner?" asked Claire, excited.

"No, miners rarely settle in one place, but the Dunloes have always had money. Jimmy runs a private bank that buys gold—he's an adventurer of the more dapper sort. He means to establish his bank here in Dunedin but also to open up a branch in the new settlement on the Tuapeka. It's rather well planned. And for the bank, he needs a representative building with business rooms and apartments. A salesroom in the building is empty right now, and an apartment belongs to it. When he told me about it, I thought at once about your fashion and tailoring business."

Claire beamed, but Kathleen looked shocked.

"But, but we agreed that there was no market in Dunedin for it," she said evasively.

Claire laughed and nudged her coltishly. "*Was*, Kathleen, *was*. Look around you. Do you see many Scots dressed like crows? Dunedin is growing into quite a wonderful modern city with beautiful women and rich men." She spun Kathleen around and bumped into Peter Burton.

"I could hug you, Reverend," she cheered, grabbing his shoulders. "We're finally getting away from the bores in Waikouaiti. Kathleen! Say something. You're happy, aren't you?"

Kathleen's face was flushed red. She did not know if she was happy. True, she would not cry over leaving Waikouaiti, especially not Mrs. Ashley and those like her. But a business in the middle of town? If Ian came looking for her . . . and if the reverend . . . if Peter was no longer there to protect her? She had to stop being so afraid. She had escaped. Ian was not looking for her. And no one had named Peter her protector.

"I'm thinking of Sean too, Kathleen. Mrs. Coltrane. He's wasting away in Reverend Watgin's schoolroom. He'll find better teachers here in Dunedin."

Kathleen nodded. Then she raised her eyes to him.

"Kathleen," she whispered. "Please just call me Kathleen. Always, not just by accident, Peter."

Peter Burton would have liked to hold her in his arms and offer her comfort. But he contented himself with taking her hand in his and pressing it lightly between his own. "Someday, you really must tell me what weighs on your heart, Kathleen," he said quietly. "But for now, I'll show you two your new business. There's an apartment over the shop—and someday it will offer an enchanting view of the jewel of Dunedin: St. Paul's Cathedral."

***

The reverend was not exaggerating. Dunloe's bank was in a new three-story building of Oamaru stone, a white limestone, and it was as centrally located as the church would someday be.

"The rent must be unaffordable." Kathleen worried, but Claire would not be deterred.

"London fashion is also unaffordable here," she laughed, managing to win over Mr. Dunloe at the same time.

The tall blond man seemed quite taken with the two women. He greeted each of them with a kiss on the hand, which made Kathleen blush. She only knew of such things from her landlords in Ireland; it was not common in her circles. Claire, on the other hand, blossomed when the banker invited them, and the reverend, too, to tea right after they met. The drink did not meet the standard of a fine house, however; the Maori maid had let it steep far too long, and she did not serve it correctly. The dark-haired, somewhat plump girl did not seem at all comfortable. She looked out the window incessantly—apparently she found the prospect of working on the second floor frightening.

"You can't find any servants here," Mr. Dunloe said apologetically.

At that Claire seized the teapot. "If you'll allow me," she said amiably. "Come along, girl. What's your name? I'll show you how to do it right."

Claire disappeared into the kitchen with the completely willing Haki. In Claire's absence, Kathleen tried to turn the conversation over to the reverend. She felt unsure of herself in the fine salon furnished with English furniture. But Mr. Dunloe was enthusiastic about her designs and would not be distracted from talking about them.

"Very tasteful, if not the latest fashion," he declared—after all, he had just arrived from London. "You need a few new magazines for inspiration. And material; you'll need to purchase material. I can give you contacts in London. Without a doubt, the business has a future. You'll make more money than most of these poor devils mining for gold. In addition to clothes, I would offer a few accessories as well. Think about it: soon a few adventurers who actually find gold will be going in and out of my bank. They'll be in a spending mood, but of course they won't know their sweethearts' measurements well enough to order a dress straight away. But a little hat, a silk handkerchief, a purse . . . Believe me, Mrs. Coltrane, here in the city, this will be the true gold mine."

Just then Claire came back in with a fresh pot of tea and Haki trailing behind her. "Then we'll name our store Gold Mine Boutique." She smiled and turned back to the Maori maid. "Look, Haki, this is how you stand next to the gentlemen when you fill their cups. Then no one will get burned if there's a splash. Don't always look out the window, child. The house isn't going to fall down." Claire shook her head, indulgently but decisively. "Mr. Dunloe, the girl is handy, but she's scared to death up here. Why don't you give us Haki to help with the store, and you can look for a maid without a fear of heights? I'll show the next one how to make tea properly, first thing."

***

Matters with the business were coming along well, but while Claire was bubbling with joy at their new opportunity, Kathleen felt empty when Peter Burton said good-bye before setting out for the Tuapeka River.

"You'll never get all of that in one go," Kathleen said unhappily when she saw all the materials he had gathered for his tent mission.

The reverend nodded. "I will, but I'll have to lead the horse. It'll be fine; don't worry. I just need a packsaddle."

Kathleen looked at the ground. She hated her shyness. She had not been like this before. But the years with Ian—whom she had never liked to look in the eye and who would punish her if she looked, even plainly, in any man's direction—had done their damage.

"If you . . . if you would do me the kindness, I'd be happy to give you my mule," she said quietly. "I don't need it anymore, after all, now that we live in the city."

Peter Burton's face brightened—not because of the mule, though it would be a great help, but rather because Kathleen was thinking of him. She was so often detached, but just now it did seem she cared for him after all.

"I'm happy to accept, Kathleen, and I'll take good care of it," he said formally. "Kathleen, would it, I mean, would you find it unpleasant? I would like to kiss you good-bye."

He did not want to admit it, but the path ahead horrified him—the filthy gold miners' camps and serving the men there. Peter Burton was an affable man. He liked all facets of the priest's office—from the clever sermons to dancing at weddings, from the sympathetic accompaniment of the dying to the baptizing of new parishioners. But he could see clearly what was awaiting him: Drunks he had to prevent from fighting, desperate men who had left house and home to look for gold and yet did not become rich. The sick, the lonely, the abandoned, idlers and dreamers, petty scoundrels, and hardened criminals. Peter Burton thought his God owed him at least a beautiful dream before sending him into this strange and hostile world.

Kathleen looked up at him timidly. "Why?" she asked.

Peter lifted his hand. He would have gladly stroked her cheek, but her gaze became even more anxious as he neared her face. So he only stroked her hair, so gently and carefully that she hardly could have felt it, though he felt the softness of her locks. That would have to do. God was not very generous.

"We'll put it off," he sighed, "until you don't ask anymore."

***

Gold Mine Boutique became a success as soon the first fabrics from London, the latest magazines, and a few selected accessories adorned the displays. The wives of the bankers and businessmen came first, then those of the craftsmen, and finally even the ladies from the grand sheep farms in the interior. Most of the sheep barons were now expanding their businesses to include cattle. The appetite of the gold seekers for steak was insatiable, and even if only a very few really became rich, that sufficed, for the time being, to create a demand for good food and whiskey.

While the gold seekers were celebrating in the taverns, cookshops, and whorehouses, higher society attended balls and concerts and met in fine hotels. Once again, Kathleen could not keep up with the sewing for all the dresses. As in Christchurch, she hired women to help and limited herself to designing. She hardly appeared in the shop. Claire managed it with the charm and assured appearance of a lady, and she enjoyed it with all her heart. With her first sizeable check, she bought a thoroughbred horse for her old sidesaddle and from then on would ride every Sunday with Mr. Dunloe, whom she also liked to accompany to evening events and matinees. Cute and lively Claire would wear the most daring designs from Kathleen's collection and was the best advertisement for their business. She flirted unabashedly with Jimmy Dunloe—which unsettled Kathleen, but she trusted that Claire knew what she was doing.

Sean and the girls likewise flourished in their new schools. Thanks to Claire's lessons, Heather and Chloe skipped two grades and grew even closer than they'd already been, because the older girls didn't welcome them. Sean no longer mentioned Ian, and the girls seemed to have almost forgotten their time on the Avon. Sean did miss the reverend, however.

"Can't we ride out to visit him during break?"

Kathleen and the Coopers heard these questions almost daily from their boys, although for Rufus it was more about seeing the gold mines than seeing Peter Burton again. Thus, the Coopers were reluctant to allow it. They feared losing their adventurous son in the miners' camps. But Kathleen trusted Sean. She smiled when she thought about how she would not have let Michael ride out there alone. He would surely have fallen for the call of the gold.

Chapter 3

"What do you think, Elizabeth? Should I ask for Claudia's hand now or once I get back from the gold mines?" Ronnie Baverly was no longer completely sober, but he asked the question very seriously.

Lizzie sighed. She had long since gotten used to her customers coming to her for advice on every possible life problem. But could she help this man?

"Ronnie, she won't take you until you lay ten ounces of gold in front of her," she said finally. "She'd rather stay in the Green Arrow. Aside from that, I can't hear the words 'gold mine' one more time. What do you all expect from digging around in Otago? None of you have ever even held a shovel."

That was an exaggeration, of course. Many of the men Lizzie had seen set out for Otago over the last few months originally came from the country, like Michael, and the handling of tools for digging was not new. However, at least in Lizzie's opinion, there was more to gold digging than two strong hands and a shovel. She had not forgotten anything she had learned about viniculture, and one of the most important things to know was that vines would not grow just anywhere. In some places there were nutrients for the plants, and in others there were not. It was the same for gold. You had to know the area, which river carried gold and why. Digging just anywhere seemed senseless to Lizzie, and digging where all the others were already doing it promised just as little success. But she could not sway her male customers with such arguments.

"In Otago, you don't need shovels, Elizabeth," Ronnie said. "The gold lies out in the road. Truly, if the Maori were so inclined, they could pave their paths with it."

Lizzie rolled her eyes. She was thoroughly tired of this story, but the men believed it. In truth, if Ronnie did not quickly find money to afford a wedding for Claudia, the blonde prostitute would move to Otago faster than he could. One of Kaikoura's three old taverns had closed for lack of customers. The men, who had once worked at the whaling station and then mainly in agriculture, moved to Dunedin in droves. Lizzie did not like to admit it, but even her business had been showing considerable losses the last few weeks. Kaikoura's population was shrinking, and Lizzie was once again struggling against fate. If things continued this way, she would not be able to maintain the Irish Coffee much longer—the more so since Michael showed little intention of sitting out the crisis. On the contrary, he, too, wanted to make his way to Otago sooner rather than later.

Lizzie was deeply satisfied with her life as a barkeeper, and so far, they had not been bothered about their distillery. Their business together brought in enough to live and afford modest luxuries. Lizzie owned handsome clothes and Michael a good horse. They had a wagon for deliveries and purchases. She was good friends with the local Maori tribe; her business had also brought the Ngai Tahu modest wealth. With Michael's direction, the Maori learned grain farming and barley malting. Thus, the distillery was independent of the farms in Canterbury. That proved a particular blessing in those weeks. The grain prices in Canterbury had soared astronomically since the gold find. It was barely possible to provide for the masses that flooded Otago.

Above all, Lizzie was respected and beloved as a citizen of Kaikoura. She was attending church again and took part in the preparation and management of charity bazaars and collections for the needy. The other women looked beyond her past; many of them had also come to Kaikoura as prostitutes, only becoming respectable after marrying this or that merchant or craftsman. The women looked at Lizzie skeptically because she had chosen another course, but her friendly manner and heartwarming smile assured her the friendship of the reverend and the most important society ladies. They had long known that Lizzie did not have eyes for the menfolk, but they were split on why they thought that was. The majority truly believed in a secret relationship with Michael, who openly courted her.

If it were not for Mary Kathleen, who still moved like a ghost through Michael's dreams, Lizzie would long ago have surrendered. She was afraid of the night in which he might call the name of the woman he loved. She could not bear that again. It would break her.

A few dreamers in the parish imagined an unhappy love for Lizzie, perhaps even with a native. After all, they knew she had friends in the Maori camp and spoke their language. Lizzie did still think occasionally of Kahu Heke, but she had not heard anything from him. At least it was calm on the North Island. The wars Kahu had predicted so far had not happened.

Lizzie heard the covered wagon in front of the tavern before Michael even arrived with the new whiskey delivery. The wagon horse whinnied excitedly. Lizzie treated it to some bread or sugar whenever it arrived at the tavern, and she went out to reward it for its loud greeting. Right away, she saw that Michael's own horse was hitched to the back of the wagon. He stepped down from the box and kissed her on the cheek.

"Sweet little Lizzie," he said with a wanton smile. "Can it be that you've gotten even prettier in the past week? Or just a little more respectable? No, it's not possible. This dress has a wider neck than the others, my dear Miss Owens—or Portland, or whatever you're calling yourself. The reverend won't like it."

Lizzie pushed Michael away, laughing. She was wearing a pretty light-blue linen dress, and lace adorned the neckline and apron. It was new, indeed, and it flattered her that Michael noticed.

"The lower neckline is simply in line with the latest fashion in London," she informed him. "It's become a bit livelier—and I learned this from the reverend's wife, of all people. Her husband has not complained so far."

"Even he likes to see a little skin," said Michael, looking rather obviously at Lizzie's cleavage. The corset for her new dress lifted her breasts a bit and made them seem bigger. In all honesty, Lizzie liked what she saw in the mirror. It seemed Michael also liked how she looked.

"But now, seriously, Lizzie, we need to talk."

From the wagon Michael lifted a crate of bottles and a small cask, which he nonchalantly carried on his shoulder. He had maintained his strength and muscles. Though distilling whiskey was not hard work, the wood needed to be chopped, and for a few weeks a year, Michael still went through the region's farms with his old shearing company.

Michael carried the bottles into the yard and set the small cask on the counter of the Irish Coffee.

"The good whiskey?" asked Lizzie, taken aback. "I thought it was supposed to sit for ten years." So far, Michael had not touched his very first batch in Robert Fyfe's barrel.

"It's been aging a few years. That's enough. And I've had enough of distilling, Lizzie. This is the last shipment for now. I'm going to Otago; I'm set on it. And when I come back we'll drink Irish whiskey from the old country."

Lizzie had suspected as much when she saw Michael's gray horse hitched to the back of the wagon and wearing stuffed saddlebags. Michael had carefully tied a collapsible shovel and a brand-new pan for gold behind the saddle, along with some blankets and his sleeping bag. What astonished Lizzie was Michael's intention to return to Kaikoura at some point.

"So you really want to look for gold, Michael?" she asked. "Isn't our profit here enough? Don't you have more than enough to return to Ireland? That's what you wanted, isn't it?"

Michael bit his lip. "Yeah, yes, sure. But I don't know what I'm supposed to do, Lizzie."

He plopped down casually onto a chair. Except for Ronnie, who was now staring into his third whiskey, dreaming of Claudia, the bar was empty. Lizzie sat across from Michael. His attitude was no newer to her than his words. Already, countless men had emptied their hearts to her after just such an introduction.

"If I go back to Ireland now—"

"Wait a moment, Michael." Lizzie knew Mary Kathleen's name would arise, and she thought she deserved a little encouragement. She tapped the whiskey cask and poured a glass each for Michael and herself. The contents tasted exceptional: smoky, full-bodied, and a little sweet.

Michael, likewise, seemed pleased. He took a second sip right away. "Look, if I go back to Ireland now, what's there for me? Mary Kathleen is gone, and no one knows where she is. Well, maybe her parents, but would they tell me? Who knows if they're even still alive? Who knows what's happened to the village and the tenants and Trevallion?"

"If I were you, I'd probably not let Trevallion or your landlord catch sight of me," said Lizzie. Though Michael's sentence would normally have long since been served, she did not know if breaking out of prison would extend it.

Michael nodded, concerned. "And if I do find out that she's in America, I'd need to take another ship. And America, it's so big."

Lizzie sipped at her whiskey. "If you really want to find someone, without an address, then you need to hire a detective or someone like that."

"Exactly," said Michael, although he did not give the impression of having thought of that before. "And for all that I need money. Loads and loads of money. I've saved a bit, of course, but not enough to buy the world."

"The world, no," Lizzie said with a pounding heart. Michael was introducing a subject she had long wanted to broach but so far had not dared to. And now might be her last chance. Once he was in Otago, it would be too late. "But certainly a piece of it. Michael, if we continue here for a couple of years, we'd have enough money for a farm. A sheep farm, I'd say, at least at first. Or cattle. Right now people are making the most with cattle."

Michael burst out laughing. "You want to buy a farm with me?"

Lizzie forced herself to remain calm. "I can do it without you too," she said. "But you're the one who knows how to farm, and you could be your own foreman. We could run it like we run this: I'll take care of the business, and you handle the production. It would be a secure life, a quiet life."

When Lizzie dreamed of her own farm, she saw a manor house made of stone, with bay windows and turrets. A little like the Smitherses' house in Campbell Town. But in this house, she'd be the mistress. She would have maids and a cook, and she would receive friends for tea. A husband and a few children fit in there as well, but Lizzie forbade herself from imagining this part of the story more precisely.

Michael took the matter up at once. "Was that a marriage proposal, Lizzie? Or are we to run the farm as brother and sister?" Lizzie glared at him, but he smiled. "Come now, Lizzie, it was a joke. A sheep farm like that would be lovely. But be honest, you're not thinking of a farm: you're thinking of something grander—a sheep baron's estate like Kiward Station, Barrington Station, or Lionel Station."

"So?" asked Lizzie. "What's wrong with that?"

"It would be unaffordable. Lizzie, I know the farms here. They're relatively small. True, the farmers have a few thousand sheep, which sounds grand, but they also work from sunup to sundown. You don't want to do that; you told me about your work with those Germans—you're not meant to be a milkmaid. And you're not suited to work fields or herd sheep around either."

"And what am I suited to, in your opinion?" Lizzie asked in a rage.

Michael thought for a moment. "For what you're doing right now," he said calmly. "You're the heart and soul of this tavern. You could run a hotel or a business. You have that enchanting smile of yours, Lizzie."

Lizzie did not know why that answer disappointed her. He was right that the work in the bar suited her and that she felt comfortable in Kaikoura. She could not expect Michael to share her dream, for him to see her as a mother and housewife—with or without maids and cooks.

"Let me go to Otago for now, Lizzie. When I come back and I'm really rich, we can decide what we want do. I've handed the distillery over to Tane. He knows how to do the work. He'll make the deliveries now. Just keep going, Lizzie. Maybe one day I'll be standing in the doorway burying you in gold."

He laughed. Then, content, he stood up, kissed her on both cheeks, and walked outside to unhitch his horse from the back of the wagon.

"Would you take the wagon and its horse to the stables for me, please? I need to get going or it won't be worth setting out tonight anymore."

***

Michael did not look back as he left Kaikoura. He regretted that it would be a long time before he saw Lizzie again, or heard her advice, or was warmed by her smile. But an adventure lay before him, and it was his to take alone.

As he rode south, he thought about Lizzie again and again. It was a tempting idea, burying her in gold, seeing her smile as he led her to the farmhouse he knew she wished for, making her dreams come true. She had led the business long enough. Now he would show her he was a man who could make his own fortune. Lizzie should finally admire him—and maybe then she would love him again, and maybe, too, she would want to live together as man and wife.

Lizzie watched the man she loved go and thought about what he had said about sheep farms in Kaikoura and the Canterbury Plains. She needed more money if she wanted to build a grand estate. Would Michael manage that on his own? Lizzie doubted it. She would give him some time.

***

Indeed, Lizzie made it a whole six months without Michael. She would have lasted longer if her business had not gotten worse and worse, but the decline of Kaikoura was inevitable. The whalers almost all left, the shepherds also tried their luck in the gold mines, and now even smaller farmers were leaving their land to chase what they believed would be easy money. Lizzie's friend, the fisherwoman with the cookshop next door, lost her husband and son to the dream. Both disappeared one day, on a small sailboat, in the direction of Otago Harbor.

"How am I supposed to live now?" asked the distraught woman. "If I have to buy the shrimp from other fishers, my prices will rise—and there are so few customers as it is."

Lizzie had problems of her own with the bar. Tane did not deliver whiskey as regularly as Michael. The Maori—their men at least—were not well suited to independent activity. Tane only distilled when he wanted to, and sometimes his whiskey made it not to the tavern but to the Maori camp instead. When there was a festival there, Tane provided liquor, and of course the tribe did not need to pay for it. Running dry twice was enough for Lizzie.

"Why don't you take over the tavern?" she asked her neighbor spontaneously. "It's not a gold mine itself anymore, but it will still support one person—with the cookshop anyway. And you're Maori; you should know how to get your tribesman in line. Honestly, I lack the right words or gestures to spur Tane to work, but I'm sure you can manage it."

The fisherwoman—who knew nothing better than kicking a man in the backside—proved ecstatic and went straight away into the mountains. In the meantime, Lizzie began to pack. She did not know if she was doing the right thing, and she wasn't at all sure Michael would be happy about a visit. But she did not believe he would succeed in getting rich without her.

Chapter 4

The road to Christchurch was not yet all that well paved, but between the Canterbury Plains and Dunedin, Lizzie made good time. There was heavy traffic on the route, since nearly all of the gold miners' food came from the agricultural regions of the plains.

She found her place in the caravan of covered wagons. She had invested a portion of the last few years' income into excellent supplies and equipment: warm clothing, a good tent, sleeping bags, and blankets. Otago was hilly. Between June and August there would surely be snow there, and it was already April. Lizzie also had bought tools of the highest quality, and she carried plenty of provisions for herself and Michael. She also brought presents for the local Maori tribe and meant to give generously to her new friends. She brought greetings from the tribe in Kaikoura, whose members occasionally spent summers in the mountains and had hunted and fished with their brothers and sisters in Otago.

"I wonder how you did not find all that gold while you were there," Lizzie said during her farewell visit to the Ngai Tahu. "Apparently everyone just trips over it."

Mere, one of the tribal elders, shrugged. "Who said we didn't find it? It doesn't mean anything to us. You cannot eat it, and you cannot make weapons from it. Jewelry, maybe, but you cannot carve it." The Maori had never learned the art of metallurgy; their jewelry and weapons were made primarily out of pounamu jade. "For us, jade is much more valuable," declared Mere.

"But now you could sell the gold," Lizzie suggested, "or the land on which it's found."

Mere arched her eyebrows, and her *moko*—her tattoos—danced as she did.

"The men who were in Tuapeka say the land is weeping. The *pakeha* are beating wounds into it to rip out the gold. The gods do not condone this."

"So gold mining is *tapu* for you?" Lizzie asked cautiously.

"Yes," Mere said, "but not everywhere. You have to ask the local *tohunga*. I cannot tell you anything. We have no gold."

Lizzie was determined to inquire specifically before she set up camp on a piece of land that was *tapu*. She did not want, under any circumstances, to offend the tribes in Otago. Surely, no one knew the land as well as the Maori. In any case, Lizzie did not intend to start digging at random.

The farther south she went, the colder it became, especially at night. While she slept in her wagon at the beginning of her journey, now she stopped at inns whenever possible. It no longer seemed advisable to sleep in the open. The roads brimmed with men, and not all of them were honorable—there were also adventurous but less savory figures around, on foot and on horse. Bearded men, their faces weathered by wind and sun; whalers and seal hunters from the West Coast; and sailors who had heard somewhere in Westport or Nelson about the gold finds and had left their ships. Every morning, she tried to find some honorable merchant or farmer whose wagon she either drove ahead of or followed behind and who would keep an eye on her. When she could, she traveled with whole families, of which ever more headed toward Dunedin.

After almost six weeks traveling, Lizzie finally reached Dunedin. She was enthusiastic about the new, vivacious city. It was wonderful to stroll the shopping streets, admiring the pretty dresses and hats in the displays; for the first time in many years, Lizzie almost felt as if she were in London again. For a moment, she thought longingly of taking a job. Without a doubt, the merchants, bankers, and high-earning craftsmen needed maids. Not having responsibility for her own business had its appeal, but on the other hand, her pay would be bad, and she would receive no thanks from her masters. She might even be preyed upon again. No, Lizzie never wanted to return to that life, no matter how attractive a warm room and cozy kitchen might be.

Lizzie shivered; in Dunedin, it was already bitterly cold. Yet the town was in a good location, and the climate was mild. In the mountains, however . . .

"Do you really want to go there?" asked the proprietress when Lizzie finally found an inn where she could rent a room. "Along the Tuapeka all alone? You're not, you're not a woman of easy virtue, are you?"

Lizzie was proud that people no longer saw that in her. "I'm looking for my man," she insisted seriously. "I don't know if he'll get by without me."

The innkeeper laughed heartily. "They all get by one way or another, and not half bad if you ask me. It's true that when Reverend Burton comes to town, we only hear the absolute worst, but I always see the wagons heading up there. Every day at least one wagon full of whiskey, so it can't be all bad."

Lizzie was annoyed she had not brought the still with her. She probably could have made more with that than by panning for gold, but that would require Michael hearing reason first. Now she could hardly wait to travel up the Tuapeka River.

***

Peter Burton had been horrified when he reached Gabriel's Gully. The terrain around the Tuapeka River had once been beautiful: green and forested, with the valleys and riverbanks covered in flowers. What the gold miners had left behind was a stinking wasteland. In the early phase of mining, no one had worried much about staking claims. The men had pitched tents and dug right where they were. Near Gabriel's Gully the gold was often just beneath the surface. Other gold seekers—especially the veterans from Australia—took to panning for gold in the streams, and the trees fell, victims in the construction of sluice boxes used for prospecting.

In the area of the first gold finds, nothing grew anymore. The earth was torn up and dug over many times. Every strong rain transformed the camp into a mud hole. Tons of dirt had washed away—and a few tents with it. At the communal camp, there were improvised taverns and primitive stores selling groceries and whiskey. There were whores, too, though only a few of the girls had come to the camp on their own. Most had come with gold miners who rented out their own lovers when their searches for gold failed.

Three such disappointed and desperate girls, who wanted nothing more than to be able to leave their men and the camp, ran to the reverend immediately after his first service. Reverend Burton fought two of the fellows—he had boxed in college—and so won unanticipated respect. He sent one of the girls to Dunedin—first to Claire and Kathleen but with a final destination of Waikouaiti. He hired the other two to help him set up his parish. Reverend Burton had known ahead of time that the men in Otago needed active, concrete help more than they did prayer. The camp needed latrines and attention to hygiene; with the current hygienic conditions, disease was inevitable.

Reverend Burton was prepared when cholera began to spread in autumn. Together with his assistants and other volunteers from Dunedin, he tended the sick for weeks, winning more respect in the camp. During this period, it was not unusual to see him in the taverns. After a long day spent washing the sick, saying deathbed prayers, and sanctifying the constant stream of coffins before they were lowered into the muddy earth, he needed a whiskey. In the end, the men began to listen to Reverend Burton. The camp became more orderly; people set out roads and latrines.

However, the men at Gabriel's Gully were just about to scatter. The land was stripped. People had found gold in other places. The men—and the reverend with them—moved on to new riverbanks and streams only to inflict the destruction anew.

***

Lizzie followed the rugged paths into the mountains. Her horse had to exert itself to pull her wagon up the inclines; mules would not have been quite so exhausted. Still, she had luck: in the bitter cold, the ground was frozen and hard rather than muddy.

When she passed Gabriel's Gully, the dead terrain of which was now frozen in ice, she understood the Maori's words. The natives must have been shocked when they saw what had happened to their land.

On the second day of her journey up the river, it began to snow. The blowing snow soon became so heavy that Lizzie could not see her hand in front of her face. Finally, she unharnessed her horse, covered it with a blanket, and tied it to the wagon. Then she crawled under the wagon, grateful she had planned well enough to purchase the wool items and tarps that were keeping her halfway warm.

When Lizzie awoke in the morning, it was as if she were in a fairy tale. The mountains and trees and anything around were under a heavy blanket of snow. Lizzie could hardly look at it enough, especially after the sun rose and made the snow shimmer like splinters of diamond. In London, snow had always been a dirty, gray mass. In the Bay of Islands on the North Island, it had never snowed. Here, however . . . Lizzie began to fall in love with the mountains of Otago.

After her third day of travel, she finally reached the new gold miners' camp. Hundreds, maybe thousands of tents stood on the banks of the river as well as around the newest discovery sites. The camp bustled with horses, mules, and oxen. Men stood around a fire trying to warm their hands, and Lizzie thought they looked more worn down and sick than optimistic. The weather was clearly taking its toll, and since the frozen ground did not permit any serious digging, they couldn't be earning much money. It seemed quite possible that some of the men were starving.

Lizzie immediately began to ask for Michael, but without any luck. It seemed the men were only acquainted with their immediate neighbors or the men with whom they were working at the time. Finally, she talked to a digger who gave her some useful information.

"You'd do best to ask the reverend, girl. At least, he writes down the names of the men who die here."

Lizzie did not find this very encouraging; nevertheless, she set off toward the center of the camp to find the reverend. She passed improvised taverns, brothels, stores, and, finally, a post office.

The postman told her where to look for the reverend: "'E's in a tent with a cross on it. You can't miss it. But now, the reverend's usually in the 'ospital. What, is 'e supposed to pray the 'ole time?"

One of the prostitutes, who looked even more frozen than the men around camp, showed Lizzie the hospital tent and pointed to a man standing on a ladder.

"There 'e is. Reverend? 'Ere's someone what wants something from you. You ain't knocked a girl up an' run off to the gold mines, 'ave you?"

The men all around the infirmary laughed. Only the reverend himself did not seem to find the matter funny. The slender, brown-haired man, whose tattered clothing and weathered skin in no way differentiated him from the diggers, was not in a good position. He hovered more or less between heaven and earth: the ladder swayed noticeably, but none of those watching moved to hold it still. Worse yet, the tent fabric whipped around in the wind, defying his attempts to secure it. In truth, he would have needed three hands to hold it in place, align the nail, and hammer. He tried hard not to curse as he smashed his thumb during a renewed attempt to nail the thing down.

Lizzie seized the ladder and then a log that lay near the entrance. She leaned the log against the wall of the tent to hold the tarpaulin halfway securely in place. The reverend realized at once what she was doing and quickly hammered in the nail. A short time later, the men in the tent were again protected from the snow and wind.

Peter Burton climbed down and smiled at Lizzie. "At least then I would have put the most handy woman in a family way," he told the prostitute who had brought Lizzie to him, drawing more howls of laughter. "Though you'd be a fool to leave this woman."

He bowed politely to Lizzie. "Many thanks, madam. Please do forgive the people here. They're of a rougher sort. I am Peter Burton, a pastor for the Church of England, even if that doesn't appear to be the case."

Lizzie now caught sight of the priest's collar hidden under his wool scarf.

"Can I assist you in some way?" he asked.

Lizzie nodded and inquired about Michael. Her heart was hammering violently. If he really had been buried by this man . . . She had not heard from him in seven months, after all.

"Michael Drury. An Irishman. He'd be Catholic, of course."

Peter Burton dismissed that. "No one cares about that here—at least not until Rome sends us a priest too. I'd be grateful for any help. Michael Drury, hmm; a tall man, dark-haired?"

"He has blue eyes," said Lizzie. "Very blue."

The reverend noticed how her own eyes brightened at the mention of Michael's, and he smiled at her. "Yes, I believe I know him. He's with one of my parish assistants."

Lizzie's heart turned to ice. That could not be. He could not have already found a girl; he . . .

"Chris Timlock," Reverend Burton continued. "A good fellow, came with the first wave of gold seekers from Wales."

Lizzie sighed with relief.

"But those two aren't here. They go their own way. They're on some stream upriver and firmly convinced they'll find gold there."

"And? How are their prospects?"

The reverend arched his right eyebrow. "Don't ask me. I'm a theologian. I have no idea when it comes to panning for gold. But they say all the streams here carry it. It's just a question of how much. Can I perhaps offer you some tea? I'm half-frozen, and you look to be too."

Lizzie gladly accepted. She soon found herself again in a warm room, likely the improvised kitchen for the hospital. There were roughly assembled tables and benches. Stew bubbled away in a giant pot set on a woodstove.

"Whenever it's possible, we offer a warm meal," explained Reverend Burton. "Only for the needy, of course, but we never have enough to make everyone full. Which encourages more illness. In autumn, we had cholera, now influenza and pneumonia. And tuberculosis. There's nothing that can be done for a few of the men. They'll soon die on me." The reverend sighed and poured Lizzie a cup of tea.

"Do people find so little gold?" asked Lizzie.

Reverend Burton laughed. "Most men here don't earn more than a laborer in the city. Often less. That's the average, Mrs. Drury."

"Miss Portland, Lizzie Portland," Lizzie corrected him.

The reverend looked at her questioningly. "Alas, Miss Portland, life here is considerably more expensive than in Dunedin or Kaikoura. Did you see the shop? They demand exorbitant prices—which is fair enough, I suppose, since they have to haul every morsel of food up here. The pubs are not running a charity either, nor are the women for sale. Add to that, men betting on everything. I preach against it, of course, but I can understand it, in a way. The boys work hard, six or seven days a week. They want to have some fun Saturday night. In any case, the merchants, barkeepers, and whores make more money here than the gold miners."

"No one gets rich?" asked Lizzie.

Reverend Burton shrugged. "Few," he answered. "The first to find a new gold source—and the good poker players. For the latter, there's plenty to make; some rob their fellows shamelessly. But they're the minority, Miss Portland. The vast majority will leave as poor as they came."

Lizzie sighed. "Then I'll drive upriver. Or do you think it would make sense to wait for Michael here?"

Reverend Burton arched his brows. "That depends on whether you're planning a visit or want to stay with your man. I can also marry you, should you want to share his name, too, and not just his unheated tent."

Lizzie gave Reverend Burton a cool look. "I have my own tent, Reverend. And I'm not sharing it with anyone."

Reverend Burton raised his hands in apology. "I didn't mean to offend you, Miss Portland. Please, forgive me. I had the impression Michael is your man."

Lizzie bit her lip. "Not in that sense," she muttered. "It's just . . . He's not mine. I, I just care about him."

Chapter 5

Michael Drury sniffled. He could not get rid of his cold, but he was doing better than Chris Timlock, who was laid up in his tent, feverish and coughing. Michael was well enough to pan for gold, and he needed to. If he did not find at least a few nuggets in his sieve that day, he could not buy anything to eat, and they had finished the last bits of their food the night before. He would have to ride to camp later, but the small amount of gold they had found so far was hardly worth the effort of exchanging.

Michael had thought about going hunting, but he was not good at setting traps, and the small game he had hunted in Ireland did not exist in Otago. No rabbits or hares, only birds with strange habits. The dark-green keas were so impudent that they would steal provisions from the tents. He had only managed to kill one with a sling. It had hardly been worth it, since the small bird hardly had any meat on it. He was better at fishing than hunting—but when he stood in the river all day panning for gold, the fish swam away.

Michael considered whether he should take a break from work to make tea. Chris could surely use it, his own boots were already soaked through again, and he couldn't risk becoming as sick as his partner.

He was just gathering up his equipment when he heard Chris call him. His friend stood at the entrance to his tent with a rifle in his hand. The men had purchased the weapon with the profits from their first, rather encouraging gold find, but in truth, neither of the two really knew what to do with it. When they had a bit of money for ammunition, they practiced by shooting at trees or bottles, but so far, they weren't good enough shots to guarantee hitting even an unmoving object.

Yet Chris must have been concerned by something to stand there with the rifle, especially sick as he was. Michael left his equipment and ran to the tent, which stood on a rise. He wanted to be able to survey his claim. So far no one else had the idea of looking for gold in this particular location, but that could change at any moment.

"Someone's coming up the way," whispered Chris when Michael reached him. He was glowing with fever, and he coughed as he spoke. "I think so, anyway."

Michael helped his friend back onto his bedroll in the tent. It was possible he had been hearing things. But from the tents, one really could hear what was going on behind the rise. And now, even Michael heard hoofbeats. He pulled the blankets up to Chris's chin.

"Do you hear it?" Chris asked.

Michael nodded, grabbed the gun, and went outside. He didn't intend on shooting, but surely the gun was good for scaring the visitor a bit first. Michael made his way to the path—and he was greeted with cheerful whinnying. Lizzie's horse recognized him at once. After all, Michael had always spoiled it—though perhaps it was just calling to Michael's gray horse, which was grazing in front of the tents. The horses had shared stables long enough to know each other well. In any case, Michael immediately identified the whinny as belonging to the Irish Coffee's workhorse. It strained up the mountain, clearly laden with a heavy load. Beside it, a woman in long skirts struggled through the snow, wrapped in wool scarves and heavy coats.

"Lizzie!" Michael ran to her and took her in his arms. He would never have admitted it, but he had rarely felt as relieved as he did at the sight of her.

Lizzie removed the scarf around her neck and hair and almost would have let him kiss her. It was good to lay eyes on him again, but his appearance confirmed all her fears. The last time she'd seen him so thin and haggard was on the prison ship. Michael's cheeks were sunken, and his eyes were red with fever. Though he did hold her close, he seemed too weak to swing her around as he often would as a greeting in Kaikoura.

But he did seem truly happy to see her. A weight lifted from Lizzie's heart.

"What are you doing here, Lizzie? Come in, come in; it's warmer in the tent. Well, not much, but a little. I can make tea."

Lizzie gave him her heartwarming smile and then began to unpack the saddlebags. "I thought I'd look for a little gold too," she said casually. "There was nothing more to do in Kaikoura, so I just hitched the horse and came here. How're your riches coming along, Michael Drury?"

Michael made a face. "We work hard," he mumbled, "but now, in winter . . ."

Lizzie nodded. "It's pretty cold here. What did you say? You have a tent?"

Michael's and Chris's tents were nothing compared to the reverend's. Fundamentally, they consisted of no more than some canvas stretched over four low poles. One could sit upright within but not stand. There were no furnishings. The men slept on the ground, which was provisionally covered with a tarpaulin. Mats and blankets protected against the worst of the cold, but they could not keep the seriously ill Chris warm enough. Lizzie was shocked when she saw him. He lay listless in his sleeping bag, hardly able to offer her his hand.

"Michael, this man has to get somewhere warm," she said. "First, pitch the tent I brought. It's small but much more comfortable than this. Down in the camp, I also have a larger one; we can fetch that sometime in the next few days. Oh yes, and see that you find a few big rocks; there are certainly plenty around here. We can heat them up in the fire and then take them into the tents with us. They should warm things up a bit. And bring my bag in. I have cough syrup of rongoa petals."

"Do you, perhaps, have something to eat?" asked Michael quietly.

Lizzie looked at him, disbelieving.

"I, I was going to ride down today to refresh our supplies. We only just ran out and . . ."

"And you haven't found enough money to pay the exorbitant prices down there, have you?" asked Lizzie severely. "Michael, what are you thinking? The boy in there is dying, and you wanted to leave him alone while you went to beg for some food? We'll cook something first, and warm him up—and tomorrow we'll take him down to the camp."

"But the claim," Michael objected. "If we leave it, someone might rip it out from under us."

Full of the pride of ownership, he let his gaze wander for a while over the idyllic little valley. It was unquestionably beautiful. But was the snow really hiding any gold?

Lizzie rolled her eyes. "Then let someone else starve up here. Michael, we can find something like this anywhere. You don't need to guard it."

"Anywhere?" Michael said. "I don't think so . . . We need only make it through winter. In the spring, when the ground thaws . . ."

Lizzie sighed. He was crazy to try to stay. Why did she keep falling for those shining blue eyes and that enchanting voice? She realized it might not even be possible to move Chris Timlock to the camp. The man was seriously ill. If he was to survive, he needed food and warmth. If she brought all of her provisions up here, she could tend to him just as well as the reverend would below.

"All right, fine," she relented. "But tomorrow you'll go to camp and try to bring up the wagon. Or make two trips with the horses—with them, you should be able to get everything here."

"You brought enough provisions to load two horses? What in heaven's name did you haul out here?"

Lizzie stared him straight in the eyes. "Everything you're missing here to live a halfway decent life. And now, get to work. I'll care for Chris."

"We, we're going to find gold, aren't we?" Chris asked with a hoarse voice as Lizzie poured the Maori rongoa cough syrup into his mouth. "In spring?"

Lizzie stroked his hair, soothingly. "Of course we'll find gold. Don't you worry."

"Do, do you promise?"

Lizzie smiled. Clearly, Chris no longer knew where he was or who was talking to him. But he needed encouragement. He was still very young.

"I promise," she said firmly.

As soon as possible, she would have to find out where the Ngai Tahu were living.

***

During her first days in Otago, however, Lizzie did not manage to find the local Maori tribe's village. There was too much to do. She did everything to save Chris Timlock's life. The young man was soon doing better thanks to Lizzie's care. Then she and Michael went about making the camp fit to survive the winter. To Michael's annoyance, Lizzie insisted they build a cabin.

"Michael, it's only June, and it's snowing every day. This will last at least three months. You can't sleep through that in a tent."

"The people in the camp can."

Lizzie shook her head. "They're either sick all the time or warm themselves at the reverend's stove. Besides, the camp there is lower down, so it's also a little warmer. And you don't have anything else to do anyway."

"I can pan for gold. That will get us something at least."

Lizzie grabbed her forehead. "Michael, in four weeks, you haven't pulled even an ounce of gold from the stream. No day laborer would hire on for that wage, not even in Ireland. Especially when you consider you're ruining your boots in the water and your shovels and spades when you try to dig in the frozen earth."

"But I can't build a house alone. And Chris . . ."

Chris Timlock had survived his pneumonia, but he was still sick in bed. Lizzie did not expect him to recover fully until winter was over. Perhaps in spring when it got warmer.

"I can help you," said Lizzie. "I'm stronger than you think, and I think it will be fun."

This latter point proved true. Though felling trees and hauling the beams was backbreaking work, Lizzie took great pleasure in fitting beams together and watching her future house go up. They made rapid progress, and after a month, they had a tiny wooden house with just enough room for three sleeping spaces, a fireplace, a table, and chairs. Lizzie partitioned off one corner of the cabin with tent canvas to have a space for herself. In the gold miners' camp, people whispered about her living with two men, but they talked more about Michael holding on to his useless claim.

The reverend never said a word about their living arrangement, but there wasn't much opportunity since they rarely made it to camp for Sunday service. Chris only managed the trip on very good days and was near dead with exhaustion afterward. So Lizzie invited Reverend Burton to come for a visit and was happy when he accepted her invitation.

The reverend gave a service for Lizzie and Chris, then drank a whiskey with Michael. Lizzie had brought the cask of Michael's first batch to Otago, and the reverend was enthused by the quality. She was pleased that he enjoyed the product of their earlier endeavor, but to Lizzie it was important that the reverend see the cabin they'd built and her private niche within. No one was to doubt her honor.

***

Spring came to Otago much later than to Kaikoura, but when nature finally threw off winter, the land exploded with fertility. Almost overnight, everything became green. Yellow and red flowers arose in the meadows and on the stream banks. These banks woke memories of Ireland in Michael, though here, southern beeches lined the path instead of oaks, and ferns dipped their branches into the water instead of willows. The birdcalls sounded strange, but other things were just like home.

Michael enjoyed the sight of Lizzie's slender body clothed only in a light dress once she'd peeled off the heavy wool layers that had kept her warm through the winter. Just like the girls in Ireland, she let her hair blow in the wind and beautified their home with spring flowers—and for the first time in years, Michael did not dream of Mary Kathleen's luscious golden locks but instead of the sunshine in Lizzie's fine dark-blonde strands. He no longer thought of Kathleen's graceful movement but cherished Lizzie's dynamic manner: her lively attempts to induce the horse to haul timber and her careful, gentle way of taking Chris out of the cabin and into the sun.

Chris talked increasingly of finally getting back to work with them, but his return was questionable. He whittled a bit on pieces of wood, trying to help Michael with the design of a sluice box, but if he even reached for the lightest saw, he was bathed in sweat and coughing within minutes.

Michael grumbled that Lizzie, at least, should give him a hand with the box, but she resisted.

"Michael, it's not worth it. This stream doesn't have any gold in it. Or too little to make any serious money. It would be better to dig a bit. After all, there might be gold veins, if you've your heart set on this claim and no other. But as for the sluice box, I'm with the Maori: before I chop down a tree, I ask Tane, god of the forest, for permission, and he only grants it when I do something sensible with the wood. Here, Tane says no. And I'll be damned if I anger him."

Lizzie had found out where the nearest Maori tribe lived. She had guessed she would have to travel two days upriver to reach their camp, and she prepared to make the journey on foot. She had laden her horse with gifts for the Ngai Tahu and did not want to add her weight to the burden. Michael offered to accompany her or let her take his horse as a mount. But Lizzie declined both. She didn't really like to ride, and his gray horse was so fiery that she did not trust herself to handle it. Although she would have enjoyed Michael's company, the Ngai Tahu would trust her more readily if she came alone. Besides, she did not want to leave Chris alone in camp.

"Nothing is going to happen to me, Michael." She laughed as Michael hovered over her, checking on every bit of her preparations. "The Maori are friendly, and I'm bringing them gifts and greetings from their friends in Kaikoura. The *pakeha* present more of a danger here. But where I'm headed, probably no white has been before."

Silently, though, she was happy about his concern. It seemed as if he was finally beginning to feel something for her.

Chapter 6

Spring brought new life to the gold miners' camp. Ships began arriving in Otago Harbor again, and thousands of new adventurers rushed toward the Tuapeka River. New gold miners, and those who wanted to become them, also journeyed by land across the country.

Two of these travelers set out from Dunedin for their spring vacation: Rufus Cooper and Sean Coltrane. After months of their begging, even Mr. Cooper had finally given his permission for a visit to the reverend—though not before Peter Burton had sworn several times over that he would send Rufus back by the end of vacation.

The two had spent hours packing their horses with every possible camping and digging tool, though it had not been at all necessary. Kathleen and Heather were going to the camp, driving a wagon filled with tent canvas and provisions for the hospital—though two sleeping bags and a couple of shovels would also have fit in the bed, as Kathleen noted with a wink.

The boys rejected this, though.

"Real prospectors don't have their mothers driving behind them," said Sean, self-assured, which drew a laugh from Kathleen.

"It might be better if some of them did," she said.

Kathleen was exceedingly optimistic that spring. She looked forward to the excursion into the mountains—and to seeing Peter Burton again, even if she would not admit it. And, against her expectations, she had settled into Dunedin well. At first she had panicked about being discovered—after all, she had found herself in a flourishing community. Dunedin had an elected city council and commercial regulations; Kathleen and Claire were properly registered, and their business was well known. If Ian had made inquiries, he would easily have been able to find her. Yet four years had passed since their escape. Ian must have moved on, and, moreover, Dunedin was no longer a town where everyone knew one another. The city was growing quickly and offered corresponding anonymity.

Kathleen now even attended theater performances and art exhibitions with Claire and Jimmy Dunloe. She had no problem affording the tickets. Gold Mine Boutique generated good profits from Kathleen's designs and from the accessories Claire ordered from Paris and London. Kathleen wondered when Mr. Dunloe might finally make a marriage proposal and how Claire might react to that. But Claire never talked about even the possibility of it.

Kathleen had admirers of her own—or could have had them if she were not so reserved. She rarely appeared in public and only answered monosyllabically when men addressed her. Her extraordinary, now mature beauty could not be hidden, however. Though Kathleen dressed more simply than Claire, her gold-blonde hair and emerald-green eyes always made her the center of attention. For the first time in her life, Kathleen had time to care for herself. Her skin was no longer sunburned, her lips no longer chapped, and her hands no longer raw and worn.

Kathleen's nightmares became rarer, and she began to forget Ian's insults and abuse. Over time, she was able to start to look people in the eye again. Nevertheless, she still struggled with feelings of guilt—more so since the new Catholic priest in Dunedin did not absolve her of them.

"You should not have left your husband," he admonished her after her first confession. "No matter what happened. What God has joined, let no man tear asunder. You should have stayed with him and tried to be a good wife to him."

Father Parrish would not hear Kathleen's objection that she had tried that long enough. He advised her to return to Christchurch, but Kathleen's submission to God did not go quite that far.

"But God didn't join you. It was pure contingency," Claire said later, in support of Kathleen's perspective. "Rather, God led you to that Michael fellow. You should have married him. Couldn't you have gone with him to Australia?"

Kathleen had never thought of that possibility, but it was too late now anyway. She now saw herself as well on her way to committing an even worse sin than leaving her abusive husband. Every time Peter Burton came to town, her affection for him grew. He made her laugh, entertained her with stories from the gold miners' camp, and always concerned himself with Sean and Heather. He was patient and never pressured her, and whenever he offered his arm on a walk, she felt relaxed and safe. When he took her hand, or when his leg unintentionally brushed hers as he climbed into the buggy, her heart beat faster. It was not the violent longing she had felt for Michael, but something was there—when Peter Burton came to town, she felt younger and lighter and danced through the day.

Sometimes, when she was sitting over her sketchbook and nothing was coming to her, she would catch herself drawing a picture of Peter Burton: His steep, somewhat crooked nose—he'd broken it boxing in college; his full lips; his oval face; light-brown hair that constantly fell over his forehead. His friendly, peaceful eyes—which could, however, flash vivaciously when something touched him. Because she finally ventured to hold his gaze long enough to study his eyes, Kathleen now knew that they were brown, the specks within them amber-colored.

Kathleen tried not to think about the possible consequences of her feelings. But she allowed herself pure joy at their reunion in the camp. She was driving up for the first time. Peter had not wanted visits in Gabriel's Gully—that is, not from a lady. But the new camp was supposed to be more civilized. A few gold miners had sent for their wives and built cabins, and the reverend was even teaching reading and writing to a few children every day.

"You'll see, Ma. After vacation, we'll be rich," Sean declared now as he trotted ahead with Rufus.

Heather snuggled against Kathleen. "Do you think I could pan gold too?" she asked.

Kathleen nodded. "I'm sure. Reverend Burton will show us how, and then we two will find more gold than all the boys together."

When they arrived, Kathleen could hardly believe her eyes. The new settlement had grown into a small city, and Peter Burton's church and community center were at its core. The women immediately recruited Kathleen: the hospital, the kitchen for the needy, the school—all needed helping hands. There weren't many women in the camp, but now there weren't only prostitutes. The helpers in Peter's parish were the wives and daughters of the chandlers, postmen, and bankers. The wives of the gold miners rarely contributed in the community because they mostly worked at the mines as well, just as hard as the men. Many did not last long, suffering miscarriages and accidents or growing too pregnant to work the mines. The first night after her arrival, Kathleen helped with two births—though she would have preferred to spend the evening with Peter.

While Kathleen and Peter had been intentionally reserved at their reunion, people were already talking about their relationship.

"My, but you'd make a lovely pastor's wife," said the wife of the general-store owner. Kathleen soon discovered the other women in the community had ideas about a wedding. She would have to be careful. It did not bear thinking about what would happen if these good women learned she was Catholic.

Still, Kathleen was happy during her days spent at Peter Burton's side in the new settlement of Tuapeka. She was hardly ever alone with him, but it filled her with joy to watch him interact with his community and to help him in whatever ways she could.

***

Peter Burton, himself, was somewhat disappointed. He had hoped to have more time for Kathleen, but while she was visiting, new arrivals were overrunning the camp. The reverend was needed everywhere at once to give advice and enforce rules for staking claims and pitching new tents.

Kathleen also worked hard, and when Peter Burton pulled up in front of the community center, he found her washing vegetables for the charity kitchen. "Now, at least ride along," he said. "The day seems made for a picnic."

Sean and Rufus had set out early in the morning to search for gold, their saddlebags stuffed with provisions, and Heather had gone along with them. Kathleen's "little girl" was now thirteen years old and not so easily left behind, and, to the boys' aggravation, she was a skilled gold panner. She had panned thirteen pounds' sterling worth of gold from rivers and streams in their first week—miles ahead of her brother, of course—and now felt rich.

Just as Kathleen looked about to make the excuse of not leaving her work undone, Peter offered up the chance at another task.

"I need to pick up wood from the other end of camp," he said. "The men have felled trees to make room for more tents, and they want to offer us the lumber. If I can find a few people to help, we'll put up a solid building for the hospital, at least for the women's section."

Finding such helpers would be difficult, since the men went off to the gold mines every morning. Still, the lumber had to be brought in, and Kathleen climbed up next to Peter on the wagon. As he steered his team safely through the camp, he chatted with Kathleen, whom he liked more every day. She finally seemed to feel safe, she liked her work, and everything seemed to be in order in Dunedin. She even laughed quite openly when he made a joke. And she was beautiful.

It was a sunny but windy spring day, and a few strands of Kathleen's hair had come loose. Peter ventured to brush them tenderly back into place. Even a few months before, Kathleen would have shied away, but now she nuzzled her face against his hand. Cautiously, he let his arm wander down around her shoulders, and he pulled her closer to him. Kathleen looked up at him, and he lost himself in her radiant eyes.

Kathleen gave the reverend a tender smile—but in an instant, her expression, relaxed and illuminated by inner joy a moment before, warped into a grimace of horror.

"Drive," she whispered to Peter. Her hands reached for the reins. "Drive, fast. Faster. I have to . . ."

It sounded so urgent that Peter spurred on the mules without asking—though not without looking over his shoulder. Something Kathleen had spied when she looked over at him had scared her to death. So much so that now she shrunk down beside him and hid her face. It seemed almost as if she wished she could crawl under the box.

Peter could not see anything that should have provoked this reaction. On the side of the street, a completely normal scene for Tuapeka was unfolding. Two new arrivals—a dark-haired man and a blond boy who looked to be thirteen or so—were starting to unload their wagon, and the man was arguing with his neighbor about the placement of his tent. None of them had taken notice of Peter's wagon, let alone Kathleen.

"What's the matter, Kathleen? Talk to me, please."

"Stop, stop the wagon, please," she mumbled. "Yes, yes, here's fine. I, I'm sorry, Peter, but I, Sean, the children. I'll, I've got to . . ."

Kathleen leaped from Peter's wagon and ran as if the Furies were on her heels.

Had he done something to scare her? No, it had to be something else. Quickly and decisively, he turned his wagon around to head back to camp.

He needed to find Kathleen and get out of her what had shaken her to her core. It looked as if she were running to the church—an indication that it was not him from whom she was running. Between the tents there were shortcuts. She would get there before Peter could with his wagon. The reverend looked once more at the place where Kathleen had frozen. The man and the boy had disappeared. Apparently, their angry neighbor had won out and they had to pitch their tent elsewhere. Could Kathleen's panic have had to do with the two of them? Or was it the neighbor? But what could she have to do with that old good-for-nothing curmudgeon from Australia? Peter Burton decided to find out later. Deeply unsettled, he shook his mules' reins and did not stop until he reached the hospital and church.

"Where is Mrs. Coltrane?" he called to the women still sitting in front of the tents, washing vegetables.

"Did you two fight?" the chandler's wife asked.

Peter did not bother to answer. "Where is she?"

"She just came past, pale as if she'd seen a ghost, and she ran to the stables. Has something happened, Reverend?" The wife of the postman asked.

Peter left his team standing there, leaped from the box, and followed Kathleen into the stables. A busy Scotsman rented spaces for horses here, earning more than most of the prospectors. Kathleen was frantically yoking her horses.

"I, I have to go," she stammered when she saw Peter.

"But Kathleen, so suddenly? Do tell me what's happened. Did I do something?"

Peter wanted to take her in his arms, or at least soothe her enough that she would look at him, but Kathleen did not stop.

"You? No, no, of course not. Peter, you must find Sean, or wait until the boys and Heather come back. But then tell him they must come straight home, will you? They shouldn't wait, just head out, even if it's at night. Maybe you can find someone to accompany the children. I'll pay. But we, we have to . . ."

Kathleen did not finish her sentence. She leaped onto the box and directed her team out of the stables.

"I'm sorry, Peter. I'm truly sorry."

Kathleen had the horses break into a trot as soon as they exited the stables. She steered them toward the road to Dunedin.

Peter remained behind, stunned.

The women were talking excitedly about how Kathleen had left without retrieving her belongings or waiting for her children. They gave him looks that were not especially flattering, but he paid no attention to them. He went back to his wagon instead. Whatever had happened, he had to pick up the wood before someone else took it. After that was done, he would look for this man and his boy, whose sight had frightened Kathleen to death.

***

Loading the wagon with the lumber was no quick task, and it was hours before Peter could head back to the church. But it was still light out when he passed the spot where Kathleen had fallen into a panic. He saw the man with whom the dark-haired fellow had been arguing and pulled up on the reins.

"Evening, Terrence. So, good day today?"

The miner shook his head. "Evening, Reverend. Poor one, actually. Didn't find much except a lot of trouble."

"I saw you were arguing with someone. New neighbors?"

"I just managed to keep them away. What goes through people's heads? A fellow needs a little room to breathe—and Lord knows there's plenty of space around here to pitch a tent. Maybe not so centrally."

That was true. The new tent spaces were farther away from the shops and taverns than Terrence's spot.

"And the fool wanted to make a trade to boot! Besides prospecting for gold, he wanted to straight pawn the two mules he had with him off on me."

Peter frowned. "What was his name? Did he introduce himself?"

Terrence shook his head. "Nah, didn't get that far in the pleasantries. Why? You want to buy a mule? Yours ain't the youngest no more. But that fellow's critters ain't, either, although he'd polish'd 'em to a shine."

"Do you have any idea where the two went off to?" asked Peter.

Terrence shrugged. "To the new tent places, I imagine. Or to make a stink somewhere else. The fellow reeks of trouble, Reverend. Better keep away from him."

Before looking any more, Peter decided to take the wagon back to the stables. There, he saddled the mule Kathleen had given him before he'd left Dunedin and made his way through the camp. On his mount, he was more mobile and might have better luck finding them. Besides, he could claim he wanted to trade the mule—the fastest means of conversing with a horse swindler.

The fellow reeks of trouble. Peter decided to trust Terrence's instincts and turned toward the nearest tavern first.

"Evening, people," he greeted everyone. "Heard there's a horse trader who wants to settle here. Anyone got an idea where he's at?"

"Fat, dark-haired fellow?" asked the barkeeper. "He was here before. Wanted to set up right next to here. But I got there in time. Now he's next to Janey's whorehouse. Janey can't say no, you know."

"Next to a brothel?" the reverend wondered aloud. "I heard he had a boy with him."

"Apparently not a soft one." The barkeeper grinned, and the men laughed. "Want a whiskey, Reverend?"

Peter was too curious for a drink, and Janey's Dollhouse was right around the corner. The man and his boy were carrying things from their wagon to their newly pitched tent. Their mules grazed, hitched to long halters over which Janey's drunk patrons would doubtlessly trip in later hours.

Peter contemplated how he should begin the conversation, but the man became aware of him on his own. With alert and hard eyes, he looked over at Peter's mule, first routinely, then obviously interested.

"Nice mule you got there," said the man. "Where'd you get it?"

Peter Burton was taken aback. If the man was a horse trader, he had to know where people bought mules. He decided to be wary.

"Bought it somewhere near Christchurch," he said. "But I'm thinking about getting rid of it. It drags a leg sometimes."

The big man grinned. "Saw that right away. Aye, someone swindled you, Mr."—he noticed the priest's collar and bowed—"oh, Father . . ."

"Reverend," Peter corrected him. "Reverend Peter Burton."

The man laughed. "Well, would you look at that? One expects Sodom and Gomorrah, and what do you know, my first business here is with the church. Pleasure to make your acquaintance, Reverend. And it'll be my honor to sell you the best mule you'll find between Invercargill and Auckland." He held his hand out to Peter. "If I might introduce myself: Ian Coltrane."

***

Kathleen's flight from her marriage had struck Ian hard—though he had not particularly missed his wife; it was more the work she did. His business required someone at the farm to care for the animals he wasn't leading across the country. Though Colin would doubtlessly have done anything for his father, he was a child. Even Ian had known that he could not leave a barely nine-year-old boy in charge of the farm, or home alone, for that matter. Thus, Colin had gotten his greatest wish: Ian no longer sent him to school but instead took him on his sales trips.

At first, Ian had tried to keep the journeys short, but his years of swindling had come back to bite him: in Christchurch and its surroundings, his reputation was ruined. People would rather travel a long way just to purchase animals elsewhere. Ian had tried finding a partner who would work the farm while he traveled. However, even in this, only dubious men had agreed to work with him. The first herded off a flock of sheep and sold them for his own profit while Ian was away. The second was dead drunk whenever Ian returned. The third caused trouble when Ian tried to cheat him on his share of a horse sale. With the fourth, things limped along for a while, but the man left as soon as gold was found in Otago.

So Ian was forced to limit his travels again—although he really should have been expanding them, since it wasn't long before even the smallest farmer in Canterbury had no need for Ian's faulty stock. The gold miners' demand for provisions earned the farmers enough to enhance their own flocks and improve their quality with sheep acquired from the bigger livestock breeders. Many sheep barons bred horses for their own pleasure or mules for work. With these, too, they helped their smaller neighbors out, for a price.

"Why don't you just work your farm?" asked Ron Meyers, the new owner of the Edmundses' farm and Ian's drinking buddy, when Ian had complained to him. "Mine runs like a dream."

Meyers raised cattle.

"Why don't we go look for gold?" Colin asked his father.

Ian had weighed his options and decided on the latter.

He had sold the horses and then the farm to Ron Meyers, who made him a rather good offer. After that, he had set off on the way to the gold mines with Colin and a team of two mules.

***

Ian Coltrane.

Peter Burton breathed deep. That was Kathleen's secret; no wonder she had been so horrified. Had she really believed her husband dead? That seemed unlikely. Her behavior over the years hinted that she had fled him, and Peter had often suspected her husband was still alive. And the boy? The reverend eyed him inconspicuously. Really, the similarities should have stood out at once: the boy was Kathleen's son, without a doubt. He looked more like her than her dear Sean.

"And my son, Colin," Ian introduced him. "Colin, show the reverend the gray mare. He's thinking of trading his old mule."

Colin looked at Peter's mount. The reverend noticed that the boy had Kathleen's features, but the expression with which he looked over the mule was his father's. Like his father, he seemed to recognize the animal; Kathleen must have had it when she escaped from the marriage. From the years that had passed since he'd first met Kathleen, Peter judged that the boy couldn't have been more than nine when his mother had fled. He wondered if Colin would blurt something out, but the boy said nothing.

"Should I ride the gray mule over?" Ian asked.

Peter decided to break off the proceedings.

"No, thank you. Not today, Mr. Coltrane. It's already getting dark. I can hardly see a thing. Hardly the right time to trade for a mule."

Ian Coltrane furrowed his brow. "Reverend, now you're insulting me. As if I would cheat you, you or the church, by day or by night. What I'm offering you, you could buy blind, Reverend. This gray one is a beauty. And not a day over eight. That's right. Yours, on the other hand, I'd say she's twenty."

Peter nodded. "And she's served faithfully just as long," he said, taking up the smug tone with which Ian had spoken to him. "Now that I think about it, it would be exceedingly ungracious of me to simply sell her in trade. No. This animal should grow old honorably in the service of the church. Many thanks, Mr. Coltrane. I hope to see you in church soon. Oh yes, and you in the school, Colin. We begin at eight. I'll be expecting you."

Colin pouted. Apparently, he didn't intend to do much more for his education.

Peter decided to play a trick of his own. He smiled encouragingly from the son to the father.

"You could also bring that gray mule around tomorrow when you come, Colin. Maybe I'll take a look at it in the light."

At least the next morning, Ian Coltrane would send his son to school.

Chapter 7

Lizzie could not give a complete *pepeha* because for the Maori, a proper personal introductory speech contained the recounting of one's ancestors, and Lizzie simply lacked that knowledge. She did her best though, giving her name and her origins in England and describing London as concretely as possible, as well as her meanderings through Van Diemen's Land, formerly Tasmania. She mentioned the ship on which she had come to Aotearoa and her travels on the North Island. In so doing, she gave James Busby's name, but it meant nothing to the Ngai Tahu. Lizzie knew that none of their chieftains had signed the Treaty of Waitangi, but most of the tribes had at least heard of it by then. That did not apply to her new friends, whose tribe was small and lived mostly in seclusion.

Lizzie had hiked two days into the mountains. She would never have tracked down the Maori on her own, but on the second day, two young hunters joined her while she caught fish with a weir according to Maori custom. The *pakeha* woman who knew traditional fishing methods interested the youths, and when she answered their questions in Maori, they brought her to the village. There she was given a complete *powhiri* greeting ceremony, and the Maori were exceedingly impressed when she answered formally with her *pepeha*. Her presents, too, were happily received—although Lizzie quickly realized there was no urgent need for the things she had brought.

It was astounding, but in this out-of-the-way village, there was nearly everything the Maori desired from the *pakeha*: the women used cast-iron pots and wrapped their children in warm wool blankets. The tribe possessed a flock of high-quality sheep, and its fields were ready for planting, a team of draft oxen having helped. Many of the people wore Western clothing, not just the chieftain and his family. Apparently, anyone here could have *pakeha* dresses or pants. The tribe was rich by Maori measures. This confirmed Lizzie's suspicion that the natives knew exactly where the gold that the *pakeha* wanted was. Yet they protected this knowledge, which Lizzie thought sensible. So she formulated her questions on the topic carefully as she helped the chieftain's sister and the other women to prepare the meal.

"My friends and I live near the new gold miners' camp on the Tuapeka River. But we were considering spreading our search for gold into your area. I've come here to ask if we are welcome."

"How many friends do you have?" the chieftain's sister asked. "Two thousand? Three thousand? And do you intend to leave our land like the riverbed they call Gabriel's Gully?"

Lizzie shook her head. "I have two friends," she said. "And one of them is sick. He can no longer work but has a wife and two children in Wales—that is next to England, where many *pakeha* come from. If he finds no gold, his family will starve."

"The woman can come here and care for her husband," said one of the younger women. "She could work the land."

"They would have to buy the land first," said Lizzie. "And there it becomes difficult. Does the tribe sell land?"

The women laughed. "If we tried, there would be war," the chieftain's sister said drily. "The *pakeha* would say the land here doesn't belong to us. We're a tribe that wanders, sometimes here, sometimes there."

"But you do have a region in which you wander?" Lizzie asked, confused.

The woman snorted. "It contained Gabriel's Gully. And the land on which the Tuapeka River camp was built. If we wanted to hold it, our warriors would have to defend it. We have twenty warriors. Should they take the field with their twenty weapons against the five thousand rifles in your *pakeha* camp?"

Lizzie sighed. "It's not right."

The Maori woman nodded. "But you and your two friends, you three are welcome," she said generously. "Our men have watched you. You know how to make a fire and catch fish. You leave the land as you found it. If your friends promise to do that, too, we'll live in peace with each other. You need not dig up all the land."

Lizzie nervously licked her lips before she made another attempt.

"It, it would all be easier if we knew where we should dig."

The women laughed again.

"You're clever, *pakeha wahine*," said an old woman who had joined the conversation. During the *powhiri*, she had let out the *karanga*, a cry meant to establish the spiritual connection between tribe and visitor. Doubtless she was the tribe's *tohunga*. "You want us to lead you to the gold stuff so valuable to you. But what guarantee do we have that you won't take more than you need?"

Lizzie sighed. "From the *pakeha* perspective, you can't have enough gold," she said. "But it really is just the three of us—in truth only two, Michael and I. Our third, Chris, is much too weak to dig here in the mountains. There's only so much gold we could take."

"So you say," the chieftain's sister retorted sternly, "but can you speak for the man? Is he your husband?"

Lizzie shrugged her shoulders. Again, this was a question for which there was no simple answer.

"He's not mine," she finally said cautiously. "I'm not married to him. Although I have, in a way, lain with him in the meeting house. On a ship, I mean. There were many people there who witnessed that we were together. But later . . . Oh, it's hard to explain."

These last words spoke for all her sorrow. She could not express in English or in Maori what bothered her, but the old *tohunga* looked at her sympathetically. Lizzie had the feeling the woman's gaze saw straight to her heart.

"Your spirits are close to each other," she said briefly. "But as you say, it's not easy. Still"—the *tohunga* turned to her tribe—"he will not betray her. It would turn her against him, and he knows that. He must know that. Nor will the woman betray us. She will swear to us. By the gods whose help she needs."

"She does not even believe in our gods," said the chieftain's sister.

The *tohunga* shrugged her shoulders. "But the gods believe in her. She's bound to us."

"I can swear by my god," said Lizzie, "or by this one here." From below her neckline, she drew out her *hei-tiki*, the small jade pendant Ruiha had given her. "Whenever you want."

The *tohunga* nodded casually. The tribe discussed the matter energetically, speaking much too quickly for Lizzie's language abilities. However, she thought she understood that most of the women supported her. A few men had objections. The old *tohunga* listened to everything calmly. Then the judgment was made.

"My granddaughter will show you the stream tomorrow," she said before standing.

The chief nodded reluctantly and then turned formally to Lizzie. "You brought us presents. Custom—*tikanga*—dictates that we give you something too."

The *tohunga* shook her head. "*Tikanga*," she said slowly, "dictates that we give her something valuable. The gold is not precious. Wait." She stepped into one of the houses, which were no more elaborate or sturdy than the gold miners' huts. When she emerged, she carried a war club of pounamu jade and placed it in Lizzie's hand. "With that, my ancestor defended the land. I pass it on to you now."

The club was decorated with beautiful, elaborate ornaments. It was valuable—and not just to the Maori. Lizzie, a bit overwhelmed by the gift, thanked her.

The *tohunga*'s present dissolved the brief tension between the tribe and its visitor. Now dinner was ready, and the women served it. Lizzie had brought whiskey with her, which the Maori drank gladly. Soon, the bottle was making the rounds, songs were being sung, and the *tohunga* began in *whaikorero*, beautiful speech, to tell the strange, endless stories of Aotearoa's past. Lizzie never fully understood them, though she enjoyed their sound.

Lizzie slept with the others in the meeting house, which she considered an honor, and prepared flatbread with the women in the morning. Then the *tohunga*'s granddaughter, a short, serious girl named Aputa, led her to a nearby waterfall that landed in a pond, from which the water flowed out in a lively stream.

"The water carries the yellow stones out of the mountains," the little girl explained in fluent English as she climbed up the slope to reach the stream that fed the waterfall. "You can catch them in pans, like the men in camp. But you can also dig. Here."

She pointed to a shallow spot on the side of the stream and reached for a large rock. Then she murmured something, likely an apology to the stream's spirits whose peace she was disturbing, and pushed the gravel and sand aside. It was simple; Lizzie supposed they had dug there often. The obvious wealth of the tribe likely resulted from this very source.

"Do you have a bowl?" asked the girl.

Lizzie shook her head. At that, Aputa pulled out an old pewter plate she had stowed in the folds of her dress. She wore a simple *pakeha* dress, unadorned but warmer than the traditional Maori clothing. She had tied up its skirt before wading into the stream.

Now she held the plate in the water and scooped some earth into it. She shook the container briefly and poured out water and sand. Lizzie could hardly believe her eyes when she looked at the plate.

"Just take it," the girl encouraged her. "Do you want to try?"

In less than an hour, the two of them panned roughly two ounces of gold from the stream—more than the usual monthly earnings for the gold miners on the Tuapeka River.

"It shines prettily," Aputa said, pleased, when Lizzie placed their yield in a bag. "What do you do with it?"

Lizzie smiled at her. "Various things," she answered. "But from this gold here, we'll have a pendant made for you. Then it'll bring you luck like my *hei-tiki* has for me."

Lizzie's departure from the tribe took almost as formal a form as her arrival. She promised to return soon and to bring Michael as well.

"You can sleep with him in the meeting house," said Aputa, giggling. "Then he'll really be your husband."

The strange relationship between Lizzie and Michael seemed to have become everyone's favorite subject. Lizzie sighed. That, at least, was something that the Maori and *pakeha* had in common.

Lizzie returned to the gold source before directing her horse home. She had memorized the location, which was not difficult—the place in question was an exceptionally beautiful piece of land. The waterfall and the pond were surrounded on the shore by five pointed rocks that rose high toward the sky. It was an unusual formation. According to Aputa, demigods had once thrown their spears there in a competition. Only one hit the target, creating the pond beneath the waterfall. The missed throws of the others could be seen in the form of the rock stacks.

By the time she was done, Lizzie estimated she'd panned seven ounces of gold—as much as Gabriel Read had brought to Dunedin after his first time in the gold mines on the Tuapeka River. She intoxicated herself by imagining the joy and surprise of the men when she returned to their cabin. With the money from the gold, Chris could send for his wife, and by the time Ann Timlock arrived, they would surely have enough money for a business together. Lizzie had in mind hardware or groceries, perhaps even construction materials or dyes, in Dunedin or somewhere where the climate was better. Chris would probably have preferred a farm to a shop, but Lizzie didn't believe he was strong enough, and Ann surely was not coming from Wales to work herself to death on a farm in New Zealand. Lizzie hoped she was a halfway good businesswoman, and, especially, that she could be a friend.

After Lizzie restored the streambed to the way she had found it, she said a sincere prayer to the spirits of the stream. Perhaps that was not pleasing to God, but Lizzie felt the Maori gods had done more for her in the last few days than the Trinity had in the past thirty years.

Chapter 8

Michael Drury met Ian Coltrane in Tuapeka at the branch location of Dunloe Bank.

Lizzie was still visiting her Maori friends, and while Chris really wasn't well enough to be left alone, he was feeling better. He had encouraged Michael to ride to Tuapeka to pick up some supplies and to redeem their meager gold finds for money. As Michael walked into the bank, he noticed a blond youth was holding a mule team in front of the building. Somehow the boy seemed familiar. Perhaps he reminded Michael of children's faces in Ireland. Kathleen's siblings? Or his own? The boy smirked when he caught Michael looking at him.

Michael turned his gaze away, entered the bank, and suddenly found himself across from Ian Coltrane. The horse trader had grown bloated and red-faced, but Michael recognized him immediately—there was something about his bearing, something predatory in his facial expression, perhaps the obvious similarity to his father too. Ian Coltrane was unmistakable.

Nor was there any hesitation on Ian's part, the less so because Michael had hardly changed. Ian looked at him, taken aback, but then a smug smile spread across his face, similar to the smirk on the boy just outside the bank. Michael's heart constricted.

"Coltrane?" he asked flatly.

Ian grinned widely. "Well, look here: Michael Drury. Didn't they haul you in chains to the other end of the world?"

Michael tried to contain himself. "This is the other end of the world," he said with effort. "And as for chains, you can throw them off. But you . . . Father O'Brien told me you, you and Kathleen, you were overseas. I had thought New York."

Ian Coltrane's laugh boomed. "Oh? Well, you thought wrong about New York."

Michael clenched his fists to keep himself from punching Ian in the face. He needed to fight back his jealousy so he could speak reasonably with Ian. *Oh God, Kathleen could be in Tuapeka.* Michael flashed hot and cold, his heart racing.

As calmly as possible, he gestured toward the front of the building. "Is that my son out there?" he asked.

Ian shook his head, the provoking smirk still on his face.

"Oh no, Mr. Drury, that one's mine. And I know that for sure. I didn't let dear Mary Kathleen out of sight after she was empty again and ripe for me."

Michael bit his lip and struggled again against the anger welling within him. What way was this for a man to speak of his wife? To speak of Mary Kathleen? And yet Michael felt almost relieved. He had not liked something about the boy out front, even if he unmistakably bore Kathleen's features.

"And where is she now?" Michael blurted out. "And where is my, where is the other . . ."

Ian became serious and a shadow crossed his face, which shocked Michael and filled him with dread.

Indeed, Ian was thinking feverishly. Should he admit his disgrace? Confess that Kathleen had left him, perhaps even to look for this rat she had always loved? And perhaps she had even come close: that reverend was riding her mule. Had he really bought it in Christchurch? Ian inhaled sharply.

"Kathleen is dead," he said, almost casually. "She died giving birth to Colin." He indicated the boy outside. "Before that, your bastard almost killed her. She wasn't made for delivering babies. Too weak, too delicate. That first boy was delivered dead. Yours isn't good blood, Drury. Mine's a model lad, however." Ian laughed again. "No hard feelings, Drury." He turned and walked out the door.

Michael stood there as if turned to stone. Kathleen was dead. Kathleen and his son. All those dreams, all those years. But that did not explain why Father O'Brien had written what he did—about the three children and Kathleen's good life. Surely the priest had not wanted to lie to him. He must have misunderstood something and then lost contact with the Coltranes. Kathleen was dead. Michael felt sick. He left the bank slowly. He did not want to encounter Ian and his son under any circumstances. Kathleen's son, Ian's son—but his own child was dead.

Michael's thoughts turned in a circle. He stared straight ahead as he rode through Tuapeka. He couldn't even answer the greetings acquaintances called to him.

Kathleen was dead, Kathleen was dead. It was too much to believe.

Michael exhaled as he left Tuapeka behind and rode upriver. But he did not want to see Chris now either. He got down from his horse and sat on one of the rocks on the riverbank. He let his thoughts drift back to the little beach on the Vartry River, the willow whose branches kissed the water. Michael took leave of his beloved, his child, and his dream.

***

Several days later, Lizzie returned.

"What kinds of faces are those to make?" she asked when she saw the men sitting, glum and quiet, by the fire in the cabin.

Chris was whittling a wooden spoon. Before Michael had gone to Tuapeka, Chris had been working on a rocking horse. He occasionally sold toys in Tuapeka, where there were now parents who could afford a little luxury for their children. In the last few days, however, Michael had brusquely asked Chris to put away the rocking horse whenever he entered the house. He could not stand to look at toys, let alone think of children.

Chris understood. The little horse reminded him of a similar one he had whittled in Wales for his children. Both men gave in to their sorrow over lost time, although Michael could at least attempt to distract himself. He worked from morning until dusk, exerting himself to wring at least a little gold from the stream near their house. That day, he had been outside until midday, but it was raining so hard that, at some point, he gave up. Now he was trying to warm himself by the fire.

Lizzie's presence seemed to brighten the cabin. She beamed as she carefully drew a pouch and a jade object from the pocket of her soaked-through coat and placed them on the table. Only then did she throw off her coat and step close to the fire to warm up.

"I don't suppose you've got the whiskey out?" she asked, breaking the somber silence. So far, the men had not been able to manage more than a curt greeting.

"Really, what we need is champagne . . . What's gotten into you two? Michael, Chris? Aren't you happy I'm back? Did something happen? Well, no matter; you'll be astonished in a moment." Lizzie took the pouch from the table and crouched between the men.

"Take a deep breath, you two," she announced happily. "Wait, one moment; close your eyes."

"Lizzie, enough with the games." Michael's voice sounded pained. Lizzie's concern grew. But this was her moment. The men would just have to cheer up. "Fine, then you'll just risk being blinded."

She gently took Michael's hand and sprinkled some gold dust into it. Then she did the same with Chris.

Immediately Chris's eyes grew wide. He couldn't believe what he saw. "But, but, Lizzie, that's gold."

Lizzie laughed. "It sure is. About nine ounces. But about two ounces of it don't belong to us. I'll explain later. More importantly, I panned it in just one day. Without breaking a sweat. Or getting up early. The spot is not that far. We just need to go west, then upstream to the waterfall. Really, it's a triangle with our cabin, the Maori village, and the gold. By my estimates we could take about a hundred ounces without destroying anything. But it has to stay a secret. That's what I promised the Ngai Tahu."

Michael stared without really seeing the gold in his hand. He was rich. Now he was finally rich. But also alone. Or free? He felt Lizzie's gaze rest upon him. Finally, he overcame himself and looked her in the eye. Lizzie was lovely with the good fortune she was so willing to share with others.

"This gold, though, is for you first, Chris," she said. "You can exchange it tomorrow and send the money to Ann. It should be enough for her passage. By the time she gets here, we should have more, much more. Michael, we'll have our farm. With maids and manor and whatever else we want."

Michael warmed himself on her smile, and he suddenly noticed his sorrow beginning to fall away. Kathleen and the child were the past. But Lizzie was there. Generous, full of life, and determined to make him happy. Up to then, he had given her back much too little. He had been trapped in an unrealistic dream.

Michael carefully slid the gold back into its pouch. Then he stood up and took Lizzie by the arms. For the first time, she did not resist, as if she also sensed that something had changed.

"Chris," Michael said, checking over his friend. Aye, he looked to be in good enough shape; he could manage the trip to town. "Perhaps, perhaps you ought to ride straight to town to redeem the gold? You could bring some champagne for Lizzie and . . ."

Chris looked from Michael to Lizzie and smiled. He, too, seemed to think himself capable of the ride. "Surely it's not good to keep so much gold in the house," he said. "Especially since neither of us could hit a barn door at ten paces with the rifle. It's stopped raining, anyway."

Chris put on his warmest clothes, took the pouch from the table, and carefully put it in his pocket.

"Maybe I'll have another drink in town too," he said with a smile and a wink.

Lizzie and Michael nodded. "And take two ounces to the goldsmith," said Lizzie. "Have him make a pretty pendant from it. Perhaps a moon and stars. Something a Maori girl would like."

Once Chris had left the cabin, Michael kissed Lizzie, and he did it with tenderness and abandon. For the first time, she felt he was really concentrating on her. It had nothing to do with lust or a replacement for Mary Kathleen. Michael was kissing Lizzie Owens alone. Even as he pulled her close, everything was different than on the ship. Lizzie surrendered for a few heartbeats to her happiness, but then doubts nagged at her again. What had happened? Had she changed or had he? Was it because the gods believed in her? Or was it . . .

"Michael," she said quietly, pulling back from his embrace. "What, what's happened? Something's different. Listen, is it, is it the gold?"

Michael shook his head firmly. "No. No, it has nothing to do with the gold. I've made a decision. Much too late, I'm afraid. I should have asked you a long time ago."

"Asked me what?" inquired Lizzie.

Michael breathed deep. But then, it was simple; it was all so simple. "If you want to marry me," he said quietly. "I, I love you, Lizzie. Have a long time."

Lizzie looked at him, pensively. "You've had a funny way of showing it until now," she said. "First I was just a whore to you, then a replacement for your lost bride in Ireland, and all of a sudden, it strikes you that I'm not just a person but also the woman you love. And all this, by coincidence, at precisely the moment I come back with seven ounces of gold. You have to understand why that makes me suspicious."

Michael sighed. "It has nothing, absolutely nothing to do with the gold," he said. "I swear it."

"You don't need to swear, Michael Drury," Lizzie said, trying to make her voice sound firm. "You need only tell me one thing: if I marry you now, Michael, can I be sure you won't call me Mary Kathleen at the altar?"

Michael lowered his head onto her shoulder. It took all his strength finally to lift it again and look Lizzie in the eye.

"Kathleen," he whispered, "is dead."

Lizzie was both friend and mother as he wept his eyes out on her shoulder. Later that night, she became his lover. And the name he called out at the climax of his joy was not Mary Kathleen's, but neither was it that of a whore.

***

Chris Timlock was happier than he had been in months as he rode Michael's horse to Tuapeka. Until that evening, he had lost his belief that he could get rich from gold prospecting. First, the claim yielded nothing, and then came his long illness. Chris had been prepared to die in the little gold miners' town.

Now, though, there was this unexpected blessing, which Lizzie shared so generously with him. If Chris had had enough breath left in him, he would have sung, but he already needed all his strength to ride the vivacious gray. The horse pranced down Tuapeka's main street. First they rode to the goldsmith's shop. That had been Lizzie's request, and Chris wanted to take care of it right away.

The goldsmith, a short, wiry man named Thomas Winslow, managed a small jewelry business next to one of the banks. He did not have many customers; most of the prospectors exchanged their few nuggets into money and scraped together just enough to live. Occasionally, however, someone struck it big, and then he'd craft an ounce of gold into a ring for one of the girls from the taverns or from Janey's Dollhouse. The business owners and craftsmen who were slowly settling in Tuapeka also ordered jewelry from time to time for their wives. There was enough business that Thomas Winslow could have lived well if he had not hit the whiskey a little too hard. Almost every night, he drank his earnings away in one of the taverns. To afford the occasional girl, he panned for gold himself on the weekend and dreamed of a big find.

Naturally, he was immediately attentive when Chris Timlock laid two ounces of gold on the table. He eyed the fine little platter of gold with desire.

Chris smiled at him guilelessly. "If I could get you to make a pendant out of that, a moon with a few stars around it, or a constellation. Sure, that would be a lovely idea: the Pleiades. And a chain for it, if there's enough."

Winslow assured him it more than sufficed—and tried to sound him out about the location of the gold.

Chris was careful not reveal anything. "My partner always believed in our claim," he said warily. "But maybe it was just luck. When can we pick up the pendant? Next week?"

Winslow nodded, but as he closed his shop door behind Chris Timlock, he shook his head. *Luck?* A one-time largish find and he was already having jewelry made from it instead of taking the money to the bank? Surely, there were men who could do that, but he did not think Chris Timlock and Michael Drury were among them.

The post office was already closed, but Chris had to have the gold turned into money before he could send anything to Ann anyway. Luckily, the bank was still open. Many prospectors took their earnings there every day, since too much was stolen in the camp. Mr. Ruland, the bank teller, kept the bank open after dark, and Chris had to line up to have his small fortune entered into his account.

"What did you just pour out there, Timlock? Just over seven ounces?" The man in line behind Chris had looked at the scale and announced loudly what he had seen.

"A few weeks' worth," he said.

Mr. Ruland looked at him, astonished. Of course, the banker had seen Michael there a few days earlier, but after an uncomfortable-looking conversation with Ian Coltrane, he had left before exchanging any gold. Mr. Ruland said nothing; he could keep a secret. It was the right thing for Chris Timlock to deposit the money rather than taking cash. There was obvious greed in the eyes of the men behind him. Ian Coltrane, especially, eyed Chris Timlock with unusual interest. Mr. Ruland shivered. He could not stand Ian Coltrane. Three days ago, the man had sold him a horse, and it was already starting to drag its leg.

Chris Timlock went to celebrate his luck with a couple of beers in one of the new taverns. He watched a few girls who performed risqué dances to entertain the drunks, but he would not be drawn into conversation with any of them. Even though the gold miners at the bar were friendly, and happy to see him again after his long illness, Chris only answered their questions monosyllabically. The story of his sudden wealth had not made it around Tuapeka yet, but he was cautious nonetheless.

Thomas Winslow and Ian Coltrane were at the same tavern, sharing a bottle of whiskey at a table in front of the stage. They were by no means friends, but Coltrane had been trying to convince Winslow he absolutely needed a mule to transport his tools from his shop to the gold mines. Naturally, he happened to have just the right animal on hand—yet so far Winslow had not quite taken the bait. That day, however, both men had made interesting observations, and they both occasionally cast appraising looks at Chris Timlock.

"A pendant from two ounces of gold," Winslow whispered to Coltrane. "That means he had the gold left over, so to speak. How much did you say he deposited?"

"About seven ounces. A small fortune. Can it be that he was lying about being sick? Maybe he's been in the mountains all these weeks discovering new gold deposits." Ian Coltrane filled his glass again.

Winslow raised his glass. "I doubt it. Jus' look at him. He's still so thin that a breeze could knock him over, and I've seen him coughing. He wasn't gone either; now and again he attended service with the reverend." Winslow also belonged to Peter Burton's church. "And when he made it there, he was definitely sick. Fellow could only stand up if his partner and Lizzie helped him. What d'y' think of her anyway? She got something with one of 'em, or both?"

Coltrane didn't answer and didn't much care. He kept his eyes trained on Timlock, as if, through a smile or movement, he would give something away. One thing was certain: the man at the bar was happy. He did not trumpet his fortune like all the other successful prospectors, seeming instead to glow from within.

"We should wait till he's drunk and then go after it," suggested Winslow. "The information about the gold, that is, not Lizzie, though she's quite a pretty l'il thing."

Coltrane shook his head. He had thrown out that idea long before. Chris Timlock was only just sipping at his second beer. He was not a man to get drunk and then blab his secrets. No, if they wanted to learn anything, they would have to resort to more drastic measures.

"Going after him sounds good," said Coltrane. "But not here in front of witnesses. We'll wait behind Janey's and interrogate him a bit."

"Inter . . . rogate?" asked Winslow stupidly.

He had already had more than three glasses of whiskey and was slowly becoming sluggish. First in his brain, which did not matter much. But if Winslow drank much more, he wouldn't be physically capable of executing Coltrane's plan.

"Oh yes, my friend. You know, the sort of questioning where you don't take no for an answer." Coltrane grinned at Winslow conspiratorially.

The goldsmith frowned and took another swig of whiskey. "But that's not very nice," he said.

Coltrane rolled his eyes. "Well, do you want to be nice or get rich?" he said. "And besides, we'll start very friendly. We're comrades, man; you don't keep secrets from your comrades."

"But if it's really his claim?"

"What do you bet no claim's even been staked? Nothing new's been registered anyway. And besides, who wants his claim? We could settle in next door. Come, Winslow. Gabriel Read wasn't the only one who got rich in Gabriel's Gully."

Coltrane was determined. Chris Timlock would tell him that very night where he had found the gold—willingly or with the help of a few well-placed blows. Winslow just needed to play along. And now Timlock was standing up and throwing a few coins for his beer on the table. Coltrane elbowed his drinking buddy.

"He's going. Come on now. Let's follow him."

"You don't even know where he's going." Winslow hesitated. After all, there was still whiskey in the bottle.

"Of course I know. He put Drury's gray in MacLeod's stable. On account of the rain—'s got a good heart, the lad. Didn't want the nag getting wet.

Now he's got to walk there, and the shortest way leads past Janey's." Coltrane fished a banknote out of his pocket, signaled to the barkeeper that he needed no change, and pushed Winslow out of the bar.

"Maybe he's going to go into Janey's," Winslow said.

Coltrane shrugged. Timlock hadn't given the girls in the tavern a second look. But it wasn't out of the question.

As Coltrane expected, Timlock walked right past the entrance to Janey's, and the two men stopped him behind the girls' tent.

"Evening, Timlock," Coltrane greeted him.

Chris nodded to him. He did not know the man, but he was with Thomas Winslow, who must have told the man his name. "Evening, Thomas."

Winslow grinned at him. "Hullo, Timlock. So, celebrated a bit?"

Chris shrugged. "Just drank a couple of beers. What's to celebrate?"

"Your gold find, of course," said Winslow. "Two ounces just for jewelry for your sweetheart. That's a bit much, my friend."

Chris waved his comment away. "'s not for any sweetheart. It's for a friend of Lizzie's. And she saved a long time for it."

Winslow and Coltrane laughed. They approached Chris, and the young man began to feel uncomfortable.

"So, Lizzie saved, did she?" said Coltrane mockingly. "And the seven ounces you still had after that? Where did they come from?"

Chris looked around nervously. "Like I said, man. A few weeks' worth."

Coltrane lunged at Chris and, with a quick movement, twisted his right arm onto his back. "Don't lie. I saw your partner at the bank just a few days ago. So tell me: Where did the gold come from?"

Chris gasped for air and twisted in Ian's grip. "It was mine. I found it over the last few weeks. Like I already told you."

"The last few weeks you've been bedridden." Ian's fist struck Chris in the kidneys. Not too hard, but enough that he groaned and bent over—which increased the pain in his shoulder. "And if you don't talk soon, you'll be spending the next few weeks back in bed. Now, out with it!"

"I already told you. I, I'm telling the truth."

Coltrane sighed as if he were sorry for what he now had to do. "Hold him, Winslow," he ordered. "It's not polite when you don't look someone in the eye while you speak."

Chris tried to use his last chance to get away from the men as Coltrane handed him over to the obviously drunk Winslow. He got his arm free briefly, but he wasn't strong enough to hit back. Coltrane tripped him when he tried to run away. Chris fell, and Coltrane kicked him in the kidneys again before Winslow pulled him to his feet.

"Had enough yet? Come, friend, just tell us where you got your luck. Then we'll let you go."

"Damn it, Timlock." Winslow now tried his luck. "It won't cost y'nothing. Where that comes from must be gold for a hundred men."

Chris said nothing as Coltrane's fists struck him again, this time in the face.

"I don't have anything to say."

Chris tried to keep his courage up, but his arm hurt like the devil. When Winslow had pulled him up by it, he must have dislocated it. The other man kept hitting him, and Chris tasted blood. His lip was busted.

"Now do you have something to say? Not even a little tiny hint, Timlock? Where did the gold come from?"

The next blow landed in his stomach. His tormentor could have been a very good fighter. His fists were like iron. Chris slumped. He tried to gain control of himself, but he had to vomit. Winslow held him by his dislocated arm as he did. Chris groaned as Winslow pulled him up again.

"Well, now you've gotten yourself dirty," Coltrane said regretfully. "And me too." Disgusted, he looked at a few drops of vomit on his boots. "You should clean that off."

Winslow pushed Timlock to the ground. "Well, do it quick."

Chris tried clumsily to wipe the drops away with his left hand.

"Now, out with it. Where did you get the gold?"

"Don't know," whimpered Chris.

"You don't know, or you don't want to say? Maybe it fell from the sky? Like in a fairy tale?"

"He, he did ask for a constellation in his order," said Winslow. He pulled Chris upright again while Coltrane struck another time. Chris persisted in silence. Then Coltrane broke his nose.

"Don't know anything."

"Maybe he really doesn't know?" The whole thing was becoming too much for Thomas Winslow. He had no objection to a few punches, but this had gone too far. Coltrane had seriously injured the man. It was time to stop.

"Oh, he knows. Spit it out already, lad. Otherwise, I'll really get unpleasant."

Chris hung, completely helpless, in Winslow's grip. He had no chance to dodge the next blow, which struck his eye and broke his cheekbone.

"My eye," Chris sensed it growing dark around him. But the pain was still there—a raging pain and the horrifying knowledge that he would not make it away from there.

"Just talk, or I'll beat the other one out too."

Winslow was whimpering. He let Chris slowly fall.

"Talk! And you, hold onto him." Coltrane ordered.

"Lizzie," whispered Chris. His last chance was to say what he knew. Lizzie would never forgive him, nor would the Maori. Chris tried to put together what he knew, but the pain made it impossible. "Lizzie," he repeated. "She . . ."

"The whore had the gold? She found it?"

Chris nodded with the last of his strength.

Then another blow struck him. "Where'd she get it? Where'd she come from, eh?"

Chris heard nothing more. Nor did he feel the rest of the punches and kicks that rained down on him. Coltrane had lost all control.

The information had been disappointing. Just another reference point: Lizzie. But really Timlock had said nothing. He had defied Coltrane. For that, he should pay. Winslow tried to yank Coltrane away from the motionless man on the ground, but drunk as he was, he wasn't quick or strong enough.

At some point, Coltrane stood there, breathing hard while Winslow checked on Timlock.

"He's still alive," he said, relieved. "Thank God, he's still alive. But for this, for this, they'll lock us up, Coltrane. We can't pass it off as a little scuffle now."

Coltrane slowly returned to his senses. He turned Timlock over and felt his pulse.

"He won't live much longer," he observed. "And it's best we put him to rest right now."

He picked up a rock, leaned back, and aimed for Timlock's temple.

Winslow grabbed Coltrane's arm. "Are you mad? You want to kill him?"

"Do you want to go to jail?" asked Coltrane. "He saw us. If he comes to and talks, we're done for."

"But, but killing him? I'll give you an alibi, and you give me one. He can talk as much as he wants."

Coltrane arched his eyebrows. An alibi that two assailants gave each other did not mean much, but if he delivered the final blow now, Winslow might turn and betray him. It wasn't worth that. He was sure Timlock would die anyway. The man's eye was crushed, a few teeth were knocked out, and every bone in his face had to be broken—and those final kicks must have shattered his ribs. Coltrane decided to take the risk. The man would probably die before anyone found him. In the meantime, he had to keep Winslow reasonably busy.

"All right, fine. Go home. Wash up and pack your things. Early tomorrow we'll ride to out to Drury's and lie in wait. When this Lizzie goes out, we'll follow her."

Winslow continued looking fearfully at the injured man.

"Shouldn't we go for help? And besides, I, I can't go. People will notice if I'm not there in the middle of the week. I have a shop, you know."

Coltrane thought for a moment. That was true, and after this incident, people would be on the lookout for any unusual behavior.

"All right, fine, then you stay in town, and I'll go alone," he said. It was probably for the best anyway. Winslow would likely stay quiet about beating the man to death—out of fear, at least. But could the drunk manage to keep a gold find secret? "For now, just go. No matter what, they can't find us here."

Winslow prayed for the man's life while he slunk back to his shop, but he couldn't bear thinking of what had happened without another whiskey. Fortunately, the next tavern wasn't far, and Winslow sat there, getting ever drunker, until the bar closed. Then he went back to Janey's. Timlock hadn't moved, but he groaned when Winslow poked him.

Winslow's conscience had pricked all the harder the more alcohol he had drunk. Finally, he dragged himself to the entrance of Janey's Dollhouse.

"Around the corner from you," he said, slurring at whoever would listen, "there's a dead fellow."

Chapter 9

Lizzie had awoken quite happy next to Michael and wanted to let him sleep while she relit the stove and made tea. When she found Chris's bedding empty, however, she woke Michael right away.

Michael tried to pull her back to him and kiss her. "I was just dreaming of you," he whispered. "But you're even prettier in the flesh. Come on, let's . . ."

Lizzie resisted gently. "Michael, Chris isn't here. Could something have happened?"

Michael laughed. "What could have happened? Probably he treated himself to a girl at Janey's to celebrate his luck. Or one from that new bar. It's supposed to have Chinese women."

Lizzie shook her head. "Michael, Chris doesn't want a Chinese woman. He wants his Ann. I can't imagine that . . ."

"Have you checked the pen? Maybe he was being considerate and set up camp there when he heard us."

That seemed more likely to Lizzie. She ran outside to check the pen, but there was no trace of Chris or of Michael's horse. In any case, the horse had not come home on its own, so Chris must have stayed somewhere over night. Lizzie felt somewhat more at ease, but a bad feeling remained as she returned to their cabin.

Michael, on the other hand, was in the best of spirits. "Do we want to just spend today at home, or do you want to look for gold?" he asked.

He had served the tea Lizzie had brewed and poured a good deal of sugar into her cup. Lizzie liked her tea sweet—and now they no longer needed to be stingy with the sugar.

Lizzie looked out the window. "You won't keep me in your bed on such a sunny day, Michael Drury." She smiled. "We'll pan a few ounces of gold, and then we can always spread a blanket out next to the stream." She winked meaningfully.

Michael suppressed his memories of the Vartry River. "But we should wait for Chris to return," he said.

Lizzie laughed mischievously. "You mean, for your horse," she teased him. Michael did not like to walk, and that beautiful horse was his pride and joy.

Michael nodded. "You know me too well, which is no good in a wife. I should be a mystery for you, and you should spend your life trying to unravel it."

Lizzie giggled. "You'd be the first man not to carry his mystery between his legs and unveil it to anyone who gets close enough. As for your horse, everyone can see that you're mad about it. I wish your eyes would light up like that when you look at me."

Michael pulled her into his arms. "You're a saucy one, Lizzie. An honest woman doesn't talk that way. An honest woman blushes when the talk is of men's mysteries."

Lizzie laughed even louder. "I've been honest longer than you've been rich," she reminded him. "Let's go, so you can finally earn some of that gold. In all seriousness, Michael, I don't want to wait too long. Who knows whether the Maori might change their minds about us collecting the gold if something happens?"

"What could happen?" asked Michael insouciantly.

Lizzie shrugged her shoulders. "Hostility between Maori and *pakeha*, for instance. Here, you don't see as much of it, but who knows what the Ngai Tahu will think of if it comes to war? I would like to be done quickly. Come to think of it, it was already a mistake to send Chris into camp with the gold. We should have mined all we needed first and then quietly left with it. In Dunedin, one might get a better price, and most importantly, we would not have drawn any attention."

Michael frowned. "You mean Chris might have gotten into trouble? He's not the kind to blab when he has a drink. In any case, I can't imagine he'd betray your trust."

Lizzie shook her head. "I don't think he would either. He's also not the kind to spend a night in bed with a prostitute. But . . . I have an uneasy feeling."

Michael chewed his lip. "Would it be better to ride to Tuapeka to look for him?" he asked.

Lizzie shrugged. "Then we lose a whole day. Listen, why don't you just go to town, and I'll ride ahead for now? You'll find the stream easily, like I told you yesterday, but I'll explain it again just to be sure." Lizzie repeated the directions to head west from their cabin, then upstream to the waterfall. She reminded Michael that everything formed a triangle: the Maori village on the river, their cabin, the gold source. "Above the waterfall, that's where we found the gold. There could also be some that flows down from there—probably is, even. But we'll pan up where the Maori gave me permission and nowhere else."

Michael looked at her doubtfully. "I don't know, Lizzie. You alone? Damn it, you already panned the first ounces alone. You can't do all the work."

Lizzie laughed and began to braid her hair. It was windy, and she did not want it blowing in her face as she panned for gold. "Oh, you'll catch up to me easily. Your gray is twice as fast as my bay."

That was true, and in contrast to Michael, Lizzie did not like to ride. Michael knew well that she would find any number of reasons to walk next to the bay gelding instead of riding it. Probably, she would load it with all the tools and supplies she would need for one or two weeks in the mountains. Then there would be no room for her in the saddle. So she could walk, but she would spend the whole day on route. Michael, in contrast, would only need a few hours if he made his gray horse trot.

"Well, all right," he finally said. "But I'll pack your horse. The last thing we need is for you to haul everything out and load it up just to walk the whole way."

Lizzie gave him her sweetest smile. "You know me too well, Michael," she said. "But don't get ideas. I still have more secrets than a little fear of horses."

***

Janey's girls had found Chris Timlock in the early morning hours and alerted the reverend, who ran, along with his assistant, to attend to the severely beaten man. There was now a doctor in the mining camp who likewise had arrived quickly. He could not offer much help though.

"I'll do all I can, but I fear he won't make it. All the facial fractures, the caved-in skull, and those ribs—so badly shattered I'm sure he has internal injuries as well. To survive that, you'd need to be as strong as an ox—and the boy is just a wisp. Any idea who would have done this to him?"

Reverend Burton shook his head. "None. Thomas Winslow, who's a notorious drunk, stumbled on him early in the morning. He's still sleeping it off, but he won't have much more to say. Otherwise, all we know is that Winslow had been at Will's Corner, but he left early, according to Will. Later he got drunker at Gregory's. That's where he was coming from when he found the boy."

News of Chris's gold find had quickly spread through town, and whoever knew something had told it to anyone who would listen.

The doctor sighed. He was a bold man, still young, and a desire for adventure had driven him to Tuapeka. Yet the rough customs of the gold miners disillusioned him a little more every day.

"Then give me a hand bandaging him. He'll lose his left eye, even if he survives. Does he have any family?"

"I don't know. Though he has a digging partner," Reverend Burton said. "Someone should inform him. They live in a cabin farther upriver, but his partner, Michael Drury, will come down on his own once he misses him. Then we'll have to ask him about the matter too. Although I don't think there can be any question of him having done it."

The doctor shrugged. "Has anyone sent word to Dunedin?"

"To the police? We've sent a telegram, and someone is riding there as well. This has to be investigated. Whoever did this can't be allowed to get away."

***

A few hours later, Michael stood, shocked, in front of his friend's bed. He would not have recognized Chris if no one had told him that the ragdoll wrapped in bandages on the bed was his friend. Chris was unconscious, his breathing was ragged, and now and again he let out a weak groan.

"You can talk to him," said the doctor. "He might even hear you. There's not much else we can do. I gave him morphine for the pain."

"Doesn't that make you weak in the head?" Michael asked.

The doctor smiled wearily. "You can become addicted. But surely not your friend. I'm sorry, but I think it's unlikely he'll survive the night."

Michael stayed with Chris and told him about Lizzie and their plans to marry. He held his left hand—the doctor had put the right shoulder back in joint and bound the arm firmly to his chest—and promised him he would write Ann and send her the money.

"Yesterday, I bet the post office was already closed," he said gently. "But if I do it right now, soon she'll be on her way to you. And when you're doing a little better, she'll be here."

Around noon, Michael thought Chris might have squeezed his hand, but he was not sure. In any case, he left Chris's side briefly to send a letter and the money to Wales.

Mr. Ruland, the bank teller, expressed his sympathy and told Michael of his concern about the other prospectors' jealousy. "I'm sure word got around quickly that he had deposited seven ounces of gold. The devils probably thought he had the money on him."

Michael nodded and felt a burning guilt. He should have thought of that. If he had not been so intoxicated with Lizzie, he would never have sent Chris to town alone.

In the meantime, a police officer had arrived and was asking the witnesses questions. Michael was concerned. His experiences with the law were not the best, after all. He decided to stick halfway to the truth, and spoke of an extraordinary gold find on their claim that Chris had made alone. He did not know precisely where, but his friend had wanted to send the money to his wife straight away. Michael had lent him his horse for that purpose. He had been at home with his fiancée, himself. Lizzie could testify to that.

The officer believed him. "Why would the fellow need to ride all the way to town to beat his partner's brains in?" the officer said later to the reverend. "He could have done it more easily up there. No one would have asked questions if this Timlock had simply disappeared. A few weeks later, Drury could have turned in the gold himself, and no one would have been the wiser."

His questioning of Thomas Winslow didn't yield anything either—the goldsmith was already drunk again. Despite that, he worked, not unskillfully, on a golden pendant that showed the Pleiades. The officer was impressed but didn't ask him anything about it.

The officer registered that Winslow looked shocked, but anyone who had found a man covered in blood might have been. Besides, Winslow had a tight alibi. He had been getting drunk first at Will's Corner, then in Gregory's Public House.

Michael's outlook grew a bit more hopeful when Chris was still alive that evening. He felt guilty when it came to Lizzie, but she would know that if he hadn't made it to her yet, it was because something important was keeping him. Lizzie would pan for gold and wait for him, at least for a day.

That evening, Thomas Winslow, completely drunk and obviously deeply upset, arrived at the hospital. He took one look at Chris's motionless body on the bed, broke into tears, and handed Michael a packet.

"Here, here," he sobbed. "It's done. Maybe he'll even be happy when he, when he wakes up. Oh, what a shame, what a shame. Such a young man."

Michael frowned and opened the packet and drew out a tiny pendant. "The pendant Lizzie wanted made. Chris gave you the order yesterday?"

Winslow nodded.

Michael dangled the pendant on its chain, admiring the craftsmanship.

"You've made it really pretty," he said. "And thank you for taking care of it quickly." Michael reached into his pocket for some money. "What do we owe you?"

Winslow recoiled as if the money might burn him.

"Nothing, no, nothing of course. I, I was happy to do it."

Winslow went away, sobbing. Michael wondered if he should speak with the reverend about Winslow. The man had obviously drunk himself out of his mind, but no minister could do anything about that either.

Michael turned back to Chris. He wet his invalid friend's lips with water—Chris could not or would not swallow, but his mouth was dry, and he had to sense the care, even if he did not react. Michael tried to remember old stories he could tell Chris, and as the night wore on, he talked about Ann and their children—he repeated everything his partner had told him in their time panning gold together. In the morning, Michael could hardly keep his eyes open, but Chris was still alive.

"You should eat something," advised the doctor when he came in around nine in the morning. "And sleep a little yourself. I'm here now, after all, and the reverend's on his way."

"Is he any better?" Michael asked, after the doctor examined Chris.

The doctor shook his head. "Not that I see. I think your friend is in a coma, Mr. Drury. I fear he won't be waking up, but no one can know for certain, so don't give up hope. You shouldn't make yourself sick though. Find something to eat and a place for some sleep."

Michael left Chris's side reluctantly, but hunger finally drove him into a tearoom that Barbara, a former prostitute now married to a prospector, had opened not long ago.

"So, they don't have any idea who it could have been?" she asked, as she placed a giant omelet in front of Michael on the spotless table. "The officer's started investigating, sure, but maybe you ought to ask around yourself?"

Michael considered it. The woman had a point; the gold miners were more likely to talk to him than a stranger from Dunedin. Many of the men in the mines had a past similar to his, and they did not trust the police.

"I think I'll start at the bank," said Michael. "It would be worth finding out who knew about Chris's gold find first. Let's see if Mr. Ruland remembers."

The bank teller did indeed remember a few names, particularly Ian Coltrane's. This alarmed Michael, but on the other hand, the other fellows were not innocent little lambs. Michael knew them and where they mined. He needed the fresh air anyway. Instead of going to sleep, he retrieved the gray from the stables and rode to the prospects.

Ian Coltrane was nowhere to be found, however, and that made Michael suspicious. Those in the neighboring claims were less surprised.

"Probably off horse trading," one of the diggers said. "Coltrane splits his time doing that. He's only here half the week at most—and I'm sure he earns more with the jades than with this gold. He's got no hand for gold mining; not a hard worker either—at least not for long. If he uses his spade two hours a day, that's enough for him. Check by his tent. Maybe he's there transforming another old jade into a young stallion."

The men laughed in chorus. Here, too, Ian had already earned a reputation.

"And the boy?" asked Michael. "Is he at school?"

The men shrugged. "Mostly he follows his dad around. But he could be, of course. The boy's like his old man: if he catches the scent of easy money, like a horse trade, he's there in a flash. But he'd rather learn to read than spend hours panning for gold."

Michael had to find out if Colin Coltrane had been in the reverend's school. But for the time being, he went looking for Mr. Ruland's other customers. It was exhausting and did not amount to anything. Though all had noted Chris's sudden riches, they said they had believed his claim that it was the result of several weeks' work with Michael.

So Michael rode back to the hospital, where Chris lay like a dead man on the bed. According to the reverend, nothing had changed. Michael had meant to take his place at his friend's side, but then tiredness overtook him. He simply had no more strength to talk to Chris. He needed sleep himself. Without anywhere else he could think of to go, Michael staggered over to Janey's.

"As an exception, could I rent one of your beds for more than an hour?"

The girls laughed. Michael's desperate vigil over his partner was already the talk of the town, like everything surrounding Chris's assault. Janey's staff found his efforts touching. The girls fell over themselves, first to make him lunch and then to prepare the "royal suite," as Janey wryly called it: a tent, but swept clean and with spotless white linens. Michael was asleep as soon as his head touched the pillow.

***

Reverend Burton kept watch over Chris Timlock and tried not to give up hope. He had helped the doctor change the bandages, but aside from a weak groan, the man had not made a sound.

The doctor was now firmly convinced he lay in a coma. "I hope it won't last too long," he said unhappily. "Please understand, Reverend. I'd be happy if the man survived. But blind, unconscious, motionless—one has to wonder what would be better."

The reverend shrugged. "We'll have to leave it in God's hands," he said. "And hope He knows what He's burdening us with."

Peter Burton took a brief break to tend to some other business, but around noon, one of the hospital volunteers ran excitedly into his office next to the church.

"Reverend," wheezed the chandler's pudgy wife. She must have run all the way from the hospital. "Reverend, you should come to the hospital. We think the boy's waking up. He's moving and moaning. Dr. Wilmers thinks you should take a look, and maybe give him last rites."

Peter Burton leaped up and rushed outside. "Is Michael with him?" he asked while hurrying beside the panting chandler's wife.

She shook her head. "No, don't know where he's hiding. Probably sleeping somewhere, the poor boy. They say he spent all morning riding around asking people questions."

"See if you can track him down, Mrs. Jordan. If Chris does really wake up, he'll want to talk to him."

The doctor stood next to Chris's bed, feeling his pulse. "Something's definitely happening. He seems to be clinging to consciousness. He wants to wake up."

Chris tried to move and opened his remaining eye. But he stared, unfocused, into the room.

The reverend took his left hand. "Chris, Chris, do you hear me?"

Chris gently returned the pressure. "Michael?"

It was but a whisper. Peter and the doctor held their breaths.

"Reverend Burton, Chris. Peter Burton. Can you talk?"

Chris pressed the reverend's hand once again, then let it go. "Lizzie, gold, warn, fern."

"Ferns, Chris? What do you mean? What about Lizzie?"

"Warn, gold, Lizzie, Mike, triangle, Maori village, cabin, cabin west," Chris sputtered out the words between his battered lips with the last of his strength.

"What do you mean, 'warn,' Mr. Timlock?" asked the doctor. "Do you mean we need to warn Lizzie?"

Chris nodded violently. "West, cabin, stream, upstre . . ."

Peter Burton looked at the young man desperately. "I don't understand, Chris. Once more, slowly. Lizzie is looking for gold in a triangle, and we need to warn her? Why, Chris? About what? Chris, who did this to you? Whom do we need to warn Lizzie and Michael about?"

Chris groaned. He seized the reverend's hand, seeming to want to pull himself up. Then he summoned all his strength. "Ride westwa, westward from cabin to stream, upst, upstream, quick!"

Chris fell back into his cushions. His eyes were closed again. The doctor felt his pulse. Then he shook his head.

"That was it, Reverend. He won't tell us more. But at least he managed that, and it was obviously very important to him. We need to find out what he meant."

Peter Burton gently stroked back Chris's sand-colored hair, which had fallen over his bandaged face. "We need to wait for Michael to come back. Maybe he can make some sense of it. Chris must have thought he was with Lizzie and both were in danger. But now . . . Michael can't have gone too far. His horse is out front."

Peter Burton stood up and looked around at his possible helpers. The men who had come for the charity meals could take the dead man to the church later and prepare his body.

"I'll hold a service early tomorrow. And it would be nice if a good many people came. Doctor, would you inform the officer? This is no longer an assault. This is murder."

***

News of Chris's death spread quickly through the town—only Michael slept through it in Janey's Dollhouse. The girls had agreed not to wake him.

"He can't bring him back to life, after all," said Janey.

Peter was just helping the sexton erect a dais for Chris Timlock's coffin when an older boy rushed into the church tent. Peter recognized him as a courier for the bank.

"Reverend, Reverend, Barbara, from the tearoom, sent me. You, you need to come right away. Some . . . someone wants to kill himself there."

Peter furrowed his brow. "One more time, Robbie: one of Barbara's customers wants to shoot himself?"

"Not shoot, Reverend. Stab. He has a knife, but he wants to talk to you before. Please, come quickly!"

For the second time that day, the reverend left his church at a sprint. He did not have far to go. Barbara's tearoom was near the hospital. As he ran past, he noticed that Michael's gray was still in front, but without any trace of its owner.

Barbara and a few of her lunch customers stood at the door of the wooden hut, highly agitated. "In there, Reverend. It's Thomas Winslow. He keeps screaming about guilt and murder and hell! The doctor's there, but Winslow only wants to talk to you."

Peter Burton peered in the door to assess the scene. Winslow had planted himself in a corner of the eatery. He had torn his shirt open and was pressing the tip of his hunting knife against his chest. If he were to thrust, he would hit his heart.

Dr. Wilmers stood a safe distance away and talked to him soothingly. "Whatever you've done, Thomas, you have to confess and take your punishment. Sticking a knife into your heart now is no solution. You should . . ."

Peter Burton walked into the tearoom.

"Reverend," Thomas Winslow whimpered. "Reverend Burton, you, you must, my sins, I didn't want to . . . I'm a murderer, Reverend. Dear Lord, Reverend, dear Lord Jesus, forgive me my sins; forgive me my guilt. I, even if I didn't want to, I . . ."

Peter Burton tried to get closer to Winslow, but the man cut his skin with the knife as soon as he moved. Dr. Wilmers gave Peter a helpless look.

"Thomas, first you should calmly tell me what happened," said Peter, trying to put strength and serenity into his voice. "Maybe it's not all that bad. God forgives—especially if you did not intentionally commit the sin."

"But it was intentional." Now he was crying. The man was obviously drunk. "We, we wanted to know where he got the gold."

Peter straightened up, alarmed. "Where he got the gold? Are you talking about Chris Timlock, Thomas? Were you part of the assault?"

"I held him still," sobbed Winslow. "And at first I thought, all right, I thought a few slaps. Nobody'd die of that. And he could just have told us."

"But he didn't?" asked Peter. "He didn't want to say?"

"He wanted to, all right," Winslow said, whining. "The way he thrashed him, he would have told us anything. But, I guess, he didn't know. You have to believe me, Reverend. When I realized he didn't know anything, I told Coltrane he should stop but—"

"Coltrane? Ian Coltrane? The horse trader?"

Winslow nodded. "But he didn't stop, he said Timlock had to know, but Timlock, in the end he said the woman knew. The woman had found the gold."

"Lizzie." Peter exchanged a look with the doctor. Chris's last words were slowly making sense. "And had she told him where she found it? Did he know where she is?"

Winslow shook his head. "No, I think he, he had no idea. But Coltrane, he wants to go up where Drury is and follow them when they go to the place. And then stake a claim there."

Peter felt cold rise up within him. Michael had said Lizzie was panning for gold. She must have gone out alone. And Coltrane . . .

"Listen, Thomas. Now you need to tell that to the officer. I'm sure they'll grant you extenuating circumstances, I'm sure of it."

"I don't want extenuating circumstances." Winslow shook his head wildly. "Don't want to go to prison. Not again. Just forgive me, Reverend. Make it so the Lord forgives me."

Thomas Winslow inhaled deeply. Then he stabbed himself, falling forward at the same time onto the knife. Dr. Wilmers went to work, but there was nothing he could do. Reverend Burton said a prayer. The doctor closed the dead man's eyes, but then quickly turned to the reverend.

"Another one," he said. "Let's go through it once more. What did Chris Timlock say about where this woman is? He did know it, just didn't tell the devils."

"A triangle," said Peter, "from their cabin to a stream and a Maori village."

The doctor shook his head. "That doesn't get us anywhere. But westward, he said, west from the cabin."

Peter nodded. "And then upstream. That's right. Where is Michael? Where the hell is Michael Drury? Take care of this here, doctor. I need to find Michael, and Lizzie."

Peter ran out into the street. His thoughts raced. Coltrane was dangerous—and he had known that before Chris Timlock's murder. Kathleen's reaction at seeing her husband again had told him enough. And now this devil was after Lizzie—who apparently wanted to keep a spectacular gold find secret. Maybe she was the only one who had ever seen the site. If Coltrane did away with her, there would be no evidence against him. Winslow's confession could pass for the ramblings of a drunk—and maybe Coltrane had no plans of returning to Tuapeka anyway. Colin had appeared at school in the morning, though. At least he was not following Lizzie's tracks into the mountains.

Peter saw Michael's gray in front of the hospital—a beautiful, doubtless very fast horse that he had often admired. But without its rider, it was useless. Unless . . .

Peter rushed into the hospital. "Mrs. Jordan, has Michael Drury reappeared?"

She shook her head.

"Mrs. Jordan, when he comes back, tell him I took his horse. I need to find Lizzie Portland. It's a matter of life and death. He's to saddle my horse and come after me. Do you understand?"

Mrs. Jordan's eyes widened, but she nodded. She was not stupid; she understood. And if not, there was also Dr. Wilmers. Peter couldn't think about it anymore. He untied the horse and mounted it, and they took off.

Chapter 10

Ian Coltrane could hardly believe his luck the morning after the assault. He had found their cabin easily enough, and he spied as Michael and Lizzie parted—Michael toward town to find his partner, and Lizzie off alone into the mountains to the west. It was easy to follow her—downright boring after a while. Lizzie was in no hurry, and she walked beside her horse, talking to the animal and letting it graze from time to time. Around midday, she began to peer behind her, which made Ian nervous at first. Then he realized Lizzie was waiting for Michael Drury to catch up to her.

Ian couldn't imagine Timlock had survived this long. True, his death would surely delay Michael, but then nothing was stopping him from catching up to Lizzie in the mountains. Least of all if he put two and two together or Timlock had talked before dying. Ian hoped that Winslow, the drunk, at least had kept quiet; ultimately Ian trusted in the man's sense of self-preservation. And on his addiction. There was no whiskey in prison.

Ian acted with more caution once he suspected Michael might be following Lizzie. But as the hours passed, he became calmer. If his adversary really were going to ride after Lizzie, he would already have caught up to her. His horse was fast. But it was probably no longer possible for him to still ride up into the mountains that day.

Of course, the police would have been summoned from Dunedin when the beaten man was found, dead or not. And with a brutal attack among prospectors, the victim's partner was always the first suspect. The officer would interrogate Michael and, with any luck, lock him up for a night.

Ian stopped worrying about Michael when Lizzie reached a stream shortly before dark and set up her camp there. He thought for a moment about attacking her and forcing her to reveal her destination, but why should he rob himself of a peaceful night? Of course he would have a little fun, free of charge, with the girl, but that could wait until the next morning. He needed only be careful as hell that his prey did not escape him.

So Ian put off the matter until the next day. Lizzie would still be pretty, and after the appropriate handling surely willing—and then, after he had the gold and was done with her, he would not need to treat her with any more care. Indeed, it would be better to get rid of her. Then he would only have to contend with Michael. Let him just try to prove Ian had stolen the claim from Lizzie.

Ian hitched his mule a few hundred yards downstream of Lizzie's camp and hoped she was not good at spotting people at night. He bound his mule's front legs just to be sure, although, naturally, it would occasionally move from one leg to another. Fortunately, Lizzie's own horse did that too, and as it happened, the sparse southern beech forest they found themselves in was populated by nocturnal birds. Their calls hardly let him get any sleep, but they also offered him the perfect camouflage of sound.

Lizzie clearly suspected nothing when she got up in the morning, washed herself in the stream, and baked flatbread for breakfast. The evening before, she had caught fish. Ian thought she was very clever; he wondered where Michael had found her.

Lizzie obviously dawdled. The sun was already high in the sky when she finally decamped. In the meantime, she seemed somewhat concerned. Probably because Michael really should have come by now.

Ian followed her farther upstream to a waterfall and a strange rock formation that thrust into the sky like needles. Lizzie seemed to recognize the terrain. With growing excitement, Ian watched as she pitched her tent at the foot of the rocks and let her horse graze. She leaned shovels, spades, and axes neatly against the rocks and brought out the weir she had fished with the day before.

Ian could hardly restrain himself from rushing her and forcing her to give up her secret, but he had to remain calm. Lizzie caught plenty of fish for two. Clearly, she was hoping that Michael would show up for lunch. She often looked back toward the trail for some sign of him, but she was too close to the waterfall to be able to hear anything but the rushing water. After she had lit a fire and roasted her catch, she looked for her gold pan.

Finally, something was happening. Ian watched Lizzie clamber up the slope. The gold site had to be past the waterfall. He made an arc and followed her at a wide distance and then saw her take off her shoes, climb into the stream, and dig along the streambed. A short time later, she began to pan for gold.

Even at a distance, Ian saw that at first try there was gold glinting in the pan. It was time now. Ian pressed silently toward the stream, but Lizzie would not have heard him anyway. She did not flinch until he was behind her, seized her, and laid his hand over her mouth.

"Many thanks, Lizzie. It was exceedingly gracious of you to lead me to your gold find."

***

Peter Burton came from a well-to-do family in Lancashire, England. Even as a child he had owned a pony, and as a young man he made a name for himself at hunts and steeplechases. Now he was using this experience. Michael's powerful, tall gray ran as if of its own will—first toward home, but it was happy to continue west too. The animal seemed even to enjoy the wild ride. Michael probably never let it dash so unrestrainedly over rocks and brush.

Peter, too, would have had fun if it were not for the burning concern that forced him to spur the horse on even more. Self-doubt tortured him the longer he rode. Had it been right to leave everything behind, take Michael's horse without asking, and follow the vague route description of a dying man? Maybe it would have been better to wait for Michael—maybe even to send a whole search party. The reverend did not even have a gun. He would have to rely on the element of surprise and his fists when he caught Coltrane. Having just seen evidence of what the man could do with his fists, the thought was not very pleasant. Coltrane was at least as tall and considerably heavier, and yet he had no choice. If he didn't find Coltrane quickly, Lizzie would not survive the day.

Many questions shot through Peter Burton's head: Was this the right way? What if he didn't make it in time? After two hours of trotting and galloping, the gray slowly calmed down, and to his relief, Peter stumbled on a camp. There was no evidence of a campfire, but the earth around a tree was upset as if a horse had been hitched at the spot. Peter rode slowly onward and thought he recognized a second camp, much less obvious; just a few nibbled blades of grass testified to a hungry horse stopping there. This discovery gave Peter encouragement. It looked as if he was on the right track—but so was Coltrane.

The reverend spurred on his horse, and the horse briskly trotted farther westward. Midday was long past, but Peter was too excited to feel hunger. If he judged his horse's speed correctly, he must have ridden some twenty miles since he had passed Drury's house. And there was a stream! Peter's heart raced as he again found traces of a camp. Quite properly covered up, though—it could almost have been Maori who had made the fire and spent the night here. Peter did not find a second camp this time, but he was no doubt headed the right way. Upstream. Peter let the horse trot a little more slowly now. It was better if Ian Coltrane did not hear him coming.

***

Lizzie tried to bite the hand that held her mouth closed, but her attacker's grip was too tight, and he pinned her upper arms to her body by wrapping his other arm around her. The gold pan fell into the water as she stumbled out of the streambed.

Coltrane looked at it regretfully. "What a shame about all that lovely gold, Lizzie. But I can pan for some more later. Before that we can chat a bit, eh, girl? For instance, about how you found this here. Do you really come this far alone, or was that Michael of yours involved?"

Coltrane took his hand from Lizzie's mouth, seizing her arms with a quick movement and pulling her backward. Lizzie screamed, but she went quiet the moment he slammed her head against a beech tree on the riverbank. Her temple was cut and bleeding. Coltrane quickly tied her hands behind her back, then threw her in the grass.

"So, girl, now we can talk—but no screaming or I'll have to gag you."

"Michael will find me, you know." Lizzie spat at him. "And Chris. They'll be here any minute." She fought against her bindings, but she didn't have much hope. This man was strong as a bear. The gruesome glint in his dark eyes did not bode well.

Coltrane laughed. "Chris might look down on us from heaven, I suppose," he scoffed, "and that Michael of yours is busy elsewhere. Now come along, Lizzie; tell me: Did you discover the claim on your own?"

Lizzie turned around on the ground. She acted as if she were still trying to free herself, but more than anything she was thinking feverishly. Should she tell him about the Maori? Or would she bring the tribe into danger then too? She cursed her impatience. Why couldn't she just have waited for Michael, ridden up together with him, and introduced him to her Maori friends first? She might be lucky. Perhaps Coltrane had drawn the attention of a few Maori hunters as he sneaked up on her. She thought that rather unlikely, however, since the Maori men would have long since intervened.

"I found it on my own," Lizzie shouted defiantly.

Coltrane nodded, content, and brushed a dark strand of hair from his sweaty face. "Very nice. But now you'll want to share it with me, of course."

Lizzie did not answer. Everything was happening too fast. She needed to take stock of the situation first. Chris was dead? Could that be true? Good Lord, if this bastard was not afraid to murder just for information, what would he do to keep this place all to himself?

"Maybe if you'd tell me your name first?" Lizzie forced herself to smile. "Who knows? Maybe I'd be happy to share with you."

Coltrane's laugh boomed. "I like you better already, sweet. Even if I don't believe a word, of course. But fine. My name, dearest Lizzie, is Ian Coltrane. And I want this claim from you as a gift if you'll give it. And if not, I'll take it anyway." He lifted her up and pressed her against the trunk of the beech tree to kiss her. Lizzie turned her head desperately to the side.

"Shouldn't we go down to my camp?" she asked with as enticing a voice as possible. "I, I've roasted some fish."

More importantly, Michael's gun was among the things she had packed—though she was not entirely sure how to fire it.

"I'll eat food later," Coltrane said. His tongue sought the way to her mouth. "First, a taste of Lizzie."

At that moment Lizzie was struck by where she had heard the name Coltrane before. This was the man from Michael's home village. The one Kathleen had married. He might even have killed her. Lizzie almost had to laugh at the irony of fate. Was Michael about to lose a second woman to the clutches of this bastard?

She had no illusions about her future. Coltrane would not leave her alive. He would kill her and claim this prospect for himself. And soon, droves of prospectors would pour over the land of the Ngai Tahu—precisely what the tribe had wanted to prevent. Lizzie would not die, but die a traitor. The Maori would never know whether she had simply sold the rights to the place or given them away. And if one thing led to another, the war Kahu Heke had spoken of would begin here. All that because she made a mistake.

Coltrane pushed her dress up and thrust into her brutally. It was demean- ing and painful, but she had survived worse. Her desperation gave her new courage. She would not withdraw into herself, sobbing; she had to defend herself.

Lizzie pretended she was following Coltrane's movements, and as she did, she rubbed her hand bindings against the bark of the tree. They were not very tight. It had to be possible to undo them. Suddenly they loosened, precisely in the moment Coltrane fell against her, moaning.

Lizzie's thoughts tripped over each other. She knew that even if she freed herself now, she could not knock this huge man out without a weapon. She looked for the gold pan, but it was in the stream. Her knife was down in her camp.

Coltrane slowly recovered and straightened himself. "That wasn't bad at all, girl. We should do it again before . . . Well, we have plenty of time, don't we, Liz?"

Lizzie tried to continue playing her role. She held her hands as if they were still bound. "I, I have loads of time, sir. I, if you don't kill me, then, I can show you a few things. Why don't we go to my tent?"

Coltrane smirked. He would not fall for just any game. Even with her hands bound, she was instinctively trying to smooth her skirt as he pulled her along.

"I think we'll go a little farther into the woods instead. What do you think, Lizzie?"

Lizzie hardly dared breathe as she felt over the pocket in her dress. It was still there, and far better than her fist. The jade war club. The *tohunga*'s present, carved for the hands of a female warrior. She had put it in her pocket before ever leaving the cabin, thinking at the time that she only wanted to keep its power against her body until Michael joined her.

Lizzie stumbled beside Coltrane toward the waterfall. Did he want to climb down here, or was he trying to throw her down? It was unlikely that she would break her neck here. The pond below the waterfall was deep enough to swim in.

Lizzie's hopes grew for a second, but then she realized that Coltrane was merely thirsty. He got down on one knee and ladled water out of the stream with his hand. He did not look at the bound woman beside him. After all, what could happen? Petite Lizzie could not even make him fall if she threw all her weight at him.

But Lizzie had the war club. And she felt its power through the fabric of her dress. What had the priestess said? It was meant to protect the tribe. The tribe and the land of the Ngai Tahu. And that was just what Lizzie would use it to do.

Slowly and carefully, so Coltrane would not notice, she drew her right hand out of the loosened binding, reached into her pocket, and felt the smooth, cool club. It was like an extension, an enhancement of her hand.

Coltrane raised his head and looked past the waterfall into the valley. As he did, he stiffened alertly as if he had spied something.

Michael? It did not matter. Lizzie had made her decision. She drew the club out, aimed at Coltrane's temple, and struck.

***

Peter Burton had spied the rock stacks from a long way off, and then he came upon Lizzie's horse beside her tent and her fire. The animal whinnied when it recognized Michael's horse, but Peter hoped the waterfall drowned out any noise.

He saw two figures atop the waterfall: a man pulling a girl behind him. But the girl did not seem beaten; alert, rather, and tense. Then the man lowered himself to drink, and the woman . . .

Peter watched Lizzie's right arm slowly rise up and strike. He knew this movement, had seen it several times when Maori girls danced a *haka* war dance. He had been a guest, with other priests, in a *marae* of the Ngai Tahu before he left Christchurch, and remembered the formal greeting very well; it also contained a sort of threat. They used it to welcome guests but also to make it clear, just in case, how well they could defend themselves should a visitor not prove worthy of hospitality. The men had wielded spears, the women small jade clubs. They swung them just as easily—almost elegantly—and doubtless aimed them as well as the woman he saw up above.

Peter held his breath. He did not hear the club's strike, but he saw the man fall as if struck by an ax. Lizzie stood straight up, and he thought her heard her let out a cry. Did they not call that a *karanga*? The cry of a priestess summoning the gods? Peter could not quite believe that he was hearing it here, in this place, from the mouth of the courageous but gentle and earnest churchgoer Lizzie Portland.

And then Lizzie saw the gray horse and ran down the slope.

"Michael! Oh my God, Michael."

Peter caught her.

"Reverend?" Lizzie's voice sounded childlike and amazed, but then fear flared up in her eyes, and her face contorted. "Is Michael . . . did something happen? My God, that man, Coltrane, he made it sound like Chris is dead. But Michael too, no . . . The gods couldn't want that."

Peter supported Lizzie as she swayed and gently shook her head. "No, Lizzie, Michael Drury is not dead. He must be on his way here. Now, tell me what happened here. Why did you kill Coltrane?"

Lizzie only slowly understood what the reverend was trying to say. And what exactly had happened.

"I?" she whispered. "I . . . somehow it wasn't me. Somehow it was all the women of the tribe. Of my tribe."

Lizzie breathed in deeply. Only then did she find her way back to reality, envisioning what the reverend had seen. He had not witnessed the attack and the rape. He had only seen how she smashed a man's skull from behind.

"Reverend, it was self-defense. He, he forced me . . ." She now felt the tears, finally, the tears she had not permitted herself to cry earlier. "You can't tell anyone, Reverend. You can't tell anyone about this place or this gold."

When Michael arrived at the camp at the foot of the waterfall a good two hours later and almost crazy with concern, Lizzie was sitting at the fire with the reverend. They had covered Coltrane's corpse with a tarp.

Lizzie rushed at her beloved. Until then, she had not truly believed he was alive, and it seemed he had felt the same about her. The two clung to each other while Lizzie told her story.

Peter Burton apologized for taking Michael's horse. "I meant to help Lizzie," he said, "but she defended herself without me." He looked at Lizzie with respect.

Michael nodded. "She has always been a fighter of a lady," he said tenderly. "Still, thank you, Reverend. You did fine with the horse. But what are we going to do now with that one over there?" He pointed to Coltrane's corpse.

Peter Burton weighed their options. "Help me throw him on the horse," he finally said with resignation. "We'll take him tonight to the cliffs above Gabriel's Gully and throw him down. Then people can interpret it as an accident—or a suicide as his judgment of himself. Winslow accused him, in front of several people, of having killed Chris Timlock. They won't be falling over themselves to investigate his death. So they won't bother Lizzie—and no one will learn of this place or this gold."

All three of them were quiet when they finally descended the mountain. Michael led the horse with the dead man on it.

"Why are you helping us?" he asked the reverend.

Peter Burton shrugged and thought once more of the scene atop the waterfall: Lizzie's dancer-like motion, her cry.

"I saw something strange," he said quietly. "Something that could not really have been. Let's say I'm following the will of the gods."

The Will of the Gods
Tuapeka, Dunedin
1862–1863

Chapter 1

After her encounter with Ian Coltrane, Kathleen had driven the road to Dunedin at breakneck speed. Only when the horses stumbled at a bend and the wagon swayed alarmingly did she collect herself long enough to reach her apartment in Dunedin safely.

When Claire came home from the shop, she found Kathleen throwing her clothing and other belongings in bags and suitcases.

"He's here," she sobbed hysterically when she saw Claire. "Ian is back. I have to go away. I have to get away from here."

It took Claire hours to even halfway calm Kathleen and, more importantly, to keep her friend from departing precipitously. "Kathleen, of course I don't doubt you saw him. But he's up in Tuapeka. That's twenty miles away. Even if he ever comes to Dunedin, he won't wander into a boutique for women's fashion. Not that he would even find you there; you hardly ever make an appearance. If he ever gets too close to me, he'll have to contend with Jimmy Dunloe. What does the reverend have to say, anyway?"

Claire shook her head as Kathleen erratically recounted her flight. "Peter Burton must think you're crazy," she said. "You could at least have talked to him."

Kathleen had stopped packing in the meantime. She sat hunched in a corner of the sofa. "I don't want to talk to anyone," she cried. "I don't know if it's right to stay here. What if he sees Sean? Or Heather? But if, if I don't go away, then, then I don't want to see anyone or speak to anyone. I'm invisible, Claire. I . . ."

***

"She's completely terrified and hysterical," Claire explained to Peter Burton.

Two days after the events with Ian in the mountains, he finally managed to free some time and ride to Dunedin. Claire served him tea and pastries in her shop. Kathleen had barricaded herself in the apartment.

"She doesn't just fear for herself, but for you too, Reverend," Claire continued. "She never wants to go back to the gold miner's camp, and you're not supposed to visit her or even be seen with her anywhere. She's scared to death because the people in camp know her name."

"But not many," the reverend reassured her. "A couple of women, the doctor, a few people from the parish. And even then, many just call her Kathie. The likelihood that one of them will mention her to Ian Coltrane is minimal."

"For Kathie, it's still unbearable," said Claire. "You should have seen her before Sean and Heather came back. She was scared to death that the children might run into Ian."

Peter Burton nodded. "She was already overcome with fear in the camp. Yet he seems to be a rather good father, all things considered. His younger son worships him."

"That boy is also . . ." Claire stopped. If anyone were going to tell the reverend about Kathleen's family relations, then it would have to be her. "He's more similar to Ian," she concluded. "Give her time, Peter. She has to get over her shock first."

Peter Burton rubbed his temples. "And here I thought we were finally getting close," he said. "She was becoming more approachable, livelier." He reached for a teacup, found it empty, and played distractedly with the spoon.

Claire poured him more tea and placed a pastry on his plate. "Here, eat or you'll get as thin as Kathie. She's lost nearly ten pounds since running into Ian. She's taking it all so terribly."

Peter bit obediently into the pastry. He, too, looked beleaguered. His eyes were ringed with red, he absolutely needed a razor, and his hair was desperate for a trim. Claire determined to send him straight to the barber, though she doubted that it would change anything about Kathleen's behavior toward him.

"In any case, now you know why she was so shy and distant," she said. "It has nothing to do with you, Peter. You shouldn't think that. On the contrary,

Kathleen loves you. I'm sure of it. But with this sword of Damocles hanging over her, how is she to see clearly?"

***

Kathleen remained completely isolated in her apartment. She drew a bit, but she did not even dare to visit the seamstresses or check on the progress of their work. If one of them had questions, she had to come to Kathleen—and would discover, to her amazement, that her boss had secured the door to the apartment with three locks.

While they were still on their school break, she hardly allowed either Sean or Heather to go outside. Sean, especially, she did not let out of sight. Heather barely remembered her father because he had traveled so much. She had been so young when they left, and she had changed so much in the last few years, that Kathleen couldn't imagine Ian would recognize her at first sight.

She did look very much like Kathleen, though. In her panic, Kathleen insisted that her daughter wear hats with wide brims when she was on the street and put her hair up instead of wearing it down or braided. Heather watched the changes in her mother with astonishment.

Sean had nothing but compassion for his mother. He remembered his father and brother well, and he knew they might still pose a danger. But he also made his mother consider that she could not hide for the rest of her life.

"Don't they have divorce in New Zealand, Ma? There has to be a way of getting rid of him without killing him, isn't there?"

Surely Sean was only exaggerating, but his question plunged Kathleen into new fears. Could her son be planning murder in order to support her?

Her heart began to race when, two weeks after she saw Ian, the doorbell rang around nine in the morning. It seemed an unusual time since Sean and Heather were back in school, the shop was not yet open, and the seamstresses never arrived before ten.

Kathleen opened the door as far as the chain would allow. She peeked out and saw a police officer on the other side.

"Did, did my son . . . ?"

The young sergeant bowed politely.

"Good morning, madam. I'm sorry if I startled you. Surely you're not used to the police . . ."

"Has something happened to my son?" screamed Kathleen.

The sergeant shook his head. "Not to my knowledge, madam. Mrs. Kathleen Coltrane?"

Kathleen finally opened the door. "Pardon me. I . . . I . . ."

"I'm Sergeant Jim Potter with the Dunedin Police, and I need to ask you to accompany me or another officer to Tuapeka today, or tomorrow at the latest."

Kathleen reeled. Could Ian have gotten the police to take her back to him?

"It's concerning the identification of a body," Sergeant Potter continued.

Kathleen caught herself on the door frame. "The, the reverend? Peter, Peter Burton?"

Sergeant Potter shook his head. "No, no; it's about a prospector. Please do sit down, Mrs. Coltrane. You look very agitated, and the news I have for you will only disturb you more. I could be . . . indeed, it is very likely that it concerns the death of your husband."

Kathleen proceeded as if in a trance as she told Claire why the officer had come and asked her to tell Sean he could ride to Tuapeka if he wanted but that she preferred he stay in Dunedin with Heather. She changed her clothes, packed a few dark dresses into her travel bag, and gathered some money and papers she thought might be necessary in regard to her marriage and Colin. By the time she followed Sergeant Potter out, she was almost at ease.

Claire wished she could go with her friend. Kathleen's sudden calm was just as alarming as her recent hysteria had been. Claire reminded herself that Peter Burton would be there. And the reverend was reliable. Before he allowed the police to contact Kathleen, he surely would have confirmed the dead man really was Ian Coltrane.

***

A few hours later, Kathleen stood in front of the Tuapeka butcher's icehouse, where Ian's body was stored. Naturally, his identity was known, but Peter Burton had insisted that Kathleen bear witness to the dead body. He was sure she would need to see Ian's corpse to believe she was truly free.

"Are you ready, Mrs. Coltrane?" asked Sergeant Potter.

Kathleen nodded and followed the officer into the icebox. Ian's coffin was among sides of beef and ham hocks. Kathleen shivered as she eyed the corpse closely. They told her he had fallen off a cliff, but she noticed there was only some scraped skin that seemed hardly to have bled. The only serious injury was to his temple. It didn't look to Kathleen as if Ian had fallen to his death; it was more like someone had smashed his skull with an extremely hard object.

"He must have fallen," said Sergeant Potter. "On a rock, perhaps. I'm sorry, Mrs. Coltrane, not a pretty sight. But is it . . . ?"

She nodded. "It's Ian Patrick Coltrane," she said calmly. "My wedded husband. And I, I would like to speak to the reverend now, before I, before I retrieve my son."

***

Peter Burton shut his office door behind Kathleen after Sergeant Potter brought her in. The reverend reached out to take Kathleen in his arms, but she pulled away from him.

"Was it you?' she asked quietly.

Peter Burton looked at her, uncomprehending. Then he understood. "No! How could you think that, Kathleen? I'm a man of God. I, heavens, I thought about it, of course, when I saw how afraid of him you were. But there would have been other ways of dealing with Ian." He put his hand on hers, but she withdrew it from him.

"Then who was it?" asked Kathleen. "Don't talk to me about cliffs, Peter. I'm an expert on beatings. Ian practiced his boxing on me for years. I know what it looks like when a fist strikes you on the temple. And I know that one usually doesn't land on the temple when thrown to the ground. I doubt it would be different if a man slipped or fell. So, who was it, Peter?"

The reverend looked at the floor. "A young woman who lives with one of the prospectors—and ostensibly with the aid of a Maori warrior spirit. In any case, with a Maori war club, and she knew how to swing it. Your husband had attacked and raped her beforehand."

Kathleen bit her lip.

"There's more. A good friend of the woman's had just died. It is an awful story, and it would not help anyone if everything became public. I can recount it to you, of course."

Kathleen declined. "So she hit him with this club. And then she . . . then she threw him off the cliff?"

"With my help," admitted the reverend. "It was self-defense, Kathleen, I swear. I'd not conceal a murderer. There's a lot resting on keeping the location of the act a secret. And the woman . . ."

"Has suffered enough," said Kathleen tiredly. "I understand. Maybe you'd tell her she has my sympathies?"

Peter rubbed his forehead. "She doesn't know that he still has family—aside from Colin, that is. And I think it's better that way. Otherwise, it would just make her think about it more. Besides, she's not here. She's panning for gold in the mountains."

Kathleen nodded. "Yes. Now I'm free?" she said flatly.

Peter nodded. "You have nothing more to fear. And I, Kathleen . . ." Peter stopped briefly, wondering if he should dare say what he wanted. There was no reason to delay, and it might comfort and soothe her. "I never asked you, Kathleen, because I did not want to press you. I knew it was a secret. But now, since there's nothing more keeping us apart, Kathleen, I love you. Would you marry me?" Peter Burton looked at her expectantly.

Kathleen's head was spinning. This was all too much for one day. And how could he rush her so? She fell back like a shying horse. "Peter, not now," she whispered. "It's, it's too soon. I, I like you very much, Peter. But you're a pastor, an Anglican, and I'm Catholic. And I have three children. Oh God, I have three children again." Kathleen braced herself. "Peter, I need to see to Colin. This is all difficult enough anyway. Give me time, Peter. I'll need time."

Peter Burton scolded himself for his haste. Of course she would not throw herself in his arms immediately. She would again need a friend, a confidant, a father for her children—but not yet.

"Come," he said, "let's look for Colin. He's been holed up in his tent since his father was found. I haven't told him anything about you so far. I'm sure he'll be ecstatic."

Kathleen followed him, but she doubted Peter was right about Colin. He would mourn for his father—and even more for the freedom he had had with Ian. He probably would not be overjoyed about returning to her.

***

Over the next few days, Kathleen took over Ian's personal effects, which consisted of an ounce of gold, two horses—worth a small fortune according to Colin, but Peter quickly placed them in the "slaughter house or charity" category—and her son. As she had anticipated, Colin proved difficult. He had no interest in returning to Dunedin with his mother, wanting instead to dig for gold and run his father's business. Of course, he was only fourteen and could not be left to do any of this alone.

So Kathleen exchanged the gold and sold Ian's covered wagon, turning over the proceeds to Peter Burton for her husband's burial and the care of the horses, which could perhaps still make themselves useful around the church. After the funeral, Peter drove Kathleen and Colin to Dunedin.

It was a mournful journey; Colin was doggedly silent, and Kathleen was lost in her own thoughts. To make matters worse, Colin gave Peter an evil glance when he kissed Kathleen good-bye. The reverend worried as he directed his horse back to Tuapeka. Kathleen was free of Ian Coltrane, but it seemed that Colin was merely biding his time to take the man's place—not in her heart, but as the source of her fear.

Only that did not prove so easy, largely because Sean had no intention of permitting his returned brother any impertinence. He clearly played the man of the house, which amused Kathleen and Claire and which at first made it easier to live with Colin. But Colin was used to doing as he pleased, and soon, he was disobeying Kathleen and earning his teachers' complaints: Colin was disruptive, arrogant, and sometimes absent entirely.

The teachers occasionally asked Sean, who remained a star pupil, to talk to his brother, but any attempt he made at this resulted in fights. Colin won effortlessly; he was far more practiced in fistfighting than Sean.

Even Peter Burton, who visited as often as he could and who tried to foster a relationship not only with Sean and Heather but also with Colin, got nowhere. Colin Coltrane did not like to be bossed around—not by teachers, not by the Anglican pastor or the Catholic priest, and least of all by his mother and brother. Kathleen knew that it was futile to keep Colin in school.

With Peter Burton's help, she turned to Donny Sullivan, the Irish stable owner, for an apprenticeship for Colin. Short, fat Sullivan—once a zealous congregant of Peter Burton's but now a member of the newly founded Catholic parish—was willing to give Colin a chance. He could sleep in the stables and assist with the horses, and most importantly, ride them.

At first, Kathleen was skeptical, since Sullivan traded horses on the side as well, but both Peter Burton and Father Parrish, the Catholic priest, reassured her. Donny Sullivan was as honest as anyone in his profession could be. Occasionally, he took a higher price from a rich city boy than the horse he sold was worth, or he shaved two years off when he gave a mule's age, but he did no outright swindling, and he never foisted a horse on anyone if it wasn't a good match. Sullivan had thoroughly satisfied customers, and he was proud of that.

That is, until he hired Colin Coltrane. After three months, Sullivan told Kathleen he needed to let Colin go.

"It's not that he doesn't know about horses, Mrs. Coltrane," said Donny. "On the contrary—the boy knows more than I do. But I always have to stop him from working on the teeth of the horses I plan to sell, to make them look younger, and from fiddling with their shoes to make them walk more elegantly. He knows all of a swindler's tricks but doesn't understand why I don't use them. I can't leave him alone with the customers. He hardly opens his mouth but he makes them think their horse's no good. Most of them want to trade their horses in right away, and usually for some half-wild young stallion that looks sharp. But I'll have to deal with it when some Sunday rider breaks his neck. I'm sorry, Mrs. Coltrane, but the boy lies like he's breathing air. Yesterday, he sold old Monty Robs—you know, that prospector who's trying his hand at farming in Waikouaiti—that little horse I had set aside for Mrs. Edmunds's daughter."

Kathleen nodded. Chloe was supposed to get a pony for her birthday, and Claire had been looking for the right horse for weeks. She thought she'd found it in Donny's little chestnut horse.

"He told Monty he could plow his whole farm with the little thing and that it'd barely eat anything."

Kathleen burst into bitter laughter. She was reminded of Matt Edmunds's donkey. Donny Sullivan smiled. He could not resist a beautiful woman, and Kathleen was captivating, but he would not keep her good-for-nothing son on just for that.

"Sure, it's a bit funny, but the man was relying on our advice, and he got cheated. If he spreads the word, my good reputation will soon be ruined. I'm sorry, but you'll have to find him another apprenticeship."

Of course, Colin did not see Sullivan's reasoning. On the contrary, he had foul words for the old man and his business dealings.

Kathleen turned to Jimmy Dunloe for advice, and he suggested she find Colin some work that had nothing to do with horses.

"The boy is quite skillful. He's just been misled, the way I see it. I can hire him as a courier. He can take a few papers back and forth and take care of orders outside the bank. When he sees how people place trust in him, he'll behave better."

Though Kathleen was grateful to Jimmy, she didn't believe his approach would be successful with Colin. After all, one of Ian's strategies had been to first gain trust and then abuse it.

"Just don't put any money in Colin's hand," she warned Jimmy. "I'm sorry to say it about my own son, but I don't trust him."

A month later, Jimmy Dunloe let Colin go. He told Colin and Kathleen it was because of the boy's unfriendliness with the clients and because his transactions were often late. However, Jimmy revealed to Claire that small amounts of money had also begun disappearing from the register after he had hired the boy.

"But we don't need to tell Kathleen, do we? She's upset enough as it is," he said.

From that day on, Dunloe stayed out of the matter. To Kathleen's relief, however, there was still the Catholic parish and the strict but thoroughly active Father Parrish. Over the course of the following year, Kathleen needed the help of the priest again and again in order to find Colin apprenticeships—first in the general store, then with a cobbler, and finally with a builder's merchant. In exchange for his assistance, she was forced ever deeper into the Catholic community, which neither Claire nor Peter Burton liked.

"Dear God, Kathie, you're turning into a regular church mouse," Claire complained as one Sunday evening Kathleen was going to Mass for the second time. "And all these requiems for Ian! How many times have you had it said? Fifty? When was the last time you talked to Peter? You need more Darwin and less Bible."

"Father Parrish rejects Darwin," Kathleen retorted, hoping to change the subject. She stood in front of the mirror, struggling to put her gold-blonde hair under a dark, unattractive bonnet. "And Ian, he was doubtless a sinner. Father Parrish says that for his eternal soul . . ."

Claire rolled her eyes. She was preparing to attend a concert with Jimmy Dunloe and wore a dark-green evening dress set with gems. "Kathleen, wake up. That only gives you a guilty conscience. He's always tried to do that. Think of how he wanted to talk you into going back to Ian, full of remorse!"

Kathleen shrugged her shoulders and threw on a black scarf. It was unintentional, but the mourning colors suited her excellently. "He's the only one who still intercedes for Colin. No one wants to hire him anymore. Without Father Parrish . . . And how does it look when I meet with an Anglican pastor? It's bad enough Colin is ruining my reputation."

Claire shook her head. Father Parrish had taken over Ian's role in Kathleen's head. He held her in a fear that grew bigger all the time, and he blamed her for what had become of Colin. In Parrish's opinion, if she had not abandoned him, Colin would be very different.

Peter Burton was hurt by Kathleen's behavior. And while she could not completely withdraw from him because Claire was always inviting him for visits, Kathleen was distant, and sometimes even curt, in her responses to him. When the wine he brought and the lively conversation with Jimmy and Claire started to break through her armor, Colin seemed to appear instantly, burning Kathleen and Peter with his sidelong glance.

Colin recognized his mother's feelings for the reverend, and he did not shy away from using his knowledge as a weapon. He taunted her for it publicly after he had been let go from another apprenticeship. His last master—a friendly old hardware store owner—tried to be diplomatic when he told Kathleen, but he could not get around hinting that Colin had dipped into the cash register.

Kathleen nodded. "My son is a ne'er-do-well. You can come out and say it. I can hardly stand to hear it anymore, but I understand what you're doing."

"And my ma does it with a protestant," said Colin, looking at her hatefully. "Sundays she goes to pray, sure. But on Monday the reverend comes in and out of our place—and they kiss."

Kathleen's reaction was instinctive. She stopped the boy and slapped him with lightning speed. Word of the whole thing would spread quickly.

Afterward, Colin slunk off while Kathleen cried to Claire and Jimmy Dunloe. "Just what am I supposed to do with him?" she sobbed. "After this, there really isn't anyone else who will take him. And what he said about Peter, I've never confessed it. What will Father Parrish think of me? I have to . . ."

"You are not really going to run to this priest now and confess that you kissed Peter three or four times on the cheek, are you?" yelled Claire, horrified.

"It wasn't just on the cheek, though, I—"

"Kathleen, whether and what you want to confess is your business alone," Jimmy Dunloe said calmly. "But as for the boy, I'd like to give you some advice. Look, every family has its black sheep. Among the lower classes, they become criminals, and Colin is well on his way to that. But in better society there are options—and thanks to your business, you can afford them. Send the boy to England to a good college, or better yet, a military academy. I can inquire about suitable boarding schools."

"But he doesn't want to go to school," Kathleen said.

Jimmy Dunloe shook his head. "It doesn't matter what he wants. And he might prefer a military education to a purely academic one. In any case, it's his last chance, Kathleen. He's sliding down here."

"But we're Irish," whispered Kathleen. "I can't send my son into the British army."

Jimmy Dunloe shrugged. "Maybe there's even an Irish military academy, although I doubt it. But I can help you get Colin in. Only if you want me to, of course."

Kathleen bit her lip and fought back tears. "That, that's very nice," she murmured. "But, the British army? He's still Irish."

Claire rolled her eyes. "Kathleen, you can't really turn down this offer. Precisely the British army. It has experience with thick-headed Irish."

Kathleen looked at her angrily. But it could not be denied. If she didn't follow Dunloe's suggestion and accept his help, Colin would end up in jail sooner or later. It was only a question of whether that was not more honorable than the Royal Army. Michael would doubtless have thought it was. And Ian? Well, he would surely have used a post in the army as a springboard to foist a lame horse on the queen. Kathleen had to smile at that thought.

"Just sleep on it," Dunloe advised amicably. "But I'll tell you now: we'll not come up with anything better."

A few weeks later, Colin traveled to Woolwich in London to enter the Royal Military Academy. He had little interest in the education but certainly more in the city of London, and a future career in the military seemed pleasant enough to him. No Irish patriotism stood in his way. True, his father had always cursed the English, but he had also always paid them a certain respect. The English were the victors. They had won, had occupied Ireland. Their queen ruled half the world. Their might attracted Colin. He, too, wanted to rule. And if he had to put on a red uniform to do so, that was fine with him.

Chapter 2

Lizzie spent the loveliest summer of her life at the Maori gold mines with Michael. They had pitched their tent above the waterfall, and in the mornings they took in the intoxicating view over the mountains and little lakes that dotted the Otago countryside. On clear days, they could almost see to Tuapeka. Life in the gold miners' town, Chris Timlock's murder, and Lizzie's revenge on Ian Coltrane now seemed very distant.

They hoarded the gold they panned in a hiding place under the rocks near the waterfall. Since no one other than the reverend and the Ngai Tahu knew their camp, there was no great risk. Besides, they knew that they would have drawn too much attention if Michael took the gold to the bank. Lizzie and Michael's gold hoard grew with breathtaking speed, although they didn't work nearly as hard as the gold prospectors in Tuapeka. Mostly they worked for the morning, then used the midday hour to make love and take a nap afterward. Lizzie enjoyed Michael's caresses and obvious affection. He belonged to her now, and her alone. Kathleen he seemed to have forgotten. Though Lizzie had not made it easy on herself.

A few days after Ian Coltrane's death, she even asked Michael if he wanted to adopt Colin Coltrane. "I have a guilty conscience because I took his father," she said, "and he's your Kathleen's son anyway."

"But not mine," he said firmly. "Ian Coltrane got what he deserved. You don't need to feel guilty about it. As for Colin: I'm sorry he lost his father and mother, but we need to start anew. And he's not the son Kathleen and I dreamed of."

Lizzie was happy about this decision, but she asked Peter Burton what had happened to the boy. The reverend told her no more than that Colin had been taken in by a family in Dunedin. He was of the opinion that Lizzie and Michael shouldn't be burdened with the memory of Ian Coltrane. Michael seemed to share this opinion. Neither of the men talked about the Coltranes when Peter visited Lizzie and Michael at their prospect, which he did every few weeks. He viewed Lizzie as his parishioner and worried about the state of her soul.

Lizzie, however, now devoted considerably more of her time to the Maori spirits than to Christian prayer. She upheld the tradition of asking the earth for forgiveness before each time she took gold, and she thanked Papa and Rangi for her happiness in Michael's arms. Michael played along willingly. Since his recollection of St. Wendelin and intercession for the sheep shearing, Michael had gotten used to the Maori ways.

Yet there were other things that clouded his love for Lizzie—especially as their gold reserve grew and Lizzie began to mention leaving the prospect. They now had almost enough gold to afford a grand farm in the plains, as well as a business for Ann Timlock, who would soon be on her way to New Zealand with her children. Chris's wife would want to at least see his grave. Beyond that, she could find greater opportunities for her children in this new country, perhaps settling in Dunedin and opening a shop.

Michael would have liked to take more gold, but Lizzie reminded him about not being greedy and not breaking their pact with the Maori. He could have given up the mine. What he found difficult, though, was his position in relation to Lizzie. He wanted to marry her; he loved her without a doubt. But had this relationship really been his idea?

He was a man. In Ireland he had been respected, and no doubt people still spoke there about his raid on Trevallion's grain. Kathleen had worshiped him, and if they had gone to America, he would have made his fortune. But since he had met Lizzie, it seemed to him, he merely danced to her tune.

She had helped him, of course. First on the ship and then with his escape, for which he would be eternally grateful. Then, years later, with the whiskey distillery. It had brought in considerably more money than sheep shearing. And now the prospects. He had worked hard, had worked with Chris like a madman. But without much success—until Lizzie took charge.

Everyone seemed to look at Michael as if he were her accessory. The Maori hardly noticed him, and even the reverend regarded him only peripherally when he and Lizzie talked about the Bible, spirits, and demons. Michael could get over the reverend. It was the matter of the Maori that aggravated him.

Lizzie visited their *marae* often and insisted that Michael accompany her. The tribe had to get to know him and accept him, she claimed, but Michael had the feeling they were mocking him. The men invited him over to their fire and were friendly, but they barely even tried their meager English out on him. In their songs and stories, Michael often thought he recognized parodies of the miners, traders, and lovers among the *pakeha*, and felt himself targeted. The Maori treated him obligingly. It was not like before with Tane's tribe, where Michael's knowledge regarding sheep husbandry and dog training were respected. Here, he was simply Lizzie's companion.

The Maori treated Lizzie with reverence. Michael had no idea whether or how they knew of her involvement in Ian Coltrane's death, but their *tohunga*, Hainga, did not tire of praising Lizzie's exertions for the land of the Ngai Tahu.

When Michael once asked about it in broken Maori, they told him that, on that day, Hainga had heard Lizzie's *karanga*—the cry as a summons to the gods. Michael could not imagine that. The Maori camp was several miles from the waterfall.

In any case, Lizzie had acquired significant *mana* and was treated accordingly. Men and women worked for her favor, they were happy when she played with the tribe's children, and the gifts she had once brought from Tuapeka— the blankets and cooking utensils—were handled with respect, as if set with gold and diamonds. Even the chieftain addressed Lizzie. He turned to her for advice regarding negotiations with the *pakeha*. Lizzie gathered even more *mana* by passing on his questions to the reverend, who then discussed them with a lawyer in Tuapeka.

For Michael, worst of all was when a friendly *hapu*, another family grouping of the Ngai Tahu, visited the tribe on the Tuapeka River. Then the tribe asked Lizzie—and her man, of course—to come to the festival. Michael felt that they wanted to lead the two *pakeha* around like trained poodles.

This again was such a day.

"Do I really need to come?" Michael asked grumpily as Lizzie told him about the invitation.

With visible pleasure, Lizzie was wrapping herself in Maori festival clothing, which the women of the tribe had given her. In winter, *pakeha* clothing suited the climate better, but for summer dances, the native women wore skirts of hardened flax leaves, which generated a strange rustling when they moved. Along with that went minimal woven upper body coverings in tribal patterns.

"Of course you do," said Lizzie. "It's a formal matter with extensive *powhiri*. It will take hours until they're done with it. But there will be food, dancing, a proper festival. We'll take some whiskey. Now don't make that face. The reverend will bring us more when he comes next. And I'll sacrifice my last bottle of wine. Hainga loves wine."

Now that Lizzie was swimming in gold, she treated herself to as much wine from Dunedin as the reverend was prepared to haul up to them. She savored the expensive bottles that mostly came from France, Germany, or Italy. She opened them slowly, decanting them as she had once done in the Busbys' house, and then shared them with Michael. He did not think much of them, however.

The last two bottles of their whiskey supply were to go to the Ngai Tahu, who never refused a drop. Michael expected that he would only get a few gulps for himself. So he was pleasantly surprised when he and Lizzie arrived at the festival and he discovered that their whiskey donation was not the only one. The visitors had also brought several bottles along. Better still was that he recognized most of the men of the wandering *hapu*. The tribe came from Kaikoura, and Tane hooted as he embraced Michael before the tribes began the official celebrations.

"We talk later," Tane assured Michael as the chieftains and elders approached each other. Tane had lived for decades among *pakeha* and would surely have preferred to limit the greetings to a short rubbing of noses and a glass of whiskey together. But he had his traditional duties for the *haka*. After everyone had prayed together, Tane reached for his spear and danced the *wero*—announcing, through special movements, that his tribe came with peaceful, not militant, intentions. This demonstrated Tane's station as the tribe's leading warrior, which made Lizzie happy. If Tane was Michael's friend, then Michael's *mana* in the tribe would climb considerably.

Indeed, people seemed to greet Michael with greater respect when he took his seat at Tane's side. During the feast, the two friends exchanged news and drank, and at the end of the night, they were the last two sitting at the fire. All the others had withdrawn to tents or sleeping lodges. Lizzie slept in Hainga's separate *tohunga* hut, which represented a great honor. Or was it that the old woman wanted to keep her from sleeping with Michael in front of the tribe? Lizzie had the feeling the *tohunga* did not approve of her connection to him.

"Clouds gather above you and this man," Hainga said when Lizzie asked her about it. "The gods do not reject you two, but I do not see a limitless blessing. Two forces fight for you."

"For me?" asked Lizzie, confused, but Hainga told her nothing more.

Michael, caught more in the here and now, and his tongue loosened by whiskey, found in Tane a less difficult confidant.

He turned to the Maori warrior for advice as the fire slowly burned down. "How do you all do it, in the tribes? With the women, I mean. You let them be *tohunga*. Nothing happens unless someone runs around screaming at one of your *powhiri*. You give them weapons, but they stay there where they belong. The men hunt and fish, the women cook and weave, and the chief lays down the law. Why isn't it like that with Lizzie? She does what she wants."

Tane furrowed his brow. "Chief does not lay down law," he corrected. "*Tikanga* custom does. Also *tohunga* lays down often—sometimes man, sometimes woman. Depends on *mana*. And chief has much *mana*."

"So, the trick is to have more *mana* than your woman?" asked Michael.

"Yes. But also woman with *mana* respects *tikanga*. *Tikanga* says man wars, women children. Depends on time, of course. When times bad, women also warrior, also fisher, also hunter. But when times good, everything as always."

So that's how it was. Michael and Lizzie had bad times behind them. Lizzie must have used her *mana*—whatever that was exactly—to get out of that. Now good times had arrived, and Michael should say how things were. As custom dictated.

As far as cooking, weaving, and hunting, the customs of the Maori and *pakeha* were more than similar. Michael decided to tackle the matter the very next week.

***

The opportunity to do so arose when Lizzie once again weighed and appraised their gold yield. She found that it was enough. As sorry as she was for the end of their dreamlike summer in the mountains, it was time to break camp.

"Good, then I'll ride to the plains and look for land," Michael said. His heart pounded with his declaration, which he hoped would not lead them to a fight.

"On your own?" asked Lizzie, taken aback. "Shouldn't we do that together?"

Michael shook his head. "Dear, with your riding style"—he smiled broadly, hoping it would take the edge from his words—"we wouldn't make it to the plains in three months."

Lizzie furrowed her brow. "But we could take our wagon. We could ride to Tuapeka and yoke my horse on again. I don't think he's forgotten how it works."

Michael laughed at this idea. "Of course a horse doesn't forget how to pull a wagon, Lizzie, but the wagon will slow us down. I'm faster alone on my horse."

"Why are we in such a hurry?" she asked. "It's only just February. Fall hasn't begun yet. It will be weeks before it's too cold and wet to drive overland. The roads around Christchurch are supposed to be well paved now, so a little rain won't be a problem. And as for the farm, you're going to commission someone for that anyway."

Anger welled up in Michael. True, he had not believed she would take his assertion completely without reservation. The fact that she had already made plans was too much. He did not need help buying land, but she probably already knew with whom he would need to talk.

"I thought I'd talk with the Ngai Tahu myself, actually."

Lizzie nodded patiently. "Another possibility. But then you really need me. Your Maori—"

"Good God, Lizzie, don't you understand that I would like to do something myself for once?" Michael exploded. His eyes flashed with rage. "If you show up to the Maori, they'll probably greet you with open arms, singing and dancing until they collapse, and then they'll lay their land at your feet."

Lizzie did not understand. "And?" she asked. "What's wrong with that? If they give us a good price because I have friends in the tribe, then that's even better. We can buy more sheep and build a lovely house and—"

"What if I want a house that's already been built?" asked Michael. He knew he was being petulant and unkind, but his frustration had grown too great.

"Then you shouldn't talk with the Maori. At most they'll have a meeting house to offer," laughed Lizzie. "What's wrong, Michael? Are you upset about something?"

"Upset? Me? You wouldn't let things get so that I could be upset. Before I can worry about something, you've long since arranged it. Can't you just stay out of something for once, Lizzie? Can't you just let me do something?"

"But Michael, we both want to live in the house. And the land is for our children. So why do you want to go alone?"

"Because that's the custom, Lizzie," Michael roared at her. "*Tikanga*, if you prefer. The man brings his wife home. The man builds the nest; the woman watches the kids. Don't you understand that?"

Lizzie furrowed her forehead. "I'm supposed to watch the kids? But Michael, so far we've done everything together."

Michael leaped to his feet. "Together, you call it? When you give the orders, and I follow? I have a different notion of togetherness." He began to pack his things.

Lizzie's patience was wearing thin. Fine, if he wanted to fight . . . "Well, my ideas haven't been all that bad," she said sharply, "if you have six pounds of pure gold to build a nest with."

"I knew you would rub my nose in that at some point." Michael stuffed clothing into his saddlebags. "But now it's my turn, Lizzie. I'm the sheep farmer. I find the house and the land. I buy the animals. I—"

"Well, I hope you know more about wool than gold. You see, I don't want to clean up after the sheep. It's enough that I always have to clean up after you. After whatever crazy plan to flee Australia in a rowboat or all the fuss about Mary Kathleen."

Michael glared at her. "You just can't let go of that, can you, Lizzie? That I had the gall to look at a girl before you. And what's more, a better one. A gentle, beautiful, virtuous girl."

Lizzie bristled. Until then, she had not granted the fight too much importance. Now she was hurt, and her gentle blue eyes sparked with fury.

"Then it's better you don't build a house, Michael. Better you take the money and start a church. Dedicated to the ghost of Mary Kathleen. Maybe you can even have her made a saint, though I'm sure that's more expensive than six pounds of gold. So you'll have to shear a few sheep or butcher whales or any one of those things you could have done to get rich without me. Go to hell, Michael Drury! And don't come back until you've put your ghosts back where they belong."

Michael bit his lip. She was right, of course. He'd gone too far. He should never have compared her to Kathleen. No more.

"Lizzie, Lizzie, I'm sorry. I do love you." He wanted to take her into his arms, but Lizzie shook him off.

"I don't believe you, Michael," she said calmly. "And I can't compete with a ghost. Just go, Michael. Find a house, build a nest, or a church, or a barn—you can take all the gold, except for Ann's share. I'll pan a little longer and then—"

"Lizzie, don't," pleaded Michael. "I didn't mean it like that. I don't want to lose you; I just want to do something myself, I . . ."

Lizzie felt the wisdom of old Hainga within her. She could not help herself from saying one last word for the road. "So go and increase your *mana*, Michael," she sighed. "If that's what you have to do. Maybe you'll increase it serving the spirits, who knows? I'll stay with the tribe a while. Hainga asked me to, so I'll do her the favor. Maybe I still have something to learn. But no more than a few months, Michael. Maybe until winter. If you're not back by then—free of Mary Kathleen's ghost—then I'll look for something else."

Lizzie did not allow him to give her a farewell kiss. She sat still and silent until he had packed his things and saddled his horse. Only when she heard him ride away did she stand up and prepare herself for the hike to the village. She thought about how the spirits were guiding her to live with the Maori; she could have done that more than ten years ago. She thought of Kahu Heke, for whom she could have been a queen.

Chapter 3

Kahu Heke had not yet been elected chief. That was largely because his uncle, Kuti Haoka, still led the Ngati Pau. It was also because Kahu Heke had passed through years of change that only rarely led him to his tribe or let him find peace there. His parting with Lizzie had left him restless. Long after their escape in the chief's canoe, Lizzie's image came to him—her soft long hair, her warm smile, and her blue eyes that were so different from the mostly dark eyes of his tribe's girls. For Kahu, the sky was reflected in her eyes, the sky on a spring day. Not yet the shining blue of summer, but still a promise. He had loved her clever manner, her courage, and her devotion. Kahu Heke had known there was another man. No girl lived as cloistered as Lizzie had in her years with Mr. Busby if she was not living from dreams, whether lovely or dashed dreams. Kahu had seen the reflection of both in Lizzie's eyes. But she had never spoken of the man, and at some point she had to forget him.

In the first years after Kahu had left Lizzie on the South Island, he had wished for nothing more than to take the place of this stranger in her heart. To be closer to her in spirit, he had returned to the *pakeha*. He applied for work on their farms, at first even in viniculture because it meant so much to Lizzie. It was not hard for him to find employment with James Busby, but when he tasted his wine for the first time, Kahu knew he could learn nothing about winemaking there, so he went on to Auckland, where the *pakeha* had already established a flourishing community. Though it pained him, he invested half a month's salary in a bottle of good French Bordeaux—and then could better understand what drew Lizzie to winemaking. The deep-red wine tasted earthy but possessed an aroma of ripe fruit, berries, and apples. It caressed the tongue, velvety as a kiss.

Kahu had gained access to the new university's library and quickly learned that the quality of the wine depended only in part on the vintner. Mr. Busby might have been doing everything right with pressing his wine, but the grapes and the soil in which they grew played a role. Indeed, everything had to fit together, the sun and rain, too, so the wine could reveal a particular taste.

It would take decades of trying different varieties of grapes and harvest times to produce a union between the soil of his homeland and a suitable grape variety that resembled the kiss of the gods. Mr. Busby lacked the patience and imagination. Lizzie might have the passion, but not the knowledge. And Kahu lacked all of it.

Handling animals suited Kahu more, and for a time he hired on to a sheep farm near Auckland and did well for himself, but in the end, he was not content to work for the *pakeha*. Above all, Kahu was interested in his people's rights. He regretted that he had not gone farther with his formal education among the whites. It would have been best to study law, in order to strike back at the *pakeha* with their own weapons of word.

Kahu was a master of *whaikorero*, rhetoric. He could trumpet his outrage at the injustices his people encountered at the hands of the immigrants from the Old World. However, no echo came from the tribes. If Maori and *pakeha* fought, it was only over individual issues, and the *iwi* and *hapu* ended the fighting as soon as they reached a settlement. The natives thought it right that the whites should govern themselves in their cities according to their customs, so long as they could hold on to their customs in the countryside.

Kahu Heke, who took a longer view and had studied European history, foresaw a catastrophe. The whites always took friendliness for weakness; that would be no different in New Zealand than in their old homeland. They let the Maori be, as long as they did not need their land. The *pakeha* numbers were growing, however. Kahu saw the ships in their harbors and their cities spreading outward; one day they would lay their hands on that land too. Kahu would have been happy to arm his people against that, but no one listened to him.

His self-appointed task of being the intermediary between the *pakeha* and the tribes kept him in contact with the Ngai Tahu, and this was how he occasionally got news about Lizzie.

Kahu had heard of Lizzie's tavern and Michael's distillery in Kaikoura. Her adaptability charmed him: if she could not make wine, she made whiskey—or got her man to do so. The Maori, however, claimed there was nothing between Lizzie and the Irish sheep shearer and distiller. Kahu wondered if that were true—recently, he had caught word that they had appeared on the Tuapeka River. Kahu no longer pictured Lizzie so clearly. He had gotten used to not having her around, and other goals had emerged for him.

Although Kuti Haoka was still in good health, he was getting quite old. He would soon have to give up his title of chief, and this was Kahu's last chance to win more influence among his people so that he might follow his uncle. Thus, Kahu returned to his tribe, hunted, fished, advised people, and told stories. He increased his *mana*, and his heart beat more heavily when the chieftain finally ordered him to come to him.

"My son," said Kuti Haoka. He led his nephew onto a plateau overlooking the *marae* and stood tall there. Kahu kept his distance—the chieftain of the Ngati Pau was *tapu*, and not even his shadow could fall on one of his subjects. "I've known you since your birth, but I still do not know what I'm to think of you. You seem unable to decide whether you want to live with us or the *pakeha*, but the priests say this is your fate. You are meant to wander between the worlds. Now the time has come for you to settle down. I am old. I will soon return to Hawaiki. Someone must lead the tribe after me, and the line would point to you. So what of you? And what of the woman you chose? The gods welcome your choice. The priests have asked them many times. Your fate lies in darkness, but the union is blessed. So, where is she? When will you bring her here? When will you take my office?"

Kahu Heke had expected something like this and hoped for it too—it was only these questions about the woman he was supposed to have chosen that irritated him.

"*Ariki*, which woman?" he asked.

The chieftain arched his brows. "The *pakeha wahine*, who else? You've given her plenty of time to herself. Soon she will no longer be able to bear children."

"*Ariki*, I have not seen her in years. She does not think of me and does not want me. When I become chieftain, I'll take one of the girls from the tribe."

Kuti Haoka shook his head—ever dignified with his long hair bound into warrior knots. "That is not what the spirits intend. You should have taken my daughter, but the gods gave me no daughter. The *pakeha wahine* is meant for you. See that you find her if you want my office. If not, there will be someone else for chief. *Kia tu tika ai te whare tapu o Ngati Pau.*"

May the sacred house of the Ngati Pau last forever. Once the chief finished his speech with the traditional words, he turned and walked away—very slowly, carefully, ever alert. His shadow could not fall on any field; no branch of a tree could touch his air. An *ariki* led a lonely life.

Kahu thought it over. It was his duty to strive for the chieftain's office. Not just to his tribe but to all his people. They would listen to the *ariki* of the Ngati Pau. In the Maori villages and the *pakeha* cities. Again, he had the idea of having himself elected *kingi*—perhaps he should court the daughter of the current *kingi*? But that was a matter for another day. The chief had given him clear instructions as to his first wife. The spirits of the Ngati Pau insisted on a union with Elizabeth. Now he only needed to convince her of this idea. As he went back to the village, he whistled to himself. It was rare that the will of the spirits and the will of a person coincided so nicely.

***

Kahu Heke did not take the chieftain's canoe to sail around the North Island this time but had a tribe of the Ngati Pau ferry him across on the shortest route to the South Island. Before that, he wandered across the North Island, speaking to the representatives of the various tribes and assuring them of his friendly intentions—now, as a visitor, and later, as *ariki* of his tribe. The *powhiri*, the ceremony that on the South Island was more of a traditional game, could become bitterly serious here. The tribes on Te Ika-a-Maui had always warred with each other. Kahu was determined to unite them now against the *pakeha*. The Maori had to strengthen their position, for better or worse, in war or peace. Kahu knew that Kuti Haoka hoped for peace. He had dedicated his life to this peace, although he had to fight often enough. Surely the attempt to bring white blood into the chieftain's line of the Ngati Pau aimed at such a peaceful solution. The eldest in the tribe were thinking more of future generations. Kuti Haoka's mention of Lizzie getting older—she might now be turning thirty—and the necessity of producing children with her as soon as possible spoke for themselves.

After his crossing, stormy this time, Kahu traveled across the South Island, visiting the *pakeha* settlements and finding them smaller and more manageable than the cities on the North Island. Naturally, Christchurch and Dunedin were growing, but in comparison to Wellington and Auckland, they were still villages. And here, there were hardly any conflicts between Maori and *pakeha*. The Ngai Tahu mostly kept away from the cities, but they were pleased with the price their land had fetched. The farmers in the plains hired the Maori as shepherds and respected their *tapu*. The land was big enough. Why should they fight about the settling, lumbering, or grazing of this or that grove or mountain?

In turn, it seemed to Kahu that the Ngai Tahu adapted to the whites' way of life. They wore their clothing, sent their children to missionary schools, and often converted—at least halfheartedly—to Christianity. Only a few of the younger generation still wore *moko*, and the strict customs of earlier times were slipping into oblivion. No one cared where the shadow of his chieftain fell. Kahu quickly saw that the Ngai Tahu were not at all likely to be talked into an uprising.

Finally, he reached the gold prospects in Otago, where he was horrified by the destruction of the land. He hardly stopped, instead continuing into the mountains. Somewhere in this region lived the tribe that had taken Lizzie in.

The Ngai Tahu village was hard to find, and although he was an experienced Maori warrior, he wandered for some time before finding it. Finally, Kahu met a Maori girl who led him willingly to her relatives. Haikina, a daughter of the *tohunga*, Hainga, had attended a missionary school in Dunedin and was on her way back to the village.

Kahu followed the tall, slender girl over paths along streams and the river. Haikina wore the clothing of the whites, but she tied her skirt up high so she could move more easily in the wilderness. Kahu soon realized that although she had learned from the whites, they had not taken her in. The two former missionary students laughed as they exchanged stories about their teachers and priests. Haikina had let herself be baptized, too, but viewed the question of the whites' gods skeptically. Finally, Kahu asked her about Lizzie, but the girl had only heard in the prospector's camp that a white woman was supposed to be digging for gold near her village. She did not know any more, since she had not been with her tribe in almost a year.

Haikina's mother and friends greeted her enthusiastically. Even the chieftain deigned to speak a few words to her. As *tohunga*'s daughter, she possessed a high rank, and many important practical and spiritual duties would fall to her. Right away Hainga gave her a decisive role in the *powhiri* ceremony with which Kahu Heke was welcomed into the village. The girl did not agree with her role, and she made the point that she had not danced the *haka* in four years, but Hainga insisted. The visitor was a future chieftain; he had a right to princesses in his welcome party.

Kahu let the praying, singing, and dancing pass over him. He would have preferred to be led directly to Lizzie's camp after arriving in the village. However, that would have been more than impolite, and on the North Island one could interpret it as a hostile act. So Kahu played along and reluctantly began with his greeting speech. Casually, he let his gaze move over the group of dancers and girls playing music—and froze. Between the Maori girls stood a *pakeha*, a petite woman, hardly taller than anyone. Kahu saw her long, dark-blonde hair, silky but easily tangled. Pale-blue eyes like the sky in spring or the sea on a cloudy day. His heart pounded. Lizzie, his Elizabeth, stood beside the girls applauding the dancers. Kahu could hardly wait for the end of the ceremony.

He was so stunned that he had to be sure he wasn't imagining his Elizabeth. "Who is that?" he asked Mahuika, a student of Hainga's. She had been permitted the honor of letting out the *karanga*, and now she handed the visitor the first bite of food.

The young priestess grinned. "Erihapeti," she said. Elizabeth. The Ngai Tahu now seemed to have an equivalent for every *pakeha* name. "And you're the reason the clouds hang over her. At least, that's what Hainga says."

"I know her," Kahu admitted. "But what is she doing here?"

Until then, Kahu had not believed the spirits interfered all that often in the lives of men.

"She's waiting," Mahuika said. "She's waiting for a man."

Kahu seized his forehead. That couldn't be. "Come now, how would she know that I was coming?"

Mahuika laughed. "She's waiting for a *pakeha*," she specified. "She is—how do you say? Engaged." Mahuika used the English word. There was no equivalent in the Maori language.

Kahu pursed his lips. "I've come to retrieve her," he said. "The *tohunga* of the Ngati Pau would like to see her at my side."

The young *tohunga* student arched her eyebrows. "Oh? Yet she sees herself elsewhere. Where her man sees her, no one knows. Hainga said it, the clouds. Her fate is unclear. There's no reason not to try your luck."

Kahu hardly dared to hope he could spend time with Lizzie that first evening. An honored visitor, especially one with rank as high as the future chieftain of the Ngati Pau, rarely came in contact with the regular members of a tribe. But to his amazement, Lizzie was also called to the circle of *tohunga* and elders. He saw from her face how embarrassing it was for her to be included. Why was it so unpleasant for her? How did she suddenly hold such a high rank? Whatever the reason, it was good that the tribe esteemed her so highly. That simplified Kahu's plans.

Kahu Heke sat next to her by the fire and handed her some food. "Elizabeth, you're just as beautiful as back when I brought you to Te Waka-a-Maui." He spoke to her in his language. "And you've become what I always hoped. Even if you didn't want to."

Lizzie shrugged. She was nervous sitting next to him. The other girls were already looking at her questioningly. Kahu should be trying for Haikina or one of the chieftain's daughters, not her.

"Hainga sees the work of the spirits here," she informed him.

Kahu laughed. "And the *pakeha* say: Man proposes and God disposes."

Lizzie smiled. She had forgotten how witty he could be—and how irresistibly *pakeha*. In the last few weeks since Michael had gone, she had missed this repartee. As a people, the Maori seemed not particularly witty to her. Their humor was bawdier and more straightforward than that of the whites. Though she still hadn't mastered their language. Perhaps subtleties escaped her.

"Since when does Kahu Heke repeat the *pakeha*'s words?" She teased Kahu. "Wouldn't you prefer to throw them out of Aotearoa?"

Kahu shrugged. "There are just too many, and my people don't see the danger they present. But now, tell me about yourself and the gods. They tell me you have a fiancé?"

Lizzie nodded, but her eyes were sad. "I hope so, but he's away." Why should she make a secret of it? Kahu would hear everything the Ngai Tahu knew about her relationship with Michael anyway. "In fact, he meant to buy a house for us, but now . . ."

"Will Kupe come back?" Kahu gave her a mocking smile.

That was the Maori expression for "You might have seen the last of him." The saying referred to Kupe, the first settler of New Zealand. He had promised his friends on Hawaiki he would come back—but he never did.

Lizzie began to brood. She had just started to feel more comfortable in Kahu's company. The other tribesmen were making music again and dancing and, at least apparently, paying less attention to Lizzie and the future chieftain.

"What is that supposed to mean?" she asked mistrustfully. "You're always talking to me about Kupe and Kura-maro-tini." Apparently she did not know the saying, even though her Maori had gotten much better.

Kahu laughed. "Because every time I see you, I feel the urge to run off with you," he teased her.

According to the legend, Kura-maro-tini had belonged to another, and Kupe had killed her husband and abducted her. It was on their flight that they discovered New Zealand—Aotearoa.

"Well, we don't see each other all that often," Lizzie said, taking a drink from the bottle Kahu handed her.

He had brought two bottles supposed to contain whiskey, and the Ngai Tahu passed them around. Until then, Lizzie hadn't had any—whiskey always reminded her of Michael. Only the spirits knew where this had been distilled.

"Tell me how you've been, Kahu Heke. Do you have a wife—or several? Any children?"

Kahu shook his head. "I've been working for the *pakeha*. For Mr. Busby first, in fact."

Lizzie's eyes lit up when Kahu talked about winemaking. For an enchanted hour, he had her eager attention.

"I tried once or twice to ask him whether other grape varieties would do better in our soil. But Mr. Busby was stubborn. He said that Riesling grew in Europe under very similar conditions to those in New Zealand. He only meant the weather. As for everything else, Hainga would say Mr. Busby doesn't listen to the whispering of the spirits."

Kahu smiled—and Lizzie noticed that his tattoos suddenly no longer bothered her.

"I may have become more *pakeha* over the years," said Kahu Heke. "But you're much more Maori. You hear the whispering of the spirits. I thought of a kiss when I tasted truly good wine."

Lizzie raised her eyebrows high. "A kiss? That must have been rather rich wine—red wine, right? It's true that Bordeaux sits on the tongue like, like a caress." She blushed. "I have one last bottle left in my tent," she continued drily. "But it's a lighter white wine, from Italy. We can drink it together. We'll see what you taste. I taste peach, maybe a little honey."

Again, Lizzie took on that dreamy expression that Kahu had only ever seen on her face when the subject was wine. Really, thinking about her man should provoke this response. Yet her supposed fiancé seemed to be more worrisome than anything. Kahu was determined to seize this opportunity.

"We'll see. I'd be happy to drink it with you. By the way, can you still catch fish, *pakeha wahine*, like we showed you?" Kahu brushed her hand lightly, as if by accident.

Lizzie laughed but drew her fingers away—not in shock, more unsure. Not a clear no. Kahu waited for an answer.

"That's not something you forget," she said. "On the contrary. I, I have much more practice now."

"I'll believe that when I see it," he teased her. "Would you like to show me tomorrow? In this stream where you pan for gold?"

A shadow crossed Lizzie's face. It wasn't just where she had panned for gold; it was where she had been happy with Michael. And now Kahu wanted to go there with her. Kahu, who apparently felt something for her. After all, he had been flirting with her since he sat down. Lizzie did not know if she was ready to show another man her prospect, but she could hardly say no. Kahu Heke was an old friend and an honored guest of the tribe.

"We could take your wine."

Lizzie stiffened. "Not, there," she stammered. "The, the way up is difficult. We shouldn't get drunk there."

Kahu hardly thought half a bottle of wine would get them drunk, but it wasn't important. She had agreed to spend the next day with him. Whether at her prospect or somewhere else, with wine or not, he did not really care. The main thing was, he would have her to himself.

"Fine, no wine and no whiskey." He smiled. "If the gods want us intoxicated, Elizabeth, we won't need drinks."

***

The day before, at the celebrations, Lizzie had looked like a Maori girl to Kahu. But now that he was alone with her, she had put on her *pakeha* clothes again and hidden her hair beneath her straw hat. Instead of dancing with swaying hips like the girls of the tribe, she moved with hurried steps past the river and then the stream. She did not say much as they went. Kahu followed in silence.

After a two-hour march, they reached the needle-shaped rocks and Kahu let himself fall into the grass. Lizzie remained standing.

"Do you want to fish now?" she asked.

Kahu shook his head. "Let's pan for gold first," he said. "Maybe we'll find a giant nugget and become rich in an instant."

Lizzie smiled. "I did not realize you were so in need. Is the chief of the Ngati Pau destitute? I do need to give you back the money you lent me long ago. How much interest do you want?"

Kahu made a dismissive gesture. "It was a present. Think no more of it. As for my people: the Ngati Pau have been selling land; they have everything they need. I think that a mistake, however. If you make me rich today, we'll take the land back."

He slid closer to her. She knew he was no longer speaking of gold; there were other riches. The gold pan seemed to vibrate in her hand. If she was going to be at the rocks, then she wanted to work.

"Have you done this before?" she asked.

Kahu shook his head and admitted he had never held a gold pan before. Lizzie sighed. She would have to show him and would hardly get to work, herself.

He was so clumsy with the pan that he almost fell in the stream. Lizzie had to laugh. She took the pan from his hands, shook it with a practiced flick of the wrist—and enjoyed his wide-eyed expression when bits of gold appeared.

"Aye, that's how I felt too," she said. "Gold, even on the first try. It's not like that everywhere, Kahu. On the contrary. For this much gold, people down at the camp often have to pan or dig all day."

"And you two did this here all summer, huh?" asked Kahu. "So, you must be rich."

Lizzie shrugged. "I gave Michael all the gold," she admitted. "For the house—or for a church." She sighed.

"For a church?" Kahu inquired, confused. "Is he a cleric?"

Lizzie laughed, distressed. "Forget it. In any case, he has the gold, and I hope he comes back with it someday—or with something worth as much."

Kahu smiled comfortingly. "If not, you can always pan for more," he said, at ease. "If I help, it'll go fast." He looked more closely at the small, pinprick traces of gold. "It's pretty, this gold of yours. It glitters. Like your hair in the sunlight."

Cautiously, Kahu reached into the pan, took a few gold flecks out, removed Lizzie's straw hat and threw it onto the bank, and sprinkled the flecks into her hair.

"Are you mad?" Lizzie laughed. "Do you know how much that's worth?"

"Not as much as a single strand of your hair," he said softly. "That hair is sacred, Elizabeth. In the chieftain's hair lives the god Rauru."

"Oh?" she teased. "Has he already moved in with you? You must be careful not to comb him out. Or do chieftains not comb their hair?"

Kahu left that open. "If I comb him out, then I have to breathe him in again," he explained. "That goes like this." He stroked her hair and then audibly sniffed at his fingers.

Lizzie giggled. "Do you want to pan for more gold or catch fish?" she asked.

"Do you want to be rich or full?"

She pretended to think it over. "Rich."

He rolled his eyes. "A *pakeha*, a typical *pakeha*. What am I even doing here?"

"Catching fish," laughed Lizzie. "Get going. You make us full, and I'll make us rich."

After Kahu fished, he roasted the catch, along with vegetables they'd brought along, on a fire he built. He used his gold pan as a grill, which amused Lizzie again. Now they sat, full and tired, beside the fire and were almost as close to each other as when they had spent day and night together in the canoe. Lizzie felt instinctively that Kahu's promise back then still held. He would not touch her if she did not want it.

"Michael didn't like that," she suddenly said.

"What did he not like?" Kahu asked without looking at her.

"That I was the one who made us rich. First with the tavern and then with the gold. He would have preferred to do it himself, and I, I was supposed to cook and manage the house. Only we wouldn't have had a house. Michael, he doesn't have much luck."

Kahu furrowed his brow. "Luck?" he asked. "A *pakeha* saying comes to mind instead, but I'd better not say it, or I'll risk your being mad at me."

"It's not that he's lazy. Only, he's, he's very honorable, very straightforward. Yes, that's it: straightforward. And I, well, once he said I have a crooked way of thinking."

"In any case, he has a problem with a woman who has a great deal of *mana*. That happens often," said Kahu.

"You think I have a great deal of *mana*?" Lizzie asked, taken aback. The thought had never occurred to her.

"Like any queen, Elizabeth." Kahu laughed. "Seriously, Erihapeti, it can't have escaped you that they celebrate you as a warrior. You have the *mana* of a *tohunga*, and your beloved cannot bear that. Like so many men—Maori or *pakeha*, makes no difference."

"But it would not bother you, at all," Lizzie said suspiciously. "That's what you mean to say with that, isn't it?"

Kahu grew serious. "With me," he said, cautiously feeling his way with what he wanted to convey, "it's somewhat different."

Lizzie thought briefly. "Of course," she said. "Because you'll be chief. Naturally, you'd marry a woman with a great deal of *mana*."

Though Lizzie knew nothing about dynastic marriages in Maori tribes, she imagined that the nobility married among themselves just as in England.

"Not quite." Kahu bit his lip. He should now talk about the way chieftains lived with their wives—or rather, how they did not. A chieftain of the Ngati Pau was always alone. His wife was only permitted to enter his house after special ceremonies. If he told Lizzie that, she would ask more questions and would never go with him or agree to be his wife. "It's just that the life of a chieftain with his wife takes a different form."

Lizzie furrowed her brow. Then she smiled. "Right, because the Maori are careful to divide the labor of men and women. Like the Busbys did. Mr. Busby had his work, and Mrs. Busby exercised her *mana* on the servants and children. Michael and I could divide things up that way too." She laughed. "Thank you, Kahu. I already feel better. I would never have thought that the problem was my *mana*. I always thought it was Mary Kathleen."

Though this was not the turn Kahu Heke had hoped the conversation would take, it at least distracted Lizzie from asking uncomfortable questions.

The rest of the day passed harmoniously. Kahu showed Lizzie how to make traps for birds, and she taught him more about the art of panning for gold. In the evening, she lit another fire, and they roasted the red-feathered bird called a weka. They did not return to the village until after dark, and when they did, the tribe members teased them about spending their day doing more than talking.

Kahu was pleased with how the day had gone. Most of all, it made him happy that Lizzie seemed no longer to shrink back from his face. If she no longer feared the *moko*, he would manage to win her over. As long as this Michael fellow did not return.

Chapter 4

Michael did not return to Otago. Not in autumn and not as autumn turned into winter. Lizzie was hurt, of course, but Kahu Heke's presence consoled her some. The future chief of the Ngati Pau was now courting her expressly, and he made it clear to her every day how much he respected her *mana*. Kahu gave her presents, and he brought her the game he hunted so she could prepare it for the tribe.

The tribe accepted Lizzie more all the time. The women showed her traditional crafts, and they tried to teach her singing and dancing, though Lizzie didn't much enjoy performing. Perhaps she did have *mana*, but she took no joy in showing it off. She preferred to let Hainga introduce her to native healing, though she looked skeptically at the many prayers and *tapu* bound up with it. Naturally, she would ask the spirits for permission to cut a plant if Hainga insisted. But why the petals of certain plants were to be harvested only after a very particular ritual and only by the *tohunga* was not clear to her.

While Lizzie had always wanted to lead a righteous life, she was not a spiritual person. Immersing herself in prayer and meditation was foreign to her. Lizzie did not like to look for the meaning of the stories her native friends told around the fire. She liked exciting adventure stories that ended with the heroine sinking into the arms of her hero. The circuitous and often somewhat monotonously presented fairy tales of the Maori still did not quite make sense to Lizzie. She even preferred the biblical parables, which were at least short and easy to follow.

Lizzie missed the reverend's company. He had only visited her once in the Maori village and seemed not to feel especially comfortable there. Lizzie suspected that ever since he had witnessed Ian Coltrane's death, the spirits had made him a little anxious. On top of that, Peter Burton seemed sad, though Lizzie had no idea why. It seemed that for the time being at least, he had given up the battle for her soul.

With all of this, Kahu's company was more welcome. He was one of few people with whom she was able to speak English, and they had plenty to talk about, including viniculture, James Busby's politics, and even the Maori and *pakeha* coexisting.

Lizzie and Kahu spent many hours together every day, and she began to find the young Maori more and more attractive. Kahu was tall and wide-shouldered. His hair was thick and dark like Michael's but straight instead of curly. When he undid the warrior knots into which he usually tied his hair, it fell long over his shoulders, and Lizzie noticed that his tension seemed to fall away too. She liked when he sang for her—not the martial *haka* but deep ballads his people seemed to have brought with them from Hawaiki, where palms rustled and where nights were warm, even in winter.

In Otago, it was now beginning to freeze. Lizzie shivered at night in her tent no matter how many blankets she piled on herself.

"I should go to Dunedin," she said one morning as she warmed herself on the fire. "To some inn with a fireplace and a bathhouse; that would be heaven."

"You can sleep in the sleeping lodge," said Haikina.

Over the last few weeks, Lizzie had become friends with her. Haikina also spoke English, and she confessed to Lizzie that, despite the strict oversight at school, she had taken several *pakeha* lovers. Like most of the frank Maori girls, she was always happy to exchange stories about the qualities of the various men and never got tired of discussing Lizzie's peculiar relationship with Michael.

"You could let me warm you," said Kahu Heke. He used increasingly clear words, even in front of other members of the tribe.

Lizzie blushed. Kahu's wooing increased her *mana*, and it flattered her, of course, that a chieftain obviously wanted her for his wife. She had also heard of Kahu's ambition to have himself chosen *kingi* of all Maori, and she sometimes dreamed of life as his queen. Naturally, she had no real sense of what that would be like, but she imagined it as rather luxurious. At least on the North Island, the life of the chief's family seemed to take place outside the tribe. She had never seen Kuti Haoka's house; it could be a gorgeous palace. Kahu gave her no clear answers when she cautiously posed questions. But she did not want to show too clear an interest and was careful not to broach the subject too often.

The first real month of winter was coming to an end, and the New Year's festival approached. The Maori celebrated their New Year—Tou Hou—on the first new moon after the appearance of the Matariki, the Pleiades, in the night sky. Tou Hou would take place in the last days of June. The Ngai Tahu expected more guests: their brothers from Kaikoura were coming back from their time in the mountains and would stay a while with them.

Lizzie thought sorrowfully of Chris Timlock when Kahu showed her the constellation. She had given Aputa the gold pendant, and the girl had been ecstatic, but the Pleiades would always remind Lizzie of Chris Timlock's senseless death, for which she blamed herself—at least in part. She should have been able to foresee how less fortunate men would react to Chris and Michael's sudden luck with their prospecting.

"The stars can't help it." Kahu comforted Lizzie when she told him the story. "Just look at how beautiful they are. Hopefully they'll shine as brightly on New Year's Eve as now."

Lizzie nodded. She had long since learned that for the Maori a clear New Year's Eve promised a warm year and good harvest. For now, though, it was cold. Kahu wrapped her in a blanket, and she even let his arm rest around her shoulder. Encouraged, he pulled her a little closer.

"We celebrate New Year's Eve with music and dancing, like you," he whispered to her. "But this time, I wish our dances were like yours. Then I could pull you to me, and we would be one."

Lizzie did not respond, but she did not reject him. It was nice to feel warmth—anyone's warmth. Beneath the starry sky, she yearned for Michael more than usual. She still nursed the vague hope of hearing from him one day soon. She was sure that Tane, Michael's old friend, would come to the festival to celebrate with his family. Afterward, he would return with his *iwi* to the sea.

***

459

Just as the first fires were burning and the *tohunga* was waiting for the moon to renew its light in the Pleiades, Lizzie joined the men with whom Michael's friend was sharing his whiskey.

Tane was already tipsy and in good spirits. He was happy to show off what he knew.

"Michael? Was briefly in Kaikoura. He talk with Fyffe, very great Michael. Now, he's rich. Gave away whiskey. We celebrate all night. Claudia from Green Arrow wants to marry him—right away."

Lizzie bit her lip. Michael was celebrating in taverns and sleeping with other women. Claudia of all people! Was she able to satisfy her old regular? Lizzie wished she could rage with anger, but in truth, she only felt limitless sadness. All that time, all that love she had devoted to Michael, and it was supposed to end now, like this?

Then she squared herself. It was New Year's Eve. She did not want to be sad anymore. What was good enough for Michael would hardly do for her.

Lizzie retrieved her last bottle of wine from her tent. "We'll drink this afterward," she said to Kahu, who looked at her with surprise.

Did he notice the tear streaks on her face? Lizzie wiped them away determinedly and smiled. Kahu handed her the whiskey bottle, which Tane had just passed around.

"Here, you look like you need a drink of something stronger than your wine. We'll drink that when the stars appear."

When the stars finally appeared in the sky, there were prayers and dancing, but Lizzie had drunk several gulps of whiskey by then and could hardly follow the ceremonies.

"Look how small we are compared with the stars," said Kahu softly. Lizzie sat, calm and quiet, beside him. So far, he had barely touched her, but now, he gently put his arm around her shoulders. "Can you still feel fear or sadness? Let their light flow into you, Elizabeth. Tonight everything becomes new."

Kahu opened the wine bottle as most of the tribesmen danced to greet the moon.

"Don't you also want to start anew, Elizabeth? On the North Island? As my wife?"

Lizzie was drunk on whiskey and wine, but not even that could really alleviate her sorrow. The music rained down on her ears. The rhythm of the *maka* may have enlivened the dancers, but for Lizzie it was only painful. She did not want to answer Kahu's question. But she did not want to be alone either.

"Let's go elsewhere," she said.

Kahu helped her to her feet and took the wine bottle. He led her away from the celebration grounds on the river, which swam in the starlight like a silver ribbon. The night was unbelievably clear. There would be frost. Lizzie's bed would be cold, would remain cold. Unless she allowed Kahu to kiss her.

Kahu spoke of a kiss like wine on her lips. He knew how to use pretty words, almost as well as Michael. Lizzie closed her eyes and snuggled into Kahu's arms. If only she could stop her thoughts. Michael and Claudia—the way that blonde whore had boasted about her regular customer. So, Michael was faithful in that way, at least. Lizzie wanted to laugh, but she could not. If she lay in Kahu's arms now, it would not be because she wanted revenge. She just did not want to be alone, not so mercilessly alone. And she did not want to be a whore. It was mad, she thought, to give herself to someone she did not really love—or did she? Lizzie laughed drily.

"What is it, Elizabeth?"

Elizabeth, a queen. That was her, what she wanted to be. Michael would marvel at what had become of little Lizzie: she was not a saint, no; not a Mary Kathleen—but not a Claudia either.

Mana. Lizzie had *mana.*

Everything spun around Lizzie, the stars, the moon, the forest on the river. But Kahu held her, safe and sound. He wanted her; he had come from the North Island just for her.

"Do you want to go with me, Elizabeth?" he asked.

Lizzie nodded, but she resisted when he led her to the meeting house.

"No, not in front of all the others, not the first night."

"But Elizabeth! Tonight should be our wedding night."

Lizzie laughed bitterly. "I haven't been a virgin in a long time, Kahu. I've had many men, more than I liked—as you know. But I've never had a man with thirty other people looking. That's too much. I can't do that."

"But you have to, if we—"

"The girls tell me you don't have to do it in front of everyone," Lizzie said. "You only need to share a bed. That's enough."

Kahu pulled her close. "Then we'll make it simple, Elizabeth. I can wait. I want—"

Lizzie pushed him away. She suddenly felt angry. "You don't even really want me, do you?" She knew she sounded shrill, and she hated herself for her hysteria. "You just want . . . what do you want, Kahu Heke?"

Kahu stroked Lizzie's hair soothingly. "Nothing, nothing. Calm yourself, Elizabeth. Of course I want you. Only you. I just wanted to do it right."

"Then do it right!" cried Lizzie. She ripped herself away from him. "Over there is my tent. Or take me under the stars like, like . . . Make me forget Michael, Kahu Heke. Make me finally forget him."

It was not the right reason to love someone, and she knew that. It was not fair to Kahu—and Lizzie marveled that he did not protest. She was drunk; she was taking him as a replacement for another. All of that should hurt him. He should push her away, let her go; he should . . .

Instead Kahu led her to his tent as if she'd never spoken the words. And he would have led her into the *wharenui*.

With her last spark of clear thought, Lizzie again asked herself what intentions the future Maori chieftain had as he carried her like a *pakeha* bride over the threshold of her tent. Then she sank into his touch and his warmth.

"You'll never leave me alone, right, Kahu?" she asked weakly. "You'll promise me that?"

Kahu kissed her, drunk on whiskey and wine himself, on excitement and disappointment. He should not have taken her that night. He knew she needed time to think, but when she thought too much, she asked too many questions. It was time to return to his tribe. The men of Kaikoura had reported, the day before, the death of Chief Kuti Haoka. The Ngati Pau would not wait forever before electing another. That night he gave in to Elizabeth's will, but the next day, their wedding would have to be officially sealed, and then he could be on his way. With the *pakeha wahine* as his wife, just as the priests had foreseen.

"I'll never leave you alone," he said. He knew in the same moment he offered her this promise that he had lied.

She would learn to accept it. She was the spirits' plaything.

***

When Lizzie woke up the next morning, Kahu had already left the tent. She had a headache, and while she knew what had happened the night before, she only vaguely recalled the details. Lizzie started to admonish herself, but there was no reason for that—Maori women took men when they wanted to, and in any case, Michael had nothing to hold against her.

Lizzie dressed, combed her hair, and went out to the women baking flatbread and roasting sweet potatoes. Her night with Kahu was doubtless the talk of all the women. She expected people to tease and congratulate her. It was unexpected when Hainga pulled her close and exchanged a *hongi* with her.

"I wish for you, daughter, that you bear your fate with dignity," the *tohunga* said. "May you give the *ariki* of the Ngati Pau children as numerous as the stars, under which you sealed your bond."

"Bond?" asked Lizzie, rubbing her forehead.

Hainga smiled. "Naturally, you must still spend a night in the *wharenui*—and they will conduct ceremonies when you first get to his tribe. Among us, all that is simpler. A man and woman make love among witnesses; then they are man and wife. But over there, well, you'll see."

The other women sat together, laughing and talking about dresses and wedding dances, presents, and customs of various tribes.

Haikina didn't join the women, and Lizzie, for whom the talk was uncomfortable, stayed close to her. She tried to remember more precisely what had happened the night before, and slowly her memory returned. Kahu had spoken of a promise of marriage, but he could not have taken that seriously. She had been completely drunk, after all. Though he had been pressuring her for a long time, and on New Year's Eve, new things should begin.

Lizzie was prepared to think the matter over. Kahu had been tender, a wonderful lover. But to marry him right away?

She was startled when Haikina suddenly whispered to her. "Lizzie?" She was the only one who still called Lizzie by her *pakeha* name. "I know it's none of my business. But I'd like to talk with you."

Lizzie was surprised Haikina was speaking English, but then she glanced at her and noticed Haikina's alert, concerned face. Apparently she did not want Hainga or the other women to understand what she had to discuss with Lizzie. The girl even seemed to shy away from Kahu, who was just then coming over to them. She lowered her head and let her long, black hair fall over her face as he sat next to Lizzie. Lizzie thought she saw Haikina blush. Was she in love with Kahu? Perhaps she was hurt because the intended chief of the Ngati Pau wanted a white wife and not a Ngai Tahu princess.

Kahu gave Lizzie a beaming smile. "Elizabeth," he said with a voice as soft as a caress. "I hope you've slept well. You did not freeze in my arms."

Lizzie nodded. He had kept her warm. She managed to smile back at him.

"And you see that everyone here is happy for us. Tonight there will be a celebration in our honor. To honor you, Elizabeth. My happiness knows no bounds."

He did not kiss her but instead put his nose and forehead against hers in the Maori way. Lizzie returned the sign of affection. She now recalled his promise. *I'll never leave you alone.* Perhaps it was foolish to hesitate.

And yet—Lizzie wanted to ask for postponement. Everything had happened too quickly the night before. She realized that the eyes of the tribe were fixed on Kahu and her. This wasn't a whispered promise between two people, a secret engagement. It seemed that Kahu had announced their planned engagement to the whole tribe. Lizzie felt dizzy. She could not back out—not without a scandal. She would hurt Kahu Heke, the man, deeply. And she would rob the Ngati Pau chieftain of his dignity. Lizzie bit her lip. She had to marry Kahu or throw herself in the river.

"I, I'm happy too," she said.

Perhaps she really would be too. At least she would no longer be alone.

Lizzie rubbed her temples. Her head still hurt. Then she heard Haikina's voice next to her again.

"Please, Lizzie," said the girl, still hiding behind her curtain of dark hair. "Please come speak with me. Maybe I don't have anything new to tell you, but . . . Say we're going to pick flowers. Or something else for the wedding. So the others will let us go alone."

Whatever she had to tell Lizzie seemed very important to Haikina.

Lizzie nodded at her friend. "We won't find any flowers in the middle of winter. I'll say we're going to weave a bridal garland."

Indeed, hoarfrost lay on the ferns and beech trees that formed the forest in this part of New Zealand. Surely it would snow soon. Plants for a garland would be hard to find; the excuse could not be very convincing.

Neither Hainga nor Kahu asked questions when Lizzie and Haikina left the village together. Everyone was busy with preparations for the celebration; a new year that began with a wedding would be especially lucky. It seemed normal to the Ngai Tahu that Lizzie would want to attend to a few *pakeha* customs before the night of nights.

Haikina and Lizzie wandered in silence up the mountain until the walking warmed them. Then they sat on a rock from which they could watch the village. Lizzie was not sure, but Haikina seemed to keep an eye on Kahu and Hainga.

"What's the matter?" Lizzie finally blurted out. "You, you're not mad at me, are you? I didn't encourage Kahu. I didn't even want to. It would, it would surely be more proper if he married you."

Haikina looked at Lizzie incredulously. "Me?" she asked. "What gave you that idea?"

"Well, because he, because he is going to be a chief, and you're the daughter of a *tohunga*. You make sense together."

Haikina laughed, but it did not sound very happy. "You think it's like one of the *pakeha* fairy tales, do you?" she asked. It could have been teasing, but it sounded bitter. "The prince rides out to find a princess somewhere in the distance?"

Lizzie nodded.

Haikina rolled her eyes and pulled her scarf tighter around her. "I thought as much," she continued, "but that's not how it is, Lizzie. The Maori rarely marry outside the tribe. That is especially true for the children of chieftains. In Maori fairy tales, the prince marries his sister."

"But that—"

"That's *tikanga*, Lizzie, since the time in Hawaiki. It's not just fairy tale. Depending on the tribe, it happens more or less often. Among the Ngai Tahu it rarely does anymore. Your missionaries saw to that. But throughout the North Island, it's still common."

Haikini waited for Lizzie to say something, but she was silent.

"If Kahu did not tell you that, I take it he did not mention all the other *tapu*," Haikini said.

Lizzie rubbed her forehead. "Kahu didn't tell me anything," she said bitterly. "Naturally, every tribe has this or that *tapu*, but—"

"There are special *tapu* that affect the life of the chieftain," Haikina said. "Strictly speaking, the whole person of the chief is *tapu*."

Lizzie frowned. "*Tapu* does mean untouchable, right?" she asked.

Haikina nodded. "For that reason the chieftain cannot live with his wife like, like the *pakeha* husband and wife, if that makes sense."

Lizzie shook her head. "No, it doesn't. What is this, Haikina? Are you trying to warn me about something? Please just tell me what you know. I, I don't feel good, and tonight . . ."

"Very well," Haikina said. "I don't feel good about this, myself, you see. I feel I'm betraying my people, but you must know what you are agreeing to if you marry a chieftain of the Ngati Pau. It begins with him not being able to live with you."

"What is that supposed to mean?" asked Lizzie, her mouth dry. She still heard Kahu's voice. *I'll never leave you alone.*

"The chieftain lives separated from all others, Lizzie. No one is allowed to enter his house. No one may touch the things he has touched. Once, even brushing past him was punishable by death. A cleansing ceremony is necessary should his shadow fall on another person."

"But, but how does he have children?" Lizzie asked nervously.

"His wife is allowed to visit him at certain times, but only after a special ceremony we call the *karakia*. You may also cook for him, but you cannot eat of it yourself, for his food is *tapu*. He cannot touch any eating or drinking vessel because afterward someone else might use it, and that would bring misfortune. So he is fed using special utensils, a calabash from which water is poured into his mouth without him touching it, and a feeding horn."

"A what?" Lizzie could not believe all this.

Haikina described the utensil to her. "And that's not all, Lizzie. His children, too, are *tapu*. You cannot wash them or comb their hair because to do that, you would need to touch them, and they are sacred. Chieftains' children are often rather unkempt until they learn to keep themselves halfway clean. And they will be taken from you as soon as possible."

"But, but how do the others handle it, the other chieftains' wives?" Lizzie felt as if she had been hit. Kahu should have told her all of this. Or did he plan to break from tradition?

"Like I said, most of them marry their sisters. They're used to it—and, naturally, of such high rank from birth that they are permitted to touch a *tapu* child. But not comb! The god Rauru lives in the chieftain's hair."

Kahu had told her that at least—but more as an anecdote. Lizzie hadn't thought he took it seriously.

Lizzie breathed deeply. "That may all be true, of course, Haikina," she said. "But don't you think Kahu will change it? He was in a *pakeha* school. He's Christian. At least—"

Haikina shook her head. "Lizzie, wake up. Is he asking you for a Christian wedding, or does he want to lie with you in the meeting house?"

"Both, both would work," cried Lizzie desperately. She felt exhausted and sad. The second man, the second betrayal.

Haikina laid her arm around Lizzie's shoulder. "Both would work, huh?" she asked harshly. "I wouldn't be surprised if Kahu also married you in a church. So that both *pakeha* and Maori would recognize the marriage."

"But then we could live together like a Christian couple," said Lizzie.

Haikina sighed. "And you will. Later. After he's first realized his will and become *kingi*. Once they invite you two to England and introduce you to the queen, or whatever else will serve the peace. But you don't really believe that Kahu will blindside all the tribes of the North Island by breaking the traditions around a chief's dignity, do you? He'll send his sons to *pakeha* schools. But in the early years, he won't let their mother comb the lice from their hair."

"That can't be true," whispered Lizzie—but she believed every word. Something had always stood between Kahu and her, an instinct that had warned her and saved her from following him straight into the meeting house.

Haikina shrugged. "Then ask him," she said. "Ask him why he's in such a hurry to make the marriage official. Ask him if engagement to you might not perhaps be a condition for him becoming *ariki*. I think I might have heard something about that. Please don't think that I mean anything bad by you. I'm not speaking from any jealousy. I wouldn't marry a chieftain of the Ngati Pau even if he was the only man I could ever share a bed with."

Lizzie pressed her forehead and nose against those of her friend. "Thank you, Haikina," she whispered. "I won't ask Kahu. Because I don't want him to lie anymore. I can't stand to hear any more excuses. I'm tired of it. Yesterday he swore that I would never be alone."

Lizzie followed Haikina into the village and retrieved her horse. She took some of her clothes and the gold she had panned over the last few weeks. She'd panned to keep busy after Michael left more than to become rich, but it was still a considerable amount. Once she exchanged it for money, she would be able to live on it for a while.

She tried simply to act and not to brood, but she couldn't. Despite all her exhaustion and headaches, she struggled with the echo of Haikina's words in her thoughts and feelings. And she started to register just how often Kahu had suppressed information and answers. He had boasted of wanting a wife with *mana*, but in truth, he had planned to bury her power under thousands of *tapu*.

With every memory of his excuses or lies, something in Lizzie seemed to die. Kahu might believe he loved her, but in truth, he only loved the *pakeha wahine*, a fitting queen for the *kingi*. And Michael had used her *mana* and then discarded her. In reality, he had only ever loved Kathleen.

Lizzie did not cry as she led her horse to the river, still unnoticed by the others in the village, who were excitedly preparing her wedding. She left her tent behind. She no longer needed it. Never again would she sleep under the stars. Never again would she think about the spirits. She didn't want to hear any more talk. No more about *mana*, no more about Elizabeth or about being a queen. No one told the truth—not the spirits; not even the *tohunga*, Hainga, had told her the truth. In the end, she remained Lizzie, the whore.

Lizzie hoped that Kahu would not follow her. She did not have any strength left to fight. That night she would sleep in her old cabin, and the next day she would continue on to Tuapeka and Dunedin. Someday, she might live and love again. But for now, she wanted to forget and to sleep. To dream herself out of this world.

Chapter 5

Michael Drury felt wretched when he returned to Otago. He hadn't enjoyed his journey at all—in fact, he had felt poorly from almost the very beginning, from the moment his anger at Lizzie dissipated. An anger for which there had been no real reason and which did not last long. Sure, Lizzie had thrown her old recriminations regarding Kathleen back at him, and he still reacted sensitively to those, but he had provoked her. Worse yet, he had behaved terribly toward her. He couldn't drink that away, no matter how he tried. He had spent a wild night with his old companions from Kaikoura, of course, but even that was not quite satisfying without Lizzie.

Michael had no more desire to drink and sleep with Claudia. The blonde whore had been a replacement for Kathleen for a short time. He had been able to bury his face in her light-colored hair and dream of his first love. Claudia was no replacement for Lizzie, and a girl with darker hair and fewer curves would not have made him happier, either. There was simply more to Lizzie— he wanted to talk to her, work with her, and argue with her. He missed her feistiness, her ambition, and her sometimes idiosyncratic understanding of morals and order.

Michael had not stayed long in Kaikoura. There was only one farm for sale in the area, and it was too small to be profitable. The broker in Christchurch knew about two farms in the Canterbury Plains, so Michael made his way there. The landscape was overwhelming: grassland green and lush as in Ireland, but not broken up by fences. The sheep of the grand farmers grazed free in the meadows, overseen only by Maori shepherds and their dogs.

Michael remembered his coup with Fyffe's dogs. Back then, he had achieved something on his own. The work with the sheep had suited him. He could do that again. Lizzie would not have intervened; she did not know what to do with livestock. But, obviously, she had wanted to choose their house. Michael had gone too far. It had simply been stupid to pick a fight. All their differences would disappear like smoke when Lizzie had her manor and he his sheep.

***

Michael had had copious time to think—likely too much. He spent most nights on his travels alone at a campfire. His path did not take him to the Maori tribes on the way, and he wouldn't stop at manors and simply invite himself in. He missed Lizzie's warmth at night, her company at the fire, her skill at catching fish. Using *pakeha* methods did not work half so well. Michael often ate only the bread and dried meat he bought in the towns through which he passed.

Finding the towns was no longer difficult. The roads in Canterbury were well paved. He could easily have driven them in a small wagon. The first farm Michael viewed was easy to reach, even though it was in the mountains. It was gorgeous, but its location was not ideal for sheep, and it was far removed from any *pakeha* settlement. Lizzie would not care for such isolation.

There was no well-paved approach to the second farm. It lay in the middle of the plains and was big and promising, but the house and stables were nothing more than primitive shacks. The owner had gotten ahead of himself with the amount of land and then had no more money for livestock or construction. Michael and Lizzie had the means for both.

Yet Michael had become unsure when he tried to envision Lizzie's desires. She had always dreamed of a manor, but did she want to build it too? Would she want to live in primitive conditions for years until everything was finally ready? He had promised her a nest. He wanted to lead her into her kingdom as a prince would a princess. He would not bring her to a piece of land on which he could but draw the outlines of her house-to-be.

So Michael rejected the purchase of this farm too, and made his way back to Otago. The broker had notified him of one other farm. It was near Queenstown, one of the new settlements of gold prospectors, on Lake

Wakatipu. The farmhouse was supposed to be lovely, so surely the property was expensive. Perhaps, the broker had said with a wink, there might still be gold on the land. Michael could hardly imagine that, but he had decided to return to Tuapeka, retrieve Lizzie from the Maori, and then travel to Queenstown with her so they could look at it together.

Naturally, he would have to make his apologies first. The closer he got to Tuapeka, the more difficult and less promising the plan seemed to him. What if Lizzie no longer wanted to have anything to do with him? What if she was no longer even in the village? He had left her waiting longer than he had planned. He had written, however. Had the reverend taken the letter up to her? Had she ridden down to check for mail? Damn it. He should have discussed all of that with her before he rode away. He never should have left in anger, and he certainly never should have left without her.

As he rode toward the cabin he had built with Lizzie, his feelings of guilt grew stronger. In his heart, he had hoped she would be there when he arrived, but the house was dark beneath an ice cold, crystal clear night sky. Michael hoped there was still wood in the shed.

At least no one had broken into the cabin and no animals had made their home there. New Zealand's fauna was limited. There were no rodents, foxes, or hares that would potentially move in. There were a few of the giant weta, and Michael swept the insects outside. Then, he looked for wood and lit the fireplace. Outside, he beat the dirt out of the colorful Maori rug, then he laid it back down in front of the fire before spreading out his sleeping bag on top of it to dry. It was much too quiet in the cabin. Michael hoped he would be able to share it with Lizzie again the next day.

***

Lizzie thought she was hallucinating when she saw light in the old house. She had hiked a long time. It was dark, and she was freezing. The whole way down from the Maori village, she had looked forward to reaching her little cabin. At least she would have a roof over her head, and with just a little work to get a fire started, the tiny house would quickly be warm and cozy. Now it seemed someone else was there; perhaps other prospectors had occupied it. People coming and going was inherent to prospecting, like whaling and seal hunting before it.

If only she were not frozen and did not dread the additional descent to Tuapeka. Though it was only two miles, if she could avoid it in the dark and cold, she would.

Lizzie decided to at least look through the window. If a family had settled there, there was no reason not to knock and ask to stay the night. If, however, it was only men, she did not want to risk that.

She led her horse closer to the cabin. Then a high-pitched whinny came from the small stable beside it. Michael's gray? Surely it was just her imagination.

"Not a step closer."

She was not imagining his voice. Nor the silhouette of the man who was stepping in front of the cabin, pointing a gun at her.

"Raise your hands, step into the light, and assure me you come in peace."

Lizzie was startled. But all of a sudden, her heart felt lighter than it had in months, in all the time that Michael had been gone. She couldn't think like that—if she did, she would make another mistake. It would have been better to turn around and flee to Tuapeka. She had written off Michael Drury's share of the gold. She had decided not to trust a man again.

But he had come back! Despite all the fighting. After all these months. And he was already doing foolish things. Lizzie could not contain herself.

"Michael," she called over to him. She tried to make her voice sound hard. "If I didn't come in peace, I'd already have shot you. If you want to threaten somebody, you should seek cover first."

Michael threw his rifle down and let out a cry of joy. "I wouldn't hit them anyway." He laughed and ran to her. "Lizzie, I know I'm a fool. But do you have to tell me all the time?"

Lizzie nodded. "Apparently. But we did agree that you don't have to put up with it. As far as I care, you can turn around and go. I'm sure your girl is waiting for you in Kaikoura." These last words sounded bitter—though she noticed immediately that Michael looked truly confused, and she felt something like hope.

"Who's waiting?" he asked. "Come in the house. You look frozen. But you really are a witch, Lizzie. How could you know that I'd come back today? The spirits?"

Should she chastise Michael more? Or perhaps it was best just to throw him out? Or should she hear what he had to say? In any case, he ought to sleep in Tuapeka tonight and give her time to think. But it was useless: his blue eyes, his smile—she melted all over again. She thought she would never see him again, but there he was, right in front of her, the same old Michael.

"In a way," she said, following him into the cabin. A fire was burning in the fireplace. The floor was swept, the bed prepared.

Lizzie's resistance disappeared. "Oh, Michael, it's so nice to come home." She looked around the room, so happy but struggling for composure. "I had not counted on seeing you here. I had not counted on seeing you ever again, Michael Drury. Where have you been? Did you buy a house or a church? Or did you just have fun with the girls in Kaikoura?"

She sat down in front of the fireplace, pulling off her boots and warming her ice-cold feet. Michael seized the opportunity. He sat down in front of her, took her feet in his hands, and massaged them.

"Why do you keep talking about girls in Kaikoura?" he asked, looking at her face, which was softly lit by the fire and reddened with warmth. "No matter what spirits whispered that to you, they don't have any idea, it seems."

"The spirit's name was Tane, and he celebrated with you," Lizzie said angrily. "He told me about Claudia."

Michael sighed, but he continued rubbing Lizzie's feet. Slowly, he worked his way up to her knees. "Aye, I saw Claudia. And bought her a couple beers, like everyone else. She's a good girl and was my friend—and yours for a long time too, if I recall. Did you two have a falling out?"

Lizzie frowned and pushed Michael's hands away. She did not want to be seduced now. "Not even over you, you charmer. So, you really mean to tell me you didn't cheat on me? All these months? And you've really come back, tail between your legs now? With the key to a palace?"

Michael gently set Lizzie's feet down. He kneeled in front of her, his hand on his heart.

"Lizzie, there are a few things I need to ask your forgiveness for. Did I already mention that I'm an idiot?"

She had to laugh against her will.

Michael raised his hand to swear. "But I swear to you, as long as we've been together, I haven't cheated on you. Not in all my traveling, and certainly not with Claudia. Do you believe me?"

Lizzie nodded. Now, all she could hope was that Michael would not ask if she had cheated on him.

Michael reported on the farms near Kaikoura and in the plains while Lizzie cooked a meal out of his meager provisions.

"You were in Tuapeka, weren't you? Couldn't you have bought something?"

Michael admitted that he had been in too much of a hurry to see her to spend any time in the gold miners' village, and that he wanted them to go to Queenstown to look at the farm there. He did not ask why she had come down to their cabin without any provisions. Her explanation for her return—that she wanted to stay once again in a properly heated house—he accepted without any doubt. Lizzie had always gotten cold easily. After all, that was why she had insisted they build the cabin in the first place. That evening, neither of them cared what they ate anyway. They were merely happy and relieved to be together—even when doubt still gnawed at Lizzie. Perhaps she should not have forgiven Michael so easily. Yet, on the other hand, his explanations sounded so plausible. Maybe he really had written her a letter and for some reason it was never delivered.

"Tomorrow, we'll ride straight to Queenstown," Lizzie said. "Or do you want to go to Tuapeka first, to get married?"

Michael laughed and kissed her. "Lizzie, to marry, we'll have to go to Dunedin. At least if you have your heart set on being married by Reverend Burton. He's finally gotten his church in civilization. He's thrilled about it. Though apparently his sweetheart left him—at least that's the way they tell it in Tuapeka."

"So you had time to gossip?" Lizzie teased him, furrowing her brow. "I guess you didn't miss me all that much."

Michael pulled her onto the bedding. "I'll show you right now how much I missed you," he said. "Oh, Lizzie, I really did. Even your snoring."

Lizzie laughed. She craned her neck toward the window.

"Come on now," Michael said, "don't look at the moon and count the days for whether it's safe or not. We're going to get married. We want kids."

Lizzie's cycle was extraordinarily regular. She could easily prevent herself from getting pregnant by paying attention to her fertile days. But she had lost track of it—Michael had been away for so long. And the night with Kahu was unexpected. Michael was right though: it did not matter now. Lizzie snuggled happily into his arms and enjoyed a perfect night. Michael dissolved every doubt she had. They belonged together.

When Michael stepped out of the cabin the next morning to feed the horses, he recognized the *tohunga*, Hainga, sitting in the clearing in front of the house, where she had made a fire.

"Surely you want to see Lizzie," he said.

Hainga looked at him attentively. "You came back," she said. "The spirits lead us down strange paths."

Michael understood only vaguely what the old woman meant. "I'll call Lizzie for you. You're welcome to eat breakfast with us, though we don't have all that much."

Hainga shook her head.

"Lizzie! There's someone here for you."

Lizzie sat up in their makeshift bed, startled. She had feared Kahu might come down and call her back. He did not know precisely where the cabin was, but someone could have shown him the way. She had hoped she and Michael would be gone before Kahu found it. Now she would have to justify herself—to both of them. She dressed quickly, and she was greatly relieved when she saw the *tohunga* in front of the cabin.

Hainga motioned Lizzie to a place at her fire.

Lizzie was thankful when Michael went off to the stable, uninterested in the women's conversation.

"I'm sorry I ran away like that," Lizzie said. "I, I should have said good-bye."

Hanga waved this away. "Coming and going; what's gone and what's coming are one."

"You say that, but I'm sure Kahu is angry with me. Haikina, Haikina got into trouble, didn't she?"

Hainga shook her head. "She only told you the truth when Kahu would not. The spirits make us come and go, speak and hold our tongues. It's all one. The spirits, Erihapeti, do not let themselves be tricked. I told Kahu that, and now I've come to tell you."

Lizzie did not quite know how to respond to that. "That's friendly," she said eventually. "So, Kahu isn't going to come, um, how do you say, demand his rights?"

"What rights? Kahu Heke is on the way back to his homeland. We received a messenger yesterday. There's unrest there. The war of which Kahu spoke has broken out."

Lizzie felt guilty about the relief that seized her. Because Kahu was gone—but also because now she had nothing for which to reproach herself. Whether the *ariki* of the Ngati Pau had married a *pakeha* or not, the conflict between the two people could not have been contained by diplomatic means.

"I'm also going away," said Lizzie, "with Michael."

The old woman nodded. "I know. The clouds have rolled away. But what the clear sky shows us does not always please us. *Haere ra*, Erihapeti. I'll see you again, when the time comes."

Hainga laid her nose and forehead against Lizzie's face. Lizzie returned the gesture. She sighed with relief when the old woman left. That, too, had been simpler than she had thought. The Ngai Tahu, at least, seemed not to hold it against her that she had rejected Kahu. And the gods seemed to be on Lizzie's side for once.

Chapter 6

Reverend Burton was grateful to Jimmy Dunloe for everything he had done for Kathleen and Colin. He paid Dunloe a visit to thank him.

"Naturally, I would have done anything to help," Peter Burton said, almost guiltily. "But it was your connections that got Colin admitted into the academy."

"Oh, it was nothing, Reverend," Dunloe said. "I just wish it had helped Kathleen more. She's just a shadow of herself. Claire is very unhappy about it."

Indeed, Peter would have done anything to help—including adopting all Kathleen's children if she had wanted that, and wanted him. But his hopes remained unfulfilled. Kathleen had been keeping him at a distance over the past few months, and she had not found her way back into her former life in Dunedin's society. She had always been more reserved than vivacious Claire, but since Ian's death and Colin's departure, she only left the apartment to go to church. Claire had told Peter that Kathleen was deeply depressed, struggling with her fate and trying to wash herself clean of her supposed guilt with endless requiems for Ian and daily attendance at Mass.

"If I hadn't left Ian, Colin might not have turned out like that," Kathleen said over and over when Claire—first sadly but, over time, with growing anger and urgency—spoke to her friend about her increasing dependence on Father Parrish.

"Of course he would have," Claire retorted angrily. "He was always the image of his father. He stopped listening to you long ago. And Sean might have turned out just like him, just to survive—after all, Ian didn't give him a leg to stand on. And Heather? Was she supposed to keep watching while her father beat and raped her mother? What would have become of the three of them if he had beaten you to death in the end?"

Kathleen could say nothing to that, but she did not accept it either. Instead, she merely wept silently to herself.

Kathleen's state was a great burden to Sean and Heather. For the first time in his life, Sean, who was happy to be free of Colin, had no patience for his mother. He refused to attend even one more requiem for Ian Coltrane. He did not care for Father Parrish's gloomy visions of hell and the draconic penance he assigned whenever anyone committed even the slightest sin. Sean refrained from attending church whenever he possibly could. Father Parrish could not accept Sean either. The boy had grown up with Peter Burton's tolerant religiosity, which had welcomed in even the scoundrels and prostitutes of Gabriel's Gully. Father Parrish upbraided Kathleen for that and for the boy's absence from church.

Heather, now almost fourteen and an extraordinarily pretty and vivacious girl, feared what her mother had become. She visited friends whenever she could and stuck even closer to Claire and Chloe. Most of all, she loved horses. Thanks to Claire, the girls were excellent riders, and Heather wanted her own horse to ride. When Kathleen denied her this desire, Heather quarreled the way her brother had with the Irish Catholic church. In Father Parrish's opinion, girls belonged at the stove, not in the saddle.

"Why don't you try to revive your womanly virtues?" Claire suggested, somewhat sarcastically, to Kathleen. "I'm thinking here of working with needle and thread. It's about time for the new spring designs, Kathleen. Now! The fashion magazines from England and France have been there for weeks, but you've yet to even glance at them."

"Pride is a sin," Kathleen said apathetically.

Claire rolled her eyes. She wanted to shake her friend. What had become of the woman who had nursed an escape plan for years? Who, through good and bad years, had mastered their shared profession with courage and determination? All the strength seemed to have drained from Kathleen. She was putty in the hands of the bigoted Father Parrish.

"What if you talked to the man yourself?" Claire asked Peter Burton desperately when Kathleen still made no move to work again. "Priest to priest. He certainly ought to take an interest in Kathleen earning money. After all, it goes into his cash box. And it's starting to get serious, Peter. We need the new designs. Otherwise the clothes won't be ready by spring."

Claire and Kathleen had made a habit of finishing one of each of the dress designs to display in the store ahead of the next season. This way, the customers had the opportunity to see the designs and could place their orders with the style and fabric tailored to suit them.

Peter Burton laughed bitterly. "How do you see that happening, Claire? Should I ask Father Parrish for her hand, so to speak? He'll notice, I'm sure, what she means to me as soon as I start. Then, of course, I'll be Lucifer himself."

"But something has to change," said Claire.

"If you ask me, you have the best cards here. Make her see that she soon won't be able to pay for her children's education anymore. Extort her with this secret she still hasn't revealed to anyone."

Claire raised her eyebrows. "What secret?"

Peter shrugged. Then he smirked. "If I knew that, I could extort her myself," he said. "But don't take me for a fool, Claire. There's still something. Something between Kathleen and Ian, even though he's dead. Why did she even marry that rat, Claire? Don't tell me he only became a swindler after the wedding. He would never have been able to pay for passage to New Zealand with honest work."

"Kathleen paid for their passage," Claire blurted out.

Peter looked at her with surprise. "I'm not asking where she got the money, but there's something there. If you see even the slightest chance to put pressure on her or to pull her out of her despair, then seize it. And I'll do the same."

Claire nodded. She knew that Peter was right.

"I'd also like to invite all of you, Claire. You, Mr. Dunloe, and Kathleen and the children, to my inaugural service in the new church. They're finally letting me come back to Dunedin. Apparently, word has gotten around that in the last few years I haven't once mentioned Darwin. At least not from the pulpit."

"Have you lost your nerve, Reverend?" asked Claire playfully.

Peter laughed. "No, I've just had other concerns. The fellows in the gold mines were not in the least interested, and Dunedin has other problems, having grown so quickly from all the people pouring into the city because of the gold. In any case, I'll be closer to you, Claire, and Kathleen—hopefully not only in terms of location. She cannot miss my first service, not after everything we've been through together."

***

Kathleen really could not say no to attending the reverend's service, but she went reluctantly and in a black dress and black hat. Despite the sad color, or perhaps because of it, she drew everyone's attention. The women, especially, whispered about Claire's business partner, who was obviously dressed in mourning. The men were busy eyeing her undeniable beauty. Peter Burton had to be careful he did not do the same. It required a lot of effort to focus on his preaching—even though Kathleen didn't once look up at him.

Nor did Kathleen want to take part in the picnic that followed the service in the garden of the small church on the outskirts of Dunedin. This almost led to a serious quarrel between her and Sean. The boy insisted on congratulating his old friend and father figure on his sermon, which had addressed several of Dunedin's current social problems.

Heather wanted to celebrate as well. She basked in Peter's compliments about how pretty she had become, and she chatted extensively with Chloe and her friends about which of the girls Rufus Cooper had looked at most often during the service.

Finally, Claire, Jimmy Dunloe, Sean, and Heather had to practically drag Kathleen into the church garden to say hello to Peter.

"A beautiful sermon, Reverend," she said with lowered eyes as Peter took her hand.

A small, cold hand. Peter thought Kathleen had lost even more weight over the last few weeks. He energetically clasped her fingers in his.

"Kathleen, what's wrong? Why don't you want to speak with me? Good Lord, Kathleen, we used to be close. I had hoped . . . Kathleen, just what's happened to you?"

He lightly put his arm around her shoulders, although she shied away as if he might hurt her. Peter gave Claire and the others a nod as a sign to excuse him for the moment. With gentle pressure, he led the reluctant Kathleen into his tiny, new parsonage.

Kathleen thought it was very nice—a cottage like the ones she had known in Ireland. She was vaguely reminded of the small house, overgrown with ivy and flowers, of Lord Wetherby's steward. Trevallion—she had hated the man but loved his house.

"A lovely house," she said, stepping into the living room, where Peter Burton's English furniture had finally found a place. She glanced out the window. "You need only add a garden. Vegetables and flowers."

"Don't change the subject, Kathleen," he said firmly. "We need to talk, and no one will see or hear us here. So they can't tell strict Father Parrish that you held hands with the Antichrist. Now, let's have it. What's wrong? Why don't you even look at me anymore? My God, Kathleen, I thought you, that you loved me, a little at least.

Kathleen shook her head violently. "Of course I don't love you. You, you misunderstood something. I, I'm not permitted. Father Parrish . . ."

"Father Parrish does not determine whom you love," Peter said firmly. "Whom you love and whom you're drawn to—only God determines that. And if you don't love me, Kathleen—if you can honestly tell me you don't love me, then at least you can tell me that while you look me in the eye."

"Maybe, maybe the devil determines it too," whispered Kathleen. Then she did look up at him. He saw how pained she was. "I'm damned, Peter," she said flatly. "I'm sinful. And I have to do my penance for that. Ian, Ian was my penance, and I did not accept that. And now, now the devil is trying to tempt me again. Please, let go of me, Peter. Leave me in peace."

"So, I'm a temptation of the devil?" Peter did not know whether he should laugh or cry.

Kathleen did not answer. She fled the house and then, as quickly as she could, the garden.

Had she gone mad? Kathleen did not understand herself anymore. Everything she'd gone through—her sins, the loss of Michael, Ian's abuse, Colin—was too much. She didn't know how to move past all of it.

Peter rejoined his guests, but he could not really take joy in his big day. Kathleen still loved him. Her eyes had told him that clearly. But unless a miracle occurred, she would never come to him. She would torture herself until the end of her days—and one of the reasons for that was this story, related to her marriage to Ian, that she still kept hidden from him. Ian was supposed to have been her penance? For what?

Suddenly a loud discussion between Heather and Sean caught his attention. Apparently they were upset by their mother's behavior. As Peter watched them, he suddenly had misgivings. Blonde Heather, dark-haired Sean . . . Colin also had blond hair. Ian had been swarthy, and yet . . . Peter never would have thought something could send him back to the prospectors so soon, but now his only thought was of going to Tuapeka to look at the church's records. At Ian Coltrane's death, he had asked Kathleen for the date of their wedding and noted it. Back then, he had not thought to compare it with Sean's date of birth.

Meanwhile, Claire was determined to produce a miracle by means of a serious talk with Kathleen as soon as they returned home.

"Kathie, it's none of my business if you have canonized Ian in retrospect. If you're determined to wreck yourself and your friendships and turn into one of those black crows we used to make fun of together, then please, by all means, go ahead. But I won't allow you to ruin our business. We've worked too hard for that. So if you don't draft the new designs soon, then I'll do it with Lauren Moriarty."

Lauren was one of the women who sewed for Kathleen and Claire.

"Lauren?" asked Kathleen. "She can't even draw."

"But she can imitate the dresses in a fashion magazine and alter them a little. That's easy, Kathleen. I can do that too: you take one dress, put the collar of another on it, and add the belt of a third. Not particularly original, but this is Dunedin, not Paris. No one will notice the designs aren't yours."

"But I, I would notice!" exclaimed Kathleen in disbelief. Slowly, she removed the hatpins from her hair and took off her black hat.

Claire ripped it from her hands and flung it to the floor. "Kathleen," she said adamantly, "you will have other worries. Because if you don't get back to work, I won't pay you. You'll have to see for yourself how to get the money for Sean's and Heather's schools. And Colin's school too. Maybe your priest will take up a collection for you."

"But, but you can't do that. The business belongs to both of us. Half of it is mine."

"Then sue me!" screamed Claire. "We'll see how far you get."

Kathleen looked at her, wide-eyed. "But we're friends."

Claire inhaled deeply. "Kathleen Coltrane was my friend," she said, "but she seems to have died. Now I live with Saint Mary Kathleen, and I don't have much in common with her. I'd be happy to bring Kathleen back to life, and if

I have to punch and kick this sniveling Mary and deny her money and throw her on the street, then I'll do it. Whether she's my friend afterward or not."

Kathleen bit her lip. "I'm going to change," she said quietly. "And fetch my charcoal. Then . . . then, I'll make a few sketches."

Claire was so happy she pulled Kathleen to her and twirled her around the room. "Well, finally! Kathleen, this time we're going to make loads of designs. Like the famous houses in Paris and London. With housedresses and afternoon dresses and evening gowns. And to top it off, a wedding dress. Don't worry about the cost. Someone will buy it, and if no one does, it will be worth the investment in advertising."

So far, there had been few brides among the women who could afford Kathleen and Claire's fashion. Most of the couples who formed the high society in Dunedin had arrived together, but their children were now growing up in New Zealand and would, without a doubt, soon be marrying each other.

"I want a wedding dress in the display window," insisted Claire, when Kathleen tried to disagree, "because one belongs there."

Chapter 7

The farm in Queenstown seemed promising. Lizzie loved its location on a small rise with a view of Lake Wakatipu. No manor house was included, but there was a spacious, homey farmhouse of solid construction and in good condition. A flock of well-bred sheep could be bought along with it. The owners' only daughter had married in Blenheim, and now they planned to follow her north.

"What would be the point of staying on here without successors?" asked the farmer, a red-faced, practically minded Scotsman. "I hear there are people who love sheep, but I've no problem leaving them."

The MacDuffs had a Maori maid who wanted to stay on, as well as a few shepherds they paid by the day. Lizzie got along with the maid at once, and Michael would be able to come to an agreement with the men too.

Michael was set on the farm, and Lizzie had no strong objections. The estate was rather far from the nearest city, and in her heart Lizzie also regretted that, at least at first glance, there were no north-facing hills for vine planting, but she did not want to argue over any of that. Michael would call her crazy— or fear anew that she was trying to order him around. Her plan to experiment with different grapes would have to remain a dream.

Lizzie and Michael promised they would transfer a payment for the farm into the MacDuffs' account once the Scots had seen to all their affairs in Otago. MacDuff wanted to make the final sale only after the sheep shearing, which Michael found reasonable.

"Otherwise, he would have worked all of last year for nothing," he explained to Lizzie, who would have liked to move in sooner.

"And what will we do till then?" she asked. "I have no desire to spend another spring in Tuapeka."

Michael laughed and spun her around. "We, my love, are going to spend the next few weeks not working in Dunedin. We'll waste a portion of our hard-earned money senselessly. We'll rent a room in a hotel; you can drink wine, as much as you want—and we'll get married, of course. In the church of that reverend of yours. Hopefully it's not still a tent."

"I'd marry you under the open sky," she said, laughing. "In any case, I'd like to have a wedding dress. Do you think we have money for one?"

Michael made a dismissive gesture. "We have money for two wedding dresses."

Lizzie wagged her finger at him and winked. "You don't really mean to court two women, do you, Michael?"

***

Lizzie found Dunedin exciting. The most important stone buildings in the city center had been finished. St. Paul's Cathedral really did hold five hundred faithful, and the octagon in the center of town hinted at future glory. Most of all, though, there were stores and markets for every wallet size. Dunedin reminded her of London in that way: there were rich citizens who strolled the streets and parks, showing off the latest fashion as well as their beautiful equipages and horses; and there were impoverished immigrants who dwelled in almshouses and tents.

Outside the city center, the streets were often muddy, no one collected the trash, and sanitary infrastructure was lacking. Reverend Peter Burton, who had taken to helping the poor again straight away, found in this a rich field for his work. Once again, he organized kitchens for the needy and care for the sick. Lizzie supported him with donations. She was happy to be counted among the well-off citizens for the first time in her life. Michael had made good on his promise and rented a suite in one of the city's best hotels. They ate in the best restaurants and attended the theater—and they planned their wedding.

Caught up in their new lifestyle, Michael wanted to get married in St. Paul's, but Lizzie preferred Reverend Burton's church on the outskirts of Dunedin.

"I'd really like Reverend Burton to marry us," she said, "and what good would a church with five hundred seats be? We don't even know anyone here."

Eventually, Lizzie triumphed, and the date was set for November 2. She would be a spring bride.

"And you'll be a baby in the fall," she whispered to her child.

She was now sure she was pregnant, and she was happy about it. She hadn't yet told Michael, however, and she hoped it would not be visible by the wedding. Lizzie wanted to be a slender and radiantly beautiful bride. So far, though, she only had vague notions of what the dress was to look like—until one day when she strolled down George Street, one of the most fashionable shopping streets in Dunedin.

The shop was small and very exclusive, and the most beautiful cream-colored lace wedding dress Lizzie could imagine was displayed in the window. Gold Mine Boutique—Women's Fashion. Lizzie had to force herself not to press her face against the window like a child. But she did not need to dream anymore. She had money. She could buy this dress.

Lizzie entered the shop. She had never been in a store like it before. But the young woman who welcomed her did not seem frightening; at most, a bit intimidating. She wore an elegantly tailored business outfit. The light-brown color of her skirt and jacket suited her walnut eyes. A pale-green blouse and a dark-green scarf thrown casually around her neck loosened the outfit and gave it even more style. The petite woman wore her dark hair up and smiled charmingly.

"Good morning, I'm Mrs. Edmunds. How can I help you?"

Lizzie breathed in deeply. "The wedding dress," she whispered.

Mrs. Edmunds beamed. "I knew someone was just waiting to get married in this dress. My business partner complained because I insisted on a wedding dress for the spring. Somehow, I had a feeling. Come, try it on. That's what you wanted to do, right?

Lizzie shifted her weight shyly from one foot to the other. She had not reckoned on such a hearty greeting.

Claire Edmunds misinterpreted her reserve. "Don't worry about the price. We'll work something out. If this design suits you . . . That is, retailoring is expensive, naturally. But this dress was intended to catch the eye, of course, and . . ."

Lizzie blushed and shook her head. "No, no, I, we, we have money. It's only I've never worn anything so beautiful before."

Claire had, by this point, taken the dress from the display window, and Lizzie ran her hand over the shimmering silk and delicate lace, marveling.

Claire beamed. "I know, isn't it lovely? There's nothing to compare it to here. Dunedin is on its way to being a city but still a long way from Paris or London—or even Liverpool. That's where I'm from. You?"

"London," responded Lizzie, trying not to let her Whitechapel accent show.

"Oh, London. You were at the center, there. Wait a moment, miss; I'll help you—putting on the dress requires an extra set of hands."

Claire chattered blithely while she helped Lizzie out of her simple afternoon dress and into the dream of lace and silk. Kathleen had based her creation on an English design that had been made for a woman of the high nobility. She did not care for it herself, thinking it overdone. Indeed, the dress would not have looked particularly good on either Claire or Kathleen.

Jimmy Dunloe had only shaken his head when Claire paraded it before him. "One would have to go searching to find you under all those flounces and that lace, Claire," the banker had said, laughing. "Decidedly too much for you, and the color makes you look pale."

The intricate dress overpowered even Kathleen's beauty. The many flounces and sashes made her slender but womanly figure look plump.

When Claire saw Lizzie in the dress now, however, it took her breath away. The rather unassuming, boyishly slim young woman suddenly had rounder body features. The flounces and lace emphasized her breasts, and the cream color perfectly set off Lizzie's complexion. Her fine hair seemed fuller as it fell over the filigree lace, and the long gloves that went with the dress hid her calloused hands.

Lizzie looked at herself in the mirror. This was no longer Lizzie Owens or Lizzie Portland. This was a princess.

"It's unbelievably beautiful," she gasped.

"Wait a moment, miss: the veil. Here, if you'll turn around, I can put it on. You can wear it short or long. My business partner designed it to be short, which is very modern. Only a few women would be brave enough. Look, the garland is made of wire and crepe and lace, but it's meant to mimic orange blossoms and . . ."

Claire placed the veil and turned Lizzie around toward the mirror again. They both fell silent at the sight of Lizzie in full bridal dress.

"It's perfect," Claire finally said. "Or almost, anyway. We need to make a couple of slight tucks, and I'd like to move the neckline up."

She quickly inserted pins and thread, but Lizzie saw only minimal differences. To her the dress was perfect just as it was.

"We can have it ready for you as soon as the day after tomorrow," said Claire. "That will be all right, won't it? And if it might be possible: Once you have a photograph of yourself in it, would you let us have a copy? Such a beautiful bride; Kathie absolutely must see you in the dress before the wedding. In fact, let's schedule a time for your fitting when she can come."

Lizzie laughed. "Of course, of course," she said happily. "But if you—if you're going to alter it anyway, the wedding is in a few weeks, and it could be . . ." Lizzie blushed but felt surprisingly few reservations in front of this woman. In a good fashion boutique, as she was just discovering, feminine secrets were safely kept. "It could be that I'll be a bit plump."

Claire beamed. "How lovely! Congratulations. That's no problem at all. There's this sash anyway. Under that we can easily make room for an additional guest if you'd like to keep it your secret for now. Oh, I'm so happy for you. Where are you going to marry? Maybe I'll come to the church. It is our wedding dress, you know."

***

"The woman is unbelievably friendly," Lizzie reported excitedly when she met Michael for dinner in the hotel that evening. She had ordered champagne to celebrate the day. "And imagine: they design these dresses themselves. Mrs. Edmunds or her business partner, Kathie, she called her. It's expensive, of course, but I'm getting a discount because Mrs. Edmunds thinks that the dress and I, that we're meant for each other, so to speak."

Michael eagerly raised his glass to her. "Dear, you and I are meant for each other. As far as I'm concerned, you could wear sackcloth. But very well, I'll take a look at this wonder dress the day after tomorrow. We'll see if I recognize you in it. After everything you've told me, it sounds like it will transform you into an angel—or should I say a cream puff?"

Lizzie shook her head, almost dropping her glass. "Are you mad, Michael? You can't see my wedding dress. That brings bad luck, guaranteed."

Michel laughed. "You're a wealthy grown woman, my dear Lizzie. That's quite a superstition to believe in." He took her hand and kissed it. "As if it makes any difference whether I see a few yards of fabric or not. What would your Maori friends say? They don't wear any wedding clothing at all, right? Clothes would just get in the way of sleeping with each other in the meeting house."

Lizzie furrowed her brow. "Even wealthy grown women can be pursued by bad luck," she said. "And the Maori certainly have their own rituals." She thought of the ceremony a chieftain's wife had to endure every time she simply wanted to visit her husband. "Don't spy, Michael. You'll see my dress for the first time in the church."

Michael nodded. Regardless, he would ride by George Street the next day and take a look at this fabulous dress. After all, what could bring them bad luck?

***

Lizzie was so excited for her fitting that she arrived at George Street a half hour too early. When she finally entered the shop at the appointed time, Mrs. Edmunds was waiting for her with two other women: Mrs. Moriarty, the seamstress, and Mrs. Coltrane, the co-owner of Gold Mine Boutique. Mrs. Moriarty looked friendly and motherly in her simple muslin dress. She seemed just to have come out of her sewing room. Mrs. Coltrane, however . . . Lizzie had been intimidated by Claire Edmunds's beauty and elegance, but she was awed by Mrs. Coltrane. Though she wore an exceedingly simple black dress without any flourishes, she was still surely the most beautiful woman Lizzie had ever seen.

Mrs. Coltrane wore her hair up, like Mrs. Edmunds, but a few locks framed her face like a halo. Mrs. Coltrane's blonde hair was like gold. Her complexion was as pale as marble, and not even the creases on her forehead—whether from concentration or worry—could mar the perfect expression of her face. All that, however, was surpassed by her shining green eyes—a color more intense than any Lizzie had ever seen before.

"Claire has told me so much about you," the woman said kindly. "She said I should come to your fitting."

"Mrs. Coltrane isn't terribly social," said Claire, "but it's about time she ventures forth more often again. We could go to Miss Portland's wedding. Do you already have bridesmaids, Miss Portland? Or flower girls? Our daughters would just love to do that for you."

Mrs. Edmunds chatted blithely while Mrs. Moriarty and Mrs. Coltrane helped Lizzie into the dress. And again the transformation took place. The woman in the mirror had been Lizzie, but now she was a fairy-tale princess, almost as beautiful as Mrs. Coltrane. With the few alterations, the dress fit perfectly. Lizzie could not look at herself enough.

"It truly is fantastic." Even Mrs. Coltrane's eyes now shone with enthusiasm. "Claire is right. Someone needs to take a picture of you in the dress—a painting would be even better. There are good painters in Dunedin. Should we ask around for one?"

Lizzie felt dizzy. A painting? She thought about the family portraits in the Busbys' house. And on the wall in the living room of her new farm near Queenstown.

She nodded. "That would be wonderful," she said. "That would be a dream come true. I would never have thought . . ."

Lizzie spun in front of the mirror, and as she did, she glanced out the window.

"I can't believe it," she groaned. "I need to take off the dress very quickly, Mrs. Edmunds. Otherwise, there'll be bad luck. Over there, on the other side of the street, is my future husband."

Mrs. Edmunds shared her concern at once. "He risked coming here?" she asked, laughing. "Sometimes boys feel they have to test fate. Come quickly, Miss Portland, into the changing room. By the time he gets here, you'll be wearing your old things again."

As Mrs. Coltrane and Mrs. Moriarty helped Lizzie out of dress, they heard Mrs. Edmunds run to the door and give Michael an earful. He responded testily.

At the sound of his voice, Mrs. Coltrane abruptly froze.

"Is something wrong, Mrs. Coltrane?" Mrs. Moriarty asked.

"No, I, I just . . ."

Mrs. Moriarty laughed. "Back home they'd say someone just stepped over your grave."

Lizzie had already put on her skirt and blouse, and she quickly smoothed her hair. Then she pushed open the door. Her face shone, as always when she saw Michael. It had been impertinent of him to come, of course, but sweet in its own way. He smiled at her, and then Lizzie watched him go instantly pale. Astonishment and confusion replaced his smile—and he stared as if something behind Lizzie compelled him.

Lizzie turned around. Mrs. Coltrane stood in the door to the changing room—and she wore the same shocked expression as Michael.

Kathleen collected herself first. "Michael," she whispered.

Michael took a step closer. Everyone but Kathleen had disappeared for him. He was in another world. Alone with her.

"I thought you were dead."

"You, you were in Australia."

"But not for long." Michael could not believe that he was standing there, talking to Kathleen. "I escaped. But you, Ian said you died in childbirth."

Kathleen's face was expressionless, a mask of confusion. "I'm here," she said. "Right here."

She held out her hand to him. He seized it. It was warm and damp with sweat. His was too.

"Do you see? I'm alive." Kathleen handed him her second hand. They stood there motionless. They were in no hurry. A circle seemed to close.

"What's happening?" asked Lizzie. "Who is this?" She did not need to ask. She knew. "Kathleen? Mary Kathleen?"

Claire did not entirely understand what was happening, but that the scene cut Lizzie to the quick was not hard to discern.

"My dear." She tried to put her arm around Lizzie, but Lizzie shook her off.

"Mary Kathleen? What are you doing here? You're supposed to be dead." Lizzie pushed determinedly between Michael and Kathleen and shoved the two of them apart. Kathleen looked at her, not comprehending.

"You were dead! Couldn't you just stay dead?"

"Michael, what's wrong with her?" asked Kathleen. She seemed to have forgotten that Lizzie was just talking about her fiancé, that Claire had been teasing Michael for his curiosity about the wedding dress.

"I'm sorry Lizzie," Michael whispered. "But now, you do see she's not dead."

Michael turned back to this apparition from his past, in which he was slowly beginning to believe. "Let's, let's . . . What do we do now, Kathleen?"

"Come, Miss Portland." Claire tried again to put her arm around Lizzie so she might usher her away. "They aren't themselves anymore. I think they know each other from another time."

"This is Michael, Claire." Kathleen's voice still lacked inflection, but she thought she ought to formally introduce Claire and Michael now. "Claire Edmunds, Michael Drury."

"Sean's father?" Claire blurted out.

Lizzie felt sick. So, the child had not died either.

"Miss Portland, come, let's have some tea," Claire said softly. "After that, everything will work itself out. Those two will come back to themselves. But I think they have a great deal to discuss. Mrs. Moriarty, please close the shop in case . . ."

In case my partner should forget to? Or run away without thinking? Claire did not quite know what she was afraid of.

Mrs. Moriarty nodded. "I'll take care of it."

Lizzie followed Claire Edmunds up the stairs into a tastefully furnished living room. But she knew that nothing was going to work itself out, that nothing would be like it was before with Michael. She had seen his expression. From now on there was only Kathleen for him. As there had only ever been Kathleen. Death had parted them. But Lizzie should have known. One could not trust in God, or the spirits—or even in death.

Chapter 8

It took Michael a long time to collect himself. Kathleen accepted their reunion somewhat more quickly. After all, she had only thought him in Tasmania, not in the hereafter.

Yet she, too, had stood there for several minutes, her hand in his, until Mrs. Moriarty finally came out with a pot of tea. "Perhaps you'd like a sip?" she asked shyly.

Michael awoke from his daze. "Really, I need a whiskey," he muttered.

Kathleen smiled. "Are you selling it again?"

"What? Oh, no. I'm, I'm a sheep breeder. I have a farm west of Queenstown. At least, I've bought one . . ."

Kathleen nodded. "I had a farm," she said. "I lived with Ian for a long time near Christchurch. But your son was born in Lyttelton. Or Port Cooper, as they called it then. Almost on the ship on our way over."

Kathleen began to tell him about it, but Michael interrupted her. "He's alive? My son?" He was in a swirl of disbelief and extraordinary joy.

"Yes, very much so. He's a good boy. And smart. He's attending high school and will soon go to university. Ian, Ian is dead, however."

Michael nodded, not wanting to go into Lizzie's involvement in the matter. Yet at that, he thought of Lizzie again. This must be a shock for her. But what a strange twist of fate. Lizzie had killed Ian. Had cleared the way to Kathleen. Lizzie had always smoothed the way for him. Michael felt a sort of melancholy and gratitude toward the woman he had wanted to marry a moment before. But Lizzie had to understand.

Kathleen took a sip of tea. Color slowly returned to her face. Her beautiful face. At first glance, Michael had thought she had hardly changed, but now he saw that her eyes were framed by tiny wrinkles. She had grown more serious and was clearly no stranger to worry and concern—but to Michael she only seemed lovelier for all that.

"What about you? Did you have a wife? Any children?"

"Me? No, Kathleen, I, I have only ever thought of you."

Kathleen frowned. "But that woman, the one buying the dress?" she asked. "Miss Portland? She is about to be your wife."

Michael made a dismissive gesture. "An old friend. We have lived through a lot together. We wanted to manage the farm together. And well, because I thought you were dead . . . We were going to marry."

"There was nothing more there?" asked Kathleen.

"Nothing you need to worry about. Kathleen, Mary Kathleen! It's a miracle. Really, it's a miracle. And our son—when can I see him?"

She looked at the grandfather clock in the corner of the room. "School will be letting out soon," she said. "We could pick him up. I, I could use some fresh air anyway."

Kathleen brushed a strand of hair from her face before grabbing her small black hat. She looked at it a moment, then dismissed her plan to wear it.

Among the accessories the shop sold was an elegant, little dark-red hat. Kathleen took it from the stand. "What about Miss Portland?" she asked as she placed the hat on her head.

Michael shrugged. "She'll find her way home," he said. "I'm sorry for her, of course. We'll see what we can do about the farm, but we'll figure all that out later, Kathleen. For now, I want to see Sean. My son!"

***

Sean was amazed to see his mother waiting at the gate to the school. And the man beside her—he was excited at first because he thought it was Peter Burton, but then he saw that this man was taller than the reverend. He reminded Sean of someone, or something. He quickly said good-bye to Rufus Cooper and walked over to his mother and the man.

"Sean." Kathleen beamed at her boy.

Sean looked at her suspiciously. Some change had taken place in her. There was a light in her eyes he hadn't seen since she was with Peter Burton. Since before his father died. *Ian.* His father? Sean was no fool. As a child, Ian's rejection and his clear preference for Colin had hurt Sean, but he had long since moved on from the man he called father. The complete lack of affection and bond had made him curious. And Kathleen's marriage certificate had not been hard to find.

Sean slowly approached his mother and greeted her with a kiss on the cheek.

"Sean," said Kathleen. "This is Michael Drury." There was an exuberance in his mother's voice that he had never heard before.

Sean offered his hand to the man. "Didn't I see you in Tuapeka, Mr. Drury?" he asked courteously. He now recalled more clearly. Mr. Drury had been with Miss Portland—and Mr. Timlock. They had sometimes gone to Peter Burton's services on Sunday. "How is Miss Portland doing?"

Sean saw his mother's features darken, and Michael Drury's face reddened. "Good," he muttered. "Very good, as far as I know."

"Mr. Drury and I know each other from Ireland," said Kathleen. "We're from the same village. And now, well, now, he wanted to meet you."

Michael stood in front of his son and looked into the narrow face where, along with Kathleen's straight nose and her high cheekbones, he saw his own features. Sean's eyes were light green, and they looked at Michael curiously.

His son! Michael's heart overflowed with emotion and love, but he did not know what to say to him.

"You, you're sixteen now, Sean?" he stammered. "And, and you're still going to school?"

Sean did not dignify this with a response. After all, it was obvious.

"Are you a good student?"

"A very good student," Kathleen answered proudly. "Sean will be going to university next year."

"University . . . when you think how we only got a few hours of education with Father O'Brien. It took me hours, Kathleen, to write you that letter. Did you get it, at least?"

Kathleen nodded and looked at him. "I still have it," she admitted, "but there was nothing I could do."

"You did the right thing, Kathleen. You did it for him. And it was worth it. A, a real good boy."

Sean was annoyed. What was that supposed to mean? His mother did not otherwise tend to parade him in front of random acquaintances like a trained seal. All of this could really only mean one thing. In which case, they both owed him an explanation.

Sean waited until he could finally hold Michael's gaze again, then held it fast.

"Mr. Drury, sir," he said with a clear voice. "You, you wouldn't happen to be my father, would you?"

***

"I'm awfully sorry, Lizzie."

Michael really did not look as if he regretted anything. Quite the contrary; Lizzie had rarely seen him shine from the inside like this.

"But you do have to understand—"

"What?" asked Lizzie. "What do I have to understand? That our engagement is over, that all our plans are overturned, that your love for me has run out from one moment to the next—all because a woman appears whom you haven't seen in seventeen years? With whom you share nothing except a homeland and an illicit past?"

Lizzie had to fight; she could not simply give up, even if at the moment she wanted nothing more. But Claire was right: Michael and Kathleen would have to come down from the clouds and begin to think again. Then, she needed to be there, and she could not look haggard and red-eyed and desperate. Until that morning, Michael had loved her. His love could not have disappeared completely in an instant.

"Lizzie, it's Kathleen," Michael said, misty-eyed. "You know—"

"Yes, I know she was your puppy love, and you even wanted to feed yourself to the sharks just to see her again. But that was half a life ago, Michael."

Lizzie laid her hand on top of his. She was sitting in her hotel room—what had been *their* hotel room. Michael had rented another—one of the things for which he now demanded Lizzie's understanding.

Michael withdrew his hand gently. "For me, it's like it was yesterday," he explained. "And she, she's the mother of my son."

"I'm also the mother of your son," Lizzie blurted out. "Or your daughter." She laid the hand he had rejected on her stomach.

"You're with child?" he sounded more disbelieving than overjoyed.

Lizzie nodded. "Does that change anything?"

Michael chewed on his lip like a schoolboy. "Lizzie, all this, all this is too much at once. I need to figure things out. First with one thing, then the other. I . . ."

"So, it doesn't change anything," Lizzie said. "What are you thinking, Michael? You don't want to marry—at least not me. I get that much. But what about the farm? What about our plans?"

Michael shrugged. "We need to think about that," he said.

"We?" asked Lizzie. "Does 'we' mean you and I or you and Kathleen?"

Now Michael really did look pained. "Both. I, we, why don't we sleep on it for now, Lizzie? Maybe—"

"Maybe I'll just vanish like a bad dream?" she asked. "The child along with me? Maybe there'll only be Mary Kathleen to think about when you awake?"

"Lizzie, Lizzie, you have to understand. I'm grateful. For, for everything. In a certain way I love you. But Kathleen . . ."

"This morning you loved me in more than 'a certain way,'" Lizzie said bitterly. "But yes, you sleep on it and talk to Kathleen about it tomorrow. Maybe she'll think of something. I'm sure she's always wanted a lovely little farm in Otago."

Michael's face lit up. He did not seem to perceive the sarcasm in her words or the hurt in her voice. "Really Lizzie? You wouldn't mind? I mean, if I kept the farm, that is? Half the money belongs to you, naturally. There's no question of that. I would only need to see if the MacDuffs would allow installment payments."

Lizzie could hardly believe it. Was he really so dense? Had he really thought she meant it like that? Or did he only understand things as they suited him at the moment? Lizzie wanted to cry, but she controlled herself. She could cry when Michael was gone.

"Well, this Mary Kathleen of yours will surely have something to contribute, won't she?" Lizzie asked icily. "After all, she's been so successful in outfitting brides—unless she happens to want the groom herself."

Michael shook his head. "Lizzie, don't accuse her of anything. She doesn't want to take anything away from anyone. It's just, it's simply fate."

Lizzie rolled her eyes.

"But you're right, Lizzie. If Kathleen sells her share in this business, we can afford the farm." Michael laughed. "You see, I wouldn't even have thought of that either. I'm really sorry, Lizzie. We, we were good together. But with Kathleen . . . well, you have to understand."

***

"And what about his bride?" asked Claire. As they did almost every evening, the two friends had sat down to dinner together with their children. Although Kathleen usually cooked, that day she had not. There was just bread, cold meat, and cheese.

"About whom?" asked Kathleen.

She still had an unearthly glow in her eyes. What had happened was incomprehensible. She and Michael were reunited. Sean recognized his father. If father and son had done nothing but embrace each other, her dream would have been complete.

Ultimately, they had tried to explain everything to Sean, who had listened to the confusing story in silence. When Sean wasn't able to take any more, he had made excuses about being needed.

"We'll talk more about it soon," Michael said.

Sean ran off, and Michael and Kathleen had walked the streets of Dunedin for a few magical hours, catching each other up on their lives but more than anything just reveling in being together again. Finally, Michael had known it was time to go; he owed Lizzie an explanation. Kathleen understood and agreed. She had returned home drunk with happiness.

But now Claire seemed to have objections.

"Miss Portland," said Claire. "The lady to whom Michael is engaged."

Kathleen made a dismissive gesture. "Oh, she'll understand. Those two are more like good friends."

"Oh?" asked Claire. "That's not what it looked like to me. I thought Miss Portland was very much in love, and Mr. Drury could hardly wait to see her in her dress, even before their wedding day. Which brings bad luck, as we've established once again."

"Bad luck?" asked Kathleen, taken aback. "But Michael and I are happy. I can't even believe he's back." She smiled at everyone around the table. No one smiled back.

"You may very well be happy, but you're not the only one in this whole wide world, Ma," Sean remarked drily. He had always shown understanding for his mother, but the events of that day had surpassed his comprehension. "I, for one, am not all that happy, and as for Miss Portland . . ."

"But you've found your father!" Kathleen said. "That's certainly wonderful. Or, or do you not like him?" Kathleen's expression turned from delight to concern.

Sean shrugged. "I don't even know him," he said. "I've seen him for a few minutes of my entire life, and there's not much to say about that. He only has eyes for you. Who knows? Maybe he's very nice."

"Oh, he's definitely nice."

"But surely not as nice as Peter Burton."

Kathleen frowned. "How can you compare them? Peter—"

Claire stood up. She had heard enough of the matter. All she wanted was to scream at Kathleen and shake her. But she had to make a final attempt; she owed it to Peter.

"Kathleen, I'll grant that at the moment you're in a—well, let's say, an exceptional mental state. But Peter Burton is a good man, and he's been wooing you for years. You grew close to him, you've been affectionate with him—and he helped raise your children. For a few months, you've both been suffering like dogs because this dreadful Father Parrish convinced you that you were guilty of all that's wrong with the world. But now, from one moment to the next, he's, well, what, Kathleen? Just 'a good friend'? Like Miss Portland to Mr. Drury?"

Kathleen looked at her, uncomprehending. She seemed to want to reply, but Claire did not let her speak.

"And what about Mr. Drury anyway, Kathleen? Will Father Parrish concede him to you? Or is there another devil in the details?"

"Father Parrish?" Kathleen had clearly also forgotten him.

"You're talking like a head-over-heels schoolgirl, Kathleen, but you're thirty-three years old," she said. "Maybe you should take some time to think. Come along, Chloe, we're going over to Jimmy's. Why don't you come, too, Heather? Your mother needs some peace and quiet."

"I'm going over to the Coopers," grumbled Sean, reaching for his jacket.

When everyone had gone, Kathleen pulled Michael's old letter from its hiding place. For the first time in such a long time, she felt no loss or sadness in reading it, only overwhelming joy. Claire was right. She felt like a teenager in love. She pressed the brittle, faded paper to her chest and danced through the apartment, and when she finally fell asleep, it was with Michael's letter against her heart.

***

Lizzie could not sleep. Everything had happened too suddenly, too cruelly. She could not come to terms with it alone. Perhaps the reverend was already asleep, but then she would just have to wake him. Her soul needed comfort, more than ever before.

Lizzie glanced through the window before knocking. She sighed with relief when she saw the reverend sitting in front of the fire, reading.

Peter Burton opened the door immediately. "Miss Portland, has something happened?"

Lizzie nodded but could not speak. She walked in and began to cry.

"Is something wrong with Michael, Lizzie?" Peter Burton ushered her toward an armchair and watched helplessly as she fell onto it. She cried and cried and cried; she couldn't remember having ever shed so many tears before.

"Do tell me! An accident? Is he dead?"

Peter could not imagine that. He was sure Lizzie would have been more composed in the case of death. This was something else, something that should not have happened.

Lizzie shook her head. In the end, Peter let her cry and went into the kitchen to make tea. But then he changed his mind and uncorked a bottle of Bordeaux. Lizzie could use a drink, and perhaps the wine would distract her. He had always liked to listen to her talk about the aromas and flavors in a given wine.

"Here, try this," he said after pouring for them.

Lizzie did indeed take a deep drink.

Peter sipped it slowly. "Tastes of cranberries, don't you think?" he asked. "Very fruity, but not as full a taste as blackberries."

"A kiss," whispered Lizzie. "A velvety taste that curls around the tongue like a kiss." She straightened herself. "Those aren't my words, Reverend, just those of another liar." She drank again. "Or silk—more like silk, lighter than velvet. I wore a silk dress this morning, Reverend, but it only brought bad luck."

Lizzie wept again, and Peter drank his wine. He could wait. Finally, she began to explain, and the reverend listened in the trained, calm manner in which he heard confessions. Lizzie knew that she could tell him anything. Yet he did seem to pay special attention when she mentioned Gold Mine Boutique.

"Yes, I've seen the dress," he said. "Very pretty; a bit overdone for, for . . . But you must have looked beautiful in it, Lizzie."

Lizzie nodded. She did not want to think about the dress anymore. She told the reverend everything that had happened at Gold Mine Boutique.

Lizzie could not judge the expression on Peter's face when she got to Michael and Kathleen's reunion—but it was unmistakable that feelings welled up within him. His fingers clutched the arms of his chair, and it seemed he had to force himself not to jump up.

"And then?" he asked quietly.

"Well, she forgot everything around her. Mrs. Edmunds said that was bound to happen. She poured me tea; she has a good heart. I did not see Michael again until evening, and by then everything was clear to him. He had even just met his son, apparently just as perfect a child as his mother is a woman."

"Sean Coltrane really is quite a good boy," Peter Burton said absentmindedly.

"How could it be any other way?" asked Lizzie sarcastically. "After all, he was born of an immaculate angel. In any case, he recognized Michael as his father at once. Must have been some kind of miracle, and now everything's going to be all right. A small, happy family."

"There's a girl too," mumbled Peter. "Heather."

"Oh?" asked Lizzie. "They seem to have forgotten about her. But then, they've forgotten everything except their wonderful summer in the fields by the river."

Peter drank his wine. Really, he needed something stronger.

Lizzie left him to muse for a while. "So, what is it, Reverend?" she finally asked. "Maybe . . . maybe you could say something. Explain to me what, what God thinks about it?"

Peter shook his head. "I don't know, Lizzie," he said wearily, "and I'm, I'm not really the right person to say something. In this case . . . in this case I'm not the best counselor."

"Now you'll be telling me you wish both of them happiness from the bottom of your heart," mocked Lizzie. "Because they're no doubt meant for each other, and because it was God's will for them to meet again."

"I certainly won't be saying that," Peter interrupted her, almost angrily. He tousled his already messy hair. If he had ever struggled with his God, then it was on this night.

"Then say something else!" yelled Lizzie. "Maybe give me some advice. I know she's beautiful, I know he never forgot her, but damn it, I'm with child, and I love Michael Drury."

Peter looked at her, and her pain was mirrored in his eyes. "And I," he said, "love Kathleen Coltrane."

Mana

Dunedin, Queenstown, Otago

1863–1864

Chapter 1

The next morning Kathleen invited Michael to breakfast. Heather and Chloe eyed him distrustfully at first, but to Michael's amazement, he found it easier to talk to them than to Sean. His son ignored him. Michael had feared Heather might be similar to Ian, but she proved to be Kathleen's double, which cheered and relieved him. He paid the girls compliments; even Claire thawed a little when he praised her pretty dress and began to talk about horses with her. Kathleen had mentioned that Claire and the girls were enthusiastic riders, and as Michael talked about his horse, Chloe wanted to talk about her pony, and Heather of her dream horse.

"But I didn't get one for my birthday," Heather said, looking at Kathleen accusatorily, "because it would be prideful, or something."

Michael laughed. "Of course it's not. A horse isn't a luxury here. Just imagine that some sheep baron out there in the plains comes to woo you. You'll have to know how to ride just to get to his farm. Not to mention if you want to help him count his sheep and all that."

"But I don't count sheep," squealed Heather.

"Or she only does when she can't sleep," Chloe said, giggling.

The girls hardly remembered their lives on the farms near Christchurch. They had grown up in the city and could not imagine anything else.

"Oh, just wait until you see the farm in Otago." Michael laughed. "It sits on a mountain, Heather. You can see Lake Wakatipu far below. And we'll have thousands of sheep."

"Perhaps Heather doesn't want any sheep," said Sean, not looking up from his plate. "I could do without sheep myself, anyway."

Kathleen wanted to reply sharply, but Michael put his hand on her arm. "No," he whispered to her, "he just has to get used to it."

He turned with pronounced cheerfulness to his son. "Just wait till you see them. I can show you how to shear them. Can you imagine? I was once the fastest sheep shearer north of Otago."

Sean shrugged his shoulders. He could not have said more clearly with words how little he cared. "I need to get to school," he said curtly, grabbing his bag.

Claire shooed Chloe and Heather out, though they would have gladly flirted a bit longer with Michael. "So, you want to take Kathleen to your farm?" she asked. "For a visit, or forever?"

Michael sank into Kathleen's eyes again. "Whatever she likes," he said. "The farm is gorgeous, Kathleen, and the area! The city is very close."

Kathleen smiled, but she did not seem to know about what. She was barely listening to Michael's words. It was enough for her to hear his voice and see his face.

Claire finally gave up. Kathleen would go wherever Michael went. At least for now. She could not, however, repress a little barb. "Doesn't at least half the land belong to Miss Portland?"

Michael smiled transcendently, passing Claire over again. "Oh, Lizzie is generous," he said, turning to Kathleen. "Always has been. It would be great if you could be friends, Kathleen. She's a wonderful person. She immediately gave up the farm, though, of course, that means we're missing some of the money. But you're not without means, right, Kathleen? If we put something together."

Kathleen nodded numbly. A farm? She did not really want a farm. But, naturally, she wanted to be with Michael.

"I thought we'd drive out there first, Kathleen. Sometime this week. We can take the children if you like. We'll do everything as you like, Kathleen."

Kathleen placed his hand on her cheek. "I'd really like to be alone with you," she said.

Claire rolled her eyes. "The apartment is all yours," she said icily. "I'm going into the shop. Someone has to earn money here, after all. Especially since the last sale was a disaster. I'll be selling the next wedding dress without you, Kathie." She left.

"What's wrong with her?" asked Michael.

Kathleen shrugged. "I don't want to be alone with you here, Michael," she said. "Not when Claire could come in at any moment or some seamstress could bother us. I need time for you, Michael—just for you, just for us. Isn't there anywhere we could ride to? To, to the river?"

Michael fetched his horse and accompanied Kathleen to the stables, where he insisted on saddling Sean's small black horse for her.

"Though it's no horse for a lady," he said, furrowing his brow, at which Kathleen laughed.

"Nor am I a lady, Michael Drury. And any horse is an improvement. I used to ride a mule." She kissed him on the cheek.

Donny Sullivan, in whose stable Claire's and Kathleen's animals still resided, grinned good-naturedly.

"Well, Mrs. Coltrane, does our Father Parrish know about this?" he teased her. "And will I be invited to the wedding?"

Kathleen and Michael both turned red. But Donny did not wait for an answer. Nor would he say anything to the severe Father Parrish. In truth, Sullivan feared the grouchy priest as much as the rest of the parish did, whereas he especially liked Kathleen. He was happy to see her smiling again.

Michael led Kathleen to the mouth of the Tuapeka River, surprised at how masterfully she handled the lively horse at a trot and a gallop. They spent the day by the river, just like on their dreamy Sundays back in Ireland. While Michael knew that Lizzie would first have searched the idyllic spot for traces of gold, Kathleen merely sat on the bank and looked raptly at the flowing water, which seemed to dance in the sunbeams. She arranged the picnic they had brought along but left it to Michael to catch and roast the fish. He did this in the *pakeha* style, so the catch was not large, but, Kathleen marveled at it nevertheless. Finally, he made love to her in the clear light of afternoon beneath a tree fern whose shadow seemed to cover them with a gentle veil. Michael only needed to close his eyes to dream his way back beneath the willow on the bank of the Vartry.

Both of them were boundlessly happy as they rode back to Dunedin.

"Will you come to Queenstown with me?" asked Michael as he parted from her with a kiss in front of her building's door. "To look at the farm?"

Kathleen nodded. She would have followed Michael to the ends of the earth.

***

When Michael got back to the hotel, Lizzie had checked out already.

"Don't keep doing that to yourself," Peter Burton had told her. The reverend had looked just as pale, hopeless, and forlorn that night as Lizzie felt. He'd let her sleep in the parsonage the first night and then offered to put her up with his housekeeper, who rented rooms. "You should save your money, Lizzie. Remember, you'll only have half of what you had if Michael doesn't see reason. You don't really mean to buy a farm with it, do you?"

Lizzie did not know. She still could not think that far ahead. But he was right. She was not a farmer.

"Kathleen Coltrane comes from a farm, doesn't she?" she asked the reverend.

Peter pursed his lips. "Yes, but I never had the sense that she longed to get back to that."

***

Sean Coltrane certainly didn't want to return to the country. He made that abundantly clear to Kathleen when she broached the subject of Queenstown. At first Heather was excited about the farm, particularly since she would have a horse, but she grew skeptical after Sean presented his arguments.

"A farm in the middle of nothing, Ma; we already had one. Where will Heather go to school? Where am I going to study?"

"Queenstown is not very far."

"And what is Queenstown?" he asked. "A better sort of gold mining camp."

"There's a school there," Kathleen said.

Sean rolled his eyes. "Sure. An elementary school where the miners' children learn to read and write. Grand. But I attend high school, not to mention I'll be at university next year. And Heather? She's in high school already. Ma, Heather has probably already spent more years in school than the girl who teaches the kids in Queenstown."

Surely that was an exaggeration, but Kathleen knew he was more than partly right. It wouldn't serve Sean to go to school in Queenstown, and the change of schools would do Heather no favors either.

"I'm sure Claire will allow you to continue living with her, and Michael can easily pay your tuition."

Sean threw his head back proudly. "Thank you, but I'll pass. I'll apply for a scholarship. I'm sure I'll get one. And I'll live with Reverend Burton. My so-called father has not cared for me for sixteen years; there's no need to start now."

Kathleen sighed. Things between Michael and Sean had not been going well at all. Michael tried to make his son understand the situation in Ireland and his actions back then, but Sean did not want to understand. Perhaps it was the influence of the passionate skeptic Peter Burton, or of the school—both had taught him to ask questions—or that he'd learned to tell truth from lies after years of listening to Claire recount fairy tales and legends. In any case, now it seemed good fun to him to play the inquisitor with his father.

"So you stole Trevallion's grain," he said, as Michael told him the story of his imprisonment, "so you could leave for America with Ma, but that doesn't make it right, does it?"

Michael shrugged. "Trevallion was a traitor. He threw his lot in with the English. And the people were starving."

"So you were starving?" pressed Sean.

"Well, not me personally," mumbled Michael. "It was more, well, it was a matter of principle. Ireland belongs to us, the Irish! Its rivers, its fields, and the grain that grows in them."

Sean frowned. "You mean, you did it for political reasons?"

Michael nodded, relieved. "In a certain sense, Sean."

Sean rubbed his temples. "So it wasn't about Ma after all?"

Michael breathed in deeply. He had to control himself. Sean was—well, Sean had lacked a father to teach him to love Ireland, no matter how far away it was.

"Of course it was about your mother. And you. But—"

"What did you do with Trevallion's grain afterward?" inquired Sean, still entirely at ease and with a steady voice. "I don't quite understand: if you stole it out of patriotism, then you couldn't rightfully sell it. Reverend Burton, he would have distributed it in the church, or the like."

Michael gritted his teeth.

"And if you did sell it, then, in principle, you profited from the famine."

Kathleen decided that for the time being it was best to steer Michael and Sean around each other. Surely it was better—for several reasons—if Sean were to stay in Dunedin should she really follow Michael to Queenstown. She still cast the move to the farm into doubt whenever she was not with Michael. In truth, she liked Dunedin, particularly now that she had awoken from the slump into which she had fallen after Ian's death.

Father Parrish had succeeded in convincing her God wanted to punish her for leaving Ian and Colin years ago, and for sending Colin to England. But if He was once angry, he seemed to be no longer. He had brought Michael back to her, and Colin was thriving. The boy wrote enthusiastic letters from England—full of spelling errors, true, but he seemed to stand out as a sharp-shooter, and he was revealing himself to be a gifted navigator.

No matter what the old priest said, Kathleen now saw Ian's death as a lucky twist of fate: her path to Michael was clear. Her marriage to Ian had undoubtedly served to send her to the same country as Michael. Obviously God loved twisting paths; Reverend Burton had always said as much.

In any case, Kathleen felt happy and free as never before, and she would have loved to celebrate that with the whole city. But Michael had little interest in any of the activities of such a city—the balls and art exhibitions, the concerts or plays to which Jimmy Dunloe took Claire. Kathleen tried once or twice to convince him to come, but he behaved awkwardly among Dunedin's high society, and people whispered about his reputation as a "prospector" and "adventurer."

Claire and Jimmy did not seem to like having Michael around. Their complaint wasn't that he wasn't as cultured as they; it was that he didn't show any particular interest in learning—whether it was about which fork to use, how to dance the waltz, or the world's political situation. It was true that Michael had had enough to do just surviving the previous years, and he had not been able to read newspapers, let alone books.

"But he could now; he could learn anything he wanted," Claire said as Kathleen once again defended her lover. "He doesn't have anything to do all day, you know, except make eyes at you. I hope he at least understands farming—otherwise you'll end up starving after all. And when it comes to being a sheep baron, Kathleen, sheep are not enough. People put the emphasis on baron, and a baron must have command of a few formalities."

"He'll get it eventually," Kathleen insisted. "He's smart. When he works a little . . ."

"That seems precisely the catch," grumbled Claire. "When I see how he traipses through life, I ask myself how he even made it this far."

***

Kathleen and Michael drove to Queenstown alone. Heather had thought about the move and had become as vehemently opposed as Sean. Naturally, her reasons were less thoughtful. She was not thinking of seeking further education yet, although Claire encouraged the girls to do so. Heather's main concern was Chloe, from whom she did not want to part under any circumstances. The girls had always been together—really, since birth. And from the time their mothers had taken them and Sean and fled, they had shared a room, crawled into the same bed after a nightmare, and shared every thought. Claire often joked that they would only be able to marry the girls off if they found twins to be their husbands. In any case, Heather did not want to go to Queenstown without Chloe. Not even Michael's promise to buy her a horse of her own as soon as they moved could sway her.

Kathleen did not know how this would all work out, but there was no reason to bring the children on the trip if they wouldn't move from Dunedin. For now, she was happy to travel with Michael to see the farm. She borrowed Sean's horse, an act he did not take well. Though Michael had suggested renting a wagon for the journey, the offer had been rather halfhearted. Lizzie's buggy, at least, was not available. Michael hardly mentioned her anymore. That was fine by Kathleen, but Claire kept making her angry by asking piercing questions about how Miss Portland was doing.

In Kathleen's eyes, Claire was behaving rather oddly anyway. Kathleen felt their friendship was fraying. With regards to this, too, it was good to get out of the shop and their shared apartment for a few days. But forever, right away? Kathleen still did not want to think about it. Her new life with Michael had unleashed her creativity. Her designs for autumn were daring and colorful, voluptuous and tight. Claire and the seamstresses had been utterly captivated. The customers started placing orders the moment they saw Kathleen's quick coal sketches, which Claire had left around the shop as if by accident. Kathleen could not really picture herself milking cows again instead of drawing, but everything would be fine. Perhaps there was a shop in Queenstown similar to Gold Mine Boutique, or she could start one. A second location; that would not be so bad. Kathleen could manage it, and she would simply mail her designs to Claire. Or they would meet a couple of times a year.

It quickly became clear to Kathleen that such a meeting would not be easy. By the second day of the trip, the road to Queenstown had grown steeper, narrower, and more difficult in every respect. Kathleen would not have braved the road by herself. Claire, who was a much better rider, would not have had such difficulty, but still, they were traveling for days, and Kathleen could not imagine Claire sleeping in a tent or wagon anymore. Her friend would insist on spending the night in inns, and for those one would have to make long detours.

Kathleen, however, liked to sleep with Michael under the stars. Spring had finally given way to a warm and dry summer. Smiling, she gave a couple of stars' names in the Maori language, but she got the feeling Michael did not like hearing them. On the second day of their journey, they started running out of conversation material. They now knew each other's life stories—at least as much as they were prepared to share with each other. And there were not many other topics they had in common—at least not ones that were easy to talk about.

The children were not a good topic. Of course, Michael liked to hear about Sean's cleverness and his studies, but he held it against Kathleen that she had largely withheld the story of his parents' homeland from him. And then there was the matter of Colin. Michael had made the harshest recriminations toward Kathleen for having sent her younger son to an English military academy, of all places.

"What else was I to do?" Kathleen had asked helplessly.

Even superficial polite speech, in which society life had long ago versed her, failed. Michael fell silent whenever Kathleen made some joke referencing art or literature. To her great amazement, he had never heard anything about Darwin or his theories. Kathleen spent two hours of the journey explaining the most important content of *On the Origin of Species* to him, but he took little interest. Only Peter Burton's exile to the gold mines as a consequence of his "heresy" provoked a reaction.

"So, that's why they exiled the poor reverend," he said. "I always wondered why he spent all those years down with the ne'er-do-wells in Tuapeka when he must have seen better days."

"I'm sure he wasn't very happy," Kathleen said carefully. She did not want to reveal too much about her relationship to Peter Burton. "He would have preferred a pastorate in the city."

"Why didn't he just keep his trap shut?" asked Michael. "He could surely have preached about something else. The Bible's thick enough, and it didn't hurt us to hear about Adam and Eve or Eden. Which makes me think: look over there, the place under the beech trees. Doesn't it look like Eden? What do you think, should we eat a few apples there?"

Kathleen laughed bashfully, but no matter how happy Michael made her over the next hour, a thorn stuck in her heart. To Peter Burton, it mattered a great deal what he preached. The reverend felt beholden to the truth. He wanted his flock to learn to think. It was not Darwin's teachings that were shocking, but their consequences, the conclusions people could draw from them. About life and death, about God and fate, all those things Michael did not think about—and never had, as Kathleen reluctantly had to acknowledge.

She remembered that even Father O'Brien had complained of Michael's superficiality. Kathleen still remembered well how the priest had wanted to send him to school in a monastery in Dublin. The anticipated course back then would have been seminary, and Michael had clearly rejected that from the beginning. He preferred to stay in Wicklow, working Lord Wetherby's fields.

Kathleen now wondered if he could not have found an alternative with a little thought, with some hard work and elbow grease. However, Michael had not even bothered. He loved the simple life. Kathleen thought with a smile of the melodies he had drawn from his fiddle. She absolutely had to give him one. He could play for her, and perhaps there was a tavern in Queenstown where he could play in the evenings. Kathleen lost herself briefly in this daydream, but called herself back. She was falling into the same immature thinking as Michael. As if a sheep baron would have any time and desire to fiddle after a day's work, and as if the farmhands would want to dance to their boss's tunes in the evening.

After three days of travel, they finally reached the MacDuffs' farm, and if Mr. MacDuff was surprised that Michael appeared with a different woman this time, he did not show it. As long as he could afford the farm, that was what mattered.

Yet the tour of the stables and shearing sheds did not go as smoothly as it had a few weeks before with Lizzie. Kathleen proved to be an exceedingly sharp observer who did not hesitate to criticize.

"The stables are rather drafty, Mr. MacDuff," she said as they inspected the sheep stables. "No wonder you had no luck with cattle—you did try cattle, didn't you? Come, Mr. MacDuff, I see the cow pies still. Of course you had bigger livestock in here."

MacDuff hemmed and hawed before he admitted that the climate had proved too rough for cattle.

"Which naturally depends on the breed," said Kathleen. "If you had decided on Angus cattle . . . But, as I was saying, you'll have to renovate this, Michael, even for sheep."

"We never lost many sheep," explained Mr. MacDuff, sounding insulted. "It was just these Merinos. They gave beautiful wool, sure, but they're so sensitive."

Kathleen said nothing more. However, she insisted that Mr. MacDuff take her to the mountain pastures to observe the ewes.

"But that's surely too taxing for a girl like you," objected Mrs. MacDuff, as she filled her guests' saddlebags with provisions.

Mr. MacDuff had reluctantly declared himself willing to present them with a young Maori for a guide. He did not want to ride into the highlands himself.

"If he's left it to his shepherds all year, that explains the reductions among the ewes," remarked Kathleen as they left the farm the next morning. "I'll bet all the Maori villages around here have a quite the flock of sheep."

"What reductions?" Michael asked.

"The losses," said Kathleen. "I took a look at the books last night while you were comparing Scotch and Irish whiskey with Mr. MacDuff. They have horribly high losses—and that doesn't just have to do with the careless Merino breeding."

"Merinos produce gorgeous wool," Michael said.

Kathleen nodded. "Fine wool, but the animals are unfortunately very sensitive. You can't just herd them into the highlands. They sometimes have difficulty lambing, don't breed so quickly, and are not hardy. They're not suited to the farms here."

"Mr. MacDuff has good-looking sheep," Michael said, trying to assure her.

Kathleen shrugged. "Could be. I just haven't seen them yet. The little rams were mediocre. Not so bad; you could certainly sell them, but . . ."

"Kathleen, the sheep we had in Ireland weren't any better."

"So? Just because Lord Wetherby didn't know anything about sheep, we're supposed to produce lower quality wool now? People moved past crossbreeding Merinos years ago. We once had a really cute flock of crossbreds on the farm, but Ian could hardly get rid of them because the breeding results simply varied too much."

Michael grinned and tried to make a joke of it. "Are you talking about your Mr. Darwin?" he asked.

Kathleen arched her brows. She looked very pretty when she furrowed her forehead so seriously, but for the first time Michael recognized more stubbornness than beauty.

"No," she ultimately answered. "I'm talking about Kiward Station, Barrington Station, Lionel Station—all of which you want to compete with, if I understood you rightly. And they have excellent breeds now: Cheviot, Welsh Mountain, Romney, Corriedale—that's a new breed."

Michael interrupted her. "Listen, I was the foreman at Mount Fyffe Run. I know . . ."

Kathleen thought for a moment. "That's the farm near Kaikoura, right? I think Ian even sold them their first flock. Decent sheep, similar to these here." In the foothills the first ewes, with their fluffy lambs, were coming into view.

Kathleen turned to the Maori shepherd, who seemed rather unskilled to her. "Can you herd them together for me?"

MacDuff's men were not usually mounted, which no doubt made the herding in spring and fall more difficult. Nor were this man's efforts satisfactory. Finally Kathleen set her own horse in motion, quickly bringing a dozen sheep together.

"Where did you learn all this?" Michael asked as Kathleen dismounted and approached the first animal.

Kathleen looked up at him, irritated. "I already told you: Ian and I had a farm, although Ian was only there every few days. He rode around selling animals. I took care of the livestock. Alone at first, then with Sean and Colin.

Sean never enjoyed it. Now, look at the wool—do you see the differences between the individual animals? Even in terms of color . . ."

Michael shook his head in disbelief. He was barely listening. It was much too hard to comprehend what had become of his delicate goddess, Kathleen. She rode for hours, herded sheep—and now was even turning a sheep skillfully onto its back to make Michael aware of this or that peculiarity in its wool.

"If you ask me, I would not buy the sheep from MacDuff. You don't know what you're getting. He hasn't even counted the livestock, and the wool quality is not uniform. The land has been overgrazed. They're not making good use of it, and the workers don't seem the best to me either."

Michael's head was spinning by the time they were ready to leave for Queenstown. Kathleen had wanted to take a look at the city, but now she was critical about the fact that it was ten miles away.

The Maori worker did not seem to feel much better than Michael about his possible new mistress, but he looked more awed than angry. "Your lady much *mana*," he said as the men briefly rode beside each other.

Michael sighed. That was the last thing he had wanted to hear.

Chapter 2

"Forgive us if we're disturbing you, Reverend." The Maori girl spoke perfect, almost accent-free English and even offered a polite curtsy to Reverend Peter Burton. "We were told you might know where to find Elizabeth Portland."

The girl was perhaps seventeen or eighteen, tall and slender for a Maori and quite pretty. Her dark-black hair was surely thick as a curtain when she wore it down. Now, however, she had bound it at the nape of her neck—a style that suited the tailored school dress she was wearing. As a missionary student in Waikouaiti, the Maori girl seemed self-assured in the whites' city of Dunedin.

This did not apply to her two companions. The man—young and adorned with tribal tattoos, which was rare in his generation—seemed nervous, almost aggressive. He looked around Peter Burton's cozy living room like an animal in a trap. The third of the trio was an older woman, who seemed only slightly more at peace with herself in the reverend's living room. She, too, wore Western clothing, but her dress was too big. The strong, stout man, on the other hand, was bursting out of his shirt and pants. He carried a spear and a few jade pieces. While Peter couldn't exactly identify them, he assumed the pieces were traditional weaponry, or related to some Maori ritual or custom. No doubt the man was a warrior, even if Peter did not find him very frightening.

Before Peter had a chance to answer about Lizzie, the girl made introductions. "I'm Haikina Hata of the Ngai Tahu tribe. My *iwi* lives above Tuapeka.

This is my mother, Hainga, *tohunga* of our village, and this is Kuri Koura, son of our chief. Kuri speaks only imperfect English, but he can write his name."

Peter wondered why she emphasized that.

"Please, excuse us, but we need to speak with Lizzie."

The reverend nodded. "How did you come to look for her here?"

Haikina shrugged. "I asked in all the hotels, so I learned about Michael . . . And my mother knew that Lizzie is a friend of yours."

"Miss Portland is staying with my housekeeper," Peter explained. "But right now, she's probably at the church. She mostly helps distribute food to the poor. There are many in need here."

As far as that went, Peter had all but come out of the frying pan and into the fire. The new arrivals often camped in the hills near his church before making their way into the mountains. They were a thrown-together heap of men from Australia and families from England, often without any means. Some erected tents; others seemed to have completely misjudged the weather in New Zealand and were trying to sleep outside without any shelter. Of course, in summer, that was possible, but when winter came, Peter and his few assistants from the still-growing parish would have to put up tents—at least to offer women and children a shelter over their heads. Most of the families had come with the notion that gold was just lying in the streets of Dunedin. The realization that they needed money to buy equipment first, and that they would have to travel miles farther to Otago, brought many to the edge of despair. Peter distributed food, clothing, and other supplies, and he wondered if he would ever lead a life in which tents and emergency provisions and care would no longer have a part.

The old woman said something. Haikina blushed but translated dutifully. Peter looked at her questioningly.

"She says people should not run after fulfillment but instead seek gold with their own tribe. They cannot expect something will grow when they haven't planted."

Peter agreed but spread his arms helplessly. "I can't change anything about it," he said.

Haikina nodded. The chieftain's son now uttered something as well, but Haikina didn't translate. "So should we go to the church to look for her? We don't mean to be a bother."

In Dunedin, people hardly ever saw a native, and the newly immigrated had certainly never laid eyes on one. If Peter sent these three to the church now—especially the chieftain's son, with his spear—chaos would ensue.

"I'll fetch her if it's all the same to you," he suggested. "You're welcome to wait here. That will surely be more comfortable for your mother, and then you can speak with Lizzie in private."

Haikina translated, and the others apparently agreed.

"It won't take me long, but how about some tea while you wait."

Haikini nodded and followed him into the kitchen so he could show her where the pot and cups were.

"Is Lizzie sad?" she asked quietly.

Peter nodded. "I hope you don't have bad news for her."

Haikina shook her head. "We just want to ask her for something," she said.

Peter saw that the Maori were not going to reveal much more to him, but he did not need to rein in his curiosity much longer.

Indeed, Lizzie was in the sacristy, where she was portioning out soup. Helping out in the church obviously provided her joy and distracted her from her worries—just as waxing and polishing his furniture seemed to. He knew she loved taking care of beautiful things, and she was able to lose herself in the tasks. Peter envied her this ability. He was always thinking of Kathleen no matter what he busied himself with. He prayed and worked until he was ready to fall over, but he could not move on from his disappointment, let alone his violent jealousy. A priest really should not be plotting murder, after all. Peter Burton was shaken to his core. He doubted his faith and the meaning of his life.

"You have visitors, Lizzie, Maori from the highlands."

***

Lizzie greeted Haikina with a heartfelt embrace, the *tohunga* with a formal but thoroughly intimate *hongi*, and the chieftain's son with a swift bow. The Ngai Tahu had long since given up the untouchability of their chieftain's children, but one still showed them respect.

Haikina handed both Lizzie and the reverend a cup of tea. Peter took this as a sign that he was welcome in this circle. It was just a shame he did not speak any Maori.

Haikina asked the *tohunga* a question in Maori. Hainga nodded and spoke a few words in the reverend's direction.

"She has nothing against me translating for you," the girl said. "You know the land near the waterfall and the five spears."

"She means the rocks that look like needles," Lizzie added, "and really she means the gold mine, not the land itself."

Peter nodded.

Hainga started speaking directly to Lizzie. "Right now," Haikina translated, "the tribe is exceedingly unsettled. The gold mines on the Tuapeka River seem to be running dry, and more and more men are coming farther into the mountains to stake new claims. Our warriors have already seen such men three times on our land, men who are moving their gold pans around in the streams. So far, they have not found the waterfall. But when they do . . ."

"If they stumble on gold, they'll overrun your land," said Peter.

Haikina nodded. "We'd like to beat them to it by offering to give the land to Elizabeth Portland."

"How much land?" Lizzie asked, taken aback. "Surely not all the tribe's land."

The chieftain's son gesticulated violently.

"We had been thinking of the land between the waterfall and the old Drury-Timlock claim," explained Haikina.

"But that's, that's well over one hundred acres." Lizzie almost choked on her tea. "I didn't even know that our claim belonged to the tribe. You never said anything."

Haikina shrugged. The Ngai Tahu were traditionally generous. If there was no *tapu* on the land and it was not turned into a wasteland like Gabriel's Gully, they did not stop anyone from setting up a tent.

"Why do you even want to give your land away?" asked the reverend. "If it clearly belongs to the tribe?"

"As long as it's just land, it clearly belongs to us. The *pakeha* don't want any trouble, after all. They accept that someone has to pay for the land on which they mean to settle. But gold mines? They don't belong to anyone. Everyone would dispute our claims."

"And they won't do that to Lizzie?" asked Peter.

Haikina gave him a look that spoke volumes. She obviously thought him naive.

"Reverend," she said patiently, "if Lizzie Portland places border markers and puts a gun under the nose of anyone who sets foot on her land, she's defending her property, and everyone will applaud her. If we do the same, it's a Maori uprising, and they send soldiers."

Peter bit his lip. "I'm sorry," he said.

Haikina shrugged. "It's not your fault. And Hainga was not happy to see Lizzie go anyway. The elders agreed to give her enough land for a farm. That was her plan after all. Michael wanted to breed sheep. The way it looks now . . ."

Lizzie looked completely stunned by the generous offer. "I, I'm happy to accept, of course," she said. "At least officially, so the land has a *pakeha* owner."

"It would be safer if you lived there too," said Haikina.

"I don't know; alone?"

"Lizzie, if you build your house where your cabin is now, then you'll only be three miles from Lawrence," said Peter. Lawrence was the new name for the gold miners' town around the Tuapeka post office. "You can't be much closer without being in town."

Hainga raised her voice. "You not alone," she said in broken English. "Baby with you. Baby welcome in tribe."

Lizzie stared at the old woman, stunned.

"How does she know?" Lizzie asked, looking at Haikina.

Haikina shrugged. "That would be the spirits—or the gaze of a practiced midwife."

Hainga looked at Lizzie. "It came to be under the lights of Matariki," she said in Maori. "A child blessed by Rangi."

Lizzie felt herself blush. What was she saying? The baby was conceived on New Year's Eve? She thought of Kahu. But then she calmed herself. Hainga had not mentioned the festival of Tou Hou, merely the Pleiades. And they still stood in the sky.

"It's Michael's child," she said to Hainga.

Hainga made a dismissive gesture. "It's a child," she said.

"It has your *mana*," added Haikina, "until it acquires its own. Are you agreed? Would you like a farm on the Tuapeka River?"

Lizzie nodded. She had been happy on the river. It was only right for her child to grow up there. And as for the farm: if she did not have to pay for the land and she lived in the cabin, she would have plenty of money for years. She would have no need to bother with sheep. And with regards to employment, she already had an idea.

Haikina asked the reverend for the address of a lawyer who could certify the sale by the Ngai Tahu of some hundred acres of farmland to Elizabeth Portland. Peter helped however he could, even calling in a justice of the peace as a double check that everything was official. Two days later, Hainga, Kuri Koura, and Lizzie carefully signed their names to a document written in Maori and English.

Afterward, the Maori left right away to bring word to the tribe.

Lizzie promised she would get to the land as soon as possible. "I can't come right away. I have a few things to see to," she told Haikina.

"Such as talking to Michael?"

Lizzie sighed. "Michael and that Kathleen of his will have a farm in Otago. I don't think there's much more left to say or do about it. But I need to go to the bank that has my money for the farm—and I have some orders to place."

"Orders?" Haikina asked.

Lizzie smiled. "Something like seeds."

***

Peter Burton opened a bottle of champagne when Lizzie joined him at the parsonage. She had spent hours studying catalogues, placing orders, and making arrangements with a transportation company. Peter had asked his housekeeper to cook, since he thought Lizzie would be too tired to do so herself.

"Just who is going to polish your furniture when I'm not here anymore?" Lizzie sighed as she fell, exhausted, into an armchair.

Peter laughed. "I'd suggest you order furniture from England and tend to your own things for a change," he replied. "You have enough money, you know. You could have a beautiful house built."

Lizzie shrugged. "What do I need a big house for? The cabin is enough for me and the baby. And I'll have so much to do outside. There'll be no household with maids." She smiled tiredly. "Kathleen surely has more of a knack for being a sheep baroness than me. Even just how pretty she is."

Peter sat beside Lizzie. "It's not my affair, of course, Lizzie, and I also understand that you don't want to discuss anything with Michael anymore. But have you thought of approaching Kathleen?"

Lizzie became angry. "Why? So she can laugh at me? If Kathleen had wanted to protect me—if I had interested Kathleen even a jot—then she would not have encouraged Michael. She knew about me. She knew of the wedding we were planning. My God, she tailored my dress."

Lizzie took a quick drink from her glass.

"She was surprised," said Peter. "Lizzie, I don't mean to excuse her, but she was surely shaken to her heart—she did think, after all, that she would never see him again."

Lizzie snorted. "That was weeks ago, Reverend. Let her come down from the clouds."

Peter shrugged. "Be that as it may," he said, "you should tell her about the baby."

Chapter 3

"So if you really want to buy this farm, Michael, then at least don't take Mr. MacDuff's sheep. Look around for well-bred stock; the big farms sell animals for breeding, you know." Once again, Kathleen was summarizing the results of the journey for Michael. For about the twentieth time—or so it seemed to him, at least. Their whole ride back from Queenstown, she had talked about practically nothing other than her suggestions for the purchase and management of a sheep farm.

Kathleen was riding Sean's little black horse, which pranced blithely as they approached Dunedin and his own stall. Michael's patience had nearly run out—no matter how beautiful Kathleen looked as she rode beside him, no matter how at ease on the horse. If he was honest, even that got on his nerves. He was nostalgic for their rare rides together on O'Rearke's donkey. Then she had laid her head on Michael's shoulder, clung to him, and given up the reins to him. Now she talked as if she wanted to take the sheep husbandry entirely into her own hands.

"But there's not enough money for that," he said, annoyed. He had said it several times already too.

Yet Kathleen simply kept going.

"Then start with cattle until you've made enough," she said. "Cattle are a safe business, especially in Otago since the gold find. Thousands of gold miners working hard, who want nothing more after all the panning for gold than a fat steak. Naturally, you'll have to seal up the barn better, but you should do that anyway. Later you'll want to hire shearing companies, and nowadays they want sturdy shearing sheds."

Michael sighed. It was best just to let her talk. Maybe she would get back to herself when they reached Dunedin.

"If you do buy the farm at all, that is; you really ought to think it over again. More than ten miles from town, Michael. And right now, Queenstown is just a better sort of gold miners' camp. Maybe someday it'll be a city, but maybe not. It's none of my business, but . . ."

Michael's ears pricked up. "Kathleen, of course it's your business. It's to be your farm too. We do mean to live there together, after all."

A shadow fell over Kathleen's face. She seemed to struggle with herself briefly, and then she stopped her horse and turned to him very seriously.

"Michael," she said, "I love you. But I don't want a farm. I don't want to herd sheep anymore or help them lamb on ice-cold nights, and under no circumstances do I want to live miles and miles from the next city. You don't know how lonely it is, Michael."

"But we would be together," Michael objected. "How can you be lonely with me there? We, we always dreamed of a farm. Even back in Ireland."

The first houses of Dunedin were now in sight. They could reach Sullivan's stables in a few minutes. Kathleen alighted and let the horse walk behind her. Obviously, she had more she needed to stay before they got there.

Michael also dismounted, and they walked a few steps side by side in silence before Kathleen spoke.

"Michael, Ireland, that was seventeen years ago. Half our lives ago. So much has happened in that time; this to me, that to you—I don't know if we can make up for that. But I know for sure that I don't want to live on a farm. Just as my children don't."

"Sean is my son," said Michael.

"Sean is almost grown, Michael. He knows what he wants. Much better than we knew back then. He's a smart boy, and I thank you for such a wonderful son. Sean was worth it all, Michael, even if I sometimes doubted it. But you can't make up those years with him. He—"

"He's sad about that reverend!" Michael blurted out. "I still haven't asked, Kathleen, but was there something between you Peter Burton?" He glared at her.

"If there was something, it's not your concern. Especially since there was also something between you and Miss Portland."

"That was different!" Michael said. "We're two halves of a whole. Between us is something holy. Lizzie is, Lizzie was a—"

Kathleen bade him be silent with a hand gesture. "I don't want to know what Lizzie is and was. Your past doesn't interest me, let alone hers. The future is what interests me. You determined my life, Michael, for seventeen years. I married Ian for your sake; I left Ireland for your sake. You did not plan all that, but it was for your sake. I did what you wanted. I raised your child with dignity. But if we really belong together, irrevocably, because God wants it, then you have to orient your life to mine. Set up something for yourself in Dunedin. A business or whatever. I would love to live with you, Michael, but I also want my children, Claire, my business . . ."

"And your reverend?" he asked.

Kathleen slapped Michael in the face. She could hardly believe what she was thinking: Michael, her wonderful beloved who had always known a way out, who had always made her laugh, who had seemed strong and good to her—he was behaving like a petulant child.

Kathleen put a foot in the stirrups and swung onto the small black horse.

"Think it over, Michael," she said calmly. Then she galloped away.

She did not care if he followed her.

***

Kathleen was dirty, tired, and sweaty by the time she had finally delivered her horse to the stables and reached her apartment on George Street. All she wished for now was to take a warm bath and then fall into a proper bed. Kathleen was tired of brooding about Michael and his farm. It was his turn. If he wanted to live with her, he would have to make a different offer.

Defiantly, Kathleen slammed the door behind her and took off her hat. She heard voices and laughter from the salon. Was that Sean she heard?

Claire opened the door to the kitchen and came out with a platter of tea and cake.

"Kathleen." She seemed surprised, and to Kathleen's amazement, she blushed. "I really had not been expecting you yet. But it's good you're here already. You have a guest." Claire gestured to the salon. "Come to think of it, though," she said as they heard a new round of laughter, "perhaps you should not intrude just yet. Here, just listen for once, would you?"

Claire pushed Kathleen into the next room and quietly opened the connecting door so Kathleen could peek into the salon. She put her finger to her lips—and yet Kathleen could hardly keep herself from crying out in surprise. Lizzie was sitting on the sofa, conversing excitedly with Sean. She was telling anecdotes from Michael's life, and for the first time, Sean seemed interested in his father.

"He wanted to make it from Australia to New Zealand in a rowboat?" Sean laughed. "Across the Tasman Sea? Didn't he have any idea how far that is?"

"In a sailboat," Lizzie corrected him, "and with three companions. One of them had sailed before."

"But he would have gotten himself killed," cried Sean. "How can anyone be such a fool?"

Kathleen frowned.

"Your father isn't a fool," Lizzie said firmly. "Just a little heedless sometimes. And then he wanted to get back to Ireland, no matter what. To your mother. And to you."

"He didn't even know me," objected Sean.

"But he talked about you all the time. He promised your mother he would come back to her. And he wanted to do that even if it meant running his head through a wall."

Sean laughed. "And how did he actually make it here? Did he swim?"

"Is that what he told you?" asked Lizzie, truly interested. She would have given anything to know how Michael had represented their passage.

"He didn't say much about it. Just that, well, it was a stroke of luck. He was able to ride on a large ship."

Lizzie snorted. Then she told him about David Parsley. Kathleen and Claire looked at each other knowingly—they could figure out what happened, even though Lizzie gave Sean a somewhat watered-down version of the story.

"That's why your father was so mad at me," said Lizzie. "He doesn't like to cheat anyone. But I'm sure nothing happened to Mr. Parsley—other than everyone making fun of him. He did not even need to pay for the voyage himself. His company or his employer did that for him. And I couldn't let Michael drown."

"I think it's very noble of you," said Sean. "Taking him along, I mean. It was a risk to ask for passage for David Parsley's wife. If there had been no more space on the ship, you would have had to stay behind, and they would have caught you."

"The ticket was in Parsley's name," explained Lizzie.

Sean nodded. "But you could have forged it."

Lizzie had not even thought of that. But it was true. She had not depended on Michael's escape in any way. Gratitude on her part was unnecessary. She, alone, was the hero of this story. She felt her *mana* grow.

"I didn't want to go without him," she finally admitted.

Sean grinned. "You were completely in love."

Lizzie blushed.

"And what happened back then in Ireland? What got my father sent to Van Diemen's Land? What happened to Trevallion's grain?"

Lizzie shrugged. "You'll have to ask your mother. I only met him on the ship."

"But Ma won't tell me anything," complained Sean. "Nothing that makes sense, anyway. Just like my father. Did he distribute the grain or sell it or what?"

"Well, if I understand correctly, he used it to distill whiskey," Lizzie said calmly. "Moonshine. You can't book passage to America for a few sacks of grain."

Kathleen and Claire gulped for air. For Claire the story was new. Kathleen was deeply ashamed. She would never have told Sean. What would he think of his father? But to her surprise, Sean began to laugh.

"My father, the Irish folk hero, distilled whiskey during the famine? I have to tell Reverend Peter. That's the best story I've ever heard."

Kathleen was grateful for all the hours her son had spent with Peter Burton. He'd imparted a deep sense of justice, to be sure, but also a sense of humor and respect for true feats of daring. It was true: Peter would enjoy the tale of Michael's "freedom fighting" immensely.

"He did not distill whiskey until later," Lizzie corrected Sean. "In Ireland, his family did it. But we had a tavern in Kaikoura."

Kathleen felt the time was right to join them. She opened the door to the salon and smiled at Lizzie and Sean. "Pardon my barging in, Miss Portland. I just got home. And I'd like to hear this as well."

***

Although Michael was not seriously considering owning a business in Dunedin, he thought about it briefly as he rode back to his hotel. A business? Maybe lumber trading or selling other construction materials. But he did not know much about wood, let alone stone. On top of that would come negotiating with deliverers, traders, and customers—maybe even bankers like the arrogant Jimmy Dunloe? No, that was not his world. Not even for Kathleen's sake. Especially not Kathleen. She was ungrateful. Here he was doing everything to make their life's dream come true. He was practically laying a farm at her feet. And what did she do? Nitpick.

He tied up his horse in the hotel's stables and walked over to the tavern on the other side of the street. The situation required a whiskey, Irish if possible. Michael called to the barkeeper and ordered one.

A few hours later, he was sitting in his third tavern, this time in the middle of the city. He looked at the newly built St. Paul's Cathedral, feeling sorry for himself. But then he saw what he at first thought was an apparition. Strolling from George Street toward the church was Lizzie. Not an apparition. Lizzie. Though strolling was the wrong word. Her movement was as deft and determined as always. She held herself upright, so she looked somewhat taller—she always did that too. Why had that never occurred to him before? She seemed at ease and at peace with herself. Completely different from him.

Michael threw a coin on the table, left what remained of his whiskey, and ran outside.

"Lizzie!"

She turned around, and Michael thought she might smile. Just as she always did when she saw him. But she frowned instead.

"Michael?" she asked, gesturing toward the tavern. "Drinking away the money for your farm?"

Michael caught up to her. Suddenly he wanted nothing more than to pour his heart out to her.

"There isn't a farm," he said breathlessly. "She, she . . . Lizzie, Lizzie, I, I'd like to talk to you. I need to talk to you."

Lizzie turned away. "I don't know what we still have to discuss," she said. "You have another life now, your 'true life.' Didn't you always think of it that way? So good luck with Mary Kathleen. If you've got something to talk about, talk to her."

She turned and began to walk again.

"But I don't even have it!" yelled Michael. He jumped ahead of her, cutting off her path. "I don't have another life. She doesn't want me. Kathleen—after everything, she doesn't want me anymore." The words burst out of Michael as if they were going to tear him apart.

Lizzie suppressed the urge to take him in her arms. Not this time. She would not make it so easy for him this time.

She stepped closer but did not touch him. "After everything?" she asked sternly. "After what? Had you done anything together with Kathleen in all these years?"

"You know very well I was thinking of her!" Michael roared. "Every damn day since I left Ireland."

Lizzie nodded and looked around unhappily. It was not good to fight on the street. She pulled Michael into the cool vestibule of St. Paul's.

"Oh yes, I know," she said bitterly. "You compared me with her every day—or rather with the memory you had of her. Kathleen the beautiful, the pure, the virgin *Mary* Kathleen. As opposed to Lizzie the whore."

"Lizzie, I never wanted . . . I didn't mean it that way."

Michael furrowed his brow in remorse, a quirk Lizzie had never been able to resist. She looked away so she could remain focused and speak in defense of herself. "Didn't mean it, did you?" she asked sternly. "Well, now it's time to grow up. Your Kathleen stripped off her virgin mantle with the name Mary, and in doing so, she sold herself just like I did. Because sometimes one has no other choice. In the end, it doesn't matter if one goes in front of the altar with a bastard so she can bring a child up with dignity, or if one goes to bed with paying customers to avoid starving. Or watches the man she loves destroy himself. Without me, Michael, they would have beat you to death as an escapee, or you would have drowned in the Tasman Sea, or you would have drunk yourself to death because your life of whaling and herding had no meaning. Of course, I needed *mana* for that, Michael, even if you didn't like it. Just like you don't like it with Kathleen now. Kathleen is just like me, Michael. The only difference is I love you. And she doesn't."

Michael, whose gaze had wandered aimlessly over the candles and the paintings of saints in the entrance chapel during her outburst, now stared directly in Lizzie's eyes. "Of course she loves me! How can you say that? Kathleen has always loved me."

"She loved the boy she kissed in the fields by the Vartry River. Perhaps even the adventurer who rebelled against his masters a little. But can you imagine Kathleen in the gold mines? And you heard her: she doesn't have any intention of giving up her cute little shop to raise livestock with you in Otago."

Michael did not ask how she knew that. He was too angry and to drunk for that.

"She thinks it now," he spat defiantly. "But she'll go along in the end. 'Where you go, there I will follow.' Are you familiar with that, Lizzie?"

Lizzie could not stop herself. She slapped him in the face.

"I live that, Michael. I've lived that for countless years. But now I've had enough. I'm doing like Kathleen, Michael. I'm doing what I want." She turned to go but then looked at him once more. "By the way, you have a charming son, Michael. I got to meet him earlier, and it was a pleasure. I hope our own child will be just as smart and thoughtful. And since I've got the money, you don't need to worry: I'll raise it with dignity."

***

"You spoke with Lizzie?" asked Michael.

It was strange to sit across from Kathleen in such a formal way. He had wanted to see her, but she had not invited him to the apartment. Instead, they met at the café in his hotel. Kathleen gracefully balanced a teacup between two fingers and occasionally took a delicate bite of a pastry. He remembered the pastry she had stolen from the kitchen of the manor all those years ago—just to share with him. Had he ever shared anything with her? Aside from love?

Michael could not forget the fields on the river. That day, the pastries had been their only real food. Now pastries were nothing but a sweet snack on a fine plate—an everyday treat to nibble on.

Kathleen nodded. "Yes. And you didn't tell me the truth. She's not an old friend. She is . . . she is your second half. Precisely what I never was."

"What you never got to be," said Michael sharply. "Circumstances were against us. But if it had worked, if we had gone to America . . ."

"Then we'd be sitting in some hole in New York now. You and Sean would be working in some factory, and I would be a seamstress. We'd be slaving away to stay alive somehow. Michael, without Lizzie, you never would have made it. We wouldn't have a farm in California or a factory in Boston or whatever else. I wouldn't have made it myself, either. Our business was Claire's idea, not mine. Together, we two would have survived, but nothing more. Precisely because we're not two halves of a whole. Your other half is Elizabeth Portland. And mine . . ."

"You want to go back to that reverend?" asked Michael.

"There can be no 'back.' I was never with him. But it's time for me to move on. Until now, my other half was Claire. But she's going to marry Jimmy Dunloe as soon as the law here finally allows her to divorce. And I'll . . . Well, I can only hope Peter forgives me. Peter's not my past, Michael. He's my future." Kathleen looked at him almost defiantly.

Michael lowered his head. "Lizzie says they're the same thing, past and future." For the first time, Michael felt no jealousy when Kathleen spoke of Peter Burton. "At least that's what the Maori told her. We always need a mountain that anchors us in the here and now; they call that *maunga*."

Kathleen smiled. "There, you see. Lizzie is your *maunga*. As much as a person can be. But I'm not. I'm not strong enough to anchor you. I need an anchor myself. We'll see if Peter can be that." She laughed. "Petrus, the rock. He must have heard that before."

Michael still did not want to give up. "But what about our love, Kathleen? It was there; it *is* there."

Kathleen hugged him. "It will remain too. Or a shadow of it will. But you don't need me to be happy. You need Lizzie—if she'll have you."

"You're not angry?" he asked.

Kathleen rolled her eyes. "I'm not angry, not that it matters. It's better to ask yourself if Lizzie still wants you."

Michael bit his lip. "It didn't seem that way when we last talked," he admitted. "Yet I feel like she still might. I don't know where she's gone though. Did you, did you know that she's with child?"

Kathleen nodded. "Yes. I do know. Make sure you find her."

Michael squared himself in his old self-assurance. "I will. If I have to turn over every stone, I—"

Kathleen lay her hand soothingly on his. "Michael, just think before you dig up New Zealand. Or decide to sail the Tasman Sea in a sailboat. There has to be a *maunga* for Lizzie too."

Chapter 4

Lizzie could never get enough of the view of her land from atop the waterfall. The forested hills undulated like waves into the valley, the rocks jutted showily into the sky, the lively stream flowed to the river, and the ribbon of the Tuapeka River shimmered in the sunlight. On an early autumn day as clear as this one, even the growing town of Lawrence was recognizable.

Lizzie was still undecided as to whether she should settle here or in her former camp. The Maori preferred she build her house near the waterfall, and they had asked her to take possession of the land there.

"Herd some sheep or whatever else," said Haikina.

Lizzie already had plans for the gentle hills on this north-facing space. There was enough sun and water here. The winters were harder than on the North Island—but surely no harder than in Germany, and a great deal of wine was made there. A few of the vine stalks Lizzie had carefully transported and placed in the moist earth, warm from the late summer, came from Germany, others from France. Time would tell how they would adapt to New Zealand's South Island.

Lizzie laughed to herself. Maybe the vines liked gold and she would begin a whole new chapter in the history of viniculture here. Since Kahu Heke had told her about the studying he'd done in Auckland, she had burned with desire to learn more about winemaking. She had ordered books on top of books, and with her slow reading pace, she had enough to read for the next few years at least. And her child would learn to read as well—when it was not sitting at the feet of a *tohunga* listening to the stories of Papa and Rangi and their divine children. Lizzie considered proximity to the Maori village to be more important in the beginning than proximity to Lawrence. She hummed to herself as she tenderly buried the next cutting in the ground.

Suddenly, some movement near the river caught her attention. Two mules were eating on the shore—and two men were unpacking their saddlebags. Lizzie looked around, without much hope though. Earlier in the day, a few Maori women had helped her with the digging, and a few men had panned for gold; the tribe needed winter stores of grain and clothing. But the Maori had gone back to the village more than an hour before.

Lizzie reached for Michael's old gun, which she had laid down nearby. She had found it in the cabin and taken it with her, primarily to show it to the warriors. The Ngai Tahu, like most of the Maori tribes, possessed enough guns for self-defense. The men had looked Lizzie's rifle over expertly, cleaned it, and tried it. Then they had given it back to her.

"It works," said Haikina, "so watch out you don't kill yourself with it."

Lizzie had promised to let the warriors instruct her in the gun's use but had kept delaying. In truth, the gun made her uncomfortable. Now she regretted her negligence. But she did not want to shoot anyone down anyway, just scare them.

She put the gun under her arm, then went down to the river and greeted the men politely. Both men had just unloaded their tents. One was reaching for his gold pan.

Lizzie approached them. "I'm sorry, gentlemen, but you can't pan here. This is private property, and the stream is part of it."

She struggled to make her voice sound firm. At first, the men, both bearlike, looked at her, taken aback.

"Since when is this private property?" grumbled the first man.

Though she was obviously fairly far along in her pregnancy, that clearly wasn't their first concern.

The second man laughed. "Hey, I know you. Aren't you Michael Drury's wife? Old Mike's supposed to have gotten properly rich. Where'd he find the gold? Here?" He pointed at the stream.

Lizzie shook her head. "Michael panned here and there. He had a claim together with Chris Timlock. But it ran dry. Now . . ." She hated herself for what she had to do now, but if she admitted that she was on her own out here . . . "Now, we're going to farm here. The land from our old cabin up to here belongs to us, legally purchased from the Ngai Tahu."

The men laughed.

"As if it was ever theirs," said the older man.

Lizzie shrugged. "The governor recognized it, as did the justice of the peace and a few lawyers in Dunedin. In any case, my sheep will graze here soon. And as for you two: you can find the next gold mining camp near Lawrence, and there are new finds near Queenstown. There's nothing for you here, literally."

Lizzie leaned on her rifle in the hope the gesture looked threatening. Her friends among the Maori warriors achieved a similar effect when they leaned on their spears. But, of course, she was neither humongous nor tattooed.

The men did not back down. On the contrary. The younger, who had recognized her earlier, strode toward her.

"Why are we being so unfriendly, huh?" he asked, smirking. Lizzie now saw how big, strong, and determined he was. "What happened to the celebrated hospitality of country gentlemen and women? Come on, little lady. Invite us in, let us pass a comfortable night, and if we're convinced tomorrow there's no gold . . ." Even now, they completely ignored Lizzie's pregnancy.

"You can just look at the deed to convince yourself this is private land," Lizzie said with a sharp tone and raised her rifle.

She aimed at the men—and would have felt considerably better if she had known whether the gun was locked and how to shoot a target. Although it did not really matter. A shot would be heard in the village. If she fired, a band of Maori warriors would arrive in short order.

"Now, be nice, Lizzie."

"That's Miss Portland to you," Lizzie replied.

"Still not Mrs. Drury?"

The men came closer. Lizzie breathed deep and pulled the trigger. Nothing happened—so she needed to unlock it. She pulled on the gun's levers and pulled the trigger again, with success this time. The gun took on a life of its own, recoiling upward as she fired the shot.

Lizzie had to keep herself from dropping the gun. Horrified, she looked over at the men, prepared to see at least one dead on the ground. But they were standing right where they had been—clearly shocked though. She had scared them a little, at least.

"Now, hold on a moment, Miss Portland," said the other. He sounded almost insulted. "We've come here peacefully."

"Then you can ride on peacefully," Lizzie spat.

She moved slowly backward, noticing that the men were moving too. They were trying to corner her. She almost had to turn her back to the one to aim at the other.

Lizzie fired once again, which was obviously not a good idea. The men noticed that she had not mastered the gun's use. They approached briskly.

"We don't want any trouble, Miss Portland," said the older one. "Give us the gun and let us do a little test digging on your land. It'd be a good deal for you, too, if we really found gold. What's that anyway?"

He pointed to the vines, distracting Lizzie a heartbeat too long. His companion leaped at her in the same moment. Lizzie struck him with the gun, but she didn't hit him hard enough. She stumbled. The man would tear away the gun in a moment, and then . . .

"What the hell is this?" Lizzie heard a loud, commanding voice she recognized immediately. "Rusty Hamilton? And Johnboy Simmons? It's been a while." Michael galloped toward them. "Could the two of you please tell me what the hell you're doing to my girl?"

The younger man—Johnboy Simmons—let Lizzie go and muttered an apology.

"No offense, Michael," said Rusty, "but the lady threatened us with the gun and—"

"The lady, I'm sure, informed you that you are on her land," said Michael. "This is Elizabeth Station, from our old claim all the way up to here. So pack up your gold pans and get going."

Michael dismounted from his gray, ran over to Lizzie, and gave her a fleeting kiss, winking at her inconspicuously. Lizzie played along, saying nothing.

Rusty Hamilton approached him with upraised hands. "But Michael, there could be gold in the stream. What if you're sitting on a gold mine?"

Michael laughed uproariously. "Now that would be a dream, Rusty, sitting here on a gold mine. But believe me, the Maori aren't fools enough to sell gold mines for pastureland. And how thick do you think I am? Do you think I didn't try the stream?"

"And?" asked the man greedily.

Michael shook his head. "It carries a little gold, of course," he replied. "But so do all the streams, even our old claim down there."

Rusty and Johnboy laughed contemptuously.

"But this here isn't Gabriel's Gully." Michael smiled. "I swear to you, boys, on my honor."

Lizzie looked at the ground.

"Well." Rusty Hamilton seemed disappointed but didn't appear to be planning any more attempts. "And you're not going to tell us where you found all that gold you bought this little sheep paradise with, are you? Elizabeth Station. Lovely. Congratulations, little lady."

Lizzie smiled. She was surprised that she managed to beam at these good-for-nothings as if they were the answer to her prayers.

Michael grinned. "Of course I'll tell you: from here, go east to my old claim, then southward to a lake that is shaped like . . . like a dead dog. That's what the Maori called it. What was its name again, Lizzie?"

Lizzie had to stop herself from laughing. She had never heard of such a lake.

"Kuritemato," she said, improvising.

"There you have it," said Michael seriously. "At the left front paw, turn westward, and then it's just a few miles to a stream—a little hidden, lots of ferns around it. You might even find our old sluice box. I just have to warn you, boys. The gold flow ran out."

Rusty and Johnboy grinned like children on Christmas.

"I don't see it that way," said Rusty. "If you ask me, you just found too much to keep looking properly. We'll take a look anyway. So then, how far is it, Michael?"

Michael considered. "Far," he said, "about an eight days march. And it's easy to get lost. There are loads of lakes there."

"We'll find it," said Johnboy, tipping the brim of his hat. "And once again: no harm meant, miss."

Michael and Lizzie waited in silence until the two men had saddled their mules again.

Michael interrupted the silence with a short question. "What are those?" he, too, asked quietly, pointing to the grape vines.

"Wine," said Lizzie. "This is going to be a vineyard."

Michael furrowed his brow. "We'll need to put a fence around it so the sheep don't trample the vines."

"We?" asked Lizzie.

"Let's talk about it later. We shouldn't argue until these fellows are gone." Michael waved at the prospectors.

"Who wants to argue?" inquired Lizzie.

She turned around and went up the hill a ways, back to her vines. One last vine had to be put in place. Carefully, she planted it.

"Admit it: you need me," said Michael, once the men had finally ridden away. He let his gaze wander over the vineyard and down to Lawrence. The view was breathtaking.

Lizzie arched her brows. "On account of those rats? The Ngai Tahu are already on their way. They heard the gunshots at the village. Soon this place will be crawling with warriors. And I'm going to learn how to aim that thing." She pointed to the gun. "You couldn't do it yourself anyway. Or why else all that with the dead dog lake?"

Michael laughed. "I'm increasing my *mana*," he explained. "*Whaikorero*, the art of talking beautifully."

"I'd work on my spear throwing first," said Lizzie, piling earth around her final cutting. "Those two won't be in such a good mood when they come back."

"Oh, they won't be back. With a little luck, they'll find some gold somewhere on the way. And if not, I sent them in the direction of Queenstown. It would be madness to turn back around instead of working the new finds."

"And what was with swearing on your honor to them?" For the moment, there was nothing more for Lizzie to do in her vineyard.

"Well, there's not much you can redeem it for anyway. If I understand you and Kathleen correctly, my *mana* won't take me very far."

Lizzie grinned. "But you could always live piously," she said, "and raise your child with dignity."

"Does that mean you'll still have me?" he asked quietly.

Lizzie sighed and changed the subject. "How did you know I'd be here?"

Michael gestured at the land around them. "It's your mountain, Lizzie. Your *maunga*."

She smiled. "And you want to let sheep graze on it?"

Michael bit his lip. "It's not about the sheep, Lizzie. We can make wine—or distill whiskey. I just want to be with you. Because you and the baby—you're my *maunga*."

"What about Sean?" she asked.

"Sean is almost grown. He doesn't need me anymore. And he has the reverend."

This last sentence almost sounded bitter. Michael accepted that Peter Burton had done a worthy job in his place.

"Is that what Kathleen said?" Lizzie smiled. "Peter will be happy. It's just a question of who will marry the two of them, the future Anglican bishop or that awful Father Parrish."

"Don't dodge, Lizzie," Michael said. "This isn't about Kathleen."

Lizzie turned her face to the heavens in a gesture of gratitude. "That I lived to see this day . . ." she said, somewhat sarcastically.

Michael forced himself to be patient. "It's about us Lizzie. And about him in there." He shyly laid his hand on her stomach.

"It could be a girl." Lizzie pushed his hand away. "One like me."

"All the better," said Michael. "I don't care either way. I'll take a boy or a girl or both. As long as it comes from you."

Kahu Heke came to Lizzie's mind, but she shooed the thought away quickly.

"And I'd like to watch him grow. I'd like to be with the two of you, build a house for you."

To Lizzie it sounded as if Michael was pleading. She couldn't be unfeeling.

"And tell him about Ireland," she teased him. "About his grandpa who made moonshine, and his grandma who prayed grandpa wouldn't get caught. And how they sent Daddy to Australia because of something to do with Trevallion's grain."

Michael nodded seriously. "Exactly," he said. "Isn't that what the Maori call *pepeha*?"

Lizzie laughed. "More like *whakapapa*, lineage. But the way you tell it, it's more like *moteatea*, fairy tales."

Michael's face took on its guilty grin. "So, will you let me?" he asked with growing hope. "May I stay with you? May I love you? May I sing the baby to sleep with good old Irish *whaikorero*?"

Lizzie turned and looked into his shining blue eyes. "As long as you never hold against our child what her mother was—or is."

Michael pulled her close. "You mean a woman with lots of *mana*," he whispered to her. "It will realize that itself soon." He kissed her, and she returned his kiss, very slowly, very tenderly: a seal on a promise.

"I'll get to work on that fence," Michael said as their lips parted. "For, for the sheep."

Lizzie rubbed her temples and smiled indulgently.

"The house first, Michael," she said gently.

Afterword

As always, I have striven for the greatest possible historical authenticity in this novel. My readers can picture the situation in Ireland during the potato blight, as well as the conditions in Wicklow Jail and on British prison ships, knowing they were as I have described them. The *Asia* truly did sail from Woolwich to Van Diemen's Land, now Tasmania, at the given time, with 169 female prisoners on board. I did, however, stow the twelve men away, and in other respects, my depiction is not quite historically correct: there were no deaths on board—the death rate on deportation ships was considerably lower than one often reads. Statistically speaking, one would actually have traveled much more safely on a convict ship to Australia than on a regular passenger ship to New Zealand or even America. Naturally, the British Crown only deported healthy, mostly young men and women, whereas the old, the sick, and many children would otherwise be on board a normal passenger ship. Though a medical examination did indeed occur, it was only cursory, and no one inspected the hygienic conditions on board. No wonder the weak quickly succumbed to outbreaks. Prison ships were considerably better overseen, by contrast, so illnesses were more quickly brought under control.

My depictions of the conditions in Australian prisons are also historically accurate, especially the female factories. The bizarre marriage markets for female convicts I described really did exist. And a prisoner really did once try to escape the prison in Hobart disguised as a kangaroo. He was caught, but that no ever escaped from Van Diemen's Land back then can certainly be doubted. On New Zealand's West Coast, at any rate, there were so many refugees from Australia that extraditions were negotiated between the two countries.

A few historical New Zealand personalities play a role in this book: James Busby, Robert Fyfe, and Robert's cousin George with the three Fs in his name. The story of the whaling station Waiopuka is as authentic as that of the settling of Port Cooper, later called Lyttelton, and Tuapeka, near the present-day town of Lawrence. The old whaler Johnny Jones really did donate the building site for the Anglican church in Dunedin, and he also resettled emigrants disappointed with Australia in Waikouaiti, New Zealand.

My Reverend Peter Burton is, however, fiction, just like all the other main characters. Also fictitious are the names and dates of the immigration ships and the ferries between New Zealand and Australia. I've fudged a bit with Reverend Burton's fatal attraction to Darwinism: Charles Darwin's *On the Origin of Species* was first published in 1859, so it is unlikely that a figure like Peter Burton would have read it by the beginning of the gold rush in Dunedin. This epochal work of science did not yet consider the evolution of humans; Darwin put forth his theories of human evolution in 1871 with *The Descent of Man, and Selection in Relation to Sex*. However, passionate discussions were already taking place in scientific and intellectual circles before the publication of *On the Origin of Species*, a text directed at interested laypeople above all. So Peter could already have heard of it and drawn his own conclusions. In any case, I ask my readers to forgive me if he is perhaps a little too far ahead of his time.

The authenticity of the all the descriptions of Maori customs and traditions is a harder question. Maori culture is very unlike my own. It is difficult to incorporate here, since it is no longer alive in the same sense. The Maori keep up their traditions, and over the last few decades they have received more and more support from the New Zealand government and tourist board. Yet the whites, their culture, and their diseases were thorough: of the original Maori population, only a fraction survived, particularly on the North Island, and their lifestyle was so incompatible with *pakeha* culture that, more or less under pressure, it largely disappeared. The Ngai Tahu on the South Island separated themselves quite willingly from the traditions and *tapu*, which they had never treated as strictly anyway. For them, the whites' lifestyle offered such a higher quality of life that they quickly assimilated.

One expression of my Kahu Heke in this book cannot be denied: the climate on New Zealand's South Island has more in common with Scotland and Wales than with Hawaiki in Polynesia. The plants and animals brought by the British immigrants thrived more, and the culture, house construction, and lifestyle of the *pakeha* were more compatible with the land than were those of the earlier immigrants from Polynesia. In my view, it speaks to the intelligence and flexibility of the Ngai Tahu that they assimilated instead of fighting the new arrivals. That they were often cheated in the process is a story for another time. In part, the courts today are still busy with restitution for tribal claims regarding deception in land sales.

If one wants to reconstruct the lives of the Maori tribes 150 years ago, there are two paths to take. One is through publications of Maori themselves, which I prefer at heart. I draw a great deal of information from official Maori sources. But Maori, too, are human: they tend to present themselves as positively as possible. Thus, Maori representatives do not like to give information about strange customs like the *tapu* around the chieftains and their families, for instance, while one can draw from them very precise accounts of harmless activities like greeting rituals, dances, fishing, and the like.

The second path is to study the publications of contemporary white ethnologists. These sources often offer more information but have their own perils. The modern studies of history and sociology were still in their infancy in the nineteenth century, particularly in the area of ethnology; the research and data gathering often fell to interested laypersons. Though they often made detailed descriptions, fundamental perceptions escaped them—for instance, that there was no Maori culture in the sense that we mean the term. Today, many emphasize the commonalities between the tribes, but back then, every *iwi* and *hapu* had its own customs, commandments, and *tapu*. *Pakeha* researchers of the day tended incorrectly toward generalization, so that, about the historical accuracy of my research, I can only say the following:

Doubtless, all the *tikanga* and *tapu* in this book existed—only, no one knows in which tribe, in which region, or just how characteristic it was. On the other hand, one can reliably say what tribe lived when and in which region. Often, even the names of the chieftains have been passed down.

For me as an author, this presented a dilemma. Kahu Heke's tribe must be an *iwi* of the Ngapuhi whose great chieftain Hongi Hika signed the Treaty of Waitangi. But could I simply impress any customs and *tapu* on the Ngapuhi just because they fit so nicely into Lizzie and Kahu's story? After thinking long and hard, I decided against it, replacing the Ngapuhi with the fictive tribe Ngati Pau. I hope they do not hold it against me, should this ever get to them. I did it out of respect for their actual history, which I did not wish to falsify: *Kia tu tika ai te whare tapu o Nha Puhi*—may the sacred house of the Ngapuhi stand forever.

In closing, one last note for purists who love to check even the smallest detail in historical novels—and thus, to my eyes, perform a benefit, since they hold an author to careful research: Claire refers to Stratford-upon-Avon in the naming of her farm in Canterbury. She is convinced that the Avon River is named after Shakespeare's place of birth. This is not true, however. The river received its name from John Deans, a Scotsman who named it as a reminder of the River Avon in Falkirk, Scotland.

Acknowledgments

A book such as this cannot be made alone.

And so, I thank everyone who has helped out, especially my editor, Melanie Blank-Schröder; my copyeditor, Margit von Cossart; and my miracle-working agent, Bastian Schlück. But also the graphic artists who designed the jacket and drew the maps, the inventive marketing department—and, of course, the sales department and all the booksellers who finally brought the book to market. As ever, Klara Decker earned her keep as a test reader, finding answers on the web when I could get no further with my research. It never wore out the horses when, while riding, I drifted off to New Zealand in my mind. And the dogs always fetched me back—at least by feeding time.

Thanks also to the AmazonCrossing team that prepared the book for my English readers, especially Rebecca Friedman and Dustin Lovett. Thank you, Gabi and Bryn—it is always nice to work with you!

With Jacky and Grizabella, Pocas and Nena on my mind,

Sarah Lark

May 2015

About the Author

Photo © 2011 Gonzalo Perez

Sarah Lark's series of "landscape novels" have made her a bestselling author in Germany, her native country, as well as in Spain and the United States. She was born in Germany's Ruhr region, where she discovered a love of animals—especially horses—early in life. She has worked as an elementary-school teacher, a travel guide, and a commercial writer. She has also written numerous award-winning books about horses for adults and children, one of which was nominated for the Deutsche Jugendbuchpreis, Germany's distinguished prize for best children's book. Sarah currently lives with four dogs and a cat on her farm in Almería, Spain, where she cares for retired horses, plays guitar, and sings in her spare time.

About the Translator

Photo © 2011 Sanna Stegmaier

D. W. Lovett is a graduate of the University of Illinois at Urbana–Champaign, from which he received a degree in comparative literature and German as well as a certificate from the university's Center for Translation Studies. He has spent the last few years living in Europe. This is his fourth translation of Sarah Lark's work to be published in English, following *In the Land of the Long White Cloud*, *Song of the Spirits*, and *Call of the Kiwi*.